Kvachi

Originally published in Georgian as *Kvachi Kvachantiradze*

First edition, 2014

Library of Congress Cataloging-in-Publication Data

Javaxishvili, Mixeil, 1880-1937
[Kvachi Kvachantiradze. English]
Kvachi / by Mikheil Javakhishvili ; translated by Donald Rayfield. -- First edition.
pages cm
"Originally published in Georgian as Kvachi Kvachantiradze" -- Verso title page.
Summary: "This is, in brief, the story of a swindler: a Georgian Felix Krull, or perhaps a cynical Don Quixote, named Kvachi Kvachantiradze. He is a womanizer, cheat, perpetrator of insurance fraud, bank robber, associate of Rasputin, filmmaker, revolutionary, and pimp. Though originally denounced as pornographic, Kvachi's tale is one of the great classics of twentieth-century Georgian literature--and a hilarious romp to boot" -- Provided by publisher.

ISBN 978-1-56478-879-5 (pbk. : alk. paper)
1. Georgian fiction. I. Rayfield, Donald, 1942- translator. II. Title.
PK9169.J39K8213 2014
899'.9693--dc23

2014026081

Partially funded by a grant from the Illinois Arts Council, a state agency

This title is made possible with the support of the Georgian National Book Centre and the Ministry of Culture and Monument Protection of Georgia

www.dalkeyarchive.com
Cover: design and composition by Mikhail Iliatov
Printed on permanent/durable acid-free paper

Kvachi

Mikheil Javakhishvili

Translated by
Donald Rayfield

DALKEY ARCHIVE PRESS
Champaign / London / Dublin

Contents

CHAPTER THREE

CHAPTER FOUR

INTRODUCTION

Mikheil Javakhishvili (real surname Adamashvili) was born in 1880 to a farmer's family. Before he became a novelist he trained as a horticulturalist. He traveled the world (in particular, France), returning home to be a prolific journalist so radical as to be exiled by the Tsarist authorities. He served in the Red Cross on the Turkish front in World War I, supported an independent socialist party in independent Georgia, but opposed the Soviet invasion of February 1921. In the terrible vengeance taken by the *Cheka* and Communist Party for the uprising of August 1924, when over a thousand people, among them Georgia's elite, were shot, Javakhishvili was sentenced to death: he was almost the only victim to be spared as a result of appeals by fellow-writers.

The composition of *Kvachi Kvachantiradze*, perhaps his greatest novel, and of *Jaqo's Dispossessed*, a shorter, but equally fine piece, were interrupted by the catastrophe of the failed 1924 rebellion. Yet, both works were completed with no sign of the trauma the author had suffered.

In the late 1920s and early 1930s Javakhishvili wrote a number of novellas and novels, of which *Arsena of Marabda*, a semi-documentary novel about a peasant turned bandit in revolt against Georgian and Russian overlords, is perhaps the finest. Thereafter, under the rule of Lavrenti Beria, censorship became harsher and the oppression far worse. Javakhishvili formed a group of writers *Aripioni* (The Good Companions) which tried to maintain an independent and principled stance. Javakhishvili, who had personal conflicts with Beria, knew he was doomed and that his immense popularity with readers could not save him. In the Great Terror of 1937, writers were forced to attend all-night meetings and denounce each other and themselves. On 26 July in the middle of the proceedings the poet Paolo Iashvili shot himself; Javakhishvili openly praised Iashvili's courage and was then condemned by a vote of the Union of Writers as "an enemy of the people, a spy and diversant." After two months' torture he was shot and his archives were destroyed: he would not be rehabilitated until 1955.

Kvachi Kvachantiradze, originally a set of sketches, was reworked into a novel in 1924. That version, published in 1925, is the basis for this translation. It describes with astonishing frankness the glories of pre-war France, the horrors of the Russian Revolution and the Soviet invasion of Georgia. In 1934 a new censored edition was brought out. Normally, the last version created in the author's lifetime should be considered most authoritative, but this second version was badly mutilated by the Soviet censor: eleven of the thirteen sections of Chapter Four were cut (clearly, the author's love of Paris was intolerable to the Soviet censor), as well as many others from later chapters (the murder of Rasputin, the myth of the origins of Russia in the marriage of a Mongol and a Scythian, the horrors of Red revolution and invasion). Racy episodes from earlier sections (e.g. the hero's attempt to rape a student) were also cut. Numerous "offensive" phrases such as "the dirt of the plebs" were removed. At the same time, Javakhishvili made changes which may be voluntary improvements, adding exclamatory and explanatory phrases, additional colorful detail: in these cases, I have added elements from the 1934 edition. In one case, Javakhishvili salvaged censored material (the orgy in *Le Moulin Rouge*) and inserted them into an earlier chapter (into the episode of Rasputin's orgy at the Petersburg *Arcadia*): this seemed a genuine improvement to the original and is kept in this translation.

In the 1934 edition Javakhishvili added three lines to his ending, the farewell to the hero. I have omitted them in this translation since they compromise the author's ambiguity (horror mixed with delight) about his hero's character. They run: "But I know that you have finally found your proper and real job. So rot in your pit without a care in the world and be in peace."

Even in 1970, Soviet editors insisted that the 1934 "revision" was not a mutilation, but "basically the same novel" made more compact, more in "conformity with literary norms." In 2011, the new 7-volume edition of Javakhishvili's fiction reprinted the 1934, not the 1925 edition, even though readers will be puzzled by references in later parts of the novel to characters excised by the censor from the middle of the novel.

Kvachi Kvachantiradze did not appear in Russian until 1999, in a free (if not loose) translation with many arbitrary cuts by Aleksandr Ebanoidze. A German translation by Kristiane Lichtenfeld appeared in the DDR in the 1980s. This English translation, it is hoped, is the fullest version of the novel in any language.

There are some linguistic and stylistic problems I have not fully solved. One is the characters' language. Kvachi talks to his closest associates not just in Georgian, but in the dialect of his native Imeretia (western Georgia) with its rather different vowel sounds; with other Georgians, he speaks Tbilisi Georgian: I decided not to attempt to render these differences by using English dialect. In the company of Russians (or of the Soviet secret police, the *Cheka*, which was staffed by Azeris, Latvians, Poles, Russians, as well as Georgians) Kvachi and others switch to Russian. Only occasionally have I indicated these "code-switchings." Kvachi's faithful Turkish bodyguard Jalil speaks a simplified Georgian in which only Turkish consonants occur: there was no way I could find to render this in English. Lastly, Javakhishvili's dialogue sometimes switches into Russian, Turkish, French, even Armenian. The Turkish and Armenian I have usually translated in brackets; the Russian I have treated as Georgian (except when the reader needs to know what language was used); the French, which is elementary, I have left in the original.

Kvachi Kvachantiradze is arguably the most spirited and

inspired work of all Georgian fiction. It is a rogue novel, mixing humour, observation and real pathos, that deserves comparison with Gogol's *Dead Souls*, Thomas Mann's *Felix Krull*, and Ilf and Petrov's novels of the rogue Ostap Bender, *The Twelve Chairs* and *The Golden Calf*; it is particularly close to Maupassant (who influenced Javakhishvili perhaps more than any other writer) and the ruthless hero of Maupassant's *Bel-Ami*. It is also the product of a writer who had more experience of life than most: the chapters on Rasputin show not just a reading of Prince Yusupov's memoirs, but personal knowledge—compare them with Nadezhda Teffi's account of Rasputin in her *Subtly Worded* (Pushkin Press, 2013). Much of the details of Tsarist and Soviet prisons, as well as of war and revolution are clearly relived personally. Moreover, it is an almost uniquely frank exposé of the Georgian character, its minuses as well as pluses, by an author who was clearly afraid of nothing, not of the authorities, not of public opinion, nor of what his own talent could reveal.

Some guidance for the reader …

Time and place Georgia in the 1890s, Russia in the 1900s, France in the 1910s, then Russia in World War I and revolution, followed by briefly independent and then "sovietised" Georgia in the early 1920s, ending in Istanbul in 1924.

Currency The rouble was stable (worth about $15 in today's purchasing power) from 1890 until the Revolution, when hyperinflation and the introduction of various paper currencies made it worthless. Finally, in 1924 a "gold" rouble was introduced; in Georgia, even after the Soviet invasion, people continued to deal in Turkish liras (then worth much the same as a Tsarist rouble).

Characters Kvachi for most of his career has a gang of faithful followers, boyhood or student friends: Beso (Besarion) Shikia, his wise, taciturn counsellor; Jalil, his Turkish bodyguard; the cowardly

Chipi Chipuntiradze; the aggressive Gabo Chkhubishvili (from *chkhubi*, "brawl"); Sedrak Havlabariani (from the mixed Armenian-Georgian Tbilisi quarter of Avlabar); Ladi Chikinjiladze.

His family consists of parents (Silibistro and Pupi) and his great-uncle and great-aunt Khukhu and Notio who foster him, and whom he calls grandparents. His many female conquests are known mainly by their first names and recur in his life so often and so colorfully that the reader will have little difficulty recognizing them.

There are many real characters—ministers, bishops, etc—from Russian politics of the 1900s and 1910s, and many prominent Frenchmen from the pre-war period. I could not identify absolutely every one of them from the transcriptions of their names into Georgian. Occasionally I have given an explanatory footnote; for the rest Google should provide the necessary information. As for the realities behind the fiction—some of Kvachi's exploits reflect those of an actual Georgian in Rasputin's circle—these will have to be the subject of future research into Javakhishvili's many sources, for he was an author as observant as he was inventive. I thank the staff of the National Parliamentary Library of Tbilisi for their generosity in furnishing me with pdfs of the early editions of the novel, and Professor Shukia Apridonidze for helping me to solve a number of conundrums.

Donald Rayfield
June 2014

FROM THE AUTHOR

Last year and this year some parts of this novel were printed under various titles in various magazines (*Drosha, Mnatobi*, and *Kartuli sitqva*). I first intended to print a series of stories under one overall title, but as I wrote, I changed my mind and decided to put them together as one novel. For that reason I have added new material to what was printed, and have corrected it and made its inner unity stronger.

In all sincerity I dare to dedicate this book to all the Kvachis, big and little, major and minor, who have always been so numerous in our blessed motherland.

The Author
Tbilisi, October 1924

CHAPTER ONE

Kvachi's Birth

On the first of April that year the weather in Samtredia was stranger than usual. A pitch-black cloud hung over the earth from the morning onwards. Snow, hail, rain and, sometimes, spring sunshine alternated; after a while there was such a gale that the whole township rattled and shook, then a calm silence would descend and you wouldn't see the slightest movement of a cloud in the sky.

So the first of April in Samtredia started in confusion: it was a deceitful, false, and treacherous day.

That day, in Silibistro Kvachantiradze's house, which was on the road to Khoni, there was a great deal of commotion and fuss: Silibistro's wife Pupi was giving birth to her first child. The whole family was up and about. The woman's labor was attended by her mother Notio, her grandmother, and the womenfolk from next door, while Silibistro and his father Khukhu Chichia were waiting in the other room, worrying about their first heir.

As midday approached, everything seemed to go dark, as if it were night. The earth stopped being calm and suddenly quaked and shook. There was a terrible storm. The whole land groaned, moaned, and thundered. The Kvachantiradzes' wooden house bent this way and that, it rattled, it lifted its eaves, as if trying to fly away. Pupi shrieked in her labor, while the others, horror-struck and frightened, ran about like headless chickens.

There was a sudden flash of lightning, so bright that it blinded everyone for a few seconds, and that same instant the heavens thundered horribly and Pupi uttered a scream, while the earth quaked, so that some of those present were petrified, some bent double, and others made a dash for the door. There was a moment's silence and then, from the corner of the room, came the cry of the new-born baby:

"Me-e ... me-e ... me-e ..."

So Silibistro Kvachantiradze's first boy fell for the first time at the feet of his first woman: his own mother Pupi.

Shrieks of joy, havoc, and bustling broke out. It was then precisely twelve o'clock. The storm fell silent and light overcame the darkness.

The sound of the baby's cry brought Silibistro Kvachantiradze and Khukhu Chichia rushing out of the next room.

"It's a boy!" the grandmother gave Silibistro and Khukhu the news they had hoped for.

"Thank the Lord!" said Silibistro.

"Glory to the Father and to the Son and to the Holy Ghost!" Khukhu added piously. "Amen."

"Amen," the others repeated; they all crossed themselves.

"I name him Kvachi," declared Silibistro in a solemn voice; the others immediately gave their assent.

Shortly after this the innkeeper's lad Bardgha rushed up from the ground floor and brought them the news that the poplar tree in the Kvachantiradzes' garden had been struck by lightning and cleft in two. Worse, the storm had demolished Zhondia's inn, which had been a serious rival to Kvachantiradze's "hotel." Silibistro dashed out to take a look at Zhondia's wrecked inn: on the way there he found a silver rouble.

An hour later the clouds had cleared and fine spring weather had returned. The sun shone overhead like a resplendent radiant crown. All Samtredia had come out to look with amazement at this crown of light, the remains of Zhondia's inn, and Kvachantiradze's split poplar tree.

That was how Kvachi Kvachantiradze was born.

In the evening of the same day Madame Notio opened little

Kvachi's palm as much as she could, read it, thought for a while, and then gave a reading to Pupi, who had now revived, to Silibistro, who was pleased with himself, to Khukhu, who had calmed down, and to Bardgha, who was giving himself airs.

"The gale and the thunder and lightning mean that Kvachi is going to have a childhood with a lot of hardship and ups and downs, but God is merciful. His clenched fist, which I had so much trouble opening, is a sign that nobody's going to take away anything Kvachi gets his hands on. The sun shining like a crown over him means that a brilliant and famous future awaits little Kvachi, bless his tiny little paws! The lightning striking the poplar tree and devils taking away Zhondia's inn is a sign that your enemies and Kvachi's—may the Cross protect us all!—will be struck by lightning and their hearts will be split in two, just as the poplar tree was cleft in two today."

Everyone found this reading reassuring and comforting. Silibistro said, "I've never heard a baby cry like him. He yells nothing but 'Me-me.' It sounds as if he's not going to let anyone else have anything and is going to lay claim to the whole world."

Everyone laughed.

"How I love my little Kvachi!" Pupi whispered with a smile, as she began to fondle little Kvachi, who had fallen asleep beside her.

Little did Silibistro, or Pupi, or Bardgha, or even Khukhu and Notio, know that their predictions and dreams had an element of truth, and that the squawking, mewling Kvachi would eventually realize all their hopes and even exceed them.

Kvachi's Parents

Now I'd like to tell you something about Silibistro Kvachantiradze and his family.

Silibistro was born in Guria just at the time that serfdom was being abolished. His father Anapodiste and mother Tsiutsia handed over the little Silibistro to be brought up by Tsiutsia's sister Notio and her husband Khukhu Chichia.

Khukhu and Notio put the tiny Silibistro in a woollen saddlebag, which they attached to the horse's saddle, and with a great deal of trouble brought him to the village of Bandza in Mingrelia, which was where they lived.

The Mingrelians didn't think much of Silibistro's Christian name: they renamed him Chipi. But this second christening was done without a priest's participation and the new name was not recorded anywhere, so that the boy ended up with two names: Silibistro and Chipi.

After about ten years, Silibistro-Chipi was taken to see his parents in Guria; sometimes he was taken in a saddlebag, sometimes in a basket, and then brought back to Mingrelia.

When the Russo-Turkish war broke out, Anapodiste enlisted in the Georgian militia and went off to capture Batumi, but he was killed during an attack at Tsikhisdziri, the city's fortifications. Barely a year passed before Tsiutsia remarried: her new husband took her off to Odessa.

So Silibistro Kvachantiradze was orphaned. Fortunately, auntie Notio and uncle Khukhu Chichia were willing to raise him and take charge of his handful of possessions.

Silibistro was not the only child in the Chichia family. In Samtredia Khukhu had a brother, Jvebe Chichia, who was widowed early in life. Jvebe had one daughter, Pupi. Jvebe was a man with little time to spare, so Pupi, too, was raised in Khukhu and Notio's family.

So Silibistro and Pupi were brought up as siblings: they were in love with each other from infancy.

When Silibistro grew up, he refused to till the soil; instead, he went off to Batumi to try his luck as a gentleman. Jvebe asked Khukhu to come to Samtredia with the rest of his family. Jvebe was ill, so he entrusted Pupi's future and his little inn to Khukhu:

then he gave up the ghost.

Since Khukhu couldn't manage the inn on his own, he summoned Silibistro from Batumi and told him:

"Chipi, son: living in your own hovel is better than serving in someone else's palace; your own dry maize bread is better than someone else's fine wheat bread. You won't get very far if you can read and write only in Georgian. There are thousands of educated people in Batumi, they won't give you a chance to get on, so my advice is: be a family man. Your fate's in your hands, strike while the iron's hot, or you'll regret it. Pupi is quite a catch. She's a good-looking, decent, and lively girl. This nicely furnished house and garden are a treasure in themselves. Everything Notio and I have will be yours. What do you say, Chipi, son?"

What could Chipi Kvachantiradze say? Fortune was welcoming him with open arms. He made a gift of his famous surname to Pupi and thus roosted in a nest made by somebody else.

Getting Noble Status from Ashordia*

Silibistro's two-storeyed, lopsided wooden house stood on the road to Khoni. The house had half an acre of land, which was called the "orchard." The orchard had a dozen or so trees—cherry, wild pear, and crab apple. There were also half a dozen rows of vegetables and herbs: radish, coriander, cress, tarragon, and celery.

The ground floor was the "hotel" where you could always be served meat and plum stew, sliced new cheese, eggs, pork sausage, fruit, and a great range of wines: Kulashuri, Sviruli, Sachinuri-Aladasturi.

There was a farmyard with animals and poultry: a dozen hens, geese and ducks, a couple of goats, a few piglets, and a loyal dog.

In the back room of the inn there were four divans, covered

* Solomon Ashordia was a notorious conman of the time; he helped many people get certificates of nobility by using forged seals and charters.

with rags in lieu of bedding. Although the house was old and on the verge of collapse, it did stand on the road to Khoni and there were a lot of customers.

There were three rooms, virtually empty, but clean and welcoming, on the upper floor. Gradually Silibistro got hold of cutlery, crockery, a table, chairs, and curtains.

Khukhu and Notio made their purchases in Bandza and contributed their share to the family's joint possessions. All four were outgoing, polite, and respectful, so that they soon built up custom: the customers enjoyed not only watery wine, desiccated sliced cheese, and fly-blown sausages, but their host's fawning smile, the latest hot gossip, civilized arguments, a thousand apologies, and constant promises to serve them better in the future.

It goes without saying that Silibistro and Pupi didn't treat everyone who came their way as an equal, but they would never let noblemen and gentry, merchants, or any decent client pass by without at least wishing them good morning, inviting them in, asking how they were doing, and responding in kind.

If Silibistro was at the station or the market, he would find out, by instinct or some other mechanism, about the arrival of this sort of customer, and he would immediately rush home, if only to make the acquaintance of a desirable customer, win him over with a few sweet words, and some time later exploit him.

When in the course of time carriages stopped taking the Khoni road, Silibistro would go to the station and the market for a thousand petty purposes. He always had a couple of pennies left over to contribute to the hotel and the family. Both family and inn were gradually developing, getting on their feet, and finding their strength.

This was Silibistro's life and family when Kvachi Kvachantiradze was born.

Kvachi grew with astonishing speed. Other babies don't learn to walk or to speak before they are one year old, but little Kvachi was barely six months' old when he babbled, "Daddy … mummy … granddad." And he learned to walk at the same age.

Notio commented, with every justification: "Believe me, when a child grows up so quickly, it means he'll turn out to be a famous and important man."

Naturally, everyone believed Notio: they began to take even greater care of Kvachi.

After Kvachi was born, even Silibistro spent most of his time at home and lost interested in trying to make a few pennies here and there. If he accumulated an extra ten roubles, he'd buy silk cocoons or silkworm eggs as a good investment, in his view.

There was only one concern, one secret thought and dream gnawing away at Silibistro's heart and mind, and he was beset, tormented by it. Silibistro Kvachantiradze was a mere commoner. Actually, I must apologize: Silibistro came from one of the most ancient and genuine noble families: the whole world knew this, but there was so far no documentary proof of his nobility. Silibistro spent countless hours and roubles trying to put this discrepancy right: he'd traveled to Ozurgeti and Kutaisi (the capitals of Guria and Imeretia) many times, he'd hired lawyers, but he hadn't been able to achieve anything. He received a lot of promises and was given a lot of hope, for which he paid equally generous sums of money, but Silibistro's identity papers continued as before to bear the shameful and despicable word: "p-e-a-s-a-n-t."

Silibistro was an upstart, a "seeker", an *ichuchi* (from the Russian *ishchushchi*, seeking). That is why some people joked about him or laughed at him behind his back. Silibistro was aware of that and it distressed him, but he still persisted in seeking, running about, and expecting victory.

Finally some merciful person gave him a piece of advice: "Ashordia!"

Silibistro went straight to Zugdidi, the capital of Mingrelia. Finally, after a lot of begging and horse-trading, a bargain was just about struck.

Several years passed. Then, one day, there was a lot of bustling about and excitement in Silibistro's family: everyone was running about, whispering, "Ashordia's coming! Ashordia!"

That evening a stranger turned up. The Kvachantiradzes met him with great awe and respect. A big feast was laid on: there was rejoicing, happiness, ecstasy. While they were getting tipsy on wine, Ashordia merely smiled and asked for his reward for bringing such good news; then he stood up and said, "Yet another respected family has been added to the greater family of the noble-born. Everyone knows that Chipi Kvachantiradze's grandfather was a nobleman, but that he was let down by chance, somehow this respectable man happened for some reason not to be listed in any document. Well, I've put right this historical injustice, and you and your family, dear Silibistro, are now confirmed as nobility. Congratulations on this great day for your family, and I wish you every enjoyment of the Tsar's grace. I drink a toast to Silibistro Kvachantiradze. Long live our newfound brother nobleman!"

Yells and shrieks of joy spurted like a fountain from Silibistro's family. Ashordia solemnly handed Silibistro the Tsar's lengthy charter, which all Samtredia read and envied the very next day.

From then on Silibistro's and Kvachi Kvachantiradze's noble status was an established fact. At supper the five-year-old Kvachi set Silibistro an example: he kissed Ashordia's hand and said, "Uncle, I'm gwateful."

Ashordia smiled back, kissed little Kvachi's forehead, patted him on the head and said, "Little one, I've cleared a path for you, I've opened every door for you: the rest is up to you. You've been fortunate: so make your parents and your motherland fortunate and famous. I drink a toast to little Kvachi, hurrah!"

There was another burst of shrieking, songs, and celebration.

The next day, as Ashordia was getting ready to leave, little Kvachi kissed his hand again and asked him, "Uncle, when you next see the Tsar, tell him that Kvachi Kvachantiradze says he won't forget what you've done for him and that when I gwow up, I'll show you how gwateful I am."

Everyone laughed. Ashordia encouraged him, saying, "Well, I'm relying on you. Don't let me down, little boy!" Then he left.

That evening Notio said, "Darling little Kvachi! Nothing will stop him now. The world will be his oyster and he'll bring us luck. Perhaps there will come a time when Kvachi can show Ashordia how grateful he is, and do even better than him."

Notio and Pupi couldn't have known then, nor could even Ashordia, nor even Silibistro, all puffed with pride, that little Kvachi would in the future completely overshadow Ashordia, really stir up the entire country, and crown his family in splendour and glory.

The dubious nobility that Ashordia had wangled for Silibistro cost him dearly. What he spent on Ashordia was equalled by what he spent on the citizens of Samtredia and Khoni who kept coming for a whole week in groups to see Silibistro and give him their sincere congratulations on the Tsar's grace and the family's admission to the nobility.

Kvachi's Youth

After Silibistro Kvachantiradze was confirmed as a member of the nobility, his character and his family took on a different nature. They all put on airs, became haughty and "gentrified." They either ignored their former neighbors, or treated them arrogantly and patronisingly: it seemed as if the bridge that once united them had collapsed and a wall had been erected instead.

Sometimes Silibistro would instruct little Kvachi, "Listen, son: this is the way the world runs. Some are rich, some are poor; some are powerful, some are weak; some are princes and noblemen, others are laborers and peasants. A gentleman's son like you mustn't sink to the level of others or follow their example. Laborers and peasants have nothing to offer you: instead, they make you less of a person. Make friends with the gentry and the rich, try and please them, and treat them like brothers. The rich and the powerful will always stand you in good stead; one can help you get on in life, another will give you presents, or a helping hand. That, little Kvachi, is how the world runs, and you must do accordingly and profit from it."

Little Kvachi was a sharp-witted and obedient child, so he found Silibistro's advice easy to understand and follow.

He was barely six years old when he began to take an active part in business. When Silibistro, Notio, or Bardgha were buying things from the peasants, Kvachi could never help putting in a word: "It's not worth it ... too dear: tomowow we'll get only ten kopecks for it." He would greet a customer with a respectful smile: "Good morning, uncle ... My name's Kvachi ... I'm six ... I'm Silibistwo's son ... We've got evewything: fwuit, sausage, sliced cheese, meat stew, eggs, and such good Sviwi wine that even a Kakhetian wouldn't look down on it."

And he'd run off to give their order, shouting "Quick! Serve the vewy best! Lay the table! Wipe it down! Wash the dishes! Hey, get a move on!"

The priest's curate started him off reading and writing. When he was eight, he was taken to Kutaisi by Silibistro, Pupi, Khukhu, and Notio. On seeing such a big, clean, wealthy, and beautiful city, they were amazed and bewildered. Silibistro realized the others were amazed and began instructing them all: "Pay attention, listen and remember: if you're bowled over by anything, don't show it, or else people will notice that you're inexperienced and make a fool of you or pull a fast one on you. If you're asked, say you've been to Tbilisi, that you spent a year there, that you've seen it all, heard it all, and tried it all."

Little Kvachi took this instruction to heart: when he was having dinner with Budu Sholia, a distant relative of Pupi's. The conversation turned to Tbilisi and he remarked with solemn serenity: "Tbilisi's all right, it's a big city, I like it ... Yes, I was there twice last year ... I like Golovinsky Avenue, the theatre, the railway station ... the inns are good ..."

He didn't blush and his voice didn't tremble, and he looked at everyone as if he was challenging them: "Well, who's going to dare tell me I'm lying?" In fact, just being in Kutaisi had astonished, confused, and excited Kvachi. But what could little Kvachi have thought then that in times to come Kvachi Kvachantiradze, using a prince's name as a pseudonym, would travel to Petersburg, Paris, Vienna, Berlin, and London and, if Kutaisi was mentioned, would laugh bitterly and say, "I feel as if I was born in a chicken-run and brought up in a pigsty; but now I've moved to a real palace."

A week later, when little Kvachi had found lodgings in Kutaisi, Silibistro took his family back to Samtredia. When he took leave of Kvachi, Silibistro gave more instructions to his sole consolation and hope: "Well, son, I'm saying goodbye to you. I shan't be able to see you for some time. We're going, but our hearts and souls are staying here with you. Be sensible, put your heart into your studies, always do as Budu and your teachers tell you. Don't have anything to do with badly behaved children or laborers' sons. If you use your brains, one day you'll be the talk of Samtredia, Khoni, and Kutaisi, you'll bring fear to your enemies and joy to your relatives. You're our hope in life, little Kvachi ... Well, it's up to you ..."

And he had trouble hiding his tears.

Little Kvachi replied, "You needn't worry ... I shan't disgrace the name of Kvachantiradze."

Everyone laughed. Then they wept, kissed each other, and departed. Kvachi stayed with Budu Sholia's family on Balakhvani Street, where the latter had a small tavern. A week later Kvachi was wearing a new grammar school uniform and diligently beginning his studies.

Kvachi's Character

Several years passed. Kvachi was by now a youth, grown up, well developed; he was turning into a tall, sturdily built, even burly, youth. Kvachi was considered one of the cleverest boys, but also the laziest, so that his average mark was mediocre. He found studying lessons and learning by heart torture, but the yoke of wisdom weighed lightly on him, for he had an excellent memory and he easily took in what he heard in class. He was not an enthusiastic reader, although he loved reading about travels, adventures, and stories of things involving dastardly adventures, big or small. He had already read Mayne-Reid, Fennimore Cooper, Gustave Aimard, Gordon's memoirs, Nat Pinkerton, Sherlock Holmes, and similar authors and works.

Silibistro's instructions were deeply engraved in Kvachi's brain. He never stopped trying to please influential people and his teachers. He made sure to circulate wherever they were, to make them like him, even grow fond of him, and to get even the smallest advantage and benefit from them. In this respect Kvachi had been richly endowed by nature: he had an astonishing and unusual ability to divine people's characters, to get through to them, to become like a brother and to win their complete trust and affection. If Kvachi was determined to get close to someone, man or woman, that person would within two weeks or so end up totally captivated by him.

Kvachi was clever with clever people, serious with serious people, frivolous with the frivolous, melancholy with the melancholy, joyful with the joyful, but submissive, sycophantic, obsequious, respectful, and ever-smiling with the powerful. But if he had to be, he was able to be humble and witty when he was in coarse or troublesome company; to be insolent, haughty, and headstrong with the weak; to be treacherous, hypocritical, and two-faced with the frank and forthright; to be unfathomably false with the treacherous; to be a reed with an oak, and an oak with a reed; to be cotton with iron, and iron with cotton.

Wherever the road ahead was barred and anyone else would turn back, Kvachi would find half a dozen sidetracks; if he found himself stuck in a room with no doors or windows, he would find a dozen cracks, so that he could get in and out of a fortress guarded by nine locked doors, like a needle going through feathers.

Kvachi had grasped and practised to perfection the irresistible and invincible power of sweet-talking, of a heart-warming smile, of meretricious praise and flattery; he had a secret talisman enabling him to win trust, to conquer and enslave someone heart and soul, to tie down and milk, shear, and exploit dozens, even hundreds of people.

When he was shearing and milking somebody, he would soothe the conscience of those around him by saying, "In this world some are born with saddles, others with spurs and whips. I prefer having spurs and a whip, others can wear a saddle if they want. That's what Voltaire is supposed to have said."

Or he'd say, "If in this world everyone were bold and brave, or stitched up their pockets with wire thread, then a man like me would have to guard other people's pockets or plough the earth."

Or even: "Remember, brother: God created sheep for milking and shearing."

Kvachi had the acute nose and instinct of a pedigree hound. He was a living barometer and could immediately sense the approach of good or bad weather, when other people had no idea that the weather might change. In Sholia's family and tavern the weather was very changeable, as it was in school, on Kutaisi's boulevard, and in city life in general. Well in advance Kvachi would instinctively sense the change and put on a different skin and different clothes, choose the appropriate weapon, and gather his strength as required: he would wash his hands of the setting sun and greet the rising sun, he would kick the fallen and proudly stand by whoever was on their feet.

"Everything has its place, time, and measure." Kvachi had learnt to perfection this simple truth, and it was an instrument that he wielded with amazing skill. The tone of his speech, the number and choice of words, using them at the right time and in the appropriate circumstances, every step, every little twist and turn, was all taken into account, calculated, weighed up, and measured: at the right time he would head for the shadows and keep away, at the right time he would come out into the sunlight and show himself; at the right time he would be patient and wait, then at the right time act and again retreat at the right time. That was his magical ability and power.

Kvachi had no equal in making money, but almost nobody ever found out the real source of this money, or the means by which it was made. In extreme cases, Kvachi would take out a loan, and in the trickiest of Kutaisi business dealings he would use a special trick of his own, which was very simple and effective: he would suddenly, by the way, casually, calmly say, in the middle of a conversation, "Lend me thirty roubles," and say the words in the right tone and at the right time, so that he was never ever refused. Whoever lent him the money would five minutes later regret it and clap his hand to his brow, while the now prosperous Kvachi would whistle merrily and stride off.

There was one habit which Kvachi had turned into a law and a custom: "Never refuse anybody anything, but only honor your promises to anyone if it's profitable for you today or tomorrow at the latest." That is why nobody ever had a refusal from Kvachi, a generous, polite, and well brought-up young man who scattered thousands of promises left and right.

"I swear on my life! You want some money? How much? Five roubles? Why didn't you tell me an hour ago? But I'll get it for you, right now."

He'd dart about here and there, he'd hide here and there, but the promise always remained a mere promise. Yet the amazing thing was that the people he let down never took offense, because Kvachi always got out of every difficulty in such a polite, sweet, and victorious way that his creditors remained sweet and would not hesitate to help him out again and again.

Over his comrades Kvachi always had a great influence. Whether he was going into class or going out on the boulevard, a big group would immediately gather round him. Friends and schoolmates flocked to him like flies to honey. Kvachi always had the right words, opinions, smiles, advice, and instructions ready for everyone. He would sort out any confusion, calm down any clashes: mediating between pupils and teachers was his speciality. Everyone said, "If Kvachi were fond of hard work, he'd have a great future." Others would add, "He'll be an important man, anyway. Mark my words."

The First Hard-Earned Rouble

Budu Sholia's tavern was on Balakhvani Street, and his living quarters were in the tavern courtyard. Kvachi would often drop into the inn, go behind the counter, and help out even with day-to-day matters. He'd keep his eyes and ears open on everything from a separate little office: he watched, took it all in, and refined his experience. Thus Sholia's tavern became a real school of life for Kvachi. By the time he was ten years old or so, he'd learnt, seen, and absorbed here more than a twenty-year-old young man would have seen or experienced.

Budu Sholia had a young wife called Tsviri: she brought up and nurtured Kvachi as if he were her own child, reassuring her husband by saying: "What do you expect me to do, you wretch? You haven't been able to give me a single child: why shouldn't I get fond of someone else's?" And she became as fond of someone else's boy as her husband was of his lucrative shop-counter.

Tsviri's inhibitions had been so lowered, as she adopted and brought up this stranger's son, that even when Kvachi was thirteen or fourteen she herself would undress him and bathe him.

Kvachi had his own tiny room. This room and the Sholia living room were divided only by thin boards, so that every word, creak, or rustle could be heard in both rooms. Budu Sholia rarely left his counter.

One evening Kvachi came back from the boulevard, read for a little while, and then went to bed. Tsviri tidied a few things up in Kvachi's room, then put out the lamp, sat on the edge of his bed in the dark, and started playing with him. The game ended as it inevitably had to: Tsviri taught Kvachi something he already knew, but had not yet fully experienced and felt personally with an actual woman.

Budu Sholia was elderly and poorly, so that night Tsviri got herself another permanent male, while Kvachi had a taste of his first real female. Little did Tsviri then think that, although she was Kvachi's first female teacher, Kvachi had a few years earlier made in the life of a neighbor's daughter, a Russian called Varia, a real variation.

The very next day Tsviri redoubled the affection and care she showed by putting in Kvachi's hand a silver rouble and whispering, "For my darling's little hand. Buy yourself something, but don't say a word, or we're both ruined."

Kvachi needed no warning: he would have kept silent about that rouble anyway, although neither he nor his friends would have laid ten kopecks on keeping the rest of the affair secret.

That was how Kvachi earned his first rouble by the sweat of his brow.

This rouble had come to him sweetly, easily, and lightly. Once Kvachi had found the right path, he so enjoyed his first easily earned rouble, he was quick to earn a second, then a third, and a tenth. Tsviri soon found out to her cost that raising and maintaining her own cockerel was very expensive, but it was too late to regret it and bite her fingernails. Tsviri found it hard to sleep and she became troubled and tense, for she found her cockerel restless and insatiable. Although he ate the chicken-feed Tsviri gave him, he would then wander off to other people's yards and act the cockerel with other hens. Tsviri thought so and reproached Kvachi.

But Tsviri had made other miscalculations: in other people's hen runs there was silver and gold chicken-feed to be had. Competition and rivalry were more than she could bear: she soon gave up trying to monopolise Kvachi. She resigned herself to her fate, queued up for her turn to be loved, and thought: "A crow can only hope to be thrown a walnut."

What else could poor Tsviri do? Everyone had their turn and their share. The crumbs from the dinnertable were not as negligible as she had first thought, and in this world a handsome man or good-looking woman would be taken over by the rich and powerful, like any other property or good fortune. Nobody should think or boast that they had exclusive possession of any of these things.

Another three years or so passed. Tsviri picked up the scent and managed to separate the neighbors' little Varia from Kvachi in good time. Tsviri loomed between the two like an insurmountable barrier; she was filled with jealousy and clung all the more tightly to Kvachi, although she was still feeding on crumbs from the dinnertable. Keeping her cockerel was getting ever more expensive, because Kvachi was raising his prices as he grew up, and it was getting harder to compete with her rivals.

Once Tsviri and Kvachi had a small, but disagreeable, quarrel. Kvachi frowned, went red in the face, and spurned the offer of over-ripe fruit and hard-earned money: for the first time he gave his mistress a taste of his razor-sharp talons.

Tsviri laughed and told him, "You must be a big fool, my little Kvachi, if you think that money comes free. When you finish your schooling, you'll earn money and pay me back. Don't be a child, take it."

After thinking a little, Kvachi replied, "I'll pay you back with interest, if you agree ..."

"Aha! As if I would lend money with no interest?"

They came to an agreement. The human soul is a mystery. Who knows if Kvachi Kvachantiradze in his old age ever remembered that he had a debt owing to Tsviri Sholia on Balakhvani Street in the city of Kutaisi? One certain fact is that Tsviri Sholia never ever counted, wrote down, or considered as a debt the money she had spent on Kvachi.

Kvachi didn't hide from his school friends that he had a lot of customers in the women's market, but he avoided mentioning the price they paid; only occasionally would he casually remark, "Only a madman or a freak would spend money on a woman." Or else, "You have to be daft or a poet to go after blue-stockings or young girls. The world is full of experienced women. They're less dangerous, you can keep your freedom, they don't take so much of your time or money. Quite the opposite, sometimes ..."

Once, when he'd got through three bottles of Qipiani's best wine, Kvachi gave his friends some rather fuzzy and oblique instruction:

"Use your wits, take a good look at life, weigh up and measure everything. I don't understand how any woman can make me so crazy or carry me away enough to lose my mind and sacrifice my freedom, youth, future, and life to some fifteen-year-old frump. As for myself, a ten-year-old kid already knows women are made just for a moment's pleasure. Take what you can from them; if you want to, say thanks, and go your own way. If there's going to be equality, it has to be in everything. Why should I carry some Sonia, Varia, or Marusia on my back for twenty or forty years? If we've given each other pleasure, then all of us can go our own way, and that's all there is to it. I'll tell you something else: life is a struggle. What you can grab from it is yours, what you can't is lost. Some women can give you a bit more than what every woman has. Any man with brains can drain a woman dry and make her carry him on her back, because, believe me, I'd rather drive someone else about than have someone else drive me. That's the way the world runs. If you have eyes to see, you'll see it; if you have ears to hear, you'll hear it; if you have any brains, you'll understand and use the opportunity."

That's how the eighteen-year-old Kvachi was developing.

Kvachi's Ordeal

Gradually Kvachi made the acquaintance, and then a close study of all Kutaisi. Kutaisi, in turn, soon noticed and singled out this handsome, capable, clever, cheerful, ingenious, and dexterous young man, for whom everyone and everything predicted great advancement and a brilliant future. Almost every family opened its doors to Kvachi, who had the magic gift of becoming one of the family within three days, finding close relatives everywhere, gaining from everyone affection, friendship, and a joyful welcome.

For the time being Kvachi stuck to friends of his own age and soon could stroll in any part of Kutaisi—Gochoura, Saghoria, Choma, or Sapichkhia cemetery—and treat it as if it was his own back garden in Samtredia on the road to Khoni. Slowly he got in the habit of visiting the inns, too. At first he went to remote little taverns where the school discipline supervisor or the police never took a look, later his older school friends took him with them and showed him better places.

When he was seventeen or eighteen, he climbed another rung in the ladder: the young party-going noblemen accepted him into their circle and submitted him to the ordeal of "Noah's vine."

Kvachi passed this test of endurance brilliantly and kept up with the drinking, the dancing, and the singing, too. Then he was taken to Laitadze's inn on the Khoni road, where the chairman of the feast and the host poured a jug of wine over Kvachi's head as a symbol of baptism and brotherhood, before making him down without a break a ram's horn containing three bottles of wine.

They feasted there until morning, as Georgians do: they got through eighty litres of wine, ate vast amounts of food; twice as much was spilled or spoiled, a lot of crockery was broken, and the sky was riddled with revolver shots; in the morning seven dead-drunk spongers were sent back to town in fifteen cabs together with the rest of the party. But that evening and the next day the feasting and Kvachi's baptism went on: first in the Levi, then the Borjomi, later in Saghoria, where the host was the bloated, obese Eremo, with whom Kvachi became close friends that evening, because it turned out that they had close spiritual—and distant physical—ties with each other.

In the middle of the feast some officer and an official arrived in a carriage, bringing two women with them. One of the women ended up sitting next to Kvachi. They caught each other's eye, laughed at one another, and exchanged a few words. The officer took umbrage. A Prince Dadiani tried to intervene for Kvachi. The men followed each other, argued, and cleared a space. Daggers and revolvers were produced. Yells, shrieks, and general panic broke out. The inn and the innkeeper were in danger of losing their good name, so Eremo took "appropriate measures" to protect his reputation, as a result of which the officer was stripped of his weapon and the official lost two teeth. Kvachi reappeared only when it was all over: up to that moment the young lad had slipped off to the bushes "to answer a call of nature." He was still learning, so they forgave him. Everyone was made to swear that if the business ever got out, they were not to point the finger at Kvachi, because things would be more dangerous for a schoolboy like Kvachi.

But the affair did get out, and there was an outbreak of storytelling, questioning, and squeaking of pens. And Kvachi's involvement came out into the open. His enemies had been waiting for an opportunity to make things up about him, saying Kvachi had organized a game of cards, that he'd won a lot of money with a marked card and swindled Seriozha Londua, and false evidence had been planted, and he'd been stitched up by more fairytales and slander from rumor-mongering, envious companions.

Kvachi's fate hung by a thread. But the police constable, the investigating magistrate, and the headmaster were all led up the garden path. Kvachi turned out to have secret protectors, and everyone had to step back. On the one hand, distinguished women were making a fuss, on the other hand there were influential civic leaders: finally Tsviri managed with great effort to gather together a big sum of money and lend it to Kvachi.

Finally, of course, Kvachi was victorious. Nobody knows the exact way in which Kvachi showed his gratitude to the women who protected him; as for the influential civic leaders, a few things have been discovered which you are invited to listen to.

His First Step

Recently, Kutaisi seemed to be inflamed by a fire that was gradually getting stronger. People were getting nervous and obstinate. Kvachi's friends would gather to discuss things, would form groups, and get ready to go to war. Many of them tried to get Kvachi involved, but he had not forgotten Silibistro's words of advice that year: "Kvachi, son, I expect you know the country has gone off its head and is crazy. They want to get rid of the nobility, bring down the Tsar's throne, and the government. They're saying they've got to take the land away from the landowners, make the rich and the poor equal, and establish universal brotherhood, so we can be free. Son, use your head! Don't lose the noble status or the property which I had to work and suffer so hard to get. Remember that these people won't be able to defeat the Tsar and the government. Half of them will rot in prison, half of them will freeze to death in Siberia. If you have any sense and if you love your mother and father, you have to swear to me that you won't get involved in this business and you won't disgrace your noble status."

Kvachi swore the oath and kept his word faithfully for a considerable time. But ideas change as circumstances change. Kvachi didn't know who would finally come out victorious, but he could very clearly see that the balance of forces was changing from day to day: the government and the school administration were retreating and getting weaker, while the people were advancing and getting stronger. Kvachi nevertheless dithered. He swayed and bent like a circus acrobat, and held out a hand to both sides: so he sat on the fence, and tried to keep a happy medium.

Who knows how this acrobatic display might have ended, had it not been for the incident in Eremo's inn, and had the loathsome gossip and inventions of Kvachi's secret enemies not poisoned everything. Further hesitation was out of the question. Kvachi took the necessary steps. He attended several secret meetings to try out his gift for oratory.

Here too he turned out to have great ability. He showed himself to have fire, pathos, aplomb, and to be clearly capable of delighting and inspiring his listeners and himself.

Things were easily and quickly sorted. In a week Kvachi became the talk of Kutaisi. But Kvachi was not particularly pleased by this sort of fame. He couldn't help overdoing things and getting himself involved up to the neck. This was very dangerous, so he had to take the appropriate step backwards, and when he had got the case that had opened against him closed and thrown the ball back in his enemies' faces, Kvachi achieved a state of complete equilibrium: he was down to the waist in one camp, and sunk up to the waist in the other.

It was then that Kvachi acquired the wisdom of the old parrot sitting on its perch, swaying from left to right and repeating a magic formula, "Not to the left, not to the right... Not this way, not that way … I want you, but I love him …"

Kvachi's involvement in politics had an unexpected consequence: the famous and respected Kolia Arevadze once asked him, "Do you know the Karopoulos family?"

"I know them very well."

"I believe you and the Karopoulos boy, Kipriane, are friends, aren't you?"

"We're good friends."

After this exchange Kvachi and Arevadze met several times in secret and whispered conspiratorially. From then on Kvachi went to see the Karopoulos family more often. Karopoulos was a Greek. He was in the coal industry, and spent more than half his time in the mining town of Chiatura, while his family lived in Kutaisi, since he sent his sons to the grammar school there. His eldest son Kipriane sat next to Kvachi in class, which is how their friendship was struck up.

Kvachi and Kipriane often went to the boulevard, the theatre, and to Sapichkhia, Saghoria, Choma, and other places for relaxation and amusement. Lately Kvachi had made great efforts to get Kipriane involved in playing cards, going out with women, and feasting, but his efforts failed, because Kipriane was his father's son: reserved and timorous.

Arevadze and Kvachi had had supper together the day before. They were both stirred up and heated; their extensive silent conversation ended with Kvachi asking, "Well then, is it all settled?"

"It's settled. One fifth is yours."

"Agreed, then, although I ought to get more, but because it's for the good of the country, I agree."

"You do understand the plan, don't you? The business won't go badly for you. will it?"

"Don't worry. I'll be there at ten o'clock precisely. Everything's ready."

"Right then, till we meet again."

"Good luck!"

The next day was Sunday. Kvachi, Kipriane, Sonia Khvichia, and Marusia Chalidze had agreed the day before to have a Sunday picnic in Saghoria forest. At ten o'clock on the dot all four were to set off in a cab. Kipriane was crazy about Sonia and consequently couldn't wait for the day to dawn.

That was the arrangement, but the next day Kvachi told Kipriane, "Last night some other people decided to come with us. They've all left. You and I are going together. The rest of them will meet us there. So, let's be off."

The two of them got into a cab and left. They paid off the cab at Eremo's inn and went the rest of the way on foot. Kvachi was telling his friend, "Let's go down here ... That's where they'll meet us ... Look, that's where they'll be ... Now go left ... to the right ... Fine, we've arrived ... Just ten yards left!!"

They walked and searched. Suddenly four strangers fell upon them. All four surrounded Kvachi and Kipriane: the four revolvers in their hands flashed.

"Not a squeak out of you! Don't move a muscle, or we'll finish you off! Follow us!"

Kvachi leapt into the bushes, but an iron hand immediately grabbed him by the back of the neck. A struggle broke out, and the bushes crackled as the two men fought. Kvachi managed to slip out of the bandit's grasp, and disappeared into the bushes. They ran for some time, laughing at each other and whispering:

"Fine, that's enough, or else you'll rip all my clothes to pieces ..."

"That doesn't matter a bit more, let's run a bit more."

In the end they lost sight of each other.

Kvachi lost his way in the forest and wandered about for some time at random: two hours later he turned up at Eremo's inn covered in scratches, his clothes in tatters, his hat lost. At the very same time Sonia, Marusia, and the others turned up. They questioned each other and realized that Kvachi must have got the meeting place wrong and had led Kipriane down some other path. There was a commotion, a lot of running about, searching for the missing Kipriane.

Several days passed. There was shrieking and wailing, weeping and mourning to be heard in the Karopoulos family. Kvachi tore his hair, struck his head, showed distress. He treated his "wounds" and hung around the Karopoulos family.

Finally old Karopoulos received a two-word radio-telegram: "Twenty thousand." He replied in two words, "Five thousand."—"Fifteen."—"Ten."—"We agree, it's a bargain."

An agreement was reached and concluded, "Nobody is to see Kipriane again in the streets of Kutaisi."

A month later Karopoulos's mines were transferred to the ownership of Saropoulos; Karopoulos and his family got on a boat for Istanbul.

Only once they were aboard the ship did Kipriane and his parents open their mouths.

Kvachi Kvachantiradze moved to a new apartment, hired a carriage by the month, bought himself a new Cossack tunic, armed himself to the teeth, brought joy to his parents, and stopped his enemies in their tracks.

Did Kvachi at any time believe that he and his companions were really concocting an action "for the good of the country" that summer in Saghoria forest? Who knows? What is clear is that the "whole country" believed that Kvachi had not intended anything more than that. So, young Kvachi won a sum of money and glory too.

Graduating from School and Rescuing a Widow

Once Kvachi had money in his pocket, he leapt ten rungs up the ladder of life in one go. He had new devilish obsessions and his heart was even more furiously ablaze. He widened his circle of friends and relatives, his life and his world became broader: everything blossomed and became sweet and agreeable for him. Kvachi began his new life, on what was a black day for Tsviri, by moving lock, stock, and barrel to Tbilisi Street, where he moved into an apartment belonging to a Russian lady, Mrs Volkova. Tsviri saw her cockerel fly off with tears in her eyes, but Kvachi showed the necessary command of the situation and firmness of character to tell his first love calmly and gravely:

"Listen to me, Tsviri, everything has a beginning and an end. You shouldn't go on about it, you shouldn't cry, or else your nearest and dearest will catch on, the world will notice, and they will see you disgraced. I'm all right, I'm an inexperienced youth, you should think about yourself. You're a woman of thirty-five, you have a family, you've been around, and you've settled down. I shan't forget your kindness and love to the day I die. I'll pay you back everything I owe tenfold. Don't let your instincts carry you away. Use your brains, and we'll both be all right. Stay calm, that room of yours won't stay empty. You know Beso Shikia? He's a nice boy, isn't he? He'll move into that room tomorrow. I expect you'll find it easy to come to terms. So: use your wits and stay calm, I tell you. Give my regards to Budu. Goodbye, Tsviri, darling!"

And she calmed down, although she still shed a few tears.

Tsviri bravely stopped weeping for her love, she really did repress her instincts, and she followed Kvachi's advice: nor did she regret doing so. Two days later she "lent" Beso Shikia three roubles and told him:

"When you have the money, you can pay me back. What do you mean, with interest? Of course! Would I lend money without interest? Beso, dear, buy yourself whatever you want, don't be embarrassed; I don't have a lot, but I can always manage to find a little bit for you."

There was no need to be wary of Beso, either, because he was even less capable than Kvachi of being "embarrassed."

That's how Tsviri Sholia calmed down and quickly found consolation.

Kvachi had rented a beautiful room: it was big, light, and had softly upholstered furniture. Mrs Volkova, a quiet, meek, good-hearted, elderly Russian widow—a real *matushka*—soon took a liking to Kvachi. She was a little vague, dim-witted, and almost deaf, and now understood little of what was going on around her; she was almost blind and could hardly see anything. They did not get in each other's way, they treated each other with respect, smiled sweetly, and lived like mother and son.

It was soon the month for the eighth form's examinations: it was May. That year was Kvachi's last at school. He and his friends were kept busy. This year was one when pupils pestered teachers and made them dance to their tune. The business of examinations was easily settled for everyone's convenience. Because the teachers were conducting the examinations in the presence of the pupils, the teachers were as soft, submissive, and pliable as eunuchs faced with a wrathful sultan. Only Siriadis, the Greek language teacher, dug his heels in and would not budge. He didn't believe in the changed balance of powers that was supposed to have happened, nor did he believe in the "Russian spring", nor in the new "committees." The pupils thought, and finally Kvachi said, "Give me three days."

On the morning of the third day Siriadis received a letter. The corners of the letter were decorated with a skull, a coffin, a dagger, and a pistol. It read: "Not a single pupil in the eighth form is to fail. If you agree, then show yourself to us on the boulevard at eight o'clock this evening. If you don't turn up, then pack your bags and leave Kutaisi within three days. Otherwise, we advise you to get your coffin ready now. Signed, The Main Anarchist-Syndicalist-Socialist Committee."

Kvachi spent a whole hour on the boulevard, but Siriadis didn't show up. Instead, Shikia, Chipuntiradze, and Chikinjiladze came.

"Trouble?"

They made short work of it.

"We beat him black and blue. We'd been keeping an eye on him. He was going to the police to lay a complaint. We kept hitting him until he yelled, 'Nobody is going to fail, nobody.' Then we came to an agreement and sorted it out."

Siriadis kept his promise and everyone, in fact, passed the exam.

That's how Kvachi Kvachantiradze and his friends graduated from school and got their diplomas.

Kvachi went to Samtredia for Easter. He was the talk of everyone: his parents, his relatives and his admirers were overjoyed, his enemies were furious. He stirred up the local girls, vexed the local lads, and put husbands on their guard, before returning to Kutaisi with instructions and warnings from Silibistro:

"Kvachi, son. The country's gone to the dogs. I've got a lot of enemies on my back. I'm getting old. If I have to, I'll sell up, go begging, but I shan't leave you without an education. You can't be a man these days without a school-leaving certificate. And I've made sure you're a nobleman; I've seen you through grammar school. I'll put a few pennies your way, but you've got to lift a finger. Cholia and Ghvichia have now both finished university in Russia, and they didn't get a penny from home. What do you say to that, Kvachi son?"

Kvachi's answer was to put a hundred-rouble note in his father's hand and to leave. There was great amazement, joy, celebration, conceit, and self-congratulation in Silibistro's family: at the age of nineteen, Kvachi was going to Russia at his own expense and yet was helping his parents out. That's the sort of son you want, for sure!

From then on Kvachi walked about, plunged in thought. He acted like a scent hound, sniffing the air as he gathered information; he befriended the widow Volkova and played *konchinka*, an easy card game, with her. He lost tiny sums each time. Sometimes he even helped her, fetching her pension from the town treasury, doing the shopping when the weather was bad, reading the newspaper to her. Because evil-doing, slander, envy, and hostility were greatly on the increase at the time, he was offering her protection from evil people.

One day the widow received a letter. The corners of the letter were decorated with a skull, a coffin, a dagger, and a pistol. It read, "Get three thousand roubles ready for us within three days. Otherwise, order yourself a coffin right away. Signed, The Main Anarchist-Syndicalist-Socialist Committee."

The terrified widow fell upon Kvachi for advice and help. Who else could a lonely old woman, who had come from Tambov to live in a remote, unknown land, turn to? Kvachi thought hard, very hard, and became gloomy. Finally, he told her:

"I'll tell you as I would my own mother. Don't say a word about this to anyone, or even Christ and God himself can't help you. These are cruel, savage people. They show no mercy to women or to the old. Just this week they've killed two women, strangled an old man with their bare hands, and thrown one into the River Rioni. Even the police are terrified. Nobody's dared stick their head outside. So you see they slaughter people like birds. Well, just the day before yesterday they murdered a policeman at the market right in front of everyone."

Some of what Kvachi said was true, some he had made up. The times really were like that. The defenceless widow knew that the country too was defenceless, so she trembled and begged Kvachi in a whisper to help her and intercede; at the same time she swore on an icon and the gospels that she would take the secret with her to the grave.

To begin with, Kvachi obstinately refused. He himself feared the danger and of the anarchist-syndicalists who "show no mercy to anyone and slaughter everyone like birds." Finally, though, he relented and gave in, because he loved the poor widow Volkova "like his own mother."

That day Kvachi got down to a task that was "extremely complicated and dangerous."

"We Georgians have this proverb: 'Thrash the uncalled-for messenger and throw him out'," he told the widow. "There's another saying, though: 'A troublemaker gets hit once, a helper gets hit five times.'"

In the end, however, he got a lead, and this is the story he told the old lady, who was exhausted and enfeebled with fear:

"May God protect you and even your enemies from this lot! What do you expect from me, why have you got me into this, what did you want me to do? Now they've got me in their clutches and they're threatening me that if I don't come up with at least two thousand roubles, they'll kill me as well as the old woman. The time runs out tomorrow evening; God, help me!"

The widow was dumbstruck and her heart began to race; Kvachi went on beseeching her:

"Please, get me out of this dangerous business. God, how have I got into this mess? What business is it of mine, what harm did I do those wolves, why have they got it in for me?"

That evening the widow and Kvachi whispered for some time before they finally decided: fifteen hundred roubles would be enough to get them out of this trouble. The widow had five hundred roubles saved up and Kvachi would borrow the rest from relatives by offering security, or he could mortgage the house, and to do that he would need to have power of attorney from the widow Volkova. The next day the widow would sign over that power to him. Kvachi would come back in the evening with everything sorted out. If he couldn't get the money, he wouldn't come back, he'd give the robbers the slip and hide in Samtredia.

The old woman didn't sleep that night, either. She prayed until morning, groaned, and made the divan, as old as herself, creak. Kvachi fell asleep at first light, for the widow's quandary had been preoccupying and worrying him.

The next day they both went to see the notary. Kvachi put the mortgage document and the complete power of attorney in his pocket and rushed to the railway station. That day was as black as night for the old widow. In the evening Kvachi returned in a joyful mood. The widow was so pleased to see Kvachi come back, as though she had increased her modest wealth instead of spending all her money. Kvachi took five hundred roubles from the widow and rushed off to see the anarchist-syndicalist committee.

That night Kvachi Kvachantiradze saved the elderly widow from certain death and the anarchist-syndicalist committee from its hundredth sin: he had got to them just in time, got them to agree to fifteen hundred roubles and handed them the money. If he hadn't got there in time, three men, already masked and ready to go, would have set off. The old lady wept with joy and fear and again got into a panic. The next day she ordered thanksgiving prayers to be said, then, as a sign of her gratitude and motherly feelings, she hung a gold cross round Kvachi's neck and as a memento put her late husband's silver tobacco box in his pocket. She told him:

"Son, if you're ever in trouble, pray to that cross. God won't forget your kindness and will help you in everything you do. I won't forget you, either, and if I survive I'll show you my gratitude again; if I don't, then ..."

Then she embraced him, kissed him, burst into tears, and nearly made Kvachi weep, too.

That was how the knight of Samtredia saved the *matushka* of Tambov from certain death.

Music Studies

This was when Kvachi was suddenly carried away by music. He'd never understood music and had no ear at all for it. He was indifferent to all musical instruments, except the grand piano which made his whole body tingle, set his heart pounding with excitement, and perturbed him. At first he wanted to buy a grand piano, but it was too expensive, so he decided to hire one. He knew someone called Maizelsohn who was going to Borjomi for the summer. Kvachi told him:

"By the way, you're off to Borjomi, aren't you? You won't be back before autumn, will you? I'll be staying in Kutaisi all that time. I've got masses of things to do. I should mention that my latest craze is music. I'm so enthusiastic that I've nearly gone mad about it. I want to learn to play. Better late than never, so would you please hire your grand piano to me?"

Maizelsohn had never ever thought about anything except his own advantage and survival, so he immediately calculated, "I'll charge you thirty roubles for three months; that'll pay for my travel, so that's fine." They agreed on the price there and then; that same evening, in his own room, Kvachi was banging with one finger at Maizelsohn's piano.

Summer was coming to an end. Any moment Maizelsohn was due to come back. Kvachi was in a hurry, even a flap. He and Beso Shikia had a whispered conversation. The next day Beso turned up at the music shop and quietly asked a shop customer, "Excuse me, you don't want a grand piano, do you? It's an urgent sale. It's a beautiful instrument, a Becker, almost brand new. It's a few doors away, not far at all. Whose is it? It belongs to a friend of mine, his name is Prince Severian Dadiani. Here we are, Tbilisi Street, Volkova's house."

In the end a certain Arutinov turned up. The piano was tried out and approved. The price?

"Seven hundred roubles."

"Four hundred."

"Six hundred."

"Five hundred."

Just for you I'll let it go at that price. Are you taking it now?"

"I have to send it to Poti today."

Kvachi frowned and thought about it for a minute. The con-trick was devised without further thought: "If you like, I'll send it to you myself."

"If you can do me the favor, I'll be very grateful. That will save me a day's work. What do you say, Siranush?" Arutinov asked his wife.

"We couldn't do better than that!"

"Right then: let's have the piano boxed up right now, sent to the railway station, and despatched. Come this evening to the Hotel France and ask for me, I'm in room number one. Bring me the railway receipt, and you can have the rest of the money; will two hundred do for your expenses and as a deposit for now?"

"That's fine. I'll get you the receipt straight away. But there's one more request and condition I have: don't say anything to anyone; don't mention my name or this piano anywhere. I'm very embarrassed at having to sell it, because …"

"Very good. That's no problem. I give you my word; you Georgians are very proud people."

"That's only too true. It's considered a disgrace for us, especially for a Prince Dadiani, to have to sell such a possession."

The Arutinovs left. Kvachi set off to the railway station. That same day "Prince Dadiani" visited Arutinov in his hotel.

"I've got everything ready for you. I managed to box it up and send it just in time. Here's the railway receipt."

Arutinov unfolded the receipt and examined it. "Despatched? From Kutaisi. Destination? Poti. Goods sent? Grand piano. Weight? 800 kilos. Name of sender? Prince Dadiani. Name of recipient? Arutinov."

"Packing and transport charges?"

Forty-one roubles, thirty-five kopecks. Here's the receipt.

Arutinov calculated: "So I owe you 559 roubles and two kopecks, right?"

"Right."

"You've received two hundred, so I still owe you 359 roubles, two kopecks. Here you are."

"Correct. Have a good journey."

"What's the hurry? Stay for a bit and have some tea with us!" Siranush Arutinova invited Kvachi.

"Many thanks, but I'm pressed for time. People are waiting for me."

"Well, if you ever find yourself in Poti, please come and see us. We live just opposite the town park."

"I'd love to … I'm sure we'll meet again. I'm very pleased to have met you. Have a good journey."

The next day Beso Shikia tackled someone called Sarokin: "Excuse me, aren't you looking for a grand piano? There's one available for a quick sale. It's a beautiful Becker grand, almost new, only a few doors away, not far at all … Why don't you come and have a look?"

Again the piano was tried out and a bargain was struck.

"I'm not local: I have to take it to Chiatura."

"Then we'll send it to you … If you like, I'll get you the railway receipt in the next two hours."

They agreed to that. Again, Kvachi set off to the station. That evening Kvachi brought the railway receipt to engineer Sarokin in the Hotel Orient: "From Kutaisi to Chiatura, one grand piano, weight 800 kilos, sent by Prince Dadiani to engineer Sarokin. Paid: 11 roubles and 29 kopecks."

They did their sums and concluded, "Good night to you," and "Have a good journey."

Beso Shikia was waiting for Kvachi in the street.

"Ah, Beso, tomorrow at the latest we've got to have everything sewn up. Have you found someone?"

"I've wangled it. Let's go."

"Who is it? Don't do anything stupid, don't tell anyone local:

not even a trader or a Jew, or else ..."

"Aha, do you think I don't know? He's a tax inspector, his name is Gertsov, he got married a month ago. He rented a flat yesterday and now he's buying furniture. He only came to Kutaisi a week ago."

The next morning Gertsov, a conceited young official, brought six workmen to Kvachi's room and moved the grand piano to his new home. The same day Kvachi Kvachantiradze and Besarion Shikia were re-baptised as students: they put on new student uniforms, showed off their new looks, and suddenly gained in prestige, value, and maturity in their own, each other's, their friends' and acquaintances' eyes.

There were two days and two nights of non-stop vortex, flurry, and shrieking in Laitadze's and Eremo's inns. Wine flowed like water, all the local chickens and turkeys were slaughtered, the heavens were deafened by revolver shots, the innkeepers and their servants were streaming with sweat, the clarinet players' jaws were breaking, Daniel the Jew lost his voice, the balalaika player's fingers were wrecked, the barrel-organ grinder wore his organ out, twenty cabbies had galloped their horses into the ground, and the women at this orgy, hardly able to stand for exhaustion and lack of sleep, begged to be allowed to go.

Kvachi, sozzled and sated, kept telling everyone:

"What is it? Money, you say? Nobody dare talk about money. I'm paying for everything. Tomorrow at ten o'clock you can all call on me and I'll settle the bill. Tomorrow you're all my guests: Eremo, Daniel, the boys, the women, and the cabbies, too. Eremo! On Sunday Beso Shikia is inviting us all. Get ready; don't let me down, Daniel! Get your voice in order! Lads. Another round of drinks! Eremo, I'm drinking your health!" And he said such sweet, friendly, brotherly things to Eremo, who was bloated and besotted, that he himself burst into tears and made Eremo cry too. Eremo's lips and cheeks were raw with all the kisses, the cellar was drained of wine, the food was all eaten, and they rushed back to Kutaisi with such banging and thunder, yelling and shrieking, that anyone not in the know would have thought the enemy had demolished the castle and, drunk with victory, had invaded the city.

When it was past midnight, a carriage left Kutaisi for Khoni. Two young men were in it. They were both wearing balaclavas, so that nobody could manage to see their faces or recognize them. The carriage thundered around Laitadze's inn at speed. The travelers huddled up and slipped down behind their luggage. When they'd left the inn well behind them, they both rose up, sat up straight, took their balaclavas off, and breathed a sigh of relief. Finally, one of them called out, "Goodbye Kutaisi!"

"Goodbye," repeated the other. "Who knows when we'll meet again?"

The next day, from ten o'clock onwards the widow Volkova had no time to do anything but open the door and reply to everyone in Russian: "They've gone! I'm telling you, they've gone. They've gone for good, for good. I'm fed up with them! Lord, they've driven me to distraction!"

Eremo, Daniel, and Laitadze were all gnashing their teeth outside the Volkova house; the organ-grinders were using the worst Tbilisi swear-words, the women were cursing in Russian; the cabbies had worn out their horses and ransacked Kutaisi, trying to track Kvachantiradze down.

Three days later Maizelsohn came back from Borjomi; at the same time Arutinov arrived from Poti and Sarokin came down from Chiatura. All three were covered with sweat from running about; then they all rushed in to see Gertsov. The four men met in Gertsov's drawing room, all four wrestled for possession of the piano, yelling together, "It's mine! Mine!"

After wearing themselves out yelling and squabbling, they sat down and told each other what had happened to them and tried to prove their right to the piano. Maizelsohn was relatively calm;

he laughed at the others and mocked them, while the other three men uttered curses and threats. The matter was finally settled by Gertsov buying the same piano again from Maizelsohn, while Arutinov went back to Poti empty-handed, the embittered Sarokin went back up to Chiatura. Kvachi, however, was left in peace, because by then the whole country was ungovernable, and searching for Kvachi, who had vanished into Russia, would have been a waste of time for anyone.

Anyway, squeezing an impoverished student would be like trying to get blood from a stone.

What can you do? Everything in this world seems to be a matter of calculation.

Buying a House

At the same time the widow Volkova received a notarized summons from Khukhu Chichia. She read it: it was a bolt from the blue. Her eyes rolled up to her forehead, she was dumbstruck, she went weak at the knees, and her heart nearly stopped beating. Thank God that her neighbor Ladi Chikinjiladze appeared in time to revive her. The elderly widow would not have recovered consciousness: her head and hands were shaking, she moved her lips but was barely able to speak. Finally, she read the summons once more and fainted again. This Chichia had written:

"On the seventh of July this year I bought your house (situated in Kutaisi on Tbilisi street) from Kvachi, son of Silibistro Kvachantiradze, who possessed a complete power of attorney signed by you, witnessed on the seventh of July this year by the notary Anjaparidze. Furthermore, on the same day I lent you four thousand roubles in cash against a promissory note signed by you, which note expires on the first of September this year. I request that within seven days you vacate the house in my favor, because I myself intend to move into what is now my house, and within three days

to pay back the debt in my favor.
Khukhu Chichia,
Samtredia,
Khoni Road, Pupi Kvachantiradze's house."

That same evening Mrs Volkova trudged off to see the famous lawyer Tvichia. He was a lawyer recommended by her lodger Ladi Chikinjiladze: what would a woman of sixty know of the vicissitudes of the law and of lawyers, when all she had heard up till now was that somewhere there existed strict judges, lawyers who saved the unfortunate, merciless prosecutors and "poor convicts, forsaken by God and man?" How could a old woman who'd lost most of her wits know that there had been a dinner that day in Sholia's inn on Balakhvani Street, at which were present Silibistro Kvachantiradze, Khukhu Chichia, Tvichia, and the widow's lodger Ladi Chikinjiladze, who brought the decrepit Russian lady so kindly and respectfully to the doors of the famous lawyer Tvichia? How could a gullible, naïve, and ignorant woman from Tambov have possibly thought or even contemplated that Tvichia was in fact acting for Silibistro Kvachantiradze and Khukhu Chichia, and that the letter which shocked her so badly that morning was written and sent that day by Tvichia?

Smiling and affectionate, Tvichia received Mrs Volkova with great respect. Sweet talk, hot tea, and rose-petal jam softened the woman's heart, enchanting her so that she was putty in Tvichia's hands.

When the tearful widow had bared her heart and entrusted herself to him, Tvichia thought hard and then told her, in a solemn and sincere tone:

"I feel sorry for you, so sorry, as if you were my own mother. But being sorry is not enough to help things. For one thing, you appear to have given the anarchists financial help. If the government ever finds out that you're involved, you'll be hanged or spend the rest of your life in Siberia. Don't be alarmed, calm down. I know that you didn't knowingly give them this money, but that makes no difference, they had money from you and profited from it. You can thank the good Lord that you've come to me. Anyone else would not have kept silence, they would have talked about it to someone and you would have been finished. But I'll give you one piece of advice, as I would to my own mother or any decent person: never ever talk again about this business to anyone. I advise you to take it with you to the grave, otherwise, I repeat, there is no way you'll avoid either penal servitude or the gallows. Now for the second thing: you appear to have given Kvachantiradze a complete power of attorney, that is, you have given him the right to sell your house. Thirdly: you also gave him a promissory note for four thousand roubles. What do you say, that it was meant to be for ten roubles? Is anything specified in the promissory note? Do you have a witness? Then there's no point discussing it further. If you start arguing about that, then the subject of helping anarchists will come out into the open, and then you can expect to be hanged or to go to Siberia."

The lawyer went on for some time instilling fear and panic into the widow, and finished by telling the dumbfounded and enfeebled woman:

"This is my advice, in all sincerity: I know this Chichia. Perhaps I can arrange for him to let you have a room in the house and whatever furniture you need. You have a small pension, you can earn a little by sewing and doing housework. That's all a single woman can ask for. I advise you, as a son would his mother, to agree to this, otherwise you end up with nothing and you won't be able to blame me. Well, have you thought about it? Fine, give it some thought and come back, but watch out: don't talk about this business to anyone, otherwise … Good night. Sleep well. Do come back …" And he showed the staggering woman to the door.

Once in the street the widow happened to come across Ladi

Chikinjiladze, who had trouble getting her back home. That evening and the next day Chikinjiladze never left the sick woman's side. After prolonged prayers, thought, groans, and weeping, she went back to see Tvichia and told him:

"I agree, but help me to get a bite to eat and a corner to stay in my house."

Tvichia had no trouble arranging that in a flash.

A week later Silibistro Kvachantiradze sold his Samtredia "hotel" by the Khoni road, packed up a few of his possessions, and moved to his own house in Kutaisi, a house which, to use his own words, he had got through hard work and the sweat of his brow from a lonely widow; he was so sorry for the widow that he gave her a little, ill-lit room under the stairs, and let her have a few sticks of furniture.

Khukhu Chichia's wife, Kvachi Kvachantiradze's grandmother, the respected Auntie Notio, on the first night they spent in the new house on Tbilisi Street, reminded everyone:

"Mark what I said the night that little Kvachi was born: the sun shone overhead like a crown. That was a sign that Kvachi could expect a brilliant and famous future. That day, when lightning struck the poplar and devils took away Zhondia's inn, was a sign that Kvachi's enemies—God protect us!—would be struck by lightning and their hearts would burst, just like the poplar was split in two. When Silibistro found a silver rouble, that meant, I told you, Kvachi would be rich. I said all that nineteen years ago. Haven't my words come true?"

Everyone recalled Notio's prophecy and they all agreed that it had come true. Silibistro recalled something else:

"Do you remember when little Kvachiko used to cry he kept calling out 'Me-me?' I said at the time, this child won't let anyone else take anything off him, but he'll get his hands on the whole world. Isn't what I said coming true?"

They agreed Silibistro was right.

"My darling little Kvachi," added his mother Pupi: "he's given me a house in Kutaisi for my old age."

"Yes, in his own house!" concluded Kvachi's grandfather, Khukhu Chichia, as he turned to Silibistro. "Hey, Silibistro? Have you been left wanting for anything? Just a lieutenant's rank and epaulettes and... would there be a marshal in Georgia better off than you?"

"It's all in God's hands, thanks to the dear Lord," said Pupi to end the conversation.

Silibistro had a disturbed sleep that night: he strutted and puffed himself out because he dreamt that he'd become Lord Lieutenant of the Nobility, wearing ten stars on his chest and a cross round his neck. His epaulettes shone brightly, and he was wearing the white, gold-braided uniform of a lord-in-waiting, while behind he was girded with a sign of the Tsar's special favor, a big gold key.

That very night his glorious, famous son Kvachi was in Batumi, buying a ticket for the voyage to Russia.

Going to Russia to Seek His Dream Woman

At four in the morning Kvachi emerged at Samtredia railway station. He was accompanied by Silibistro, Pupi, and Khukhu: they were all moving permanently to Kutaisi. The officials at the station were amazed to see Kvachi, because about ten years before there had been a persistent rumor in Samtredia that Kvachi had gone to the theological seminary at Kazan. Samtredia's womenfolk were virtually in tears, lamenting:

"Oh, poor man! Isn't it a sin to bury alive such a handsome young man? Kvachi in a monastery?! Oh no, his poor mother Pupi: I hope she doesn't end up in a convent, too! There must be something behind all this!"

When Silibistro sold his house the Samtredia gossip became

a real phenomenon.

"Didn't I tell you Pupi is off to be a nun? And they say Kvachi is going to Kazan or somewhere to be a monk. That was too much for Pupi, so she's going to Bodbe convent; that's why she's divorcing and why Silibistro's sold his house and, they say, is going to be the Lord Lieutenant in Kutaisi."

That was pretty well the Samtredia gossip when Silibistro's family had gathered at the station; while they waited for the train, they all had tea with lemon and pastries. Silibistro told three or four of his friends:

"I'm fed up with living here. I'm going to Kutaisi for good. I've had enough of the respect I get in Samtredia, now I'll see what I get in Kutaisi ... The house? Yes indeed, I've bought a little house, but I had to pay dearly for it. Becoming Lord Lieutenant? Well, I'm not thinking about that, though I was asked ..."

Thundering and puffing, the train from Tbilisi came in. They all rushed around lifting Kvachi's luggage into the carriage before they themselves got in. They hugged Kvachi, kissed him over and over again, wept, and gave him endless bits of advice. Finally Silibistro, too, embraced his one and only consolation, saying:

"Well, Kvachi, sonny, now we're going to be far away from each other. You've now got more learning and experience than I've ever had, you manage things better, but I'll say a couple of things all the same. You're going into the world, son, I expect you'll settle in in a couple of days, but you could come to grief, so be very careful. You'll meet thousands of different people in Russia; there are more desperate rogues there than there are clever, respectable people. Mix with important people and avoid having dealings with troublemakers, hail-fellow-well-met, wretched peasants. Keep away from wine, women, and cards, because they'll put you on the road to ruin. Don't forget your mother and father, and write to me about it all. Well, son, we rely on you ...It's up to you ..."

Everyone burst into tears again. The train moved off and

disappeared in the murk. Kvachi's eyes drooped.

He woke up when they got to Kobuleti and the coast. Dawn was breaking. To the right, the Black Sea was spread out, boundless, gray-blue, glittering, and crystal-clear. The train sometimes rushed along the seashore, sometimes veered a little inland to the left. The sea murmured gently, moaned like a fabulous dragon, hissed, rustled. The sea followed the green avenue of bracken, sometimes on one side, sometimes on both. On the left the train rushed past rocks clothed in ivy, hills covered in dense forest, neat and cosy country houses. One superannuated student was talking to two other passengers:

"That giant whitish tree is a eucalypt. Mosquitoes hate it, because they can't stand the scent ... And those trees with bunches of pink flowers hanging down are rhododendrons, they're called European rhododendrons. The dense thick undergrowth here is Chinese and Japanese bamboo. It's very useful: they make furniture, huts, and thousands of things out of it ... This is the local fir tree, *Abies nordmanniana* ... That's an Italian pine ... That's a conifer called Biota: a handsome, neat plant, isn't it. That's a cypress, sorry, you already know that, I expect ... it's our plane tree. That's an aspen. That's what we call an *ieli*, or 'black mane': others call it an azalea ... Those are lemon and orange orchards ... That's a tea plantation ... We've reached Tsikhisdziri now: in 1871 Russians and Georgians killed an awful lot of people here, but the Ottomans wouldn't surrender it. Now we're at Chakva. There's a famous botanical garden here, it's the second greatest in the world ... What's the greatest? Melbourne botanical gardens are the greatest, in Australia ... Now we've reached Makhinjauri. Here is where the forts are. Over there, on top of the mountain, is Egre Fort, after it comes Hamidiye, before it is Megruli, and on the right, on the seashore is Bartskhana."

The train rushed noisily through Bartskhana. Listening to the student had made Kvachi giddy. In his own homeland, apart from

Samtredia and Kutaisi, there seemed to be thousands of things that he did not yet know about or had never seen.

The passengers crowded the carriage windows, staring at the bewildering panorama to the left and the right of them, loudly expressing their delight and amazement. Kvachi was very impressed by the orchards and country houses, but he could never understand or share some of the passengers' joy and childlike clamor at the spectacle of the eye-catching natural beauty or the boundless, restless, and furious sea. The sea was beautiful at a distance, but Kvachi intuited its treachery, its changeability, and in anticipation he was filled with fear, trembling, and distrust.

After flying through Bartskhana, the train slowed down and solemnly slipped into Batumi station. Kvachi came out onto the platform, strolled about, and met about ten students from Kutaisi. There were a lot from Tbilisi, too. They got to know each other, asked each other about their lives, and decided to see the sights of Batumi. They left their luggage at the station and set off for the town centre.

The ship was leaving at midnight. Kvachi was followed by a few of his newfound friends. They walked the streets, saw the city park, and strolled for some time along the seashore, toured the Buruntabiye lighthouse and guns, and the Aziziye mosque, and finally reached the sea port, which was full of ships, sailing boats, and steamboats. Here the long, tall, and handsome *Pushkin* was docked. The travelers had already gone up to stroll on deck. The ship was still loading and being washed: smoke came from its funnels and it was getting ready to depart.

Some of the travelers were amazed by everything: the clean city, the handsome boulevard, the exotic vegetation, the enormous sea, the sailboats and ships; but Kvachi was unmoved and inspected everything so casually and cursorily as if none of it was unfamiliar or new to him. In the evening he bought a second-class ticket and boarded.

It was a warm evening. The seashore was brightly lit with a string of electric lights: the seaport was illuminated by red, green, yellow, and white fire. The pitch-black sea glittered in bands reflecting this fire. The seaport was slashed every now and again by ships and from them came the sound of Russian and Georgian singing and yelling, laughter, and giggling.

Suddenly ten or so cabs packed with students came up to the ship. They stormed the ship with such shrieks, yells, and roars that they seemed to be taking it captive. They rushed aboard and occupied the deck as if it were their own back yard. Soon they gathered again at the ship's prow. Flutes were blown, drums were banged, there was a burst of applause, and they started a crazy Lezginka dance, shouting, "*Tashi-tushi, tashi-tushi!*"

The captain tried to quieten them down, but turned back thwarted. He muttered his resentment to the other passengers, "They're savages, real savages! I know they'll wreak havoc if I say anything; they could knife me in the belly."

Kvachi smiled and chimed in agreement, "You're right, captain. They're real savages. I know their sort only too well."

The passengers and the captain turned to Kvachi, "Aren't you a Georgian, too?"

Kvachi hadn't got his answer ready, so, a little embarrassed, he stammered, "Hmm ... I am, but ... I'm Georgian by origin. My father was Gurian, my mother Mingrelian, but I was born and grew up in Imeretia. We're related to Georgians, but ... all the same ... Mingrelians and Georgians don't understand each others' language."

The captain and one official took what Kvachi had said the right way: they loosened their tongues, rolled up their sleeves, shed their reserve, undid the muzzle of politeness, and for a whole hour they rolled Kvachi's friends and their relatives in the dirt. Kvachi expressed his agreement by nodding every other second, saying:

"Yes indeed ... it couldn't be truer ... they're all drunks, robbers, terrorists, and blackmailers ... Yes indeed, you've seen through them. Half of them never graduated properly from school. Either their certificates are fakes, or they got them by extortion, or bought them for cash ... Who knows how many of them are robbers, pimps, or kidnappers?"

He gave them half a dozen examples, some true, some made up, and then added:

"You're aware that the most important thing is family, upbringing, tradition, religious faith. They don't have families, they don't believe in upbringing or tradition, or God, or the devil."

Once Kvachi's listeners decided he was a man of their mind and beliefs, they were more drawn to him, they felt less inhibited, shared their interests and their intimate thoughts with him. Finally the captain asked Kvachi:

"I do apologize ... I'd like to get to know a young man as clever and decent as you are. My name is Sidorov."

"I'm delighted to make your acquaintance, delighted! I'm Prince Kvachantiradze."

And Silibistro's son shook everyone's hands with genuine princely dignity.

The words "Lord Lieutenant" had been on the tip of Kvachi's tongue for some time: as nobody had ventured to ask him any pointed question about his social standing, he seized the moment and suddenly blurted out:

"My father couldn't bear being among such depraved people any more, and several times he gave up his official post—he happens to be Lord Lieutenant of the Nobility—but he was virtually forced to take it up again. Now he's serving for no salary. In fact, he's spending a lot of his own money on the post. That's nothing: everyone demands countless fraudulent things from him: exemption from military conscription, false witness, and thousands of other swindles. But my father comes from a very different sort of family and has a very different concept of service to the Tsar, the fatherland, and the nobility. I can remember several examples ..."

And "Prince" Kvachi gave them several examples of the "Lord Lieutenant of the Nobility's" loyal service, his Roman strictness, his rare decency and the depravity, the moral slough, the savage mentality, and boundless ingratitude of the Georgians. Finally the dinner bell just about rendered him speechless. They all made off towards the dining room, ejaculating as they went, "Terrible people, terrible! Leave them to their devices for just a day and they'll eat each other like wild beasts ... We do live in dangerous times ... God help us! God protect us!"

At supper Kvachi sat between a well-built, fair-haired young beauty from Odessa, and Captain Sidorov himself. When the passengers learnt that Prince Kvachi was going to Odessa, they were all very pleased, especially the blonde and Captain Sidorov, who finally told Kvachi:

"If you'd do me the honor, I'd very much like to let you have one or two rooms with my family. I don't need the money, but for a clever boy from a distinguished family, like yours, I'd do a lot. Times are bad, these are dangerous times. We don't have any men in our family and if a lad like you moves in with us, I'll have peace of mind."

How could Sidorov have known then that letting Kvachi into his family would be worse than introducing a wolf? But if everyone knew with whom they were dealing, prodigals like Kvachi would not get anywhere in this world.

Kvachi suddenly broke off his talk about being a prince, about Silibistro being a Lord Lieutenant and the people being depraved, because the passengers at the dinner table had been joined by a dozen or so students: they used all their strength, their sharp wits, politeness, honeyed speech, and expressive eyes to storm the blonde beauty, and within an hour they had captured the outer fortifications of the castle of Odessa.

When supper was over, they all went up on deck again. The ship's whistle blew three times and those who were disembarking got off, while the last passengers and travelers who had all but missed the boat got on. The gangway was put away, the anchor was weighed, and the ship, moored by a cable as thick as a man's leg, was set loose.

Finally the ship's propeller began to turn. It churned the water and the engines started clattering. The ship gravely freed itself from the quay, very slowly slipped into the middle of the harbor, turned round with difficulty, and then pointed its prow into the middle of the sea.

The noise of the engines grew louder. Then they started banging, emitting fire like a hissing dragon, groaning and rumbling. The ship shook a little, drank in the murk with majestic greed, and swished as it cut through the pitch-black bottomless and boundless sea, which barely groaned, lapped, and splashed in the darkness. The string of lights over Batumi harbor was now almost out of sight. Two big electric lights hung from the two masts lit up the ship's deck, which was now silent.

In the east, Mars glimmered. Kvachi stood all alone on the ship's prow, listening to the swishing of the sea, the loud vibration of the ship, the thumping of the engines; he stared at the black, infinite space, the countless glimmering stars fixed to the heaven's dome. It seemed to him, he thought, expected and sensed that this gigantic and boundless world had been created for him and for him alone, that this world was impatiently expecting him, the son of Silibistro of Samtredia, Kvachi Kvachantiradze, that everyone and everything in mysterious and infinite Russia was prepared for him, longing and waiting, like an unhappy woman for her brilliant fairytale prince. There would be marble palaces, slaves, and servants with bowed heads, the best ancient wines and liqueurs, French chefs, English and Arab horses. Shining automobiles, all sorts of fabulously beautiful women of every race, shape, and color, his own ivory carriage, a ship furnished with satin, damask, and velvet—a yacht and ducal rank, a court marshal's post, a ministry under the Tsar and … money, money, money, an inexhaustible, incalculable flow of money, because Silibistro's son was firmly, deeply, unshakably convinced that the axis and mother-pillar of this world was money alone, and that anything else that existed— the soul of the world, hearts, and flesh—everything without exception was only money's dust, its subservient lackey, which could always be bought, like the change of underwear he had bought that day in Batumi.

Kvachi saw dawn break and stared at the breaking light; Mars and he then smiled at each other like old cronies.

"Ah, my star! Ah, my patron and traveling companion!" Kvachi exclaimed silently, waving his arm: he greeted his heavenly friend, who cast Kvachi a glance, encouraged him, gave him faith and hope that his dreams and longings would soon be achieved.

With this firm belief and deep hope Kvachi Kvachantiradze sailed at speed to his new kingdom, where an unseen, unknown, fairytale beloved, an immaculately beautiful woman was waiting for him.

Making Friends and a Little Money, and Finding a Dream Woman

In the morning Kvachi came up onto the deck. The ship was docked at Poti. Kvachi strolled about, taking a look at things, but suddenly rushed back to his cabin and sat with the door locked until the ship sailed. The reason for his panic was simple: on shore he had spotted engineer Sarokin, to whom he had in Kutaisi sold Maizelsohn's grand piano.

When he'd escaped danger, he went back to the deck. He was nicely dressed. The sunlight generously spread an agreeable smile over the sea and landscape. The captain offered him a friendly handshake. An elderly official respectfully bowed his head; the women gave him smiles of pleasure, their eyes lit up as they tried to attract him.

The captain asked him, "I do apologize, what's your name, and your father's?"

Kvachi's birth certificate read as "Anapodiste son of Silibistro." But the Christian name was unfamiliar to almost everybody. Kvachi had long been tormented by his everyday name: "Kvachi" struck a Russian ear as obscene, so he renamed himself on the spot: "Napoleon, son of Apollo."

Everyone was overjoyed to hear this name. The blonde beauty liked it: "I don't know about Napoleon, but you're certainly an Apollo." And she devoured Kvachi with her eyes.

Kvachi immediately responded in kind: "The only thing Apollonic about me is my little finger, but you are an Aphrodite from the hair on your head to your toenails." And they went on like that, covering each other in glory.

From that day on Kvachi kept his new name whenever he was with strangers. Some people called him Napoleon, others Apollo: women turned that into "Apollonchik."

The ship's deck gradually filled up with students who had sobered up. They were no longer as rowdy as the day before, and they stopped leaping about. But they were the only people on deck and the only people whose voice was heard. They gathered in groups, joked, enjoyed themselves, laughing at the sea and the sun.

Kvachi joined one group, greeted those he already knew and told those he didn't, "Let me introduce myself: my name is Kvachantiradze."

"Really? You're Kvachantiradze? Well, I've heard thousands of good things about you in town. Well then! I'm Sedrak Havlabariani. I'm glad to have met you."

"I'm Gabo Chkhubishvili," an uncouth buffalo of a man yelled, as if he was calling out from the bottom of a clay amphora.

"*Sabah hayır olsun* (Top of the morning to you), Prince Kvachantiradze!" a strapping Jalil called shyly in Turkish and bared his teeth like a horse.

"Jalil, you here too? Where are you off to?"

"I've been to Tbilisi, bought some goods."

"How are you, Kvachi?" asked Ladi Chikinjiladze, who had joined the ship at Poti.

"All right, neither one thing, nor the other."

"Really: you walk about as if you were on top of the world."

"Thank the Lord, I'm not as on top of the world as my friends want me to be, but not so badly off as my enemies would like me to be."

The student, Tedo Qoranashvili, who had been throwing out all the Russian-Latin botanical terms like confetti, was also hanging about. Now he took up the thread of the group's conversation.

"I've used this summer to good advantage. The year before last I climbed the Arkhoti pass; last year, I climbed Qazbeg; this year I climbed the Mamison pass, and also, I've explored Svanetia. My collection has doubled in size."

Kvachi listened to the young traveler's words and tried to change the subject of the conversation. But he was unable so far to take over from the student.

"There's no mountain on earth so beautiful as Mount Ushba. How high is it? The highest mountain is Mount Elbruz, which is 18,410 feet. The next highest is Dikh-Tau, 17,054, then comes Ararat, then Kashtan-Taun, the fifth is Mqinvari, that's followed by Gistola, while Ushba is the seventh, it's 15,408 feet high, but it's the beauty of the Caucasus chain, the crown. I had military maps on me and in some places I could correct them ... I found a new variety of fir tree, I gave it the Latin name of *Abies nordmanniana georgica* ... Next summer I'm going to climb the Glukhori pass ... Traveling? No, that's not what I'm interested in. I've been looking for traveling companions for three years and I haven't been able to find a single Georgian. So it's foreigners accompanying me … That's why the Germans, English, and Russians have come to know Georgia better than the Georgians. No Gurian will go to Mingrelia, no Mingrelian goes to Kakhetia, or Kakhetian to Imeretia, while neither eastern nor western Georgian ever takes a look at Borchalo, Javakheti, Meskheti, or Adjaria-Chaneti. We have just a tiny patch of land, we're just a tiny bunch of people, but we don't yet know ourselves and we wrestle with the whole country and we want to ransack it."

Kvachi was bored listening to this walking encyclopedia. His talk and his opinions were alien to Kvachi's heart, and his brain would not take it in, so he went off and joined another group, where half a dozen young men were attacking each others like cockerels and going for each other with bitterly venomous and poisonous words: "Federation … autonomy … socialization … nationalization … municipalization … monism … materialism … idealism …"

Others stood aside. Some listened, some chatted. Among them was Beso Shikia, who had come aboard at Poti.

Kvachi quickly made a move to join this third group. Here was a congregation of well-fed and happy students. Their easy-going laughter, bass laughter, endless joking, and fish-market cursing was deafening. Kvachi felt he was immediately back in his proper setting, with kinsfolk and comrades of his own age. He wasted no time mingling, joining in, while Sedrak Havlabariani let loose a torrent of talk, with a great range of stories about many things, stories of boys' and girls' relationships, of street pedlars, pickpocketing, and debauchery.

When they got to Sukhumi, Kvachi was again subjected to Qoranashvili's information on Abkhaz-Georgian history, on Pitsunda, on the Sinop gardens, and on Sukhumi which was once called Dioscurias.

It was a hot sunny day. Saturated in heat haze, the purged sky seemed to burn. The sea slept. On the right the Caucasus chain towered into the sky. Its dark, misty green slopes rushed down to the sea, looked at their reflection, and inspected themselves. The water was a very dark greenish color. The ship was followed by dolphins which kept leaping up into the air before diving back and swiftly swaying and cutting the water with their sculpted noses and grabbing at whatever was thrown to them from the ship.

A great number of white sea birds—albatrosses, gulls, pelicans—circled round the ship.

That morning another passenger joined the students: he was a middle-aged, medium-height, well-dressed swarthy man. Beso Shikia whispered to Kvachi, "That man wants a game of whist: so give him a game."

They whispered some more, went down to the cabin, and asked for some paper. Four men played, drank wine, and snacked on fruit. Kvachi, Beso, and Ladi Chikinjiladze kept uttering in Georgian, as they played, "Big spade … little diamond … one of clubs … Hang on, I shouldn't have played it."

As they played they used their feet to signal to each other under the table.

Kolia Zhuria looked into the cabin for a short time, listened to the conversation, and said in Georgian to his friends: "Ladi, you ought to be ashamed."

"It's none of your business … What is there to be ashamed of, we've only just got the salmon in our hands … Clear off, brother, don't interfere in other people's business. Go for a walk, or read a poem …"

The game came to an end. They added up the winnings and the losses. The stranger was the only loser, the others were all in pocket. The loser calculated his losses at twenty roubles, but the winnings came to five hundred.

"Wait a bit, how much were we playing for?"

"A fifth of a kopeck a point," the stranger said in Russian.

"Not a fifth of a kopeck, five kopecks," explained Beso.

The others confirmed this.

"Then your winnings equal my losses. So be it!" said the stranger, taking out five hundred-rouble notes. They divided these winnings into three and rose to leave. At that very moment Qoranashvili came in and asked the stranger in Georgian:

"You're here, are you? Have you finished? Who lost?"

"Yes, we've finished in fact. I lost a bit. Have you missed me?" replied the stranger in perfect Georgian, as he got to his feet. Then he turned to the dumbstruck students: "Lads, thanks a lot for helping me pass the time. Let me introduce myself. I'm Bagrat Davitashvili," he said, offering each of them his hand and adding: "I'd like you to do me the honor of having dinner with me. Today all the students are my guests. Goodbye, gentlemen."

The three amazed students stayed behind in the cabin. They turned as white as mistletoe, and they muttered: "I thought he was a Jew ... I thought he was a Russian ... He understood, he understood everything, but he never said a word ... And he paid up in full ... What should we do? How should we take it?"

They squabbled and argued. They blamed each other, they were so ashamed they broke into a sweat. Finally all three went to see Davitashvili and offered him a muttered apology and their winnings: "There's been a misunderstanding ... We didn't think you were a Georgian ... We were playing a bit loosely ..."

Davitashvili smiled and gently reassured them: "Don't give it a thought. The game ended as it should. Put that money back in your pockets, you need it. I've got so much that a sum like that is just a drop in the ocean for me, while you will be buying books ... No, no, don't bother yourselves ... Don't offend me. It's time for dinner, let's go."

The dining room was filled with students, with the warbling of a shawm, the banging of a drum, yells of "*Tashi-tushi*", the song "Live for ever" being belted out, the crashing of crockery, roars of laughter, and witty remarks.

Finally, Kvachi asked for permission to speak. He praised their host to the skies, he stirred everyone up and fired them with his own enthusiasm:

"Gentlemen! Friends!" he called out at the end. "Life involves all of us, it weighs on us, it burns us, it tramples us down, it makes us weep blood and tears, but in one thing it can't defeat us, can't bend us: we're Georgians, we have from birth an innate chivalry and bravery, noble blood flows in our veins, we imbibed with our mother's milk a perception and feeling for respect, brotherhood, and comradeship. We have flesh and bones saturated with a feeling of pure duty to each other and our fair motherland. A wretched life deprives us of everything, withers the flower of our youth and blots out our sunlight, but chivalry, bravery, respect, and nobility are things that we can't be deprived of. Never ever, I said! Friends! Gentlemen! Comrades! I ask you to drink a toast to the best representative of this respect, this bravery, chivalry, and nobility, to our host today, the magnanimous, thoroughbred, and generous Georgian Bagrat Davitashvili! Hurrah to our glorious compatriot! Hurrah to his manly manliness! Hurrah to Georgia which has given us such a son!"

"Hurrah, hurrah!" roared the packed room.

The shawm played a flourish; there was a crashing of wine glasses. Everyone rose to leave and mingled. Some went up to Davitashvili to kiss him, others kissed Kvachantiradze, others one another. A lezginka dance followed the flourish, then a slow folk dance which everyone joined in.

That evening the notorious north-west gale of that part of the Black Sea blew up. The drunken ship creaked, groaned, and pitched like a splinter of wood in the water. After all that food and drink, the gale defiled and polluted the brightly burnished *Pushkin*. The sailors could barely keep up with washing it down and, as they did so, they swore as only Russians can.

The next day everybody blamed the misfortunes of that

evening on the gale and nothing else.

In the morning the *Pushkin* docked at Novorossiisk with great trouble, yawling and rolling and pitching. When the gangway was lowered, Chipi Chipuntiradze from Kutaisi turned up on board. People were amazed, stunned, and swarmed around him: "How are you, Chipi? Chipi, how are things? Chipi, what are you doing here?"

"Curse and damn me, body and soul! The last thing I want! Even the devil can't make out what's gone wrong!"

"What's the trouble, Chipi? What brings you here?"

"Well, I was supposed to go to France? Man, I thought Berlin University was in Paris, and Paris University was in London?! When I was in Russia, Moscow University was supposed to be in Kiev, so Kiev University's probably in Warsaw."

"What's going on, man? Explain it to us! What's wrong with you, what's happened to you?"

"God knows who thought that up. Man, did anyone think that Novorossia University would be in Odessa?! I'm not saying that Moscow University is probably in Chokhatura or Bandza. I was told Novorossia University would be in Novorossiisk so I came to this city."

The guffaws of forty students could be heard in the city.

"What are you laughing at? Have I said something wrong?"

Another round of guffaws rocked the ship.

"You can laugh, man, you can laugh! I'm cleaned out, even if you're all right! How are you, Kvachi? If it weren't for the thought of you coming, I'd have given up and thrown myself in the sea … Well, did you think I was staying in a hotel? Or I spent my money on that? I went to see the school headmaster, he made me look a fool. Was that a time to embarrass me, I said, I need money. He gave me twenty roubles, that's all he could give. He wrote down my address. What about that? He can wait, my grandfather will send him the money: what are you laughing at, you scum? Shell out something, couldn't you find two roubles for me? I could do with a bit more ... I'm not so crazy worrying how I'll repay it. What's going to happen next, God knows."

Qoranashvili was enlightening one group: "Over there is Tuapse. It used to be called Nikopse. It was the boundary of Georgia. The chronicler writes, 'From Nikopse to Derbent ...'Gelendzhik is nearby, a colony of Tolstoyans ... Over there's a cement factory ... Beyond it is the Abrau-Dersu estate ... Fine wine and champagne are produced there."

That night Kvachi pursued the blonde. Her name and surname? Rebecca Isaakievna Idelsohn. Where from? From Tbilisi. Identity? Rebecca hesitated for a little, then spoke up, because Kvachi had such charming and trustworthy eyes and such a sweet tongue, that it would have stirred a heart of stone and made it speak.

Rebecca had a husband. Middle-aged, rich, an Odessa merchant. The gendarmes suspected him of providing revolutionaries with a lot of money. Idelsohn fled to Tbilisi, but they traced and arrested him. That's why Rebecca had been in Tbilisi, now her husband was being sent overland under police escort to Odessa, while Rebecca was returning by sea ... No, Rebecca had plenty of money, she owns personally three large houses in Odessa, but ... Rebecca is alone in the world and inexperienced. She needs someone to advise her, to help her, she seeks consolation and friendship ... Rebecca shouldn't cry? How can a woman left alone not cry, when she's worn out and without comfort! Not cry?! But isn't Kvachi here, a fearless knight in shining armor? He will help a poor woman, he will offer her friendship, he will see her through her trouble to the end, devote himself to her and stay with her until the temporarily widowed Rebecca gets her beloved husband back. So Rebecca need not cry! Her eyes that glitter like stars shouldn't cloud over, or Kvachi too will burst into tears ... Kvachi too feels his strength failing ... Kvachi, too, has tears in his eyes ... Kvachi is weeping … He weeps as he puts an arm round the tearful Rebecca's waist and kisses her soft downy arms and comforts her.

And he comforted her like a real man: first he captured the second row of fortifications, then with a ruthless attack he broke down the last tower and the helpless blonde castle was completely subdued.

"Aha, congratulations!" Jalil smiled at Kvachi the next morning. "It's very hard for a man to get a *matushka* like that!"

"How do you know, you Turk?" said Kvachi in amazement.

"Jalil sees things that happen at the bottom of the sea," said a smiling Jalil.

CHAPTER TWO

Founding a Group of Comrades and Settling in with a New Dream Woman

Once in Odessa, Kvachi moved into Captain Sidorov's apartment, where he was given a nicely furnished room. Sidorov was constantly at sea, always traveling: once a fortnight his ship, the *Pushkin*, returned to Odessa, and three or four days later left again for Batumi.

Sidorov had three daughters, all fledged and ready to fly the nest. His middle-aged spouse had only two things to worry about: looking after the family and marrying off her daughters. Kvachi was received and lodged by the family as though he were the family's loyal defender and senior member.

Sidorov's youngest daughter Vera was a short, full-figured, blue-eyed, and lively girl, always bustling about with a swing of her hips and laughing for no apparent reason. She ran off to classes in the morning, then helped her mother, and spent her evenings with students.

Vera completely accepted Kvachi's authority in the family: within three days she was thoroughly used to him. She laughed and joked with him and wasn't embarrassed if she found Kvachi not fully dressed, or in bed. She would bring him tea or coffee, sit by his side, fix her bright blue eyes on him and chirp away, as carefree as a sparrow. Kvachi would rub his sleepy eyes, yawn, and his hands would fumble and grope around him. Vera would calm his hand movements, tell him off for being a "Caucasian devil," and feel conscience-stricken. But she would torment Kvachi and then, blushing and dishevelled, would finally rush out of the room.

Kvachi had decided to study law. This was the faculty—advocacy, the law, and finance—for which he was best suited and had a natural affinity; it also fitted in with his aims. The day after they arrived, Beso got Kvachi enrolled in the faculty and made him buy so many books that Chipuntiradze had every reason to say afterwards: "It was a pile of books too high to jump over, let alone read and study."

Kvachi's friends lived in the same block of buildings as Kvachi. Not a day passed without the lads from Tbilisi and Kutaisi getting together. They soon got the hang and the measure of each other, became good friends, and in no time a secret force united and fired up the six of them.

Jalil constantly passed with his hawker's tray, shouting "Rahat lakoum, rahat lakoum!" When Kvachi and his friends caught his eye, he would doff his hat and bare his shining horse's teeth, saying: *"Sabah hayır olsun* (Good morning), princes! Going to a feast, are you? Come and have a nougat."

The friends gave Jalil their blessing and helped themselves to so many sweets that they lost their appetite for the whole day. Whenever they went to a Georgian inn to eat shashlyk and drink Kakhetian wine, they made sure Jalil sat at their side, and they joked and made him roar out Turkish laments and melodies.

For the time being they all took their studies seriously. They were punctual, attending every lecture and, when they got home, tried to get down to their subjects. But they were Georgians and their enthusiasm gradually waned. They ran out of energy and lost their joy. The road to mastery of a subject turned out to be far too long, in fact impossible, for them. Eventually they slowed down, got behind, and joined the mass of idle, freeloading students that spend a dozen years calling themselves students in the hope of finally getting a degree. They threw their books in a corner and set off for the boulevards, for inns run by their countrymen, for European restaurants, Fanconi's coffeehouse, amusing themselves with playing cards, the circus, wine, clowning about, and pursuing cheap whores.

Kvachi waded up to his neck into this quagmire, but he felt revulsion and disdained the dirt and the smell, because he was by nature more fastidious and discriminating than his comrades. But he stuck to them, as they did to him, because he was trying his luck, seeking a fabulous beauty. But Kvachi felt the nasty smell and a bitter taste emanating from the dirty lower storeys of this pursuit and search for the woman of his dreams. He turned his back on cheap brothels, stopped heading for basement drinking dens, and aimed at the upper storeys. There he could breathe clean air and wash off the dust and dirt of the plebs. He guided his comrades away, too, from the drinking dens, the dark streets, and stinking cellars. If Kvachi climbed two rungs up life's ladder, he managed at least to bring his comrades up one rung, but some of them backed down, and often dragged Kvachi down with them.

Kvachi was generous to his friends, and his pocket was always open for them, although he never let them dig very deep. Mostly it was Chipi Chipuntiradze and Gabo Chkhubishvili who slipped their hands into it.

Eventually Kvachi and his comrades had a common kitty, which Sedrak Havlabariani took over as treasurer. Once Sedrak felt he had power, he became domineering and mean: no day passed without him telling off his comrades and reading them a long lecture: "This is no game: we're not Mantashov's bank, so don't shout 'Give, give!' Hang on to your money, can't you?"

"Your job's to get the money in," Chkhubishvili told him. "You can send the lectures to your father in Sighnaghi."

"Leave Sighnaghi out of it, you think of your Gori, where you trick people into buying your wild pears and crab apples."

"Bring in the money, you cheap wine seller," Chipi Chipuntiradze would attack. "Get it in. We elected you, we can throw you out."

Sedrak Havlabariani didn't raise an eyebrow: he reacted calmly "If you throw me out, I tell you, you might as well throw out the Tsar. Be grateful I'm working for nothing for country bumpkins like you."

In the end Kvachi ended the argument by donating five roubles to each comrade, while backing and praising Sedrak.

When there was an election for the leadership of the Georgian community, Kvachi and his friends went around lobbying, caused a rumpus, and made sure that Beso Shikia was elected treasurer. After that the group got its second wind, relieved by Beso's ability to extract money for himself and for his comrades from an empty kitty. Only Kvachi and Beso knew the secret of how it was done.

Kvachi liked to say that because God gave Georgians as much wit and capacity for hard work as appetite and ability to imitate, they were a people who could turn the world upside down.

This saying was incarnated by Kvachi and his three or four closest friends. Providence seemed to have endowed them generously with a bloodhound's nose and the ability to observe and absorb. Kvachi never walked the streets without noticing something new which he could emulate the next day. If he was struck by the sight of some snob or idle dandy or spick and span aristocrat, then the next day he would be transformed into a fine copy of this model. He immediately caught on how one should hold a Russian cigarette with fingers just slightly parted, let the smoke out of one's mouth and one's nose, how to twirl a stick in one's hand, at what angle to wear a student's hat, to nod, bow, smile, cross one's legs, or flick one's finger at a waiter and in a casual nasal tone mumble, "He-e-ey, garçon!"

So, in a very short time the handsome and striking Kvachantiradze grew in leaps and bounds and easily found a place and a welcome in a society of a breed which, unless guided by its own nose, would ignore and disdain anyone.

Isaac's Liberation and Kvachi's First Love's Flight

Kvachi was pursuing Rebecca Idelsohn. An extremely prudent woman, she concealed her affections. She had a lot of relatives and acquaintances and was anxious to avoid any gossip or tale-telling. They sometimes met at Kvachi's lodgings, sometimes at Rebecca's.

Rebecca lived on Langeron Street. Her husband was back in prison and his temporary widow was guarded by a score of relatives, some hers, some her husband's. But Kvachi immediately laid hands on a powerful key which could open a fortress protected by nine locks: every time he came to see Rebecca, he slipped Rebecca's maidservant and concierge three roubles, easily reassuring the nervous widow and warding off the attentions of her guards.

This was an expensive love affair for Kvachi, entailing suppers, bouquets, sweets, and dozens of minor expenses.

Finally, after two months Rebecca's husband Isaac Idelsohn was repatriated from Tbilisi to Odessa prison. When Kvachi heard about this, he was reanimated, and told Rebecca:

"I've got to know Pavlov, a gendarme: we seem to be old acquaintances. He used to work in Kutaisi: he's dealing with your husband's case. I asked him about it: he says that things are looking very bad, but they're not altogether hopeless, either ..."

Rebecca unexpectedly leapt for joy: the fact that Kvachi and Pavlov knew each other gave her courage, for she had long known that her husband was in serious danger ... From now on Kvachi played a careful and masterly game. He really had renewed contact with Pavlov, thanks to an Odessa constable called Dvalishvili: he offered the gendarme hospitality and then suddenly asked him at the dinner:

"Tell me, how's the Idelsohn case going? What's he charged with?"

"Being a member of the party and giving it help."

"What can he expect?"

"If the charges stick, then hard labor in Siberia; if they don't, then just deportation."

"What do you think: will the charges stick?"

"I don't think so."

Kvachi changed the subject.

"Aren't you planning a holiday in Europe?"

"That's what I dream of, but who'll give me the money for the trip?"

"There's no need to worry about money. Would a thousand roubles be enough for you?"

"A thousand roubles would be enough to see half of Europe and have a really good time."

"Excellent: to seal our friendship, please accept my gift of a thousand roubles."

Pavlov was neither amazed nor shocked. He instantly grasped where the money came from. A little later Kvachi mentioned Idelsohn again:

"I do have one small request. I believe Idelsohn is going to be sentenced to deportation, so could you possibly arrange for him to have permission to travel abroad instead of deportation to Siberia?"

"That's easy. I can promise you I'll sort it all out in three days."

"No, no, leave him where he is for the time being. When the time's right, I'll let you know myself."

An hour later, when they were both quite tipsy, Kvachi said, "One more request: don't tell anyone that Idelsohn can get out of it so easily; instead, frighten him with the prospect of hard labor in Siberia, and …"

At this point Kvachi's fingers made the sign of a noose round a neck, then he added: "That's very important for me, I'll be very grateful to you."

Pavlov laughed: "I understand, I understand all too well. That's no problem, so let's do that. I'll frighten his blonde beauty, too, so that she doesn't dare come near me again. The rest is up to you."

The next day Kvachi responded to Rebecca: "My queen! This is very hard for me to tell you: your heart isn't strong, and I'm afraid."

"Tell me, don't be afraid."

"So you won't be frightened? Do you promise me? Let me warn you now that something can be done about the danger, but ... Oh, my God! Why have I been singled out to take on this dodgy business? All right, all right ... I'll tell you. The fact is, that ... Pavlov's got hold of a document which proves everything against your husband ... And if you ask me what that is? I think you've already told me ... That's the document that's come into his possession, but it hasn't yet been included in the prosecution papers ... Pavlov said he'd wait for a bit ... He asked if you'd like to leave with Idelsohn for Europe ... Otherwise? Oh, my God! Really, I shouldn't be getting mixed up in this. After all, I'm in no great hurry to get Isaac out of jail, since ... Well, you can guess why not, can't you? Fine, darling, fine, don't get upset. Don't cry, or you'll make me cry ... All right, I'll tell you. He's asking for an awful lot: five thousand, he says ... You agree, then? Give me something with your husband's signature on it, I've got to compare it with the document. Is this it? This is a love letter he's written, isn't it? Aha! Let's see how much the old man loves you ... Five thousand is a lot, an awful lot, but what can I do? You've agreed to it, so there's nothing I can say! Right then, till tomorrow, my darling."

Kvachi put Isaac Idelsohn's letter in his pocket and left. The next day Rebecca's relatives held a discussion. Meanwhile Kvachi had carefully studied Isaac's signature, imitated it, and taught himself to copy it.

That night Kvachi and Pavlov came to terms and arranged things.

"That's agreed: it's no problem. She can come tomorrow," said Pavlov, "and I'll tell her ..."

The next day Rebecca and Kvachi were in each other's arms having a conversation. "Pavlov must be a real gentleman: he treated me with great respect when he saw me. He told me it was either the gallows or Paris. It will be decided in a week's time, his fate will be settled by one document. He suddenly mentioned your name: he said, 'Napoleon Apollonovich is my best friend, he's a completely reliable and careful man'."

"I told you so, my beauty. I said the case was sorted! Now tell me who that letter was written by. I expect you know. I'm amazed that Isaac, an experienced man like him, could be so stupid ... Fine, tomorrow morning I'll hand you back that letter ... I'll see you at ten in the morning at home ... You'll pay half then, and the rest when they let Isaac out ..."

The next day Kvachi collected half the sum and burnt the document in Rebecca's presence. A week later Rebecca and Isaac Idelsohn, who had been given ten days to get ready, rushed into town to get passports and packed for their departure. At the same time they said nothing to each other or to their closest relatives: they kept everything secret and trembled with fear.

Meanwhile Kvachi deposited several thousand roubles in his current account at the Azov Bank.

Kvachi and Rebecca spent their last day together. It was beyond description, a day both black and fiery, of separation and departure, when threads of love were snapped, two hearts inflamed with passion were split, two united bodies cloven, and two fused hearts ripped apart.

There were floods of tears, there was sobbing and shrieking and wailing, there was the tearing of injured flesh: a taste of gall and of honey, melancholic sadness, consolation, promises, and oaths of eternal love.

That night Kvachi went to see Rebecca and Isaac off at the station, although, as he told Rebecca that morning, he was frightened that he might unintentionally reveal his own grief and own heartbreak.

Kvachi met Pavlov the gendarme on the station platform.

"Are you off abroad, too?" Kvachi asked him.

"Yes indeed, I'm traveling to Paris."

"On Idelsohn's money," thought Kvachi as he followed Pavlov.

Rebecca and Idelsohn had already taken their seats in their compartment. By chance Pavlov had been given a seat in the same compartment. The two men got in and were only slightly taken aback.

"You needn't worry," Kvachi intervened. "Magistrate and prisoner encounter each other again by chance. You needn't be enemies, because you now have a fine conciliator here."

And he kissed Rebecca's hand. The three passengers drowned their anger and embarrassment in a bout of jocularity.

Shortly after that Isaac led Kvachi out into the corridor and told him, "I shan't forget your kindness until the day I die. There's not a lot I can afford, but ... no, no! Take it, you've absolutely got to accept it."

He thrust a package into Kvachi's hand and rushed back to his compartment. That moment Rebecca came out, took Kvachi's left hand, and put a large diamond ring on his middle finger.

"Rebecca! I'll never forget you! My darling friend!"

Rebecca, deeply moved, wiped her tears away and murmured, "Have it as a keepsake ... Don't forget your Rebecca ... your sincere friend Rebecca. Goodbye."

They looked all round them, seized the moment, and kissed each other fiercely, melancholically, and for the last time.

The third bell rang. Kvachi and the departing travelers' relatives said their farewells and left the carriage. The train moved off. Rebecca and Kvachi waved and blew kisses to each other until all sight of the train was blocked by another train.

Madame Lapoche

The same night that a train was rushing Kvachi's beloved Rebecca off, he was dispelling his sadness with his friends in a *café chantant.*

"Fine, thank you very much," he ruminated sluggishly, lazily, with an aristocratic lisp. "No more of this petty-bourgeois stuff for me. What's Odessa, what can life here do for you? There's nothing to be studied here ... I'll go either to Moscow or to Petersburg. I'm bored drifting about in this filthy backwater. There's no room to swing a cat ... For me Odessa is a straitjacket, I can't find room to move in it ... It's a cramped staircase, it won't let me take off and spread my wings ... When am I going? In a month, or sooner. You come, too ... I'll help you, why shouldn't I? What do you say? Kutaisi? Oh no. Don't even mention Kutaisi. It's a bog, a stinking bog. But take even Georgia, for example ... My God, don't go on about it. Oh no, it's a lie. Not even a hundred people on earth have even heard of Georgia. And what is our great Georgia? If you lay down your head in Batumi, you'll have to tread on Kiziqi with your feet; if you sneeze in Sukhumi, they'll call out 'Bless you!' from Sighnaghi. If Daniel the Jew starts playing 'Live Many Years' in Kutaisi at Laitadze's or Eremo's inns, all Qazbegi will sing along and Levana the folk-singer will belt out 'Thanks' from Telavi. If you take out a cigarette in Borjomi, twenty hands will reach out from Poti and say, 'Give us one.' If you find a stinking towel, the whole of Georgia will come running, yelling, 'It's mine! Put it down!' Don't talk to me about it. Garçon! Another bottle of Louis Rederer champagne. What did you say? Beso, you'd rather have chartreuse? Seriozha, you want sherry? Garçon, bring us all three, and lobsters, pineapples, oranges, and mandarins to go with them."

Then Kvachi offered his guests his gold cigarette case and invited them to take a cigarette as thick as your finger. The cigarette case was decorated with monograms. In the middle the inscription read: "To Prince Napoleon Apollonovich Kvachantiradze a token of Rebecca's undying love," and the cigarettes had gold letters and a prince's coat of arms printed on them: a knot made of Kvachi's initials and his motto, "Me ... me again ... only me ... mine ... for me ... about me ..."

"Kvachi, what's the sense of this pattern?"

"You can understand it any way you want. That way or this way."

And he showed his guests his expensive ring, his watch, and his gold-handled stick. All three were decorated with jewels and pearls, and they were all inscribed with the same motto by which he lived.

"Garçon, this champagne hasn't been properly chilled. Disgraceful! I never get served properly in this restaurant. And the pineapples are no good, they're too small ... Beso, old boy, go and give the orchestra a twenty-five rouble note and get them to play my favorite waltz, 'Maria Theresa'."

Suddenly Kvachi's eye alighted on the queen of the season, the prima donna of this *café chantant*, the brilliant star from Paris, Madame Lapoche, who'd only just lit up the restaurant with her entry.

"Sedrak, here's my visiting card: invite that woman over quickly before other people carry her off."

Sedrak broke through a circle of men.

"Prince Napoleon Apollonovich Kvachantiradze and his friends ask you to do them the honor of accepting their invitation."

The other men dispersed, grumbling enviously.

With wan langor Kvachi greeted the beauty and reverentially kissed her hand.

"*Charmée de votre connaissance* ... Prince Kvashantiraze."

"*S'il vous plaît, madame ... Garçon! Chère madame, voulez-vous choisir ...*"

Kvachi and Sedrak struck up, smashed, defiled, and polluted

the soft and pure French language.

His eyelids drooping langorously, Kvachi was swimming in waves of intoxication. He had a momentary vision of his submissive Rebecca, smiling reproachfully at him, her blue eyes alighting on him, but the blurred hallucination and momentary phantom immediately melted away, faded, and was swallowed up in the glowing embers of the Parisian prima donna's eyes. Those eyes were slowly burning him and setting fire to Kvachi's faint heart.

Soon Kvachi was in the power of those eyes, soon he had mounted a wild beast with its face stained with blood; he was swimming in waves of intoxication and had galloped like a bolting horse into a conflagration of fornication and passion.

When dawn broke and Madame Lapoche had finished her third "number", a lanky Frenchman came in and took possession of the prima donna. Madame Lapoche took her leave of Kvachi: "*À demain, mon chat.*"

Kvachi was stunned: "What did she say? Am I supposed to let you go off with that man? Never!"

"*Il est mon mari, mon chat.*"

Kvachi was left dumbstruck, but from that moment he could not come to terms with the fact that this man was her husband, and he could not forget the woman.

He went home seething with fury and lay down. A servant woke him for lunch. In the dining room he found only Vera: the rest of the family had gone to see their relatives.

Kvachi seized his opportunity and added to his lunch a bottle of chartreuse which he had been keeping for his friends.

Whenever Vera downed a little glass and put it down, she said as she did so: "That's enough, I shan't have any more, or I'll get tipsy."

When Kvachi poured her another glass, he told her: "This is the last one. I shan't let you drink any more."

But Vera swallowed one more and said again: "Enough, that's

the last one. I shan't drink any more, or else I'll get tipsy."

But "the last one" was the last only when the bottle was empty. The wine went to the girl's head; her eyes started to shine, and this plump girl burst into song and became fidgety. Her speech was slurred and she began talking nonsense: "You're my Napoleon … You're my Apollo, too …"

"And you're my Venus, you funny little thing!" Kvachi responded as he embraced her plump waist.

"You're handsome, but you're wild, too … Wait, you can't move that fast! Yes, I was telling you I loved you, but I'm scared."

"Why are you scared, my girl?"

"I don't know, I'm just scared."

And the tender, scared child again pressed her scared heart and head against Kvachi's chest.

"What's got you so scared? There's no need to be afraid of me: I don't bite and I'm not a robber … Let's sit on this sofa and get started."

They sat down and got started. Kvachi didn't in fact bite, but Vera's broad body and slender bones creaked, groaned, and bent in his iron arms.

Two weeks passed. The pursuit of Madame Lapoche and paying bills day and night was making Kvachi's flesh and wallet melt away. The obsessive passion unleashed by the swarthy Madame Lapoche was released by an embittered Kvachi on the blonde little Vera.

Kvachi's friends, spurred on by Shikia, swore an oath and confronted Kvachi. Ladi Chikinjiladze, the group's "philosopher", casually ate his fourth bunch of grapes and ruminated as he ate: "I do understand your passion, Kvachi, old man, but there are limits. If a man doesn't rein in his passions, sooner or later he'll be ruined. Listen to your friends, all they want is whatever is best for you."

Chipi Chipuntiradze, who had voluntarily taken on the job of spy and "Kvachi's look-out", supported Chikinjiladze. Chipuntiradze tended to be fidgety and hot-tempered:

"I've got it all written down," he said cuttingly. "The last two weeks, you spent 723 roubles in the *café chantant*, 8 roubles on flowers, 145 roubles on cabs, and 1,242 roubles on various presents: total—2118 roubles. That really is overdoing it, isn't it?"

"It really is," said the others in amazement.

"How do you know my expenses?" Kvachi asked.

"The reason you call me your lookout is that I have to find out everything. Anyway, you told me: 'What are you doing spending so much on a woman?' Would I throw away that much money? God, no! If Silibistro found out, he'd give you hell."

"Pri-i-ince, what's all the fuss about?" Sedrak wondered in all sincerity. "You're a man, aren't you? Well, who doesn't love women? I love women and boys … Hey, what are you laughing about? Why shouldn't I love them? Aren't we all Christians? Why should a man spend more than a rouble on a woman? Even if she's a real beauty, at the very most three roubles and that's the limit. Better spend your money with men friends. Learn some sense from Chkhubishvili. When he's short of cash, in the evening he'll go out to Richelieu or Deribas Streets and see a sight for sore eyes. There are flocks of them there, each one better than the last. You just have to follow behind, the way a wolf follows a fat-tailed sheep. When you get the urge, just call me. You can shut your eyes and follow me. If you have to spend more than three roubles … Hey, why are you laughing, you wretches, aren't I talking sense to you?"

"Hey, come to your senses, Kvachi. Who are feeding when you spend so much money? When you shower her with a thousand-rouble ring, who are you being so generous to? When you hire a carriage by the month, who are you hiring it for? You spend two hundred roubles on each supper: who are you giving this money to? You hang about here day and night: who are you doing it for, why? You might get a crumb, that's the sum total: we're here, so what are you going to tell us?" Gabo Chkhubishvili attacked Kvachi roughly and directly.

The person actually behind this attack, Beso Shikia, had his nose in a newspaper and was too embarrassed to say a word.

Kvachi was so ashamed that he was covered in sweat; he tried to justify himself. In the end he gave his friends his word of honor that he would leave Madame Lapoche alone. But the very same evening he sent Madame Lapoche another bouquet and some confectionery, and at midnight he was back in the *café chantant*, where he roasted until morning in the fire of his passion.

The flint had struck the steel, the irresistible force had met the immovable object. The steel had sent sparks flying and blunted the flint's teeth, without doing any damage to itself. Kvachi Kvachantiradze was the son of Silibistro from Samtredia, while Madame Lapoche was born in Paris and raised on the milk of Montmartre, and behind her stood a Belleville apache, whom some called a pimp (others just used the Russian term "tom-cat"), while Madame Lapoche passed him off as her husband.

"*Mon mari vient … mon mari est ici … il est là … mon mari se fâche,*" the Parisian prima donna would repeat with fear and trembling.

Monsieur Lapoche vanished when needed, appeared when needed, smiled or flashed his eyes when needed and, after a while, even gnashed his teeth.

Kvachi's patience was exhausted. He had become heated and highly strung. He tried to achieve his final aim with obstinacy and firmness, he expected his rightful share, and demanded that the debt be settled.

Recently Madame Lapoche had been "not at home" or had been chained to her *mari*. Finally a Major Baron von der Schlimpen Hohenstaufen intercepted Kvachi and blocked his path like a wall.

One evening this baron, a tall, twenty-stone titan with a moustache as wide as his hand, put his hands on his hips, rolled his walnut-sized eyes, stood over Kvachi, and asked with a voice like a trumpet from above:

"Who do you want to see? What? Madame Lapoche? I'm the one she's invited this evening ... What? Tomorrow, the day after, the day after that ... What did you say? Yes, she's mine. She's mine permanently, I said. What was that? I haven't lost my temper yet, but if you make me, God protect you: even your enemies will be sorry for you. What did you say? It's nothing, did you say? Then we agree, do we? Fine, that's better ... What? I said I haven't lost my temper yet ... What did you just say? Goodbye. Sleep tight."

The next day Sedrak was saying:

"Pity that blessed baron didn't turn up a month earlier, my God, he would have been a godsend ... What? Did he come too late? That's not what I'm saying. It's just as well, since now it will teach him some sense. Pri-i-ince, can't you trust Sedrak that much? What they say abut you is that you're a smart lad. You just wave a hand, and money comes from Baghdad ... What? Really! Just because we call you a prince doesn't make you a real prince, does it? Do you now believe you are? Really? You want me to lend you a hundred roubles? Is that how things are? You're that broke? Then I'll do what I can and borrow the money ... Me? If Sedrak had a hundred roubles of his own, then he'd open a shop in the clothes market ... Fine, fine: I'll see you this evening, now let's go and have a shashlyk each. What do you say?"

"Let's eat," they all agreed quickly.

"To hell with it," Kvachi exclaimed in Russian, nearly smashing the table. "Arutina's inn is better than that damned *café chantant*. Enough. It's over."

"I really like that. Before now you used to spit on it as if it were the devil. Ask anyone what Arutina's is. It has turtle-doves worth ten of your madames. True, they do smell a bit of soap and vodka, but that's all right, you just have to shove cotton wool up your nose for five minutes, anyway. The 'main thing', as the Russians say, is that you won't come across any baron there."

An hour later the five of them were sitting in a damp darkened cellar loudly singing "Live for ever." The dubious wine from Ganja was passed off as Kakhetian. The dirty tablecloth was strewn with forlorn, demeaned Georgian cheese, smoked belly of sturgeon, radishes, a baguette, and green herbs. The shashlyk was sizzling over the grill, saturating the cellar with its smell and smoke. Arutina, from Sighnaghi, was bustling around, pouring his customers drinks, drinking himself, and reassuring Sedrak:

"What? Didn't you say you wanted Marusia and Katinka? They'll be along any minute. I sent a lad to fetch them an hour ago. Don't worry, my boys. Drink and buy me a drink ... Hey-ho! Hey, long live the prince: here's to him."

"Jalil, a Turkish song!" Kvachi ordered.

Jalil coughed, cleared his throat, and bawled out: "*Ata mindim başı yok, çayları geçtim taşı yok, ortı sardım yanımda tadaşım yok.* (I got on a headless horse, I crossed streams with no stepping-stones, I got into a bed with no woman by my side.)"

Once he was drunk, Kvachi couldn't dampen his ardour. Befuddled by wine and saturated with "Marusia's soap, at dawn he toddled off to Madame Lapoche's apartment. At the hotel door he was again intercepted by the baron.

"What's this? What did you say? You're going to see Madame Lapoche? It's all above board, is it? What? What did you just say? I said, clear off. I'm giving you the option. What, what did you say? Clear off and don't come back. She's leaving today. What, what did you say? Then goodbye to you."

And Kvachi was about to trudge off home.

"*Mon chat,*" a fatigued Madame Lapoche called out, opening the door to Kvachi. "Wait a moment ... In a second. Just wait over there for a little. My husband's not at home today."

She locked the door and went back into the room. Kvachi looked through the keyhole and saw Lapoche's husband thrusting a pillow under his arm and running into the next room. Madame Lapoche opened the door again, let Kvachi in, and told him again, "Come in, *mon chat*, come in! You're in luck today. My husband's not at home. Try your luck ..."

When Kvachi woke up, neither Madame Lapoche nor her "husband", nor their luggage were in the room. He got dressed and left the room. He meant to give the hotel servant a rouble, but he couldn't find a single penny in his pocket. He tried to collect his wits and he recalled that he had put four hundred roubles in his pocket the day before, but where he had spent them or lost them he could no longer remember.

When Madame Lapoche vanished from Odessa, she disappeared from Kvachi's heart, too. All that was left was a bitter memory of three thousand squandered roubles and his friends' endless complaints, whines, and reproaches.

Beso Shikia kept silent and looked after the Georgian communal kitty. Sedrak could not settle. He constantly moaned:

"Oh dear, oh dear! That's a really stupid waste! For three thousand I could have bought half Sighnaghi or I could have got you three thousand women. Don't laugh. The rule is that a woman is worth one rouble. It's a fixed tariff, isn't it? Now, if you're really not going to be offered a princess, you won't mind running off to the whorehouse, will you?"

"That's what love does to a man," Chikinjiladze interjected.

"I believe in a one-night stand: that's an end of it," Chkhubishvili spoke out.

Finally Jalil nodded and said, "What can I say, prince? She was a very captivating girl, but it's a great pity you spent three thousand on her. Three roubles would have been the right price."

Kvachi put an end to the debate.

"Enough!" he decided firmly. "It happened, and it's over. Nobody is to mention Madame Lapoche again."

A Jinxed Love Affair

The next day Kvachi caught sight of a group of Georgian students in the gardens of Odessa University. There were women among them. He went up to them, greeted them generally, and listened to the conversation.

In this group he encountered for the first time an educated girl: she was tall, slim, elegant, as white as snow, clear-skinned, with jet-black hair and black eyes, enchanting and witty.

Kvachi and the girl caught each other's eye. Then she averted her gaze and devoted all her attention to a rather strange debate between Leo Shavidze and Sandro Arsenashvili.

Certain words recurred: "Impressionism … symbolism … entity … essence … permanence … being …"

Kvachi meant to get a word into this debate, as a device for attracting the girl's attention, but when he considered the content of the debate, he changed his mind: to hell with it! Georgians couldn't resist blathering on about politics or philosophy. Which ever subject it was, he knew these "isms' were French, but what the hell were "essence", "being", "entity"? Or "reflection", "Ibsen"? "Vrubel" must be old Georgian for "trouble." But what about "Verlaine", "Maeterlinck", "Annunzio"?

Nadia Armeladze and Verichka Kaloshvili detached themselves from the group. Kvachi followed them. They asked after each other like old friends.

"What's happening, Kvachi? You shun everyone these days, have you forgotten us all? That's not right, is it?" Nadia reproached him.

"An unlicensed priest can't have absolution," Verichka added.

"Oh, that's not fair," Kvachi defended himself. "I've been

swamped with lectures and haven't had any time."

They laughed and joked. They each had a coffee with a pastry, recalled the past, and passed on the latest gossip and stories. Finally Kvachi asked:

"Who is the girl who was standing there in the gardens? Sophie Shivadze? I haven't seen her before … Do I like her? I wouldn't say no, but … Does she have a lot of admirers? Oh, Kvachi's not afraid of them … Good, introduce me. Where? When? Today, can she be at your place at seven? I'll come … All right, I'll bring chocolates."

That evening Kvachi got to know Sophie Shivadze.

The girls were talking about chemistry. Kvachi couldn't contribute. Then they moved onto their professors. Kvachi waited. They turned to literature. Kvachi bore it, just looking at this gazelle-like girl, getting intoxicated by her. Finally, he managed to divert the conversation onto lighter topics, and Nadia followed suit. Sophie listened to them, smiling shyly, but not sharing in the jokes.

"So you don't like circuses?" Kvachi asked her. "Or wrestling? It's a fantastic sight. I really must show you Zaikin, Bambulla, Ono Okitoro, Kosta Maisuridze, Bull, Vakhturov, and the 'Red Mask' … So you like theater and opera? No, I haven't been yet. But why don't we go tomorrow? You're too busy? You have to go now? What's the hurry? You'll catch up on preparing for lectures tomorrow … I'll see you out … Nadia, let's take a walk."

They went out. Sophie was in a great hurry. As they crossed the street, Kvachi took Sophie by the arm. Sophie carefully freed herself from his hand and walked even faster. At the door to her lodgings she thanked the two of them and then disappeared.

Kvachi felt offended. Nadia consoled him: "She's cold and proud, but she has a very good heart. She just doesn't get time, she works very hard … Come on, Kvachi, you know you needn't be embarrassed, though …" she laughed as she teased him.

From that day on Kvachi went more often to lectures. He tried to catch Sophie's eye in the lecture hall, in the doorway, even in the nearby streets. Kvachi gathered all his store of politeness, experience, intuition, and talents in order to captivate and enchant that girl's heart.

Sophie neither avoided him nor sought him out; she gave a hint of a smile and a laugh, sometimes she even had a flirtatious expression, as if she was responding and trying to attract him, even lead him on, but she still kept a barrier and a distance between them. A boundary had been set and she would not cross it nor let Kvachi come any closer.

Several times Kvachi tried by word or gesture to cross that barrier, but he could not break the ice of Sophie's remoteness and inviolability.

"Sophie, I swear by God and all I hold dear that I have never met a girl like you before."

"There are hundreds of thousands, millions like me."

"Something strange is happening to me, I've been bewitched."

"You've bewitched yourself. Just wake up."

"I try to, but nothing works. I can't sleep properly, I've lost my appetite … I can't do anything … I'm in torment, take pity on me …"

This was the time and point at which Sophie had drawn her circle of ice: "Stop it, Kvachi, let's put an end to this … I'm in a hurry … Goodbye … Calm down."

Her tall figure swaying elegantly, she quickened her gazelle-like pace, looking back from time to time, her big black eyes smiling and flashing out magical fire.

"Show me some pity, Sophie: can't we go to the opera or the theater?"

"Thanks, but I'm too busy."

"Let's take a stroll on the boulevard."

"I never stroll on the boulevard."

"Let's take a boat trip."

"I don't take boat trips ... I don't want to, and I'm too busy."

Kvachi would bring her flowers and confectionery.

"Don't bother ... don't spend so much money."

Finally he sent her a poem:

> Your black eyes have dimmed everything for me,
> I can't sleep, I lie in love's red flames,
> If you revive me God will reward a womanly deed,
> If you kill me, do not kill my song of praise.

That was the end of Kvachi's quatrain, into which he had woven, poured, and strewn his fire of courtly love, his tears of exaltation, the groans of his heart, the hopes and faith he had in his ordeal, and Sophie's mercy. But the ice did not thaw, nor did the sun disperse the clouds.

Kvachi got more heated, more insistent. He intensified his pursuit and put more determination into his attacks.

Once the two of them came across two hideous paupers who were nervously and angrily groping passersby, demanding alms: "Christian people, give alms to a cripple, give alms! Can't you hear? I said, give! Have pity at least on two cripples, you ruthless tightwads!"

Then they started cursing in Russian.

Kvachi and Sophie both laughed.

"Napoleon, don't you think you and that beggar are rather similar?"

"Both of us are begging. He's begging for money, I'm begging for love."

"Not quite right: the two of you are demanding, not begging: your begging is nasty, persistent, and menacing."

Kvachi's feelings were hurt; he did not reply, but coldly took his leave and went home. But in his heart he had decided to bring forward his final attack.

From then on he didn't ask, he demanded. He pleaded for

Sophie to show mercy and give in, he implored her for alms and pity, he made himself look pitiable, he wilted, he groaned, he suffered, and he said he would kill himself.

His comrades—Sedrak, Chipi, and Ladi—inquired every day: "Hey, how are things going?"

"Leave off, and put a stop to it somehow!"

"Oh, if you win, don't keep it from us; don't keep all the winnings to yourself.

Kvachi made a friendly bargain with them and promised a banquet to mark any victory.

The whole city had heard of Kvachi's infatuation, his love, and new obsession, so that conquering and captivating Sophie had become a matter of self-esteem for him. Everywhere and in every circumstance it was easy for Kvachi to manage to direct his walks at the right time, to lurk in the shadows at the right time, to be patient, to choose his time and place, even to retreat, but Sophie seemed to be able to nullify and ruin all his ploys.

A considerable time passed. Kvachi's comrades were urging him on, but the enterprise showed no signs of succeeding.

Kvachi lost patience and decided: "Either today, or never."

That evening he got on his knees in front of Sophie, wrung his hands, and said tearfully: "My dove … My beauty … My god and my icon! I can't take any more, I haven't got the strength left … Put an end to all this torment and torture … Have pity and show some pity … My Sophie, Sonechka, Sophochka …"

Kvachi had almost made himself believe in his love: tears welled in his eyes and suffering had furrowed his face with wrinkles.

Sophie stepped back. She was bewildered and lost for words.

"Napoleon! Napoleon! Get up! I'm sorry for you, but … Stand up, get on your feet … I can't take any more, I really can't."

Her voice, too, began to tremble and tears welled up in her eyes.

Kvachi let his head droop, covered his face with his hands,

collapsed into an armchair and sobbed like a child, with hopeless grief he mumbled desperately: "I can't take any more, I can't take any more. Now I know everything, I know it only too well ... I've got nothing left ... It's all over, everything's finished."

Sophie was even more confused. Fear, sympathy, and pity melted the ice and softened her heart, overrode her caution, and broke her resolve. She lost her self-control, softened, and weakened. She sat next to Kvachi, ran her crystal fingers through his curly hair, fondled him, calmed and consoled him, while she herself became more and more perturbed, and her voice trembled:

"All right, that's enough ... You must stop now ... Calm down ... Don't torment yourself, don't cry. All right, darling, enough, or else ..."

Kvachi seized her hand and scalded it with his tears. Then he ran both his hands over her shoulder and very slowly drew her closer.

Sophie offered just a little resistance; Kvachi pulled her closer very gradually, and then used more and more force. Then he embraced both her shoulders, and the girl was in his arms, clasped to his chest and entangled in an embrace.

Sophie took fright and became faint; first she pleaded, then she fought.

Kvachi met force with force: he insisted, he grew determined, then fiery and then ferocious. Groping hands became blundering paws, blundering paws turned into a battle, which itself turned into an unrestrained, vicious, and crazed bestial attack.

A blouse was torn, breasts laid bare; white underwear and bare feet became visible; quiet bellowing, groaning, and moans could be heard.

A jaw was lashed by a slapping hand. A torn clump of hair fell onto the floor. Sophie was worn down, enfeebled, and broken. Kvachi had almost mastered and subdued the girl and final victory seemed to be in his grasp, but then an infuriated Sophie sank her teeth into his wrist.

Kvachi uttered a shriek of pain. They both went for each other. Sophie grabbed a long, sharp-pointed paper knife as she wiped her blood-stained lips and covered her exposed breasts. Breathing heavily, syllable by syllable she fired out the words:

"Quick! Get out of here quick! Scoundrel, scum! You loathsome … horrible creature."

"Forgive me … Sorry! I apologize," Kvachi mumbled, grimacing with pain and wrapping his bleeding wrist with a handkerchief.

"I said, clear out of here!" She stood over him with the knife and her eyes blazed fire. "You filthy beast! You're a wild animal! Quick, I said."

And she pursued Kvachi to the door: he mumbled as he went.

Cured of his love, Kvachi went home, taking with him the poison and bile of a stallion that had been jinxed and frustrated.

The next morning Kvachi was visited by his friends. He turned over in his warm bed, stretched out, and smiled.

"How are you?" asked Chikinjiladze.

"Heavens, it's noon, time you got up!" Sedrak advised him.

"I expect he found a way in last night," decided Gabo Chkhubishvili. "That's why he's smiling and stretching himself with such pleasure."

"Hey, is that true?"

"Suppose it is?"

"Kvachi, spit it out; don't hide things from us."

Kvachi didn't spit anything out. He had his lips firmly sealed, he kept his secret double-locked, he was protecting a woman's reputation and honor, guarding them as a real knight and man should do. He just smiled slightly, rolled his eyes devilishly, and stretched out lazily, while his face expressed the greatest possible sweetness, happiness, and bliss.

"I swear by the grace of St Sergius, the business is over."

"Congratulations, Kvachi, congratulations! Dinner today is on you."

"Yes, that's what I said, let's stop at that."

Kvachi became stubborn, refusing to speak or blurt anything out: "Oh, I can't possibly talk about it … Dinner? Supper's better than dinner. You're all my guests, don't argue."

He stretched out again blissfully, rolled his eyes, and spread a victory banner over his lips.

When Sedrak saw that Kvachi's wrist had been bitten, he finally believed in Kvachi's victory and shared his belief with the others: "Well, just look at that, will you? She must be a very tough woman; you've got to hand it to her."

That evening they drank several toasts to Kvachi, wished him further victories, called him a womaniser, and even mentioned Sophie's name.

Kvachi gave another ambiguous smile, keeping the banner of victory on his lips, but refusing to confirm or deny his friends' belief.

From that day on an invisible, silent, and intangible poisonous fog hung over the Odessa students. Miss Gossip slowly circulated, hissing like a snake, slithering into everyone's ear in a subtle surge, leaving a little venom before it left, moving from one house to the next, and so on.

It poisoned, rotted, and polluted Sophie's heart and her saintly reputation. Miss Gossip had left a tiny drop in some ears, a big drop in others, and a stinking pool had accumulated.

Ending Two Love Affairs

Vera had lost weight and become very pale, thanks to her secret love affair with Kvachi. He had nothing to gain from appearing in public with her, so that Kvachi avoided her and gave as his pretext the possibility that Captain Sidorov or his wife or one of their many relatives might prematurely expose their love affair. Did Kvachi intend to marry Vera, or not? Of course he intended to! There was no need even to discuss it, but Vera would have to obey the Georgians' unalterable rules and laws, or Kvachi would never be able to darken his parents' door again and wouldn't get a single rouble from Silibistro's pocket, whereas they could count, he said, on getting at least a million. Kvachi would have to get his parents' permission and blessing, and he was expecting that any day now. Of course, they would consent. Silibistro and Pupi had before then begged Kvachi to marry a woman who was wholly Russian, and definitely an educated girl. So Vera needn't fear anything. She could calm down and wait without worrying for a letter to come from Silibistro.

For the tenth time Vera felt reassured and patiently waited for the Lord Lieutenant of the Georgian nobility, Silibistro Kvachantiradze, to give his consent and blessing.

On one occasion Vera rushed in a panic to see Kvachi, put both arms round his neck, and whispered to him in fear and trembling: "Listen to me … I have to tell you that … that it's just moved. Look, here …"

She was shaking, clinging to Kvachi's side and waiting for him to advise and comfort her.

Kvachi broke out in a cold sweat. He was bewildered, he was numb and speechless, overcome with fear. Vera reminded him: "Tell me what to do, will you?"

"Wait … Wait a bit, let me think."

After furrowing his brow, he thought of something:

"I mustn't stay here any longer. It's like a prison for the two of us, we can't see each other and we can't talk freely. I've got to move out. You'll come to see me often … if you have to, you can move in with me … that's the best thing to do."

Vera was obsessed with Kvachi's idea:

"Move out today … don't leave it too late. That's by far the best thing to do. We'll rent two or three rooms until your parents' blessing comes, we'll stay as quiet as mice."

The very next day Kvachi moved out, but he couldn't give Vera time to meet each other in private or talk about their future, or embrace each other, or even forget for ten minutes tomorrow's fears and worries. Either Kvachi was not at home, or Sedrak or Beso or Ladi was sitting there with him, or they'd all gathered there with no intention of departing. They treated Vera like an old friend, they entertained her, and saw her out politely.

Once, Vera came at a time specified by Kvachi, but found Beso Shikia there instead of him. He greeted her amicably, sat her down, and began sweetly:

"I know you well, as a friend; you're a serious and intelligent woman. So I can be bold and speak to you openly."

"My God! What's happened? Nothing bad has happened, has it?"

"It has, but nothing special. Please stay calm. What I have to tell you is that Kvachi has had a reply from his parents."

"So? What then?"

"In principle they agree and they're pleased that Kvachi has chosen someone like you, educated, respectable, from a good family. They're sending their blessing straight away, but ..."

"But?"

"But their letter says that he can marry when he finishes university."

The girl was nonplussed; she murmured:

"Fine ... I understand, but ... but I ... What am I to do? How can I wait three or four years? I ... I'm pregnant and ... and very soon I'll have a baby."

"That won't be a problem. Kvachi will support you, he'll give you fifty roubles a month ..."

"I don't know ... I can't come to terms with it ... I have to think ... I have to work it out."

"That's what I said: you're a clever woman, I said." Beso replied joyfully. "Have a good think; I'm sure you'll think of something. Goodbye, then. Don't upset yourself, think it over seriously."

Drained of color, the girl staggered towards the door; she came to a halt, remembered something, and turned round.

"Really, I'd forgotten: where is Kvachi? Why didn't he tell me all this himself?"

"Kvachi's gone to see his uncle. His uncle came from Tbilisi to see him yesterday."

"Fine ... Good."

She turned round again and, staggering, left; she crashed into the door, and, weak at the knees, it was all she could do to carry on.

Vera came several times afterwards to see Kvachi, but she never found her fiancé at home.

Once they bumped into each other in the street. Vera put a hand on Kvachi, led him aside, and tearfully whispered to him:

"What are you doing, what are your plans for me? My mother's found out everything ... The day before yesterday they threw me out of the house. A friend has taken me in. I don't have money even for a crust of bread."

"Calm down, it will all be sorted out. This isn't something we can discuss in the street. Here's five roubles for you to spend; at seven this evening come and see me, and we'll talk there."

"I've been to see you ten times, but I never find you at home."

"Can't be helped, darling, I haven't had any spare time. People are expecting me today, so take it easy, don't upset yourself."

That evening, instead of Kvachi, it was his friend Chipuntiradze who met her, invited her into the room, and went onto the attack:

"Why do you keep pestering Kvachi? Aren't I just as good a man as him? A girl as good-looking as you can always get a man to stick around, so she can live without worries."

Chipi put his arm round Vera and drew her towards him. Vera turned her face away and let out a sudden hysterical sob. Chipi took fright, quickly had someone fetch water, and with great difficulty calmed her down when she recovered from her faint.

That is how Kvachi freed himself from a girl he had "hooked as a joke", but two weeks later the student community told him that Miss Sidorova had laid a formal complaint against him. Kvachi became pensive, but then asked:

"Will the matter be discussed publicly?"

"Of course it will."

"I agree."

That evening Kvachi had a word with Beso.

"Ah, Chipi won't agree to do that, nor will Sedrak, nor will Gabo."

"If they won't, what do I care? What sort of friends are they if they won't stand up for me when I'm in trouble? If they won't budge, tell me and then I'll sort it out myself ... Go and explain everything to all three of them and tell them what to do."

That day was set for the Georgian community's court of honor. Sidorov's daughter told her story, in a confused way, to the student body, alternately blushing and turning pale with shame. She stammered out that he won her affections, made her love him, swore he would marry her, and then deceived her. Finally the mother of Kvachi's future first-born and the object of his past amusement burst into tears like a vulnerable child.

"What has comrade Kvachantiradze got to say?"

"It's all true, except for one detail I have to correct. I don't know whether the baby is mine, or ..."

"What do you mean you don't know? If you've been sleeping together ..."

"I find this hard to say, very hard, but since this girl hasn't been too ashamed to make this business public, I am compelled to say everything."

"Tell us."

"The fact is that this girl has had other men …"

Vera blanched and interrupted him: "What, what did you say? That I had other men? Who? What others?"

"Let me speak, miss, and I'll refresh your memory. Now tell me, do you know Chipi Chipuntiradze and Sedrak Havlabariani, or not?"

"I know them … you introduced me to them yourself … they often came to see you. So what are you implying?"

"What I'm implying, miss, is that these gentlemen went to see you more often than me. You used to visit them. Now I'll say nothing more. Mr Chairman, you can ask my witnesses about anything else."

"Me?" Sedrak gave his evidence. "Of course, I used to go, and she used to come … Well? It's embarrassing to say so, but I mustn't hide things, I must tell you the truth … well? It certainly happened, everything happened, of course it did … When? It would be just eight months ago; Proof? Sorry, I can't offer you written proof, bless you all! I can give you a sign: that woman has in that place there a big pink birthmark. If you like, look for yourself …"

Chipi Chipuntiradze seriously, firmly, and without budging, repeated the same evidence.

Sidorov's daughter was lost for words, petrified and frozen. Then she started shaking all over, she banged her little fists on the table, and in a choking voice shrieked:

"It's a lie, it's a lie."

Then the yell was mingled with laughter, and she gasped for breath. She staggered away and fell into the arms of Sophie Shivadze. The case was over. Sidorov's daughter was carried into an adjacent room.

There was uproar among the students. Then the eternal student Vano Shivadze, a giant of a man, came in: his eyes were lackluster, his brow furrowed, and he clutched a big gnarled stick. He looked all round the room and then headed straight for Kvachi.

"I've got a couple of words to say."

"Go ahead, sir."

"You've been spreading the most horrible rumors about my niece Sophie … What rumors? Do you mean to say you don't understand?! Let me remind you …"

And he did.

"My God, God forbid! The things they say! When did I say that? How could I have? Oh, Mr Shivadze, how could you believe such a thing? God forbid!"

"If that is really how things are, say out loud to these people that you refute these vile rumors."

"That's easy."

"Attention! Please listen! Attention!"

"Comrades! Friends! Some scoundrel has been spreading vile rumors about me and the very reputable Sophie Shivadze. I declare publicly that there has never been anything between us, nor have I ever said there was … I and Miss Sophie Shivadze do not talk to each other, because I once behaved recklessly … But nothing of that sort has ever happened … That's all."

He stopped and joined the students, who were pale with shock. He was muttering: "If I ever meet the swine who passed on those rumors … Lies. It's all lies!"

The court delivered its verdict. As comrade Miss Sidorova was unable to prove that comrade Kvachi Kvachantiradze was the sole person who could be the father of her unborn child, her complaint should be left unpursued.

Sidorova fainted and her girl friends stayed put, but the rest of those present left the court. Kvachi was worked up, and reproached his comrades: "How could we have spread rumors in such a way that both the girl and her cousin would hear about them … Because

I used that word? But what was I supposed to do? Confirm what she said and destroy myself because of that girl?"

"Well, at least you get away unscathed, what more do you want?"

"I got away, but let's stop talking about that now. Sedrak, where to?"

"Well, Arutina's expecting us, I told him to this morning."

Kvachi, now acquitted, set off to the sounds of merriment in the company of his five loyal friends for the dock area, to the inn run by his fellow-countryman Arutina, where they would enjoy shashlyk, smoked sturgeon, and Kakhetian Ganja wine.

So ended Kvachi's first and last real love.

Bankruptcy and the Boxwood Spoon

Kvachi was distressed, extremely so: his money had run out.

The consequence of running out of money was that he lagged behind his friends and fellow-students, and his influence waned. Friends no longer fawned on him as they used to. The women had dispersed. Getting credit had become difficult. His tailor, shoemaker, and launderer were complaining; his cab-driver threatened to sue him: a penniless Kvachi was like a fish in a drought, stranded on the bank, gasping for air.

Finally he informed Silibistro of his dire straits. The reply he got from Kutaisi was a mere eighteen roubles and the same amount of paper covered with remonstrations and rebukes.

Once again Sedrak came to his aid.

"Oh dear, you're skint, are you? Do you want me to show you how to get money? Then pay attention and trust me completely. Nadinka Armeladze and Verichka Kaloshvili are good friends of yours, aren't they? Invite me to a good supper. You'll have a good time and you'll win fifty roubles … All right? Leave the rest up to me."

The next day there was a supper, attended by a Greek, by Sedrak, Kvachi, and two women, in a nicely isolated private room in the *Olympus*.

After midnight had struck and the diners had got quite tipsy, Sedrak caught Kvachi's eye and gave his foot a gentle kick. Kvachi sneaked unnoticed out of the room, put on his hat, and headed off home.

When it was already light, Nadinka and Verichka left the *Olympus* by the back door and went back through the deserted streets to their lodgings.

"I felt very ill that evening, I was on the point of collapse, so I left," Kvachi told the two women when he happened to meet them in the street.

Nadinka, blushing furiously, turned her face away and murmured: "We left too straight after you … We didn't stay more than ten minutes … We didn't want to stay there with strangers once you'd gone."

Fifty roubles were hardly enough for Kvachi to draw breath, but he soon got deeper into things.

Silibistro's son used to dine in the *Europe* hotel. Once, when he had finished his dinner, he deftly slipped a silver spoon into his pocket and then left. The same gesture was repeated the next day and the next one. The restaurant manager lost patience: he gathered all the waiters and told them outright:

"Every day we lose a silver spoon. My restaurant has never known anything so disgraceful. The thief is either one of you or one of the customers. If you haven't found the thief in three days, I'll fire the lot of you. So go and look for him."

And he deducted his losses from the waiters' earnings.

From then on the waiters never took their eyes off the customers, not even for a minute. That was just what Kvachi wanted.

One day Kvachi behaved extremely boldly: when he'd finished eating he picked up a silver spoon and right under the waiter's eyes put it in his breast pocket. The waiter was astounded and joyfully ran to fetch the restaurant manager. Kvachi chose his moment and furtively slipped the silver spoon to Beso Shikia, tipping him off:

"Now watch me and see the trouble I'm going to get that idiot into. Take that spoon quickly and hide it somewhere."

The restaurant manager sent an employee to summon a policeman, while he respectfully went up to Kvachi and asked him, with a smile:

"I have a small request to make: would you like to come to my office for a minute?"

A few minutes later, when the policeman entered the office, the restaurant manager pounced like a bear on Kvachi:

"Thief! Robber! Spoon thief! Pickpocket! Give back my spoon. Search this rogue right here and now. He's stolen ten spoons from me ... Look, he's just put a spoon in that pocket."

Kvachi listened patiently to this torrent of curses and abuse and then turned to the policeman: "Search me, I agree to it, but ..."

The policeman apologized. He searched Kvachi and removed a boxwood spoon from Kvachi's left pocket.

"Is this your spoon?"

They all stared at each other dumbfounded. Kvachi calmly sat down, crossed his legs, and gravely addressed the policeman:

"Would you please now draw up a statement? As for you," he turned to the restaurant manager, "I'll see you serve six months in prison for slander."

The restaurant manager ran his fingers through his hair and groaned: "The scoundrel has got me, he's got me."

"Please include those words in the statement," Kvachi asked the policeman.

The policeman was now writing it down.

"Statement of what? What statement?" shouted the restaurant manager, turning to the waiters. "Get out of here, you wretches, you fools." And when they were all gathered round, he ripped the statement from the policeman's hand, tore it to pieces, and said submissively: "No need to waste paper. Why don't you just say straight out how much you're asking?"

Kvachi curtly replied: "Three thousand."

Some razor-sharp bargaining and haggling began. The manager's starting offer was two hundred and he wouldn't budge above one thousand. Finally, after a lot of squabbling, with the help of Beso Shikia, Kvachi just managed to get him up to fifteen hundred roubles.

Kvachi took the money, threw it on the table, and said:

"Look at these easy winnings. One boxwood spoon and my own wits have won fifteen hundred roubles. If I was really desperate I could have got three thousand roubles as easily as three."

Beso told his starving friends all about the boxwood spoon. They burst out shrieking and yelling in praise of their leader, whom they longed to imitate. Then they started attacking each other and complaining. Sedrak demanded repayment with interest of their debt to Arutina; Chikinjiladze wanted a hundred roubles, Chipuntiradze two hundred. They added up the sums and shared out the money.

Beso Shikia barely managed to hold on to five hundred roubles for Kvachi, money which ran out in two weeks.

Shortly afterwards Kvachi was again on his uppers.

Again Sedrak came to his aid. Trembling, his eyes shining, he'd brought a pile of new money: "Hey, prince, be careful or you'll be in terrible trouble and get me into it, too. Don't try to change it in a big shop or good restaurant. Go to small traders, buy a bagel or a cigarette, or take a cab ride. A quarter of it is yours. But be careful, or else ..."

In two days Kvachi had changed the money, but he only just avoided disaster: on two occasions his money had been refused. Sedrak warned him:

"I did tell you not to go to anywhere good, but you couldn't control yourself: you tried to pass those notes in Fanconi's coffeehouse. Well, that's it: there's no more. Get it? I said there's no more, it's finished."

Kvachi once again could hold his head high, but very soon he was downcast again.

"Sedrak, help me!"

"What? You want me to help you? I do help you. Like a brother helping another, any day. But how can I get it over to you, prince? Dangerous jobs end with accidents. Go and try your hand at something clean. You're a clever and ingenious man. You're cut out to be a salesman. I have a job for you, so pay attention."

Kvachi Becomes a Salesman

A few days later Kvachi was going from family to family and shop to shop. All the patter made his jaws ache, his tongue numb, and his head dizzy. Ever since the beginning of May he had been selling the novel *Helios* stoves. He praised the goods, puffed them, exaggerated their merits, and gave his customers lectures on chemistry and thermodynamics.

"Bear with me and pay attention. You pour the oil in here … Then you pull this down: this is your thermoscope … Half a pint of oil will heat five rooms for a day … You can work out the savings."

"We're not interested! All five of our rooms have fine stoves … May's a funny time for selling stoves! I don't have time for this."

"Bear with me! Just give me five minutes of your time … Work out the savings …"

Kvachi's calculations implied that one only needed to buy the stove, and it was being virtually given away, then that using it to heat five rooms for a whole year would only cost two or three roubles.

So he managed to sell a dozen stoves in a week.

Finally he encountered a man called Hofstein. They got into an argument and confronted one another. Hofstein received Kvachi coldly, refused to buy, and would not budge; in fact he picked up his hat as if about to leave, and finally shouted at Kvachi: "I don't want it! I said I don't want it."

Kvachi dug his heels in. He ignored Hofstein's hat, Hofstein's loss of patience; he implied: "You've got to buy this stove, and that's all there is to it. Until I've sold it to you, I'm not moving." Without waiting to be asked, he sat down and made himself comfortable.

Hofstein slipped out to the next room. Kvachi followed him.

Hofstein started reading a newspaper. Kvachi waited patiently. Finally, Hofstein was tired out. He softened, broke down, and meekly asked: "How much are you asking for it?"

"Seventeen roubles and twenty-five kopecks."

"Fine, and now leave me alone."

"Here's your receipt. Good day to you."

Hofstein caught up with Kvachi on the stairs:

"Wait a minute … I've got a few words I want to say to you. Come in; sit down … Now you can listen to me. Take this document: the cat has more use for that stove than I do. Install it at your place, or sell it, or throw it away, or give it to charity. Nobody's ever sold me anything so worthless and completely unusable before. I have nothing but praise and respect for your persistence, energy, and skills. You must have real flair and talent for salesmanship. Do you know anything about insurance? No? You don't even need to. I can teach you the lot in an hour. Now pay careful attention. I'm an insurance inspector. I work for the *Salamander* company. We're the biggest and richest company in all Russia … Our capital is a hundred million … We make ten million net profit … Our nominal share price is a hundred roubles, on the stock exchange we trade at 341 roubles. Well, take a look at today's paper … *Salamander* is out-buying and out-selling *Russia,*

Anchor, The Northern Society, Volga, Moscow. We'll appoint you as an agent for life and accident insurance … The salary? Nothing. You'll work for commission … Some agents make two thousand roubles a month … Yes sir, two thousand, I said. Now I'll explain how agents work, the rules and techniques."

Kvachi dined with Hofstein that day, then had one more lesson; in the evening he returned home laden with tariffs, placards, and tables of charges.

Once home he came across his landlord, the seafarer Kulidis.

"You mean to say that you still aren't insured? A seafarer with no insurance? Everyday you face the danger of drowning or catching some disease, or old age … then what do you expect your widow and orphans to do? How will you be able to face them in the next world? Are you telling me that you don't intend to die? That's all very well. If you live another twenty or just fifteen years, you get your money back with interest. Insurance is a way of increasing and accumulating wealth. Whether you die or stay alive, you'll still be in the black … You're telling me that you've had plenty of persuasion but they've never got you to agree? Are you afraid of death? All the better, you'll die a peaceful death, you won't have a problem with your family being reduced to beggary … But you're afraid of death?! That's silly. You'll have to pay five hundred roubles a year? That's a lie. Don't look at other people, quite the opposite, you should set others an example … Let me give you some information: in America 99.7% of the population is insured, in England it's 97.9%, in Germany 94.3%, but in Russia only 0.1%. That's how badly we lag behind developed nations. So this is yet another example of our lack of enlightenment and civilization. In fact, sir, I have been sent as a guardian angel for your family, and I shan't let you go until I've enrolled you. You're in a hurry, are you? Don't worry, I shan't make you late … You haven't got any money? That's all right, a hundred roubles will do me for now, the rest can wait for when they send the policy from Petersburg, then you can give it to me. Doctors? You'll be examined tomorrow. Now I'll write it all down ... Your name? Your surname? Date of birth? You'll be insured for ten thousand roubles ... Here's your receipt. Sign here, please ... Now let me have a hundred roubles ... Many thanks. You can go now ... Have a good day."

In half an hour, Kvachi had "done over" Kulidis, a man whom other agents had been pursuing for ten years.

Kulidis sent Kvachi to see Ivanov, Ivanov sent him to see Petrov, Petrov sent him to see Pavlov, and Pavlov sent him to see Smirnov.

"What? You still aren't insured? Amazing! Astounding! Yet another example of how backward we are. In America 89.7% are insured, in England it's 81.3%, in France 79.4%, but in Russia just 0.7%."

He persisted, he pestered, he pursued, he wore his victim down and, once he had marked him out, gave him no rest until he had signed him up and tied him down.

Kvachi rushed about, bustled about, ran about from morning to night, repeating the same spiel, which he had learnt by heart, and adding quite a few lies. Some he frightened with talk of death, others he lured with promises of making money. He wrote applications and receipts, collected money, handed his clients policies, and constantly cursed rival agents and firms:

"*Russia* company? Any day now it will go broke. *Volga*? It's already bankrupt ... *Moscow*? It doesn't pay out. Karpov the agent? He's a pickpocket. Katsmann? He's a swindler. Sikhovich? An embezzler. Don't trust them. Keep away from them. Trust me, or you'll regret it."

Kvachi was a member of everybody's family, a friend of the house.

"Ah-ah-ah, so it's Prince Napoleon Apollonovich I see! How are you doing? How are you? Come and see us, prince, do come."

Kvachi would do Peter the honor, and then Paul; sometimes he dined with Ivan, sometimes he had supper with Sidor, sometimes he feasted with Kuzma: in two weeks he put all his weight back on, and became a handsome well-built man.

He got himself a dozen sub-agents, hired a carriage by the month, paid back what he owed Sedrak, and got his other friends involved in his work.

But Kvachi still had one sore point; there was a troublesome thought, something that gnawed at him: he didn't have any surplus funds.

What he was earning was earned by hard work and toil. What he earned the day before was spent today, but for tomorrow, the day after, and the day after that he still had to run about finding new clients, inventing a new spiel, winning trust: in a word, it needed constant worries, bother, work, sweat, toil, and diligence.

Kvachi dreamed of an utterly different life; he demanded more of this world. He expected liberty, free choice, and sheer pleasure. But the first, second, and the rest could only be had through money, as he very well knew, and the money had to be huge, beyond counting, enough to require a bank account. Meanwhile Kvachi merely had to write out cheques and sort out things all round him. Kvachi didn't have that much money, and this was what worried and grieved him.

"Why don't you take out a policy yourself?" Hofstein once asked him.

The same day Kvachi asked himself; "Indeed, why haven't I taken out a policy? Why shouldn't I enrol Silibistro?"

And his brains started working overtime from that day on.

Insuring a Life and a House

Kvachi continued to be on the move, running about all the time, thinking and thinking, measuring, weighing, assessing, and calculating. When he'd finished calculating he wrote:

"My dear father, my noble Silibistro! Fill in correctly this printed form which I am sending you with this letter: you can get Kolia Tsalikadze to write everything. I've got to insure you for ten thousand roubles. Don't ask me why, I'll be seeing you soon and I'll tell you everything. In Kutaisi there's an agent for *Salamander*: his name is Volodia Sharidze. Go and see him and he'll do all the rest for you. Tell him that Kvachi the agent said so, so don't pay him any commission. I'm sending you three hundred roubles. Give a hundred to the agent, have a hundred for yourself, and the other hundred you can give to the agent when you get the policy from Petersburg. When you get the policy, send me a telegram to say so. Then I'll come and fix everything for you.

"I'm well, you needn't worry about me. I was sorry to hear about Tvichia's death. I'm very glad you managed to get a junior officer's rank.* You deserved better, but that's fine: the rest can wait. I still owe a bit to Eremo and Laitadze and Daniel the Jew. Give them all my regards and tell them Kvachi is coming soon to pay them back. Anyway, you know, don't make any mistakes.

"I wept bitter tears at not being able to see my beloved Pupi, Khukhu, and Notio. Kisses to you all. Who knows: with luck I may be able to move you from the filth of Kutaisi to Tbilisi. Pray to God and he'll help us. Your son Kvachi.

"P.S. Tell me, is the Volkova woman, whose house I sold you, still alive? I've done two years of university, I've got two more to do. Don't tell anyone I'm coming. Your Kvachi."

Meanwhile Kvachi presented Hofstein with a declaration addressed to Salamander, saying that he, Kvachi, wished to insure himself against accidents for twenty thousand roubles.

"Don't you want to insure your life?"

"I'm afraid to ... I don't want to, I'm still young, but I could have a bad accident ... I walk a lot and I could be hit by a railway carriage, or a cab could run me over, or a brick could fall off a

* In Russia, members of the aristocracy and retired government officials were given the rank of at least second lieutenant and allowed to wear épaulettes.

house and strike me."

Two weeks later he had a policy, and then he received a telegram from Kutaisi, saying: "Received policy. Silibistro."

After a few days Kvachi suddenly announced to his friends that his father Silibistro had fallen ill and that he was off to Kutaisi the next day.

Kvachi and Beso hurriedly boarded a ship and on the fifth day they surprised everybody by entering Kvachi's own house, where he had spent his last school year and which Silibistro and his uncle Khukhu Chichia had bought "at great expense."

There were shrieks and yells of joy from Silibistro's family, kissing, embracing, and rejoicing. Kvachi's mother Pupi nearly had a heart attack from sudden joy; the elderly Khukhu and Notio burst into tears, while Silibistro smiled and strutted about, because his burly shoulders were adorned by a lieutenant's resplendent epaulettes.

When they had asked after each other's health and their initial burst of emotion had subsided, Kvachi, Beso, and Silibistro locked themselves up in his study and whispered, conversed, and pondered for some time.

It took them three days to measure, weigh up, and calculate the job. Kvachi had learnt by heart the details of Silibistro's life policy and house insurance policy. He was extremely proud and pleased that a house worth four thousand had been insured by Silibistro for ten thousand roubles.

On the fourth day Silibistro declared himself unable to get out of bed: his innards hurt, he groaned, and he complained.

Two more weeks passed. Doctors examined Silibistro and diagnosed malaria, then a stomach inflammation, then diabetes, then cancer.

"Oh what's the point of trusting a Kutaisi doctor with anything?" Silibistro and the members of his family said. "Thank God, Kvachi has got here in time and he can take his sick father to Odessa or to Tbilisi."

Kvachi and Beso meanwhile ransacked Kutaisi once more, once more behaved like madmen, not forgetting to revisit the swollen Eremo, Laitadze, Daniel the Jew, or Sholia and his loyal wife Tsviri.

Sholia was not at home when Kvachi called, not that Kvachi minded: instead of her husband, Tsviri met him and was too overjoyed to be able to stand. Once again Tsviri and Kvachi revisited and recalled past times and once more they had a taste of the scrapings of a love that was now moss-covered and mouldy.

Beso had not forgotten Tsviri, either, and he remembered delightful and profitable past times with his former landlady.

When the widow Volkova heard that Kvachi was back, she locked herself in her dark, damp room, and all the time that Kvachi was carousing in Kutaisi she spent praying and fasting. She was so anxious to avoid Kvachi and so abhorred him, as if it were she, a demented woman, who had deceived, robbed, and destituted a poor little Kvachi.

Eventually Kvachi wrapped up the debilitated and confused Silibistro warmly and took him off to Tbilisi.

They rented a three-roomed house in the suburb of Didube and got down to work the very next day.

Kvachi got his nose into action, wore out his eyes, sniffed the air, ran about, collected information; he was searching for something and he finally found it, pursued what he'd found and pinned it down.

One day Kvachi went to see a forty-year-old Russian.

"Are you the owner of this house?"

"I am, sir."

"Does an Ovanes Shaburiants live here?"

"He's my neighbor. He's very ill."

"He's ill, is he? What's wrong with him?"

"It'd be about two weeks ago he was struck down by paralysis.

He's lost the use of his right arm and leg and he can't talk any more."

"My God, why didn't someone tell me before? I might have been able to help. Don't look so surprised: we're old friends. Once I got into deep water and nearly drowned: Ovanes rescued me and got me out ... He saved my life ... He nearly drowned himself ... since then we've lost touch. I've only just got back from Russia and I happened to hear that Ovanes was staying with you."

"You'll be doing a godly deed if you can somehow care for him. He hasn't got a single relative in the world, nobody to look out for him, nobody to help him. He's a refugee from Turkey."

"I know, I know, Ovanes is an Armenian ... His family were massacred in Turkey ... my God, how could this happen to me? How could I come so late? For the love of God, take me to see the poor man."

"Do come in. I've been nursing him myself, I don't know how I can cope or look after him. Today we meant to go to the hospital and ask if we can get them to take him in."

"No, don't do that. I'll see to him myself."

In a dark, damp, and dirty cellar they came across a motionless corpse wrapped in stinking rags.

"*Bari luys* (Good morning), Ovanes! How are you? I expect you recognize me! So I've come ... I had trouble finding you ... Once upon a time you saved my life, now it's time I repaid you ... Well, you've got to come with me ... Don't be afraid, I'll have you on your feet in two weeks ... Well, where are his identity papers and documents? Do you have them? Let me have them."

They brought along some workmen, put the stunned Ovanes in a cab, and took him off to Kvachi's lodgings.

All three were very pleased and satisfied: Kvachi Kvachantiradze, the elderly Russian, and Ovanes Shaburiants.

That same day Kvachi called in a doctor.

"Doctor, help me! For the love of God, help me! Such a terrible thing has happened to me! Why is God so angry with me?" Kvachi whined tearfully.

"Calm yourself, my dear sir, calm yourself and tell me what's happened, how it happened? Who is the patient?"

"It's my father, Silibistro Kvachantiradze … we moved to Tbilisi a month ago, he was a well man then, there didn't seem to be anything wrong with him … Perhaps you remember that about ten days ago a grenade went off in the market?"

"Of course I remember, I remember it only too well."

"My poor father and I were there. The grenade almost fell at our feet. Only God knows how we survived. We were saved by a real miracle. We'd got into a cab and left at that very moment. Ever since then my father's had the shakes. I meant to call a doctor, but he wouldn't have it: he said he'd never in his life been to the doctor's and he wasn't going to start now. But today he's suddenly lost the use of his limbs and he can't speak. For God's sake get me out of this mess. God, I wish I were dead!"

"Calm down, don't upset yourself; I'll examine the patient, there may be nothing much wrong with him."

The doctor examined the patient. Ovanes's eyes showed his astonishment as he watched the two of them; he moved his lips as he thought to himself:

"*Astvats Ter oghormian* (God, merciful Lord)! Who is this young man? What does he want of me? And why has he brought me to this house?"

Kvachi's heart was racing with fear: he thought the sick man might any moment get his speech back and start talking.

Finally the doctor spoke: "I shan't hide anything from you: you're a man, so gather your strength and prepare yourself. Your father may not last long, although it's also possible that he'll live for some time to come."

The doctor's consoling words alarmed and scared Kvachi: he ran his hand through his hair, groaned, and collapsed onto a chair: "My God! Great God!"

The doctor wrote a prescription, gave some instructions, and left. Then Silibistro came in from outside.

"How are things?"

"Very good. The doctor said he should pass away soon. He said I'm a man and should gather my strength and prepare myself."

They smiled and laughed.

"Don't give him anything to eat, or any medicine."

"Ah, as if I'd spend money on that! Though we've got to get some medicine, the doctor's coming again ... I'm off to the pharmacy ... Tomorrow I'll take you to the hospital and you'll pretend to be sick, pretend you can't talk ... just put up with it for a week."

"Fine, fine! You go and get the medicine, and come back soon."

The next day in one of the big hospitals they noted: "Ovanes Karapeta's son Shaburiants, aged 45, from the town of Van, an Ottoman Turkish citizen ... symptoms of paralysis."

Two weeks later one of the Georgian newspapers printed an announcement in black borders:

On the 27th of September of this year in Tbilisi, after a short illness, the sudden death is announced of Silibistro Kvachantiradze, which his widow Pupi, his orphaned son Kvachi (Anapodiste), his father-in-law Khukhu Chichia, and mother-in-law Notio Chichia announce with the greatest sorrow. The body will be laid to rest today at 12:00, and taken from the deceased's lodgings (Didube, 84, Saguramo Street).

There was a slight misunderstanding: thanks to the inefficiency of the newspaper's editors, the bereavement announcement was not printed until the day of the funeral. Because the paper came out in the evening, the couple of distant family acquaintances that the family had in Tbilisi were unable to come to the requiem and the burial of the late Silibistro.

The unfortunate "Silibistro" had been firmly locked and nailed in his coffin from the day after his death: Kvachi explained this by saying that for unknown reasons Silibistro had begun to decompose and smell bad within twenty-four hours.

The priest and deacon dragged out the dreary funeral hymn lazily, barely opening their mouths:

"Lo-o-ord, give eternal rest to the soul of thy-y-y deceased ..."

" ...now and for ever and ever, for all eternity-y-y, a-a-men ..."

Pupi, arrayed in widow's black, and Notio were both tear-stained, deeply sorrowful, exhausted, and weakened. Their hair was dishevelled, "their cheeks were faded and their eyes were like pools that never dry." Khukhu and Kvachi stood with their heads bowed. Their faces were sullen, their brows furrowed, their eyes swollen and red from excess of grief, exhaustion, tears, and lack of sleep.

When the requiem mass was over, "Silibistro's" coffin was put on a palanquin and hurriedly carried off to the Kukia cemetery.

The mourners moaned, groaned, and lamented as they followed the coffin, but kept furtively and anxiously looking round, examining the passersby. Sometimes they fell silent, sometimes they loudly mourned:

"Silibistro, son! Why have you abandoned us? What pained you, what hurt you to make you leave us so soon?" Notio complained, covering her face with both hands.

"Chipi, son!" Khukhu took up the lament, "why has the Lord robbed me of a man like you? Whose shoulders are going to wear your officer's epaulettes now? Who is going to lead the nobility as their Lord Lieutenant? Why have you put out the fire in our hearth? Why have you pissed on my candle?"

"O, wretched me! O, ruined me!" yelled Pupi. "Who's going to market now? Who will buy meat for the shashlyk and green herbs? You loved them so much, Silibistro-o-o! Who will now close my wretched eyes that you loved so much? We've lived together all this time, we should have departed together from this li-i-fe ... That's what we'd agreed, Silibistro, my faithful husband."

"God, how wretched I am," Kvachi shouted as he struck his head. "Who'll care for me now? Who'll pay for my education? Who'll see me through university-y-y? I'm a ruined miserable wretch."

Beso Shikia, his head bowed, also followed the mourning family: he was laughing behind his little moustache.

They ran at a brisk pace into Kukia cemetery, put the coffin in the grave, covered it with earth and, their heads bent, went home. That same evening "Ovanes Shaburiants" was discharged from hospital and left for Navtlughi railway station. Kvachi saw "Ovanes" off.

They whispered for some time in the dark, then they exchanged kisses and parted.

A few days later a clerk in the Vladikavkaz police wrote in the police register:

"Ovanes Shaburiants, aged 45, Ottoman subject, has arrived from Tbilisi. Is lodging at 16, Bazaar Street."

Making a Profit from Insurance

Filed.
To the district inspector of the *Salamander* Insurance company, Apt 2, 21 Vera Rise, Tbilisi.
A declaration by Kvachi, son of Silibistro Kvachantiradze.

With respect I inform you that on 1 October this year, at nine in the evening, I was returning by bicycle to Didube. When I was passing by the church, a carriage struck me in the darkness and knocked me off my bicycle. The appropriate statement was drawn up at the time, and I am sending you a copy with this letter. My right arm and right leg have been injured. I am insured against accidents by your company, policy No. 124392 of 11 May this year.

In addition, I inform you with great sadness that on 25 September this year, at 4.30 in the morning, in my apartment in Tbilisi my dear father Silibistro Kvachantiradze passed away. His life was insured with your company, as well, for ten thousand roubles, under policy No. 475663 of 4 June this year.

I am sending you with this letter three certificates: namely, 1) treatment of the illness; 2) death; 3) burial.

I request that you carry out the procedures prescribed by law.

With respect, Kvachi Kvachantiradze.

Following the rules of his profession and existing legislation, the district inspector for Transcaucasia visited Saguramo Street and personally stood by Kvachi Kvachantiradze, who was confined to bed.

"Are you Mr Kvachantiradze? I am calling because of your declaration."

Everyone—Khukhu Chichia, his wife Notio, and Kvachi's mother Pupi—was stirred into action and alarmed. Kvachi tossed about in his bed and groaned.

"I am very pleased you've come, sir … Please sit down … sit down here … No, over here you'll be more comfortable …"

Khukhu offered him a cane chair, Pupi moved a small cushioned chair towards him, while Notio tried to drag an armchair over.

"Don't bother, ladies and gentlemen. Thank you very much."

"I know you by reputation, my dear sir. I've heard a lot of good things about you. Everyone speaks well of you," Kvachi began.

"Thank the Lord!" interjected Khukhu. "If they don't say anything bad, that means they speak well."

"A good name is more important than anything, son!" groaned Notio.

"If you've got such a good reputation when you're so young, all Russia will be talking about you when you're old," moaned the "widow" Pupi.

That was the reception the Kvachantiradze family gave the inspector: they laid on flattery with a trowel, spoiled him, and perfumed him with praise.

The inspector's only shield against this sword of respectfulness was to say:

"Don't believe a word of it. If anything good is said about me, it's all rumor and exaggeration. If they say just one bad thing, they're hiding a hundred more. I know you, too, by reputation, Mr Kvachantiradze: let me remind you that two years ago you and I traveled to Odessa."

"God, I must have gone blind!" Kvachi said, coming to life instantly. "I remember, I remember very well. You were going abroad at the time, weren't you? The whole ship was talking about you then. There wasn't an engineer as good as you to be found in all Russia!" Kvachi was lying, for the inspector knew no more about engineering than Kvachi knew about astronomy or Sanskrit.

When they had stopped enquiring about each other and kowtowing, the inspector spoke out:

"Let's get to the point. What's wrong with you? What happened to you?"

The family burst into tears and moans. They kept interrupting one other.

"What's happened to us, sir? You wouldn't wish on your worst enemy what happened to us ..."

"God must be angry with us for all this to come down on our heads at once."

"We've been destroyed, we've been wiped out! The whole family and everything has been ruined."

Pupi began to cry and left the room, while Notio dried her tears and Khukhu bowed his head.

"Our family had everything," Kvachi continued, now calmer. "We never had any illness in our family. The day before yesterday my father died. He passed away so suddenly that he couldn't say a word. The next day our house in Kutaisi burnt down. Now I've had a bad accident."

"Wasn't the house insured?"

"Oh, don't talk about it! Last year I was offered forty thousand for the house, but I refused. And now I'm only due to get ten thousand. If I weren't mourning my father, I'd let the devils take the house and this arm and this leg, too."

"Are you badly injured?"

"Oh yes, take a look yourself."

With great care Notio revealed and spread out Kvachi's bandaged limbs; he was groaning, suffering, and gritting his teeth.

His wrist and ankle were blue and swollen.

"This is my poor father's policy. We're due to get ten thousand or so."

"I'd rather he hadn't died; I'd rather instead pay that insurance company a hundred thousand," murmured Khukhu.

"And this is my policy. I'm insured for twenty thousand or so. It wasn't worth the trouble, I didn't want to, but the Odessa inspector tricked me into it. Do you know Hofstein?"

The inspector examined the policies and the other documents.

"Indeed, I do know him."

Everything turned out to be proper and in order.

"Who's treating you: who's your doctor?"

"Dr Bedov. You can't find a better doctor in all the Caucasus.

Do you know him?"

"I don't: I've never heard of him. The insurance company has its own doctors here. I'll send you one of them."

Kvachi's eyes came alive: "Which one? Who?"

"Why not Rodenbaum? He's a well-known doctor."

"Oh, no, please. Don't do that."

"Why not?"

"He's incompetent. It's not easy for me to say this, but …"

"Say it."

"Do you know Rodenbaum's wife?"

"I've seen her, but I don't actually know her."

"Well let me tell you, but give me your word of honor that nobody else is going to hear this."

"Fine, I give you my word. Speak."

"I was going to call that doctor to take a look at my father. He wasn't at home when I called. His wife saw me. I left my address with her and went home. An hour later, instead of the doctor, his wife came and … I won't say any more about it … Oh, don't ask me, I shan't tell you any more. Now tell me how I can let myself be examined by a doctor I don't respect. Send Ghabidze, I think he's one of your doctors, too."

"He was one, but he isn't any more … Why not? I don't know. Shabishvili's been appointed to take his place, I'll send him to see you. We'll be back to see you very shortly."

"Oh, that goes without saying! But, my dear sir, why are you in such a hurry to go? Bear with us a minute, we can have coffee … Why don't you do us the honor? Give us just another five minutes or so of your time."

"It's not that I don't want to do you the honor, of course I do. I'm in a hurry, otherwise I'd love to be your guest."

"Mikheil" Kvachi pleaded. "Get this business dealt with as soon as possible, don't keep me on tenterhooks, or I'll spit on the money and go my own way: what good will a few pennies do me?

They aren't worth all this torment and time-wasting."

"Don't worry yourself, Kvachi. I'll send your father's death certificate to Petersburg today and in a month's time I'll hand you ten thousand roubles. As for your arm and leg, you'll have to wait a bit. When they're healed, we'll calculate each day's sickness at twenty roubles and give you the money then."

"Suppose they don't get better."

"Well, how can you think that? Of course they'll heal."

"But, all the same, suppose they don't? There have been plenty of cases when a man's arm or leg withers for no great reason at all."

"If you have a withered arm or leg, of course, we'll give you the entire sum assured. So, you can be calm and free of worries."

"Goodbye and thank you, sir, goodbye! We'll see you again, sir, we shall ... We shan't forget you, sir, please do us the honor of coming again ..."

When the inspector had left, they exchanged looks, and their eyes questioned one other. Finally, Khukhu mumbled into his beard: "Ah, a man like that can't understand anything."

"He can't understand anything," Kvachi agreed in a low voice.

Doctor Shabishvili was telling Inspector Javakhishvili:

"I can't make any sense of Kvachantiradze's arm and leg. Whatever I do, someone else, I don't know who, undoes. I put ointment on them and bandage them, and I always leave a secret sign. The next day the sign hasn't been touched, yet the limbs are weaker and more bent. It's obvious that someone else must be working on them.

"I have information that our previous doctor Ghabidze is visiting Kvachantiradze at night. What's more, Kvachi's granny Notio Chichia has got a hand in this: that woman might well know about traumatic injuries. She's supposed to be very skilled at crippling limbs. Clients come flocking to her, because a lot of men want to get out of military service. We have the right to have Kvachi moved to a hospital and have him subjected to twenty-four-hour observation; but I shan't resort to such extreme measures, because it will cause a lot of gossip. Agents of other insurance companies will exploit this business, will get rumors circulating about us, raise the alarm, and damage our reputation. Just visit every day and keep an eye open, and let's see how things go from there. We'll somehow give Kvachi the hint that we've rumbled him … Does he already know that? Have you let him realize that? Then you've done the right thing … Fine, it's better that way … Goodbye, then. Until we meet again."

A week later Hofstein, the inspector, and Doctor Shabishvili suddenly turned up at Kvachi's. Kvachi was astounded, utterly taken aback, and he turned alternately red and pale. Over that week he seemed to have taken a turn for the worse; he was jaundiced and emaciated.

"Greetings, Napoleon Apollonovich!" Hofstein called out joyfully.

"We have come to see Mr Kvachantiradze," was the inspector's solemn greeting.

"Hello … good morning … sit down … pull up a chair …"

The family bustled about, and the visitors were at a loss.

"How are you? How are you feeling?"

Kvachi complained as before. He became tearful and moaned:

"I'm finished, I've had it … My father's died … My house has burned down … My family is broken up … Now I'm ruined."

"I know, I know everything, I know more than you think!" Hofstein interrupted him emphatically and distinctly. "Doctor, undo the bandages on the injured limbs."

Kvachi began moaning again and then yelled. They undid the bandages and examined the limbs. Both arm and leg were emaciated, withered, and looked like dry sticks."

"Ah, that's what it is. It's exactly what I've seen. I know what that is!" Hofstein interjected syllable by syllable. "Bandage them up!" Then he turned away and, while the doctor was bandaging Kvachi's limbs, he calmly tapped at the window and watched the clouds passing. Then he turned back and began speaking in a steely voice:

"Now let's get to the point. In short, in a nutshell, let me tell you straight: let's put an end to this game of hide-and-seek. It's embarrassing, we're not children any more. First of all, I must remind you that I've been entrusted with settling your three claims, haven't I?"

"And the claim for the house?"

"Yes indeed, the house fire, too. I'll begin with the beginning. First of all: you ran away from Odessa without settling your accounts, you took up to a thousand roubles with you … Hang on, sir, bear with me: we don't recognize Shikia, or Chikinjiladze, or Sedrak Havlabariani, or Katsmann. You're the only agent we recognize and you're the only one we have been dealing with. Secondly, you have misled so many clients that you are now the talk of Odessa … What, you say, who have you misled? Well here's a list, kindly read it. In your absence we have returned everybody their money, a total of 2,675 roubles. Thirdly, last year your father mortgaged your house with the bank for 1,400 roubles. The bank valued it at two thousand, but you've insured it for ten thousand. The agent is in my hands. Your great-uncle or grandfather, this old Khukhu Chichia, is not going to get away with it … hang on, I said, slow down and keep your temper. Fourthly, I'm a doctor and I used to be an inspector. I've spent my whole life working for the company and pulling the wool over my eyes is difficult, impossible in fact. I've seen thousands of tricks and I'm thoroughly experienced. I've even seen arms and legs with the same injuries. It's amazing, such a thing doesn't often occur. Just tell me one thing, how did you fall so neatly that you injured the inside of your ankle, but the outside of your wrist? It's amazing! It makes no sense! Apart from that, why should your limbs lose flesh and dry up? We'll leave the hospital to find out why. Tomorrow you have to be transferred to the clinic … What did you say, you don't want to? Don't you worry, there'll be two supervisors keeping an eye on you day and night … What was that, you don't like the idea? You won't stand for it? But you know we have the right … And you still don't want to? What do you say, you'll raise a furore? You'll move heaven and earth and get the newspapers talking? That's your business. If you don't care about your name, or this old man, or the Kutaisi agent, then our being here isn't necessary, and we'll leave."

Hofstein got to his feet.

"Wait a bit, let's talk it through … Perhaps we can come to terms," said little Kvachi, lifting himself up.

"Fine, let's see if we can. Let's cut it short. Right, you see this money?" said Hofstein, taking a pack of five-hundred-rouble notes from his breast pocket. "This money goes into your pocket right now if you behave sensibly and show some moderation."

Kvachi's eyes started to burn and gleam, his throat went dry: he fidgeted and then moved his lips:

"I'm … I'm not a greedy person, and I don't like arguments … I hate squabbling, and I'm not one to make a fuss …"

"Then let's settle up. You are owed ten thousand for your father's death, that's not in dispute."

Kvachi felt a wave of relief, as if Hofstein had removed a 150-kilo rock sitting on his chest.

"Your house, if we push things to the maximum, was worth four thousand. Here's five. That makes fifteen thousand. Next, you have your arm and leg insured for twenty thousand. We dispute that sum, even if your arm and leg really have withered. I give you my word of honor and I assure you that neither your arm nor your leg are going to wither. In one month they will heal so well that you'll be able to hop about on either leg. That would be worth about four or five hundred roubles. I'm offering you ten times more: accept five thousand."

"So, instead of forty thousand you're giving me just twenty, right?"

"Yes indeed, twenty thousand. Either accept the money now, or move to the clinic, or … or we'll hand it over to the prosecutor's office."

"It's not enough: I refuse."

"Right then, goodbye."

"Hang on, don't be hasty. Give me three days to think it over."

"I can't do that. If you like, I'll give you an hour. I'll go out, have a walk in Mushtaid park, and come back."

"I don't have any alternative, so I'll give in, but I protest."

"Right, goodbye for now. I won't say farewell."

The three men left, and the four family members stayed behind. There was an outbreak of shrieks, heated discussion, adding up on fingers. An hour passed, the men who had gone out came back, and—

"Have you thought it over? Have you decided?" Hofstein enquired.

"I'm still owed thirty-five thousand, but I'll agree to thirty."

"Is that your last word?"

"It is."

"Then we can't come to terms. If you regret this, don't blame me. Goodbye!" And the three men went out again. As they were going down the stairs, Pupi rushed after them:

"Wait a minute! Come back! Please don't be angry, please bear with us. There's a couple of things we need to tell you."

They came back again.

"I can't go one rouble lower than twenty-eight thousand," Kvachi declared in a faltering voice.

"Then there was no point our coming back."

"Wait, where are you running off to? Twenty-five."

"Twenty. Yes, or no … I know, I know everything, there's no need to go on talking. Yes, or no? In that case, goodbye."

They left again. At the end of the street Khukhu staggered up to them:

"Please don't hurt our feelings, gentlemen … If we've offended you in any way, forgive us. Come back … Kvachi is going to agree."

Again they went back.

"I hope there's going to be no more haggling. We settle at twenty?"

"Fine, but could you prepare an account for me, that's not something you'd charge me for, is it?"

"We won't charge you: let's break it down. Ink and paper!"

"All right, settle it," and again Kvachi began whining in a squeaky voice. "I'm ruined … I've had it … How could I do business with them! No respect, no conscience, no contract. But how can I drag on and chase them through the courts for two or three years? That way I'd receive twice as much."

Hofstein wrote out an extensive document.

"All four of you, sign this."

They read and signed it, then they squinted and grabbed hold of the money which Hofstein counted out for them.

"I'm ruined … I've had it," Kvachi whined again as he shoved the money under his pillow.

"Now goodbye. May God help you spend that money wisely."

"Goodbye, my dear sir, goodbye."

They saw their visitors off to the staircase. Hofstein muttered:

"I let myself be tricked, I overdid it. He would have agreed to fifteen thousand."

In Kvachi's house they all grabbed each other. Khukhu and Pupi were extremely pleased and cheerful, but Notio and Kvachi shrugged their shoulders and grimaced. Then Beso came in and joined them.

"Beso, where've you been? Where did you disappear to? Why hide away when you're badly needed, man?"

"When Hofstein left you the first time, that's when I arrived. But I turned back and followed him to Mushtaid park and eavesdropped on their conversation. I found out that they weren't going to give you a single rouble over twenty thousand, and I passed that onto you through Pupi. What did you say? My opinion? We ought to offer an icon to the church as thanks for not going to prison."

After Beso's speech they all started chatting, overjoyed and relieved. They took off Kvachi's bandages, bathed his limbs with something medicinal, and anointed them with a new ointment. He had no more pain and he stopped groaning.

Then he sat up and composed a telegram:

"To Shaburiants, 16 Bazaar St., Vladikavkaz. Settled at twenty. Sending you five. Sell house. Coming soon. Anapodiste."

"Send this money and the telegram to Silibistro," he told Khukhu. "And tomorrow get ready to go to Kutaisi. Sell whatever we have left there—property and furniture. What's that? What should I let the Volkova widow have, you ask? Oh, so I have to drag that old woman around until she dies, do I? Give her a hundred roubles; that will be enough for her. Tell everyone that we're going to Warsaw … Wait a minute, buy some Martell cognac, Rederer champagne, marsala, sherry, or port … one bottle of chypre or chartreuse … Victoria cigarettes … don't forget what they're called. Beso, write it down for him. Bring some fruit, a pineapple, too; what did you say? You're an old man and you still don't know what marsala, sherry, chypre, chartreuse, and pineapples are? Beso, old friend, you go instead and buy it all for me. Get some Cailler or Suchard chocolate. If there isn't any genuine chypre or chartreuse, bring some abricotine and Benedictine. You could do with some really good presents, but I'll buy them myself for you. What did you say, Notio? You'll have me on my feet in ten days? Then it's up to me to thank you … Now let me rest for a bit … I'm tired … I need to get some sleep."

Worn out by hard work, but relieved at achieving a hazardous enterprise, Kvachi surrendered to an all-devouring and calm sleep.

Two weeks later the inspector caught sight of a handsome, well-built, nicely dressed young man at Tbilisi station.

"So I'm seeing Mr Kvachantiradze!"

"Greetings to the much respected Inspector Javakhishvili!* How are you doing? How are you and your lady wife?"

Kvachi offered the inspector a firm handshake, from a hand which two weeks before had been emaciated and withered.

"Thank you, and how are you feeling?"

"So-so … Not as well as I'd like, but not as bad as Hofstein would have liked. I'm all right: I'll come across that scoundrel again somewhere. Goodbye, then."

"Have a pleasant journey," the inspector responded, and watched Kvachi, as the latter swiftly walked off, his back erect. Then he smiled, shook his head, and went his way.

* Mikheil Javakhishvili did at one time work as an insurance inspector and thus gives himself a walk-on part in the novel

CHAPTER THREE

Studying Banking and Panicking an Associate

While Khukhu Chichia was in Kutaisi selling a building plot and all his possessions, Kvachi was using the opportunity to tour Tbilisi.

Although he was still limping and he had one arm bandaged, he still managed to go to the clubs, theaters, and other places of entertainment.

He was acquainted with only a few people, but he sniffed out everyone, assessed them, and put a value on their notional usefulness and exploitability.

Until his right arm and fingers had healed and he got his dexterity back, he had no luck at cards. Afterwards, however, three rounds of cards were enough to turn his luck round, recover his losses, and take away five thousand or so roubles in profit.

True, there had been a slight unpleasantness on the final night: their host, who was in charge, drew him aside to his own room and said some stinging words to his face, but this didn't embarrass or even pain Kvachi. He was leaving for Russia shortly, so didn't care what a dozen or a few score men said about him in a city where Kvachi was virtually unknown.

Playing cards, Kvachi got to know someone called Nazimov, an official in the Azov bank, a gambler, gourmand, big spender, and heavy drinker, bankrupted and destituted by card games. Several times he had been given credit, but finally he was told to pay up in cash and nobody would deal him a card. He looked all round, then turned to Kvachi:

"Prince, lend me ten roubles until tomorrow."

Kvachi retorted coldly, "Ten? I can't lend money to strangers."

"If that really is your reason for refusing, then let me introduce myself: I'm Nazimov, an employee of the Azov bank."

Nazimov offered Kvachi his hand and Kvachi felt obliged to respond.

"Now that the obstacle's been overcome, you owe me ten roubles."

Kvachi was so taken by Nazimov's response that he was happy to hand him ten roubles and, as he did so, an idea flashed across his mind. Smile followed smile, words followed words, ten-rouble notes followed ten-rouble notes: that night the new friendship was baptised in wine and crowned with beautiful women.

It was a meeting of two hearts and souls. Nazimov was Kvachi's guest two or three more times, and was loaned a little bit of money: they became good mates and on easy terms with one another. They whispered conspiratorially a couple of times. After this Kvachi suddenly declared he was in a hurry and hurried up his family. Pupi indicated with her eyes that she wondered why. Kvachi understood and answered her query:

"Tbilisi is a peculiar city. You can't do profitable business here. In any case, it's full of our own people. I'm going to leave and disappear. The country is big enough: no rumors will reach here from Russia. Who knows what the future has in store for me, what trouble I might be in, when and how I'll need this city, and how useful it can be for me."

His family got the gist and wasted no time packing and getting ready.

Kvachi and his household set off on the overland route to Rostov.

In Vladikavkaz, at Beslan Station, they met up with Silibistro, who was disguised as a European, having shaved off his beard and moustache and re-baptised himself as Ovanes Shaburiants. They only just had time to ask after each other and express their affection.

The family turned off into Vladikavkaz to be with Silibistro, while Kvachi and Beso headed for Petersburg. The morning after, Kvachi, Beso, and Nazimov, who had taken time off from work, arrived in Rostov. They had a short discussion at the station, drank coffee, and then entered a bank.

At first Kvachi was hesitant and fearful, but later he quickly recovered, gathered his strength, wits, and courage, and his face expressed firmness of purpose; he casually opened the door to the manager's office, went straight in and told him, without a care in the world:

"Let me introduce myself: I'm Prince Orbeliani."

He put a passport in this name and a banker's draft on the table. The banker's draft read: "Azov-Don Bank … Rostov branch. Please pay Prince Nikoloz, son of Pavle Orbeliani 37,435 roubles against this bank's Tbilisi branch account.

Manager N.

Accountant B.

Cashier Z."

The manager called in a clerk, handed him the draft, and ordered him:

"Find the letter of advice." Then he turned to Kvachi:

"Is this your first time in Rostov? Whom do you know here?"

"I've passed through three or four times. I've been in these parts before, to stay with a friend of mine for a few days—Senator Denisov's son, Count Notbeck, Baron Tiesenhausen. We were brought up together in the Tsar's page school. Now I'm going to stay with Notbeck … His estate's called Kalinovka, if I'm not mistaken, isn't it? It's about twelve kilometers from here … It's possible that I'll be his brother-in-law in a week's time."

The clerk came back and handed the manager some papers. The papers were inscribed with the word "Payable." Kvachi was given back his passport and the conversation turned to the page school.

Kvachi skilfully changed the subject to Odessa. The others followed suit and chatted. Finally, Kvachi got to his feet:

"I'm very glad to have made your acquaintance. I'd be happy if you could come to my engagement party. I'll let you know by letter. Goodbye and thank you."

Until Kvachi had finished "fixing" the bank manager, Nazimov was overcome by a fit of trembling: his lips moved with fear. He either distanced himself from Beso Shikia and stood aside, or whispered in his ear:

"If there's any trouble, then I don't know you."

Then Nazimov slipped away, walked towards the street, and suddenly said to Beso: "I'll wait for you outside ... don't forget, I don't know you."

Five minutes later Kvachi put the money away in his breast pocket and looked all round. Nazimov was nowhere to be seen.

"Where's that drunk?" he asked Beso.

"He ran off. He said, if anything happens he doesn't know us. He's waiting in the street now."

Kvachi frowned and headed for the doors. He had his hand on the door handle when he suddenly paused: his face lit up with a new idea. He suddenly spun round and whispered brief instructions to Beso. Beso immediately rushed outside: Nazimov was lurking by the doors.

"Quick, run for your life!" Beso whispered to Nazimov and lowered his head before quickening his pace.

The petrified Nazimov staggered after him.

"What's happened? What's going on? Did they rumble us?"

They turned off down a narrow lane.

"We're lucky to be still here ... Things are bad," Beso gabbled at him in a quivering voice. "The letter of advice was there, but the manager is dithering and won't give us the money ... He says he doesn't know us, that the numbers are wrong, and that he has to telegraph Tbilisi ... The manager and accountant went to the next room and started whispering something … They were on the phone … I told them I'll drop in tomorrow and made a dash for it. We're finished if we don't find somewhere to hide right now. Anyway, let me tell you that I don't know you, either."

Nazimov was overcome by a trembling fit and he raved through clenched teeth:

"What will become of my wife and child? I don't have the money to get home … How am I going to get back? I'll be arrested; I've had it!"

"I'll give you the fare, but you've got to go back right now. Here's a hundred roubles, make do with that much. Go on, be quick about it!"

Nazimov, empty-handed and panicking, left for Stavropol where his aged parents were expecting him. Meanwhile Kvachi and Beso, both smiling with joy, got into a first-class carriage and set off for the north.

"If Nazimov gets arrested, they can search for me in Kiev … He really thinks I am Dadiani … I've covered our tracks well," Kvachi told his loyal friend and first secretary Besarion Shikia.

Kvachi and his Friends Move to Petersburg

More than a year passed since Kvachi and Beso settled in Petersburg. Kvachi summoned Jalil from Odessa, and he was eventually followed by Sedrak Havlabariani, Gabo Chkhubishvili, and the rest of the gang. The Odessa family was up and running again. None of them looked in very often at the temple of learning, but they were often to be seen anywhere where there were crowds of young people feasting, whores, and dubious entertainments.

Kvachi was expanding, maturing, and blossoming by the day, for here the arena for work, observation, emulation, and spreading his wings was far more extensive than in Odessa.

Kvachi, Beso, and Jalil lived in the same apartment; the rest were dispersed nearby. The friends' work by its nature divided them into two camps. Kvachi no longer wasted his talents on details and active work He would "fix" some big job, give support to his associates, and divide the loot among them fairly; otherwise, when Chikinjiladze and his camp were pursuing small game, Kvachi would issue instructions and supervise them from afar.

A long period of working together had honed their skills and trained them well. The laws of natural selection had aroused and brought out in all of them their naturally born talents and inclinations, skills, and intuition.

Beso was as taciturn as ever. He either refrained from giving an opinion, or gave it only at the end, and a dozen words whispered by him could sometimes completely turn a job round, shed light on a complicated tangle, and illuminate the darkness. Beso seemed to be invisible in any joint enterprise, yet every thread nevertheless led back to him.

Chipi Chipuntiradze never stop clowning; he competed with Sedrak in gossiping and telling jokes. He had no peer in setting up agencies and spying out the land, but at the same time he had no equal in causing uproar and chaos. If he thought he saw a shadow or heard a mouse squeak, instead of showing steadiness and coolness he would make his escape at the worst possible time and raise the alarm by screeching:

"We're in deep trouble! We're finished! Run for your life."

Chipi often unravelled a nicely set net with his premature cries of alarm and frequently frightened off the salmon that were about to take the bait. He often got told off by Kvachi and the others, but even so, he couldn't break his habit of panicking. Finally, when Kvachi thoroughly understood his nature, Chipi was kept out of any job involving dangerous actions and was restricted to keeping a look-out.

Sedrak was now more fearful and timorous than he used to be. He was good at setting up a job, working out a plan, and sharing the loot, but at times of danger he either fell ill or invented something urgent, or came too late and excused himself with a joke:

"Oh dear, what sort of man do you think I am, what use am I to you? Anyway, I wasn't needed, was I? If you needed some who can box Gabo knows as much about boxing as I do, and if it's a knife-fight, you're far better at using knives. I'm the treasurer. I'm good at my job, and Gabo's good at his."

Ladi Chikinjiladze hadn't changed either: he chewed and munched, he was always eating but still complaining he was hungry. On a "job" he never put himself forward, he always dawdled at the rear, but if circumstances put him in the front of the action, Ladi didn't retreat or hide behind the others: he took his full share of the action.

Gabo Chkhubishvili had been whittled and planed down, but he was still like a buffalo that had never been broken in or harnessed. His rude directness, his lack of tact, and his pushiness often caused confusion and chaos in the gang. He was always grumbling and complaining, but he bore his yoke faithfully and obeyed Kvachi like a child.

Jalil never demanded anything. He was always submissive to fate, always looked Kvachi straight in the eye and said:

"*Allah sana hayır versin* [God give you luck], Prince! You're a real brave man, you're really clever."

Providence gave Kvachi so much extra, he demanded so much more, he resented fate and yet pestered it, gnawed at it, and he kept trying to open new doors to paradise.

Eventually he broke down yet another such door and found somebody he had been eagerly searching for.

Beginning a New "Job"

Kvachi has a flat on Vasilevsky Island: a bel-étage with seven rooms, expensively furnished, decorated very tastefully. He has a dining room in dark oak, *nature morte* by old Dutch and Flemish masters, a rich collection of very old wall plates, Sèvres porcelain, and Venetian crystal.

His hall is resplendently bright, with four ceiling-high mirrors. Gold-lacquered chairs line the walls. In the corner stands a yew-wood concert grand piano. The windows and door are embroidered with silk brocade and hung with thick satin curtains. The walls too are covered with satin and silk, and hung with paintings by Serov, Levitan, Makovsky, Repin, and Shishkin: here and there are a few nudes obtained from a Paris *salon*.

The study and the lesser halls are furnished either in Persian, or in European style. Turkish and Khorasan carpets, French tapestries, old Burgundian velvet, fine Kashmir and Indian gold embroidery, a rich collection of weaponry, and a thousand expensive artistic baubles. Every room is strewn generously with crystal glasses, mirrors, bronzes, marble and yew, furs and brocade, animal skins and silver. All the rooms are furnished with works by the immortals: Cellini, Canova, Rembrandt, VanGogh, Ruysdal, and many others.

Two carefully insulated rooms have been turned into a library and a billiard room.

A servant dressed like a magpie in black and white occasionally slips into the rooms. A doorman, as colorfully dressed as a parrot, stands rigidly to attention at the front door.

Prince Napoleon Apollonovich Kvachantiradze is sitting in his study, wearing an expensive Bukhara gown, perusing a newspaper, and smoking a Havana cigar.

On a tiger skin spread out at his feet sprawl an intimidating black English mastiff and a gigantic honey-colored Saint Bernard.

A long-tailed and long-haired white Persian cat is catching flies on the window sill, relishing the sun, and chasing its own tail.

On his desk crouches a monkey no bigger than his hand, wearing a miniature silk coat and top-hat: the monkey is smearing ink over its face and grimacing at Kvachi.

This room and Kvachi's heart are enjoying perfect peace, perfect comfort, and perfect relaxation.

Kvachi's personal secretary and loyal follower Beso Shikia came in on tiptoe.

"Ah, Beso, it's you, is it?" Kvachi lazily mused. "Anything happening? Any letters? What do they want? Begging again? Throw them in the basket."

"Yes, but Princess Golitsyna is putting on a big masked ball for her charity and is asking you to take charge of things."

"Fine, put it down there … Let's see, let me have a think. If I don't go, send her a letter of thanks and five hundred roubles."

"Prince Coburg-Hottel is inviting you to supper."

"Oh, he bores me stiff … Tell him, thank you, but I haven't got time."

"Prince Volkonsky is selling his Arab horse and is asking you …"

"Don't bother me with that. I've got ten Arabs as good as his."

"Tomorrow there's a special supper at the yacht club in honor of the Ottoman prince Muhtar Aziz."

"Fine. Remind me tomorrow."

"Smirnova is dancing at the opera tomorrow and …"

"You go, give her my regards and take a bouquet for her with you."

"There's another letter here: Tania Prozorova writes to say that 'he' will be at her place tonight at ten o'clock."

"Quick, show me."

And Kvachi snatched the pink silk envelope from Beso's hand. He read it, became animated, smiled and stirred himself:

"Just in time, Beso, just in time! I've been waiting a whole year for this. Beso, do you know who the 'he' in this letter is? You don't? Then I'll tell you: no, wait, I'll tell you later … Later, later …"

Kvachi anxiously paced the room. His eyes were burning with

purposeful thought, he was racking his brains, and his heart was pounding against his ribcage.

"Right ... Fine ... This is a new stage ... Well, Kvachi, fate is knocking at your door: if you're a man, seize the moment ... Good, very good ..." he was murmuring, as he stoked the fires of new plots, wove new nets, and smiled at the prospects. Then he turned to Beso: "Ring and get them to bring the Daimler-Benz round for me."

"It's beautiful weather; the landau would be better."

"All right, the landau then. Don't have the black horses harnessed: they're too highly strung. Harness the grays or the bays. But do it quickly. Call my valet, too." Then he reached for the telephone. "Hello, Elena, is that you? Yes, it's Kvachi ... I kiss your divine hands this morning ... Last night? I won twenty thousand or so ... What's that? But you've been told lies about me: someone wants to make bad blood between us, so you mustn't believe it ... No, it wasn't me who saw that woman off, it was Prince Wittgenstein who took her away ... Me? I swear on my life, I've not been anywhere, I went straight home ... All right, we'll drop the subject. Elena, I've got something important for you today. Last night you took a liking to a pearl necklace: I'll give it to you tomorrow if you're a clever girl ... What did you say, nobody must find out?! What do you think? That they have a Georgian in Petersburg listening to the phones and understanding what we're saying in Georgian? Fine, fine ... I understand ... Right, wait at home for me to come; I'm on my way. Goodbye, darling!"

Then he turned to his valet Jalil: "Right, Jalil, get me dressed."

While Jalil was dressing him, Kvachi fidgeted like an unbroken colt, talking to himself or to Jalil:

"It's a lovely day, it's a beautiful day ... Wish me the best, Jalil, so I pull this job off ... It's a magnificent day ... I'll see that old man, that holy man, let's see if he's man enough to stand up to me! See if he can resist my Elena ... I don't want this tie, nor the other one: give me that one."

Jalil raised his arms and said piously: "*Allah il-allah*! God give my prince and Jalil victory!"

A Kazan Tatar announced: "The landau is ready."

Two English thoroughbred grays, harnessed English-style, sped the landau along with a clatter of hooves. Jalil, sitting straight-backed, dressed in a Circassian tunic, sat next to the driver. They drove out onto Morskoi Boulevard, then down Nevsky Prospekt. Passersby stared at the brilliant landau, the gray thoroughbreds, and the handsome young man, who scattered to the left and the right polite greetings and a charming smile. The pavements resounded with comments:

"What, don't you recognize him? Prince Kvachantiradze, Napoleon Apollonovich ... A fine name, isn't it?"

"He's got unbelievable wealth: oil, manganese, copper; he owns five hundred thousand hectares."

In another group someone was asserting: "They say he has a marble palace in western Georgia which is so fine that people come from America to see it."

Someone was assuring a third group: "He's of royal blood. His blood is as pure as the Chinese emperor's."

"They say that he has ten of the most beautiful women living in his house: they sit there cutting out share certificates for him."

"Three days ago the jointstock company *Anglo-Russe* had its Annual General Meeting. Just imagine, Kvachantiradze got the majority shareholding of the company, so the whole company fell into his hands. What? You say the *Salamander* and *Cosmos* went the same way? I'm not surprised ... He's a big financier, a rising star."

"They say he's been invited to become director of the state bank, but he's not so crazy yet as to say yes! He's buying five banks of his own, after all."

"Apparently there isn't a single beautiful woman in Petersburg he hasn't ... Don't you remember the Duchess of Catalonia? They say there wasn't a woman in the world more beautiful or respectable than her. She came to Petersburg last year. You know what happened next? She couldn't hold out three days against Kvachantiradze. Believe me, I know this for a fact. Her husband found out ... A duel? No, he wouldn't have dared. Kvachantiradze can shoot a fly out of the air."

"He's already challenged three men to duels: he got all three in the ankle."

Kvachi's friends and agents, whom he had hired, trained up, and instructed, were working for a considerable time to create all these rumors and to puff up his reputation.

The landau stopped on Suvorov Avenue; five minutes later Kvachi was kissing a young widow's hands. She was a Georgian beauty, with the figure and face of a real queen.

"Good, that's enough from you, you madman ... Go on, tell me where you were last night? I'll bet you were unfaithful to me."

"I swear to you, Elena, that ..."

"Don't swear any oaths, I don't believe them. Now tell me what scheme you've thought up. What? From now on I'm supposed to be your cousin? You wicked man, why do you need me to be your cousin? Aren't I yours, anyway? Ah, I understand: I've got to pretend I'm a relative of yours? And then? What, what did you say? God, anything but that! How could I sink so low? Have I got to throw myself at that beast, at that dirty peasant?!"

Kvachi explained his scheme to Elena briefly and succinctly; he revealed to her the prospect of a brilliant future. Elena relented and let herself be seduced by his dream.

"Of course, the money is good, and the present, too ... Mixing with the *crême de la crême* ... is very nice, too; but ... well, they say ... he's a big man ... they say he's a saint, but ...Aren't you all I want? What? He's better than you? In what way? How? All right, shut up, don't be foul-mouthed ... Ha-ha-ha! Are you serious? It must be just gossip, or else … Was that really the way you found an opening? My God, anything but that! It's beneath me to have anything to do with a pig like that, but since you've got such a big scheme going … Let's see … You mean, today? Do you mean to get away with it that cheaply? If you've already started the job, then at least buy me the little house I've taken a liking to. You remember the one, don't you? Well, I'm listening, so tell me what to do."

It took Kvachi a whole hour to give Elena her instructions, then he tested her on them, held a short rehearsal, and, thoroughly delighted at Elena's aptitude, made her a thousand more promises and left.

Getting to Know a Holy Old Man and Other Men of Power

On the Neva Embankment there was a modest little house, painted in mourning colors. Here lived Kvachi's patron, an elderly widow who was a very influential member of the upper classes, a "Dame of the Empire of every conceivable order", Anastasia Prozorova.

Kvachi was such a familiar visitor to her drawing-room that he called her "Tania" and treated her as if she were a close relative, while she called Kvachi "my little Apollo": she seemed to be a real guardian angel sent to him by fate.

Who can count the times this divine creature had guided little Kvachi across a tightrope, had retrieved him from dark, stinking pits, how much she had spent on him, how many times she had dismissed him, and how many times had brought him back?

If you'd been listening, who knows how much gossip and poisonous rumors you'd have heard! It was even said that Kvachi had to visit his "sister" twice a week, that, apart from confectionery and flowers, Kvachi sent her thousands of bills, that "Tania" was fed up with seeing to these bills, so that she set aside a fixed monthly sum to pay for these "relations", that Kvachi's apartment had been furnished by her efforts and at her expense, etc.

In a word, there were so much "supposedly" and "allegedly" involved, that even the most idle gossipmonger couldn't make sense of it all.

People who knew this "Dame of the Empire" naturally refused to believe even a hundredth part of the gossip. She was such a quiet, meek, and pious woman, so devout and modest, so godly and so reserved that no carnal or spiritual fault, let alone fornication, could ever find a place in her withered, elderly, feeble body, or her soul, which was infused with divine grace.

Her house was adorned with icons and imbued with the scent of candles and incense: it was visited only by a senator, who was bent double, a toothless court chamberlain, a sixty-year-old lady-in-waiting, court ladies, and equally decrepit bishops and archbishops, none of whom could climb the stairs in the house unaided. "Little Apollo" was the only young person among them, but this was the only exception to the rule. In truth, no speck of dirt could come near this holy place, but ...

At nine thirty that day, Kvachi and his "cousin" Elena arrived in the covered landau at the widow's house, which was plunged in darkness. They offered their hostess confectionery and flowers. The guests were having tea; Anastasia introduced Kvachi and his relative to them.

"His holy reverence the Tsar's chaplain and inspector of the theological college ... the most worthy abbot of the Tsaritsyn monastery, Iliodor ... the Bishop of Saratov, Hermogenes ... General Lokhtin's widow ... The Senior Procurator of the Holy Synod, Lukianov ...His deputy, Sabler ... The Minister of War General Sukhomlinov ... Lady Kurakina ... Baroness Noden ... the Minister of the Interior, Makarov ..."

Kvachi and Elena offered their hand to all the other guests and introduced themselves: some they kissed on the hand; to others they bowed in reverential greeting. Then they sat down and inspected their new acquaintances.

Among the guests were both former and actual ministers, as well as would-be ministers: some were yesterday's men, others today's, tomorrow's, or the day after tomorrow's.

In the widow's ecclesiastic salon bishops sought to be archbishops or metropolitan bishops, major-generals sought to be lieutenant-generals, lieutenants—to be adjutants; provincials aimed to get to the capital, merchants sought leases, bankers—concessions; women lobbied for husbands and lovers, and everybody was trying to get closer to the throne, aiming to rise at least one rung higher.

Deep in these people's hearts an invisible, maniacal, ruthless, and cruel battle was raging, but their faces and tongues showed only imperturbable sweetness, fraternity, friendship, smiles, Christian meekness, and angelic submission.

The widow Lokhtina, the "Virgin Mary", resumed the interrupted conversation. Kvachi watched and listened to this odd widow with astonishment. Dear "Tania" had just told him who this strange woman was. Lokhtina was an elderly widow, extremely proud, clever, well-versed, of good family and parentage.

A few years earlier this widow had transformed herself into the first disciple, and into an obedient and meek slave of "Saint Grigory"; she had given up everything else—family, property, pride, womanly dignity—to follow selflessly her new Messiah, master, and god. This deranged woman was Saint Grigory's confidante, handmaiden, and the best propagandist for his spiritual and physical purity, and for his fornication and raving utterances. In the end, this sick woman had opened a path for the "savior" to enter the unfortunate family of the unfortunate Tsar: not knowing what she was doing, she had brought that old man to the throne.

Since then she had given up her place at the Tsar's court to the younger, prettier, and more elegant Vyrubova, but she hadn't abandoned the court, or her views, or her enslavement. As before, she tailed the "saintly old man" Rasputin all over Russia, writing down in her diary every step he took and every word he said.

Everyone was now looking at her. "The Virgin Mary" was bare-foot and dressed in a strange yellow and white dress more like a cassock than a woman's garment. It was decorated with silk and satin patches in ten different colors; on her head she wore a weird gaudy hat with a golden inscription: "All forces are within me, Hallelujah."

Every now and again she began sooth-saying:

"The day before yesterday I saw our savior for the third time," she said with ecstatic eyes and trembling voice. "You will know that evening 'he' was traveling again, coming from Moscow, but his soul was here and made itself known to me. Our holy man was dressed in white from head to toes, God's light shone above him, he was holding a cross in one hand and a fiery sword in the other."

"Lord have mercy on us!" whispered Sabler as he crossed himself. The others followed suit.

"He appeared to me and told me, 'Repent your sins. Orthodox people! The Day of Judgement is coming! Tremble and quake, ye unbelievers, you Jews, and you who corrupt others' souls!' I fell prostrate at his holy feet. He laid his hand on my head and pardoned my sins. When I opened my eyes, my savior was flying off to heaven. The next day our holy man came down from Moscow. I told him everything and he said to me, 'Sister, truly I was with you in spirit at the time.'"

Everyone crossed themselves again as they moved their withered, flabby lips: "Wondrous, Lord, are Thy deeds."

"The Day of Judgement is at hand!"

"Have mercy on us, Lord, and forgive us our sins."

"Hallelujah! Hallelujah! Hallelujah!"

The woman rose to her feet, lifted her eyes to the heavens and, raising her voice, spoke with ardor and inspiration:

"What they tell you is true: he is our holy savior, sent to us by heaven to free this sinful world, our holy Russia: to judge sinners, to annihilate the unbelievers, and to establish a life of eternal bliss." Then she turned to the Tsaritsyn monk Iliodor. "This is his immaculate and martyred son, and I am their sinful and unworthy disciple, and the Virgin Mother Mary. Tremble and repent your sins, o Orthodox believers."

Iliodor the monk frowned and fidgeted; the others again moved their lips and, each whispering something, bowed to the "Virgin Mary."

Sabler and Makarov kissed her hand. Kvachi and Elena did the same, crossing themselves and whispering piously: "Lord, have mercy on us."

The "Virgin Mary" clutched all four to her breast and gave them all sisterly Christian kisses.

"Dostoevsky's prophecy has truly been realized," Sabler, his eyes full of tears, told her. "Dostoevsky said that it would be some humble, lowly, blessed, and crazed peasant, chosen and sent to us by the Lord from the common people, who would save Russia from great turmoil and strife."

"Russia, once it has been cleansed by such a peasant, will brand the whole world of unbelievers with a hot iron, will cure it of the devil's ideas, and will impose our holy faith on the entire globe at the point of the sword," added General Sukhomlinov.

"There have been two Romes, the third is Russia, and there will be no fourth!" Lukianov repeated the ravings of the new Byzantines.

"The filthy Jews and their hirelings the socialists have been trying day and night to fulfil their dream of destroying our Rome," lamented the monk of Tsaritsyn.

"The third Rome will last for ever! It is impossible to destroy it! Don't be afraid. Orthodox believers, God is with us," declared Sabler, the devious old fox.

Kvachi saw his opportunity: "His excellency has spoken wisely. Don't be afraid, don't believe in the destructibility of the third

Rome. It is immortal. The filthy infidels have shown their heads in the Caucasus, too, but ..."

"Are you from the Caucasus?" Makarov asked him.

"I am, sir: that's where I was born and that's where I come from. There too the holy name of our holy Russia has been besmirched and defiled. Everything that Russia has built over a hundred years, that feeble and senile Vorontsov-Dashkov has destroyed in two years. It's time we got rid of that secret freemason. We have a very true saying: 'There are two Vorontsovs in the Caucasus: one is always in heaven, the other always in bed.' But just because he's lying down, doesn't mean that he's idle: he's slowly destroying all Russia's achievements in the Caucasus."

The great and the good giggled with toothless smiles, and Kvachi continued: "Thank the Lord. Apart from that feeble covert freemason, our greatly worshipped Tsar has many other faithful servants in the Caucasus: Alikhanov, Vostorgov, Tolmachov, Martinov, Griaznov, and thousands of others. If we combine our efforts we can cut the head off the dragon of revolution. So you can set your minds at rest and relax."

Tania whispered something to the two people by her side. They both became instantly animated and amazed.

"It's not possible! Really?" they said, turning to Kvachi. "Tell us, young man the story of how you were wounded."

"It's hardly worth telling. It's nothing much, but if your excellencies wish ... Because I wouldn't let the Jews and the revolutionaries get away with any more and because I'd silenced them, they put a price of ten thousand roubles on my head. I'd wrecked several of their most treacherous plots. When I got too much for them, they began hunting me down, but I turned out to be a better hunter than those curs. They threw a grenade at me once. I survived and went after them, killed three of them, wounded two, and arrested two more. Another group pointed their rifles at me. I gave them worse than they gave me. Later they tried to poison me and they bought off my servant. That didn't work, either. Well, I won't go on about it, I just wiped out the filthy swine and showed them no mercy. Actually, I was wounded in the foot, but they suffered a hundred times worse."

Tania was about to show everyone Kvachi's wound, which actually was a dog bite from Samtredia, but she stopped herself in time and calmed down.

Kvachi had quite a lot more to say and he won the hearts of the company and entertained them with his boasting, titivation, and flattery.

The Lokhtina widow wrote down Kvachi's name in her notebook; the others committed it to memory. The sound of car tires was heard from the street.

"He's coming! Our saint and our savior is coming!" shrieked the "Virgin Mary" reverentially as she jumped to her feet.

While the others also rose, the hostess and the widow Lokhtina rushed towards the stairs.

Two minutes later the "holy savior" Grigory Rasputin burst into the room. Kvachi ran his eye over this man, the most powerful man of the times, and recalled the character description he had just read in a secret newspaper: "obscure, a simpleton, a fool, completely ignorant, conceited and arrogant, filthy in mind and body, a fornicating, depraved Siberian peasant ...." Other papers wrote: "a saintly old man, free of sin ..." "a heaven-sent prophet", "the linchpin, the conscience and the leader of dark Russia", "the all-powerful real patriarch, the autocrat, and the soul-searcher of an errant people."

Everyone was on their feet, their heads bowed in submission, every face wore God's grace, reverence, purity, and a filial smile.

Rasputin paused for a moment in the doorway.

He was of middling height, thickset and sturdy. He had a long black head of coarse hair, casually combed and oiled, with a parting down the middle. His lips were thick, sensual, and blue. His forehead was high, his nose was flat, and his beard seemed to have been swept with a broom and his moustache stuck on. He had shaved under his lower lip, his facial skin was swarthy, chapped, and greasy. His long hands seemed covered in rust. His fingers were twisted and his fingernails were musty and black-rimmed. His eyes were strikingly odd: deep, bluish, restless, they flashed and seemed full of some secret and invisible power which both drew and penetrated one; they were caressing, sincere, and at the same time devious, distant, and chilling.

He was wearing a Russian gown of cornelian satin, hand-made by his "mother" the Tsaritsa, and adorned with blue silk. His waist was girded with a belt woven from silk and gold threads, with a heavy fringe. His broad velvet trousers were tucked into wrinkled lacquered boots.

The holy man seemed to laugh: "Peace and God's blessings be upon you."

Then with a hop, skip, and much writhing he hurriedly greeted everyone, grimacing, fidgeting, and waving his limbs like a circus clown. He spoke a strange, unintelligible Russian, constantly inserting religious terms at the most inappropriate moments.

He left nobody out: he clutched each person to his breast and gave them a powerful, lip-smacking kiss. Some he kissed once, some twice. He clutched Elena, bent her double, took her breath away, chapped her lips with his kissing, and was reluctant to let go of her.

Everyone kissed his hand with reverence and worship. Rasputin blessed them and addressed a few words to each. He asked Sukhomlinov: "Have you made sure God's sword is sharpened?"

He responded to Archbishop Hermogenes, "God is with us."

He remarked to the monk from Tsaritsyn: "The Jews can't interfere with us, they will perish."

He told Makarov brusquely: "It's time it was all over."

He offered Elena comfort: "Seek healing from me, sister, and

I shall show you mercy."

Kvachi sniggered. Finally, his turn had come.

"Seek and ye shall find," the holy man encouraged him.

Rasputin turned to Lukianov, the Procuror of the Holy Synod. The Procuror's deputy Sabler fell at Rasputin's feet, sobbing and muttering: "Bless me, Holy Father. Bless me and show me grace."

The "Virgin Mary" disciple and preacher knelt down with Sabler, embraced the holy man's knees, and kissed the toe of his boot. Rasputin raised both to their feet, wiped away their tears with a kiss, comforted them both: he himself was crying and making the others weep. The spectacle led one to whisper to another: "Lukianov's going to be moved, Sabler's going to get the Procuror's job."

Then everyone sat down to enjoy the confectionery and uplifting conversation.

The holy man had his disciple sit down on one side of him, and the regal Elena on the other side. He put his hand on Elena's knee, then let it creep up her thigh. Kvachi's eye caught Rasputin's hand: he smiled under his moustache and thought: "He's taken the bait, it's started."

The disciple put her arm round her teacher's waist and rested her dizzy head on his shoulder.

Elena was embarrassed at first: she bowed her head, half-closed her eyes, and held her breath. Sometimes her almond-shaped eyes cast a glance at the holy man's blue, bean-shaped eyes and flashed at them, then she would flirt by looking away and use her eyelashes to cloud and curtain her gaze, and then make her black eyes as dark as night.

Finally, she plucked up courage and put her divine head on the holy teacher's chest; her eyes were closed and she seemed to have dozed off.

Everyone looked reverentially at this trinity and smiled immaculately. They were all reminded of the Holy Trinity, to which they compared this spectacle: the savior, Mary, and Martha.

"Elena looks more like Mary Magdalene than does the Lokhtina widow," thought Kvachi and began plotting a love affair. Suddenly the holy man pointed his black twisted finger at Kvachi and asked: "And who are you?"

"Prince Kvachantiradze, Holy Father."

"So you'll be a Caucasian, then … I don't like them; savage people … always got their eye on a dagger, they're Muslims."

Kvachi sweetly explained to him: "I'm a Georgian, Holy Father, and Georgians are Orthodox believers."

Rasputin was stunned: "Really, Christians? What's your first name?"

"Napoleon Apollonchik."

"Napoleon? Apollo?" Rasputin was again astounded.

His disciple, the widow Lokhtina explained the two names to Rasputin.

"So they're both pagans, devils I suppose. The cross protect us from them!" Rasputin called out, and he made the sign of the cross over everyone. The hostess whispered in his ear.

"That young man and the young woman Elena are cousins. You may remember we've talked several times about the lad."

Rasputin suddenly yielded: "Ah-ah, Apollonchik! You fought in the Caucasus for the Tsar of holy Russia, didn't you? I like your name. Come closer. Do you drink wine?" And once again he kissed the "cousins."

Kvachi refused the offer of wine, saying he didn't drink: his temperance was widely approved.

The topic of conversation switched to the fate of Russia, the Jews, revolution, the third Rome and its mission to rule the world.

The young Kvachi used the opportunity to demonstrate in full to the Holy Father his intelligence, his sophistication, and his loyalty to the church and the throne: Stolypin and Shcheglovitov were the strongest pillars of holy Russia … mutiny had not yet been completely eliminated, its roots had not yet been fully torn out ... the monster of filth was still breathing fire... the snake of destruction was still writhing ... our precious homeland had been disabled ... there were still secret agents of Jewry in the government ... there were still a lot of unbelievers in the church ... our fair land and holy church had to be purged and cleansed immediately, otherwise we couldn't sleep peacefully in our beds.

Kvachi went on at length on this topic. He had poured oil onto the flames and the company, already alarmed, became even more perturbed.

The widow Lokhtina, the "savior's" disciple, took over Kvachi's preaching, flaring up as she spoke: she fell at the holy man's feet again and shrieked: "We are perishing! Help us! Holy Father, help us!"

Sabler started muttering. The others were excited and leapt to their feet. There was another burst of embraces and noisy kisses.

That evening decided the fate of a number of ministers, senators, ambassadors, provincial governors, bishops, and archbishops. Some came tumbling down, others climbed up the greasy ladder.

One by one the guests departed.

The holy man smuggled Elena into the room on the right, while Kvachi and his hostess Tania slipped into the room on the left.

An hour later all four were reunited, calmer and satisfied. Elena's face was burning red, and her hair was tousled; her eyes had a film of oil. The hostess and the holy man had a short whispered conversation.

"Come here," Rasputin then called to Kvachi. "I like you. Do you want to be friends? What's more, you can be my bodyguard, because the Jews and devil-worshippers have got it in for me. Do you want to? Look after me well. Tania, bring the icon and we'll swear an oath."

Did Kvachi want to be friends with Rasputin? Of course he did. That had been his sole desire for a whole year: he had spent a year blazing a trail to this old man and had been seeking him by torchlight all that year, because he knew very well that he was the real Tsar and Patriarch of Russia and held complete power in that boundless country.

An icon and a gospel was brought for them to swear eternal brotherhood and friendship. Then Rasputin recalled something: "The Jews and devil-worshippers have raised the question of myself in parliament. I'll show them what a question is."

He got to his feet in his temper. His eyes flashed fire, he was at times shrieking in a woman's voice, stamping his feet and slobbering:

"Ah, the bitches. Ah, the scoundrels. Ah, the despicable curs."

Then he demanded ink and paper, sat down and spent half an hour sweating hard, groaning and moaning, until he had written a telegram to the Tsar and Tsaritsa, who were in the Crimea:

"Livadia, to the Tsar and Tsaritsa.

Dear Daddy and Mummy,The accursed demon is gathering strength. And the Duma is on his side: there are many devil-worshippers and Jews. What do they care? The quicker God's anointed is overthrown, the better, they think. But Mister Guchkov is their creature, slandering, and fomenting rebellion. Demands. Daddy! You own the Duma, do whatever you want. How can they make demands on Grigory? This is Satan's business, you must give orders. Yes! No demands need be made. Right! Grigory. Yes."

He handed Kvachi this scrawl, which looked like a goose's footprint, and told him: "Send this telegram today. Off it goes, straight home. Hostess, my sunlight: thank you. God give you everything good."

Rasputin kissed his hostess, then turned to Elena: "Lenochka, my sister! Come to my place."

And he almost carried Kvachi's gift to the stairs. Elena clung hard to the holy man's neck and hid her tired, bewildered face in his long beard.

They all three got into a car.

"That's no good, sister: come, sit over here! Sit here."

Rasputin put Elena on his knees, since there wasn't much room in the car. When they got to the old man's house, Rasputin announced to Kvachi: "Apollonchik, you wait here a bit; Lenochka, you see me to my room. Both of you come tomorrow, I need to speak to you."

While the holy man was "trying out" Elena upstairs, Kvachi waited in the street. A whole hour passed. Finally, Elena came out and they both got into the car.

Kvachi's feelings were hurt and he was sulking. Elena was smiling.

"Quite a remarkable old man, that Rasputin: he hasn't got a single gray hair, has he?" murmured Kvachi.

Elena didn't answer. They went home, neither of them saying a word.

Kvachi accompanied Elena to her room and sat down.

"That's going too far," he finally murmured.

Elena smiled again.

"Did he try you out all the way? What did he say? Did he ask what was wrong with you?"

"He's still better than any other doctor," Elena retorted venomously.

"Better than me?"

"Than you? Don't make me laugh. You're still a child, my little Kvachi."

Kvachi was upset: "Well that's a lie."

"When the husband went to war, the wife told him all about the battle. So you don't like it? You want to use me for one of your jobs and keep me at the same time? Chase after two rabbits and you won't catch a single one … What was that? What did you say? So you're not jealous, are you? That's better. You're a clever man and you should understand."

"Don't start anything without my say-so."

"I won't, you needn't be afraid, he's not going to get away from me. We started this together and we'll work it out together. You'll use your brains, and I'll ... use my eyes and smile. So come back tomorrow and we'll talk. Don't forget the pearls you promised me. No, no, it's out of the question now. I said I can't do it today. I want to sleep ... How about tomorrow? What? Have it your way: I can't and I won't ... Or put it this way, I'm completely sated ... Fine, don't be silly. Go away, get some sleep, by tomorrow you'll have forgotten all about it ... What did you say? Is he better than you, or not? Didn't you tell me this morning that he's better than a lot of your kind?! I said you're still a child. Go away, go ... Good night, sleep well."

Half berserk, Kvachi rushed out of the house. He was choking with rage. One bull had taken the other bull's cow. And how! Elena had deliberately and sincerely preferred Grigory Rasputin to Kvachi, who was young, a handsome lad, strong and fiery.

"It wouldn't be so bad if he deserved her!" thought Kvachi bitterly. "An obtuse, dismal, simple-minded, utterly boorish, dirty, and elderly peasant! What did Elena tell me? That he's better than me? That I'm a child compared with him? How? In what way? What does someone like him have that ... I expect," and he thought for a while. "Didn't I take her myself, didn't I introduce her to him? Didn't I give her instructions? If it hadn't happened today, it would have happened tomorrow, does it matter at all? Why should I worry, why should I beat myself up about it? If she prefers him, let her. There are plenty of good-looking women in the world; but I mustn't let go of Elena, or a nicely planned job will go wrong on me and I'll be ruined."

Then he turned his mind to his endless plans and pursued a multitude of new ideas. A new land and boundless virgin fields spread out before him, all for Kvachi's benefit, to adorn as he saw fit and to reap without having to plough them.

Elena vanished into the darkness and there was not the slightest trace left of little Kvachi's recent anger or his damaged pride.

For a while he had raged, but that same night he slept as he always did: peacefully, innocently, and serenely.

The Holy Man's Secretary and Bodyguard

The next day Kvachi summoned his colleagues to give each one his instructions and tasks. He gave the holy man's address to Gabo Chkhubishvili, Beso Shikia, and Jalil, telling all three to be there at noon precisely and wait for him by the entrance. Then Kvachi the leader toured Nevsky Prospekt, made a few purchases, and then went round to Elena's house with a present of pearls and flowers.

Elena seemed to have blossomed that day: she was even more beautiful. Straight away she put the expensive present round her neck. She could barely stay upright for joy: she posed in front of the mirror or clung to Kvachi's neck, laughing, fidgeting, and burbling:

"So, were you annoyed about yesterday? You naughty boy, wasn't I doing as you told me to? All right, you're not annoyed any more? You've calmed down? That's better, forget all about it. What I said to you was on purpose, to make you angry: how could that boor be better than you? Apart from anything else, that peasant is twice your age … Ugh! Dirty, never washes! Ugh! He stinks of candles and oil … shall we go right now? I'm ready."

Ten minutes later Kvachi's Mercedes turned into Gorokhovaya Street and stopped outside the holy man's apartment. Beso and his assistants were waiting by the door.

They all went upstairs. The staircase was packed with people. Others were in the street waiting their turn.

The holy man was scolding a general. When he caught sight of Kvachi and Elena he broke away and clutched both of them to his chest.

"Sit and watch, I won't be long," he told Kvachi, and abducted Elena to an adjoining room, telling Kvachi: "You'll be my secretary. Can you think of anyone more important and better?"

Kvachi got down to his secretarial duties; he employed Beso Shikia as his deputy, while Jalil was put by the door, and Chkhubishvili and the other gang members were entrusted with reconnaissance duties, for the holy man had a thousand enemies and was always in danger.

Nevertheless a hundred men and women passed through Rasputin's study that day. All sorts of people from all sorts of places for all sorts of reasons had come to see this miracle-worker, From Vladivostok and Warsaw, from Mt Athos and Tashkent, from the Solovetsky Islands and remote backwoods came generals and governors, monks and merchants, bankers and lawyers, peasants and nuns, priests and officials.

Some sought promotion, some—subsidies, some—transfers; many sought justice or investigation. The holy man saw to the gentry and the beautiful women first, and then ran down the stairs, thrusting a rouble coin into some hands, or a three-rouble note into others, shouting as he went:

"Pray for the Tsar's family and for me. I don't have the time. There's my secretary, tell him if you need something."

After that he fell back exhausted into a satin-upholstered armchair and groaned: "Ugh, these striped devils! Bitches! They're the death of me."

That day Kvachi witnessed a lot of amazing spectacles. That coarse old man revealed astounding guile and sophistication. He could tell at a glance who was strong or weak, who was good for something or for nothing, and treated all according to their deserts. Some he received with joy, respect and hugs and kisses, some with a reverently bowed neck, flattery, and grimaces; others got barely two harsh words. Rasputin never let a good-looking woman go without words of comfort: he would give her a close brotherly embrace. If a woman complained of being ill, he would lead her off to another room to examine and treat her, or else get Kvachi to write down her address. Sometimes it took Rasputin half an hour to write down a dozen words, and the result was an illegible scrawl as if chickens had dipped their feet in ink and run across the paper to write down their cackling.

Beso had thoroughly grasped Kvachi's instructions and carried them out in a week: from that day on a "human tide" overwhelmed Kvachi's house. This "human tide" consisted of Rasputin's clients.

Kvachi used his wits: in one week he cut off the irrigation water from Rasputin's garden and diverted it to his own.

The clients understood that the road to the holy man passed through Kvachi's apartments. First they came to Kvachi for a certificate and paid him a large amount for prayers and shriving, and then went to Rasputin's house with Beso's certificate to receive prayers and blessings.

The friends took turns guarding the holy man: they rivaled the government's secret agents. The suspicious and timorous old man could now for the first time sleep peacefully; he wondered how he could thank Kvachi, who, astute as ever, in less than two weeks had concrete proof of that gratitude.

Cracking New Big Jobs

In no time Kvachi's and Rasputin's new friendship became the talk of the town. Government ministers and businessmen were the first to hear of it. A "human tide" flooded Kvachi's apartment, and the elite, the great, and the good, ascended the marble staircase to wait their turn on gilded chairs.

The banker Ganus was the first to head for Kvachi's apartment. First he had a whispered conversation with Beso, then he went in to see Kvachi and came straight to the point:

"I'm a businessman and I value my time very highly. I know you're pretty busy, too, so I'll get down to business straight away. I've got a dozen deals in the making. I know you can offer me assistance and bring off these deals for me, and for that ... obviously ... your work certainly has to have a price."

They got to work and in two hours had weighed and measured these big and complex deals. Then they signed an agreement, shook hands, exchanged smiles and compliments, and wished each other success.

Beso brought in a second businessman: a certain Gintz, an elderly Jew whom he himself had found. Gintz left Kvachi's room three hours later.

After that Kvachi took the opportunity to have a word with Rasputin about irrigation canals in Central Asia.

"How much are they worth to me?" Rasputin retorted to Kvachi. "Will they bring in three thousand?"

Kvachi was pleased Rasputin could be bought so cheaply. Rasputin picked up the phone. He summoned a government minister, then called another one, telling them both:

"Mama and papa are both very anxious about this holy cause. Apollonchik's coming to see you, he'll tell you, and you do as he orders. Yes. That's what I want. Yes ... What? To the Caucasus? I'll write a telegram about that to papa and mama."

He sat down and groaned and sweated for half an hour. The first telegram read:

"Livadia. To the Tsar's family.

Dear Papa and Mama, You get no peace about who to send to the Caucasus. Now our dear bishop of Tobolsk Aleksei is just the man. He's what the Caucasus needs. Send him. I very much want that. He's kind to me. He understands a holy cause. He needs to be honored. He's loyal, always loyal. And in the Caucasus he will be our friend. Yes, it's me. Grigory! Yes."

The second telegram read:

"Darling. Demons have attacked father Ivan Vostorgov*. He needs that icon. Don't you listen? It may be a market icon, but it's still holy.

"How else do we take it, anyway? Reward Vostorgov with Caucasus and Siberia. Let his enemies weep. Yes, me! Grigory. Yes."

Rasputin entrusted the despatch of both telegrams to Kvachi, remarking:

"You see how nice I am to Caucasians. But Vorontsov is a scoundrel, he likes devil-worshippers, Jews, and Armenians. I'll sort him out. Don't show the telegrams to anyone, and don't talk about them, or watch out!"

Rasputin waved a finger at Kvachi to warn him. Once more Kvachi swore an oath of loyalty, praised and glorified Vostorgov and the bishop Aleksi, and went to see Sukhomlinov and Krivoshein.

Rasputin detained Elena, telling her she needed more treatment.

The next morning Kvachi went to see the banker Ganus.

"It's all ready for you: here's the letter, and now let's agree terms."

They agreed terms, wrote and signed the agreement, and Kvachi reached for the telephone.

"Hallo. Who is that? Your excellency? It's Prince Kvachantiradze speaking ... What did you say? You don't know me? You must know me, our Holy Father spoke to you yesterday on the phone about me. You remember now? I have a letter for you from our Holy Father ... Yes, indeed. Very good, I'll be with you shortly."

Half an hour later Kvachi was standing in the finance minister's study in front of a map of Russia. He spoke enthusiastically:

"This used to be the empire of Timur Lang; today it's Turkestan. Once upon a time it was flourishing and feeding a hundred

---

* Ivan Vostorgov was accused of palming off a forged icon as an antique.

million people. But now it's a desert and unable to feed five million. Now take a look at this boundless stretch of desert. There's room for five Frances. It has to be irrigated, ploughed, and we'll make it flourish, and we'll settle our people there. Everything will grow there: tobacco, cotton, rice, wonderful fruit, export-quality wine, hemp, peas, raisins, and silk. First, we import raw materials from America and Persia, then we'll be exporting ourselves. Turkestan can easily take two million people. We'll populate the region, make it blossom, we'll russify it and enlighten it. In two or three years we'll correct our trade balance. As for ten or twenty years' time: who can calculate? But we've got to irrigate the land first: for that we need four hundred million. The treasury doesn't have that much money, but we do and we could start work tomorrow. Let's talk it through and come to an agreement ... Yes indeed, we've got it all ready, a memorandum, plans, and draft contracts, too."

Kvachi spoke at length and his gift of the gab, together with Rasputin's scrawls, almost convinced this clever, grave, and reserved minister. Finally the minister told him:

"I like it, I like it a lot. I'll study the material today and I'll arrange a session for the day after tomorrow. The ministers of agriculture and of war will have a lot of influence in this business. If they don't oppose it ..."

"You can be quite sure they won't oppose it!" Kvachi interrupted: he had already prepared the ground.

"If the Tsar is willing ... the minister responded cautiously.

"He will be, there's no doubt about it," said Kvachi with conviction.

"In that case, the project is virtually settled. Good day to you. Give my regards to the Holy Father, kiss his hand for me, and tell him that his wish is my command."

"I'll be seeing him today and I'll pass all that on to him. Actually," Kvachi casually informed the minister, "the Holy Father and

I visited a certain family yesterday. Witte was there too: he did all he could to charm the Holy Father, but … don't you worry, I and Anastasia Prozorova took the appropriate measures and we made sure that your position is completely unassailable. Good day to you."

"I'm very grateful, prince, very grateful. Don't forget me, prince, come and see me at home, it will be a great honor for me."

They shook hands and Kvachi headed for the stairs, smiling as he made his apologies and expressed his thanks.

The Holy Man's Character

It was Saturday evening, so Kvachi went to pray at the seminary church. He prayed very sincerely and piously. When the service was over, the monks surrounded Kvachi: he knew them from Tania's salon. The court chaplain Feofan invited Kvachi for tea in his cell.

Iliodor, the monk from Tsaritsyn, and the bishop of Saratov were there too. In the corner Kvachi spotted a hideous and old cripple. He was a one-armed hunchback, almost mute and deaf, bent double and horrible to look at.

"It's our holy fool, Mitia Koliaba," Feofan explained to Kvachi.

Mitia made rasping, burbling, and bellowing sounds, and twitched his face, eyes, shoulders, and feet.

"He's one of us. He's good! He's one of us," Kvachi found it hard to make out what Mitia's mewling and bellowing meant.

Everyone was pleased by Mitia's praise of Kvachi, because this hideous creature was their medical expert.

They sat down and started an edifying spiritual conversation. Kvachi said not a word. That evening he heard much that was new; many secrets were revealed in a room where the curtains were lifted from much that was unfamiliar and uncanny.

Among other things he had insight into the fundamental idea behind the holy man's telegram about Vostorgov.

The monk Iliodor told him: "Vostorgov is a great scoundrel, that 'great patriot' is a debauched monk. He's very fond of money, gossip, and blood. Everyone knows that, but they still give him promotion and presents every day. Some time ago Vostorgov gave Aleksei, the heir to the throne, an icon and told him the icon used to belong to Vostorgov's family and was very precious and old. Then Doctor Dubrovin proved that Vostorgov had bought the icon a day earlier on the Apraksin market. There was a terrific scandal, Vostorgov put a price of twenty thousand roubles on Dubrovin's head, and nearly had him killed. After that Vostorgov took a back seat. If our Holy Father Grigory hadn't interceded, he certainly would have been unfrocked ..."

"What sort of man is the bishop of Tobolsk?"

"He's no better than Vostorgov. In fact, he's worse. A bribe-taker, thief; he plundered the bishopric of Pskov. He's been proven to be a thief. He should have been unfrocked, but our holy man helped him. Now he's in Tobolsk, where the dog should rot like a dog. Why do you ask: haven't you heard?"

"No, yesterday I was told about them. I'd like to know whether what I heard was true, or whether it was slander."

"What they said was true, but there's a lot they're not saying."

"Who is this Mitia?" Kvachi asked about the cripple.

"Mitia is a real man of God, he's holy. He's a prophet. Before the Siberian holy man appeared at the palace, the Tsar and Tsaritsa had him as their adviser and as an intermediary with God's providence. Then Rasputin took his place, but ... we'll see ..."

Kvachi pricked up his ears, but no more was vouchsafed.

"Napoleon! I've got a request: see that I never come across your cousin again, otherwise ... she's too pretty, far too pretty. I don't want to damn my soul in my old age," an elderly archbishop joked with Kvachi.

They laughed and talked of beautiful women, their eyes watered, their tongues wagged as they raked over the ashes of an extinguished fire.

Mitia walked around the table, twitching and whimpering, bellowing and mumbling.

That evening Kvachi realized that there was a plan to build a church for St Grigory and that four million roubles had already been accumulated for the purpose. Kvachi immediately thought: "If we calculate the profit is only ten percent, that makes four hundred thousand."

He immediately asked Feofan: "Who's building it?"

"There are thousands who'd like to. Whoever the Tsaritsa chooses will build it."

Kvachi made a mental note of this information, committed it to memory, and privately resolved: "Then I'll be the one that builds it."

In the end, the talk turned to Russia's saints and Rasputin in particular. They asked each other who this holy man was. Was he really a saint, or was he a devil? An old man without sin, or a hellish monster? A prophet or the Antichrist? Whose disciple or whose precursor was he—the holy Savior's, or accursed Satan's?

They all looked at each other askance, nervous, even afraid of one another.

"Father Grigory is a holy man!" announced an archimandrite tentatively and through clenched jaws.

"Devil! Devil! Devil!" the crazed Mitia began howling, getting excited, ever more clamorous and angry. Feofan had trouble calming him.

The others furrowed their brows and stayed silent for a long time. The monk Iliodor was very upset. Hermogenes winked at him, but Iliodor could not take any more.

"I speak to you from afar," he began in a highly emotional tone. "I'm a sinner, I must confess to you. My patience is exhausted."

Then after a short pause he continued: "Our holy man is a Siberian, as you well know. His father Efim was a simple peasant, a drunk, a thief, and a horse trader. The son followed in his father's footsteps. His real surname is Novykh. The neighbors called him Rasputin, because that means "dissolute, debauched, lecherous": that's the origin of his present surname Rasputin. The neighbors often thrashed and beat this future holy man because he chased their wives and daughters. He was flogged several times on the public square on the order of the local magistrate.

"Then he found himself a guardian angel, Meleti, who is now bishop of Barnaul. Our holy man once took this bishop from one village to another; on the way Meleti discovered that Rasputin had the great abilities, intuition, and talent needed for a monk and a spiritual career. And Rasputin believed him.

"He was working on the threshing floor once, when he suddenly stopped work and said: 'That's it. God is calling me. I have to sacrifice myself to his mercy and name. Goodbye.' He abandoned everybody and everything: his wife and child were left without support, and he just left.

"Since then he's been walking and roaming the length and breadth of Russia. He hasn't missed a single church, monastery, priest, or monk."

"Or woman, or woman!" shrieked the holy fool Mitia.

"Everywhere—villages, towns, hamlets—he's been preaching, talking in parables, he never stops talking about the holy Savior and the Gospels. He's drawn to the humblest, simplest folk; he hates educated people, he loathes them like the plague. He's tireless, hot-headed, uncontrollable. He has a powerful temper; his feelings are tempestuous, hot, and inflammable; his daring has no limits; his dreams are wild and go beyond this world.

"That's why he has bewitched so many followers among simple believers. Rasputin has gradually found strength, won himself a name, and got powerful protectors. He's moved imperceptibly from preaching to prophesying, now he's started to be a clairvoyant and he's also made himself a miracle-worker. Rasputin is a real *khlyst*, a flagellant."

"True, true!" Mitia responded like a parrot.

"Iliodor, my son, stop talking," Hermogenes warned the monk reproachfully.

Everyone else exchanged glances. Iliodor got to his feet, even more worked up: "It's true, brothers and fathers! Rasputin is a real *khlyst*, as I said. I have sinned before you and before God, because I saw and understood all this before, but I said it and exposed him too late: like you, I was afraid. Now I have really seen through his holy deeds. He's no holy man, he's a devil."

"Devil, devil!" the crazed Mitia began chattering again.

"We have walked a lot together. He's visited us at Tsaritsyn monastery several times. I've been to his birthplace. God, the things I saw and heard! That Satan Rasputin started his healing and his miracle-working at the bottom: with nuns and wandering pilgrim women. Since then he's been working his way upwards. Wherever he's been, he's polluted and debauched the family or the clergy. Anyone he sets eye on or rubs up against he plunges in mud and slime."

"Yes, yes, yes," the crippled Mitia chimed in.

"Then he wormed his way into Petersburg. He stayed close to father Feofan, took control of him, led him astray, found his way to the Tsar and Tsaritsa, and got all doors opened to him."

"You're a sinner, a sinner!" squawked the hideous Mitia, challenging Feofan, who was hanging his head. "Repent! Repent!"

"I'm a sinner ... I'm penitent, very penitent. Lord have mercy and forgive my sins," Feofan mumbled as he crossed himself.

"Ioann of Kronstadt also befriended Rasputin and claimed to find in that filthy soul a disciple of God, and blessed his journey towards the helm of our church and state. So this beast has got into the company of the helmsmen of our fate, a company that even before he came was full of freemasons and spiritualists. Now he is deciding the fate of our orthodox church; in fact these people serve the devil, not God the Father; instead of servants of God we have spiritualists, and they seek hope and blessing not from a church, but from occultism and theurgical spell-casting.

"So this is the time when the devil's disciple turned up in the royal palace. He had no trouble enslaving and subduing our Tsar, Tsaritsa, and their family. They are annoyed and bored with the flattery, sycophancy, hypocrisy, and disloyalty of the courtiers. So they took a liking to Rasputin for his straight talking, simplicity, simple-mindedness, and stupidity. Since then the Tsar's household and family have been torn apart and destroyed, so have the church and the state. Things are so bad, that a debauchee like Rasputin has been foisted on us as Russia's actual patriarch and real autocrat. So that's what your Rasputin is! A genuine devil, Satan's disciple, and hell's servant."

Mitia, the holy fool, was stirred into new ravings. Kvachi had trouble making any sense of his mumbling: "Rasputin boasts the Tsaritsa is his wife … He calls her 'my old lady' … Devil, devil, devil!"

"Brothers, we've been patient too long. From now on staying silent will mean serving the devil. If we are serving the church and the Russian people, the time has come for us to do our sacred duty. From now on I declare war without end on Rasputin. Anyone who can do so should follow me. This war will be a people's Christian war, a war against heretics, freemasons, Jews, and a government which is enslaved by them. They have all united to dig the grave for our church, Tsar, and motherland."

Iliodor, Mitia and some of the other senior clerics went on working themselves up and protesting for a considerable time. Finally they decided to set a cunning trap for Rasputin.

Kvachi understood what needed understanding, gathered what needed gathering, tidily stored everything in his mind and left, giving these conspirators vague hints that he was with them heart and soul.

On his way home he thought hard, searching for the fundamental idea, the knot, the essence, and the prime cause behind this "rasputiniade" and the fabulous powers of this loutish peasant. But he couldn't make anything of it, his intuition couldn't perceive, nor his senses detect, nor his intellect grasp anything. So he decided:

"Oh well, it's all a load of lies and idle talk. It's a simple battle for a crust of bread and for the good life. Rasputin is preferable to Mitia Koliaba; the Vyrubova woman puts the Lokhtina woman in the shade; Vostorgov has knocked others out of the way; Aleksi has taken the Exarch's chair from Feofan; Makari has stolen a metropolitan bishops' mitre from someone or other; Iliodor's been played a dirty trick, that's all there is to it. So it's all philosophizing and hot air, that's all there is to it!"

Intimidating the Holy Man, and Spying on Others

As soon as he got to know Rasputin, Kvachi devised a trick: every now and again he pointed out some passerby to Rasputin and told him:

"That man is keeping an eye on you, so watch out for him."

The holy man would panic, stick even closer and cling even tighter to Kvachi, while Kvachi would reassure him and give him courage:

"Don't you worry, Holy Father, the detectives I've set on the job won't miss anything. Only I ask you very humbly and reverently not to go off anywhere of your own accord or to let anyone take you anywhere."

The holy man did as Kvachi ordered and would neither receive anyone nor go with anyone without Kvachi's say-so. People all over Russia transported the Holy Grigory with the same reverence as the Iveria Icon of our Lady, and that brought in the appropriate income and profit for Kvachi to enjoy. If Rasputin showed any boldness or obstinacy, then Chipuntiradze would walk up and down past his apartment and watch it, as if he were spying on the holy man, while Kvachi would lead Rasputin to the window, show him Chipuntiradze and tell him:

"Look, that's the man who's spying on you, but don't be afraid, Holy Father. I've arranged things so that not even a fly can get into this apartment. Just don't go anywhere today, or else ..."

The holy man would obey Kvachi like a child and live according to his dictates.

Once Kvachi whispered into Rasputin's ear, as part of his daily dose:

"My dear teacher. I've given my oath of loyalty, so I have to warn you: bishops Iliodor, Feofan, Hermogenes, and many others are hostile towards you and want to see you ruined."

This was a mixture of rumors he had collected and of real facts.

Rasputin seethed and exploded with fury: "Ah, the bitches. Ah, the scoundrels. Ah, the outlaws. Little Iliodor, I'll show you! It's me that brought these snakes into society, brought them to the Tsar's court. Think of all the presents I've got people to give them. Twice they were to be sent to a remote monastery, and both times I saved them. God, what ingratitude. God, the reptiles. I quarrelled with Stolypin and made myself unpopular for their sake."

Then Rasputin sat down and wrote something:

"To Tsarskoye Selo. To the Tsar and Tsaritsa.

Dear Papa and Mama! Our dear bishops are possessed by devils. Those rebels against God's anointed have been punished. And quite right too. Now they should be treated gently. Reward them. But not all of them at once, just one, and after him another, or those dogs Hermogenes and Iliodor will start barking. Yes, that's necessary. It me, Grigory, writing. Yes. For noble deeds they have to be encouraged. Yes."

Kvachi realized that Rasputin intended to reward the obedient members of the Holy Synod and punish the disobedient clerics.

"Send this telegram off straight away. That's just one thing, there'll be a thousand others. I'll see them all rot in remote hermitages. I'll have them starved so they'll wish they could eat dog flesh. And you, Apollonchik, you keep your eyes open. Go and see them, get them talking, and find out everything ... What did you say? You want to build a church? And that'll cost five thousand? Fine, I'll sort that out by tomorrow. Get ready, tomorrow I'm going to present you to the Tsar and Tsaritsa ... Apollonchik, did you ever think you'd be so lucky? I'll bet you didn't. Take it to heart and value me. Don't treat me like that ungrateful Iliodor has, or else ... you look out!"

Kvachi dutifully kissed his hand, then let the petitioners in. This was followed by the usual fawning, kisses and embraces, servile kneeling, praise and glorification, lamenting and tears, attacks of shrieking and preaching, offerings and ... treatment of beautiful women, chasing out of demons and sick spirits.

Kvachi went home after that was over.

"Beso, what's the news?"

"All quiet. Today we've had two hundred people coming for their tickets."

"Anything else? Hasn't Ganus or Gintz been?"

"Gintz phoned you to say you were to ring him when you got back."

"What else is there?"

"Our reporter Knulman is getting on with gathering information from the newspapers and forging share certificates and banknotes."

"Hire a good-looking woman. I need someone to read things. She might as well be good-looking, or I'll get fed up with the sight of her ... What else?"

"You remember Qoranashvili from Odessa? He's supposed to have written a book, and wants it published."

"Send him a thousand roubles, but my name must be on the

title page."

"Four students are asking for scholarships."

"Send them each three hundred ..."

"There's a request for restoration at Gelati monastery ..."

"Send them a thousand ..."

"*The Russian Cause* is printing denunciations and threatening us. Look what's written here."

"I don't have the time to read some scribbler's rubbish. Find out who wrote the article and stuff his mouth with three or five hundred. If he's obstinate, tell him that he'll be sent off further than Siberia. But for now just thump him in the neck a dozen times."

"The Georgian children's magazine *Morning* has got your portrait in it with a lot of nice things under it."

That was an article that Kvachi did read. It made his face twitch and his heart pound, although he must by now have got used to being lauded and puffed, because his praise was sung in print every day, thanks to the ingenuity of Knulman. This article was generously spiced with unctuous and encouraging words: "rising sun", "genius, financial wizard", "inexhaustible energy" and "magnanimous, educated Maecenas, a patron and friend of the arts, of literature and science."

"Send the paper some sort of declaration and a thousand roubles. And tell the author ... What does he write?—that he wants to go to Paris to further his education and would like to have his travel costs paid? He's pricing his services too cheap. Three hundred. What else is there, Beso?"

"There's a letter from Tbilisi saying they want to start up a cooperative to publish a Georgian newspaper and books, so ..."

"Aha!" Kvachi interrupted, waving his hand several times. "Into the bin with it. Wasting time on corpses!"

"Your father Silibistro has written; he's fed up with living where he is, he's always worried, he daren't go out ..."

Kvachi leapt to his feet and frowned.

"What can I do, Beso, what can I do? If I'd known earlier ... But now it's far too late. What can I do now? It's one thing to hand back double the money to *Salamander*. But how can I let the world see that Silibistro's not dead?"

"People already suspect and are starting to talk."

"I know they're talking, but how can I let them see a dead man resurrected? They'll laugh at me. The whole world will make fun of me."

Then he became pensive, pondered hard, and finally decided: "Ah, I know how. There's no question of going back to Kutaisi. Write and tell him: nobody seems to know here: if they want, they can come and live here, but Silibistro's still got to stay dead, so he's got to live using Shaburiants's papers. When they get here, I'll give them instructions about everything. Beso, you find lodgings for him in some nice cosy suburb. Go and see *Salamander* and find one of the local agents so you get him to realize in good time, if they hear of anything in Petersburg, not to start any case ... I'm not worried, I'll pay them back the money with interest straight away and shut them up, but it'll still be better if you let them know first. So do it. Now leave me alone for a bit."

He lay down on a chaise-longue upholstered in lambs-wool felt, collected his thoughts, racked his brains, spinning one thread, and then another, eventually a tenth, and soon a net of new plots was spread out and unfurled.

"I'll get a million the day after tomorrow from Ganus; I'll place it on the stock exchange and buy *Anglo-Russe* shares ... and at the same time I'll buy on the quiet and put together a controlling packet ... I'll find some way of dealing with *Cosmos*, and get the newspapers talking about it. I'll get the share price up, puff it, and then sell ... I'll use Rasputin, too, and I've got to pass a thousand shares or so on to Tania, or else ... Gintz will help me, so will Ganus and Mendelsohn ... They'll put money in my account, and

I'll fire the shares at them ... The Caucasian railway won't have been sold off, Tania will know for certain. The shares are down because of fears of selling off the railway ... I'll buy a hundred or so tomorrow ..."

He devised and assessed a lot of other plots, worked out plans of action, and sorted everything out in order.

"Hallo! Who is it? Gintz? Am I talking to Abraham Moiseevich? You said ... What? Not possible? Then leave me a hundred shares, at least. What did you say? Incredible! Aha. Tomorrow in the *Arcadia*? Fine: I'll see you. And Elena? When are you going to get old and calm down?! Fine, fine, I'll bring her to you, but you'll let me have Klava in exchange, won't you? Fine ... Abraham Moiseevich, you're not building churches, are you? What, you've already built twenty! A Jew building churches? Aha. What? You're building an icon factory. You're going into the icon business? Then start making myrrh and open a theological seminary, too. You'll make money ... What can we do, that's always been the way business works. Yes, we've got to build a really big church. What's more, the army needs two million sets of underwear, a million blankets, and thousands of other things ... It comes to over twenty million in total. Right, tomorrow we'll talk it over. Give my regards to your dear Susanne Markovna, kiss her hand for me. Good night, my dear friend."

At the same time Knulman's and Beso's efforts in Gintz's and Ganus's circles, in the newspaper world and elsewhere had increased the amount of frequency of Kvachi's publicity, so that he ended up believing in his own financial genius.

A schoolteacher published a manual of accountancy and printed in his work: "The author dedicates this work to the supreme financier and generous Maecenas Prince N. A. Kvachantiradze." Thanks to this little dedication, the teacher published a second book, and Kvachi could once more gratify his greedy soul and his thirst for advancement.

One magazine printed a full-page portrait of Kvachi with the caption, "Our Morgan."

Another wrote: "Recently stock exchange circles have been very excited over the unprecedented rise in 'Gintz and Kvachantiradze' shares. A one-rouble share was being bought for five hundred yesterday."

A third paper gave a detailed account of the Turkestan concession. The article ended: "Only Kvachantiradze's firm hand could cope with this concession. We sincerely wish him success."

Printing articles like these cost Kvachi a lot of money, but whatever he gained in one day, thanks to the publication of some minor stock-exchange information, was enough to buy a whole newspaper.

Recently Kvachi had been regretting that there were only twenty-four hours in a day. He had a hand in so many enterprises: Silibistro's offspring was in such a flurry that Elena once joked to him: "You're utterly exhausted: you only remember about me once a week at most ... If I weren't getting help from the Holy Grigory I'd leave you."

"All right, don't talk nonsense," Kvachi retorted.

But there was a grain of truth in what Elena had said. Overwhelmed by running all over town, by frantic work and sleeplessness, Kvachi really had become weak and exhausted. The old fire had vanished from his eyes and his blood no longer rushed like a fountain in his veins as it used to. He couldn't let go of threads he had stretched out until he had cracked three big jobs; every day he had to devote several hours to his holy teacher, then he had to receive a herd of visitors in his apartment, after that rush to the stock exchange to see Ganus or Gintz; sometimes he had to mix with their families and give their wives consolation; yet twice a week he had to fulfil his brotherly obligations to Tania, without forgetting Elena and giving orders to sort out a thousand minor matters.

But Kvachi wouldn't surrender: like a stubborn horse he galloped towards his lucky star, which twinkled in the distance to its chosen protégé, encouraging him and luring him on with a wave of its finger.

Saving the Holy Man

Kvachi's full-speed gallop towards his lucky star came up against an invisible wall. The Turkestan concession was bogged down in a quagmire, Rasputin's church project was gathering dust in the archives, while someone had stolen the army supplies contract and other plans were put on ice or allowed to rust away.

The newspapers and magazines had stopped printing pictures and eulogies of Kvachi.

Ganus turned on Kvachi with a stinging reproach and Ganus's beautiful wife declared herself to be ill and became too haughty even to allow Kvachi access to her bedroom.

Gintz was snarling: he was losing his grip on the stock market. Tania had become distant and even Elena had become sullen.

Kvachi pondered the situation hard. It was clear that Silibistro's offspring was in deep trouble. But it took more than this to depress Kvachi. Once again he racked his brains and a little scheme was born.

"Right, now I know. Beso, come here."

He sat his faithful Beso down beside him and whispered just a score of words into his ear.

"All right, I understand ... I'm off right now. I have just the sort of man."

He went and asked a destitute former student: "Are you hungry? Are you thirsty?"

The tramp actually had a full stomach, but he still swore: "I haven't drunk a drop for three days now. I'm in agony."

"Well then, come with me and I'll relieve you."

They dropped into a bar and had a few drinks. When the tramp was tipsy and worn out by all the chatter, Beso asked him: "Would you like to earn a hundred roubles?"

"God in heaven! For a hundred roubles I'm ready to jump into the River Neva."

"It won't be as hard as that. Can you fire a revolver once or twice into the air?"

"Never mind a revolver, I'll fire a cannon if you like."

"Well, we've got an agreement, then. Here's twenty roubles. The rest comes afterwards. Now follow me."

He took the tramp to Kvachi's apartment and told him: "Here's some clean clothes and underwear for you. Settle here and then put on the clean underwear and have a sleep … I'll tell you the rest afterwards. Jalil! Come here. Look after this man. See he has a bath now and then goes to sleep."

Then Beso went to see Kvachi and told him: "I'm ready."

Kvachi picked up the telephone: "Holy Father, the Lokhtina widow has been pleading with you for the past month. Show her some mercy and see her … Yes, this evening … What? Dangerous? There's no danger at all. I'll send our lookouts there now … Fine, I'll be with you in an hour."

Kvachi and Beso had another short whispered conversation and then left.

When it was already dark Rasputin and Kvachi came out of the widow Lokhtina's apartment and got into their carriage.

Very soon this carriage turned off into a quiet sidestreet. Two shadows appeared in the dark and there were then two loud bangs. Kvachi immediately leapt from the carriage: "Stop! Don't move! Stop, or I'll shoot you," he yelled as he pursued the two shadows.

One shadow immediately stopped. In an instant Kvachi had fired his revolver at the shadow three times in succession, and, when the victim was sprawled on the ground, shot him again in the temple. Straightening up, Kvachi leapt back into the carriage and called to the driver, "Move on."

An hour later, Rasputin was being congratulated on his escape by countless prominent and celebrated persons, while Kvachi received expressions of deep gratitude. A police inspector came up with the identity papers of the unknown assassin and said, "We know that scoundrel. He's a notorious terrorist. Finally we're rid of him."

When Rasputin finally recovered from his panic and bewilderment, he gave Kvachi a bear-hug, burst into tears, and mumbled: "You've given me back my life. I don't know how to thank you ... Ask me for whatever you want."

Kvachi seized the moment and made his request.

"Certainly ... certainly!" growled the holy man. "Let's go the day after tomorrow to see 'Papa' and 'Mama' ... I'll congratulate them on their return from the Crimea and I'll settle the business. Come and let me hug you again, my Apollonchik, my loyal brother and friend."

From then on all doors to the high and mighty were open wide to Kvachi Kvachantiradze.

By evening Kvachi's telephone was worn out with all the ringing. Almost everyone in Petersburg now realized that Kvachi must have climbed to the highest rung of the ladder. That evening several new bankers, ministers, senators, senior clerics, and generals came to see Kvachi. His rooms and staircase were packed and resplendent with hundreds of different uniforms, raiments, top hats, peaked caps, French and Cossack hats.

Some came to congratulate him, others brought requests, some came to thank him, others to give advice and instructions.

The secretaries were worn out and streaming with sweat as they wrote down the names of all these people and their queries and recorded the amount of money contributed. Kvachi himself could barely stay on his feet.

"Well, is this St Sarkis's feast in Armenia, or Ascension Day in Georgia?" asked Sedrak Havlabariani.

"Clear off, Sedrak, before it's too late!" advised Chkhubishvili, who looked very fine in his black monk's habit.

"Nobody else is to slip in; put the money box where everyone can see it. How many times has it been filled up?" asked Chikinjiladze.

"It's been filled four times. There's a lot of gold and paper money today. Some people are putting their rings in, or earrings, or gold chains."

Eventually the wine ran out and the rooms and staircase were deserted.

"Right: let's add it all up."

Although tired, Kvachi gave the telephone no peace:

"Hello! Elena, is that you? Have you heard? Is Rasputin there? What, he's promised to make you a lady-in-waiting? Oh, so you've been promoted. Yes, of course, I'll say a word or two. Well, it's been quite a day for you. I know what you're worth. Aren't you a vassal of the Kvachantiradzes … After all, I'm a nobleman, but … What? Fine, darling, don't overdo it. You yourself are fake Ashordia nobility, but a Kvachantiradze was one of King Bagrat's generals. Aha! You don't seem to know your history, apparently. Well, remember my words: if I don't manage to become a genuine prince tomorrow, then my name isn't Kvachi. Goodbye for now. Is Rasputin busy chasing out devils now? Keep up the treatment, keep it up. You've got a good doctor, you don't need anyone better … Goodbye, my dove. My lovely friend. Goodbye. Till we meet again. Till tomorrow."

Jumping to the Top of the Ladder

A gleaming train came to a halt, with a whoosh of steam, groans, and creaks, at Tsarskoye Selo station. The platform and the station square were resplendent with hundreds of different uniforms.

Rasputin and Kvachi had trouble getting through to greet the royal couple. Jalil, armed to the teeth, let his eyes run everywhere and muttered:

"Och, if they're all going to see the Tsar there won't be enough horses."

Several dozen landaus and motor cars with gold coats of arms filled up with ministers, senators, and courtiers. Rasputin spat at a motor car:

"Ugh, the devil's work. Satan's box. You won't get me in one of those. Hey, you, little parrot, get me a horse-drawn cab."

They got into the cab, stretched out on the cushions and with a loud clatter of hooves set off for the palace. The broad marble staircase and the entrance were crowded with people: uhlans, hussars, horse-guards, chamberlains, pages, lords-in-waiting, the court marshal, the head groom, and officials of countless familiar and unfamiliar ranks and seniority.

The court commandant General Voyeikov was listening to an inaudible command from the court minister and just as inaudibly giving the appropriate instructions to the right and the left of him.

Rasputin and Kvachi entered the palace. Kvachi looked round the enormous hall. His eyes blurred, his mind went blank; he no longer knew what to examine, where to begin, where to look: the crystal, the bronze, the marble, gold and silver, the silk, the tapestry, the pictures, or the sculpture.

The grandees, lined up in their gold-threaded uniforms, stood like monuments; these living monuments wore dozens of different colored sashes and pearl-encrusted crosses, medals and stars round their waists, on their chests, and round their necks.

At the sight of Rasputin the grandees bowed their heads low and their faces set in a reverent smile, before freezing in their previous expressions. In the autumn sunlight the hall, packed with dazzling precious stones, shone and burned like a miniature sun.

Everyone was in his appointed place, but each nevertheless

was trying to poke his nose if only an inch further to make sure that he was seen by the others and that the others could take a good look at him.

"Well, Apollonchik, you're enjoying it, aren't you? Your eyes are popping out of your head. Never mind, stay with me and I'll see you through," Rasputin told Kvachi, who was bewildered and embarrassed.

Doors opened: "The Tsar and the Tsaritsa are coming."

The guardsmen drew their swords, the cavalrymen put their hands to their temples, the others bowed their heads, and everyone bent their bodies as low as they could.

The Tsar, the Tsaritsa, and the heir to the throne appeared in the doorway. The Tsar was in the middle, the Tsaritsa strutted to his left, and on his right the young Tsarevich Aleksei was led in, followed by his tutor, the sailor Derevenko.

All three were dressed plainly and simply, which left Kvachi dumbfounded. All three looked to their left and their right and gave a barely detectable smile. Suddenly something odd and puzzling happened: holy lunatics and seers leapt or rolled out on all sides—cripples, hunchbacks, and other deformed men grimaced and pranced, shrieked and yelled, raved and ranted as they pursued the royal couple. Rasputin whispered:

"The holy lunatics are blessed devils. Do you think they're going to upstage me? You're joking! Apollonchik, stick to me. Keep your wits about you. Why are you gawping?"

He darted forwards, dragging Kvachi off with him. The Tsar and Tsaritsa turned round and, following the old Russian custom, gave a solemn greeting to the buffoons and cripples, the dumb, the one-armed and one-legged men of God, and the holy lunatics. Then they smiled at them all, placed a hand on their heads and stroked them.

The living monuments all around also smiled, but some found it hard to repress their anger that the Tsar's doors were open to buffoons and the "men of God", before being open to them, ministers, and other grandees.

The master of ceremonies knew what he was doing: as soon as the Tsar and Tsaritsa had left, he halted the lunatics and lepers with a kindly smile, but greeted Rasputin and Kvachi and opened the door for them. Rasputin took Kvachi by the hand and rushed him into a room where the Tsar and Tsaritsa had taken refuge.

"Holy Father!"

"My dearest! Mama, Papa, Aliosha!"

They embraced, kissing and reluctant to let go of each other.

"Well my darlings, you've brought me and God joy. What was your journey like? And mama is well. And so is Aliosha. And you, Nicolas dear, you're not quite right. God grant, God grant! Well, I've brought my guardian and savior prince Apollonchik to show you. He's good, oh so good. And he prays so hard, he prays so lively. Darlings, be nice to him, that's what I want. Yes, me. Yes."

The he turned to the heir to the throne:

"Aliosha, come here."

And he sat the little prince on his lap, kissed him, tickled him, laughed, and made the prince laugh.

The Tsar and Tsaritsa held out their hands to Kvachi and offered him their ardent thanks for saving the holy Rasputin. Kvachi reverentially kissed both their hands. Nicolas was smiling, as if embarrassed at something which he felt was not quite proper.

"What is your surname, prince?"

Kvachi immediately plucked up courage: "It's Kvachantiradze, your majesty."

"What's going on in the Caucasus?"

"A lot of disorder and confusion, sire. The Jews and the devil's disciples have made themselves known among us, but we, your loyal slaves and vassals, are not afraid of them: we have fought them, overcome them, and slaughtered them, and pushed the survivors so far into the backwoods that even the devils won't find them again."

Kvachi went on to describe his heroic deeds to the Tsar and Tsaritsa: how a bomb was thrown at him, how bullets rained down on him, and how he had nearly been poisoned, and yet Kvachi—Thank God! Glory to the Lord!—had been saved by Providence from all perils, for the Lord probably wanted to test further his loyalty to the throne and to Russia.

"Well, the Lord tested you again yesterday, didn't he?"

"Yes indeed, your majesty, but I am ready, if need be every day, to show my deepest loyalty and sacrifice myself."

"I'm grateful, prince, thank you very much. I shan't forget your services. Now tell me: in your opinion, has the Caucasus now quietened down?"

"Not altogether, but ... You needn't be afraid any more, your majesty, or let your courage fail you. There are a lot of us in Holy Russia who are loyal to you and to God, so rely on our strong backs. They're mighty and powerful. We will move on and carry you gently forwards."

The morose and downcast Tsar embraced Kvachi closely, shed a couple of tears and, reassuring his timorous and frightened heart, expressed his thanks again:

"I'm grateful, prince, grateful ... Look after our Holy Father well. Watch out for him. We have many enemies."

"You're quite right, Nicolas dear, I said he deserved your affection," Rasputin intervened. "Give Apollonchik his princely rank back, Nicolas dear. You yourself have just called him prince. The Tsar's word is law, you can't take it back."

Nicolas blushed. Kvachi reassured him.

"Your majesty, the Kvachantiradzes have been princes since the seventh century. In the eighth century my ancestor was commander in chief of the Georgian army. Since then fourteen Kvachantiradzes have served Georgian kings as viziers, ministers, and catholicoses. In the eighteenth century the Ottomans seized our castle and palace, demolished them, and burnt them down ... That's when we lost our documentary proof. The whole of the Caucasus knows that we were princes, so our grandfathers and their fathers didn't need to provide proof. We still kept our rank as nobility, and I haven't sought anything more."

"Good … so be it!" the Tsar muttered and wrote down something.

"Ashordia, you're not worth anything any more," Kvachi exclaimed to himself. Then the conversation turned to state matters. The Tsar and Tsaritsa stared at the holy man's eyes like Jews staring at Moses when he came down from Mt Sinai and announced the ten commandments God had dictated to him. Whatever Rasputin wanted or uttered was always accepted and acted upon. Just once the Tsar, shy and embarrassed, put a word in: "My heart tells me one thing, my mind another."

Suddenly Rasputin raised his fist and struck the table with all the force he could muster. The whole family was dumbstruck and trembling. White as a sheet, the Tsaritsa rose to her feet; the heir to the throne burst into tears; the Tsar shuddered with astonishment.

Rasputin caught the Tsar's eye, stared hard at him for a time, and then stung him with a question: "Well then, you've missed a beat, but where: here or there?" He put his finger on his chest then on his forehead. "That's what I mean: when you think about something, don't trust your mind, but ask your heart. The heart is better than the mind."

The Tsaritsa seized Rasputin's hand: "Thank you … I'm grateful, holy teacher."

"Good … that's how I'll act," the Tsar conceded.

Derevenko had trouble calming the weeping heir to the throne. Then they spent a long time assessing, weighing up, and deciding the most important and complex matters of state, not to mention the appointments of ministers. That day some grandees were demoted and others promoted. Finally Rasputin ended the audience:

"Well, let's clear off now, Apollonchik! Papa, don't mess things up! What are you so miserable about? God forbid! Hold on to your throne and don't let the Jewish devils have their way. Crush the outlaws without mercy. Make the devils sick! That's right. Well, good health to you. And, papa, I've got a few more words for you later. I'll be here with our Tsaritsa and your daughters."

The Tsar and Tsaritsa took affectionate leave of Kvachi, entrusting Rasputin's treasured safety to him, and invited him again "for a glass of tea and for godly conversation."

Rasputin and Kvachi left. Instantly, the holy lunatics rushed in, yelling and shrieking, whimpering and laughing, to see the Tsar and Tsaritsa.

"You wait here, I won't be a moment," Rasputin told Kvachi, and trotted off across the hall and slipped into an adjoining room.

Ministers, senators, courtiers, and other grandees—some of whom Kvachi knew, some of whom he didn't—crowded round him with greetings and questions.

Kvachi realized that he had risen very high. So he made the appropriate changes to his speech and posture: he stood like a ramrod, gave himself airs, and conducted the interview in an offhand tone.

"I'm glad to be able to record that our most precious sovereign, his spouse, and the heir have come back from their stay in the Crimea significantly improved in health. They all seem to be in the best of spirits … And changes to be expected in policy? Nothing in particular. Probably measures against the Jews and other filth will be intensified: they have been making themselves a nuisance recently … War? War with the Ottoman Empire is not desirable at the moment because we shall need our strength and our forces for still greater causes in the near future … Against whom? I can't discuss that with you at the moment … You'll be told soon … The State Duma we shall have to restrict a little. We'll have to filter the ministers and senior officials a bit, too."

Many of his listeners had their hearts beating faster after these words: some from fear, others from hope.

That day Kvachi had accomplished his exploration of the top floor of Russian society and ascended to a rung that no ordinary Georgian had ever set foot on before.

That was what Kvachi himself thought, as he waited for Rasputin and so generously distributed grace and hope among the grandees and the dignitaries who fawned on him and tagged after him with the intention of making him one of them and using him as a friend in the complex and hazardous game that constantly was played around the court in the pursuit of victory, success, and the good life.

Once again Kvachi now perceived and absorbed a fundamental principle, as he had when he ran around Samtredia with no underpants: in this most august hall he made the most of his precepts, his natural intuition, his trained hound's nose, and all his ingenuity in order to please everybody, not to incur disapproval or make enemies. But, at the same time, he knew very well that his appearance in the palace and his sudden promotion had disadvantaged many and made many others envious and hostile.

The circle of dignitaries and grandees was broken by the Minister of the Court, the tall, handsome old Baron Friedrichs. With his honeyed tongue he reminded Kvachi:

"Prince! Their imperial majesties have by grace and favor asked you to come to dinner today."

Kvachi bowed as low as he could.

"My most hu-u-umble thanks and de-e-epest joy are unbounded and beyond words."

That day, of all the grandees and dignitaries, only Kvachi and Rasputin were to experience this boundless honor and highest bliss.

This really was the highest rung in Kvachi's wondrous ladder, and he had now reached it.

Saving the Throne and Russia from Turmoil

History always lies. But the exception proves the rule.

This is what happened when that old gossip history unintentionally blurted out the truth and in its ravings assigned and set out in golden letters a place and role for Kvachi Kvachantiradze in the vital historical deeds done on that unforgettable day by Rasputin and Kvachi.

These deeds of long-lasting and universal importance, which turned back the wheel of Russia's and the world's fortune, are inscribed in gold in Russia's history, and Kvachi's globally important service has been correspondingly acknowledged and valued. But Kvachi is mentioned in this matter only by a one-letter pseudonym, K, because he, as we have shown countless times, was an extremely reserved and shy young man who always avoided publicity or puff. Nevertheless you might find a very few people who were jealous of Kvachi and would assert that this "K" was not Kvachantiradze at all, but the grand duke and poet Konstantin. But, thank the Lord, the famous historian Gossipmonger* has completely dismissed this version and has reassigned Kvachantiradze the place he merits in the global events described below.

Apart from the Tsar and Tsaritsa, their heir and four daughters, only Rasputin, Kvachi, the courtier Vyrubova, and the minister Baron Friedrichs were present at this historic dinner.

After dinner, when the younger generation had left the table and the spiritual conversation and edifying discourses were over, the Tsaritsa, worried and trembling, spoke:

"Holy Father, you've always been our loyal friend and reliable adviser ... Everything you've said has been a prophecy come true, everything has turned out to be right: losing the war with Japan, defeating revolution, giving birth to an heir to the throne, and

---

* The literal meaning of the name of the Russian historian Spletnev.

many other things. That's why, as you well know, we dare not decide anything without you."

"That's very sensible of you," retorted Rasputin.

"This is a business that can't be put off. When you were in the Crimea, Holy Father, Nicky wanted to say straight away what was grieving us, but I made him put it off. Now, however, is the time to reveal the greatest secret, but you must know and not forget that this secret has to be buried under six other secrets. If it comes to light too early, the state will be in terrible danger."

Kvachi raised a finger to show that he swore silence.

"Don't worry, prince," the Tsaritsa addressed him. "There's no need to swear an oath. It's quite impossible for our holy man's chosen friend to turn out to be a chatterbox. Now let's get down to business ... You will know that about five years ago, when Russia was in the greatest chaos, we decided to abdicate and seek refuge abroad. But then we and Russia were saved by our holy confessor, who changed our minds and almost forced us to keep the throne."

"Well, didn't my prophecy come true?" asked Rasputin.

"It did, Holy Father, it came completely true. That's why we pray in your name and that's why we think that we should build a church in the name of St Grigory while you are still alive. But the trouble is that Nicky still hasn't abandoned the idea of abdicating."

"What are you saying? What do you mean?" exclaimed Rasputin and Kvachi as one.

"He's been thinking about it all the time: we're in the most terrible danger, we're all doomed, Russia will collapse around our heads ... On my own there's no way I can do anything, I can't influence him. Help me somehow, Holy Father. And you, too, prince. Advise us, let us know what God wills, father. Our redeemer, our holy man, help us! Advise us."

The Tsaritsa burst into tears and sobbed. Nicolas had his head in his hands. Rasputin thought for a while. Everyone was silent for some time, waiting for Rasputin to speak. Finally, his brow furrowed, the holy man stood up and said piously: "Let us pray to the Lord."

They all got up and kneeled before the icon. They prayed piously, from their hearts, and prostrated themselves. Then they rose to their feet and gathered round Rasputin. He stood in front of Nicolas and asked him sarcastically: "What did God put in your mind while you were praying, what answer did he give you?"

The Tsar, his head bowed, said nothing. Then he shook his head and whispered: "He didn't deign to answer me."

"The reason he didn't deign was that you're an unworthy sinner. Repent your sins, cleanse your heart of evil, and then God our Lord will open the door of wisdom to you."

There was a lengthy session of advice and instruction given to the torpid and despairing Tsar. Rasputin frightened him by warning that abdication would bring about terrible chaos, anarchy, the collapse of the state, war, fire, and bloodshed, that God would hold him alone responsible if nobody else could inherit and hold on to the throne.

Kvachi gathered his wits and summoned his eloquence, but to no avail. The downcast Tsar, his head drooping, sat down and said not a word: he only kept shaking his even more bowed head as a sign of denial.

Rasputin suddenly lost his temper and turned nasty. He shivered as if struck by a strange fever. His hands and lips quivered, his face turned deadly pale, his nose seemed to be honed, and his eyes lit up with an uncanny blue fire. Suddenly he fell upon the Tsar and began scolding him and yelling at him, stamping his feet and waving his hands under the Tsar's nose.

"What? You don't trust the people or even the Lord?! Have you forgotten that he who disobeys the Lord must be excommunicated from the church and driven out! Anathema, anathema to any Tsar who forgets the Lord, his congregation, the church, and his duty!"

When he heard the threats and the word anathema, the Tsar stood up and staggered in fear. Rasputin turned up the thunder and lightning:

"Who gave you the right to destroy Russia? How dare you leave so many people to perish? Do you understand that you're encouraging devils and Jews to gather round the throne? If so, you have let devils into your soul. If so, you must be a disciple of hell. You're not a Tsar, you're the Antichrist! Antichrist! Antichrist!"

"Lord have mercy upon us," groaned the Tsar, as he made a sweeping sign of the cross with his shaking hand.

"I'm telling you, watch it! I, Grigory, am telling you, watch it!" yelled the furious Rasputin. "Get on your knees! Get on your knees and beg the Lord to pardon your sins. Pray to the Lord, pray for the evil spirits and hellish devils to be chased out of your heart."

And he stood over the Tsar, who was prostrate in front of the icon, and he made the sign of the cross praying at the top of his voice: "Holy God, holy and mighty, holy and immortal, have mercy on us! In the name of the Father, the Son, and the Holy Ghost, amen."

All six once more spent some time kneeling before the icon, praying loudly, fervently, prostrating themselves, shedding tears, groaning. Finally Rasputin rose and said: "Arise, Tsar. Arise and tell us what the Lord has put in your mind, what he has advised you."

The exhausted and enfeebled Tsar suddenly fell at Rasputin's knees. The Tsaritsa and the court lady Vyrubova kneeled next to the Tsar; all three clutched at the holy man's feet, coat-tails and hands, greedily kissing them, generously watering them with tears and, as they clutched him, raving and shouting in breaking voices:

"Holy Father! You are our savior. You are our Christ. You are our redeemer and lord. Show us mercy and have pity on us,

Holy Father."

White as a sheet, Rasputin stood as if ossified.. He had flung his head back. His eyes, frozen but flashing, stared at the icon. His whole body quivered. Then he put his left hand on the Tsar's head and made a broad sign of the cross with his right hand, whispering with trembling lips:

"Thank you, Lord, for saving Holy Russia, its Tsar, his family, and your orthodox church from turmoil and hell … Lord, have mercy upon us. Hallelujah, hallelujah, hallelujah! Amen."

Then the Tsaritsa swore an oath before Rasputin's icon: "I swear by the Lord God, Saint Seraphim of Sarov, by my children and my husband, that I shall never abandon you, never, even if the whole world makes war on us. Until the day I die I shall be with you on this earth. I swear loyalty and obedience to you."

They gradually calmed down and settled their spirits, which had been inflamed by prayer, and their racing blood. Finally Rasputin lifted the half-unconscious Tsar to his feet.

"Arise, Tsar. Arise and rule Russia with glory. Gladden the holy church, console the people, and trample down your enemies. And let the angels in heaven and every orthodox believer on earth rejoice … Get thee behind me, Satan! Be gone, Satan!"

Nicolas, in tears, held Rasputin to his chest.

"Amen, amen! Get thee behind me, Satan! Be gone, be gone!" the others murmured, trembling with fear.

Then, weeping for joy, they took turns to embrace and kiss their redeemer, the savior of the church and all Russia, the holy savior Grigory Rasputin.

Kvachi's Award, A Woman's Apology, and a Few Other Things

"You saw? Are you convinced now?" Rasputin asked an astounded Kvachi in the Tsar's railway carriage.

"Wondrous are thy deeds, great teacher and miracle-worker! I saw, I understood, and I believed."

"Once again I've saved Russia, the church, and the Tsar from the greatest possible peril."

"You deserve the greatest possible monument, great teacher, redeemer of our country. I'll start building the church of St Grigory tomorrow."

"I've got you that business, too: the Tsaritsa has given an additional million, as well as the four million we had, to mark this day; now you know what a magnificent church you are going to build. Five million will pay for a big church, won't it?"

"I'll build you such a church that it will put Aghia Sophia and Rome's St Peter cathedral in the shade. With God's help I'll take on this project for posterity. I have the knowledge and experience to do it."

"I did make sure you were given a prince's rank. I gave you the irrigation canal concession in Turkestan. You got the contract to provide twenty million sets of underwear for the army. And I got you an aide-de-camp's uniform, too."

"Immortal are thy works, Holy Father!"

"You owe me ten thousand."

"I'll give you them tomorrow, Holy Father."

"We've got Elena accepted as a courtier. We've made her a lady-in-waiting, a lady of honor, and a dame of the Tsar's order. So she better not get above herself, or forget a favor, or else …"

"No, Holy Father, no. Elena is not that sort of woman."

"We've changed the synod membership and got rid of the obstinate ones: we've sent that dog Iliodor and that stubborn mule Hermogenes out to the wilderness, we've appointed new ministers, we've given bishops who support us presents. Rejoice, ye orthodox! Quiver and tremble, Jews and devils! Don't fool with us."

Suddenly his eye hit on a good-looking woman. He slipped off to close in on her. Five minutes later Kvachi followed. There was a noise in the distance.

In the doorway to a compartment a furious Rasputin was yelling: "Why are you digging your heels in, bitch? The Tsar and the Tsaritsa kiss my hand, and you squirm and twist?! What? You don't know who I am? You don't recognize Grigory Rasputin? I'll show you then who I am. You stuck-up cow, you slut, you ..."

He abused her with words that made the whole carriage blush red.

Kvachi had to beg and plead with Rasputin to get him to come back to their compartment: the great teacher refused to calm down and started threatening people with hard labor in Siberia.

Ten minutes or so later the woman and her husband, an important assistant and friend of the minister of justice Shcheglovitov, tiptoed into Rasputin's compartment and meekly asked for forgiveness. Rasputin wouldn't deign to speak to them. The husband, both offended and afraid, went out again. Kvachi followed him.

"Apollonchik! Stand outside the door and don't let anyone in," Rasputin called after him.

Kvachi leant against the outside of the compartment door and wouldn't let the woman's husband in. He tried to console him:

"Don't worry, calm down. I promise you that in a few days you'll be given a medal and the highest possible promotion."

The husband tried to push in. But Jalil grasped his arm, pulled him back as if he were a child and begged him: "Please, sir, please, you mustn't. Your lady will come, then you can go in."

The official took Kvachi's remonstration to heart: he went to his own compartment and sat down to read a newspaper.

When the train reached Petersburg station and the woman, red-faced, dishevelled, but looking pleased, emerged from the compartment, Kvachi asked Rasputin: "Did you forgive the woman? Did she apologize?"

"I forgave her; I made her apologize several times and I absolved her sins ... What else could I do? I'm a Christian. Here, write down her address."

"Thank God! Glory to the Lord!"

"Apollonchik, today I'm your guest at the *Arcadia*."

"I'm not sure I can take so much happiness at one go, Holy Father!"

"They must get everything ready, hire a curtained-off private room. We'll go at midnight on the dot. Bring Elena, too. Go now and get some rest. I need a rest too. It's been a terrible day, terrible. Lord, have mercy on us and forgive us our sins!"

How could Kvachi possibly find time to rest? He had a lot of things to see to, sort out, and finish off that evening. First of all he had his *Berliet* driven to Ganus's.

"Congratulate me! We've won ... We've got it confirmed!" he babbled at the stunned banker. "Tomorrow at twelve o'clock they'll pay my account ... I've been all day at the palace ... I barely had time to manage. They asked me to stay to dinner and wouldn't let me leave ... There are so many new things you can't count them ... A lot of changes ... Aide-de-camp appointment."

As he spoke he made much of the day's adventures and "a sworn secret of the greatest possible importance." He added some gossip. Kvachi's talks constantly repeated: "We've appointed ... We've transferred ... We've decided ... Russia was perishing and it was all I could do to save it ... Rasputin and I did ... They've entrusted everything to us ... They'll do it all for us ... Bring it on now, whatever business you have ... Do it quick, tomorrow, right now, or else, who knows what will happen, who knows how things will turn out ... Tomorrow at ten a.m. I'll come and see you, we have to go and get the signed contract. May I use your telephone? Thank you."

He ran like a young goat to grab the telephone: "Hallo! Beso, is that you? Get hold of my brokers. Do it quick. Find them wherever they are. I'll be with you in an hour ... Fine, fine, so be it. Tell them they're free to go ... Hello! Elena, a thousand kisses, and congratulations on being a lady-in-waiting … What, don't you believe me? Tomorrow or the day after you'll get it in writing. Won't you believe me then? What? Rasputin did it? Yes, Rasputin and I sorted it out for you. What? You shouldn't be embarrassed, Elena. Ha-ha. Fine, fine … Don't go anywhere today, I'll be with you at ten, I've got something big on … Ha-ha-ha. Is that true? Should I believe it? All right, fine, tell him he's free to go."

"Hello! Is that the Gintz residence? Abraham Moiseevich, is that you? Congratulate me, I've won all the business. That's all I have to tell you. I'll be with you in half an hour. Get your engineers and architects on the job … Right now? All right, I'm on my way."

He turned to talk to Ganus: "Right then, my dear friend. You owe me a nice present! Until tomorrow morning … Kiss your spouse on my behalf. I'm sorry I haven't seen her."

He rushed off to see Gintz, showered him with talk, boasted of his achievements and of Gintz's too:

"Rasputin and I did it … We've been dining all this time … We've dismissed … appointed … transferred. I've been entrusted with building a church. Can you do the building? Will you take it on?"

"I'll take anything on. If they contract me to build a railway to the moon, I'll say yes."

"Well, here are the plans, here's the contract, here's the Tsaritsa's letter …"

"I'll examine it … I'll see … I'll do an estimate."

"We need twenty million sets of underwear for the army, blankets, and a thousand other items. Here's the list and the prices. Give me five percent and take the job."

"I'll have to do some calculations. I'll give you an answer tomorrow morning."

"In that case, goodbye! Until we meet again. I've got a thousand other things to do … Ministers and dignitaries are waiting for me at home … Greetings to your spouse: I kiss her hand … Goodbye, dear friend."

He found his stairs crowded with people.

"Send them packing. Don't let any more of these petty clerks in. Look at the time! I've been given a job so big that it isn't worth counting these people's money. Beso, call the stockbrokers."

Kvachi locked his doors and gave his brokers full instructions, had them write down what he said, and sent them home.

"Sedrak! Choose the better-off people and let them in, send the rest home … Chipi, run to the station, meet Silibistro and Pupi, and find them somewhere to live. They're not to come here until I tell them they can. Look after them, see they have what they need. Gabo! Take this letter for prima donna Volzhina at the opera. Buy her a big bouquet and give her my apologies for not being able to come. If she wants to go, take her off to the *Arcadia*. She doesn't like motor cars? Book a horse cab then. Get moving, then."

He went back to the telephone: "Hallo! The *Arcadia*? Prince Kvachantiradze speaking. Keep the first or second private room for me, arrange flowers … Get everything ready …"

He turned away: "Beso, is that you? Who's waiting for me? Bring the list. Senator Shubin, Archimandrite Makari … Governor Tiesenhausen … Kochubei, chairman of the senate … Good, good, let them wait a little … I'm tired."

He lay down to rest and revised his network of devious plans, which was so well constructed and calculated … As long as Gintz didn't let him down, Kvachi wasn't afraid of the rest. "Fine, we'll see … tomorrow, we'll see."

"Beso, call in whoever is there."

An hour later Kvachi's 60-horsepower Mercedes was flying down Suvorov Avenue. When he went up to see Elena, he came across Rasputin. He thought:

"He's got in before me, the bastard!"

"Apollonchik, is that you? Are we having a party tonight? Is it all ready?"

"We are, great teacher, we are! It's all ready. We're expecting you at midnight precisely."

Depressed and offended, he went in to see Elena. She was dishevelled and her face was red, and she looked at him with pleasure; she was caressing and affectionate.

"So that peasant got in before me. Really! Did he tell you everything?"

"My darling Kvachi, don't be jealous. Don't try and have everything. Be content with the money, being a prince and a courtier, or else you'll regret it."

"What do you mean, trying to have everything, sweetheart? For one thing, I've let Rasputin have you. It's killing me, but what can I do? Anyway, it's time I got dressed."

Again, he pounced on the telephone: "Hello! Tanechka, is that you? A thousand kisses … you're well, I hope? Would you like me to show you a place of mortal sin? Our spiritual leader will be there … You won't regret it, don't be afraid; if you like, you can wear a mask. What, you're afraid? I said you needn't be; I'll take you to a private room where even the devil won't be able to see you … Elena is coming, too, so is the singer Volzhina, we're all from the same crowd … So you agree? Well, get dressed quickly, and I'll come and fetch you."

Holy Grigory's "Passport", and Flogging a Fornicator

It was now two in the morning. The *café chantant* was wild with drinking and eating, dancing, singing, music, and flirtation. The enormous hall was ablaze with light. The clusters of crystal chandeliers hanging like countless necklaces shone like diamonds. You could hear the clatter of Sèvres porcelain. The champagne, chilled in silver buckets and wrapped in serviettes, sparkled golden bubbles in crystal bowls. From a bulbous decanter dribbled honey-colored curaçao-chypre liqueur. Muscat, marsala, Benedictine, Bordeaux, and burgundy sparkled red and yellow. Burning chartreuse emitted blue flames in the Baccarat glasses. Dozens of colors are exuded from all the exotic fruits: pineapples, oranges, and mandarins. French pears, St Germain and Duchesse, melt in the mouth.

On a table, as white as cotton, there is a generous spread of red-blushed peaches, Calville apples, yellow and black grapes, rare roses and other flowers.

Shiny crabs and lobsters are splayed out, as if about to crawl away.

Roasted and baked poultry are laid out with their browned breasts and legs upwards.

Food with dozens of different seasonings lies around, some nibbled at, some untouched.

Bare shoulders, chests, arms, and legs showing through translucent lace are generously displayed in every color, shape, and racial form.

Brocade, satin, velvet, and fine silk are everywhere in profusion.

The eye is drawn by Venetian, Genovan, Valence, and oriental embroidery, textile and golden needlework. Jet-black, chestnut, mousy, straw-blonde, and golden hair is combed up and decorated.

The eye is dazzled by diamonds, rough and cut, rubies, turquoises, emeralds, amethysts, pearls, balas, and lapis lazuli.

Tobacco smoke curls like blue snakes, rises up to the ceiling and deposits its soot.

The spicy unguents spread, irritating the senses.

On the stage there is an uninterrupted succession of Frenchmen, Spaniards, and Algerian Jews. There are Tunisian Arabs, Japanese, and dancers from every corner of the globe.

There is a maddening frenzy of unbridled Spanish dancing,

Hungarian csardas, and Polish mazurkas. There is shameless squatting cakewalk, the *Maxixe* dance breaks all bounds, a lecherous tango twists, and a passionate belly-dance strips off. Shins and thighs of every color and shape leap about, brocade dresses rustle, and white underwear flashes.

Young men and women are locked in a tangle, intoxicated and dizzy with each other's breath and flesh, as they slide and leap in waves of dancing, uninhibited and ecstatic.

There is infatuated whispering, jocular hints, and excited peals of laughter. The hall is transfixed by frequent flashes of eyes inflamed by lust. Naked bosoms heave with ominous arousal. The flame of naked desire trembles on blood-colored lips and brilliant teeth. Honed by drugs and tipsy after burning drinks and food, flesh seeks assuagement and boiling blood urgently demands appeasement and cooling. The overheated hall is enveloped in flames and fumes of passion. Raging and on fire, the wild beast of whoring and fornication is growling and prowling, its face covered in blood, its teeth sharpened. In an uncontrollable blaze of depravity and lust, the hall burns, melts, and is swallowed up.

In a spacious private room, curtained off, Rasputin, Kvachi, Elena and Tania are feasting; every now and again they take a quiet look at the stage where one after the other a Russian troupe, gypsies, negroes, Tyroleans, Frenchmen, and Spaniards are singing and dancing. Rasputin, already drunk, periodically gives orders:

"Put on a cakewalk for me! A *Maxixe*! I want that Spaniard to dance again! Call back the gypsy women! I invite them all! Tell them, Grigory Rasputin is having a party and wants them to come. They'd better not let me down, or I'll wreck this nest of devils."

There's a button torn off Rasputin's silk gown, his sleeves are rolled up, his hair is dishevelled and falling over his eyebrows, his eyes are bloodshot, his head overheated and foggy.

His oily and glowing eyes have a beast swimming in them; his heart is on fire, and he knows no peace, but is as excited as a wild animal in a cage. He lets his hands wander everywhere and drinks anything he can lay his hands on; he bellows out filthy songs as well as hymns; like a gun, he shoots out incomprehensible words and street language, and these strike Tania, Elena, and the women singers in the heart like arrows. He is constantly falling upon one or the other of the women:

"Why are you acting up? Why are you behaving like an unbroken filly? If we're having a party, then let's do it our way, the peasant way. Undo your buttons. Show me your breasts. Take off your clothes."

Then he mingled with the actresses, behaving like an oaf and ripping a button off one of them. The women started shrieking. Some were laughing, others lost their temper and tried to get away, but Rasputin got only more querulous and nasty:

"Why are you being so high and mighty, bitches? What's all this nonsense? I've seen hundreds of women like you naked; dozens of better women than you come to see us in the baths. The Tsaritsa is nice to me, so who do you think you are? Look, this gown was made by my old lady personally. Yes, the Tsaritsa herself made it for me and embroidered it, too. Apollonchik, leave me alone, I said. Tania, you shut up! Today the Tsar and the Tsaritsa kissed my feet, so who do you wretches think you are?"

Kvachi tried to calm the now rabid Rasputin, while Tania and Elena were bright red with embarrassment; others were calling for the police and the restaurant manager. People gathered round their private room.

"What's all this? Aren't I Grigory Rasputin? Don't you believe me, then? If not, listen to me. Take a closer look and make sure!" He unbuttoned his trousers and took out the best proof he had of his identity.

"Don't you believe me even now? Don't you recognize Rasputin now? Look, that's my ID! See and believe. Have a good feel."

Tania and Elena shrieked and rushed out; several women followed them, swearing and cursing. Those who stayed burst into loud laughter. Someone tore down the curtain from the private room and revealed this beast to the eyes of the enormous hall packed with people. Uproar and commotion broke out in the hall, the dancing and singing on the stage broke off, and the music fell silent. Someone called out: "Grab him! Throw him out!"

Someone else shouted: "It's a lie! He's lying! That isn't Rasputin!" Then everyone and everything was thrown into chaos.

"Take a good look! See! This is my ID. This is my proof!" Rasputin was shouting as he stood up in the private room.

The hall was in turmoil. Some were guffawing: "Ha-ha-ha, ho-ho-ho."

Others were yelling: "Throw him out! Grab him! Draw up a statement! Call the police! Send him to the madhouse."

They all buzzed around the private room, like bees to a hive, with threats, laughter, and alarm calls.

Jalil was propped like a rock against the doors of the room. He had his hand on his dagger. He rolled his equine eyes and begged the people:

"Please, sir, please. Don't come closer. Or there'll be blood."

The restaurant manager and a police officer rushed into the room. Someone covered up the room with the curtain that had been torn down and thus shut down this extraordinary spectacle. To calm everyone and to distract attention, the chorus of singers strained their vocal chords and the band shrieked as loudly as it could.

Rasputin calmed down, came to his senses, and threatened the police officer:

"If you write a statement, I'll see you rot in a Siberian prison and I'll have your flesh fed to the dogs. Yes, that's what I'm telling you. Me, Grigory Rasputin. Leave me alone, I'll go of my own accord; Apollonchik, throw these dogs some money, a hundred roubles each, and that's their lot. Now let's go. Where are Tania and Elena? They've made a run for it? To hell with them. I said, don't write a statement, or else ..."

Kvachi finally managed to get the drunken Rasputin away. They were followed by laughter, threats, yells, and whistles. Half-way home, Rasputin lost his bearings: "Turn right! Now left! Now straight on. Stop!"

They drove the car to a brothel.

"Teacher, what are you doing? We'll be recognized, the Tsar and Tsaritsa will find out."

"Apollonchik, shut up. Who's going to find out? My old lady? You're still wet behind the ears, you don't understand anything yet. If she finds out, all the better, she'll love me all the more. You don't understand anything about women's souls and characters. Come, follow me."

The drunkard pushed his way into the hallway and called out: "Here we are, mademoiselles! Dance me a Komarinskaya, then."

Nimbly, boldly, and neatly he danced a Komarinskaya to the sound of the piano, and a few of the girls joined him. Then he gave each girl five roubles and ordered twenty bottles of wine and vodka. There was an outbreak of shrieks, giggles, dancing, embraces, and groping. Wine was drunk, glasses were smashed, and the whole place was trashed.

Finally Rasputin chose five girls and took them off. One girl virtually dragged Kvachi off, and Jalil chose himself a hundred-kilo blonde.

After half an hour there came the sound of constant shrieking and Russian cursing from one room. Kvachi was now ready to leave and was waiting for his teacher. Suddenly a woman's prolonged shriek was heard from the room where Rasputin was entertaining himself: "He-e-elp! He's ki-i-illing me!"

Kvachi leapt to the porch and then let himself out to the street. By the main gate he bumped into a completely naked and dishevelled girl who was running, yelling, and shouting, towards the street. The great teacher was pursuing her. He too was naked. He was lashing at the naked woman with a braided belt as he ran, shouting: "You bitch! You slut! You lowlife. Take that, take that!"

Every time she was hit the woman shrieked, twisted her body, leapt aside, and ran on further: "Help me. He's killing me."

Kvachi and, after him, two yardmen went in pursuit, then others came to help. They lifted up the woman, who had now fainted, while others fell on Rasputin and blocked his path: "Hit him! Grab him!"

Jalil appeared from nowhere. He had half drawn his dagger and he pleaded with the mob: "Please, go away, please …"

The police came rushing in. Rasputin was afraid of nobody and gave no quarter: "I'll defend myself and then I'll see who dares to hurt Grigory Rasputin. Constable, chase these dogs away, or I'll see you rot in a Siberian prison. Go on, quick."

At the sound of Rasputin's name there was a burst of laughter and a general commotion.

"True, it's true. It must be Rasputin. Just take a look at him."

"I told you to disperse," yelled the policemen.

Meanwhile Rasputin had gone back into the house; ten minutes later he came back dressed. His path was blocked by the police officer.

"What do you mean, a statement? Are you bored with life? Do you have a wife and children, or not?"

"No, sir, I … nothing … I just wanted to catch a sight with my own eyes of the holy Grigory … Nothing else … I'd see you home, but …"

"There's no need. Apollonchik, thank the officer. Give him twenty-five. What's your name? Come and see me tomorrow or the day after."

Immediately after that the motor car moved off.

The Holy Man's Penitence, and Crashing the Stock Exchange

Rasputin had a small room full of icons and religious objects. This was his prayer-room.

Stumbling and staggering, he entered the prayer-room. Jesus, dimly candle-lit, looked at Rasputin with merciful eyes, as though gently reproaching him.

A broken, lustful, and sinful Rasputin fell prostrate and lay before this icon. As he lay he bellowed out a list of his sins:

"Holy God, holy, almighty, holy, immortal, have mercy upon us! Lord almighty and merciful, pardon my sins, unworthy and evil that I am, and send me the punishment I deserve."

Daylight had now come. Rasputin stood up to pray. The damned saint once again prayed with prostrations, groans, moans, and burning tears, yet pronounced the prayers clearly and distinctly, sometimes reciting hymns, striking his chest hard with his fist and tearing at his kneecaps.

After midday Kvachi came running in to see his teacher. A servant told him: "Father Grigory is still at prayer. Since last night he hasn't left the prayer-room or touched food or drink, or seen anyone."

Kvachi was amazed, but not offended, for that day he had a dozen "jobs" to be fixed. The next day he dropped in again, and the servant told him the same thing: "Father Grigory is still at prayers. He hasn't been out since yesterday and hasn't touched food or drink or seen anyone."

"What's going on?" wondered Kvachi, as he entered a room next to the room where Rasputin had now been praying for two days.

In this room a dozen or so men and women were standing by the doors leading to Rasputin's prayer-room and fervently repenting the teacher's sins. Kvachi saw among them Tania, drained of strength; he knelt by her side. Her head drooped, her hands and eyes were fixed on high, and she was moving her lips. The teacher's now weakened voice could be heard from the prayer-room:

"And they stripped him and placed a crown of thorns on his head … and they began to mock him, saying Hail, King of the Jews! And they smote him on the head with a reed and offered him worship. And after they had mocked him and robbed him of his garment and put his own raiment on him, they led him away to crucify him."

Rasputin broke off his reading of the Gospels with sobbing: "Enough! Let it be finished! Let this suffice!"

The others also rose to their feet and burst into tears. Kvachi led the exhausted Tania into another room, finally calmed her and then, because he had a couple of "jobs" to attend to, leapt into his motor car and went to see the banker Ganus. That evening he phoned to ask after Rasputin:

"Hello! How is the Holy Father? What, he's still praying? He hasn't had anything to eat? He doesn't want to see anybody? He's still behind locked doors? God almighty, what's going on? Fine, then I'll drop in again tomorrow."

On the third day he again dropped in to see Rasputin at vespers. He found the door to the prayer-room still locked. Even more disciples had gathered in the anteroom. This time Tania was nowhere to be seen. Rasputin's loyal disciples and followers were about to break down the door, but the Virgin Mary Lokhtina stopped them: "Give the Son of God some peace and pray for his soul. Do not mourn: our holy savior is able to fast for forty days at least."

A whole week passed. Rasputin's drawing room was packed with dignitaries and grandees, as well as his disciples. Some were quietly praying; others were inspired to preach and were uttering strange and meaningless ravings. Suddenly the doors to the prayer-room opened. The servant let Kvachi in, before anyone else, to see the holy man. Worn out and drained, Rasputin was lying on the bare floor.

"God almighty! Holy teacher!"

"Apollonchik! My faithful brother and friend!" said Rasputin in a barely audible whisper. "Don't worry, I'm all right. Try to understand and remember: God rejoices when sinners repent their sins. So, when God sends us the devil, we have to do as he says, we have to fornicate and err, so that we have a reason to repent our sins. If we don't commit sins, we can't repent anything. A saint is always damned, because he is without sin, and he who is without sin cannot repent anything, because he has no sins to repent. Do you understand? Do you grasp what I'm saying?"

"I do and I'll remember. Unfathomable and boundless is thy wisdom, o holy one."

Rasputin became calm and then continued:

"Apollonchik! You're as innocent and sinless as a child, because you still don't know much. It's still early days, you'll grow up and understand everything. Today I'll just tell you one thing: there's no devil in the world as sinful as me. Spending seven days on my feet praying is nothing. I remember the first time I ran away from my family, I dug myself a cave in a hillside and I didn't leave that cave for three days. I didn't touch anything except dry bread and water. I had scabies; I was itching with mange. I stood in front of the icon without changing my clothes or washing. Once I was so weak I nearly passed out, I fixed my eyes on the icon of the Virgin and I clearly saw: the Virgin was weeping bitter tears. Then she told me: 'Grigory, Grigory! You are cleansed of your sins. The world is perishing in the devil's clutches. Arise and go to save and heal your people.' So I went. Since then I have walked about serving Christ our Lord. Who knows how many times I have distanced myself from this sinful world for two or three months? Now the time has come for us to distance ourselves, my Apollonchik."

Kvachi was so shocked that his heart missed a beat: "Where to, Holy Father? Where are you going to go?"

"A long way away, very far, to Jerusalem. I have to pay my respects to the holy places, prostrate myself at the Lord's grave. Finally, I have to bathe myself clean and repent my countless sins."

"Holy Father, what are you doing to me? Who's going to help me when you leave? What? I'm to come too? I'm ready for the journey. But I need to think about it. Holy Father, put off this terrible journey at least for two or three months."

"I can't do that. The icon announced to me last night: 'Grigory, in three days' time leave here for Jerusalem, because your sins are beyond counting.' Now go, my Apollonchik, and send Elena or Tania to see me. Tomorrow at ten in the evening be here, there's somewhere we've got to go to. I'll show you something that you could never even dream of."

When Kvachi got home, already downcast and in a very bad mood, he had to deal with a number of unpleasant events.

Since he returned from Tsarskoye Selo, Kvachi had felt he was the happiest of men, because that day he had achieved everything: princely rank, a place at court, wide-ranging influence, power and wealth which would any day now find its way into his pocket: a part of that wealth he had already realized, and he had made his mark on the stock exchange.

Recently Kvachi's mouth had uttered a limited range of words: "money on call, promissory notes, coupons, shares in Putilov steelworks, Lena gold mines, *Salamander* ... exchange premium, I sold, I bought, I lost, I won," and so on. But the fact is that Kvachi said "I lost" more often, and that was why he was downcast. Beso and the broker Chainstein now had more bitter and hazardous news for him. The broker told him: "I've deposited 120 thousand on call in your current account at the Azov Bank. The Lena shares have lost almost half their value. *Anglo-Russe* keeps falling. *Russe-Perse* is going bust. Yesterday you told me to sell *Uralplatinum* at four hundred, today it's gone up to five hundred. We've lost almost three hundred thousand trying to get the price of these shares down, and we've only recuperated one hundred thousand or so. If we don't invest half a million tomorrow, our mortgaged shares will be sold for peanuts."

Kvachi finally realized that someone was looking at his cards when he was playing and he saw that he lacked the power to turn back the wheel of fortune at the stock exchange: in fact, Kvachi had ended up becoming someone else's plaything and victim. But it was too late to bite his nails about it. He didn't have the strength, the alertness, the caution, the willpower to retreat. Once he had waded into the quagmire of the stock exchange, he went on doing so and ended up swimming into the heart of the whirlpool, which would bring him either complete bankruptcy or enormous wealth.

"Tomorrow morning you'll get my instructions, but now I want you to run down to the exchange and get this advertisement printed in the *Stock Exchange Chronicle*. Good day to you."

Then he rang his friend, the banker Gintz:

"Hello! Is that you? Listen carefully. If we've got an agreement, when will you let me have the money? Tomorrow? What? You've got the contract ready? And if I don't agree? What? You'll drop the price you pay me? Fine then, I agree. Being friends with you is costing me a lot, but what can I do? Let's leave it at that ... Until tomorrow morning, then."

Then Kvachi turned to Beso.

"What should I have done: wait and spend five years building a church? Take six months to supply sets of underwear? If I'd carried these deals through to the end, I'd make three times as much, but I need the money now, or else ... No, I'm not going under. When I throw another million at the stock exchange tomorrow, you'll see how I can blow the whole thing apart. Don't receive anyone on Rasputin's business: the man is off his head. In his old age he's off to Jerusalem to save his soul. To hell with him! He's got so much filth and so many sins on his conscience that it'll take a thousand angels and saints, not just Jerusalem, to scrub him for a year, and even that won't wash him clean."

Then Kvachi picked up the phone again:

"Actually, I forgot! Hello! Elena, is that you? Rasputin is expecting you, he says his soul needs treatment again, he needs a reason to repent his sins. What? You're too busy? What are you up to, woman? Find a bit of time for me. What did you say? You want to go to the operetta? Fine, get ready, I'm on my way now ... I'll send Tania instead to Rasputin ... All right, I'm coming."

The next day Kvachi handed over the church-building and the underwear contract to Gintz, and gave his broker some very complicated instructions "to crash and destroy the stock exchange."

The broker invested Kvachi's money and shares in the exchange, but this raid ended the same way: Kvachi's pocket was emptied and his brow was furrowed, while Gintz and his secret agent Chainstein profited and gained even more. But the joy of having cashed in his business overshadowed the grimness of the losses, so Kvachi barely noticed what he'd lost that day and didn't raise an eyebrow.

The Last Supper

That night, at midnight, Rasputin took Kvachi, Elena, and Tania to a Last Supper for "men of God."

Rasputin and Kvachi had put on white gowns, Elena and Taniawhite dresses, broad, free-flowing, and long. This was what the rules and customs of the martyrs demanded, since the color white was a symbol of their devotion, brotherly love, and purity.

At the edge of the city, a "ship of flagellants' was already assembled in a low-ceilinged house. A spacious room held about sixty men and women, more young than old. They, too, all wore white. Kvachi's comrades were huddled in one corner: thanks to their leader, they had been given permission by Rasputin to be present at this Last Supper.

The "Virgin Mary" Lokhtina widow stood by the table at the back of the room: she too was in white, adorned with countless baubles; her hair was loose and was covered with a strange headgear with the inscription: "In me is every power. Hallelujah."

As always, the "Virgin Mary" was barefoot. The service had already begun. The "Virgin" was reading the prayers. When she saw Rasputin, she darted forward, yelling: "Aha, behold the son of God. Aha, behold Jesus Christ! Behold God's messenger! Our holy man, prophet, and teacher has come! Verily I say unto you: arise and worship him, for he is worthy, as the son of God, of glory and worship."

She fell at his knees, kissed his hands and feet and then the hem of his gown. Everyone rushed round their confessor: some fell at his feet, some kissed his hands and body. Rasputin gave everyone a brotherly hug and a slobbery kiss and then followed the "Virgin" to the table. The "Virgin" began to sing a hymn. Everyone joined in magnifying the Lord God and the Holy Ghost, who, they believed, was now present in the room; they sang many more hymns and finally began to announce "Christ has risen!" They sang harmoniously, ecstatically, and reverently, raising their voices ever higher, straining their vocal chords, and working themselves into a mystic exaltation. When they finished praying, their leader and son of God began preaching.

Kvachi was standing in a corner listening attentively to Rasputin. Kvachi had trouble understanding the holy man's language. Sometimes it was quite beyond him, because Rasputin colored his Russian with a mass of obscure peasant and Church Slavonic words.

Rasputin now reminded his flock of their leader's twelve commandments:

"I am the son of God, sent among men to redeem their sins, and there is no other God than mine.

"Whatever you have once set out to do, you may not abandon.

"Do not drink intoxicating liquor, commit no carnal sins, do not fornicate.

"Do not marry; if you have a wife, divorce her. If you have a wife, live with her as with a sister.

"Do not curse or steal, for in the next world a copper coin will be placed on a thief's skull and he will not be forgiven until the coin melts."

He then made gibberish of this commandment, or rather annulled it as far as conjugal or sexual relations were concerned:

"The soul is good, the flesh is bad, so we must torment, weaken, and beat down the evil flesh: for that reason we must observe fasts, not eat meat, not drink intoxicating liquor, not smoke tobacco, not play cards, not dance, and not lust. Marital relations are a sin. Through the mass and praying every day the Holy Ghost will give everyone a spiritual spouse. Between such spouses carnal intercourse is not considered a sin or fornication; relations with another's wife will not be considered a sin, for 'such love is only the cooing of doves.'

"Our soul is immortal, eternal: it always has been, but we do not know for how long and in what animal it has resided. After our death, if a 'man of God' has truly fulfilled God's commandment, his soul will be transformed into an angel, and if he has been a sinner, his soul will become that of the appropriate animal or of a child who is considered unclean, until he is baptised according to our custom.

"God is one, but He and His son Christ are often incarnated as one or several holy men. Jesus Christ was mortal as we are, he died a natural death and was buried in Jerusalem."

Then Rasputin discussed his Lord God, several saints, Jesus Christ, father of the church, and martyrs: Filippov, who was supposed to have gone straight to heaven, Ivan Suslov, Prokopi Lupkin, Andrei Petrov, Tatarinova, Avvakum, Kopilov, Atasonov, and many other men of God who had sacrificed themselves for the holy and true church. Finally he talked of himself:

"Once I saw the heavens open and the spirit of God descending like a dove towards me; and it came and stood over me. And there was a voice from heaven, which said: 'Grigory, you are my beloved son whom I have blessed,' and the spirit took me straight to a desert and I was there for sixty days and I was tempted by the devil and I was surrounded by wild beasts, and angels served me. And I ate only locusts and wild honey."

Then he talked of temptations that besieged his soul, of devils, women, and sorcerers "who had come to destroy Grigory" and of many other miraculous things:

"In Kazan I saw many lepers and sinners possessed by devils, and I said to one of them: 'Open your mouth and go hence from him.' And the unclean spirit surrendered and made a loud noise and departed from him."

And the news of Grigory's chasing out of devils spread to every village and city in Russia:

"In Saratov a nun was stricken with fever and I was told about it. And I came and laid my hand upon her and raised her up, and the fever left her immediately, and she arose and became my servant. And when it became dark and the sun was setting they brought to me all the sick and the possessed. And every city and every woman had gathered before me and I cured them all of evil sicknesses and from every kind of illness, and I did not forgive the words of their devils, so that they should know that I am Christ. And I said to my disciples: come and travel the nearby villages and towns, so that you may preach there and drive devils from their bodies, for this is why I have been sent. And I preached to their gatherings and to all Russia, and freed them of devils."

Then the holy Rasputin taught his disciples:

"Since the time has come and the reign of God is approaching, repent and believe in me: I have come and stand before you and have made you fishers of men, and I baptise you in the name of the Holy Ghost. And I shall cure you of all evil diseases and will relieve you of devils and will strike down unclean spirits and will strengthen your souls—my mothers, brothers, and sisters! Eternal peace, the bliss of paradise, heavenly delights, brotherly love, and filial affection."

And after a silence the holy confessor looked round his seated disciples and said:

"Aha, my mothers, and my sisters, and my brothers, for whoever does my will, does our Lord's will, and is thus my brother and my sister and my mother. Dear mothers, brothers, and sisters of mine! Delight as if in heaven, for the son of God and the Holy Ghost is with you! Love one another, as in paradise, and coo like doves, for I say unto you truly: there is no sin or lust or whoring in brotherly or filial love. May all devils, lepers, sinful diseased souls depart from us!"

"Depart! Depart!" the men of God responded as one.

The holy Rasputin became strangely inflamed, stood bolt upright, and reached for the heavens. His disciple and loyal friend Kvachi remembered this day when Rasputin gave advice to the Tsar and prayed for him. He also remembered Rasputin's sincere penitence, and was astounded by today's holy man's celestial flights, his exalted body, fiery eyes, thunderous voice; he perceived the holy man's unique strength, his boundless influence, and overwhelming power. Meanwhile the holy Rasputin continued speaking in fiery tones:

"Let there be established between our souls and flesh divine love and eternal bliss!"

"Amen!" roared the assembly once again.

"And let us become one flesh and one heart, and let us rejoice and sing and magnify the Lord our God!" he said, ending his sermon with a hymn: "Hallelu-u-u-jah!"

The men of God rose to their feet. And they took each other by the hand. And they started a round dance and a brotherly celebration. And they sang hymns like heavenly birds and angels, with heavenly voices, with dove-like hearts and pure hearts: "Hallelu-u-u-jah!"

The son of God had Elena attached to him on one side and on the other the "Virgin Mary" Lokhtina.

Kvachi had Tania standing on his left and a plump blonde on his right. Kvachi's comrades each chose a well-rounded woman and joined in the round dance.

The round dance of linked partners began moving gravely, gently, and sluggishly, while hymns were sung at the same tempo; but gradually the dancers became more heated and their ardor stepped up.

In the middle of the dancing circle a number of young men and women started spinning like tops on one leg, then the round dancers changed position, formed a "wall", split up into several groups and intensified both the rhythm and the singing. Very soon the "wall" disintegrated and became a "ship's crew", following one another like a flock of cranes, becoming ever more fiery and quick-stepping. When they began to tire perceptibly, they formed a cross and moved as two intersecting lines, even more heated and wild. Finally, Rasputin shouted:

"Spin, spin!"

They let go of each other's hands and whirled on the spot like tops.

The men and women of God were all blushing bright red; their hair was tousled and hanging down. Sweat streamed off them. They were dizzy and giddy, their hearts were pounding wildly, yet they kept spinning like a tornado, waving their heads and limbs wildly; instead of singing hymns, they were blurting out fragmentary nonsense in cracked voices charged with emotion, and they uttered strange words. They were all crazed, bloated, and dazed. One would occasionally stagger forward and collapse, like a hewn-off block of wood, to be followed by a second, and a third, and eventually a tenth. There was a constant sound of crashing bodies. The floor was strewn with white dresses, shirts, and gowns.

Those still standing during this mad tarantella were now losing their strength, but they still staggered about yelling and hissing, instead of singing hymns; the fallen were scattered like shrouded corpses, uttering weird and incomprehensible words and prophesying. Here and there you could hear them, drained and enfeebled, deliriously muttering, shrieking, whispering, or mumbling:

"The son of God is with us! Men and women of God, rejoice and enjoy! Ours is the Holy Ghost, sisters and brothers!"

"I am the dove of heaven and the mother of God," mumbled the "Virgin Mary" Lokhtina. "Come and show me grace, beloved brothers. In me is every strength and love that has no bounds, for this is why I have been sent. Hallelujah! Hallelujah! Hallelujah! Holy Father, I am stricken by fever. Come, lay your hands on me and cure me of evil sicknesses ..."

"I can see the open heavens and the soul of God descending like a dove over me. Lord have mercy upon me."

"The time has come and the reign of God approaches. Repent, fathers and brothers, and believe in me."

"Jesus Christ, you are my brother. Come to me and establish within my soul brotherly love, heavenly affection, eternal delight, and the bliss of paradise. Come, brother, come to me," mumbled Tania, holding out her hands to Kvachi. Kvachi didn't yet dare fall down, but staggered to the left where the blonde he had been pursuing was lying supine.

Finally Kvachi caught Sedrak's eye, and Sedrak immediately fell down to lie next to Tania. Suddenly the tarantella lamp went out and Kvachi could collapse at the place he had been aiming for.

The scene was now plunged into pitch darkness. And the brothers and sisters, fathers and mothers, beheld the heavens open and the spirit of God descending like a dove over them.

And in the room there was brotherly love, heavenly affection, filial delight, and the bliss of paradise.

And as the sky grew light and the sun began to rise, there was heard a continuous cooing of doves and singing of magical birds and angels, and the lowing and bellowing of wild beasts and the howling and shrieking of apes, and the whimpering and moaning of devils and unclean spirits, which had been expelled and forced out of the hungry and the sick and sent to the furthest outpost of hell.

That night the sisters and brothers had come in to the rooms, and the brothers had changed sisters and the sisters had changed brothers, and they had found new loves to cherish.

So ended the Last Supper of the men of God.

In the morning they assembled again and re-elected Rasputin as the son of God, the widow Lokhtina as the Virgin Mary and twelve men and women of God as the twelve disciples: these included Kvachi, Elena, Tania, and a number of dignitaries and grandees.

Then, with icons and hymn-singing, they all headed to the station to see off Grigory, son of God, who was going to the Holy City to atone for his own sins and the sins of his sisters, his brothers, and mothers.

As they progressed, their holy imprecations were joined by those of many sympathisers, followers, and disciples who were singing sacred hymns and rejoicing at the forthcoming blessing of the son of God: they shed many tears, for the time of parting was approaching.

And at the station there was much sobbing and much moaning, groaning, and shrieking, tearing of hair, ripping of cheeks, and countless slobbery kisses.

And the disciples had pallid cheeks, and their eyes were inexhaustible pools of tears.

And the locomotive of the devil issued a soul-piercing shriek and a loud noise.

And the devil's locomotive took away the son of God, the holy disciple, the leader, patriarch, and autocratic monarch of all Russia—Grigory Rasputin.

And his disciples immediately left and scattered in order to preach the doctrine of the holy teacher, to repeat the Last Supper, and to magnify the son of God. Amen.

CHAPTER FOUR

The Break-Up of the Comrades' Lair

When Rasputin set off for Jerusalem, Kvachi Kvachantiradze and his friends definitely felt that they had been orphaned and abandoned.

The ground seemed to have crumbled beneath Kvachi's feet; his right hand felt as if it had been amputated. He felt like an eagle with a broken wing. The abandonment was painful, and he asked himself:

"What is happening to me? I've got lots of money and I have people I know who will protect me. I didn't need Rasputin to keep me. If my enemies wake up and go for me, don't I have the Tsar and Tsaritsa and a thousand dignitaries and grandees who only last night were hoping to get a smile from me and were clinging to my coat-tails?"

Such thoughts enabled Kvachi to find peace again, but an intangible fear still haunted him and gnawed at his heart.

When he got back from the station, there was nobody to meet him except Chainstein's agent.

"What's up?"

"Bad news, very bad news. The banks are demanding payment of the full amount on call; they threaten they'll sell your shares. If they unload that amount of shares on the stock exchange, the price will go down even more and tomorrow you'll have to pay even more on call."

"Sell the *Anglo-Russe* shares and put the money in the bank: there's no alternative."

"The outcome will be the same. The share price will fall."

"Then what are we to do? Where can I lay hands on so much cash?"

"Mortgage your share holdings with Ganus or Gintz."

Kvachi and Chainstein spent the entire day with the banks, the stock exchange, and the financiers, but everywhere they came up against secret and insurmountable obstacles.

Finally, tired of flailing about in this mysterious trap, Kvachi obeyed his adviser Chainstein, who was leading him down a path marked out by Gintz. He mortgaged some shares, sold others, cashed in some and even bought a few, but he still ended up short of money; he was still drowning and unable to wade out of the bog and find any peace of mind. The shares he sold rose in value the very next day, while the shares he bought went down in value. As day followed day, losses followed losses and Kvachi found himself more and more entangled in an invisible web which would finally end with visible bankruptcy. In the final days he heard more and more often the words: "Pay up the difference … Pay in … Transfer …"

Kvachi was flailing about to no purpose and with no sense in a net of bankruptcy, repeating like a parrot: "Sell! Mortgage! Buy! Redeem! Pay in! Pay out!"

Finally he opened his eyes, saw things for what they were, and realized the truth. He cried out: "Help me. I'm ruined! Help me."

But it was too late. Instead of help, people rushed him even more from all sides and made his life worse.

Kvachi turned first to Elena, then to Tania, but after the public scandal in the *Arcadia* and Rasputin's departure, the two of them had quietly gone abroad. They left Kvachi a brief note:

"Dear friend, After what happened in the *Arcadia*, we can't stay here any more. We're going to Europe for a while; we advise you to remove yourself, too. We haven't yet decided what city we'll stay in. Goodbye. May God stretch out a protective hand to you, but … we both have lots to tell you, but we'll put it off for another time. Your Tania and Elena."

Gintz and Ganus poured a bucket of cold water over him. Kvachi convulsed a few more times, waved his limbs about a couple of times, and quietly died as far as the stock market was concerned.

Kvachi the businessman, Kvachi the financier, Kvachi the shareholder was stripped and divided up by Gintz, Ganus, and their agents.

Silibistro's son and heir sat plunged in gloom, hitting his head with his hand and thinking, "They stripped me of my raiment and played dice for my tunic."

That day Kvachi was surrounded by his comrades: "Sedrak, help me!"

"What? You're broke? Will a hundred roubles be any use to you?"

"Get lost!"

"You've squandered millions, so how can Sedrak help you now?" Chkhubishvili reproached him.

Chikinjiladze intervened: "You deserved it, trusting those conmen with anything. Tell us what we're supposed to do."

"Things have got more complicated," Beso said gravely, opening the newspaper for Kvachi. "Read this."

They sat down and read: "*The Russian Cause* has been breathing fire because the building of the largest Orthodox church has been entrusted to a Caucasian, a Mr K—, who handed the job to Jews."

Another newspaper asserted that K. K—dze used false identity papers to infiltrate the Tsar's palace, that Kvachi's nobility was dubious, and that Kvachi wangled his prince's title thanks to a "certain holy man's" underhand machinations with the Tsar.

A third newspaper announced that Kvachi was bankrupt and gave an sketch of his biography, with the threat that in a few days they would reveal this young man's full identity, name, surname, and previous record.

Kvachi turned as pale as mistletoe; he felt embittered. He tore the newspapers into shreds, fell into an armchair, and groaned: "It's over! That's it! Everything is dust and ashes."

They were all silent for some time. Kvachi, exhausted, his eyes closed, lay down and rubbed his deadly pale forehead; then he suddenly leapt to his feet and stood bolt upright; his eyes were full of fire and there was iron and steel in his voice:

"Oh, it's all a big lie! Kvachi Kvachantiradze is not that easy to destroy. Sedrak!"

"What is it?"

"Go right now and get a dozen foreign passports made. One passport should be in the name of the heir to the Emir of Afghanistan, the others in the names of his suite. You can invent the names. Everything's got to be ready by tomorrow morning, get it?"

"All right? I've got it, fine."

"Well, get a move on! Chipi, Ladi, Jalil, Gabo! Now go to the newspaper offices and make sure they all shut up: you can threaten some, pay others. Tell them the man says he's left town and gone to Palestine to be with Rasputin. He wants to be left alone, and for them to shut up, and if they don't do so but scribble more of their rubbish, he'll come back and make every mother's son of them wish he'd never been born. Take two or three lads with you, in case it's necessary, to smash up the place: bash a few faces if needed until you're too tired to do any more. Right, get a move on! Have you understood everything?"

"Hey, this is a really easy job! Don't ask me to do anything different, because that's work for the bruiser Chkhubishvili."

"Beso! Right, get into action. Find someone rich and sell him everything we have by tomorrow. What? It all belongs to Tania? I know, but there's no time to sort that out when a man is in real trouble. Yes, the furniture too; sell the horses, the motor car, everything, the lot. Get ready for a long journey ... Don't let anyone know we're leaving. Right, get moving. I've a little job to attend to ... Jalil, get me dressed quickly. Call for a *Berliet* lorry. Be quick about it. Get a move on."

Then Kvachi went to see a minister:

"Their excellency has no time to spare."

He ran off to see a second minister:

"Their radiance is not at home."

He visited the metropolitan bishop:

"Their holiness is indisposed."

He did the rounds of five or six more dignitaries and high-ranking officials, but found all doors were closed to him, and all had turned their backs on him: they had forgotten his graciousness to them.

"Very well," exclaimed an embittered Kvachi. "As they've blocked all my paths and shut every door in my face, I'll lean on one last set of doors, and if I give someone a punch in the nose it won't be my fault."

That same day he went to see Ganus's wife and told her:

"Listen to me, my lovely. My enemies are trying to bury me alive. Your husband is mixed up in this dirty business. I'm a decent respectable man, but I'm not going to my own funeral of my own free will. All my paths have been blocked, and you're my last hope: you've got to help me, or else ... or else I'll come and see your husband with your letters, yes these letters here, and ... Don't get upset, calm down and listen to me. I helped your husband to get hold of five wagon-loads of gold; now it's my turn, now I need help. What? How can you help me? You've got to lend me money ... What did you say? You can't get hold of that much? Dig deeper, and you'll get it. You've got enormous property of your own, you can run rings round your husband. If you want to, you can get the money back from your husband's pocket. You don't want to? Well, if you don't want to, don't. Give me my share and sort out your old husband any way you like. So I can come back tomorrow? We have an agreement, then: goodbye until tomorrow."

At the same time Gabo Chkhubishvili led the other comrades round the newspaper offices. At one newspaper they placed a one-thousand-rouble advertisement announcing a public auction at Tsarevo-Kokshaisk, and also had a correction printed to a report the previous day, saying that the report referred to a non-existent Prince Konstantin Kimuchadze. The next newspaper was easily dealt with, but the third had an obstinate editor who had an inflated self-esteem.

"If that's the case, then name your seconds for the duel."

"What: a duel? Hmm, that's a solution for savages."

"Then it will be your fault if we shed any blood."

The gang reached for their revolvers. The editor and his colleagues panicked and immediately relented.

"What's the problem? Why should you need to use firearms?"

"You Georgians are a strange lot, you immediately resort to weapons."

"Just because of an ordinary report? What does it matter if a simple correction is printed? Hey, it wouldn't come to more than twenty lines."

"Well, let's write it and settle at that."

They wrote the correction and settled the matter, then exchanged ingratiating smiles, clapped each other on the back, and parted.

In three days Kvachi had "sorted" all his business and then took a seat in the Warsaw train.

Meeting the Emir and Kvachi's Muteness

The leader had wrapped himself in an expensive Asiatic gown, donned a turban, and shod himself in expensive oriental slippers. His followers were sitting in nearby compartments, and they were just as exotically and ornately costumed.

Kvachi's pocket contained the passport of Prince Rabibullah

Abdul Rahman Sheikhal; his briefcase held a supply of half a dozen passports of dukes, barons, and princes of various nationalities: "Who knows where I might need them?"

Kvachi's friends were equipped with similar passports, though of lesser rank and quality, as appropriate for a dignitary's underlings, adjutants, secretaries, and valets.

When the conductor saw Kvachi's identity and realized he was dealing with an emir, he informed a gendarme. The gendarme sent a telegram to inform Warsaw, and himself informed the governor-general.

When they arrived at Warsaw station, a resplendent officer came into the carriage and politely asked Chipi Chipuntiradze:

"Would you happen to be their radiant highness the Afghan prince's secretary? Please inform the noble prince that the governor-general's adjutant would like to meet him."

Chipi rushed in a panic to Kvachi's compartment: "We're finished! We've been caught ... They've realized!"

Kvachi seemed not to be perturbed; he furrowed his brow, though, became pensive, and then gravely gave orders:

"Don't panic, stand up straight! Remember I don't know Russian. Sedrak, you're my secretary and interpreter. Beso, you're my doctor. Show some courage. Something's up. Just be careful. We don't want to come across anyone who knows Georgian. Talk in our code. Right, ask him to come in!"

Kvachi lounged in his seat and puffed at his amber pipe.

The adjutant greeted him politely: "I have the honor to inform you that his excellency sends his greetings and asks you to do him the honor of dining with him."

Everyone breathed a sigh of relief. Sedrak translated the adjutant's greeting and request in coded Georgian for Kvachi: "Well-tee, he-tee in-tee-vite-tee you-tee."

All these tee-tee-tee coded words warmed up the atmosphere in the carriage. Kvachi smiled subtly:

"I told you that there was nothing to worry about, didn't I? Thank him on my behalf and tell him that my doctor has forbidden me to leave the carriage, because he says I'm not well."

Sedrak translated this, and Beso played along. The adjutant expressed his regret that the heir to the Emir should be unwell and informed Kvachi that important officials were waiting on the platform to see his Highness.

"Ask them to come in."

Like geese in a row, the governor, the chief of police, the mayor, and many other seekers of awards came in. Smiling, with heads bowed, they stood before Kvachi and wished him a pleasant journey; they enquired after one another, examined each other, exchanged smiles and news, nodded and bent double at one another.

Kvachi gave them all gracious warm smiles and vaguely promised them protection and assistance, had his secretary write down the names and medals of the officials, as a sign that one day, when the prince got back home, the officials could add Afghan medals to their list of awards. Then after more hand-waving and smiles they all filed out of the carriage. The Afghan prince and his suite were killing themselves laughing.

"Ah, that really is very dangerous. We don't want anyone tripping us up. We've got to cover our tracks, or else ..."

They quietly changed to the Krakow train and diverted to Austria.

When they were approaching Katowice, a gendarme took the travelers' passports to examine them and to issue visas. Before the train moved on to the border station, two gendarmes entered the carriage. From the door of his compartment Kvachi could see that the gendarmes were asking each traveler his name and surname, then picking out and returning the passport from the pile of passports they had examined. Finally they reached his compartment: "Your surname and name?"

Kvachi was petrified: he burst into a cold sweat. His mind

blurred, he turned deadly pale, then bright red and began to shiver. Suddenly he had remembered that an hour ago Beso had picked out one of Kvachi's six passports, the first he laid hands on, and handed it without a glance to the gendarme.

"My surname?" Kvachi thought as quick as lightning. "How do I know which passport he handed over? If I start talking Turkish, it might turn out he was given Baron Tiesenhausen's passport. If I start talking Georgian, perhaps the gendarme is holding Prince Trubetskoy's passport."

"Your surname and name?" the gendarme asked a second time.

Kvachi was now swimming in his own sweat, his eyes were squinting senselessly as he looked now expectantly at Beso, now towards the door. The gendarme's expression was full of suspicion.

"Your surname and name, I said. What's going on? What's wrong with you? You're not dumb, are you?"

"What, haven't I been struck dumb? Of course I have." Yes, this gendarme has got it right: he's realized Kvachi is dumb, mute from birth.

Kvachi was relieved; he smiled and howled. "Mmm … mma … mmiii …" he mumbled, put his hand to his mouth to show he was mute, and reached out for the passports. The gendarmes smiled.

"So he really was a mute," one of them said, thrusting the pack of passports at Kvachi. "Well, find your passport yourself."

Kvachi raked through the stack of passports.

"Got away with it. Thank God!" he exclaimed to himself and held out one passport to the gendarme to say, "Here's my passport."

"Prince Irakli Bagration-Mukhransky!" the gendarme read out loud and smiled, as he relaxed and fawned. It was then that Sedrak and Beso looked into the compartment.

"These wretches are bound to give me away," it occurred to

Kvachi; he rushed towards them, thrusting his passport in their faces, stamping his feet, waving his hands in sign language, and bellowing: "Mmm … mmmaaa … mmmuuu …"

The two of them stared wide-eyed and open-mouthed at him. "God, has he been struck dumb?" wondered Sedrak.

Kvachi was overjoyed and nodded his head so vigorously that he nearly tore a tendon in his neck: "Yes, yes, I'm mute, I'm mute."

Sedrak caught Beso's eye: "It looks as if he's been struck dumb!"

"Poor prince!" one of the gendarme's remarked. "So young, so handsome, and mute?"

"And look at his surname!" added the other one. "Bagra-tion-Mukhran-sky, Irakli, son of Giorgi!"

"Quite right!" Beso Shikia confirmed. "He's been mute since birth, so we're taking him to a famous doctor in Vienna."

The gendarmes handed back Sedrak and Beso's passports and left. Kvachi and his friends immediately locked the compartment doors.

"What's going on? What's happened?"

"It's so bad that I hope the devil takes Beso, head and body." And he told them everything.

"Oh-oh, ah-ah. Oh!" Sedrak and Beso exclaimed.

"Why are you laughing, you idiots?" said Kvachi in fury. "I've just pissed myself and I thought I'd had it, and you were no help."

Then he recalled how he had become mute and found it funny himself; by the time they crossed the frontier, they were leaping about like calves and whinnying like fillies.

They passed through Krakow; in the morning they were in Vienna; they took four rooms in the best hotel and prepared to see the sights.

Going a Little Mad in Vienna and Visiting the Capital of the World

After an hour, the hotel owner, manager, and maître d'hôtel came in to ask after the great Prince Bagration and pay their respects. Then a Russian Jew, indispensable everywhere, omniscient and widely traveled, introduced himself.

"I've come to see the prince. I'm a guide. I've been living in Vienna for twenty years … I'll show you everything … I cost just ten crowns a day."

They went out to see the sights.

Five days passed. The guide kept taking Kvachi to historic monuments of art, he wanted to show him museums, the university, St Stephen's cathedral, the Hofburg theater, the stock exchange, the Academy of Art, the Town Hall, the palace and a thousand other noteworthy places, but Kvachi was so tired and exhausted after visiting just one museum, that he used a headache as a pretext to put off everything for another time, apart from the enormous Ringstrasse and Prater, where night was like day and day was like night. These gigantic streets, avenues, gardens, squares, the English grove, the aquarium, the menagerie, a thousand different restaurants, cafés, beer halls, wine cellars, fairgrounds, puppet theaters, carousels, and countless other entertainments were always full of people, especially women, the famous Viennese women. They seemed to have been specially selected: tall, good-looking thoroughbreds with golden hair, emerald eyes, soft and chubby, with fair skin like a glacier slightly reddened in the setting sun.

These living irises disoriented Kvachi somewhat; they disturbed his sleep, dulled his appetite, bewildered his mind, and so excited his heart and soul that he forgot some of his neatly devised plots and put off carrying them out, on the pretext that he would soon be visiting Paris where he could "pull off" these jobs.

In a few days Kvachi was quite intoxicated, overcome, and

exhausted with an animal, overpowering love for this fair tribe. In response to these fair-skinned women he revealed for them to sample the heat of Black Sea blood, the impulsiveness of a country bumpkin, the burning desires of a jet-black-moustached Georgian with salty predatory eyes and unbridled passionate sinews, hardened by sun and by time.

Sedrak and Beso had trouble tearing Kvachi away from the demonic nets of these blonde women and dragging him off to Paris.

The Orient Express rushed along the banks of the limpid Salzhach, the Inn, and the Danube.

"Kvachi, we've reached Salzburg. Baedeker says good things about this old city. Let's get out and take a look."

"Oh, I'm bored with the sight of old things, they remind me of the dead."

"Kvachi, we're coming up to Munich: the capital of Bavaria. It's supposed to be very clean and tidy. They say it's got the world museum of architecture and art. There's a lot to see, apparently: Greek propylae, the Siegestor, Wagner's theater, the Odeon, the glypotheca and ..."

"And beer, black Munich beer! Right, Beso, bring a couple of dozen bottles. Quick! The devil take all the other antiquities!"

"Kvachi, we've arrived at Strasbourg. Take a look: that cathedral there is said to be world-famous."

"Oh, that isn't even worth getting out of bed for!" said Kvachi, continuing to examine albums of naked women which he had bought in Vienna and Munich.

At ten that evening Beso told him: "In exactly half an hour we'll arrive in Paris: take a look, you can see it already."

Kvachi leapt up, as if a snake had bitten him, and rushed to the window.

Far off, in the darkness the vault of the heavens was colored red for as far as the eye could see, as if the edge of the world were on fire and the fire was reflected in the sky. Their winged iron bird still wouldn't rest: whistling, rumbling, and shrieking, it flew towards this conflagration. Finally it rushed into the city, went on running for some time, and with groans and moans stopped at the Gare de l'Est.

The ubiquitous Odessa Jew did not fail to appear: "I've been living in Paris for twenty years. I know it all like the back of my hand. I speak nine languages. I cost twenty francs and my meals and drink per day."

Kvachi took a good look at the Jew: "Isaac Abramovich! Isaac Idelsohn!"

When he heard this name, the Jew stared at Kvachi, then gave a wide smile and exclaimed: "Napoleon Apollonovich, is that you? Good God!"

"What are you up to here, Isaac?"

"Oh, I'll tell you later. I'm broke now, Napoleon, I'm broke … I'll tell you later …"

"And Rebecca? How is she?"

"She's fine, fine, but … I'll tell you later, I'll tell you everything. Just follow me for now."

All four got in a motor car and headed for the best hotel on the Boulevard de Strasbourg. Kvachi ordered the car to drive down tree-shaded streets.

"We've turned onto the Grands Boulevards," said Isaac Idelsohn, showing them the metropolis. "This is Boulevard Saint-Denis … That's Bonnoir … That's Poisonnière … There's the famous Montmartre … Now we've come onto the Boulevard des Italiens … There's the famous opera and the Avenue de l'Opéra … That's Boulevard des Capucins … There's the extraordinary Madeleine church …"

Kvachi listened offhandedly to Isaac's flow of talk, full of foreign, unintelligible words. He understood nothing of his guide's speech, because impressions had suddenly overcome his wits and muffled them.

Kvachi and his comrades had plunged into the heart of the world's capital and were instantly confused, disoriented, and baffled. The sides of the enormous boulevards were lined with two seven- or eight-storey walls of brightly lit buildings. An unending river of people was going up and down this channel. It seemed impossible to cross the street, which was crammed with open and closed carriages, double-decker omnibuses, trams, motor cars, and all sorts of carts. Policemen stood at the intersections, imposing order with short truncheons and, like irrigation channel managers in Georgia, stopping the river of traffic on one street and heading it off down another channel, then for five minutes damming it up and releasing it down the first street.

The cafés were brightly lit and full, both outside and inside, of well-dressed, nicely turned-out people. Thousands of different advertisements struck the eye from above: red, yellow, blue, and green electric inscriptions flashed from thousands of places in the sky. The city's mysterious noises, its roar, its murmuring, and its vibrations, its breath, groans, and moans hampered Kvachi, irritated his nerves and confused his mind.

"Hey, Beso, doesn't it remind you of your Samtredia and Kutaisi?" he said with a smile.

"It's better than Samtredia, but no comparison with Kutaisi," joked Beso Shikia.

"And what about Tbilisi?" giggled Sedrak.

They turned off at the Madeleine and got out on the enormous Place de la Concorde, crossed this spectacular and strange place, and rushed to the Champs d'Elysées with its five lines of shady trees. They got to the splendid Hotel Elysée on the Place d'Étoile. Here they took seven rooms on the first floor, as befitted a great prince of great Russia, an Afghan emir, a baron. and his suite.

Touring the Modern Babylon and a Short Discussion

Kvachi, his friends, and Doctor Qoranashvili, whom they found a day before in the Latin quarter, were at the top of the Eiffel Tower. The three-hundred-meter iron tower seemed to hum, tremble, and sway. The travelers felt slightly dizzy. Paris, the jewel of the country, the beautiful capital, the first among the first, the core of the world and the sun around which all places and peoples revolved, stretched out beneath them.

Beyond the bounds of Paris, in every direction, as far as the eye could see, there were countless towns, big and small, villages, and hamlets, which seemed to be fleeing from or hovering around the heart of the country, as if surrounding a precious beauty, guarding and serving her.

Over the hills of the Marne an enormous red ball was emerging from the morning haze, dyeing pink the green hills surrounding Paris. The morning mist lay like a veil covering the wrinkles in this boundless space, the slopes of the hills and the copses of the towns and the Seine.

Paris slowly removed its veil of mist, waking up gradually, sluggishly stretching its limbs, and smiling its morning smile. The haze, like steam or breath coming from this city of the sun, eventually gathered on the hills, retreated to the west and settled down in the area around Saint Germain-Argenteuil and in the lower bends of the Seine.

This center of the world spread out and blossomed in the eyes of the fortune-hunters: combed and washed, nicely and immaculately turned out, smiling and laughing, radiant and brilliant, boundless and infinite, dwelling places and temples, the desire and dream of all clerics, scholars, and artists of this world.

The Georgians were three hundred meters above ground. They stood there trembling at the height and the beauty.

Very far off, to the south and the east wound two limpid

rivers, the Seine and the Marne, uniting and embracing at the edge of Paris, at Charenton, before crossing the city and turning south again. Then at Saint Cloud and the Bois de Boulogne they turned north, and at Saint Denis went south yet again, once more winding to the west and disappearing in the enormous misty forest of Saint Germain.

Convoys of ships and small boats went up and down the river; from high above they looked like flies and worms crawling over a distorting mirror. This mirror of a river was crossed by two score iron and stone bridges and split and divided by a score of green islands. Out of the eye's reach there were three rows of forty or so guard and sentry posts, half buried in the ground, armored with iron and steel, bristling with a thousand cannon: they included Charenton, Mont Valérienne, and Saint Denis, looking angry, menacing, and frowning towards the Germanic lands.

This pretty panorama was pierced in all directions by a dozen railways, which transfixed the heart of the country like arrows; it was also encircled by several belts of railways, artillery emplacements, boulevards, broad, deep moats, and thick high walls of cut stone. Several dozen trains breathed steam and smoke as they twisted like black snakes, heading off in various directions. Countless villages, towns, buildings, roads, and canals seemed to have been deliberately carved, painted, and stitched into an unending green carpet. Paris's lungs—forests, gardens, and groves—were still exhaling the morning heat haze. The great forest of Vincennes, dotted with lakes, stretched out in the east; in the south, equally large, were the forests of Meudon, Saint Cloud, Sèvres, and Versailles, and in the west—Boulogne and Saint Germain. The center of Paris seemed covered in green liquid: the Tuileries, the Luxembourg, the botanical, Monceau, Trocadéro, Montsouris, Elysées parks, among many others, groves and tree-lined avenues.

Les Invalides's golden dome seemed to be on fire.

From the sea of buildings there stood out the Panthéon, the

new Sacré Cœur church, Notre Dame, Saint Germain des Prés, Saint-Sulpice, the Madeleine, the Louvre, the Palais Royal, the Grand Opéra, the Sorbonne, the stock exchange, the Trocadéro, towers, palaces, museums, and many other prominent monuments and new buildings.

At this height they could clearly hear the fabled city's roar, murmurs, groans, commotion, and breathing.

Kvachi was impervious to the beauty of nature: it left his heart and soul untouched. He was never excited, enchanted, or moved by mountains that reached the sky, or the boundless sea, or colorful valley scenes. But now, staring down from three hundred meters at the beauties of Paris stretched beneath his feet, he experienced a dizzy, all-enveloping bliss and the beauty of a metropolis which had been made, who knows when, how or by whom, out of all that stone, iron, steam, and smoke.

Kvachi was tone deaf: he couldn't distinguish one note from another, so he disliked and failed to understand music. But now, at a height of three hundred meters, he was captivated, intoxicated, and exalted by this city's mysterious roar, rumbling, and heavy breathing.

Then the morning breeze brought the smell of coal and heavy oil from Belleville to the Eiffel Tower: it hit Kvachi's very sensitive nostrils.

They stood for a long time in silence, utterly absorbed in these exalting and unprecedented feelings. Occasionally Doctor Qoranashvili would point a finger to show them some new treasure:

"Just in front of your hotel where that gigantic arch is, you see twelve streets and avenues lit up by beams of light: that's why that place is called Place d'Étoile … that's where the Elysée Palace, the president's residence, is … There's the Bourbons' palace, today's parliament … Look, right beneath us you can see the military academy … There are the Grand and Petit Palais of the Arts and Sciences."

"Well, Paris is like a living beauty, a naked Frenchwoman lying for all to see on the banks of the Seine, and she's there for anyone from anywhere to come running and see. What else would make a bankrupt from an Imeretian village or a stuck-up country squire come running all the way here?" exclaimed Kvachi.

Sedrak disagreed: "Nobody but millionaires live in Paris! Any bank or trading house here could buy and sell all Georgia three times over. Wherever there's honey, you'll see flies, nobody's mad enough to come from America, Japan, or Tbilisi just for beautiful women. Show your money, and you can get beautiful women anywhere."

"Beautiful women come here because there's a lot of money in Paris," whispered the taciturn Beso.

"There's more money in London and New York than in Paris," Qoranashvili interjected. "But beautiful women and other people, with or without money, are more drawn to Paris. Apart from present company, not even a hundred thousand beauties would bring me such a distance."

"Then why are people drawn from so many countries to Paris?" asked Kvachi.

"Beautiful women are only one side of Paris; to my amazement, I must tell you that there are far more handsome men than beautiful women. The women here say the same thing. Paris has other, many other, sides. It'll take some time to explain this to you. Anyway, you may understand what I say, but you won't feel it. You have to live here and take a good look at everything first before you'll grasp and feel the magic and the enchantment. Then you'll be convinced that everyone really has two homelands: his own, and France."

They took the lift down to the second floor of the tower, where there was a restaurant; they had breakfast and went off to see the Louvre.

When they stepped on to the Alexandre bridge, Kvachi examined the splendid ornamentation with amazement: statues, pillars, marble, gold veneer, wrought iron, and bronze. Then turned to his comrades: "You can't find anything to match this in all of Georgia."

"It reminds me of the white bridge in Kutaisi, ha-ha."

"There's no bridge like this in Europe or in Russia," declared Qoranashvili.

The gigantic eight-sided Place de la Concorde once again aroused Kvachi's enthusiasm. It was adorned with sculptures of France's eight great cities. As a sign of mourning, Strasbourg was wrapped in black. There were two fine pools in the middle of the square, as well as thirty thirty-meter columns, and the Luxor obelisk which Napoleon had brought back from Egypt.

"During the revolution the guillotine stood on this square," Qoranashvili informed them. "This was where Louis XVI had his head cut off, and, probably, several thousand others."

Kvachi was overcome by a fit of shivering and quickly turned away.

They toured the former kings' gardens, the Tuileries, the Arc de Triomphe and entered the Louvre.

First they looked at the sculptures on the ground floor. They went from hall to hall, epoch to epoch, one country's culture to another. Kvachi paid almost no attention. He singled out only naked women among the countless statues, especially Canova's. He went all round the nudes, examining them, and feeling more and more delight and respect.

When they entered the ancient Greek hall and looked at the divine Skopas, Miron, and Praxiteles, and saw the heavenly Aphrodite and the Venus of Milos, mutilated, legless, armless, and eyeless, Kvachi was extremely disturbed and exclaimed:

"Who could have created these beautiful women? Beso, just look at this broken Venus with no head or arms. Put a hand on her thigh and see if she's alive or made of marble. What, you're not allowed to touch? Fine, but God help us! How did some

Greek stone-carver make these women here, when this stone has the smell and the warmth of living flesh! Beso, go, old chap and find out what they'll sell this Venus of Milos for. She must have been someone, I suppose the wife of some Russian or Polish Milosky. If they'll let it go for no more than a thousand francs, I'll buy it and put it on the stairs to my apartment, and I'll have the broken arms repaired. I'll put flowers or a drinking horn in one hand and I'll have an electric lamp fixed to the other. I'm telling you, it will be an asset to the Kvachantiradze palace, won't it?"

Then they went deeper into the enormous building and ran about it for three hours at breakneck speed, dazed and with blurred eyes. Only Qoranashvili was calm, because he'd seen and digested it all ten times. They covered the Apollo galleries, the Lhorloge, the flowers, and the old Tuileries.

In the Apollo hall Kvachi was physically fascinated by one glass cabinet and couldn't tear himself away: his eyes blazed and glazed, his heart pounded, and his whole body trembled. The cabinet contained several white diamonds the size of pigeon's eggs, Napoleon's sword, also covered in diamonds, and many other treasures beyond price. The cabinet sat there glittering, just like Kvachi's eyes then. Kvachi immediately looked all round. There was one guard calmly strolling about the hall. Kvachi became unsettled and restless. He rushed towards Qoranashvili, then fell upon the guard: "*Combien coûte cette chose, s'il vous plaît?*"

"*Sais pas, m'sieur: on dit quarante ou cinquante millions.*"

Kvachi found it hard to leave the treasure. From then on he walked about bewildered, obsessed, and pensive, as if devils had invaded his head, as if an idea was maturing, as if a plot was taking shape and thickening.

"Look at these masterpieces, these select examples of world art," Qoranashvili continued. "Let's begin with the Italian renaissance ... Here's Correggio ... That's Titian ... That's Peruggio ... There's the tender, romantic Botticelli ... Ah, the divine Leonardo da Vinci's Gioconda, too."

"Is this the Gioconda?" wondered Kvachi. "The one that was stolen last year? Only an idiot would steal it. What's the picture worth?"

"It's beyond price, it's not for sale. Connoisseurs value it at a million. The Venus de Milo would be worth the same."

"Heavens, how many idiots there are in the world! I wouldn't give ten roubles for it. Just look, Beso, at the way she's rolling her eyes. They must all be fools, or who'd be daft enough to pay as much as a hundred roubles for some stuck-up frump in a picture? I bet for a hundred roubles I could get five living good-looking women today, so why should I pay more for that picture."

"Hey, look over here and see what's going on!" Sedrak interrupted Kvachi from the door to the next hall.

They went round the French art hall: its walls were hung generously with naked women.

"Rosa Bonner ... Prudhomme ...Delacroix ... Watteau ... Meissonnier ..." Qoranashvili continued. But nobody was listening to him now, all three had gathered in a corner by the Ingres naked maidservant, bloodless, boneless, plump, and soft as dough.

"Hey, just look at her haunch," said Sedrak, fidgeting, his eyes moist.

"The woman and the picture are both good, a live woman like that is worth a thousand roubles, and so is the picture."

"Forget about the live woman, for a thousand roubles they'll do you a copy. Look, there's an artist here."

Three artists were at work, all making copies.

They asked one, agreed terms, gave their address and went on.

"Now we've got Spanish art ... Murrillo ... Velasquez ... Goya ... This is the English school: Reynolds ... Ruskin ... Here we have the Flemish and Dutch: Van Dyck ... Ruysdael ... Rubens ... And now the genius, Rembrandt ..."

Gabo and Sedrak were fired and enthused by Rubens's women,

all well-fed, plump, monumental, red and white, like wine with a touch of milk. Kvachi was at the end of his tether; his eyes were drooping and he was dragging his feet.

"We've done about a third. Let's just quickly look at the rest. Then, if you want to remember at least a little bit of it, you should go round it for two weeks," Qoranashvili advised.

"Oh no, no, no," Kvachi said, waving his hand. "I'll never manage that, that's not the reason I came here. Let's go, I've had enough."

They left. They passed through several courtyards, crossed a square, and looked back at the half-mile of masonry of the Louvre, which was criss-crossed with streets; buses and motor cars were passing in the courtyard and by the main entrance.

"I wonder whether France would exchange all these treasures here for the whole of Georgia?" Kvachi said, as if to himself. They stopped a taxi and drove round Châtelet and Bernard's theater, Saint-Jacques tower, the city council, Notre Dame, from where they went to the Latin quarter.

"That's the Sorbonne … That's the Collège de France … Sainte-Geneviève library … The famous Panthéon. Where the bronze monument is, that's France's famous sculptor Rodin's work. It's a man who's thinking."

The bronze giant of a man was seated. His legs were crossed. His jaw was resting on a fist, and he was thinking so deeply, so obstinately, and wilfully that the sinews in his leg were tensed, as if the thought reached the sinews, giving them strength and support. Kvachi looked hard at the bronze man and said:

"That man is thinking up some great plot, I know. I wish I could meet him, he'd be a good comrade."

"Here's the Luxembourg and Cluny museum, let's take a look."

"No, I'm tired, I've had enough. It's time we went to a good restaurant and had dinner."

They went to Duval's. Kvachi objected: "What's this? This

is no good. It looks like a students' canteen. Isn't there anything better around?"

Qoranashvili didn't know the difference between a good and a bad restaurant, because he dined, and only occasionally, in one-franc diners.

"Well, let's go to our hotel ... What, you're embarrassed? You don't have the right clothes? Then goodbye for now, we'll see you tomorrow."

And they left by taxi, while Qoranashvili, who was now hungry, went back to his attic.

The Thoughts of the Worldly Idelsohn

The friends put on formal jackets; each put a chrysanthemum in his lapel before going down to dinner.

The hotel owner and manager immediately approached their new guests, humbly enquired after their health and their impressions. The restaurant was quiet and peaceful, conversations were whispered and restrained; there was no loud partying, no toasts, no singing.

When they finished eating, a depressed-looking Isaac Idelsohn appeared in the doorway. The three of them quickly took him prisoner and bore him off in a taxi: "*À Longchamps, s'il vous plaît.*"

Idelsohn gave Kvachi a short account of what had befallen him. Driven from Odessa, the couple had come to Paris; Isaac had brought a lot of money.

"I was living comfortably on that money, but the trouble is I'm a Jew and, even if you give me millions, I can't bear to spend a day idly. So I didn't stop working. I went and opened a great big shop selling gold. I lost money. I couldn't stop in time, I dug my heels in and went on to the bitter end."

"Are you telling me that Isaac Idelsohn went bankrupt?"

"I did. I managed to keep just enough for Rebecca to open a

small workshop."

"So Rebecca is working now?"

"We're both working. I've got an orphaned niece who works too. Rebby is very pleased you've come."

"I'll come and see her, I certainly will."

They went down the Grande Armée avenue, crossed the Bois de Boulogne, and arrived at the Longchamps racecourse, which was already packed with people, and how many, and what sorts! Kvachi worked out that there must be twenty thousand people. They were Paris's *beau monde* and *tout Paris*.

The boundless field was garlanded with living flowers; it buzzed with swarms of bustling bees. Kvachi's greedy eyes spent two hours drinking in an inexhaustible sea of women. But when the races were over, Isaac showed him a trick: at the edge of the road through the Bois de Boulogne was the big Armenonville café-restaurant. The *beau monde* had to pass this way, and Parisians who wanted to celebrate would inevitably take an apéritif, so as to show themselves and be seen.

First Kvachi bought himself a thoroughbred riding horse which had won a race that day, and then he headed for the restaurant. They sat down, asked for ices and took endless balm for their excited hearts and sweet water for their greedy and thirsty eyes.

Tout Paris really was parading before their eyes, several thousand riders, cars, fiacres, landaus, carriages, and hansom cabs passed in front of Kvachi, who feverishly stared, examining this cream of the cream, these extremely beautiful and well turned-out women. He mentally undressed them and used his monocle so neatly and nimbly that his teacher, the minister of the court Baron Friedrichs, would have been envious.

Isaac, now a well-trained guide, showed them where to look: "See, President Poincaré ... those are the ambassadors: Russian ... German ... English ... There are the ministers and former ministers—Sarrienne, Cayot, Cloumans ... Now the millionaires: Chauchat … Rothschild … Hirsch … Duval … He's the steel king … the housing king … the banking king … That's General Halifé on horseback. You've heard of Halifé's trousers? He's the man who shot several thousand communards … That's Duke … Prince … Marquis … Baron … Count … over there are the professionals and the journalists: Stanley, Marcel Prévost … Calmette … Sara Bernhard … Rogeant … Lausanne …"

At the same time Idelsohn was telling them about his adventures and intimate stories, then he turned to the people who had come into the restaurant:

"Now these women are models. The fashion shops dress them free of charge, send them everywhere, and that's how they show the whole country the latest fashions and their dressmaking … That's Baron Grévy's mistress … That's Condé's mistress … And she …"

And he pointed out a dozen quite mature ladies and named just as many millionaires.

"What?" asked Kvachi, amazed. "Elderly women like that? Couldn't the millionaires get young ones?"

"Ah," smiled Idelsohn. "I can see you're still young and inexperienced. The Paris demi-monde won't receive silly young women who are unsophisticated, untrained, and haven't learnt their trade. A young woman like that, frivolous, easily carried away, flirtatious, uncontrollable, giggly, and fiery, learns her trade in student cafés. In that sense Paris is split into two: the other side of the Seine and this side, the Latin quarter and Montmartre. Young women begin south of the Seine and end up north of the river. There she is baptised, here she is matured and sets root; there she ploughs and sows, here she reaps; there she's a girl, here she's a woman; there she's taught love by students, here she is the professional and the professor. In the Latin quarter woman's love smiles and giggles meekly, sometimes cries tenderly and follows her heart's desire or her whim. But in Montmartre a woman laughs and guffaws loudly; her sorrow bellows, her love howls, her passion roars … Across the Seine the caresses are a breeze; this side, they're a gale; there, passion is a flame; here, it's smouldering coals. A silly little flirt smells of roses and violets, a Montmartre woman or a millionaire's mistress smells of marinade and … of camembert and Roquefort cheese, or worse … what, you've haven't tried Roquefort? Garçon! Bring two Roquefort's and a nicely mouldy camembert … What was I saying? Who has the millions? The old men. So, the very best women are theirs. Apart from neat lips and beautiful eyes, women need to have wits and the right character. Men of my age don't like flirtatious fools, gigglers, frisky, whimsical, tearful chatterbox jackdaws; we prefer serious, quiet, experienced, mature, calculating, and wise ravens. Yes, let me tell you: I'm an Odessa Jew, a well-rusted Idelsohn who's spent half a century wandering this earth and has seen, understood, and experienced and gone to the heart of it all. There's not a square yard of the earth I haven't seen. I speak nine languages, I've tried nine trades. Ah, they've brought the camembert and Roquefort. Now try it and smell it … The smell is a hundred times better than Houbigant or Coty L'Origan … Taste it, don't wrinkle your nose … When you get used to it, you can't get enough of it. That cheese smells of woman, doesn't it? It does, doesn't it! There you are … Well, as I was saying, I've tried nine trades. In Odessa I was a watchmaker, then a revolutionary. Don't be so surprised, it's a trade, just more dangerous and less rewarding. Twenty years ago I escaped from Siberia to America. In Boston I had a factory that reused rubbish and old rags; in the Klondyke I panned for gold, in Virginia I started a cotton plantation, in Cuba I grew sugar cane, in Greenland I fished, in Alaska I hunted, in Pretoria I dug for diamonds, in Zanzibar I traded in ivory, and in Ceylon I dived for pearls at the bottom of the sea. I had a dozen other jobs. Finally I went back to Odessa; in my old age I lost my wits and joined the revolutionaries. Ha-ha. It was only thanks to you that

I got out of hard labor in Siberia. I was lucky to end up in Paris instead of Siberia and I got a lot of my money out, but ... Yes, I was telling you. I've been a millionaire five times, I've gone bankrupt ten times, and now ... now I tag along after decent people like you and work to get my family a crust of bread."

Astounded, open-mouthed, Kvachi and his comrades went on listening for some time to the aged Isaac, who really had seen, heard, and experienced everything.

They got into a taxi again and rushed off to various areas outside Paris: Sèvres, Saint-Cloud, Courbévoir, and Clichy. In the evening they sat in the veranda of the Café Riche and each had a grenadine. They drank through straws and watched the Grands Boulevards. The sun was setting. A strange cloud appeared in the sky over the Madeleine; it was rushing over to them like a fabulous red-winged bird with its wings outstretched. This fiery bird seemed to hold in its beak a gigantic red ball, the red sun which dyed the endless boulevard—the tall buildings, the lines of trees, the flashing sea of people, and various carriages—the color of flames.

Here and there the large panes of the house and shop windows glowed red and gleamed with blood; the air was imbued with a golden haze through which living waves of young men and women swam.

All sorts were swept up in the waves: rich, poor, rentier, and worker, family men hurrying home and idle promenaders, snobs, and beggars, the careworn and carefree French and—who knows where from, why and on what wave—Russians, Indians, Arabs, Englishmen, and fortune-seekers from every corner of the globe.

Kvachi felt an odd mental unease and surge of desire: he was watching everything around him eagerly and trying to make sense of this incomprehensible exaltation and bliss. Finally, unable to solve the mystery, he turned to Isaac:

"Isaac, I've often been at evenings like this on Nevsky Prospekt; I've see the Vienna Ringstrasse and Prater; the weather was just as fine, there were just as many people, but yet … I can't understand what makes these boulevards so especially attractive."

"Ah," Isaac laughed. "I've seen ten times as much: Berlin's Friedrichstrasse, Rome's Corso, London's Piccadilly, Madrid's Prado, New York's Fifth Avenue, Delhi, Cairo, Tonkin, north, south, east, and west, but I've never come across a city as magical as this. Why? I've been searching for the answer for twenty years, and I've finally managed to find it. Ah! Look at those buildings. Have you seen anything better anywhere?"

"Vienna's got better buildings, they're newer, more colorful and neater."

"That much is true. Now look at that sky, breathe the air."

"Vienna has a clearer sky and cleaner air, it's softer."

"That's true, too. Take a look at the people."

"People in Vienna are just as fine, just as neat and well turned out."

"Yes indeed, neater and finer. Now compare the women. Women are the attractive thing about any people, they are the garden rose in a bouquet of wild briars; they are the dawn against a star-studded sky; they are the most beautiful ornament in any family, city, or nation. Now compare the Viennese women with the Parisians."

"Viennese women? They're better looking with better figures, they're thoroughbreds, but the women here are more … more …"

Unable to find the right word, he waggled his fingers. Old Idelsohn came to his aid:

"They're livelier, more coquettish, and prettier, aren't they? Parisian women have unquenchable fire, pepper, good taste, charm, sharp wits, a sense of beauty, and savoirfaire: it's all in their eyes, in the way they walk, and in their blood. So what's the secret of Paris's charm? I'll tell you: the air and life here are intoxicants, imbued with something magical with mysterious powers to bewitch.

What can you call this bewitchment, this magic? The people's soul and blood: that's the simple key to the secret."

"So the French have different blood!" Kvachi exclaimed ironically.

"Certainly. Believe your old Isaac. If everyone had the same blood, they'd have the same language, laws, bodies, religion, morals, and customs. Idelsohn may be no scholar, he never went to secondary school, but he has been round the world; he's got eyesight, hearing, observation, and brains; he's seen, heard, and understood everything. You'll benefit if you trust old Idelsohn, I say … Hmm, as I was saying, when God created the Frenchman he put hot blood in his veins, a burning heart in his chest, and well-scrubbed brains in his head, gave him savoirfaire and an instinct for beauty, and threw in a bit of pepper. This nation has used this instinct, ability, hot blood, and spirit and taken it abroad, spread it everywhere and, as you see, imprinted it for all to see on this boulevard, the buildings, and the air. That's it for now. I'm old Isaac Idelsohn and I'm telling you. Yes, take it from me, there's no more to be said."

Old Idelsohn went on for some time instilling sense into Kvachi; he kept pointing out passersby:

"Over there is the famous artist Mounet-Sully … There's the mad Lebaude, the king of the Sahara, a bankrupt millionaire … That's the *Folies Bergères* primadonna; There's Gouldie, the American billionaire who's lost his wits betting on dogs, horses, and races … That gentlemen with shaven cheeks is Shackleton, the greatest English explorer …" Isaac suddenly leapt to his feet and shouted: "Rachel, Rachel. Wait, my child, wait, I'm coming." Then he addressed Kvachi again and said: "She's my niece, a remarkable musician. Did you like the look of her? I'll introduce you, certainly I will. But now I must go. Goodbye. Until tomorrow!"

And Isaac's tiny figure was suddenly swallowed up by a sea of people. With amazed eyes, Kvachi and his friends watched Ra-

chel walk away and then exchanged glances. Finally Kvachi said:
"A girl like that would drive grandfather Khukhu mad. Old Isaac's got something in mind, I fancy. We'll see."

Visiting Nightclubs and Renewing Old Affections

The friends dined in the Grand Hôtel and then went out to see Paris's night entertainments.

They began in the Latin quarter. They looked into the American bar, *Souffleau, Darcourt*, then went down the Boulevard de Sébastopol, from where they came to the *Folies Bergères*. They ordered a *consommation*, saw heavily made-up women, and watched the day's *revue*, of which they understood little, because it was based on puns and they needed perfect French to grasp them.

As Kvachi watched the dancing and swaying he was reminded of the Petersburg *Arcadia*. He compared them and said: "I'm reminded of the polar bear and the gazelle."

They left early, headed for the *Olympia* and then slowly climbed Montmartre, which didn't come to life until midnight. They had a look at the cabarets, each time knocked back a drink and then intoxicated themselves with yet more spectacles. They visited a dozen cabarets, saw the *Monaco* and *La princesse* and ended up at the *Moulin Rouge*.

The colorful doorman, the maître d'hôtel, and the waiters, wearing white-fronted coats that made them look like magpies, greeted them with smiles and deference, led them into an enormous hall filled with people and gave them a special box. That moment the orchestra struck up the Russian anthem "God save the Tsar." Everyone stood up, straightened themselves, and turned to look at Kvachi's box.

"*Vive la Russie! Vive la Russie!*" the whole hall cried out, with thunderous applause to Kvachi, who was also bolt upright: people all over the audience sent him generous presents: flowers, confectionery, champagne, marsala, Benedictine, and many other drinks.

During the flow of presents and the enthusiastic applause, Kvachi nodded at everyone, smiled and waved his arm to show his gratitude. Then he turned to give the orchestra a signal. The orchestra struck up a fiery Marseillaise. Again everyone stood up straight.

"*Vive la France!*" Kvachi called out loudly, once the Marseillaise was over.

"*Vive la France! Vive la France!*" the audience thundered and roared.

"Please give the orchestra three hundred francs and ten bottles of champagne," Kvachi ordered the maître d'hôtel. "And those who kindly gave me presents must have double back: flowers for the ladies, drinks for the gentlemen."

He gave the deferential maître d'hôtel with his instructions a whole pack of cards to pass on to the audience; they were inscribed in gold:

Prince Irakli

BAGRATION-MUKHRANSKI

aide-de-camp to the Emperor of all Russia

They took their seats and ordered food and drink. Suddenly Kvachi turned pale: in one corner of the hall he caught sight of two eyes, smouldering eyes which transfixed his heart like burning arrows.

"It's Madame Lapoche. Beso, Sedrak! Madame Lapoche!"

They recognized each other and smiled; eyes met and heart reached out to heart.

"Sedrak, invite her over quickly, or … Quick!"

Five minutes later a half-naked, ivory-skinned Lisette Lapoche was presented by Sedrak to Kvachi, and this ivory skin, the jet-black stack of hair, the blood-filled lips, and eyes like burning coals ignited, lit up and enhanced Kvachi's box.

An old wound was reopened, the stitches came undone, a doused fire came to life, and dried-up fountains of untimely interrupted desire and love burst forth.

They squeezed each other's hands, reproached one another sadly, and recalled past times in Odessa. Then Kvachi asked her:

"*Où est-il votre mari*?"

Lisette moaned sadly: "*Il est mort, mon chat.*"

"Well, that was good of him!" exclaimed Sedrak.

"It was stupid of him to take so long about it," Kvachi added.

Gradually they got into a party mood: they made themselves at ease, warmed up, and were soon quite tipsy.

The enormous hall blazed with light. Crystal candelabras sent out countless diamond rays of light. There was a clatter of Sèvres porcelain, and the sound of a game of baccarat.

Kvachi was carried away by this conflagration and gave into the beast with blood on its lips, he swam off into the drunken waves and bolted like a horse into the vortex of lechery and passion. For a fortnight he drowned in that sea and roasted in that fire.

He saw and tried everything: hell and heaven, Apaches' cellars and whores' shelters, suburban gardens and secret trysting houses, love hired by the hour; he experienced the female rut which delighted and intoxicated exhausted eunuchs watching through keyholes. All that a dizzy, bestial Kvachantiradze could hear around him was the roar of vicious passion, the shrieks, convulsions, and moans of sensual delights laid bare. In the world's capital all that Kvachi saw and felt was a naked beast kicking its legs, endless feasting and partying, entertainment, pampering, and relaxation.

Kvachi sincerely thought that this wonderful city and all of France spent their lives and used up all their strength exactly as he was doing. Silibistro's son the aide-de-camp did not know, however—how could he, or would he have ever thought or believed it?—that, while he was turning day into night and night into day in a fire of passion and a whirlwind of the senses, ninety-nine percent of the enormous population was working day and night, breaking their backs, bustling all their lives, exhausting themselves in relentless toil, just to earn food for their families and those they cherished.

Resurrecting Old Love and Finding New Passion

Three days after Kvachi arrived in Paris Isaac invited him to his home. The Idelsohns had a neat small flat in the Latin quarter; Rebecca was seductively dressed, blushing and nervous with joy. In just five years she had filled out a little and become even more beautiful. Kvachi and Rebby asked after each other and devoured each other with their eyes. There were just three of them at dinner.

"My niece Rachel works a long way away," said Isaac. "So she has dinner there and comes here to sleep. Somehow I must introduce you, she's a fine singer."

After dinner Isaac got up: "I must apologize. I've got a very good client and we agreed to meet at eight. You go on chatting or take a walk, but I must rush."

"We'll take a walk, too," Rebby told her husband as she saw him out; then she spun round and clung to Kvachi's neck: "My Apollo! My Napoleon!"

"My Rebby! Rebecca. My darling!" And the old love was revived with sweat and groans.

From then on Kvachi devoted two days a week to Rebecca. On the Champs d'Élysées he rented a *hôtel-palais*, furnished in Parisian style. Apart from himself, all his friends, his secretary, and his French teacher Susanne also settled there. Beso had found

Susanne, a short, chubby, vivacious, nimble, and cheerful Frenchwoman. There were also half a dozen maids—*grisettes*—and a dozen or so male servants: doormen, footmen, cooks, a gardener, a groom, and a chauffeur.

Kvachi found French easy to learn, he quickly found his way about town and soon became familiar with the morals, customs, habits, and laws governing the local rentiers and flâneurs. Susanne sometimes taught Kvachi French love as well as language; she was very pleased and happy at her apprentice's progress and vigor. Nearly all Kvachi's friends and acquaintances had a prince's, duke's, count's, marquis's, or baron's title, while the others were at least all rich and well brought-up.

Early in the morning Kvachi would take his groom with him to ride down the Champs d'Élysées and round the Bois de Boulogne; then he breakfasted on the Grands Boulevards, lunched with his friends in his palace. At five he would have five o'clock tea at the *Carlton* or the *Angleterre, Madrid*, or at the *Elysée café*. At seven he would dine at *Maxime* or the *Grand Hôtel* or some other elite restaurant, while the rest of the evening and the night would be spent in *cabarets-chantants*.

He often had guests or was a guest himself at cafés and restaurants. Because his new friends and acquaintances were foreigners and lived in hotels, Kvachi could not at first surmount native French caution and reserve and get the natives to open the doors to their families.

In the museum of the Republic he saw Napoleon's golden dinner service: "Well, am I any worse than him? I have his name!" And he bought gold crockery for himself.

Kvachi found himself a place everywhere and never missed an occasion: a private view of an exhibition, the opera, a promenade, the races, variety theatre, *Folies Bergères, Olympia,* and every festive spectacle and entertainment.

Once at a private view in a Paris salon Kvachi unexpectedly

exploded: "It's been four months since Elena and Tania made themselves scarce after the scandal that Rasputin caused in the *Arcadia*. Since then they've both been living in the avenue Faubourg Saint-Honoré, but they still aren't aware that Kvachi is in Paris."

Prince Wittgenstein had come to Paris in pursuit of Tania and of Elena in particular, for he was by now himself bankrupt and Kvachified. Kvachi concentrated his mind at once. True he already had to look after Lapoche, Susanne, Rebecca, and Elena, but that same day he "managed" to sort out a new problem:

"Really, there's no need to hesitate! Tania's got so much money that she can help me keep twenty women and settle all my other expenses."

There was just one thing that Kvachi couldn't decide: whom to devote the night to—Tania or Elena. Finally he solved the dilemma: "I'm very sorry I can't devote the whole evening to you, my darling! I'll have to leave you soon. Tonight I've got to go to Châlons to see a friend, Viconte Choiselle; we're going hunting tomorrow."

Since Kvachi was walking between Tania and Elena with a hand on each of their arms, he squeezed their arms in turn, gave them a look, and said everything without words. Then he kissed their hands and went off on his own. At nine he was walking down the Faubourg Saint-Honoré. There was a light in Tania's window.

"Suppose you'd met Elena here?" asked Tania an hour later.

"I'd have told her I missed the train," replied Kvachi.

"If Tania sees you tomorrow morning, what will you tell her?" Elena asked Kvachi that night.

"I'll tell her I missed the train."

So the web binding all three, broken four months earlier, was woven again. But because the insatiable and exhausted Kvachi was still seeking and finding new objects, the old truism soon applied: Kvachi fed and clothed his mistresses, and others, known and unknown, paid for them and helped Kvachi out.

Despite this truism, Kvachi deliberately turned a blind eye because he was using Tania Prozorova's deep pockets to pay for dressing and undressing his mistresses, feasting, and keeping a *hôtel-palais*.

It was at this time that Isaac Idelsohn turned up when Kvachi was slurping a grenadine through a straw on the balcony of the Café Riche. Isaac rebuked him: "You've found your way about, have you? You don't know old Isaac any more, don't you? Should old acquaintance be forgot like that? The day before yesterday we bumped into each other, I said 'Hello,' but got no answer. Is that right? You're too important, are you?"

"No, Idelsohn, no! I didn't recognize you: seeing you and having a chat is always a pleasure for me. You're a clever man, clever, and experienced, so I'd like a talk."

"Clever, experienced and decent!" added Isaac.

"True, you're a decent man. Well, come and sit next to me and tell me how Rebecca is."

"Very well, thank you, but she's bored when she doesn't see you. I'm not alone here; my niece Rachel is waiting for me."

"Really? Then call her over … Ask her … Do me the honor …"

"Rachel, come, my girl, come! Here, let me introduce you: the generous, clever, respectable, and noble Prince Bagration-Kvachantiradze."

"Please take a seat … Order whatever you fancy … Garçon!"

"As good as the royal family of Georgia, the Bagrations," Isaac told Rachel. "He's a descendant of the biblical King David."

"Really? Truly? How? In what way?"

"Yes indeed," Kvachi confirmed the ancient legend, which he now repeated to Rachel.

Isaac suddenly slipped away: "I'm off right now. I have something to see to." And he went up to someone.

First Kvachi eyed Rachel up and down, then sat so close to her that their thighs and shoulders warmed, burned, and branded one another.

Rachel was a woman of an entirely different race and breeding compared to the other women in Kvachi's harem. She was tall, slim, white as cotton, slightly freckled, red-haired, with green eyes and a long face, and was so captivating, attractive, and desirable that people seated or passing nearby couldn't take their eyes off her.

The Museum of Art

Suddenly Kvachi caught sight of something odd. When Rachel bent forwards, she revealed her chest and showed she had a blue drawing on it.

"Mademoiselle, what have you got there on your chest?"

"Oh dear! You saw it? It's nothing, for God's sake, nothing!" Rachel murmured with embarrassment, using both hands to hide the drawing which had in any case vanished when she straightened up.

"All the same, tell me. I beg you, tell me."

"It's nothing special, I tell you. When I was ten we lived in Ceylon. There was a famous artist who painted people's bodies with ink. My mother liked the women he painted so much that she had him paint my body too. That's all there is to it."

"Please tell me just one thing: did she have a lot of painting done?"

"A lot ... My whole body. Here ... And here ..."

"Would you give me the pleasure of seeing the drawings? I should tell you I'm a great connoisseur of art."

Rachel went into peals of laughter, replying: "No-one's seen them yet."

"A hidden treasure might as well not exist. Actually, your uncle told me that you give singing lessons. Is that true?"

"It is."

"Take me on as a pupil."

"It costs ten francs a lesson."

"Even if it cost a hundred times more I'd easily manage the expense."

Rachel burst into laughter again: "Suppose it cost you ten times more?"

"Then let's settle up. But I'd better tell you that you'll have to come to me."

Rachel examined Kvachi cannily and laughed.

"All right … I'll come … The price is twenty francs."

That same evening Rachel tapped on the piano with one finger as she tormented Kvachi: "Do-o-o … re-e-e … mi-i-i. Mi! Mi! Oh my God, what a dim useless pupil you seem to be! Mi-i-i: mi-i, mi-mi!"

Kvachi strained and forced himself and nearly tore his vocal chords, but he couldn't distinguish one note from another.

Rachel lost her temper and finally told him brusquely: "You and that chair have the same ear. Let's stop. I'm going."

"Bear with me, I haven't begun yet."

And he began. The battle was heated and short. Kvachi stormed the museum of art and inspected every detail of the famous artist's handiwork. Although Kvachi knew no more about art than about music, he still discovered an archaeological treasure. In various parts of Rachel's body he uncovered and read the names of several of Rachel's clients: Jean, Paul, Eugène, and Pierre.

Only a few weeks later did Kvachi Kvachantiradze find out, by chance, that Rachel worked in a "house" and earned ten francs an evening for showing her museum and … for entertaining the clients, whereas just one visit by Rachel cost Kvachi … but who knows and who can count Kvachi's expenses and income?

The Break-up of Kvachi's Harem

Rachel's first visit was nevertheless no great event in Kvachi's life, but he would never forget that day, because a minor cause had the very greatest consequences.

When Rachel left Kvachi's house, he told himself: "Rachel is number six. I don't want any mix-up here, or ..." And, to stop things getting confused, he took out his pocket book and wrote down a timetable:

Monday	Madame Lapoche
Tuesday	Rebecca
Wednesday	Elena
Thursday	Rachel
Friday	Susanne
Saturday	Tania
Sunday	rest day

When he'd written their names he added their addresses. Kvachi usually kept this book in his breast pocket or left it on the desk, or in a desk drawer. He knew his timetable by heart and the rest of the entries were so unimportant that he left the book on the table and forgot about it.

After some time his French teacher Susanne came one Friday for her share of attention. Kvachi was out, and Susanne waited for a long time for him to come, then couldn't help reaching out for the pocket book and perusing it. As she perused it, she came across the timetable. Susanne had a trained nose: she worked everything out.

Women and men often share love, but such sharing is not easy to tolerate. Susanne suspected some of Kvachi's infidelities and knew of others, but once she had stumbled on this timetable she flared up in anger. She quickly copied the timetable and the list of addresses on a sheet of paper, put it in her pocket and left.

Two days later Kvachi's mistresses received notes: "Darling! I can't manage our usual day, so please come and see me on Saturday at five precisely."

Susanne knew that Kvachi would not let Tania down or let anyone stop him seeing her, so it was Tania's day and time that she specified.

On Saturday Tania was the first to arrive. Straight after her came Susanne, Rebecca, Elena, Rachel, and Mme Lapoche. Tania had only just undone a button on her blouse when Jalil knocked at the door to announce Susanne's arrival. Ten minutes or so later, Tania was dressed again and left the study for the drawing room where all the other women had by now gathered.

Kvachi was pacing about like a confused turkey-cock, mumbling: "Allow me to introduce you … Please sit down … Yes, it's beautiful weather … Last night I was at the circus."

Then one woman seized the opportunity to draw Kvachi aside, and she was followed one-by-one by the others. They all had the same question to ask:

"You sent me that note, didn't you? Just tell me why."

If Kvachi said yes, he was in as much trouble as if he said no. He strained himself hard, racked his well-exercised brain, yet couldn't devise an answer. The poor man was trapped.

"Beso, get them to serve tea right away. Do a sort of 'five-o'clock' for me. Invite them all, then come in and keep these women amused, or I'm finished."

The women were deep in a mysterious whispered, snorting conversation. Kvachi noted that Susanne was fussing about more than the others. He realized that Susanne had a hand in all this, but he was tongue-tied and bound hand and foot. Meanwhile Kvachi's comrades came in to rescue their leader. Six men took on six women. They each talked a woman round, and Kvachi was left with Susanne. Kvachi sat down next to her, asked after her health, and pinched her arm so hard that she almost shrieked. He pinched her again and whispered to her: "I'll show you what a scene is! Just wait … wait a minute …"

"Jalil!" Susanne instantly called out: Jalil looked through the doorway. "Jalil, come here! Come and sit down ... How are you? Today you're going to entertain me. Go on, tell me what you think of French women." Susanne made Jalil sit next to her and take part. A great smile broke out on Jalil's face and stayed there. His inch-long white teeth flashed, his French was horribly broken, so he spoke by wagging his fingers, and he was dripping with sweat.

"Jalil, what do you think of this woman?" asked Kvachi.

"I like her a lot, sir, a lot! Jalil loves fair-skinned women."

"Then take her as a present from me."

"I'm grateful, prince, but ... she won't go with Jalil."

Kvachi went from one woman to another, but all of their lips were sealed: nobody would speak to him, and they all turned their backs on him. When tea was brought, they suddenly all rose, shook the hands of Kvachi's friends, and made for the door.

"What's the hurry? Where are you off to? Have some tea."

Kvachi kept inviting them to stay, but they neither spoke to him nor shook his hand: they left.

"What's all this about?" the comrades asked each other.

"Susanne did this to me," said Kvachi. "I've been ruined and disgraced."

"Sometimes trouble is good for you," Beso tried to console Kvachi.

"Yes, you're right, Beso!" Kvachi agreed. "I'll get some rest and I'll have more time for new business."

That was how the pert Susanne wrecked and scattered Kvachi's harem.

A Conversation and Three Comrades' Return to the Motherland

Kvachi and his gang had settled down in Paris. At first they were helpless infants, barely able to stand on their own feet, looking around timidly, walking the streets shyly, living off what they had brought from Petersburg. But then they gradually plucked up courage and became bolder, breaking into a canter like stallions given free rein. And why shouldn't they have cantered off? They'd learnt enough French to get by, they'd adopted French morals and customs, they'd learnt the code of conduct, they wore top hats, followed people's steps, and got on with life.

For some time Kvachi and his gang had circled round French families and banged at their doors and windows, finally trying to get access and do some "business." But they soon realized that a family in France was as tightly closed as a fortress in Georgia. This realization didn't bother them. They gave up on families and concentrated on the boulevards where they found plenty of gullible victims with too much money.

Kvachi and his gang had been hunting and fishing for nearly two years in this bottomless, boundless ocean. Who could count or describe Kvachi's sleight of hand, heroism, refinement, wariness, and instinct?

There came a countless flock of hunters,
Russian, British, German, all seeking Kvachi
To become Kvachi's vassal, whoever is the sharpest.
Here is a hand and heroism and a tireless arm!
They ran across a field, they sat the flock in front of them,
They reaped what wasn't sown, they sweated with their "business":
Spectators called Kvachi, "Like a poplar, the tree of Eden."

Once the gang pulled off a couple of big "tricks" and made so much money that it seemed like chaff. They shared out the "chaff" between themselves in a fraternal and friendly way. Then they sat down, opened a bottle of champagne, and started chatting:

"Prince, you know what? We must come to our senses!" Sedrak began.

"What are you saying, you insolent pup? That I'm out of my

mind?" Kvachi objected.

"Believe me, you know whether you're in your right mind or not. We've done a good job. Your father Silibistro and my father Galusta could never even dream of so much money, it'll take more than a week to count it. Why don't we use our brains and stop there? I know you mean to do nothing but party for a while. But this money is going to run out, isn't it, and then we have to begin all over again. It'll all be the same, but we'll die as crooks. Then what? We'll hate all this like poison. We're up to our necks in money. We've done all the foreign parts. If you want, let's roam about just a little more. We've had so many parties, we've"tried out" all the women on earth, now let's settle and live a decent life. That way we're safe from prison, we can do a bit of good, we can have a family, and start a business. Well, do you get what I say, or not?"

"Oh dear, our Sedrak's quite the bourgeois!" exclaimed Kvachi. "So I'm to leave Paris and go running back to crappy Georgia! I've got to leave the beautiful princesses here and attach myself to some frump in the backwoods! I've got to leave a palace and go to live in some chicken shed in Samtredia or Tbilisi!"

"I've got to give up the *Olympia, Moulin Rouge, Café Riche* and get used to going to Daniel the Jew's, Laitadze's, and Eremo's inns?" said a stunned Chipi Chipuntiradze.

"I prefer the Apache cabaret and a walk down the Grand Boulevard to the whole of Georgia!" Chikinjiladze joined in. "Sedrak's off his head."

"What do you expect, what have you got back there in Georgia, you idiot?" asked Kvachi.

"I've told you a lot, I'll tell you what else I've got: you know what I have? Elderly parents worried sick about me; poor relatives looking to me to feed them and waiting for my return like manna from heaven ..."

He was interrupted by the rest of the gang's laughter.

"As I said, he's quite the bourgeois now."

"What have I got there? Everything, I'm afraid: vineyards in Telavi, the panorama from Nadikvari park, the breeze up on the Gombori pass; Kakhetian wine, our black-eyed girls, my loyal mates ..."

Jalil interrupted Sedrak: "Mates are fine, so are rolled red kebabs, so are lamb stew and mutton soup, Hazira's Turkish songs, a nice blonde Russian woman. Hooray, Jalil! Your turn now, Gabo."

"Oh what can I say?" Gabo Chkhubishvili responded: he was agitated. "What have I got to go back to Gori for? Gori castle—my respect to its builder! Me and my mates will picnic up there and roast kebabs on skewers and sing a feasting song and play sweet tunes on our shawms ..."

Sedrak took the floor: "When an oboe player gets up on a hill at dawn, strikes up an aubade to greet the sunrise ..."

Then they talked over one another: "When a raft floats down the Mtkvari with a banquet laid out and we rush downriver like an arrow ..."

"When the attendant gives you a good rubdown in the bathhouse, then you eat your fill of fat sheep's tail and go to sleep ..."

"When you're working in the vineyard, dripping with sweat, then you sit down in the shade of a gigantic walnut tree and get down to cold cucumber, chicken stew, and yogurt ..."

"In the evening when you bathe in the Liakhvi then channel a bit off and catch fish; and then you get a fire going and boil it alive ..."

"When Jalil wakes up and gets Hazira to sing, then you hear a broken melody, a shikasta ..."

"At harvest time, when you stuff yourself on sweet Budeshuri grape, then you get down to goat kid with quince, with young Saperavi or Rkatsiteli wine to wash it down, and Levan, bless him, sings a Kakhetian song ..."

"When you spit-roast a woodpigeon or a hare you've caught

in the grove ..."

"Then you go and lose yourself in thick forest to cool off ..."

"Good God, what's got into these insolent pups?"

"I thought these are men who've become European, educated, and civilized: actually, they're still complete Asiatics!"

"They gave Darwin the idea for his law of atavism. A grafted fruit tree can go mad and suddenly revert to the wild: it's been struck by atavism."

"What do these milksops understand about atavism?" asked Kvachi, who confused atavism with atheism.

Gabo went on justifying his desire and longing to return home and recalled his motherland. The very word provoked a response.

"The whole world is my motherland!" said Kvachi. "I can live in any developed country. I love culture, civilization, progress, clean streets, a nice tidy apartment, really good entertainments; I like a well-starched shirt, a top hat, patent-leather shoes; I love women of good breeding who are scrubbed and bathed, wear silk underwear, and change it at least twice a week; I can't understand how anyone can live in a town where there aren't several colleges, a dozen theaters, arts and sciences, a town where intellectual life is extinguished or never existed."

"My motherland is anywhere where I can get a tasty bite to eat," Beso added.

"What use to me is a homeland of poultry keepers, shepherds, and market gardeners?" wondered Ladi.

"Eh!" exclaimed Gabo. "So you mean, if my mother is very old, poor, and ugly, I have to hit her, forget her, and abandon her, do you?"

"No, of course not," intervened Jalil. "Shame on me, if I did that to Jalil's father Soin Emin-oglu and mother Khanum. It's out of the question, prince, Allah will punish you. That won't do, *olmaz*, prince, *olmaz*."

"Or another thing," Sedrak interrupted him. "Only if my parents are young, handsome, healthy, educated, and millionaires, will I be a good son to them? Shame on you, my old man Galusta! Shame on you, my toothless mother Marta! They sacrificed their lives and their youth so that an ungrateful Sedrak could turn his back on them in their old age, leave them to someone else's charity?!"

"He can talk, can't he?" Gabo intervened. "You play with words: why bring Kvachi's parents into it?"

They changed the topic and got down to eating and drinking; then they followed Sedrak who had found a little Mediterranean restaurant in the Latin quarter. They went in and turned the Greeks' refuge upside down. They took over themselves and together concocted and laid out a banquet of cheese, herbs, red Cypriot wine and Greek brandy, fried chicken and pilau, rolled kebabs with flat bread, shashlik with onion, smoked sturgeon, sliced curds, lamb stew, turkey with walnuts, and raw fish.

They feasted until morning like real Georgians, made the Greeks join them, got them drunk and laid them out on the floor. Then Gabo, Jalil, and Sedrak got ready to depart and a day later they were on their way back home.

Those of the friends who stayed in Paris heard several months later that Gabo had bought a large flock of sheep, a farm, arable land, forest, and mountain pastures, while Sedrak had opened a big business in Telavi, added three vineyards to his own, and had developed a money-lending business in Tbilisi; Jalil had opened a fruit and confectionery business in Tbilisi and taken a lease on a bathhouse.

The three returnees had fulfilled their ambitions: they'd made their parents happy, they'd made a wide network of friends, and built themselves warm nests. Gabo and Sedrak were toiling hard, resting under walnut trees, feasting to the sound of shawm, lute, and oboe, occasionally bathing, fishing, and hunting. They often made shashliks and lamb stew, washed down with red Kakhetian wine, they sang feasting songs, and pursued black-eyed maidens.

They often recalled the past and spoke warmly of their former comrades, they stumbled and mumbled as they told stories of Petersburg, Vienna, and Paris. Jalil worked and feasted. Instead of chicken stew and fried chicken he dined on mutton pilau and full-tail-fat mutton stew. Sometimes he would invite the minstrel Hazira, more often he himself would sing a *shikasta* or other Turkish song and ... he was very drawn to Russian blondes whom "Jalil is very fond of and likes a lot."

Kvachi's words came true: Gabo and Sedrak had reverted to being Asiatics, they lagged behind the world and lost their civilized habits: they hardly ever touched soap now, they rarely changed their underwear, they looked askance at white collars and gloves; they never touched a newspaper now, nor went near a theater; they shunned decent city folk whom they found odd. On the other hand, they were living in their own country, breathing its air, ploughing its soil and, feeling and sensing its mystery, they suffered its griefs and enjoyed its delights.

Kvachi, Beso, and Chipi began rushing round Europe again, breathing the Grands Boulevards, living in cafés, wearing themselves out in cabarets and restaurants, relaxing with women, acting like gentlemen, princes or marquis, and occasionally pulling off a few "jobs."

Who can know or understand which of them was the winner and which the loser: Kvachi and his two friends, or Gabo, Jalil, and Sedrak?

Lady Harvey's and Kvachi's Passionate Affair

A few days after little Susanne had sent Kvachi's harem packing, Kvachi, having pondered the way things had developed, went to see Tania that same day. She refused to see him, but he stayed outside her door until she took pity on him and opened the door herself:

"What do you want? I don't know you any more ... Everything between us is over."

He began to swear oaths and to plead, implore, and vow, he recalled the past and promised the future. Kvachi knew very well that his quarrel with Tania had to end as it had before: by forgetting the past and swearing to the new. He also knew that the best way to reconcile lovers who have quarrelled was a soft warm bed: so this row too ended in bed, and Kvachi's credit was renewed.

The next day Madame Lapoche came back to Kvachi of her own accord, but the others stopped enquiring after him.

Kvachi now had a taste for, and the habit of European ways; he had the appetites, manners, and lifestyle of an idle man with a lot of money. He had a nice *hôtel-palais* in Paris, a very pretty villa in Biarritz, a yacht in Nice, a special railway carriage at the station, three motor cars in his garage, six horses in his stables, and a cheque-book in his pocket.

That summer Kvachi relaxed in Trouville. In the evening he went to the beach where the women bathers liked to expose their naked bodies. Kvachi inspected this exhibition with a professional eye. He was excited and satisfied by this new and rare spectacle. Women of every race and breed were stretching their bodies, barely concealed by patches of jersey of various colors: there were tall, stiff, sinewy, reddish, touch-me-not, wan Englishwomen; there were rounded, broad, big-shouldered, big-hipped wobbly Flems and Dutchwomen, as plump as geese; there were well-built, proud, and fair-skinned Scandinavians and Germans; there were languid, lean, nimble, proud, black-haired and bronzed Spaniards; there were Italians and Frenchwomen of various color and shape—nimble and coquettish; swaying and elegant; fiery and impetuous; flirtatious and haughty; shy and bold; tall and short; full-figured and thin; blonde and brunette; mademoiselles, mesdames, miladies, misses, mistresses, donnas, and maidens, and married women of every other title, weight, race, color, and breed.

Here, from the waves, emerged an unearthly foam-colored Aphrodite, a beautiful ocean nymph, an irresistible sorceress: cypress-like, elegant, big-breasted, with strapping thighs and narrow waist, fine-boned, long-necked, red-haired, and blue-eyed. This magical being seemed not to have noticed Kvachi. She stood at the edge of the water, put her white arms round her neck, bent forward, and stretched with pleasure.

"Great God!" Kvachi exclaimed to himself: he was instantly inflamed and confused, and he blushed. "Well, a living, new-born Aphrodite! A real jewel of the earth! No ordinary girl or woman! God, help me! God, give me a helping hand and serve me: I swear to You, Lord almighty, that I'll build you a church and will keep a candle burning for You forever."

At this moment the magical being looked round. Her big blue eyes alighted on Kvachi. The gates of heaven were opened by those eyes, the spell-casting smile and the pearly teeth; he became a knight engulfed in fiery flames, burning and fainting. Then she quickly shielded her eyes, stretched back her neck, rushed to her bathing hut with a couple of fawn-like leaps, and burst into peals of silvery laughter.

An hour later Kvachi moved to the hotel where the Aphrodite was staying. He slipped a gold coin into the doorman's hand and asked for the name of this goddess.

"Lady Harvey," replied the doorman. "The widow of Lord Harvey, who was torn to pieces by a Bengal tiger when hunting in India last year. Lady Harvey is fond of swimming, playing roulette, rare steaks, hunting, fishing, flowers and … men with thick black hair, like you."

All that night Kvachi hung round Lady Harvey at the casino. The roulette clattered as it span, the croupier called out with his practised and familiar phrase "*Mesdames et messieurs, faîtes vos jeux! Rien ne va plus.*"

The cashiers raked in their gains with little wooden shovels and distributed what the players had won. Winners smiled, losers frowned, but everyone was tense, heated, and fidgety—some openly, some secretly.

Lady Harvey had next to her her companion Miss Hopkins, a wan, myopic, tart, and elderly Cerberus; she also had a fair-haired youth of about twenty, as tender as a girl, a shy, chubby, and innocent Briton.

The men couldn't take their eyes of Lady Harvey; they followed her like shadows, they licked their lips, their eyes were moist: they lusted after her. Lady Harvey lost a couple of thousand francs, Kvachi—three thousand. The girlish youth every now and again took some money from his pocket and silently put it in Lady Harvey's hand; Miss Hopkins fidgeted, Lady Harvey frowned divinely and wouldn't let anyone but her chubby young man come near her.

Finally she stretched out her swan-like neck, lit up her surroundings with heavenly rays, gathered the hem of her silk dress and, strutting like a peafowl, swept out of the hall, followed by the smiles, oily eyes, and the concupiscence of the men.

Kvachi followed her out and ordered the hotel doorman:

"Tomorrow morning give Lady Harvey a bouquet of the very best flowers and send her this too." He handed over his imperial visiting card.

The next morning Kvachi was handed on a silver tray a little note on satin paper. On one side it read: "Thank you. I'm very fond of flowers when I'm traveling. Don't look for me." On the other side, in print, it read: "Lady Elizabeth Harvey, London, West End, Charing Cross, 276."

"What has she written? Don't look for me? When a woman tells me not to look for her, that has to mean the opposite, and I have to look for her. Now I need to know where she's gone, and when. Beso, pack the luggage! Quick, don't dawdle! What, she's gone to Le Havre by boat? Fine then, I expect she's off to London. Beso, hire a motor boat at once. The weather's good. I'll catch up with her, or I'll be in time for the boat to England."

They got into a large launch and made for Le Havre. As they approached Le Havre, a big steamship passed by them. Kvachi caught sight of Lady Harvey leaning over the railings: she recognized Kvachi, laughed, and kept waving her handkerchief at him. Kvachi asked the launch's owner: "Where's that ship going to?"

"It's going round France and Portugal, then following the Spanish coast to Marseilles."

"Can I catch up with it?"

"Only by rail, via Brest or Saint Nazaire, if you catch the express."

An hour later Kvachi was speeding along in a specially hired railway carriage, pursuing his new fortune as it sped ahead. The locomotive had the wings of a hawk. Other trains stopped at stations to yield the way to Kvachi's furious progress. They rushed through Rouen, Le Mans, Angers, Nantes, and early in the morning arrived at Saint Nazaire.

"Has the *Bordeaux* docked?"

"It's due to leave in one hour."

"Thank the Lord! Beso, move."

Two hours later, as the ship moved into the ocean, Lady Harvey lit up the upper deck like a second sun. His head bowed, Kvachi stepped forward to meet her: "Milady, please be gracious and forgive me! You wrote to say I mustn't look for you. I couldn't obey your first command."

The lady seemed lost for words, she was so astonished and stunned.

"How? Where? This ship left Le Havre, and that was where you were going."

"I got a special train to overtake you, milady."

"But you still disobeyed me."

"If you'd ordered me to throw myself into the water, I'd have found that easier to accept than losing you."

The Englishwoman's icy heart was captivated and thawed by Kvachi's courtly exaltation.

They both disembarked at Biarritz on the Franco-Spanish border, in the Basque country.

While the ship was docking, Kvachi, using his binoculars, pointed out to Lady Harveya pretty Mauritanian villa perched on top of the rock and asked her: "How does that seem to you, milady?"

"It's beautiful. Life at that height would be paradise. It's got a big garden. I wonder if it's available: then we could rent it."

"It's at your disposal, milady. The villa belongs to me. Do me the honor, and make me happy."

"It's yours? Really? Living there will be the greatest pleasure, but ..."

Kvachi immediately understood her point: "Don't worry, milady. I shall be staying at another villa."

They settled the matter, and Lady Harvey jumped for joy. For a few days and nights they thoroughly enjoyed themselves and relaxed. They would go to the beach and bathe, or take a motor launch out into the ocean, or walk round Bayonne, or follow the Pyrenees ridge by motor car. Sometimes they stayed out all day and spent the time with the Basques.

A Basque café owner once told Lady Harvey: "We are the oldest people in Europe. We descend from the ancient Iberians."

"Iberians?" said Kvachi with amazement. "I'm an Iberian, a Georgian Iberian."

Both were puzzled. They stared at each other for some time, asked each other a lot of questions, compared their languages, found that some words coincided, but couldn't find any closeness or family relationship. All that Kvachi understood was that at one time the Basques had been outstanding seamen and pirates, that they had explored the Arctic ocean, that they had once had a powerful kingdom, that they had eventually evaded both Roman and Spanish domination, that at times Basque rebellions had set the Pyrenees on fire and that they had watered the Pyrenees with blood for the sake of freedom. Now schools and courts were forbidden to use the Basque language, but every Basque was still proud of his blood and love of freedom; their proud necks had never borne the yoke of serfdom. There were about a million of them, many had emigrated to Mexico, Cuba, and Argentina to earn a crust of bread.

Kvachi noticed that the Basques were more burly, better looking, and more nimble than the Spaniards or French; they were clean-shaven, they wore a red or blue beret, a belt and a short tunic; they liked ball games, dancing, singing, and popular entertainments; the women were considered excellent wet-nurses and carried out the heaviest manual tasks.

Something deep was gnawing at Kvachi's heart: he sensed a very distant, mysterious rush in his blood; he felt a momentary affinity, closeness, spiritual oneness with this people, but the flame quickly died down and went out. Soon he forgot everything, because Lady Harvey found this a boring, annoying waste of time.

Kvachi and Lady Harvey spent the evenings strolling in the wooded parks, listening to concerts; then they would have supper in one or another casino and gather round the roulette table, where they either won a little or lost a lot.

Lady Harvey's icy heart had desiccated and destituted Kvachi, weakened, exhausted, and withered his burning heart. Once, after supper, in the dark, Kvachi embraced Lady Harvey in his villa garden: she had had a little to drink. They both became inflamed once more and were incinerated in a fire of passion; Kvachi fell at her feet, imploring and begging her, while he clutched her coquettish feet to his chest and wet them with his tears. Laughing, Lady Harvey slipped from his grasp and rushed to the house.

Thwarted, Kvachi hung about the dark avenue, struck his chest with his fist and murmured: "Right then … I know what to do … I know …"

When the light went out in Lady Harvey's bedroom Kvachi crept up onto the balcony and opened wider the window, which was already open.

"Prince! Sir! How dare you? Come to your senses. I'm going to shout … Miss Hopkins! Miss Hop …"

Kvachi silenced the frightened woman with his lips, clutched her tight, and overcame her. After five minutes the sound of slippers and of Miss Hopkin's sleepy voice came through the door: "Milady! Lady Harvey! Did you call me? Is there anything you need?"

Gasping for breath, Lady Harvey had trouble making Miss Hopkins hear her broken whispers: "Nothing, Miss … Nothing … I've found it … I've found it …"

"You've found something; I've not come away empty-handed, either," Kvachi whispered in her ear, muffling his laughter.

"Shh. Be quiet, you madman," the transformed Lady Harvey whispered in turn through heated lips; her long, powerful arms stopped him breathing, tore the sinews in his neck, and choked the prince, who was by now calm.

For three days and nights nobody caught sight of either Kvachi or Lady Harvey—not in the casino, nor on the beach, nor in the parks. A blissful Kvachi was so grateful that he presented Lady Harvey, who was sated with sensual delights, with his Mauritanian villa; he decorated her tall marble breasts with a necklace of pearls as big as hazelnuts. Then they both went mad with nymphomania, satyriasis, and frenzied traveling.

They couldn't settle anywhere or cool their boiling blood. Once a week they ran to the station and, inflamed with passion, sped off to one of Europe's resorts: "Vichy … Ostende … Karslbad … Trouville … Aix-les-Bains … Montreux … Vévey … Lugano!"

Finally they put down roots in Nice, in the *Hôtel Nebraska*, where they cooled down and rested.

The Story of a Really Big "Job"

Monte Carlo casino is blazing with light. Everything gleams, burns, and shines with gold, bronze, silver, marble; there are precious pictures, tapestries, carpets, brocades, there is velvet and satin. From every corner of the earth people have come to try their luck; they crowd the hall like flies. A hundred languages can be heard and a hundred races seen: blonde northerners—Russians, Scandinavians, Germans, and English; fast-moving, hot-blooded black-haired Frenchmen, Italians, and Spaniards; generous, taciturn, and imperturbable Yankees; heated, tense, and nervous Mexicans, Brazilians, and various mulattos; Arabs and Turks, Persians and Indians, Chinese and Japanese, Asia and Europe, America and Africa—all gather here, spinning the wheel of fortune, hoping for wealth and fame.

Everyone's face reflects their wins and losses. Some smile for joy and laugh, carefree and relaxed; others mourn their losses, sulk, turn sour and bilious. Some, now bankrupt and finished, give in to despair and start begging and sometimes spill their own blood right here or in the fabulously laid-out park. Some are so used to this palace of tears and fortune's smiles that they graciously grow old here. They know the secret of gambling; they have sounded out the way to win. They have discovered the way to get rich. They hold the secret key in their hands: differential calculus, mathematical formulas that occupy sixty pages, faultless, precise, and authentic, the fruit of lost fortunes and five to ten years' observation. If you want to win, trust yourself to these people. The cost is quite small: any losses are yours, but you hand them part of your winnings, or give them a hundred francs or so for a change of linen and shoes—that's all they ask for, because it's easier to die of starvation in this casino than to gain admission in a dirty shirt; fresh clean clothes, faultless manners, and unspoken submission are what the management of the casino demands from this breed of people in exchange for letting them in free of charge.

Every night Kvachi and Lady Harvey tried their luck in the casino; sometimes at *trente-et-quarante*, sometimes at *rouge-et-noir,* sometimes at *petits-chevaux*, or other games. Over a period Lady Harvey had drained her fortune gambling. Kvachi tried to help her out, but couldn't change her luck or win back her losses. They gradually sank deeper and deeper until they were overwhelmed; sometimes they used their wits, sometimes they relied on the advice of the bankrupts, but every day brought them closer to ruination.

One day the bank bounced one of Kvachi's cheques and told him his account was empty. He became completely dispirited: "Beso, go to Aix-les-Bains today, sell my villa before the week is over, and come back ... What? I know, there's no alternative."

Beso brought the money, which Kvachi handed over to the croupier.

"Beso, go to Biarritz and sell my villa."

"The villa you gave away to Lady Harvey?"

"Yes, but when I get back my losses, I'll buy back the villa."

Two weeks later he asked Beso for more help:

"Beso, go to Paris today, sell my *hôtel-palais* today and come back ... Fine, fine ... I know that I'm finished, but there's no alternative ... Don't be afraid, by the time you're back I'll have sorted out a job."

Meanwhile Lady Harvey's brother Lord Brouxton had come over from London for two weeks. He was a young *bon-vivant*. They won a little, but lost it all. In the end, the lord told Kvachi:

"Prince, come and stay with me in London."

"All right! Thank you!"

"Shall we travel together?"

"Yes. Beso, get everything ready."

They arrived in Paris, and Kvachi invited the brother and sister to his *hôtel-palais.* It wasn't his any more, but he hadn't yet moved out. They stayed a few days. Kvachi went wild once again and amazed his guests with his spectacular palace, his décor, the number of his servants, his influence, and his genuinely aristocratic tastes and manners.

Before they departed, Kvachi gave Ladi Chikinjiladze secret instructions. Beso and three of the servants were sent with a lot of luggage to London three days in advance; four servants were retained by Kvachi.

When they disembarked at Dover, Beso had a special train ready for them. Lord Brouxton reproached Kvachi:

"Prince, you're going to too great expense."

"There can never be any expense too great for my friends!"

"But you are my guest."

"Let's discuss that when we get to London."

Beso had arranged in advance for Kvachi to have seven rooms in the Hotel Astoria, as well as motor cars, a landau with a coat-of-arms, riding horses, and reporters.

The next day the newspapers printed news of Kvachi's arrival: "A Caucasian prince of royal origin has come to England ... a great friend of England ... a supporter of Anglo-Russian friendship ... accompanied by a brilliant suite ... the prince is staying at the Astoria ... seven rooms ... a personal friend of Lord Brouxton ..."

A day later Lord Brouxton and Lady Harvey took Kvachi to see the sights of London. They showed him Piccadilly, the West End, Trafalgar Square, Charing Cross, Saint James, the Tower, Waterloo, St Paul's, and many other amazing spectacles. At Westminster Kvachi was met by the speaker, at the British Museum by the director, at the admiralty by the Admiral-in-Chief.

That evening Brouxton held a big dinner at his palace in honor of Kvachi; the next day Kvachi was invited to the Yacht

Club, and the following day to the Sports Club. After that he was showered with invitations in all directions and had no time to relax. Two weeks later Kvachi expressed his thanks to everyone by putting on such a fabulous feast that his guests still frequently recall its extent and its strange spectacular beauty. There were more than three hundred present, all from the elite of London society: lords, viscounts, dukes, Indian rajahs, bankers, factory owners, and many other wealthy, distinguished, and prominent figures. Three of the best orchestras played. Specially invited famous singers—Caruso, Battistini, Nelly Melba, Maria Haye, and Tito Ruffo—sang from all sides. The huge building was decorated with rare flowers and tropical plants ordered from the Riviera. Oriental and western art and tastes were both called on to entertain and delight Kvachi's guests.

The next day all London and the press were talking about it. That was just what Kvachi wanted. When Kvachi arrived in London, he sent a telegram for ten thousand pounds sterling to be sent to him that day. Beso wired the money back to Chikinjiladze in Paris. The third and fourth days the same money was wired to London and returned to Paris. Beso's skills and timing were excellent: he passed on the telegrams about money transfer to Prince Bagration in the presence of his master's guests.

Kvachi apologized to his guests: "Gentlemen, please excuse me: it must be an urgent telegram ..." Then he gave Beso directions:

"Take these ten thousand pounds now ... send forty thousand to my manager in Tbilisi ... give my banker in Paris instructions to give my chief secretary Prince Trubetskoy in Paris a million francs every month, and inform my head office in Petersburg that they are in charge of all business; I don't want to be bothered ... I'm fed up with it."

"Your highness's yacht is on its way to London."

"Good."

"The Tbilisi office is asking how much they should spend per month on charity."

"Three hundred thousand roubles."

"There's one more telegram: Count Orlov agrees to your price: he'll sell you the Siberian gold mines for three million roubles."

"I accept. Hand the telegram to head office. Leave the rest for later ... I must apologize again, dear friends, for interrupting our conversation so rudely."

This was roughly the dialog that Kvachi and Beso had in the presence of distinguished lords and bankers. Kvachi knew very well that talking business in front of guests was considered "shocking." But he also knew that his guests would not hold it against Kvachi: they just smiled and said: "*Voilà un prince étrange et ... exotique!*"

Kvachi's friend Lord Brouxton defended him: "Every nation has its customs."

But nobody knew what Kvachi had in mind. Two weeks passed after that still unforgettable dinner. Kvachi was perusing the morning paper. Suddenly his eye was caught by a report printed in inch-high letters: a postal strike had started in Paris. Kvachi dropped the newspaper and pondered the situation very deeply; for a long time he trembled with a hot creative fever. Then he scrawled a note in pencil and called for Beso: "Here's a list of my friends and acquaintances in London. Send them all a letter like this. I must have a reply from each one in a day's time. Read it ... You understand?"

Beso smiled: as if he didn't understand! The plan was simple and straightforward.

The very next day about sixty lords, gentlemen, and bankers received the following:

"Dear Lord (or Mr, or Sir) X., Tomorrow I have to send a rather large sum to my head office in Petersburg to cover all the costs that cannot be put off. I have most of this sum in hand. The rest I am transferring from my Paris manager. But today's newspapers inform me of a very regrettable fact: because of a strike the French post and telegraph are not working. This somewhat interferes with my accounts and hinders my usual financial operations.

"That would not matter, but you will understand that tomorrow or the day after the English postal system could also go on strike. Such a possibility forces me to ask, deeply respected Lord (Mr, or Sir) X, if I may benefit from your generous hospitality, trust, and friendship. Five thousand pounds sterling (to some he wrote three thousand, some—two, some—just one) will release me from an awkward situation. In any case, I shall give you a promissory note falling due in ten days' time. Today I am sending one of my secretaries to Paris with the money, because I fear that the strike may continue. From now on I shall hope for a chance to reward your generosity and hospitality as it deserves. I offer you in advance, dear Lord (Mr or Sir) X, my heartfelt gratitude for your help and my regret for any inconvenience.

"Please accept my sincere salutations and deepest respect.

"Irakli Bagration-Mukhransky, Prince and Aide-de-Camp to the Emperor of all Russia."

Kvachi's calculations proved accurate. About a dozen addressees were not reached in time, but the others received the letters and almost all of them gave him the money. Lord Brouxton personally visited Kvachi and gave him double what he asked. Lady Harvey seemed to understand Kvachi's predicament: she pawned the pearls and precious heirlooms Kvachi had given her, summoned him by telephone, and forcibly thrust the money into his hands with passionate caresses and generous affection. How could the poor lady know that this frenzy would be their last?

Beso and Kvachi sat down that evening and spent two hours counting the money. Then they packed a few things and called for the motor car. Beso explained to the hotel manager: "His highness is off to Birmingham to see the arrangements at a number of factories which he might buy. We'll be back the day after tomorrow, so we'll keep the rooms."

They went up and down London's narrow streets, and headed along the Thames towards the sea. The next day Kvachi and Beso turned up, not in Birmingham, but in Antwerp.

Jewels, a Madhouse, a Duel, a Motion Picture, and Many Heroic Deeds

From now on Kvachi Kvachantiradze, under a dozen different surnames, was racing round the world. Sometimes he was Prince Bagration, sometimes the Afghan emir's son, sometimes Count Tishkevich, sometimes a Persian Qajar prince. Who can assess or describe his sleight of hand, his versatile handiwork, his subtlety and astuteness?

In New York he hit upon a woman with wits and experience equal to his own. They began with a modest experiment. Kvachi went into a shop to buy diamonds; he chose half a dozen stones as big as hazelnuts. He tossed all of them in his hand to assess them. Then his new woman assistant came in and engaged the shop owner in conversation at the counter. Kvachi deftly dropped one of the diamonds, and it fell so softly on the carpet that nobody heard a sound. The woman moved her foot to cover the stone, then ended the conversation and left with the diamond stuck to the sole of her foot.

The shop owner noticed the disappearance of his precious stone and looked askance at Kvachi. Kvachi took umbrage and demanded that he be searched. He was taken to a side room and undressed. Then he received an apology: a distressed Kvachi was seen out to his car, with several thousand dollars in his jacket pocket, to soothe the place where his self-esteem had suffered, since a formal complaint of assault had been torn up and thrown away.

In the diamond-cutting city of Antwerp Kvachi sent his girlfriend to a newly opened private lunatic asylum.

"Do you know Monsieur Vermet?" she asked the asylum director.

"I'm afraid I don't. I'm new to Antwerp."

"Vermet is my father, the poor man's demented. He's obsessed with diamonds and pearls and raves about them. He has a small suitcase he won't let go of, he thinks it's stuffed with diamonds. Sometimes he goes so crazy that we have to use force to calm him. You must accept him as a patient here."

"With great pleasure, Madam."

"All the jewellery I had he's taken from me and put in that suitcase; he says he's going to open a shop. I warn you that he will fight very hard if anyone tries to take away the bag."

"That's nothing, we'll cope. Are you going to bring him yourself?"

"Yes, certainly: today or tomorrow."

Then this crafty woman went off to Monsieur Vermet's shop. She chose a fine pair of earrings, a large diadem, and a beautiful necklace of large pearls."

"How much does that come to?"

"That will be a hundred thousand ... This is sixty ... That is eighty."

They haggled: "Ninety is my final price."

The woman looked at her watch and gave in: "I must confess, Monsieur Vermet, that I'm getting engaged today. Papa has given me seventy thousand and he's letting me choose my presents myself. I like that necklace a lot. But I'm twenty thousand short. Papa won't grudge the money, he'll make it up, but I'm afraid of being too late. By the time I get home, get a cheque written, and go to the bank, the bank will be closed. See it from my point of view, and come with me."

Monsieur Vermet thought hard: he might miss out on a substantial profit.

"All right, let's go."

"Take the three pieces, perhaps Papa may choose the earrings or the diadem. I like the necklace, but you never know …"

Vermet put the chosen pieces in a little bag. They both got into a motor car and arrived at the asylum, which looked more like a palace than a madhouse.

They were met with respectful smiles: "Do come in … please sit down … it's beautiful weather … could you bear with me for a little?"

The woman behaved as if she were at home: she gave orders to various people and then went straight to the director's office. Monsieur Vermet was waiting in the drawing room.

"I've brought him … he's got my jewels in a little bag … I warn you, he'll resist and start raving. But take the bag off him."

"Don't worry, we're used to all that, we've had a lot of experience."

The director came into the drawing room with the woman.

"Monsieur Vermet, bonjour! It's very good to meet you … please come over here …" And Monsieur Vermet was led into a third room.

"Papa, how about my things?" the woman exclaimed as she snatched the bag from Vermet. Nobody could work out who this "papa" was: Vermet or the director.

Vermet was alarmed by the furnishings of this room and the servants' different clothing. He jumped back in confusion and clutched his bag, but the woman snatched it from his hand and rushed out. Vermet tried to pursue her, but the feeble old man was instantly seized by the director, who'd been warned in advance, and by a well-built employee.

"Let me go! Bandits! Robbers! My bag! My pearls! My diamonds!" Vermet shrieked, flapping about like a bird and trying to make for the door.

"Calm down, Monsieur Vermet, calm down! Your diamonds

will be safe … don't get so worked up, we're not bandits. I'm a doctor, let me introduce myself … you are in a clinic … you'll stay for a short while and then return to your family …"

"What? A doctor? A clinic? A lunatic asylum? Who's mad here, me or you? Aha, I understand, I understand … Let me go! Let me go! My diamonds! My jewels!"

"I told you to calm down, Monsieur Vermet. Your daughter's got your pearls."

"What? My daughter? Are you raving mad? What are you going on about? That scoundrel is your daughter, yours."

"Mine? I don't have a daughter."

"Nor do I. So … so …"

He suddenly realized what had happened and almost went genuinely mad: "Get it into your head, you lunatics and idiots: that pickpocket has tricked both of us … Get hold of her … Get hold of her … Catch up with her … Quick, quick!"

The director and his employees were seized by panic; it took five minutes babbling for Vermet and the director to tell each other everything. They quickly telephoned the police and private detectives, but it was too late: the earth had swallowed up Kvachi and the woman.

In Rome this same woman persuaded a dealer to take a lot of pearls and other jewels to her "fiancé" and her "father", who was in fact Kvachi.

"The prince will see you now."

The "prince's" daughter and the dealer sat down in his office. The woman took out the jewels and began inspecting them. Then a servant of the prince reminded the woman: "Marquis Palavacic is waiting for you."

"My fiancé! My God! I don't want him to see this present before the wedding."

In an instant she put the jewels in an iron safe which was fixed to the wall, and slipped the key into her pocket.

"Ask him to come in."

Kvachi entered, kissed his "fiancée" reverently and asked how she was. Then the servant looked in again.

"Princess, your father wants to see you for a moment."

"Forgive me … I'll be with you in a moment …" she said as she left.

Two minutes later the "Marquis Palavacic", Kvachi in fact, also left. The house was enveloped in the silence of the grave. Ten minutes passed, then fifteen, then twenty … The dealer became fidgety, he got up, moved about, coughed several times, then went into the next room.

There was nobody there.

He looked into another room. There was nobody there, either. He went back to the adjacent room which was next to the drawing room, where he and the woman had been waiting for the prince. All he saw was that the doors of the wall safe were open. He looked into the safe. He was thunderstruck: these were the doors to the safe in which the woman had locked up the jewels she had taken from the first room.

The panicking and maddened dealer tore his hair, ran round the empty room, and shouted: "Police! Help! I've been robbed! I've been fleeced."

The earth had swallowed up Kvachi and his "fiancée."

In Vienna Kvachi targeted a rich Jewish baron. He jostled the Jewish baron as if by accident in a club, but called out: "Careful! Manners! Oaf!"

"Sorry … I … I …"

Kvachi interrupted him by flicking two fingers under his chin. There was an uproar and general commotion, which ended with Kvachi and the baron exchanging addresses. The next day Kvachi's seconds, Beso and Chipi Chipuntiradze went to see the Jewish baron and informed him: "This is going to end in bloodshed."

Then they added, casually: "Don't do anything hasty, baron.

Don't send your seconds yet ... Wait until tomorrow ... The Afghan prince is a famous crack shot ... he can shoot down a fly ... If you want, you can see for yourself ... Today at five o'clock the prince will be at the Prater shooting range: send someone to see for himself. We'll visit you again this evening and have a talk. Perhaps we can avoid bloodshed, that is, if you agree that ..."

"There has to be a duel!"

"Yes indeed, there will definitely be a duel, but ... things could be arranged so that ... there's no bloodshed ... Give it some thought ... We'll be back at nightfall ... We wish you good day."

From five to six Kvachi used his pistol to demolish the Prater shooting range. The man the baron secretly sent came back and convinced him that the Afghan prince really could kill a fly in mid-flight.

"The prince gives the word of honor of an Emir's son," Beso told the rich baron that evening, "that he swears by Muhammad's holy name that he won't spill your blood, if ... if you arrange to fire two or three times in the air, then be reconciled and become good friends."

"Let's get to the point. How much do you want?"

"Your life is beyond price. You're said to have ten million. One million will be enough for us."

"I'd prefer to leave Vienna today."

"You can't get away from the disgrace wherever you go. We'll let the whole country know of your cowardice."

"We Jews have never boasted of our heroism, and a man's good name isn't worth such expense."

"Don't forget that you are a baron of the Austro-Hungarian empire: *noblesse oblige*.

"Let's stop this. A hundred thousand."

"Nine hundred with blood and eight hundred without."

"I don't understand"

"You will inflict a slight wound on the Afghan prince."

"I still don't understand!"

"The duel will end with the prince being slightly wounded ... how we arrange that is up to us."

The baron rather liked the idea of a duel with blood: "If the duel really ends with the prince losing blood, then I'll go to two hundred thousand."

"Eight hundred!"

"I can't go above two hundred."

"Then we expect your seconds tomorrow at the duel. Good evening."

"Wait a bit. Three hundred, that's the most I can do. And that's on condition that the prince's blood is shed."

They finally agreed on half a million and took half the sum in advance. Kvachi and the rich baron agreed terms in writing.

Two days later, early in the morning, Beso scratched Kvachi's right arm, bandaged the wound, and took him off to Schönbrünn forest where the baron and his seconds were ready for them.

"Fine, begin! One, two ... three!"

The baron and Kvachi calmly fired their pistols. Kvachi threw down his pistol, clutched his right arm, and tore off the bandage before the doctor could get to him. The baron puffed himself up with conceit.

"I wounded the heir to the Afghan throne ... I got him in the arm ... I've taught him to be polite!" the baron is still exclaiming to this day.

That evening the baron and Kvachi settled accounts, returned each other's signed notes, and held a reconciliation banquet in the same club. The baron was even more conceited and told his friends:

"Thank God my friend the prince got off so lightly. Prince, let's drink Bruderschaft. You've been lucky ... Yes, I tell you, you must be a lucky man. I aimed at your heart first, but I felt sorry for such a fine man and ... aimed at your arm, and I hit it."

Kvachi smiled, drank, and every now and again clapped the

baron on the shoulder in a friendly way.

Time passed, and the heir to the Afghan throne got through this money, too. He was in trouble, deep trouble. Because of the trouble he had another attack of creative fever. Like a woman giving birth, he sweated and strained for a long time, before devising a neat plot. First he knotted the threads to plait a net, got everything ready, and then went to see the manager of a bank:

"Let me introduce myself. I'm a representative of Pathé films, and I'm making a film about a bank robbery. I've got heavily involved: we've chosen the bank, and we've got the actors. We want you and your employees to play a part, you will immortalise yourselves on screen and you'll be paid for it."

The manager liked the idea: "Very good ... we're grateful ..."

He called in his colleagues and told them the news. They all became eager, being secretly convinced of their artistic talent.

"Tomorrow or the day after we'll tell you what to do and hold a little rehearsal," Kvachi said. "Yes, in fact, we'll tell the police, too, in fact I'll come in person and talk to them."

The manager reached for the telephone: "Hello! Monsieur Grade, is that you? This is to inform you that our bank is going to be robbed tomorrow or the day after."

"What did you say? Who? What are you saying?"

"Calm down, dear friend, calm down. They're making a motion picture ... Yes, yes, you'll be in it too. Pathé's manager is coming to see you right now."

The next day Kvachi and the police inspector did the rounds of the policemen in the area near the bank. The inspector told each one of them:

"This man is shooting a cinema film about a bank robbery. They're deliberately causing mayhem in and around the bank. You'll be in the picture too, but don't move a step and don't try to stop the mayhem until this man gives you the order ... Understand? Tell the others, too ... Order people not to be alarmed and not to chase the actors. Fine, good men!"

Then Kvachi and his suite entered the bank and set up his camera.

"Right, action! Take your places ... Put all you've got into it. When the robbers come rushing in, everyone has to be scared ... You hide under the table ... You run into the manager's office ... That's right, there, over there ... You won't have time to lock up the till: raise your arms and open your mouth with fear ... That's all ... We'll film you chasing the robbers in the street ... Right, take your places ... You move to the left, and you—to the right ... Don't look outside, turn your head this way ..."

Then Kvachi went into the manager's office: "This robber will rush in to your office and aim a pistol at you, you'll be too frightened to move. He'll cut the telephone and ..."

"The pistol isn't loaded, is it?"

"No, don't worry ... Well, let's begin with this scene. First robber, start."

Chipi Chipuntiradze rushed into the manager's office, frightened the manager to death, and actually cut the telephone wires. The cameraman calmly went on turning the film.

"That's the end of the manager's scene. Now let's go to the cashier."

The performers went to the main hall and went on shooting.

"Right, take your places! Everyone, sit where you're supposed to be. Now we're filming the till. The others will get their turn next. Right, second, third, and fourth robbers, start!"

Chipi Chipuntiradze, Ladi Chikinjiladze, and Beso Shikia attacked the till. Kvachi was running about, shouting:

"Raise your hands, raise them! Open your mouth, you! Don't smile! Turn your back, turn your back! Beso, take it out! Chipi, rake it in! Ladi, very good! Right, run for it, lads! Cashier, turn your back, turn your back!"

While Kvachi was giving orders, the cameraman was turning the camera, the cashiers were acting, and everyone else was smiling stupidly, Chipi and Ladi really had raked and packed the money and run for it. The manager and some of the others began to have their doubts; they gradually got uneasy, then alarmed and panicky:

"They've taken the money ... They've actually taken it ... Hey, help us!"

The cameraman pointed his camera at the panicking employees and Kvachi, delighted by their acting, yelled:

"Yes, that's good! That's good! Beautiful! Excellent! ... Pure genius! Now we'll film the street scene. Robbers, follow me!"

The manager picked up the now useless telephone, the other employees chased after Kvachi, but two robbers blocked them in the doorway: "Stop, or else!"

"Help us! They've robbed the bank! Arrest them! Lock them up!"

"We know, we know," the policeman smiled serenely into their moustaches, not moving a muscle. "We know you're acting ... We haven't had our orders from this man."

"I'm telling you they really have robbed us."

"Go tell it to the marines, I know my job."

Finally they were persuaded of the truth and went into action, but ...

They're still looking for the Pathé film director.

Easy come, easy go: Kvachi spent all the money and was down to his last penny. There were no big jobs, and the little jobs brought little in.

Occasionally Kvachi got a letter from Silibistro. Silibistro wrote: "Dear son Kvachi, I can't understand what makes you keep running God knows where. Come back to your parents and to Rasputin, who's back from Jerusalem. I hear that the holy man is asking after you and other people are looking for you. As for us, we've aged, my Kvachi, and we'd like to see you a little in our old age, otherwise it feels as if we never had a child. Pupi and Notio cry every day; they're waiting for you, there's no sign of you, why couldn't you send a letter in all these years?"

Silibistro wrote a lot more and he wanted an answer. But Kvachi had no time and he didn't get round to sending a single letter.

Kvachi learned by chance that Tania had settled in Baden-Baden, and soon he too turned up there. He swept away the ashes covering their old friendship, washed off the rust and the cobwebs, and by his enthusiasm and persistence won back the old trust and the position he once held.

But how could a free soaring eagle of this world be satisfied with just board, lodging, and clothing? Kvachi needed a great deal, a very great deal of money. But Tania, having had her share of grief and experience, allotted Kvachi just a monthly allowance and not a single rouble extra. Kvachi tried hard to get round this aging female, but this divine woman turned out to have a heart of stone and will of iron.

"Fine!" an enraged Kvachi said at one point, telling Beso: "Beso, you have a few days to learn the art of photography."

A week later Beso reported to Kvachi: "I've learnt photography and bought a camera."

They sat down to a whispered conversation.

One day, when Kvachi and Tania were carried away by mutual affection, Tania suddenly became alarmed and afraid: "The door curtain moved … What's going on?"

"You're mistaken. I expect it was the breeze. Calm down, my love."

After that Tania saw nothing of Kvachi; instead it was Beso who came to see her the next day: "We need money, and we need it badly."

"Who are you?"

"That doesn't matter, but …you might well guess. Yesterday, when the curtain moved in Kvachantiradze's room …"

"Get out of here!"

"All right, I'm going, but there's a memento I must leave you." And he left her a photograph.

Tania gave a little shriek and covered her face with her hands; she blushed, she was burning hot with shame.

"Good day to you."

"Bear with me ... wait a bit ... What do you want? How much are you asking for?"

"Three hundred thousand now, and forty thousand a month."

"That's not possible ... Even if I sold everything, I couldn't pay that."

"We wouldn't be depriving you of anything. Think about it. I'll drop in tomorrow."

It took a month for Tania to sell her estate. Then she handed Beso three hundred thousand, received the negative, and vanished from Baden-Baden. But she couldn't possibly evade Kvachi's eye and nose. In Italy, or in Spain, or even in Egypt she would find waiting for her the same photograph, with menacing threats and demands for millions. Tania gave him all she could, ten times getting from Beso his word of honor that he no longer had the photograph or the negative.

When her money was finally exhausted and her hopes were gone, she vanished from sight for ever. Some said that she had gone to Tasmania, others to Ceylon, others named a convent on Mount Athos.

Kvachi spent some time searching for his milch cow, but, unable to find her, plaited new nets and set them.

Then World War One began. Kvachi was immediately transformed: he changed fronts, invented new nets and traps, disguised his face to seem a different animal, put on the armor the times required, and girded himself with new weapons.

CHAPTER FIVE

A Secret Obligation and the Return to Russia

"Kvachi, what do you think? Just because someone killed an Austrian archduke, will there be a war?" Beso asked.

"I've been thinking about that all day. If those two countries stand up to each other, the whole world will get involved."

"Read the newspaper, will you? Russia is backing Serbia, and Germany is backing Austria."

Kvachi read the paper and paced the room. He flared his nostrils for a while; he could not settle. Then he turned to his friends, prophesying:

"Beso, Ladi, Chipi. Remember my words and let history have them later: before two weeks are out, Russia will punch Germany in the nose, and Germany will do the same to Russia. Then war will break out and the wrath of God will be let loose. England, France, Romania, and Italy will take Russia's side … Yes, yes! Italy will oppose Germany and side with England and France, they say. Austria, Bulgaria, and Turkey will join Germany. In the end, America will get involved and the whole world will be covered in blood. If I should perish, let history know what I said. Well, friends, we really do need to keep our wits, to be vigilant and careful."

He spoke, got dressed, and went to the Berlin stock exchange, which was like a madhouse. Some had staked their happiness and their property on war, others on peace. Shares, bonds, and thousands of valuable and valueless papers were somersaulting through the air: some landed at the top of the ladder, others plunged into the deepest pit.

Kvachi bet on war: he had an eye on metal and munitions

shares. He seized the moment to join a secretive group which was lowering the price of these shares and bought cheaply Schneider-Creusot, Skoda, Armstrong, and Krupp shares. He used up almost all his available cash.

Then he joined a crowd of three hundred thousand and yelled furiously in the streets, the newspapers, the coffeehouses, and salons: "Nach Paris! Nach Moskau!"

A few days later he left Germany for France and wore out his voice there, too: "À Berlin, à Berlin."

After that he returned to Russia and yelled there, wherever he could: "To Berlin! To Constantinople!"

Time passed. A spark lit by one man somewhere in Sarajevo set the whole world ablaze. Just one princely bullet caused such a whirlwind and storm to break out in every corner of the world that its thunder reached the very heavens. A drop of blood turned into a river, then broadened into a boundless sea: twenty or thirty million trained warriors set upon each other with fury and frenzy. The rest of mankind abandoned everything else to back up soldiers stretched over a thousand kilometers and to join in the service of blood-loving Mars, while all with malice and reverence yelled: "God is with us!"

They crossed themselves with blood-stained fingers, begging the Lord of their souls to join their military alliance: "Death to savages! Victory to civilization. Victory to liberty, fraternity, and equality of the peoples."

The angel of death had so far got wet only up to the ankles in human blood, but soon he was wading in it up to the knees, and then he entered the red lake waist-deep, until finally he swam into a bottomless whirlpool in which he would splash about for five whole years.

Both earth and hell had turned deaf and blind, as they drowned countless human beings, white and black, red and yellow, from all corners of the earth, rich and poor, men and women, in blood and tears, with wailing and lamenting, bellowing and shrieking.

And Kvachi Kvachantiradze with his little guild also swam and moved in the sea of blood and tears, the storm of fire, the vortex of global grief; he ran and flew about, embittered, frenzied, and he fought, not sparing himself: "Sell Schneider-Croesus shares! Buy Krupp! Mortgage the Armstrongs. Get rid of the Skoda. Bring down Cunard Lines. Stockpile sugar! Get the price of flour up!"

French law confronted him: "Kvachi, enlist in the army!"

Kvachi in the army? Kvachi at war? At Verdun or in the Ardennes? Were they out of their minds? Who for, what for? For the French? What harm had the Germans ever done him? In what way was Paris any better than Vienna or Berlin? What had it to do with Kvachi if either of them went under or soared up? Suppose a bomb fell right by Kvachi, or a bullet whizzed past and spilled his blood! Were they out of their minds?

Because a trip to London was too dangerous, because he'd already kvachified the city, he and his companions headed for Manchester. But soon the law, even in England, caught up with him: "A fit adult male! Everyone to the army!"

"Beso, they're out of their minds here, too. Right then, to Rome."

But it turned out all the countries were now out of their minds. Italy soon took action and Kvachi once again heard the crazed yells: "Adult fit male! Everyone to the army!"

They're not going to get you! Kvachi hasn't yet gone so mad as to shed his blood for the macaronis.

"Beso, to Geneva."

Finally Kvachi had reached an oasis of peace: he climbed the alpine peaks and from this island of peace he calmly and serenely looked down on the raging fire of war, telling himself several times: "Remember what I said to you in Berlin: it's all come true."

Finally a letter from Rasputin reached him after traveling all over Russia: "My brother Apollonchik, why are you hanging about that wicked Europe? Come back here, it's boring without you, and there's a lot of business. You'll find peace here, calm, fame, money, and divine grace. And bring Elena and Tania along with you. That's what I want. Yes, me. Grigory. Watch out, don't delay. Yes, Grigory."

Frightened but pleased by this letter, the Russian ambassador managed without delay to arrange for Kvachi an uneventful journey by land and sea. He begged Kvachi with a grimace:

"Drop a few words about me to the Holy Father and to the minister Sazonov. Give them my sincere greetings. God grant you a safe journey."

Beso managed to track down Elena and bring her back.

Who knows if it was a person's hand or providence's grace that arranged what occurred on the day Kvachi boarded a ship: immediately, Kvachi came face to face with Rebecca on deck. "Rebecca, my Rebby!"

"Apollo, my beloved!"

They embraced,; they rekindled an extinguished fire, and reheated their cooled blood. Their parting was something that neither Kvachi mentioned to Rebecca, nor she to him. From the depths of the ship emerged Isaac Idelsohn.

"I'm bankrupt and I'm finished," fretted Isaac. "I'm going to Petersburg to stay with my uncle Gintz."

"Gintz! Gintz is your uncle? Why didn't you tell me before? What: do I know him? Of course I know him. We used to work together."

In the ship's dark corners Kvachi laid hands on Rebecca several times, but his Rebby persisted in responding: "No, no ... It's out of the question here. Let's get away for a day when we get to Stockholm and ... Don't be so woe-begotten, we'll be there in a day or two, and ..."

Accompanied by cruisers, the ship arrived in Bergen. Everyone changed to the train, crossed Norway, and went to Stockholm.

Kvachi had only just changed his clothes in the hotel when

Idelsohn and a German came in. They took a good look at the room, locked the doors, sat down and made Kvachi sit down too, then had a quiet conversation with him. They chatted conspiratorially for two hours, constantly looking at the corridor. They examined the whole area and then went on with the "business' they had begun. Finally they came to terms, gave each other masses of instructions, and parted. When they had left the room, Idelsohn came back for a moment and told Kvachi:

"From now on, you and I don't know each other, and we never did. The only person you know is your French teacher, Rebecca. Don't forget anything, or ... you know! We'll communicate with each other through Rebby. Goodbye."

The same evening Isaac Idelsohn sent Kvachi a message via Rebecca. Kvachi took on a task so complex and difficult that he needed all night to listen to what Isaac had to tell him and to take Rebby's instructions. The next morning Kvachi met some Georgians in Stockholm. They whispered a secret to him: "It's better for us if Germany wins."

"That's impossible. That's treason."

"Then work from outside, perhaps we'll get autonomy, like Poland."

"Autonomy won't do Georgia any good."

"Then what's the point of all the blood we've shed?"

"It's for greater Russia. If Russia wins, we win too. As for the rest—language, national culture, political power—that's just a chimera. Why be so crazy about tiny Georgia, just a handful of people? We're choking in that pit, there's no room to spread our wings, no air to breathe. Look at great Russia. A sixth of the globe, two hundred million people. If you have strength, talent, or ambition, spread your wings and soar in boundless space."

They went on whispering for some time in this safe house. Finally, Kvachi gave them cause for hope:

"Don't take sides. Be cautious and submissive. Don't annoy

anyone, don't antagonize anybody. I'll get news to you, and you inform me about everything. Change your password once a month. Go safely."

What he really thought was: "Who knows, maybe something might come of all this."

"Brother Apollonchik! Sister Elena!" Rasputin, overjoyed, said two weeks later as he clasped the two of them to his breast.

After not seeing one another for two years, it took two days to ask after one another and to relate their adventures. Kvachi told Rasputin a lot about the madness, immorality, and depravity afflicting rotten Europe. He emphasized church and spiritual affairs, although he hadn't heard or read a word about either in Europe.

There was a great commotion of joyful shrieks in Silibistro's family.

"Was that right, you scoundrel? Aren't you ashamed of yourself?" Silibistro reproached Kvachi.

"Son, it's wrong to forget your mother ..." said Pupi, as she clasped her estranged son to her heart.

"Do they know about your insurance business?" Kvachi finally asked Silibistro.

"The whole country's heard about it. I've been hung out to dry!" grumbled Silibistro.

"I'll pay *Salamander* ten thousand roubles and the interest, and that'll be the end of it," decided Kvachi.

While Rasputin and Elena sated each other until they were bored, Kvachi once again picked up the threads of his affairs and re-knotted them. After two weeks or so in Petersburg, he had nicely spun and woven a new wide net, cleared the old paths and canals, and blazed new ones. He got round conscription by dressing up in a "home guard" uniform, putting spurs on his boots, a military tag on his hat, and gold epaulettes on his shoulders, with aiguillettes too: a ramrod-back prince was back again on the boulevards, with the horses, motor cars, bankers, restaurants, courtiers, powers-that-be, and society beauties, who had after two years become even more numerous and attractive.

The "Good Samaritan" and Kvachi's New Success

One day an enormous new office opened on Nevsky Prospekt: it had a gold shop-sign: "The Good Samaritan Society for Aid to War Wounded and War Dead."

Its president and patron Kvachi Kvachantiradze had nine secretaries, the same number of assistants, and up to two hundred employees, chosen from the same source, the "home guards." Apart from the handsome mechanics, there was one woman involved: Kvachi's secretary and French teacher Rebecca Idelsohn.

Kvachi had gathered all his old friends, except Gabo and Sedrak who had been marched off as rank and file soldiers to capture Constantinople. Later, Kvachi got both of them released, because they were badly needed specialists in his complex and "patriotic" business: he was expecting to see them any day. Finally, that day dawned and they, too, joined him.

"Well, prince, have they made you a general?"

They embraced one another and that same night celebrated the family reunion in the *Arcadia*.

Every day Kvachi issued a hundred orders: "Let the second corpus have a hundred horses ... Give the Don district army a hundred wagons of barley. Get two hundred wagons of flour to Warsaw ... Give ten thousand sets of underwear to the fourth army ... Give quartermaster Ivanov a hundred thousand ... Sell! Buy! Sell off! Mortgage! Demand!"

Kvachi was swelling with profits. He often added a zero to the accounts that he received. He worked all day, but devoted his evenings to Rasputin, society beauties, and dignitaries.

Sometimes he handed Rebecca a little bit of information coded on cigarette paper, and would get from her a short order. Rebecca stuck any message given to her in her hair, which she wore piled up. She then left.

Sometimes Rasputin was depressed and dispirited. He prayed a lot, he complained to God, he could not rest and was often in tears.

"My esteemed teacher, is something bothering you, is something grieving you?" Kvachi enquired of him once.

"Brother Apollonchik! My heart tells me something bad. God refuses to bless this war. We are going to lose it, we shall perish, we shall be destroyed. God, save us from the devil. God, forgive us our sins. Apollonchik, pray: you pray, as well! The whole of Russia has to pray. The churches must stay open day and night, services must be held every day. The Lord God must bless our victory, or else … Though … Apollonchik, when the war started I fell on my knees to the Tsar, I warned him and I begged him with tears in my eyes: 'Nikolasha, don't make war! You'll ruin your people, you'll destroy Russia, you'll lose the throne, you'll perish and leave us to perish too.' At first he refused to listen to me: my advice didn't get through to him. The impure and the crazy turned out to be more powerful than us. We stood to one side, because we were afraid of being reproached; now we are being blamed for their defeat and their incompetence. Things are going very badly, Apollonchik. Our army is being defeated. Defeat leads to terrible things: revolution, anarchy, mass slaughter, famine, the break-up of Russia, and the destruction of the throne. Prince Meshchersky, the one they call the old fox, is the cleverest man in Russia. The way he talks is like the raven of fate cawing. My whole body has the creeps and my head is full of black fog. The devil in hell arranged the alliance of holy Russia with infidel France. What do we have in common with those people? They don't believe in God, they have no morals, they don't even have a king. Depraved, rotten, and degenerate people is what they are. Yesterday I was praying all day and all night and I begged the Lord again: 'Lord, Lord, cleanse my soul of evil, forgive me my sins and open the doors of the future to me.' The icon closed its eyes and spouted tears again. My icon is always crying, Apollonchik, it's crying. That's a sign that Russia is going to perish. Apollonchik, I'm just an ignorant peasant, I don't even know how to read and write properly. I'm uneducated, but God gave me good peasant wits, a penetrating eye, and sharpened instincts, so I understand this country better than many learned men. Apollonchik, remember my words: if the war doesn't stop right now, we shall perish and Russia will be destroyed. Come, Apollonchik, come and let's pray to the Lord again and plead with Him for Russia."

Kvachi agreed with Rasputin utterly and promised to work for peace. But he felt and saw only too well that it was premature, even dangerous to be concerned for peace, because the mangy, sharp-fanged bloody dog of war had found so many unexpected supporters and allies and blazed such a trail, that an embittered and blinded dominant generation would rather kill itself than break its oath or betray its country.

Rasputin had moved to live on the English Embankment. His influence and power had doubled, although he was always fretting that nobody trusted him any more or asked his opinion.

Once, when Rasputin and Kvachi were out walking, at three points various passersby would fall at Rasputin's feet and kiss his hand, embrace his coat-tails, and piously implore him: "Jesus Christ, our Savior! Pray for our sins. God will listen to you. Pray, for we are doomed."

"In the name of the Father, the Son, and the Holy Ghost. Have faith, brothers and sisters, for the time of Christ's coming is near. Be patient and remember his suffering." Then Rasputin dried his tears and turned to Kvachi: "Our cause is ruined ... We shall perish."

A few days later Rasputin showed Kvachi a telegram written

by the Tsaritsa and sent to Rasputin, then in Siberia: she could no longer bear to pass a day without him. She was constantly suffering from fainting fits and nervous fevers, and the heir to the throne was having more frequent bleeds from anywhere he hurt himself. The best doctors were powerless to help. When Rasputin got back from Siberia, the Tsaritsa calmed down. The Tibetan doctor Badmaev, whom Rasputin brought with him, stopped the heir's bleeding. From then on the Tsar and Tsaritsa remained in Rasputin's hands and would not let him or Badmaev out of their sight.

Then Rasputin's enemies again tried to get rid of him. In response, Rasputin went to the palace and in the presence of the highest in the land berated the Tsar and Tsaritsa: "I know that my enemies are digging my grave. Don't listen to them, don't lose sight of me, otherwise in six months you will lose the heir to the throne and the throne itself."

The Tsaritsa knelt down by Rasputin, exclaiming: "We can't part with you, holy man! You're our only protector and friend. A blessing, Holy Father, a blessing!" After that nobody now dared refuse Rasputin anything. There was hardly ever a day that he didn't speak or write to the Tsaritsa: "Dismiss so-and-so … appoint … transfer … move … promote … demote …"

The Tsar took no step without asking the Tsaritsa; she wouldn't move or make the most minor decision without Rasputin's say-so.

Once Rasputin and General Sukhomlinov visited Kvachi's office and with great ceremony, gratitude and prayers and blessings and loud kisses, conferred on him the Tsar's gracious honor: a cross and a medal for Kvachi, and a cross for each one of his colleagues.

That very day Beso Shikia brought two large books published abroad and generously illustrated. First, Kvachi responded to Rasputin and Sukhomlinov with a fiery, lachrymose speech, then he presented each of them with a book. They perused the books; one was entitled: "General Sukhomlinov's Life and Achievements".

The other was entitled: "The Life and Achievements of the Holy Father Grigory". Both were printed in 72-point fonts and published by their Imperial Majesties' Aide-de-Camp Napoleon Apollonovich Kvachantiradze.

There was another burst of ceremonial words, gratitude, embraces, and loud applause. When General Sukhomlinov realized that Kvachi had published the same books in English and French and had sent several thousand of them to Europe, he swore brotherhood to Kvachi and promised to return the favor.

Then Rasputin told Kvachi:

"Apollonchik, listen carefully: our enemies are trying to convince France that I have asked for the war to be stopped immediately. It's true that this is what I believe, but *papa* and *mama* want me to reassure the French ambassador. Take this letter and give it to the ambassador."

He sat down, strained himself, and scrawled:

"God let us live according to Russia's example, not the example of a deplorable country. Any moment God will show his strength. The army will see His force. Victory with you and of you, Rasputin."

This mystical raving was given by Kvachi to the French ambassador Maurice Paléologue. Nobody—not Kvachi, nor the ambassador, nor anyone—could make sense of the letter's contents.

That same evening Kvachi settled up finally with the journalist Knulman for the biographies of Sukhomlinov and Rasputin.

A few days later Rasputin and Kvachi entered an important person's palace, which had been turned into a military hospital, and handed presents to the wounded soldiers.

In a large ward Kvachi and the French ambassador met.

"May I introduce the two of you? Grigory Rasputin ... the French ambassador Maurice Paléologue."

Rasputin suddenly turned red and became embarrassed:

"I very much wanted to see you. Apollonchik, translate for me. Russia is falling apart. The people are being crucified. It's time we stopped, or we too will be finished, or the people will finish us off. Yes indeed, it's high time. It's me, Grigory Rasputin, saying this. Yes, me."

Then he suddenly fell upon Paléologue, clasped him to his breast and, without waiting for an answer, rushed out, yelling and waving his arms:

"What's politics got to do with it? I'm a peasant and I like to be direct, like a peasant. This is no time for politics, when the people are about to stone us to death. Peace! Peace quickly, or else we shall perish!"

How a Major Military Job was "Pulled"

Time passed. Rasputin was back in power. Kvachi was a frequent guest of the minister Sukhomlinov, since his *Good Samaritan* was closely linked to the war department, to which he gave countless pictures, horses, sets of underwear, and a lot of military material. In any case, thanks to the Sukhomlinov biography and a common friendship with Rasputin, Kvachi and General Sukhomlinov had become firm friends, almost brothers.

As always, Kvachi held in thrall numerous newspapers which used any pretext, or none at all, to puff him and the war minister, their abilities, their inspired activities, their prescience, and their fabulous organization.

As a sign of his gratitude and profound trust, Sukhomlinov gave Kvachi two more crosses and told him:

"Napoleon Apollonovich! We have a very important matter of state to entrust to you, and there's nobody we can rely on but you. You are to go to America and order from their factories high-power weapons, bullets and explosives and bombs. Do you agree?"

"This is something that I find hard to do, very hard, but there's no way I'll avoid serving my motherland: tell me what to do."

"But remember that we are entrusting you with the most

important and dangerous job. Nobody may know about it, or ..."

"You watch out, Apollonchik," added Rasputin, wagging a crooked finger under Kvachi's nose.

Kvachi left for America a few days later: he had instructions, money, and a stack of thick, wax-sealed packets. At Stockholm station he was met by a general he knew: "You are going to America on a secret mission ..."

There was a whispered conversation, a prolonged argument, and a session of bargaining. German forgers sat down to work on Kvachi's packets, copying them so well that nobody could tell the copy from the original. There was only one minor alteration made in the transcription: the mathematical sums were diminished a little. The next day Kvachi was handed back his packets, wax-sealed as before, together with a cheque; he was wished a pleasant journey, while the agents set off for Berlin.

A British cruiser got Kvachi to New York a week later; there the Russian military attaché invited factory owners over. They negotiated and came to terms. When Kvachi signed the contract and laid hands on yet another cheque, he could breathe freely and get down to his own business.

Very cheaply he bought a dozen ships and loaded them with provisions and military material. He sent the ships to Archangel, to the Russian military department. He himself toured nearby cities: Philadelphia, Washington, Boston, and Chicago, doing "business' in each one of them. He gave their chilly women a taste of hot Georgian blood, then he crossed the whole of America, traversed the Pacific Ocean, looked in on Japan, tried out the geishas, and got back to Petersburg via the interminable Siberian railway.

He brought back expensive presents for Rasputin, Elena, his friends, and the men of power: he put them all in his debt and tied them even closer to himself. He presented the bill to General Sukhomlinov:

"They had weapons and bombs of this quantity and quality

ready to sell as a lot to other buyers. I paid a little over the odds. But we are going to get half of the goods immediately, and the other half will come three months later. We've gained time."

The huge amount of rotten goods from America was bought by the military department.

Kvachi was sent to Tsarskoye two weeks later. In the presence of Sukhomlinov, Rasputin, Friedrichs, and many dignitaries, senior figures and prominent persons, the Tsar and Tsaritsa gave Kvachi their deepest thanks, granted him a Lord-in-waiting's uniform, and hung three more different crosses round his neck.

At dinner the Tsar had Kvachi sit next to him and tell him all his news. Kvachi loosened his tongue and related what he had seen or not seen, heard, or not heard, with fire, wit, clarity, and courtesy. Finally, after a pause, he lowered his voice:

"I know that your Majesty would find it agreeable to know the opinion of a prominent American about this terrible war."

"It would be very agreeable, very."

"I saw a lot of ministers and the presidents, the present and the former. I met them all privately and informally: Taft, Roosevelt, Wilson, Hughes, Edison, Morgan, Rockefeller, and a lot of ministers, billionaires, senators, and prominent people. To put it in a nutshell, they all very much want us to be victorious, but …"

"But?"

"But … I can't hide anything from my Tsar, it seems to be my absolute duty to tell the truth, even if it is unpleasant. Almost all of them very seriously insisted that this war will go on for one or two years more …"

"God almighty!"

"Victory will certainly come to the allies, but if Russia … if Russia can't hold out to the end …"

Everyone stopped talking: they now frowned. But Rasputin caught Kvachi's eyes to signal his encouragement.

The Tsar became deeply pensive, bowed his head, and didn't

touch his food any more. There was a silence in the hall, as if it were somebody's funeral wake. Then all rose without a word. Only the Tsaritsa gave Kvachi a look of gratitude and offered him her elegant hand, which Kvachi, overcome with shyness, eagerly kissed.

"Good man, Apollonchik, good man!" said Rasputin approvingly. "Now the cross of St George would look very good on you. I don't want you to go away, but what can I do? Go to the front for a week, stroll about there, and come back with a St George's cross, what do you say to that?"

What could Kvachi say? He was well aware that if Rasputin or Sukhomlinov wanted, he could fire a gun just once, a hundred kilometers from the front, and get a St George's cross round his neck for it.

"Don't be afraid, Apollonchik!" Rasputin ordered him reassuringly. "General Sukhomlinov will write to the commander-in-chief that you're to be looked after like the apple of his eye. Hang about not too close, not too far. Get a sniff of the front, fire a gun, and come back."

That was agreed. On these conditions Kvachi would dare to earn himself a St George's cross.

Silibistro's hope and consolation now headed for Georgia.

Doctor Qoranashvili bumped into Kvachi at the Petersburg station; the doctor, too, was off to the Ottoman front. He was wearing a military doctor's uniform. They asked after each other. Kvachi invited Qoranashvili to his compartment. It took them a week to get to Erzurum. All that time Qoranashvili never spoke a word about medicine or about anything similar: for seven days he stuffed Kvachi with archaeology and history. From morning to nightfall he buzzed like a wasp in Kvachi's ear:

"Urartu ... the Nairs ... the Alarodians ... Phasis ... ancient Erzurum ... Nicopse ... Archaeopolis ... the Hittites ... the Sumerians ... Adarnase ... the ancient Ingush and Chechens ... Odrzqe and

Gurji-Bogaz."

In the end Kvachi confused all the names and all the eras and blurted out: "Oh, I can't understand a word. History's never been my thing."

Kvachi's Amazing Transformation, and a Lost Battle Won

After ten days Kvachi reached the Russian army in Turkey and presented himself to military headquarters. The staff officers were no fools and immediately realized who Kvachi was and why he'd come for a fortnight or so.

One week was spent partying. The senior staff officer and Kvachi kept to the motto: "You scratch my back, and I'll scratch yours." They supported each other, then the staff commander handed Kvachi over to a drunken divisional general, gave them their separate instructions, and sent them off to the front. Kvachi brought with him three wagons loaded with wine, brandy, vodka, and all sorts of edible supplies. They were accompanied by his faithful followers—Gabo Chkhubishvili, Ladi Chikinjiladze—and two experienced Russian soldiers.

They traveled for two days on horseback.

The road was busy with carriages, lorries, carts, cavalry and infantry, artillery and cases of shells, as well as the wounded and the sick.

Everyone slouched along lazily, reluctantly, often resting at the side of the road. The drunken general was generous with his elaborately foul curses, he gave occasional orders, sending couriers in various directions.

One evening they entered the burnt-out ruins of a town. Every one at headquarters worked until late, receiving and issuing orders. Then they sat down to a generous banquet.

Eventually they got round to the drinks, became merry and livened up, becoming so heated that they sang "May you live forever", "Let's drink to that" and the Russian soldier's song "My very last day", as well as many other martial songs and songs of consolation. As they sang, every now and again they pointed their fists at invisible Ottomans, uttered words of wrath and threats, and with stiffened jaws growled: "To Istanbul! We'll annihilate them! Hit hard! Go for it!"

After midnight, the thoroughly drunk divisional general announced: "Right, friends, let's get some sleep. A fighter who hasn't had a night's sleep is useless. I drink the final toast to tomorrow's victory. Hurrah!"

"Hurrah!" they all roared with gritted jaws, smashed their glasses, and went their separate ways.

Kvachi went to bed without undressing. He shut his eyes and pondered the forthcoming battle. A devil stirred in his heart:

"There's going to be a battle tomorrow ... There'll be bloodshed ... They'll be mutual slaughtering and mutilation ... Some will lose an arm, some a leg, some other body parts. I could be left wounded on the battlefield. Nobody will come to my aid. I'll die of hunger and thirst ... A burning-hot piece of shrapnel could get me in the stomach, or a bullet could go through me, I could be hacked down with a sabre, or a bayonet might stab me in the side ..."

Kvachi could now really feel the pain of having his side pierced by a bayonet, then his torn stomach burned from shrapnel and his head, hacked off by a sword, went fuzzy, and his innards, ripped apart by a bullet, felt as if they were frying.

"No, you poor wretch, you're not fit to be loose, you're crazy," he told himself. "Who dragged you all this way for some George medal?! What, who are you getting yourself killed for? Are you so puffed up, so fat, that you can't stay in your skin any more? What were you missing? What are you looking for? You've got money to make, countless women, a lord-in-waiting's uniform, princely rank, unlimited power, a palace and servants, respect, a decent life:

all you could ever want is now yours or is promised. What more did you want? What are you after, what are you seeking? When the goat is fat, it decides to wrestle the wolf: that proverb applies to me. I'm supposed to be clever, a man. What nonsense! Would any clever man leave a regal life to sacrifice it for some one-rouble cross?! Rasputin and Sukhomlinov promised me I wouldn't even hear a rifle being fired. And here they've landed me in the middle of a battle. I'll be lucky if a bullet just gets me in the thigh or in a soft part of my body. But suppose a grenade tears off an arm or a leg, or turns my guts inside out …"

Kvachi's shrapnel-ripped belly gave him no rest: the pain got worse and worse. The devils in his head began a round dance, they lit hell's bonfire there and poured molten iron over him. Kvachi spent a lot of time tossing and turning in his overheated bed: finally he leapt to his feet and rushed out to the veranda.

The ruined town's dogs were barking horribly. From below he heard horses whinnying, carts creaking, artillery roaring. The camp was waking up and on the move. Suddenly, a rifle fired, then another, then more.

"What's happened? What's going on?" asked Kvachi, rushing to his Russian batman who had just emerged.

"Nothing," the batman tried to reassure Kvachi. "The ruins here are full of homeless dogs. They hide by day, but come out to hunt at night and annoy the soldiers. They go for the wounded and the dead. The soldiers get upset and kill these dogs. That's all that's happening."

Dawn began to break. They broke camp and moved off. The headquarters followed. Suddenly, in the distance, a cannon thundered. The thunder filled the entire valley: the noise was repeated.

"It's started," said someone.

The devils now crept into Kvachi's heart. He looked all round him. The others were calm. Some were even smiling. The soldiers were strolling so carefree that they seemed to be coming home from the fields, rather than going into battle.

"I suppose it's not as frightening as some people say it is," said Kvachi, turning to Chkhubishvili.

"Put a brave face on it. Those Turkish bastards won't even bother us," Gabo encouraged Kvachi. "We've shown them at Hasan-Kale, at Erzurum, at Van, and everywhere else. I was afraid the first time round, then I quickly got used to it."

They climbed to a mountain valley. The commander's camp was pitched in a small gorge. They dismounted and clambered up to the peak.

The field of battle was spread out below for Kvachi to see.

Following the mountain contours was a twisting plethora of trenches and dugouts. The Russian troops were hidden in the crannies of the northern slopes of the mountain range. Along the mountain you could see a dusty and interminable road, packed with troops.

On the side of a deep gorge a detachment of cavalry was wending its way, like a black snake, to the right. On one steep incline the horses and soldiers had great difficulty dragging the cannon. Couriers were galloping off in all directions over the grassy plain.

In the south, crossing the first chain of mountains, there was a second chain, still shrouded in morning mist. It too was bare and stony. In between the two chains was a long, narrow meadow, with half a dozen ruined villages, scrubland, intersected by gullies and former orchards.

Through his binoculars Kvachi saw the enemy swarming like ants at the top of this mountain ridge. Suddenly he heard a wasp buzzing in the air. In an instant the buzzing turned into an uncanny whoosh and then a thunderstorm of iron. This storm hit the top of the steep slope like a crazed flash of lightning and an arc of fiery iron flashed. A minute before this lightning bolt, everyone ducked. Faced with God's wrath, some just bowed their head, some bent double, some squatted.

Kvachi couldn't help falling face down onto the earth. At the same moment this lightning strike exploded horribly by the camp at the bottom of the slope. A pillar of flame, smoke, earth, and rocks was flung up into the air, mushrooming out as it hit the sky.

All round some were now laughing, but others stared with panic-stricken eyes. Kvachi, deadly pale, could barely stand. He was bewildered, looking in all directions, mumbling something unintelligible.

"God is angry ... I was quite scared ... I nearly perished."

"The first time is always the worst," Gabo consoled him. "You wait and see what's coming, this was just the 'hallo.'"

"They've got our range," one man called out.

"No, it was just a lucky strike," responded another.

"If that shell was just a lucky strike, what will a properly aimed one be like?" Kvachi wondered.

"Open fire," ordered the commander.

The couriers moved into action. The telephone wires spread over the ground began to hum.

Miniature mountain cannon bark like a lapdog.

Field cannon groan and roar.

Mortars bellow and thunder.

Howitzers bang and rumble.

Machine guns cackle like hens.

Rifles clatter like chickpeas thrown on the floor.

The sky weeps white, yellow, and pink clouds of shrapnel.

The earth is scutched by fire, smoke, and columns of rocks and earth. The air is saturated with roaring thunder, rumbling and banging, buzzing and hissing, the groans and moans of the dying and the wounded, rasping and cursing, shrieks of fighters, the laments of the fleeing, bellowing, galloping hooves, neighing, and a hundred unsettling cries and voices.

Periodically, narrow lines from one side or the other make forays, like long waves, against each other. Sometimes they attack each other and force one another back, sometimes they turn round halfway and are swallowed up in the ravines and gullies.

It was now after noon. The divisional general, worn out by cursing and shouting, decided to have lunch in the shade of a wall. The others, too, took refreshment.

"The Demir-Tepe position is in deep trouble," the staff officer reported. "The fourth brigade is almost wiped out."

"Send in the third," replied the general, curt and unconcerned.

"Half of them are lost, too."

"Make up for the lost half with two regiments and tell them that the outcome of the battle depends on Demir-Tepe peak."

The battle in the center grew less intense, but the left flank was embroiled. A constant, uninterrupted thunder came from Demir-Tepe.

Suddenly a number of black waves came out of the crannies and gullies on the other side of the mountain.

"It's an attack. Their cavalry is charging!" men called out on all sides.

Everyone grabbed their binoculars and focussed on the enemy.

The black snakes had crawled out of their holes, come together in a big field, and turned into one monstrous dragon.

"Cease fire," ordered the general, examining this dragon with an ecstatic smile and canny eye.

The cannon, machine guns, and riflemen gradually fell silent. The commanding officers were busy tying up loose threads, closing up their scattered ranks, and getting ready to meet the enemy.

The black dragon stretched out, tensing its limbs, gathering its strength for a leap.

The staff officer reported again to the commander-in-chief: "Demir-Tepe is in very great danger."

The general pointed his arm at the dragon: "See the thunderbolt that's going to strike us? I can't send a single man from here to help. Bring up the reserves, and send this order to Demir-Tepe:

everyone at Demir-Tepe is to die killing the enemy. Anyone who retreats is to be shot on the spot."

"General, that is an order which …"

"I've spoken and that's it."

He spun round and took another look at the charging Ottoman ranks.

After studying them, he rose to his feet with delight, ruffled his hair, and stirred into action: "Fine men. Fine men, you Ottomans! I salute your courage! There's a spectacle for you, that is military art at its best! But I'm going to exterminate you in half an hour, I'll wipe out the lot of you, destroy you, annihilate you. But I still admire you, you hopeless infidels."

He was shouting like a madman, waving his arms about, jumping up and down, waving his fists at the enemy, and firing off order after order:

"Aim all the cannons! Get all the case-shot ready. Not a rifle is to fire until they get close! Stay calm, take up your positions, take cover."

The Ottoman cavalry division spread out. In the middle were Arabs wearing white burnouses and Kurds with their strange headgear. They were preceded by the Muslim scholars bearing green banners and seeing the army off with prayers and blessings. Then suddenly the air was filled with the groans and laments of the dragon: "*Allah il-allah*."

They moved off and slowly emerged, gradually quickening their pace. Then they broke into a gallop and came like the wind. Green banners and flags fluttered in front of them. Countless sword tips shone in the sunlight. Whirlwinds of dust rose up behind them. The whole earth trembled. The roar and shouts reached the heavens: "*Allah il-allah*!"

Suddenly every cannon thundered out against the enemy, and the proud dragon that had attacked was instantly engulfed by a tornado of smoke, stones, and dust. The dragon was slightly taken aback, it started twisting and slowed down. Then it stepped over the mass of the slain and wounded, rushed into the haze of smoke and dust, and went on coming.

The roar, clatter, and rattling of every kind of artillery, machine gun, and of several thousand rifles became one long unbroken thunderclap.

The heavens broke and struck the earth with terrible lightning.

Suddenly the dragon fell like a hailstorm on the steep slope; its teeth bit the trenches and dugouts.

"Hit them! Go on! Hack at them."

"*Allah il-allah*!"

"Aim at them! Fire at them! Reload!"

Everybody and everything was plunged into chaos: cannons and rifles, swords and bayonets, cavalry and infantry, enemy and friend.

"We're doomed! We're beaten! Run for your life!" Kvachi raved in delirium, as he ran about aimlessly, looking like a mouse for its hole: but there was no horse to be seen. He had no idea where to go. He hid behind bushes, tumbled into a trench, or blundered into groups of fighting men.

"Prince Kvachantiradze!" the general yelled in the ear of the petrified and paralyzed Kvachi. "Take this order down the hill and give it to the staff taking cover in that ravine. You can see that hill, can't you? It's called Demir-Tepe. Tell them word for word that this hill is the key to the battle; if they let the enemy take it, not a single man will come out of this hell alive. We'll all be killed by Ottoman bullets. The telephone line's severed. So the fate of the army depends on you. Be quick! Goodbye!"

Kvachi had trouble rounding up his suite. They mounted their horses and spurred them on. They spotted from afar an ominous band of cavalry.

"We've been cut off! They're Ottomans. Go left."

And they turned their horses aside. In a ravine they came across a corps of medics. The doctors wore white and their sleeves were rolled up. Qoranashvili was among them; they were working away with saws and knives at the wounded. The whole area was drenched in blood, and strewn with amputated arms and legs, with wounded and crippled men, some bandaged, some not yet.

When Kvachi saw all this blood he was overcome with giddiness, his eyes dimmed, and his heart nearly failed him. One of his suite put a shoulder under his armpit and led him away from the hellish sight.

Kvachi came to his senses. He leapt back on his horse and dug his spurs in. He flew off at random, pursued by the thunder of battle.

The galloping horse circled a rough crag and suddenly ran into the middle of an Ottoman band. The unexpected onslaught unnerved and scattered the Ottomans, but they were blocked to their right by bare rock and on their left was a deep ravine. The panicking Turks clung to the rock and left a path open for Kvachi before they could grab their rifles.

"If I go ahead, I've had it; if I go back, I've still had it," Kvachi thought in a flash; suddenly he tugged the horse's reins so hard that the horse reared up on its hind legs.

That instant Kvachi drew his saber and looked behind him. He saw his companions, who had come round the crag at the same time.

"Stop!" Kvachi shrieked to his suite in a stentorian voice. "The first squadron stops behind the rock; the second comes down from the top of the crag and quickly joins the third squadron taking cover ahead of us. Go on, be quick about it. Hurry up!" At the same moment he addressed a Turkish officer in French: "Captain, if your bravery and bloodshed had the slightest sense, then I wouldn't advise you to surrender, but ... you do see, don't you, that you've fallen into a trap. Not a man of you can come out alive. So throw down your weapons."

The captain replied: "I can see I've fallen into a trap. What can I do against several squadrons? You've ambushed us so well that we don't know who to fire at. Here is my weapon."

And he flung his weapon onto the path. The others threw down theirs with a clatter of falling rifles.

"Pile up your weapons together," Kvachi ordered the Ottoman captain.

The captain passed on the order to his soldiers and five minutes later there were a hundred rifles piled in the middle of the path.

"Gabo, take two Russians and escort these Turkish prisoners. Ladi, you and I will follow behind."

Three men led off a hundred Turkish soldiers, and two followed.

"Well, captain, get your army moving!"

"At once, but what about your army? Where are your squadrons?"

"If I had any squadrons, I wouldn't have taken just you prisoner, I'd have taken the whole army corps."

The Turks struck their heads with their hands and muttered bitterly: "What a scoundrel, what a swine! A devil, a captain-devil."

Kvachi and the Turkish captain were laughing, one sincerely and in delight, the other with tears and bile.

Kvachi's band of men suddenly ran into a large group of soldiers running bareheaded and panic-stricken, yelling: "They've surrounded us, they've cut us off! Run for your life! Run for it!"

An unknown general, his head bandaged, his face as pale as death, staggered forth and confronted Kvachi:

"Help me, captain. The Ottomans have taken that hill there, they've taken our staff officers prisoner and wiped out almost all our officers. I'm the only one still alive. If we don't get that hill back right now, the whole army will be captured by the Ottomans. You're our only hope. Think of our motherland, our Tsar, our duty. Try … Help us!"

The wounded general collapsed in the dust.

What happened that moment to Kvachi's inner self? What devil got into him? Who transformed him out of the blue, and how, is beyond the comprehension of Kvachi himself, or any outsider.

"Stop! I said, stop, you rabble!" Kvachi screamed at the mob of deserters; placing his horse in front of them, he blocked their escape.

"They've surrounded us! Run for your life!"

"Stop, I said, or else …"

And he pressed his revolver against the chest of the first man. His suite quickly handed over the Ottoman prisoners to others, took their stand next to Kvachi, who was now maddened, and drew their swords.

Something inexplicable and unprecedented had occurred. That instant had reversed and aborted Kvachi's life and character and endowed him with something miraculous and otherworldly. The old Kvachi had died; another one, unfamiliar and new, was born a moment later, as proud and unbending, courageous and fearless as Leonides at Thermopylae, Alexander the Great, or Erekle King of Kakhetia, or Napoleon at Arcola.

Kvachi suddenly had the wings of an eagle and the body of the archangels Michael and Gabriel, who had put their fiery swords in his hand. In his chest a lion's heart was beating, in his soul hell's chief devil was at work, with a thousand gremlins serving him. Kvachi, already a tall man, suddenly grew half a foot taller; he burned the flock of frightened sheep with his eyes and deafened them with his thunder:

"Stop! Join ranks!"

About a hundred mindless soldiers ran off. Like an eagle of the fields, Kvachi pounced on them and felled seven men with seven bullets. Then he calmly straightened up in the saddle, looked the others over with a smile, and scorched them with divine fire:

"Brothers, the fate of the army is in your hands. Our exit is blocked. We shall all rot in prison camps and we won't be able to look anyone in the eye again for shame. Brothers! Several thousand of your comrades, the Tsar, and the motherland are watching you and asking you to do your duty in a brotherly, comradely, and patriotic way. There are no cowards among us. Anyone who betrays us by running away will meet the dog's fate of those I've just slaughtered with my own hand. I shall lead you, and don't you lag behind me. Come on and let's do our duty."

"Let's go! Call on us! Lead us on!" two thousand battle-hardened trained men roared out.

"Warrant officers, step forward! From now on you are officers. Begin sorting your men into squads."

Half an hour later a force of two-thousand had become one of four-thousandin three groups.

"Come on. Follow me."

And he moved off at a solemn pace towards the hill.

"Keep in ranks! Move fast! Keep together!"

Ladi Chikinjiladze led the left flank, Gabo Chkhubishvilithe right flank. Behind the three of them came a moving wall of iron, a forest of untamed, unbending, and fearless bayonets. All were bending forwards and had their right arm and a bayonet thrust ahead.

"Keep in ranks! Move fast! Keep together!"

Initially a commotion broke out on the hill; a hail of bullets followed. But nobody stopped advancing, nobody lagged behind, nobody fired a shot.

The silent high-speed march filled the enemy with horror and froze their veins. Pallid, the Ottomans whispered: "The devil's madman! *Allah il-allah*!" and their quivering hands fired their rifles into the air.

Straight as a ramrod, tall and handsome, Kvachi led the iron wall on, sometimes looking behind him, heating up this wall once again with his fiery eyes, then waving his saber and calling out once or twice:

"Keep in ranks! Follow me!"

The iron wall ventured up the hill without a word, clambering up like bears until it reached the top, and crashed down onto the Ottomans.

"Go on, stab them, hack them!" shrieked Kvachi, crazed with unearthly madness, whirling about in the middle of the fire of battle.

His saber flashed like lightning and his fiery eyes seemed to look down on everyone from above.

A brief, ferocious battle took place. They fought with swords, bayonets, daggers, revolver and rifle butts, hands, feet, and teeth.

"We give up, we surrender!" the Turkish soldiers said loudly.

"We've won! We've got the better of them! Hit them! Go on!" Kvachi thundered hacking off one Ottoman's arm and slicing through the sinews of another's neck. He clove in two another Ottoman's chest, sliced off a fourth's ear, and aimed his sword at a tall Arab's brow. He aimed, but …

Suddenly fire flashed in Kvachi's eyes and bells tolled in his ears, and a black fog enveloped his mind. He suddenly clutched his chest with his left hand, and flung his right hand out. His sword clanged as he let it fly off and, like a felled tree trunk, he sprawled on his back.

A Strange Delirium

Abandoned by all, Kvachi Kvachantiradze lay on his back in a desolate field. He was surrounded by nothing but yellow sand. The desert reflected the sun's heat. The air was saturated with a baking haze.

Lying all alone on the hot sand, Kvachi was burning up with the heat and dehydration. A black raven perched on his blood-stained chest, its awl-like beak pecking at his wound, its hot talons tearing at his guts and raking through his inner organs. At times, the raven thrust its beak in one of Kvachi's eyes, then calmly rested and haughtily examined the desert.

Not far off, a horrible, shaggy, black-faced hyena was crouching. It was waiting for darkness, for it knew that at night Kvachi would be its to devour, and by dawn all that would remain on this sandy spot would be not Kvachi, but gnawed bones.

A golden chain came down from heaven, and down the chain climbed a demon bringing red wine in a crystal decanter. This clown swung from the chain and poured red wine over Kvachi from above. The wine missed Kvachi's mouth. Kvachi opened his mouth wide like a baby bird, trying to get just a drop of wine down his throat, but he couldn't move his feeble limbs or move his feverish head an inch. The demon spent some time tormenting Kvachi: it fooled about, it laughed, it grimaced, made faces, and suddenly climbed up the chain back to the skies.

All of a sudden the desert came strangely to life. Kvachi could clearly see Paris boulevards, avenues, gardens, cafés, squares, and people, strangers and acquaintances.

A drunken Rasputin was making a bare-breasted Elena run at a trot.

Lady Harvey, Kvachi's London mistress, was strutting like a peafowl.

Madame Lapoche's sparkling eyes were setting fire to all around her.

Blue-eyed Rebecca was swaying her hips as she floated past.

Tania, Susanne, Isaac, Vera, Sedrak, Beso, Ladi, Chipi, and a thousand other men and women whom Kvachi knew, passed by carefree, relaxed, laughing, smiling happily.

Not one of them cast a glance at Kvachi; nobody noticed him.

The black-headed hyena was still waiting for the dark, the black raven was still pecking at Kvachi's heart and aiming at his eye.

"Water, water!" Kvachi yelled silently: nobody could hear a thing.

Kvachi made an effort to gather strength; he tried to cry out, but no voice came, and he could not move a muscle.

The city had vanished, together with the people. The black raven cawed again and the black-headed hyena was still waiting for the dark.

Suddenly Dr Qoranashvili stood over him: he was oddly dressed, armed with bow and arrows, wearing chainmail armor and a helmet.

"Kvachi, arise and follow me."

They both mounted winged Pegasuses and flew off.

The black raven pursued them; the hyena galloped over the ground.

"Our Pegasus gallops, flies us away, while a black-starred raven caws after us," sang Qoranashvili, who then told Kvachi: "Ah, see? Julamerki peak, now the Giavar range ... Ravanduza ... Khanikin ... Samara ..."

All around armies were bustling. The slain were strewn about, lying face up. Ravens pecked at the corpses, and wild beasts devoured them. Kvachi and Qoranashvili recognized many of the living and the slain.

"Brothers, what are you after up there? What's brought you so far?"

"We don't know. We were following our fortune, trying our luck."

In Iran they recognized both the living and the dead, their forefathers and their ancestors.

"Brothers, why have you deserted your motherland for this desert?"

"This earthly life has made us do it."

In Afghanistan the walls of Herat and Kandahar were ruined. The slopes of the Hindu Kush were stained with the blood of their parents. Their ancestors rose up from their graves.

"Brothers, who stained Central Asia with your blood?"

"Fate did. We were followers of Nadir Shah. We were the first to storm the walls of Herat and Kandahar."

They crossed the Soliman range, the Punjab,the holy Ganges and reached Delhi, the capital of India, once called Shah-Janabad. Everywhere they came across their relatives' spirits and skeletons flying along with them, clutching at their Pegasuses with bony fingers and pleading:

"Take us with you! Bring us home! Reunite us!"

"Who brought you so far?"

King Erekle II, "the little Kakhetian lad", stepped forward and said:

"I brought some, others brought others."

"What were you seeking? Whom were you pursuing?"

"We were pursuing our fortune. Some of us sought fame and loot, some were borne off by others' powers."

Kvachi and Qoranashvili flew on to Arabia, Egypt, Assyria, Babylon, and lands both new and old. Everywhere the dead arose: countless Mosokians and Tibarenes, Makrons and Mosoniki, Nairi and Colchideans, Mamelukes and Janissaries, spirits and skeletons of close relatives rising up with laments and groans, pleas and demands, chasing after them like a hundred thousand bees emerging together from a hive.

The skeletons' pursuit and howling complaints wore out and deafened Kvachi: in the end he was so tormented that he bellowed at Qoranashvili:

"What do you want from me? Why are you dragging me through this hell? Get me out of here. I can't take any more of this torture."

Qoranashvili asked him: "Kvachi, why did you want to come

all the way to Turkey? Who made you come? What were you after?"

"God only knows what I wanted: I don't. Water, give me water! Just let me have a drop!"

The demon clambered down from the sky again and poured a jug of wine over Kvachi's face, but not a drop reached his tongue. Once again, everything vanished.

Kvachi was lying in the gardens of paradise. The raven perched on his brow again, the hyena lay at his feet. He thought everything was familiar: the skies, mountains, meadows, vineyards, and buildings of his motherland. He fancied he saw Samtredia, Batumi, Kutaisi, and Tbilisi.

In the distance countless people were moving about: Kvachi's parents and friends, acquaintances and relatives, Rasputin and Tania, Elena and Gintz, dignitaries and grandees, madmen and holy fools, simple people and courtiers. They were all pointing a finger at Kvachi and milling about.

"Bury him! Put him in a coffin! Put him into the ground!" some were yelling, herding Kvachi's parents, relatives, and friends towards him.

Others were pitting their strength against these madmen, pleading tearfully with them, asking for mercy. The battle went on for a long time. Finally, the Tsar and Tsaritsa appeared and commanded: "Bury him!"

Everyone sprang into action and rushed towards Kvachi. Some did so with a yell of victory, others with laments and mourning. The Tsar and Tsaritsa, the grandees, dignitaries and senior clergy recited Kvachi's funeral rites. Then Rasputin, Mitia Koliaba, the madmen and holy fools, the disfigured and crippled started a crazy round dance around Kvachi. Everyone was leaping, somersaulting, grimacing, spitting, and yelling: "Let's take him to paradise, to paradise!"

"I don't want to go to paradise, I don't want to!" Kvachi

shouted, but nobody heard him.

Then a terrible roar broke out. Everyone instantly rushed to Kvachi and laid him in a big coffin.

"Mother, father! What's wrong with you? I'm alive! I'm alive! Beso! Sedrak! Help me! Help me!"

Some were weeping, others rejoicing. Those at the back pushed to get to the front and shouted:

"Is little Kvachi going to paradise, to paradise?"

"Mother! Father!" Kvachi pleaded. "If you can't help me, at least keep back. Don't let your son's sins fall on you."

Pupi was weeping as she whispered to him: "It's all right, child, it's all right! It will be better this way, believe me."

The raven had perched over him again, and the hyena had lain on his knees. A black snake slithered into the coffin and wrapped itself round Kvachi's throat. People stood at the head of the coffin and nailed the lid down. A nail went through Kvachi's forehead and came out of his temple. Kvachi, no longer breathing, was put into a bottomless grave; to the sound of victorious yells and joyful shrieks they saw him lowered into the ground; then came the patter of falling earth. The noise gradually faded and then stopped.

Kvachi was lying in black earth. He could hear himself breathing and the raven pecking at his eyes, the snake slithering in his mouth, the hyena gnawing at his chest, and damp worms writhing in his wounds. Kvachi was lying in the black earth, baking, choking, and thinking as he lay there:

"Oh, you've made a big mistake … I'm not going to die, because I don't want to die, and fate has not decreed my death, either. All the worse for you!" And he stood up once again.

Instantly he had the strength of a hundred demons. He tensed himself. He stretched upwards, shifted the enormous gravestone, which was as thick as a wall, as if it were a sheaf of hay and surged out, stretched his full height and matched the height of the mountains.

At his feet ant-sized gravediggers had sat down to an endless feast, his wake. When they saw Kvachi, shrieks of terror, yells, and screams broke out. Kvachi stepped onto their banquet and squashed Rasputin, Mitia Koliaba, the madmen, and a hundred or so dignitaries like ants.

At that moment an invisible force grabbed hold of his arms and legs.

"Let me go!" he yelled, tossing as he lay there, his eyes wide open.

"Calm down, Kvachi, calm down," Doctor Qoranashvili was telling Kvachi in a sweet voice.

The stretcher-bearers took firm hold of Kvachi's arms and legs.

"They've killed me! They've buried me! But I've come back to life. I've risen from the dead. I've annihilated them. I've beaten them! I've destroyed them!" Kvachi lapsed back into delirium.

The raven flew in through the window, and the hyena, its tail between its legs, lurked by the door, while the snake slithered into a crack in the wall. Kvachi, covered in sweat and void of all strength, fell back on his pillow and examined his surroundings with blurred eyes.

"Water ... if you have any mercy, water!"

Doctor Qoranashvili poured a thimbleful of wine into Kvachi's mouth and said in a firm voice: "He'll live." He then left the ward.

The only person standing over Kvachi is an angel in white, a princess disguised as a sister of mercy; she has a red cross pinned to her white chest. She softly strokes Kvachi's sweaty brow and curly hair with her downy hand, sings him a courtly song with her firebird's voice and whispers tales of manly valor.

Kvachi's Quarrel with People at the Top

White with fury, Sukhomlinov was foaming at the mouth.

"Prince, what's going on? We began the new offensive relying on your shells. But the shells were the wrong caliber and the cannon exploded. We lost the battle, the loss of life is incalculable. We've got no more shells. Now we're retreating and all we've got to fend off the enemy are cudgels. So I'm asking you what's going on?"

"I don't know, I'm no artillery expert," Kvachi replied calmly, smiling as he toyed with the three St George crosses dangling from his chest.

"I smell treason, prince! We'll have you jailed. We'll shoot you."

Stretching to his full height, Kvachi scowled: "Be careful, general."

Rasputin interposed himself between Kvachi and the general, trying to calm them down.

Kvachi wagged a finger under the general's nose: "If you weren't a minister of the Tsar, I'd ram those words down your throat. When you're fired from the ministry, I advise you to keep out of my way, or I'll riddle you with bullets."

Kvachi slammed the doors so angrily that the window panes nearly fell out of their frames.

Things were getting more complicated. The military prosecutor summoned Kvachi for questioning: "What's this? Kvachi sold documents? He handed them to the Germans? Where? In Stockholm? What's all this nonsense? Who's making up all this gossip? Kvachi saw nobody in Stockholm, he had no meetings with anyone. Ha-ha. It's absurd, it's just a joke. What did you say? That Kvachi has nothing to joke or laugh about? Forget about Kvachi, it's probably the prosecutor who's joking. No, it'll need more than these documents to ruin Kvachi."

The prosecutor drew up a statement and told Kvachi: "Anyone

on such serious charges would normally go to prison. But out of respect for our Holy Father Grigory, who is standing guarantee for you, you are free for the time being. Please sign this undertaking not to leave Petersburg."

Kvachi signed, left, and rushed off to see Rasputin.

"Holy teacher, what's all this about? They don't seem to be joking. Help me somehow, or our common enemies will destroy me and then it will be your turn, too."

Rasputin whined: "Listen to me, Apollonchik. You're as good as a brother to me. I've spared no efforts to do everything I can for you. Wealth, princely rank, uniform, crosses, a place at court. I've got you respect and power, but now times have changed. I don't have the power I used to have. Our enemies are winning. Your name is on everyone's lips now, everyone wants to see you shot, because they blame you for our recent defeat. I don't know who is right and who is lying. The court will decide. I've helped you as much as I could. They won't put you in prison until they find more proof. Meanwhile, make yourself scarce, don't go anywhere now, stay quiet and live in the shadows for a little while. That's my advice. Don't ask anything else of me."

Kvachi really did stay at home and lock the door. Ladi's trained nose and hands kept him brilliantly well informed. Every day he had reliable information from a dozen various sources. Just in case, he sold Gintz *The Good Samaritan* and a lot of his real estate and other property; he handed the cash for safe-keeping to Silibistro, who was also living in Petersburg.

Several newspapers went for Kvachi, smearing his good name. Kvachi sent the appropriate response to his own newspapers. Just three papers printed them as brief corrections, but other papers rejected them.

"Things really must be bad," Kvachi concluded.

Meanwhile Beso, Ladi, and the agents had nothing encouraging to report.

"Things aren't going to go well," the taciturn Beso summed up.

"Make yourself scarce," advised Chikinjiladze.

"Oh no, that's no good. Things aren't that bad yet," responded Kvachi. Once again he tried his luck: he paid visits to the ministers, dignitaries, and grandees he knew. Everywhere he got the same curt refusal:

"He's not at home ... He's too busy ... He's unwell."

Rasputin's response was as before: "I've done all I can do."

Everyone avoided Kvachi, shut their doors in his face, and washed their hands of him.

"Make yourself scarce," Beso and Ladi repeated their advice.

"Oh no, never!" Kvachi decided, and issued a threat: "I'll soon see who'll be pleading with whom. You'll have to wait a long time to see Kvachi go under, you'll go under yourself first."

The next day a despondent Chipi Chipuntiradze came running in:

"We've had it! We're wiped out! The Idelsohns have been arrested."

"Both of them?"

"Both. Isaac and Rebecca. Quick, run. Hide. Get away! Quick!"

Kvachi retorted curtly and seriously: "Now the time really has come."

He tore off his epaulettes, removed his crosses, threw them away, and went into a fury: "I've had enough of their injustice! Now they'll get a taste of my revenge."

That day he turned the battlefront round 180°.

A Change of Direction and Kvachi's Prophecy

For a while Kvachi, disguised and wearing make-up, habitually visited three down-at-heel apartments. Every now and again paupers and other dubious persons would meet Kvachi in remote suburbs and engage in long, whispered conversations.

"Step up your work in the army, in the army," insisted Kvachi. "Everyone else has been ready for a long time."

Kvachi gave more invitations and held more banquets. His guests were exclusively officers. He spread his money about generously and talked a lot of gibberish. A few subordinate adjutants reported to him daily and took instructions for missions on his behalf.

Kvachi was busy with covert work. Beso, Ladi, Chipi, Jalil, Sedrak, and many old and new friends and acquaintances had trouble keeping up as they ran round the whole city, the barracks and the outer suburbs, holding secret meetings, selling weapons at bargain prices, and getting ready for a final battle.

"Everything's ready, and we're all prepared!" Kvachi's secret military junta finally declared. They had worked out a plan of action and set a date.

One evening Elena sent Kvachi a message via Beso: "Come and see me straight away. You won't regret it. It may be of use to your cause." Half an hour later Kvachi climbed Elena's stairs.

"Let me introduce you!" said Elena, presenting to Kvachi a bald man with a black beard: Purishkevich.

Kvachi was astonished and pleased. He thought that Purishkevich might really be of help. They got to know one another, took each other's measure, and had a long whispered chat.

The next day Purishkevich introduced Kvachi to Grand Duke Dimitri, Prince Felix Yusupov, Captain Sukhotin, and Doctor Lazovert. Supper and a quiet conversation lasted until daybreak. They worked out a plan, swore each other loyalty, and then parted.

Kvachi immediately summoned his junta, told them everything and ordered: "Pass it on."

When everyone else had left, he smiled venomously and told Beso and the others close to him:

"The hunter has been hunting the beast, but the beast is going to turn the tables on him. Those idiots will get what they deserve.

They must be completely mad to be so stupid. They're digging their own graves, pulling down the roof over their heads, working hard to saw off the branch they're sitting on. Fish starts stinking from the head: that saying was written for these people. We've been meaning to turn the world upside down from below; they think they're doing it from above. Ha-ha! They've been begging me, saying they have to kill themselves, so please help. Fine, gentlemen, I really will help you do this noble thing, I certainly will. The crazy lot don't know that just one drop of their blood shed by their own hand will become a deluge in which they'll be the first to drown; they don't know that the breeze they start will become a whirlwind and blow away their very memory, like yesterday's snow melted and swept away by the wind. Ha-ha! Beso, isn't it a ridiculous sight when your enemy, whom you've been chasing for the kill, puts a pistol in his own mouth and begs you to help him? Jesus Christ taught: help your neighbor in times of trouble. Our humanitarian duty teaches me the same; self-interest says the same, and intuition dictates it. Ha-ha! Fine, gentlemen, fine! I'll help your cause and do so with pleasure and joy."

Kvachi's finger was threatening someone in the distance; he was prophesying like the raven:

"Just you wait. Give me a little time. The time will come and you will bitterly regret it, you will hit a wall, drink your own blood, and tear at your own flesh, but you have only yourself to blame for everything. It will be too late to bite your fingernails, strain your neck, and gnash your teeth!"

Suddenly he stood up straight, tensed himself, and rose up, as when he was sprawled beneath Demir-Tepe. His voice trembled, his eyes blazed:

"Comrades! Remember my words and, if I perish early, tell the whole world and history that I, Kvachi Kvachantiradze, on 27 December 1916 said: on 14 July 1914 today's Russia, by getting involved in a World War, cut its own throat. That's one thing. In a few days, a group of dignitaries and grandees will saw down the pillar that holds up the house of Russia. That's the second thing. In two months or so this group will support the secret forces of dissent and join them in tearing down the barrier holding back a bottomless and boundless dam which has been accumulating for ten years. That's the third thing. This floodwater will come like God's wrath and sweep today's government to hell. That's the fourth thing. Then it will gather strength and tear down the new government in a roaring gale and rip off the heads of half those who are demolishing the dam wall and sawing away at the pillar of their house. That's the fifth thing. Then a time will come, terrible and furious, merciless and cruel, ferocious and remorseless in which the heads of the other half will be cut off. This terrible time will come ten months later. That's the sixth thing. The torrent will become Noah's deluge, the gale—a whirlwind, the pure saints—vicious wild beasts, roses—henbane, angels—hellish monsters, and the harmless silkworm—a venomous snake. Brother will attack brother, father—son, and they will not be sated by one another's blood. The flames from the fires will reach the heavens, rivers will run red, and the groans of the dying will deafen the land. A new earth will be born: alien and unfamiliar, strange and puzzling. Both outsiders and its own inhabitants will attack this land, a terrible and unrelenting war will break out. Vicious and angry, rabid and crazed, all Russia will become a lake of blood; a white wave will reach red cities, but … The reds will overcome, they will exterminate the whites, throw them into the sea, and establish their own power. This is the seventh and final thing."

Kvachi was speaking to a distant audience. His eyes blazed with a mysterious fire, his voice with a strange, otherworldly inspiration. He was now unaware of anything, he looked at nobody, he was in a medium's trance and shackled to some invisible force.

"Comrades!" he continued. "I have a great number of enemies. I know that they are trying to undermine my work and eliminate me from history, but I shall always find plenty of friends like you. Who knows if I shall perish, or not, but you will not let historians throw my name on the rubbish-heap of oblivion."

He went on raving and ranting for much longer, but his comrades could not remember any more than what we have already described, and thus they have deprived history of an invaluable treasure.

One thing alone is clear beyond doubt: that evening Russia's Moira opened the book of Russia's fate through Kvachi, but the doomed did not believe him.

But I've already told you that history is a lying gossip. This simple truth has yet again been proven in the case of Kvachi. In the last ten years enough books have been written about Russia to fill two hundred carts. A bookworm may read them all from beginning to end, but—typical of the world's ingratitude—he'll never come across Kvachi's name anywhere. Others have ascribed to themselves, misappropriated and redistributed his glorious cause, his inestimable labors, and invaluable good deeds. But, thank God, Kvachi has many living witnesses: just to name a few—Beso Shikia, Sedrak Havlabariani, Ladi Chikinjiladze, Gabo Chkhubishvili, Chipi Chipuntiradze, Jalil Emin-oglu, and many others who can confirm what is said above and below. Just try and disbelieve them!

Giving Thanks and Distorting History

The next day Kvachi, Purishkevich, Yusupov, and others met again.

"Let's kill him with a revolver," said one of them.

"Let's poison him," advised another.

"Let's drown him," exclaimed a third.

"That's pointless," Kvachi finally said. "We've got to remove the axis on which today's Russia revolves." The remark delighted everybody.

"Let's remove it, remove it," they yelled, talking over each other.

Then they studied Kvachi's plan, weighed it up, and left for home.

"Great teacher, Holy Father!" Kvachi said to Rasputin that same evening. "You've done so much for me, so I want to show my thanks in a small way; if you're in the mood, there are five beautiful girls in the bathhouse who'd like …" And, smiling, he whispered a few words in Rasputin's ear. Rasputin beamed and his eyes became oily.

"Where? When?"

"Tonight, at Prince Yusupov's. Felix and I are inviting you because we both feel we are in your debt."

"Are they good-looking?"

"All five are real beauties, the first has jet-black hair, the second …"

Rasputin stopped them in mid-word and hugged his grateful friend and loyal defender to his chest.

When midnight was drawing near, Yusupov and Kvachi brought Rasputin by car to a house and went up the stairs.

"No, I can't do it," Felix, who was deadly pale, suddenly whispered and leant against a wall.

"Shame on you, prince!" Kvachi exclaimed and took the stumbling Yusupov by the elbow. "Summon up your courage: you're not a bride at the altar, are you?"

"I find it hard … It's treachery … I'll kill him here, but luring him into my house … No, there's nothing manly about that."

"I said shame on you, prince. You should've thought about it before."

"You're right," said Felix, recovering his spirits; he rushed upstairs and knocked loudly at the door.

They both embraced Rasputin, who was nicely dressed in his finest clothes. Forcing himself to smile, Kvachi called to Rasputin:

"Right, Holy Father, let's go to the holy place."

Rasputin seemed to have an inkling that something was wrong: "Your kiss, Apollonchik, feels like Judas's."

He eyed both of them, and a flash of mistrust lit up his eyes: he sensed danger. The two of them disguised their treachery, hypocrisy, and double-dealing behind a mask of laughter and joking.

"Apollonchik, I'm your sworn brother ... I've put a lot of trust in you ... if you're hiding anything, think of God and don't touch me, or ..."

"Great teacher! Holy Father! You're joking, if ..."

Kvachi spoke with such heartfelt sincerity that Rasputin's glimmer of suspicion died away.

"Are you mad? Can't you take a joke?" explained Rasputin and flicked two fingers at Kvachi's chin. But he looked again into Kvachi's eyes and threatened him: "You look out ..."

Twenty minutes later all three were sitting on the ground floor of Yusupov's palace. They were having a pleasant chat with sweets and lots to drink. Kvachi and Felix were drinking champagne and telling Rasputin for the fourth time: "Holy Father, have some of your favorite marsala: why aren't you drinking any?"

"I don't feel like it, I don't want to."

The noise of a gramophone came from the first floor.

"The guests haven't left yet ... My mother-in-law is up there ..." Felix told Rasputin for the third time. "They'll go any minute, then it will be our turn ... I've hidden the girls nearby ..."

Suddenly Rasputin downed two glasses of marsala and ate two small cream pastries.

"Why aren't you eating them?" asked Rasputin, offering them a cream pastry each. They both turned pale and exchanged glances.

"No thank you, father ... I don't like them."

"I had them made for you, Holy Father ... I know that it's your ... your favorite ..."

Each pastry was dosed with three hundred milligrams of

cyanide, the strongest and surest of poisons. Rasputin's drink was also poisoned.

Kvachi and Felix were anxiously waiting for the poison to work, but Rasputin showed no ill effects.

"He's not dying." they both thought, looking Rasputin in the face. "He must be a strong dog, or the poison is no good."

Rasputin was getting tipsy: "Pour me some more!"

Kvachi refilled his glass, and poured himself another glass of champagne. Rasputin downed two glasses one after the other, and followed them with two more pastries. Again, nothing happened.

"They don't work on him," the two assassins thought; they turned pale and gave each other furtive looks.

Rasputin's mood improved: his face relaxed and he started talking; he was looking forward to the pretty girls and stamping his foot impatiently like a stallion, whinnying: "Pour me some more."

He drank another two glasses. Nothing happened.

"It's not working ... he's not dying ... there's enough poison to kill five buffalo ... the man's made of iron," Kvachi thought and exchanged glances with Felix again.

The gentle Felix was utterly pallid. He was being underhand, but turning pale because he could no longer keep up such a hypocritical act; he looked cadaverous, his lips trembled, his left eyebrow twitched, and rose and fell. Suddenly he got up and ran his hand round his collar, as if he were choking.

"They're late ... I ... I'll go ... I'll be back in a minute ... I shan't be long ... In a minute ..." he mumbled as he staggered out of the room.

Upstairs Purishkevich, Grand Duke Dimitri, Captain Sukhotin, and Dr Lazovert waited for it all to end. They were all in shock and confusion.

Felix came into the room groaning and shouted hysterically: "I can't stand it ... I can't stand it ..."

"What's happened? What's going on? What's wrong?"

"He won't die ... It doesn't work on him ... He's eaten a dozen pastries and had a whole bottle of marsala, but he won't die."

"I overdid it, I put in too much poison," murmured Dr Lazovert.

"Prince Yusupov! Go back at once and give Prince Kvachantiradze a hint that it's his turn now. Let's get on with it! And put this in your pocket, it may come in useful."

Felix, revived and encouraged, put a revolver in his pocket and went back downstairs. Rasputin was just belching. Kvachi was pouring him more wine and handing him glass after glass. Felix laughed joyfully, but not opening his mouth.

"The girls are here ... Prince, it's your turn ..."

Had Kvachi's turn come? Well, then. Kvachi would do his duty. He turned to Rasputin:

"Holy Father, great teacher! The girls are shy and they're religious; they won't drink with us. Let's go, the girls will come in later. The bathhouse is right by here ... We'll be upstairs. If you need us, ring the bell."

The two assassins left. Five girls, shy and meek, all angelic, came in to see Rasputin. They came in one after the other and started a religiously edifying conversation. Then Rasputin warmed up and became inflamed. He went for them, striking his chest with his fist and shouting:

"I'm holy! I have nothing to do with filth and impure passions. Test me now! I'll show you! Come closer!"

And they all went into the palace's heated bathhouse.

"Whether you lie on top of me, or lie next to me ... See, you see that I show no signs ... Tumble all over me, I won't feel anything ... My blood stays cool ... Well, you've had a good look, and you can believe it ... But now, now the holy ghost has left me and now I'm a human being again, now ... Well, let's begin."

That moment a razor glinted in the air and a bestial bellowing shook the palace itself. The girls instantly rushed out of the bathhouse and bolted the thick doors from the outside. Rasputin's bellowing, moans, and roar shook the palace again. Like an enraged buffalo he rammed the doors three times. The fourth blow broke the oak doors and a naked beast burst out, roaring and thundering, from the bathhouse. Hunched, he sped off, leaving a trail of blood behind him.

A commotion and uproar broke out on the stairs: "He's got away, he's escaped."

The naked Rasputin pounded at one set of doors, then another, until he broke down a third set and burst into a room. Yusupov blocked the naked beast's path and fired his revolver three times. Rasputin groaned again and folded up.

"He's dead ... it's over," they all decided, leaving the room to discuss what to do.

Not long after, Kvachi went back to the first room and stared at Rasputin, who was lying face down. The corpse suddenly swung its arm and gripped Kvachi like an iron hoop.

"Help me, help me!" croaked Kvachi, as he struggled in Rasputin's grasp. Rasputin suddenly let go of his arm, got up, bent double, and tumbled into the corridor. The conspirators panicked again and went after the immortal holy man, shouting at each other:

"We're finished! Follow him! Hit him! Kill him!"

Felix's and Kvachi's guns fired.

"Quick, or he'll get away."

Rasputin had rushed into the palace gardens. Leaping like a panther, Kvachi went after him, and an ashen-faced Yusupov followed. Dawn was about to break. The path was just visible, but where had he run off to? Left, right, or straight ahead?

Kvachi heard a weak moan behind him. He looked back. Felix staggered off and fell down. Purishkevich came rushing out: "Help him, he's fainted."

Purishkevich took Felix's revolver and came running towards Kvachi.

"Where is he? Where did he run off to?"

A shadowy figure emerged from the bushes onto the snow-covered path: "He's on the move … Quick!"

At twenty paces Kvachi aimed and fired.

"Apollonchik, you too?" groaned Rasputin. "Is this how you show your gratitude?"

It took Kvachi a few leaps to get within five paces; he fired twice more. Rasputin shook, fell on his knees, and then headlong into the snow. Then he rose up again and ran off like a lynx, growling like a bear:

"I'll have the lot of you hanged tomorrow! Scum! Bandits!"

By now Purishkevich had caught up.

"Shoot him, shoot him!"

They fired again, riddling the body with a dozen bullets. Rasputin bit and clawed the earth with his iron teeth and fingers; he writhed, groaned, and called out strange words. One last time he rose up onto one knee.

Suddenly Felix, who had revived, appeared.

"Hit him, shoot him, kill him!" the demented Yusupov yelled wildly, and smashed a bronze candle-holder into the dying man's head. He had crushed Rasputin's head, covering himself in blood. Kvachi and Purishkevich had trouble pulling the frenzied and shaken Felix off Rasputin's corpse.

"Prince, enough! Rasputin's dead … Let's go, or we'll catch cold."

"Let me go! Let me have him! Hit him, kill him!" Felix went on yelling and got back to Rasputin, who was now still. Then Felix fell silent, let go, and became quiet and dazed.

"Right, now let's throw this carrion into the Neva."

They dressed the corpse in its sheepskin jacket and boots, threw it into a car, and drove off. They straightened out the corpse in the car, to make it look like a third seated passenger. Kvachi held it up under one elbow, and Lazovert took the other.

"Drive faster! Quick! Get on with it!" Kvachi shouted to Captain Sukhotin who was driving like the wind.

The crazed motor car flew through the sleeping city, rushing Russia's axis and pillar. That night Kvachi had lifted the dome off the Russian state. Hissing and groaning, a cold wind struck the travelers' heads and stung their faces. Kvachi bent down, huddled, and shifted into the nest-like depths of the motor car. Suddenly, Rasputin's arm poked out of that nest and wrapped itself round Kvachi's neck. Kvachi sat up as if a snake had bitten him, but the arm had grown as stiff as a piece of iron or wood; then Rasputin himself bent forwards and lay on him like a heavy rock, pawed him like a bear and made him groan. Rasputin growled strangely.

Several times Kvachi, entangled in fur coats, tried to get up.

"Help me! He's choking me! Help me!"

The driver couldn't hear Kvachi's groans. The car flew on like a storm wind. Doctor Lazovert was struggling as the car jolted him.

"Help me! I'm suffocating! Help me!"

Finally Kvachi managed to get free and sit up: "Stop the car! Stop!"

Completely demented, Kvachi leapt out of the car: "I don't want to … I'm not going … You go …"

What was going on, what had happened? Kvachi was quivering, gnashing his teeth: "I don't want to … I can't … You take him."

"Prince, shame on you! Come to your senses."

"I can't do it … This is too much."

"Prince, come to your senses! Get a grip on yourself. Yusupov is a weak youth, you're a real man. Cowardice like this doesn't suit the hero of Demir-Tepe, a knight of the order of St George, or any Georgian! Shame on you."

Demir-Tepe? St George's cross? Georgian? These words hit Kvachi like a hammer. He was shaken and startled, he tightened his sinews and rid his heart of the fear that haunted it.

"Ha-ha-ha," he guffawed heartily, jumping back into the car and grabbing Rasputin's collar. "Move on, get going, drive like hell! And you, Holy Father, calm down and rest for ever, or ..." The corpse convulsed and swayed from side to side. Rasputin ground his teeth and nodded at Kvachi, as a sign either of agreement or menace.

They stopped at a small bridge on Krestovy island and dropped the body through a crack that had opened in the ice that morning. They left one of Rasputin's boots at the edge of the ice.

Nobody noticed.

The first thunderbolt had struck Tsarist Russia: Rasputin was murdered. "Amen! And that won't be the worst of it," exclaimed Kvachi with excitement. That evening he summoned his junta.

"It's happened! We've got rid of the pillar holding up Russia. The building is cracked and on the verge of collapse. There's no hurry, the rest will come about of its own accord. If by any chance I'm put in prison, start a fire; if they decide to shoot me, set fire to this stinking, rotten, mouldy country and blow it sky-high. My last request is this: don't let them kill me, blow the place up in good time, because I want, if only once, to celebrate and see with my own eyes the destruction of those people who are so ungrateful as to throw on the rubbish heap their loyal sons." (Kvachi meant to say "like me.")

"Kvachi, it wasn't you, was it, who shed Rasputin's blood?" asked Sedrak.

"Me? Who knows ... That will become clear later," replied Silibistro's heir with a hypocritical smile.

Kvachi was congratulated on carrying out a deed so important for posterity: they bowed their heads before his magnificent character and self-sacrificing personality.

Three days later Rasputin's corpse was found in the Neva. The whole country was abuzz with the news. Russia reared up on its hind legs; Petersburg was in uproar. People congratulated and kissed each other for joy; believers said prayers of thanksgiving and burned large wax candles. Nobody could talk about anything but Rasputin's death.

The murderers, Purishkevich, Dr Lazovert, and Sukhotin, found refuge at the front; Grand Duke Dimitri was sent to the Persian front, Prince Yusupov was deported to his estates, and Kvachi hid with Silibistro.

The Tsaritsa took possession of Rasputin's corpse. She had it taken to Chesma convent and entrusted it to Rasputin's friend, the nun Akilina. Rasputin's wife, daughters, and close relatives tried to see the body to take leave of him, but the Tsaritsa had ordered everyone to be kept away.

Akilina washed the body, filled its wounds with balm, dressed it in expensive new clothes, put it in a coffin, with a cross on the chest and a handwritten note from the Tsaritsa. The note read: "My dear martyr! Grant me your blessing to accompany me on the thorny path that I have to walk on this earth; may I be remembered in heaven by your holy prayers."

The next day, when Russia was blessing the killer's right hand and offering thanks to the Lord, the Tsaritsa and her best friend, lady-in-waiting Vyrubova, were standing over Rasputin, his body swollen by the Neva, in the little Chesma chapel. Mourning with pious laments and bitter tears, they prayed for their hope, their saint, their fortress and friend, the country's savior. Exhausted and tired out with weeping and grieving, they took Rasputin's blood-stained shirt and left. This shirt, a holy relic, a sacred reminder, and a talisman for the Tsar's family, was turned by the Tsaritsa into an icon she would pray to.

Kvachi was hiding on Elagin Island. A lot of threads linked him to the outside world, which (as Kvachi clearly and rightly saw) was swelling up and would at any moment explode. Beso brought and took away any news. None of the others had any idea where Kvachi was living. He was avoiding them and was afraid of their carelessness, saying: "They might, without meaning to do so, bring a spy along or show people where I am."

Nevertheless, he couldn't escape danger.

Falling into a Trap and Getting out of It

Disguised, wearing make-up, Kvachi once went to the Okhta area to see members of his junta and to give them instructions. He had finished his business and was going home, pleased with himself. Beso was a few steps behind him.

Suddenly someone put cold metal against his temple.

"Stop. Hands up! Are you armed? No? Now put your arms behind your back. If you move them, I'll kill you here and now. Right, move."

Unmasked, Kvachi was so taken aback that he gave in without a word and walked on in front of the stranger. Then he collected himself, took courage, and started a dialog with the stranger:

"You're local, who are you?"

"A secret police agent."

"Name?"

"None of your business."

"I recognize you: you're Bekarev."

"So we know each other, but why ask my name if you know me?"

"I also asked you why I'm being held. Aren't you looking for someone else? Haven't you made a mistake?"

"No, I haven't: I was looking for Prince Kvachantiradze and I've found him, too."

"I don't deny it, you've got your man. But, old friend, tell me one thing: how big a bonus do you get for capturing me?"

"None of your business."

"You're quite right, but … All the same … Are you looking for a cab? Be patient, don't be too much in a hurry. Let's talk a bit, you won't regret it. Yes, I said you won't regret it. So: for capturing me you'd get a bit of promotion and … about a hundred, even two hundred roubles."

"What business is it of yours?"

"It is my business. Let's agree a sum."

"Shut up, or …"

"I'm not joking: how about a thousand?"

"Don't fool with me! Move!"

"This is no time for fooling about: just remember that any day now the times will change, you'll be needing a friend … Think about it."

A thousand roubles and future danger settled the matter: the agent pondered. The ice gradually thawed, finally cracked, and broke away.

"I wouldn't soil my hands for a thousand roubles."

"Then two thousand …"

"Five. And pay up now."

"Fine, but I don't have it on me. Let's go somewhere, have a bite of supper, and then go to my house."

The agent pondered again. But he overcame his fear and agreed.

They entered a little restaurant, sat in a corner, and ordered food and drink. In came Beso and took a table not far off. The restaurant was empty. Kvachi and Beso made signs to each other and looked round the restaurant. Then Beso went out the back door into the yard and came back ten minutes later. They exchanged signals again.

Beso later wrote half a dozen words on a piece of paper, went to the counter, and asked for a vodka. Kvachi stood up at the same time, taking the agent with him, and also stood at the counter. In an instant Beso's note was in Kvachi's pocket.

They had a drink or two and got tipsy. The agent unbuttoned himself and became chatty. They paid the bill and left. When they reached the door, suddenly the electricity cut out, plunging the whole room into darkness. In an instant Kvachi evaded the agent and hid behind the door. That was when Beso ran round the room banging his feet everywhere.

"Stop, stop, or I'll shoot!" yelled agent Bekarev, running round the room and the yard. The shadow behind the door slipped out into the street.

The lights came on again. Beso was sitting at his table without a care in the world. Kvachi was nowhere to be seen. The agent's voice could be heard in the yard:

"Arrest him! He's escaped! Arrest him! Constable!"

Bekarev ran back into the restaurant. There was chaos as he ran about. Beso blocked his path:

"What's up? Lost your prisoner? Have some sense! How can you broadcast something like that? What are you and a prisoner doing in a place like this? You'll be put in prison and dismissed."

The agent eventually understood what Beso had said. Having grasped it, he felt afraid and begged those present: "Don't ruin me … keep quiet … I have a family … Say that it was a drunk shouting."

In the doorway a policeman bumped into the agent.

"It's nothing, man, nothing … Let's go … Some drunk was shouting … Let's go, or … come and let's have a vodka each."

They each started with a glass to calm their nerves, then went on until they saw the dawn in. Beso had crept out on tiptoe, then turned left to be swallowed up in the darkness.

Getting Trapped Again, Avoiding the Noose, and the Country's Explosion

Kvachi met Beso at an agreed meeting place.

"Well, I can't go home tonight," said Kvachi. "Let's go and meet the others as soon as it gets light. Go and see Silibistro and find out if my hideout's been discovered. If everything is all right, I'll go home."

They went to the group's lodgings and quickly got everyone together. There was a loud commotion and some joy.

"*Shukur Allah*, Thank God!" exclaimed Jalil. "Allah has saved our prince once more."

"I swear by St Karapet I've never been so happy to see you as I am today," declared Sedrak. "Right, Jalil. Lay the table! Come on, get busy."

Everyone deftly got to work and soon they were having a banquet with plenty to drink. It was daylight when Kvachi began prophesying:

"Comrades! In three days' time it will all explode. Who knows whether we'll be buried under the ruins. This may be the last day we see each other and the last time we dine together. Whatever happens, there's one thing you should know. My enemies are determined to bury me in silence and secrecy. But, friends, you must swear to me that you won't forget the story of my life and will let the whole world know it."

"We swear, we swear," the comrades roared out.

"Comrades," Kvachi continued. "On 27 February, in three days' time, you will come to see me at this apartment; if I don't turn up, then you'll know that Kvachi Kvachantiradze is dead."

"You'll turn up, you'll turn up," the comrades yelled.

"Yes indeed, as long as I'm alive, so wait for me here in three days' time and if I don't turn up, go straight to the church and have a requiem mass said. Beso, you're back? Nothing going on at my place? Then I'll go there. Well, goodbye, comrades!" And he embraced and kissed each of them and left.

He'd passed down one street and turned into another, when he bumped straight into agent Bekarev on the corner.

"Stop! So this is Prince Kvachantiradze! Are you going to get away from me this time?"

"I've got no choice. Let's go; just my luck."

Kvachi and the drunken agent got into a cab and left.

"Take me home and get your five thousand," Kvachi haggled again.

"Ten thousand, and no argument."

"While Kvachi and the agent were haggling, the cab was approaching the police court. Suddenly a second cab caught up and a cheerful voice cried out from it:

"Hey, my regards to Prince Kvachantiradze! How are you, how are you doing?" Gendarme Pavlov leapt out of this cab and stopped Kvachi's cab. "What's happened to you? Cat got your tongue? Never mind, we'll get you talking again. So, kindly change cabs."

Pavlov grabbed hold of Kvachi by the arm and pulled him out, while Bekarev, faced with going home empty-handed, gnashed his teeth as he saw the two of them off.

Twenty minutes later Kvachi, bathed in cold sweat, was sitting opposite a happy Pavlov.

"Fancy meeting you like this!" said Pavlov, offering Kvachi a cigarette and a glass of tea. "Ten years ago we were good friends, but now ..."

"What about now?" asked Kvachi, looking Pavlov straight in the eye. "Can't we be friends now?"

"No, we can't." Pavlov replied icily.

"But I reckon we could be a hundred times closer than we were then."

"A hundred times? Hmm! I understand, but ... I'll be straight with you: any friendship between us is out of the question. The

Tsar's palace knows about your case. Apart from that, we have such good evidence that your case is an open-and-closed case for us. So, let's get down to business. I advise you from the start not to be obstinate: it makes no difference, denials won't help you. So let's begin."

For two hours they sweated and tormented each other. Kvachi dug his heels in and forgot every word in the language except "no."

"Bring in Isaac Idelsohn and his wife for me," Pavlov finally ordered.

With pounding heart Kvachi waited for Idelsohn to enter the room. Ten minutes stretched out like ten hours.

Rebecca and Isaac appeared in the doorway. Kvachi could barely recognize his blonde beauty. They had both withered and seemed to have aged ten years. Neither Isaac nor Rebecca looked at Kvachi. Their heads bowed, they edged round him, sat down, and stared at the wall.

"Do you recognize each other?" Pavlov asked Kvachi.

"Perfectly," Kvachi replied at once in a firm voice. "Isaac Idelsohn and I are sworn enemies, and Rebecca used to be my mistress: I left her because she was unfaithful."

Kvachi concocted such a neat story that for five minutes or so they all stared at one another with gaping jaws.

"Have you forgotten Paris?" Kvachi asked the Idelsohns. "You've forgotten so soon? Rebby, tell me the truth, were you or were you not my mistress? Speak, not that I care whether you confirm what I say, or not."

"Well … I was … Yes, I was, but …" mumbled Rebecca, but before she could finish speaking she started sobbing. In those five minutes Isaac became even more withered and elderly.

The three men and one woman tormented and tired each other for another two hours, but nothing could make Kvachi say "yes."

"Take them away. Get them out of my sight," Pavlov finally

called out, sending all three of them off to cold, dark cells.

In the evening Pavlov summoned Kvachi again and took a pair of pliers to his mouth, but he couldn't pull out any of Kvachi's well-rooted teeth. For a time he tried being nice and kindly, even flattering, smiling, and promising to show respect; then he attacked angrily, beat him on the soles of his feet and threatened him with the gallows. Kvachi just went on repeating "no" and forgot the very word "yes."

"All right, leave it like this," Pavlov said. "Go away. I don't care if we hang you in the morning in two days' time and throw your corpse to the dogs."

"In two days' time, in the morning?" Kvachi smiled. "The day after tomorrow? Fine, we'll see who hangs who."

"What? Are you threatening me again? What are you hoping for?"

"We'll discuss that in two days' time. Keep me alive until then, and you'll see for yourself. I'll be off now. Good day to you."

He nodded politely to Pavlov and went back to his cell with a smile.

The next day Kvachi was not interrogated. The following day, as midnight approached, all three prisoners were put on trial by a military tribunal. A captain was appointed to be Kvachi's lawyer. It took ten minutes to read the indictment and then the three of them were advised:

"Admit you're guilty of the crime."

"Never," Kvachi replied categorically.

Isaac and Rebecca revealed everything, then burst into tears and began to plead.

"When you left here for Stockholm, whom did you meet at the station?" Kvachi was asked.

"Nobody."

"Who gave you the next day cheque No. 137429 for a million kronen?

"Nobody."

"Look, this is the cheque with your signature. Confess."

They showed him a photograph of the cheque, inscribed, "Received, Prince Kvachantiradze."

Kvachi blushed, but boldly retorted: "It's a forgery."

In half an hour it was all over. A toothless general, the chairman of the court, pronounced the sentence: "Prince Kvachantiradze, Isaac Idelsohn, and Rebecca Idelsohn are to be deprived of their civic rights and are sentenced to be hanged."

The judges immediately slipped out of the courtroom. Rebecca gave a shriek and collapsed. Isaac made not a sound, but suddenly fainted. The color drained from Kvachi Kvachantiradze's face, but he didn't twitch an eyebrow. He ran his eye over the courtroom, and called out with a smile to his comrades and Elena: "Goodbye, friends! I'll see you the day after tomorrow, in the morning."

Beso tried to revive Elena. The others had turned the color of the courtroom walls.

Kvachi was taken to Peter and Paul fortress and thrown into a dank cell. He sat on an iron stool and began to think. The thought took a day and a night, and reached a conclusion the following night. What had the toothless general said? Prince Kvachantiradze is to be hanged? Silibistro's son Kvachi? Little Kvachi?!

He secretly thought: "Oh, what idiocy, sheer idiocy!"

But an imp began to gnaw at him and scratch at his innards; it giggled: "Do you suppose they wouldn't dare do it to you?"

"Would they dare do it to me? The Tsar's godson, the right hand of the throne?"

"Hee-hee," the imp rasped merrily. "For once, be frank with your conscience. Who are you shy of now? Well, be bold ... Start. Don't be so secretive all the time. Show yourself your real heart ... So you're the Tsar's godson? You're a loyal servant of the throne, are you?"

"Demir-Tepe hill? Who saved so many people from death

and shame?"

"I did, it was me! Yes, me! The flesh was yours, but the spirit was mine. You were running away in panic. You were fainting with fear. I got inside your soul and took you to the top of Demir-Tepe. The whole country was amazed by your heroism, because they knew you only too well and didn't expect such selflessness from you. Your achievement amazed you more than anyone else."

"What sort of wretch are you to claim my heroism for yourself?"

"Me? Hee-hee. You still don't recognize me: I'm Kvachi Kvachantiradze, Silibistro's son."

"Don't be silly. I'm Kvachi."

"I'm Kvachi Kvachantiradze, and I'm not fake Ashordia gentry, or a fake prince, or a fake lord in waiting, nor a pickpocket, pimp, or traitor."

"Why are you pestering me? What do you want from me?"

"I want just once to hear from you a word of truth. Any moment you're going to be hanged. At least now you can stop double-dealing."

"Leave me alone! The past is the past. Why the hell do you want the truth? Anyone can tell the truth—idiots, savages, and babies."

"A sincere heart?"

"I'm not a saint."

"Loyalty?"

"Loyalty to Tsar Nicolas and Rasputin?! I haven't gone mad yet."

"You've changed recently, you did show those people some loyalty."

"Shut up. Be quiet. Clear off!"

Kvachi struck out angrily at his double, but his blows hit only air.

"Hee-hee-hee," the imp giggled, squeezing into a narrow crack in the door.

Kvachi banged at the door, using both fists.

"What do you want? Why are you banging?"

"A cigarette. Just one cigarette, quick."

"What?"

"A cigarette ... just one."

The guard calmly turned away without a word, his boots clumping on the floor. Kvachi span round and suddenly bumped into Rasputin. Nodding his bloodstained head, the holy man said: "So that's how you show me gratitude ..."

Kvachi, deadly pale, flung himself back against the wall, then struck out at Rasputin, but again hit only the air. The figure of Vera Sidorova emerged from the dark depths of the cell, then came the Volkova widow, followed by Tania, Elena, Lady Harvey, Lord Brouxton, Sophie Shivadze, Inspector Hofstein, Nadia Armeladze, Vera Kaloshvili, and Kvachi's many victims, whether known to him or not. They all fell upon him, at first one by one, then all together. Some pulled him one way, some the other. Some spat on him, tore at his hair, guffawed, and yelled: "That's what you were asking for! Today you'll be hanged. You'll be hanged. Good riddance! You deserve it!"

Kvachi hit out at one, chased another, knocked down a third, and sat on him or her. Then he whirled like a spinning top, waving his arms and legs, yelling and roaring: "Help me, help me!"

"Why are you yelling?" asked the guard as he entered the cell.

His face white, his hands bloody, Kvachi lay senseless on the iron bed. He was revived by cold water and the guard rubbing his ears.

"Don't shout, shouting won't do you any good. Hang on another hour and then it will all be over," the guard advised him gravely before leaving.

Kvachi's troubled soul gradually calmed down and resigned itself. He thought some more:

"So they're going to hang me? My comrades aren't going to

help? They won't start on time? Perhaps they'll be late? Then, suppose? Stupid of me! I can't believe it, I can't! How dare they? I expect they're trying to frighten me. They want to crush me, or … who knows … They may be putting the gallows up now … God almighty, almighty God!"

The moment he mentioned God some invisible being flew into his soul: "The time has come for things to be fulfilled. Repent your sins. Very soon you will stand before your Lord."

Kvachi froze. He surrendered his resigned heart to an invisible being and followed it. Suddenly he realized that in a few hours there would be no Kvachi in this world, that Kvachi would die … He would emigrate to eternal darkness and nothingness … There wouldn't even be darkness there, nor time, nor space, nor nothingness … So what would there be? Nothingness? There must be something if there was nothingness … So I'll be living in this nothingness … So … What, I shan't exist any more? How stupid! What nonsense! There'll be no more Kvachi in the nothingness? That's utter nonsense! It's impossible."

"You will exist!" the invisible being whispered sweetly. "You are immortal … humans are immortal, eternal … I shall take you there, to Him, and your life will be eternal, unending … for ever and ever … pray and you will be forgiven … ask and it will be given to you."

"Our father, Who art in heaven," Kvachi whispered with trembling heart, raising his hands high. "Who art in heaven … Hallowed be Thy name; Thy kingdom come; Thy will be done …"

Suddenly he stopped praying. He didn't know what to ask for, or whom. His resigned heart contracted again and became as hard as flint. The invisible being fled his soul.

"Oh, that's all stupidity!" Kvachi muttered and paced about like a maddened beast in a cage. Then he pounded at the door again:

"A cigarette! Just one cigarette. I'll give you anything you ask for a cigarette."

The guard's toothless maw uttered just one word: "Soon."

And he clattered off, as indifferent as ever. Ten minutes later the iron bolt clanged and the wrought iron doors creaked open. The elderly guard, a simple, one-eyed veteran, was holding a cigarette in one hand and a pair of pliers in the other. His black pit of a mouth opened and closed and just audibly uttered: "First give me a tooth."

"What? What did you say?"

"I said, give me a tooth."

Kvachi looked round the cell: "Tooth, what tooth? Which tooth?"

"Yours, your gold tooth."

"You aren't mad, are you?"

"Me? No. I'm in my right mind." And the pit of a mouth grimaced as if it were smiling; the guard screwed up his gray, bean-sized eye.

"You're new, so you don't get it. Why do you need your gold tooth? You can't take it with you. Anyway, in an hour's time you'll be hanged."

"So?"

"So, I was asking why you need your gold tooth? Are you going to take it to the next world? Oh, I can't say how many gold teeth I've taken out here with these pliers. People are amazed at first, but then they let me do it. Don't be afraid, I've had a lot of experience pulling teeth. I'll pull it before you even feel anything."

"You sell a cigarette that dearly?"

"I give some people a cigarette, sometimes … I take a last letter to send to their parents."

"You take it, then tear it up. It doesn't matter, no-one will find out."

"Never on my life!" the old man whispered fearfully, smacking the lips of his pit of a mouth and crossing himself. "God forbid! God forbid I should commit such a sin! A last letter is something so sacred that …"

"So you'd send my letter, too?"

"Of course! As soon as we've buried you, I'll go to church and pray for you, then I'll put the letter in the post."

Kvachi's eyes were shining and his seething brain was working on an idea at lightning speed.

"Fine … I agree … If you take the letter personally to my father, he'll give you a hundred roubles … he lives quite close to here. Give me a pen and paper."

"In a minute," the old man mumbled.

Kvachi quickly lay on the bed; the old man brought pencil and paper.

"Put it on the table," Kvachi said calmly.

The old man came into the cell and made for the corner where a tiny metal table was fixed to the wall. That instant a tiger sprang from the bed, and a short rasp "Hhht" was audible in the cell.

In an instant Kvachi had thrown the old man over his back, put his right hand behind and was throttling the guard's throat, while his left hand also went back and clutched the old man's convulsing feet. Kvachi stayed crouched for some time, holding the waist of the old man, who was bent double and suffocating. Then he lowered him onto the bed and pressed his fingers into the guard's windpipe.

His face bloated, the old man stared feverishly at Kvachi with his frozen bean of an eye, while the grimacing pit of a mouth complained of Kvachi's ingratitude.

Five minutes later, Kvachi, changed into the guard's clothes, crept towards the yard gates. Dawn was already breaking. It was freezing cold. A motor car crawled into the courtyard, stopped, and sounded its horn. A military man in a fur coat got out of the car and went into the prison office. Kvachi recognized his prosecutor at the trial, the man who had demanded the death sentence for him. The car turned round and stopped again. The driver got out and entered the barracks. Kvachi ducked down and ran across the courtyard.

A minute later the car headed towards the main gates. The sleepy sentry instantly opened the gates and only later rubbed his eyes.

Panic broke out in the courtyard. The horrified driver ran around waving his arms and shouting: "Stop him, stop him!"

The car crossed Trinity Bridge a moment later, then like an arrow it shot across the Field of Mars, lost itself in the turnings nearby, and stopped at a corner. Kvachi jumped out, ran left, then right, then left and rushed to his comrades' lodgings, where he called out: "Comrades! Get up! Get up and come. Quick, quick, I said."

Still undressed, alarmed and confused, his friends rushed out instantly to meet their leader, who stood as tall as the central pillar of a house and now looked exactly as he had when he stood on the peak of Demir-Tepe.

"I've kept my promise and come to the appointed place at the appointed time."

"Long live the leader of the revolution! Hurrah!" his army shouted as one man.

"The day of judgement has come. Arm yourselves."

In ten minutes they were all armed to the teeth.

"Summon the others!"

In half an hour Kvachi's junta had gathered around their leader. The silence of the grave fell on them for a while, then Kvachi uttered in an awesome whisper the key word: "Be-gin!"

This happened on 26 February 1917. It was the anniversary of Austerlitz. Two eternal enemies had met head-on.

That day Kvachi's deeds proved fully worthy of his famous forebear Napoleon, whose name he had casually misappropriated a decade earlier.

Never had any commander issued such a short, wrathful, and

clear order: "Begin!!!"

That was it. Nothing more.

This one word was followed straight away by an unprecedented catastrophe: that very day wrath and thunder like no other broke out on the old, moss-covered, corrupt, and rotten empire. The gigantic building which a hundred million people had built with their sweat and blood suddenly quaked and collapsed with horrible crashing and roaring, and its tenants, protectors, and guards all fell with it.

This was Kvachi's response to base ingratitude. This was how he acquitted himself of his debt to that ungrateful empire which blamed Kvachi for its own profligacy and its defeat on the battlefields of Poland, alleging that Kvachi had imported from America useless dud artillery shells for the Russian army.

Those in power had just as easily forgotten Kvachi's invaluable and immeasurable achievements: bringing calm to the Caucasus, saving Rasputin from a hundred pitfalls, providing clothes for the army, building an enormous church, realizing half a dozen concessions, keeping the Tsar on the throne, winning Russia a reputation in Europe, the boundless success of *The Good Samaritan*, planting the Russian flag on Demir-Tepe, arming an army that had no weapons and no munitions, as well as a thousand benefits, beyond count, which Kvachi had conferred on a moribund and ungrateful regime.

Ingratitude is not, however, a vice unique to the dead. This disease seems to afflict today's generation too. Read modern history, in print or not: you won't be able to read in any book, newspaper, or manuscript even two words about Kvachi's exploits in Russia's great revolution. True, historians do concede, but only in private conversation, that Kvachi helped with money and advice, but they have denied outright the most important fact: that Kvachi gave the signal for rebellion and issued the unforgettable order: "Begin!"

But a future objective generation will discover this black ingratitude, will wipe out the fabulous injustice, and will give the real author of 26 February the place he deserves, for it was he who prepared the way for that day and what followed. He issued the unforgettable order at the right time. Yes, the right time: not an hour too soon, not an hour too late.

Kvachi didn't expect an unbiased opinion of his achievement from the generation of his day, because he had many personal enemies. What can you do? Fate showed no mercy to poor Kvachi.

Yet, whatever Kvachi's enemies might say, one thing is clear and certain: on the morning of 26 February 1917 Kvachi gave a laconic and categorical order to his staff: "Begin!!!"

And it began.

This has always and everywhere been confirmed by Kvachi's staff: Beso Shikia, Ladi Chikinjiladze, Chipi Chipuntiradze, Jalil Emin-oglu, Sedrak Havlabariani, and Gabo Chkhubishvili.

CHAPTER SIX

The Society of Defenders of the Revolution and Founding the Free Socialist Party

"Begin!" Kvachi ordered on the morning of 27 February, then sat down in his armchair and reached for the telephone.

For two days and nights he didn't leave the armchair or the telephone. His comrades watched the country shake itself to pieces and shed blood either from the main gates or through the windows; sometimes they poked their noses into the street, sometimes, when things fell silent nearby, they even crept out to the corner, questioned passersby, sniffed the air, and brought news back to their leader.

Chipi Chipuntiradze would rush in panic up to Kvachi and tear his hair, shrieking: "We're finished … They've beaten us! Run for your lives."

Beso would come in smiling to say gravely: "Keep cool, Chipi. Everything's going well. I think we'll win."

Jalil never left the window, sometimes telling Kvachi: "A lot of army is going. They're all laughing, I expect the Tsar is losing."

"Oh God, won't it ever end?" asked a faint-hearted Sedrak. "I feel so terrible! I wish I was home, in my native Sighnaghi."

Two days later, Beso, ducking as he went, ran round half the city. He came back and reported to Kvachi: "It's all over. We've won."

Kvachi passed on to his comrades a plan he had spent two days working on, and spread out the net he had just woven. Then he got up and said: "Right, now we should really begin. Follow me."

He left and took his comrades, who were armed to the teeth.

Jalil went first, waving a strange gigantic flag.

"Citizens, follow us! Do your duty. Long live the revolution! Down with tyranny and slavery!"

Kvachi suddenly caught sight of agent Bekarev, who had arrested him five days before, among his band of men. They shook each other's hands, smiled and laughed as if they were the best of friends. Kvachi noticed that Bekarev's voice had cracked from shouting.

An hour later, under Kvachi's leadership, two thousand men were standing outside the Taurideam Palace. Sentries blocked the mob, but Kvachi and his comrades attacked the tall-hatted sentries: they yelled, they kicked at them, they rattled their weapons, they called out "revolution" in the name of the people and by threats, bluff, and brazen intimidation they managed to storm the White Hall.

"In the name of the long-suffering people and the sacred revolution I have risen to bless freedom ..." Kvachi began his speech, so ardent that it fired the whole palace and made his listeners shed tears. His speech ended: "The revolution has given this hall as shelter for its sacred purpose: we shall live here. We shan't leave it and we shan't entrust its defence to anyone. Comrades, am I right, or am I not?" Kvachi addressed his party.

"Right! Right!" two thousand throats roared in agreement.

An hour later the mob dispersed just as it had gathered. Kvachi and his comrades took possession of five rooms in the Tauridean Palace, filled them with furniture and left roughly scrawled signs on the walls and doors: "Society of Defenders and Helpers of the Revolution. Membership and Donations." On the doors of the big office was written: "Chairman of the Administration"; on a desk in another room Beso Shikia stuck a notice: "Department of Mandates and Permits." Here and there were palm-sized scrawled notices: "Supreme Committee of the Free Socialists Party."

Sedrak Havlabariani manned the till, Chipi Chipuntiradze

took on the job of intelligence, Ladi Chikinjiladze was secretary, Gabo Chkhubishvili would manage the future warehouse, and Jalil Emin-oglu, armed with rifle, Mauser, and dagger, was stationed by Kvachi at the entrance to his office. Bekarev was content with a minor role for the time being: he sat at the party table and took over the enrolment of members.

After a few days, work was so intense that the comrades were covered in sweat, working fifteen hours a day, struggling to keep up with issuing strange and very varied mandates and permits, and counting the donors and the money. But the ministers' doors, double locked, were always open for Kvachi: he could enter the leaders' rooms without asking, boldly take a seat, cross his legs and casually, but firmly and cockily report:

"The Society of Defenders and Helpers of the Revolution, and the Party of Free Socialists, which now has up to four hundred branches and two million members, is maintaining vigilance day and night, guarding the people. But we lack clothing, provisions, weapons, and ... money. The Society demands of you, citizen minister, tha-a-at ..."

That was the moment when he put forward his report and pronounced the word "tha-a-at" with such menace and gave the minister or the leader such a look that the latter at once signed the report unread, "Approved."

Kvachi and his comrades grew more powerful every day. The Society and the Party soon spread, expanded, and swelled up. The membership was claimed to be "nearly five million" and there were sixty people working in the administration office and up to two hundred in the warehouse. The queue of people waiting to pay at the till snaked in four lines and there were sometimes a hundred men at the doors of the mandates department.

Kvachi's Party took wings: its left wing reached Archangel, its right wing—Tbilisi, its beak—the Vistula, and its tail—Vladivostok. From all over the country came torrents of donations: they became rivers, and these rivers headed for Petersburg and poured such a deluge into Kvachi's till and pocket that he and his comrades nearly drowned.

Agent Bekarev was given a second job: he took up his former trade and became Chipi Chipuntiradze's assistant.

"Don't trust everything he does, but don't be too wary of him. He's an excellent spy. If need be, he can set up a very nice bit of provocation. Help him, he's a useful man," Kvachi told Chipi as he handed Bekarev over to him.

Gendarme Pavlov was now thrown into the very same cell in which Kvachi had spent a terrible and unforgettable night.

Once Kvachi remembered Rebecca and Isaac Idelsohn and asked Bekarev what had happened to them.

"They're still in prison," Bekarev replied. "They're hoping you'll show them mercy."

"Me? Those scoundrels betrayed me. Am I supposed to rescue them?"

"No, it wasn't like that," Bekarev smiled. "I should have said, but I couldn't find an opportunity. Someone else betrayed you: guess who."

"Gintz? Knulman? Chainstein? Then who did betray me?"

"What did Gintz or the others know about your dealings? Let me tell you. There was a banker by the name of Ganus, your colleague, the one you made rich with the Turkestan concession."

"So? So?"

"Once his wife, who was your … what do you call it …"

"Mistress, mistress! So?"

"Yes … You apparently borrowed a bit of money from her and …"

"And I didn't pay it back. So what did the old man know, and how?"

"Hmm. That old man was considered in Petersburg to be a German agent, but he was our agent, too. So he often went to

Stockholm and we entrusted him with giving false information to our enemies, while he brought back genuine information."

"What do you mean?"

"Of course, in fact, it worked the other way round."

"Ah, I understand, now I understand. Ganus, old man, I pity you if I ever get my hands on you! Fine … thanks … And Isaac and Rebecca?"

"They were exposed by Ganus. We made Rebecca and Isaac give us your name. Don't be angry with them. If they'd been made of iron, Pavlov would still have broken them."

"Fine … I'll think about it. I'm grateful."

Soon the old fox Gintz made his way to Kvachi's office and whined:

"Let's put the past behind us and bury the axe, prince. Let's make up."

"Let's make up," Kvachi greeted him with a smile of agreement. "Please sit down, old friend, and tell me what you're up to. I can't imagine you'd come without a good reason."

"Of course not! Poor old Gintz is always running about doing business. You know very well, Kvachi," (Gintz had decided to be familiar with the prince), "that you're a very important person now."

"Am I? Really?"

"Of course you are, and you know it. You're more important than you were, to hell with everything that happened before. I have some business for you. Though, wait, let me show you first."

He opened out for Kvachi an illustrated weekly magazine. The whole of the first page was taken up by a portrait of Kvachi, captioned "The loyal defender and ever-vigilant guard of the revolution, N. A. Kvachantiradze." This was followed by a twelve-page biography concocted by Knulman. Kvachi perused the biographical sketch and smiled. For one thing, there was no mention of Kvachi being a prince or an aide-de-camp, nor was there any mention of Rasputin or anything which would harm Kvachi now. For another thing, Kvachi's revolutionary past was emphasized as a reason for his fleeing abroad. Thirdly, Kvachi was said to have returned to carry out secret work, to found a socialist party and, as a result, the authorities had decided to hang Kvachi, but the "lion of the Caucasus" had broken through the walls of the Peter and Paul fortress, killing seven and wounding ten, so as to be in time to help his beloved cause, the revolution.

"Whoever wrote this essay is a clever man," said Kvachi. "Who owns the magazine?"

"I do, but from now on it's going to be ours. You let me use the name of your Party and Society, while I ..."

"And you (Kvachi was calling Gintz by his first name, too) will give me half the profits, won't you?"

"You've got my gist. Are we finished?"

"We are."

"Good. From now on the magazine will be subtitled: "Organ of the Free Socialist Party and of the Society of Defenders of the Revolution."

The contract was signed and the magazine's advertising, size, contents, and print run were increased.

Not a day passed without a former minister or former dignitary coming in to see Kvachi, bowing as low as they could, making a donation, and asking Kvachi for protection and help. Kvachi recalled the time after Rasputin left for Jerusalem, when he himself, with his tongue hanging out, went to these dignitaries begging for protection, when some had no time for him, others were not at home, or apparently had stopped knowing him. Remembering this, Kvachi treated these dignitaries differently from the others: he taxed them and burdened them "for the benefit of the revolution," thus nearly working some of them to death or bankruptcy.

But with Ganus he was putting off settling accounts to a later time.

Silibistro, Pupi, Khukhu, and Notio were now as used to Petersburg as they had been to Samtredia and Kutaisi. The four of them dressed like Europeans and gave themselves even more airs, proudly, even haughtily boasting: "Our little Kvachi's got far too big for his boots," Silibistro said, "I'm afraid the poor lad will burst or something else will happen to him."

"Oh no, you don't know little Kvachi," Notio reassured Silibistro.

"I'm very fond of him," said Pupi, who was now fifty years old but still called "Little Pupi.""The man who can ruin him hasn't been born yet, but only God can tell what's in store."

"All respect for the grace of God," Khukhu concluded. "He is our protector and Kvachi's, otherwise we'd have been ruined ten times over."

One evening Beso told Kvachi: "Someone came to see you. He said they're going to burn Rasputin's body and you ought to come."

"Hmm, but I've heard that hooligans and oafs are visiting his grave to pray. So we'd have to burn him or the coffin will be snatched and it will be dragged all round Russia and he'll be declared a saint."

It was past midnight when Kvachi and Jalil arrived by motor car at the edge of a forest where kindling and firewood had been piled up. Soon the coffin was brought and with great difficulty lifted onto the firewood. Then they poured a big canister of petrol over the wood and the coffin and set fire to them. A thousand tongues of flame began licking the wood and the coffin. The fire soon took hold of the coffin. The smell of a roasting rotten carcass hung in the air all round. Everyone went round to the side of the fire where the night breeze was blowing. There they started chatting about Russia's past and future.

The fire crackled, rose up in a pillar and in its light the forest, the small clearing, and the twenty or so men present were dyed the color of blood. The sky in the east turned dove-gray.

Kvachi stood aside, watching flames engulfing the coffin; he was thinking of his own past and future. Drowsily he felt his own colorful past burning up in the fire with Rasputin's corpse, while a new Kvachi was being born, purified in the crucible of the revolution, baptised by the people, to whom, loyal and respectful, he now dedicated himself.

The fire was now out. They poured water on the embers, threw the ash and coals into a sack and left the area spick and span. The coals, the ash, and what was left of Rasputin, they threw in the Neva before returning to the city.

"Beso!" a sleepless Kvachi said to his faithful comrade. "I've had enough of this demeaning life. I'm fed up with it. From now on I don't want to hear about anything that might smear me. From now on everything belongs to the people and we have to serve the people honestly. Tell this to the other comrades."

"Fine," Beso retorted, telling himself: "I wonder what's got into him? He's heard someone preaching and believed them, but ... Well, I know this won't last even until tomorrow, and then it will all start again. We'll see ... We'll see what comes of some monk's teachings."

The First Command, July, and Building a New Bridge

Tiny little human figures were moving around outside the huge building, bustling, walking on their hands, thinking with their feet, and using their fingers to fortify Mount Qazbeg, which was about to collapse. But the mountain refused to stand properly or to bend to the right. Its left flank was leaning over and, like a stubborn child, it was trying to roll over only onto that left side. That obstinate child, history, seemed unaware of the sea of human figures, the sky-high mountains of their corpses, and the bottomless torrent of their blood. History couldn't feel the fingers digging into its flanks, it couldn't even hear the peoples' shrieks, moans, and wails, fear, hope, urges, and joy. History was striding blind and deaf into pitch-black space: nobody knew the secret ways of its will and movement.

Kvachi's mysterious intuition felt and saw a blind state and stubborn history following different paths: they were in conflict, and this senseless struggle had to end with the annihilation of the crazed little humans.

Kvachi also sensed the utterly inevitable and relentless outcome of this battle, and every now and again told his disciples so:

"Comrades! Anyone who embraces a madman goes mad himself: if you cling to a corpse, you become a corpse yourself; if you clutch a drowning man, you too will perish. Mademoiselle Kerensky will flap about and squawk for a few more months, and then tumble into the pit of history. Today's state is doomed. It's digging its heels in, but it might as well try to bore through the Caucasus mountains with its nose. They won't make a hole, but they'll break their nose: we can't follow madmen like them. But the Mademoiselle's death is not close enough for us to abandon it yet and take refuge with the new power. When the time comes, I shall give you further instructions. But I tell you now that Russia has been pregnant with twins. February's baby boy turned out to be a runt who will kick the bucket any day now, but his mother is giving birth to a second child. We must tie a little thread to this second child who is now kicking in his mother's belly, about to break out and be born prematurely. So trust me with this task. In good time this thread will become a bridge to lead us over a torrent of blood, tears, and fire to the other bank."

"Go and summon us!" exclaimed the disciples. "Wherever our leader is, we shall be too."

Kvachi had just demanded for the tenth time from a minister ten thousand sets of uniforms, provisions, and twenty million roubles for the army of the defenders of the revolution. The minister was in a bad mood and had reduced the amount demanded by half. That wouldn't have mattered—Kvachi would easily have dealt with it and made up the deficit twice or thrice over in two weeks—but there was no way Kvachi would endure and put up with any defeat or loss of face. Since the revolution began, Kvachi had been affected by an insurmountable lust for power. His heart itched for domination and command and would not be sated or assuaged. He had spent a lot of time in high-power circles and tried to get himself appointed deputy minister in several ministries, and then asked to be director of the agricultural department, but he couldn't turn the right wheels. Finally, Kvachi got so carried away that he would have agreed to move to the provinces, if he was appointed governor-general of Finland, Turkestan, or Georgia. Kvachi presented a plan to the government—written by God knows who—for giving autonomy to provinces on the border. To Beso Shikia he explained his subterfuge.

"It's a question of tactics, Beso, fifty million people will be on our side. That's how we weaken and overthrow the Provisional Government, and then ... then the tactics will change."

When the minister halved the amount of goods and money requested Kvachi saw that his hopes of a governor-generalship were shattered.

"Fine!" said Kvachi: offended, he was menacing the government. The drop of poison in his heart was followed by a whole jugful. That day he gave Gintz for the tenth time the goods he had received from the minister and bought jewels with the millions he got from Gintz. In the evening he went to a meeting and told himself: "Kick anyone who's staggering, he'll fall more quickly; smash his head in when he falls, you're doing him a favor; strangle anyone who's doomed, you'll benefit the people."

At the meeting Kvachi asked to speak: he read his first order for the army. The meeting was in an angry mood anyway; now it became uproarious and explosive. Kvachi's order told soldiers to stop saluting officers and to set up their own committees. Kvachi and his followers knew very well whom they were targeting; they understood what would ensue if the army's foundations were undermined. Indescribable scenes of chaos and riot ensued. For three days and nights a thousand men at the meeting of workers' deputies strained every sinew and fought ferociously, going without sleep or food, bathed only in their own sweat. Kvachi, who was now used to winning, finally won again and the next day his order spread like lightning all over Russia, bringing anarchy and disorder.

"Let them have a taste of this medicine," Kvachi told his friends. "Let them feel the consequences. This is nothing compared with what's next. I've sprinkled such poison on this drowning regime that its army will be paralyzed from tomorrow. So they needn't give me any more money to defend the revolution, and they needn't liberate the poor Finns, Georgians, Ukrainians, and Tatars."

From that moment Kvachi grew a foot taller in the eyes of the left wing, while the state bent and gave way under the pressure of his influence and powers.

Meanwhile July was approaching, and the wild unborn baby could not be held back in its mother's belly, it was raging wildly, kicking and trying to tumble out. The air was imbued with the smell of a storm, the sky was weighed down with lead-colored clouds, auguring any day now an explosion and global destruction. Darkness fell all over Russia. Here and there ominous thunder and crackling lightning periodically slashed the sky and the ground with deadly arrows.

One evening the minister who oversaw Kvachi summoned him and informed him with a trembling voice:

"The revolution is in very great danger from the left. The day after tomorrow the Bolsheviks are starting an armed uprising. The time has come for the Society of Defenders of the Revolution to do their sacred duty by the nation and justify the unlimited money and goods that have been spent on them. The day after tomorrow your army must come out in the morning and defend both sides of the Winter Palace."

Kvachi listened to the minister's appeal and instructions with his right ear, but his left ear let it all out again. He left, and that evening gathered his junta, telling them:

"The Bolsheviks intend to come out on the streets the day after tomorrow, before they were expected. I've tried many times to persuade them to put it off until October. I told them that the baby should stay the full nine months in its mother's belly, that the second revolution conceived in February should be allowed to ripen until October. But they won't take my word for it. That lot are so bossy that they don't believe anyone but themselves. If they're defeated the day after tomorrow, they needn't blame me for anything. I've said what I had to say, and that's it: they can repent at leisure. That's not important, but our cause has got a bit more complicated. Just now I told the government that the Society of Defenders of the Revolution had twenty thousand men here. Today the government has ordered me to bring twenty thousand men out onto the street the day after tomorrow."

Kvachi cast an eye over his comrades. They were all sitting there dazed and pensive.

"Don't be downcast, comrades! Listen to me and carry out all my orders. I'll take care of the rest."

Kvachi explained to everyone his plan of action in detail; he gave everyone their mandates and money, and sent them off to work.

On the appointed day the air became so dark and stuffy in Petersburg that friends and enemies could not tell each other apart. People flooded and scattered; two opposing waves struck one another.

"War to the end! Law and order! A constituent assembly and democracy!" one crowd shouted.

"Land, bread, and peace! All power to the Soviets! Down with treason, speculation, and secret diplomacy! The revolution is in danger!" yelled the other crowd.

While lightning and thunder struck the streets, Kvachi and his friends were sitting in a cosy refuge and tossing coins to predict whether Mademoiselle Kerensky or the Bolsheviks would win. Once again, Chipi Chipuntiradze was running about in panic and shrieking in despair:

"We're doomed ... Run for your lives ... Quick, turn left ... No, I was wrong, I meant turn right, right."

"Don't get so excited, Chipi," Kvachi soothed Chipuntiradze's distress. "Whoever ends up winning, we shan't go under. I've got one foot in the right camp and the other in the left. If Kerensky wins, I move my left foot straight away to the right; if the Reds win, then I instantly move my right foot to the left and turn red myself. That won't take any time or need any thinking about. It'll take us five minutes to wipe the white paint off our faces and put on the red. That's all there is to it."

Beso arrived that evening and calmly announced: "Kerensky's won."

"I told you so, the Reds should have waited till October. The Bolsheviks wouldn't believe me, so they can't blame us for anything," said Kvachi, rising to his feet. "Well, comrades, you've been given your jobs and positions. So go and assemble as you were told to."

The comrades divided into three groups and advanced from three directions on the Winter Palace.

"Citizens!" they shouted in each group, herding the people on the pavements into the middle of the street. "Citizens, support the Provisional Government! Join us! Come on. Do your duty."

The people joined the winning groups and merged into one common river. Each group of twenty was joined by twenty more, forty became eighty, three hundred—six hundred, a thousand—

two thousand, and five thousand—ten thousand. Torrent joined torrent, river—river. Everyone gathered round the Winter Palace: they became a sea of people. In the middle of the sea Kvachi and the white and red flag of his Society rose like an island. From this island the leader's voice thundered:

"Citizens! From now on you can sleep soundly. Your sleep is watched over by the Society of Defenders of the Revolution and the Free Socialist Party, which has today freed you from the red devils and has taken on the frightful danger itself. Citizens! Our Society and Party are once again ready to shed their blood as a sacrifice for the revolution, but at the same time we hope that you will show some concern for us and will give us a little help. Citizens," Kvachi ended his stentorian and fiery speech, "We offer our deepest thanks in advance for the donations which we shall be accepting every day in the Tauridean Palace."

Kvachi was lifted up by his disciples and a "Hurrah!" deafened the whole district. Ten minutes later, the leader rushed to the palace, burst into the minister's office and called out:

"Congratulations on our victory. Hurrah!"

The dignitaries greeted him with exclamations of childlike joy. The chairman solemnly addressed Kvachi as the savior of the revolution, while the others' thanks, loud acclaim, and handshakes seemed endless.

"Prince, help the government actively: take on a post," one minister asked Kvachi.

"That's difficult, very difficult, but … if the motherland demands it …"

"What area is it easiest for you to work in?"

"Either the department of credit, or else the Caucasus."

"Fine, since I have your agreement, we'll talk to the other ministers and let you know their answer. In any case, the government values your heroism today very highly."

After a few days Kvachi's unforgettable achievements and

deserts were rewarded: by government decree he was thanked, and that was all ... Kvachi burst into the minister's cabinet at once.

"Is that all?"

"It is."

"Then goodbye to you, too. You may talk to me in a conqueror's tone, but in three months' time I shall reply to you in the tone of October."

"What did you say?"

"You won't understand what I said until October. Goodbye."

The next day Chipi, as head of information, informed Kvachi:

"We're ruined ... Let's make a run for it! In two days the auditors are coming to see us."

"Get Gabo for me," Kvachi replied.

Kvachi whispered just a couple of words in Gabo's and Beso's ears.

The same day twenty lorries shifted provisions and property from the Society's warehouses to an unknown destination. That night an unexpected disaster happened: for mysterious reasons the warehouses caught fire, and the fire didn't go out until the last splinter of wood had been burnt up. The auditors inspected the scene, sniffed about, took measurements, and went home crestfallen. The leader reassured and consoled his downcast comrades:

"Don't lose courage, comrades! October is coming. Those who are coming will value your loyalty more highly that those who are departing. The Reds are bringing fraternity, equality, and justice, this lot are taking with them to the grave their ingratitude and black hearts. Now is the time to get down to work, before it's too late."

The very next morning a gigantic machine set up by Sedrak and Beso got to work. Two thousand beautiful girls, the same number of young men, boxes, and lorries set off for the capital. But Beso had miscalculated: the three huge warehouses he had leased could not cope with all the donations that had come in on just one day: it took the five cashiers the society employed not three days, but a whole week to count the money.

At the same time Kvachi was edging towards the Smolny Institute, where the Bolsheviks' headquarters were encamped. He circled it for some time, collecting information, inspecting and sounding out the area. Then, lowering his head, he attacked the entrance like a fighting ram.

"Where the hell do you think you're going?" asked a hirsute sailor, blocking his way.

"What?" Kvachi answered with menacing astonishment. "Can't you tell a brother from an enemy? I'll show you …"

Just then Ivan Ivanych, a Red whom Kvachi knew, turned up. Ivan was Red to the marrow of his bones, absent-minded, clumsy, cross-eyed.

"What's going on? Let him in, comrade, I know this man."

Kvachi stuck to Ivan Ivanych like a fly to honey, flattered him, and did all he could to keep him happy, patted him on his red head. After ten minutes he could twist this naïve man round his little finger.

"I've finally come to think that Kerensky is leading the people to ruin … Only your path will lead the state to a point where it can create and blossom. So my Party, my enormous Society and I stand with you with every fiber of our being. Put us to work and use our power and strength."

"I'm very glad that you have changed, and my comrades will be too."

"From now on you can rely on our Society and, if you don't mind … accept a small contribution from us."

He handed Ivan Ivanych the list of donations.

That evening Kvachi added just one word to all his Society's signs and announcements: the next morning it was the Society of Defenders and Helpers of the Red Revolution, while the Party was baptised as the Socialist Party of Land, Soviets, Peace, and Returning Home.

Kvachi and the Comrades Turn Red and Prepare for October

"Comrades," Kvachi instructed his disciples as October approached. "Politics is like a cow. Some people take the cow out to graze, others milk it and get milk and butter. A clever man doesn't shed blood or sweat chasing after a cow. Yes, madmen chase after it, take it to graze, and look after it, but we just have to milk it and get fat on its butter. Milking the cow is no trouble, you just have to be nice to it and tame it. Well, that's the only clever sort of politics. Don't bother about the color of the cow, whether it's black, white, red, or green. Don't upset it, or it will kick you and won't let you milk it. If other people attack the cow, stay out of it, and just pick up the loot after the battle. If two people are quarrelling, the third man profits. But you've got to keep an eye open to join the winning side, spit on the loser, and congratulate the winner all in good time. Now look at the situation in Russia. Russia's intellectuals know as much about the people, as Chipi or Ladi know about Zulus or Tahitians. The intellectuals have taken to European food and are trying to force it on Russian stomachs. Well, think what would happen if you made a wolf eat hay. The wolf will throw up the hay. I tell you, comrades, that is what Russia's people are doing. Any day now it will spew out this foreign food and Mademoiselle Kerensky, the Duma, and democracy with it. They'll roll a huge rock from a mountain peak and block the path of these spineless bookworms, short-sighted intellectuals, and bald lawyers. They'll block them and stick two fingers out at them. But I tell you that the rock will roll and destroy all those fingers, will squash the bookworms like bugs, and throw them on the scrapheap of oblivion. Remember my prophecy: if it doesn't come true, then dismiss Kvachi Kvachantiradze from the leadership and appoint Jalil or

Gabo instead. I've said it before and I say it again: Russia is pregnant with twins. The first was a premature runt; the second now seems so forward, lively, rough, wilful, and bold. So the inferior, uncouth Russian peasant in the forthcoming battle will certainly beat his senior European brother: he'll thrash him and stove his sides in. We have princes and gentry, merchants, priests, officials, Cossacks, and bald lawyers, all on the same side. On the other side are Russia's workers and peasants, who are now armed to the teeth. Don't assume that today's government is on the side of the Russian people, while the Reds are selling the people. Believe me, it's the very opposite: the Entente has drained Russia of blood for its own purposes and brought the country to the grave. Anyone who shouts 'War to the end' is a deliberate or unwitting destroyer and traitor to Russia: the Russians have so far never had a national force so loyal to the Russian people as the Reds. I, Kvachi Kvachantiradze, tell you: if you don't believe what I say, then leave our Party right now, or our paths will cross one day soon and we shall certainly disown one another. So, friends, I am absolutely convinced that, as always, unity is in our flesh and bones, as always. The old comradeship and our traditions have been forged and tempered by great struggles and many deeds which will in the future help us and rescue us from danger and disintegration. So, friends, if you want a good life and a peaceful outcome, go on following and trusting me. Wherever I am, there you must be! What I do, so must you."

"Call on us and lead us on! We'll follow you … Long live our leader and commander," shouted the disciples: their vows and loyalty heartened their commander-in-chief. Then they received their leader's orders, rolled up their sleeves and, making ten times as much effort, groaning, dribbling, sweating, and moaning, went back to attacking the building that had been marked out for destruction.

Lately Kvachi had been visiting the Reds' headquarters more

often. Sometimes he brought donations, sometimes he passed on information he had from Chipi and Bekarev, sometimes he gave advice, and sometimes even conscientiously carried out missions for them.

The Smolny Institute buzzed like a fabulous hive and boiled like a giant's cauldron. The building where hitherto the powers-that-be had educated countless girls for the glory and the benefit of the Tsar and the fatherland had now become a peasant palace. Instead of the old perfumes and unguents, it now smelled of pitch, sweat, pickles, and borscht; the once sparkling clean floors were now rust-colored, and the doors and the walls were adorned with weirdly drawn placards, fierily composed proclamations, and clumsily scrawled announcements. The huge building and its air were saturated with literature meant to rouse the people, with dynamite, hand grenades, squashed noses, four-kilo boots, and fair facial hair. Anyone dressed in clean European clothes would have been treated in this hive as if he were a bear that had crept in. So when Kvachi went to the headquarters he put on a dirty greatcoat, made sure his face and hands were filthy, and changed his speech and gait so that he would be taken by everyone for a soldier who had just come from the trenches.

"Greetings, comrade," he would confidently address Ivan Ivanych. "How are things going for us?"

"Badly, very badly," Ivan Ivanych would reply. "We're being hounded, arrested, accused of treason … but victory will still be ours."

"Of course it will," said Kvachi encouragingly. "Remember my words: by the end of October we will get our hands on power."

"You're in a great hurry."

"I tell you we will."

"Let's see, let's see. But now we've got a little job for you. There's a little meeting for the soldiers and you have to say a few words."

Kvachi didn't need to be asked. He was looking for a pretext to address meetings and to make speeches. He had always had the gift of the gab, and now that gift grew wings: his tongue itched, he had developed a lust for hot air and for stoking fires of rebellion. His scent-hound's intuition made it easy for him to find the Russian peasants' sore point, and he could scratch it and then anoint it with balm:

"Forty months have now passed since the loathsome Entente started sucking the Russian workers' and peasants' blood. The blood we have shed for the foreign bourgeoisie has irrigated Russia's fields. Today the Vistula, the Neman, the Dniester, and the Euphrates have been dyed red with our blood. Comrades, who are we fighting for? Who are we shedding our precious blood for? For our own people and for foreign bourgeoisies who are slaughtering us, while they are nicely protected, earning millions, and starving our families to death."

"True, true," agreed the mob, worn out by war and roused by fury.

"Your anger is just," Kvachi continued fanning the flames. "We firmly demand peace without annexation, without contributions, and with the right of peoples' self-determination."

"Peace, peace!" roared the warriors, fed up with waiting for peace.

"We also demand land and freedom," said Kvachi, rousing the people.

"We want land, land," shouted the inflamed peasants, who had been captives for centuries, who were famine-stricken, and longed for land.

"But you must know, comrades, that you will get peace, a low cost of living, freedom, and land only by struggling and by your own hands. Comrades, the revolution is in danger. We must defend it with weapons and blood. Long live the proletariat and its government, the Soviet of workers, peasants, and soldiers."

"Long live the Soviets, long live the Soviets!" thundered the people, aroused by the prospect of peace, freedom, and land.

"Down with today's bourgeois government! Down with treason, profiteering, and the lackeys of the Entente."

"Down with them. We don't want them! Long live the Soviets!"

The next day Kvachi presented Ivan Ivanych with a resolution that was full of arrogance, threats, and fire: he had a copy sent to a German who expressed his thanks. Ivan Ivanych had a high opinion of Kvachi, because he was conscientiously carrying out the tasks he had been given and had a rare talent for rousing, inflaming, and exciting a people who had suffered from a pointless war.

Some time ago Kvachi had noticed that paper money was losing its value, so he quickly ordered his comrades not to pile up paper money. The stockbroker Chainstein therefore converted Kvachi's income every day into gold. As October approached, Kvachi told Sedrak to convert the Society's property and gold into jewelry. That was done in a few days.

One day Kvachi went to see Elena. No sooner had he entered her drawing room than he bumped into Pavlov, who was on his way out.

"Ah, Napoleon Apollonovich! Greetings. How are you?"

Kvachi stared with astonishment at the man who'd tried to destroy him and then, willy-nilly, offered him his hand. Pavlov sat down again.

"Who let you out of prison?" Kvachi asked Pavlov.

"The revolution did, my friend. As you see, I'm in civilian clothes now, but I still work in the same job."

"I understand and see. All the February revolution changed in the old regime was the clothes, am I right?"

"In the old regime and ... in you, too," Elena added.

"I don't give a damn about February and March. I'm utterly convinced that Wilhelm will help us again, and his NCOs will bring us peace, bread, and rule of law," said Pavlov.

"Rule of law, bread, and slavery," added Kvachi.

"But Wilhelm's laws, bread, and slavery are better than today's lawlessness and famine," Elena intervened.

"Supposing Wilhelm doesn't come?" asked Kvachi.

"In that case we prefer the Bolsheviks," said Elena

"Really? Surely not. What do you say?" Kvachi turned to Pavlov.

"Yes indeed, we prefer the Bolsheviks," said Pavlov, agreeing with Elena. "Yes, I said I prefer the Bolsheviks. They will bring blood, famine, and anarchy, but they will be followed immediately by a Tsar, the old regime, the law, peace, and plenty."

"Your wishes will soon come true," Kvachi consoled the two others. "We'll see what you say after that, but you can forget about the Tsar. Do you really not know where the Idelsohns are?" Kvachi asked Pavlov.

"Because of your escape, their execution was put off for a day. You helped them both, because that day Russia had its revolution. Now they're both back in Peter and Paul's fortress."

"But the revolution didn't do you any harm either, I see," said Kvachi, teasing Pavlov.

"It did me no harm, and it made you important."

"What makes you think that?"

"You must think that I've been asleep. I know everything about your life. For example ..."

Elena left the room.

Pavlov then gave a detailed account of Kvachi's life in recent times.

"I neither confirm nor deny your information. All I want to know is, if the information is correct, why you don't arrest me."

"Because ... it must be obvious to you why. For what reason or purpose? Who needs it? Who would I do a favor for? Who'd value my loyalty? Russia has nobody in charge, so nobody will give me any thanks. Why should I arrest you when it does me no good? Who knows where we'll meet again, and what we'll mean to each other."

"Clever men always make clever choices. You deserve to be hanged for arresting me, but I'll repay you some day for your kindness today."

"You can repay me today."

"Please say how."

"You go every day to the Smolny Institute and you work for Ivanov."

"True."

"Tell him that tonight I intend to arrest twelve Bolsheviks. They all have secret apartments, but I've got the list of their new addresses in my pocket. You can write down the list of those to be arrested now. If you do as I ask and say a few kind words to Ivanov about me, your debt to me will be paid off. I was going to send Bekarev, but since I've met you ..."

"You're in touch with Bekarev even now?"

"No, not really ... we meet very occasionally ... I'll have some information for Ivanov later. So you'd do well to get him to meet me in secret. Write down the list."

Kvachi wrote down the list, took his leave of Pavlov and told himself:

"I shan't send Ivanov to see you. I'll be the bridge again. That way will be better, I'll have both of you in my clutches."

Pavlov left. Elena treated Kvachi coldly. Their bridge had gradually collapsed and crumbled with time's ravages. Kvachi was so carried away building new red-yellow bridges that he barely spared time to see Elena once a month. She had built new bridges and paths to new Kvachis.

"Elena, have you known Pavlov for long?"

"Six months, I think."

"So he's a close friend, is he?"

"What business is it of yours?"

"Don't I have the right to make it my business?"

"You forfeited that right yourself."

"You're right, Elena, to say that I see you hardly more than once a month. What can I do? It's not my fault. That's how my life has turned out. But you've still got your nice arrangements … Those pictures … I've seen them somewhere."

"They're Tania's. You remember Tania?" Elena asked venomously.

"True, Tania! Poor woman. How could she disappear like that without anyone knowing what happened to her?"

"She disappeared from your life, but not from mine. She's here now, and she's due to arrive any moment. I'm expecting her."

"Really?" asked Kvachi, just a little perturbed. "It must be five years since I last saw her. It would be very nice to see her, but …"

"Nice, you say? I don't think so. No need to go away in such a hurry. Tania will be here in five minutes."

Kvachi looked at his watch: "Oh no, I'm terribly late. Goodbye, my dear. Actually, there's a piece of advice I ought to give you. Sell everything you have, otherwise … any day now there'll be a knock at the door and you'll lose the lot."

"I sold it all ages ago and spent the money, too. Tania did the same."

"You both did the right thing. So, goodbye, dear friend."

Kvachi ran down the stairs as if he was escaping from somebody. Once he was in the street he caught sight of Tania's carriage in the distance. He darted into a shop and watched from inside. Two chestnut horses were speeding her landau along. Tania was dressed in black. She'd aged, and looked even more bedraggled and withered. For a minute Kvachi had a flashback to their colorful past, but the doors of memory slammed shut. He called a cab and in half an hour was at the Reds' HQ.

"Greetings, comrades," he called to Ivan Ivanych. "I've got

something very secret to discuss with you. There's nobody about, I hope? Fine, then listen. Here's a list. Read it ... Have you finished? These people will be arrested tonight ... Don't you believe me? I tell you, their secret addresses have been discovered ... How do I know? Sorry, I can't tell you that."

"Suppose the information is false?"

"Then shoot me. But suppose it turns out to be true?"

"Then ask us for a reward."

"All right, let's shake hands on it. Tomorrow morning you'll know whether my information is true or not. But take action now. I've done my duty to the revolution, and I'm off. Goodbye."

He went to a secret meeting and satisfied his itch for speechmaking; he repeated himself a hundred times and added something that the deserters liked to hear:

"Comrades, Russia's peasants have lost patience. They have started taking the land back and sharing it out themselves. They've already shared a lot out. I tell you, comrades—and you must tell others—that anyone who dithers won't get his share of land. So to hell with the front! Leave the service, rip off the government's epaulettes, and go back home at once to your family and your land, or you'll be late and landless. Long live our slogan: home to our houses and our land!"

"Home, to our houses!" they bellowed even louder, hungering for land, worn out by war, sweeping like a torrent after the red banner on which was written in fire: "Peace and bread! War against palaces, peace to the cottages! Land to the peasant and power to the Soviets."

Kvachi's words came true. That night Pavlov raided two dozen apartments, but failed to arrest a single person on his list. The next morning Kvachi's reputation and trustworthiness had risen ten times in the eyes and hearts of the Reds.

As October approached, Kvachi told Silibistro:

"Very soon such hell will break out here that even the devil won't be able to escape. So I advise you: pack tomorrow and move to Georgia."

Everyone agreed, except Pupi, who didn't want to part from her son. Finally, however, she too gave in to Kvachi, and three days later he put his parents on a train and saw them off to their motherland.

Red October

Once upon a time, and what could be better, there was a fair-haired giant called Ivan. Ivan's mother was a Scythian, and his mother was a Mongol. The Scythian lived in the boundless steppe, the Mongol in the unending taiga, around Lake Baikal and the Hindu Kush. They met and became one on the banks of the Volga. The Mongol overcame the Scythian and they married. From then on their realm expanded so that they themselves did not know where it began and where it ended.

The Scythian was a big monster, white-faced, blonde, freckled, hairy, blue-eyed, and pug-nosed. The Scythian had a steed the size of two buffalos, stern and heavy. The horse's thick mane came down to its knees, and its tail swept the ground. When its hoof struck the earth it raised dust and smoke, scattered fist-sized stones, and left potholes behind it. When the Scythian rode this horse, he bent its back and made its knees tremble.

The Mongol was smaller than the Scythian: round-headed, black-haired, swarthy, a little yellow, with bristly hair, a bobbing chin, widely separated temples, broadly slit gray eyes, a squashed nose, and flared nostrils. The Mongol's horse was peculiarly small, powerful, and quick.

They were both wanderers, unable to stay in one place for long, unable to settle or make a permanent home. They spent half their life in a big cart roofed with felt; the other half was spent on horseback.

Every now and again the hairy Scythian mounted his unfortunate horse, flung his bow and arrows over his shoulder, struck his horse's head, ran his hand through its mane, and flew off like the wind through the endless steppe. Sometimes he attacked the Sarmatians, sometimes the Agorites, sometimes the Nevrians or the Anthropophages, or the Budins and Gelons, or even the Savromats. His steed sometimes drank the waters of the Boristhene, sometimes of the Hipanides and even of the Tichas, once it even crossed the turbulent Mtkvari, then the rocky Araxes, the Euphrates, and the Tigris. Then the Persians' and the Assyrians' women saw their black-bearded husbands confounded and had a taste of blonde moustaches and white arms, and the heat of the south was cooled in the northern ice.

The Scythian hunted his neighbors as well as game. Sometimes he made human sacrifices to his god of war, or followed the great rivers, seeking their sources, or headed for the eternal oceans.

The Scythian and the Mongol lived like this for a thousand years. Finally the Mongolian lady grew old, broke down, and submitted to the Scythian she had been forced to marry.

The Scythian and the Mongol had two children: the elder was called Ivan, the younger Peter. The brothers lived together fraternally at first, but then the younger began to defy the elder. Once Peter put on iron sandals and an iron hat, picked up an iron stick, and went off west. He walked for nine months, nine weeks, and nine days, crossed nine mountain chains, nine seas, and after nine years returned. When he got back, he said: "From now on I'm called Europe."

Peter had changed remarkably: instead of a long coat and gown he wore narrow trousers, high boots, and a short-tailed jacket, while his head was covered with a bent and folded piece of broadcloth; he'd shaven off his forefather's lordly beard and put on a very long, curly piece—a wig—of somebody else's hair. Ivan could have borne this much shame, but ...

"I'm called Europe," Peter announced and demanded that Ivan, too, should renounce himself and also call himself Europe. Ivan shook his hairy head and brusquely retorted: "No."

"No's no good: yes!" Peter counter-attacked.

"I said no."

"I said yes."

They attacked each other. Ivan was stronger than Peter, but Peter had learnt some devilish tricks when he was overseas. These tricks and devices helped Peter to throw Ivan to the ground and tie him up. Then he produced a razor and cut off Ivan's long beard. That, however, didn't satisfy him. He made Ivan wear peculiar clothes and told him:

"From now on you're called Europe, too."

"Fine, so be it," replied Ivan, giving in to Peter, but his heart filled with the poison of shame and the venom of vengeance.

Two hundred more years passed. Peter's oddities knew no limits. He brought all sort of odd clowns and idlers in from the west, kept on hiring new ones, opened the doors that his father the Scythian had kept tightly locked, and turned the Scythians' tracks into roads. The things Peter and his sorcerers invented and transformed and adopted! They launched ships and boats, dressed their armies in strange uniforms, and gave them new weapons, they moved New Year's day from 1 September to 1 January, made war on their neighbors, set foot on the Black, Caspian, and Baltic Seas, founded new cities, moved the capital from Moscow to a Baltic swamp, turned the Scythians' slack life upside down, and adopted so many new customs and names that two hundred years were not enough for Ivan to remember them: a nonsensical Synod and Senate, regulations and Tables of Ranks, mayors and town halls, magistrates and an academy. Of a thousand new words Ivan could manage to remember and understand only a few: flogging-canes, police, gendarme, general, regulations, hard labor, prosecutor, march, guard, statement, and a hundred of other similar awkward concepts which made Ivan's skin creep and his blood boil when they were mentioned. But the most fearful and terrible things that Peter had brought from the west, among other devilish things, were smoke and gold. He'd started up factories, laid railways, founded banks, adopted double-entry bookkeeping, and saturated and darkened the country and Ivan's head with a fog of nonsense and with stinking fumes.

Confused, Ivan rather like the smell of the smoke, and the fog of bookkeeping; he was pleased by the gold, and got money from the banks, he became good at wielding hammers and rode the iron devil with joy, but ... the fruits of his sweat by some mysterious and incomprehensible sorcery ended up in the pockets of Peter and the western sorcerers.

Ivan thought for two hundred years, seeking the tubes and cracks through which his sweat was swallowed up and lost. Finally he found out and realized: banks, capital, bourgeoisie!

Once he'd understood and had a good look round, Ivan learnt, apart from "march", "prosecutor", "statement", gendarme" and "police", the words "proletariat", "capital", "dictatorship", "bank", "finances", "class", "exploitation", "bourgeoisie" and "pauperization."

From then on Ivan waited for the right circumstances. However long the wait, the time finally came. Once Peter and his good-for-nothing friends summoned Ivan:

"Ivan, the country, humanity, and civilization are in terrible danger. The Huns want to make slaves of you and fleece you. So, go and attack those savages. For the Tsar and the fatherland! Off you go!"

They gave him a rifle and pushed him on. For four years Ivan trudged from sea to sea, from mountain ridge to mountain ridge, from river to river. Sometimes he went for a week without eating, sometimes in mid-winter he was up to his waist in snow, sometimes he was stuck in mud for a month. Ivan prowled like a wolf and fought like a bear, while Peter and the good-for-nothings gave him orders from the rear:

"Fire!"

And Ivan fired. Meanwhile thousands of his brothers were being slaughtered every day.

"Go on! Attack! God is with us!" Ivan heard once more. He went on fighting, muttering to himself: "Go to hell, you and your God. I'm tired."

"Hands on swords, souls on God," Peter and his friends shouted yet again.

Ivan could barely stay standing. He waved his sword perfunctorily, again muttering: "Why don't you risk your own life? I'm too tired."

"Go on! Hack them down! Attack!" Peter and his allies call out again. "For Tsar and fatherland."

Ivan stopped. He had shed a sea of blood, but still couldn't see the point of the struggle. The words "culture", "God", "Tsar" and "fatherland" did not appeal to his heart or stick in his mind.

Finally Ivan was fed up swimming through blood, firing his rifle, waving his sword about, shouting "Hurrah!", suffering hunger, cold, and non-stop thunder and roaring. One day Ivan heard the news: the Tsar has been dethroned. Ivan was at first in shock: he couldn't work out whether dethroning the Tsar was good or bad. "I expect it's a good thing," he thought, "because everybody's pleased." So he himself rejoiced. He put his sword in its scabbard, his rifle across his back, turned home and said:

"I don't want to make war any more, I've had it."

Peter and his friends were astonished and afraid.

"Ivan, you'll perish!"

"I shan't perish. If you want to, you can fight on now."

"Ivan, the Huns will make slaves of you, they'll turn you into a serf."

"They can't touch me," Ivan retorted gravely.

"Ivan, remember your country's culture and God."

"I don't give a toss about your culture. I have my own."

"Ivan, how about freedom?"

"I'm free from today on."

"And your fatherland?"

"I have my peasants' and workers' fatherland. It's in no danger as long as I'm around."

"Ivan, how about Constantinople? There's no finer or richer city on earth."

"God protect whoever it belongs to. I don't even know where the city is, and I can't remember what it's called."

"Ivan, remember your brothers, the Czechs, Hungarians, Ruthenians, Slovaks, and Poles."

"Those names mean nothing to me. I don't have brothers like that. I do know the Poles. Peter enslaved them, using me to do it. Now God has given them peace, they can go and look after themselves."

"The Huns? Ivan, the Huns? They are your mortal enemies!"

"That's a lie too. The Huns never came to Tambov and they won't, either."

"Ivan, we gave an oath that together we'd fight to the death."

"To my death, you mean? I don't want to die. You've spilt a lot of my blood, let that satisfy you."

"We gave each other our word of honor that ..."

"Then you can go and kill each other; I told you before your word of honor isn't worth a penny to me, because nobody asked me anything."

"Ivan!"

"I said I don't want to make war. That's all."

"Ivan, where are you going?"

"Home. I need to take a bit of land off the masters. The factories and banks don't bother us."

Peter and his friends blocked Ivan's path: "Ivan, wait! Hang on for a little bit, until we've thought of something and worked things out. Don't open the doors to the enemy."

"All right, I'll wait. I have a lot of patience, but I tell you now that it's running out. If you don't make peace very shortly and if you don't allot me a little bit of land, I'll deal with it myself. So, get a move on."

Time passed. There was no sign of peace, of land, or of a break. Peter and his friends went on calling as before: "Hey, Ivan, attack! Go on, attack once more! Go for them! Go on! Fire!"

Ivan fired a couple of more rounds and just waggled his sword. In reply, the Huns let loose such thunder and lightning that he spent a week trudging through his brothers' blood. Then he stopped to remind Peter:

"Where is peace?"

"Any moment ... We'll get it to you any day now. But you must attack once more. Go on, fire! Attack! Go on!"

Time passed. Ivan was fooled a dozen more times, believing Peter's promise, exhausted in a trench full of blood and ice. Then he opened his eyes and it was all clear. Ivan had long been searched for by his many younger brothers scattered in the towns and villages: they called on him to come home, promising him white bread, land, peace, and power. Ivan found it hard to grasp that Peter and his foreign friends could not bring him peace or give him land or power. But when he did grasp it, he came out of his trench and set off home. Peter and his army intercepted Ivan:

"Ivan, stop!"

"Get out of my way. Peace and land!"

"Ivan, go back! The Constituent Assembly and war to the end!"

"Peter, get out of my way, I said. Peace, land, and the Soviets!"

"I told you to go back! War to the end, and then buy the land."

"Peter, don't make me sin against a brother. I tell you: peace, land, and the Soviets."

"Ivan, don't force me to spill a brother's blood. I told you to go back, or ... God, help me!"

Peter then unpacked a thousand different rifles, pistols, cannon, aeroplanes, tanks, armoured vehicles, and many Satanic weapons. He then aimed them at Ivan. Ivan then brought up the weapons which Peter and his friends had given him to annihilate the Huns, to conquer Istanbul, and to liberate the Hungarian-Ruthenian-Slovaks. Brandishing these weapons, Ivan aimed them at Peter and revealed what Peter and his allied army didn't have: a gigantic, gnarled, twisted oak cudgel.

The two brothers grabbed each other by the arms and overcame their fear: Peter crossed himself and announced:

"I believe in God on high, holy Russia, the Constituent Assembly, the sale of land, democracy, war to the end, Aya-Sofya and the liberation of Poland, the Hungaro-Russians, the Slovaks and all our brothers. Amen."

Ivan waved the red flag and shouted out what he had to say for every corner of the globe to hear:

"Everybody, everybody, everybody! Peace to the cottages, war to the palaces! Eternal peace without annexation or contributions! Freedom of the peoples. Dictatorship of the proletariat! Confiscation of capital! Land to the tillers, and power to the Soviets!"

These words uttered, they started punching one another so hard that the earth shook. A terrible storm of thunder and lightning broke out. Flames came from thousands of places and reached the heavens; the clouds of smoke, the thunder, the heat of battle frightened and stifled the birds and animals. Rivers and seas were dyed red and filled with corpses. The world gasped, held its breath and, trembling with hope and fear, followed this contest of the Goliaths, and listened to the earth quaking.

Peter was wearing a European morning coat, a starched shirt, and patent-leather shoes. He had put on a tophat and white gloves, while he wore a monocle for his eyes. He couldn't stand firmly, because his European upper body was held to his Scythian thighs by pegs and the bones wouldn't knit. He was as white as a sheet, because the two bloods in his veins hadn't merged properly or got used to one another; he was short-sighted, because he had someone else's eye inserted in his monocle; he was bald, because his Russo-Mongol head couldn't grow Franco-English hair; he was toothless, because his horse's tooth couldn't be fixed in a wolf's mouth; his hair was neatly combed and his face clean-shaven; his head and body were generously anointed with cosmetics, Coty, Houbigant, and Chypre perfumes.

Ivan's body is coarse and uncouth, as gnarled and twisted as an oak root. Unlike Peter, he has iron bones and steel muscles. He's almost naked: he wears a torn gown, one foot has a bark sandal, the other a worn-out boot he's found. Ivan's face has never known a razor, his bristly hair has never been touched by a comb, his body has never met soap.

For three years, three months, three weeks, and three days Peter and Ivan fought. Peter went for Ivan and cast him into a bare field. Peter sat in his coat in a warm house, but for odd reasons still quivered and quaked.

Ivan walked naked through the Russian winter. He spent the nights in the fields, the days in the dark forests, keeping an eye on Peter's house, thinking grim thoughts, scratching the back of his neck, and calling out casually: "Never mind!"

He thought and he thought, then tore up by the roots a nine-branched oak tree, waved it about and thrashed Peter's city so that half the city was demolished, and Peter was cast into bare fields.

Peter constantly received weapons and clothes, food and drink from the west. That day the cocoa and chocolate was three hours late getting to Peter: this cowardly brother nearly fainted from hunger. Ivan had run out of food. For three years, three months, three weeks, and three days he had lived and fought like this: the oak tree which hadn't eaten or drunk for three days swallowed three pickled gherkins in three days and washed them down with three glasses of moonshine, then went out on sentry duty into the winter blizzards for three days, leaning on his cudgel and muttering to himself: "Never mind!"

Ivan thrust his bayonet at Peter's guts. Peter leapt back in time, but still lost a dozen drops of blood. He yelled hysterically and went to bed for nine weeks and nine days. Then he got up, crept up to Ivan, and struck his three-sided bayonet in him so hard that it went in to the hilt. Ivan barely gave the wound a look, just scratched it, wiped the snot off his face with his fist, spat hard, and coolly murmured: "Never mind!"

Ivan had lost nine liters of blood but he kept standing and didn't take to his bed.

Peter aimed a nine-barrelled cannon and fired it. The shells threw Ivan back nine yards, spun him over nine times, and the nine fragments made nine holes the size of a fist. Ivan, still on his feet, removed nine bullets from each of his nine wounds, scratched the back of his neck again, and once more said: "Never mind!"

Peter circled him from the sky, snatched Ivan into the sky, broke through the clouds, and dropped him headlong into the sea. Ivan flew for nine minutes and nine seconds, spent nine times nine minutes without breathing at the bottom of the sea, then turned upright, floated to the surface and came ashore, spitting out salty water and calmly saying, "Never mind!"

Peter tried one last trick. He waited for his chance, and then used some machine to throw Ivan into the devil's furnace. Ivan baked for nine minutes and nine seconds in molten pitch and iron, then broke the furnace pen, came out red-hot and singed, reached for his cudgel, and lost his temper: "Now wait for it, you bastard!"

Like a bear stung by a wasp, he spun round in fury. The thump, bangs, hammering, and racket of his cudgel was loud enough to reach the heavens. The shrieks, squawks, groans, and moans of Peter and his friends were heard by the whole gasping country. Tornados, flames, smoke, and dust swirled all over Russia. Wherever

Ivan set foot, the earth cracked open; whatever his cudgel hit, crumbled; wherever his arm hacked, a storm broke out. If he blew on a city, the city would burn and turn to ashes. In panic and dismay, Peter ran from the Arctic ocean to the Caucasus, from the Vistula to Sakhalin, pursued by a frenzied Ivan who was yelling: "Go on! Hit him! Exterminate him. Drown him!"

They were both burning in fire and choking in blood. The gigantic country was scorched with flames, suffocated by the smell of corpses, red with blood, and weak and on its last legs with famine.

Finally, Ivan won. He swung his cudgel a bit longer, burned a few more enemies, and set them scattering to the ocean. John Bull and Jacques de Paris were good swimmers, so they supported Peter's armpits and reached the other shore. Ivan settled down on his side of the sea, everyone sat down to anoint their wounds, bandage their battered heads, patch their torn clothes. They started talking:

"Everybody, everybody, everybody!" roared Ivan. "Hey, brothers and comrades. Proletariats of all countries, unite! Unite and overthrow your bourgeois!"

"Shut up, *sans-culottes*," John Bull and Jacques de Paris shouted back at Ivan from the far shore, watching him, shaking with fear and suspicion.

Ivan looked down: he really wasn't wearing *culottes*. All he had for trousers were rags clinging to his body. But Ivan was neither ashamed nor embarrassed by the laughter coming from the far shore. He scratched the back of his neck and called out:

"Never mind! I tore my trousers fighting. I'll get some new ones made soon, or your brothers over there will take off yours and send them to me. Hey, proletariats of all countries, unite. As for you, you dirty robbers, this is what you're worth: pooh!"

And he spat out such a gob of spittle that Europe still hasn't been able to wash it off its face.

"Hey, you, Ivan," John Bull shouted. "You'll die of hunger."

Ivan's stomach actually was twisted up with hunger, but he threw one of his three sacks of flour to John Bull, with the words: "Never mind! You're hungry, too. So, take it. If you like, grab a bit for yourself, but give the rest to my hungry brothers over there. And you, you loathsome scoundrel, take it and enjoy: pooh!"

And again he spat such a gob that John Bull's and Jacques de Paris's ships were sunk by it.

"Shoot him, I said, shoot while Ivan is still hungry. Attack him before he gets his fill of food, while he's still too weak," squealed Peter, who had been thrashed and battered.

"Hey you," Jacques de Paris squealed. "Pay me what you owe me! Give me back my factories, or else ..."

"Or else you'll have my guts?" retorted a revived Ivan with a laugh. "If you're man enough, come and take them. If I owe you anything, you owe me three times as much. You pay me back for my losses, or ..."

"That's all lies, lies!" croaked Peter, whose head was bandaged and limbs were broken. "I said shoot him, shoot him."

"Hey you, scoundrels. Leeches! Robbers! Set my brothers free over there, or I'll make you wish you'd never been born. I'll smash you, I'll exterminate you, I'll slaughter you. Hey, brothers and comrades! Unite! Overthrow them! Attack them!"

John Bull and Jacques de Paris rolled up their sleeves again, but, on looking round, they halted; Karl Müller, Mahmud Hassan, Ching Chong-Chung, the negro Bambulla, Rabindranath Gora, the Egyptian Zaglul, the Moroccan Abdul Kerim, the Persian Saad Reza Sepahi, the Afghans, Africans, and a thousand different continental and island peoples were rolling up their sleeves, loading their guns, sharpening their swords, and roaring: "Self-determination and freedom of the peoples! Get out! Down with intervention and occupation! Long live Ivan!"

Ivan felt heartened. He gradually raised his voice and shouted for all lands to hear:

"Ching Chong-Chung, liberate yourself! ... Karl Müller, don't pay those leeches any debts! Mahmud Hassan, lock your doors tight! Negro Bambulla, hit back! Rabindranath Gora, throw John Bull back into the sea! Brother Zaglul, attack from behind! Moroccan Abdul Kerim, attack from the left and hit at Jacques de Paris! Saad Reza, attack from the right and fire! Right, brothers and comrades, together! In line! Attack! Proletariats, arise!"

John Bull and Jacques de Paris went after Ivan again, but not only their slaves and vassals, their own families scattered in confusion. The proletariats heard Ivan's thunder and rose up. They rebelled and, dressed for war, struck John Bull and Jacques de Paris on the arms and legs.Red flames burst out in some places, in others a red flag fluttered, or there was thunder and lightning: Jacques de Paris and John Bull trembled in feverish fear. The Irish O'Grady, the Egyptian Zaglul, the Afghans and others, took the chance to break free of the ropes that bound their hands and feet.

This shrieking and shouting, rioting and clashing went on for seven years, seven months, seven weeks, and seven days. One day Giovanni Giraldini called over from Rome:

"Iva-a-an! I recognize your strength and right to exist: give me your hand!"

Ivan spat on his right hand and proffered it, but it was met not by one, but two hands, one from Rome, one from London. John Bull then growled:

"Ivan, I recognize you, and admit that you exist and are my equal. Here's my hand."

He put his other hand behind his back: that hand had a nice dreadnought and several rumbling tanks in it. Ivan held out his hand again, but meanwhile Giovanni Giraldini and John Bull had attacked each other.

"I was the first to tell Ivan I recognized him," declared the offended Tweedledee Giraldini, "so I'm the one who should offer him my hand."

"No, I was the first to say so," replied the offended Tweedledum John Bull.

"No I said it first!"

"Not you, it was me who said it."

"Liar, I said it! Liar, pirate!"

"Liar yourself, macaroni-eater!"

"Then let's ask Ivan."

"Let's do that."

"Ivan, who was the first to recognize you, me or John Bull?"

"Ivan, who was first, me or Giraldini?"

Ivan looked them both up and down, scratched the back of his neck, and reassured them both: "You're equal scoundrels. I don't care whether you're black or white dogs, you're both dogs and sons of bitches."

And he burst out in such a loud guffaw that Giraldini's *bersalieri* hat and John Bull's tartan rug were both carried away by the force of Ivan's laughter. Then a cawing, croaking, and clamor was heard from every corner of the world: "Ivan, I recognize you! Ivan, I recognize you, too! I do, I do, I do! We recognize you! We recognize you!"

And hands were proffered from everywhere, Ivan's head began to spin. People interrupted each other, jostled, squabbled as they foisted their goods on Ivan and whispered in his ear:

"Brother Ivan! Don't let that villain John Bull deceive you. I, Jacques de Paris, have been since the day I was born your closest friend. Here's the proof: see the cosmetics, perfumes, ointments, champagne, and liqueurs I've brought you. Buy them, Ivan, buy them. I'll let you have them very cheap. Just pay me a little of what you owe, give me back some factories and then you, I, and Mahmud Hassan will give John Bull something to worry about and trim his claws, or that bulldog will take over half the world. Buy my goods, Ivan, buy them, they're cheap, I'll let you have them at rock-bottom prices."

John Bull pulled Ivan away from Jacques de Paris and took him aside:

"You must be a remarkable boxer, brother Ivan. To mark our brotherhood, let's divide the world in two and leave Jacques out of it, or he'll get too big for his boots. Look, cars, textiles, colonial goods, opium, morphine, poppies, and hundreds of different sweet drinks, spices, and injectable drugs. I'll let you have them for practically nothing. Just promise that you'll pay me what you owe and give me back my factories. Ah, Ivan, let's come to terms and give Jacques de Paris a bit of a licking, since he's got above himself."

"Macaroni, beautiful macaroni! Wonderful macaroni!" whispered Giraldini. "Ivan, it's cheap! Dirt-cheap! Almost free!"

"All right," Ivan finally said. "Let's agree. Let me have the goods on credit and lend me a bit of money, too. I don't want a lot. A billion will do me for now."

"First promise to pay the old debt, give us our factories back, compensate us for the damage and then …" said Giraldini, John Bull, and Jacques de Paris.

Ivan just stood there scratching himself. Then he said:

"Never mind! I'll think about it, it's better to sleep on these things. There's no great hurry, it'll still be there in the morning. Tomorrow."

Ivan waited first for John Bull, then Jacques de Paris and Uncle Yankee to forget about their debts, factories, and damages. He waited and again calmly said: "Never mind. Tomorrow."

Jobs Botched While Ivan Burns in October's Fires

While Ivan was in a frenzy, rearing up, whirling his cudgel, running from one side to another, the cunning Kvachi was darting like a rat about the inflamed city, "milking his cows." His trained nose and intuition soon told him Ivan had won, so he clung with both hands to Ivan's torn coat-tails and waded into the red maelstrom, all the time quietly egging Ivan on by talking into his ear: "Go on, Ivan ... Hit them ... Fire! That's right, I love your right hand, that's right!"

Kvachi had exercised his jaws and his ears so much that, without noticing, he began to believe in and agree with the fiery slogans and bloodthirsty phrases. But he was still the same old Kvachi, and he periodically instructed and urged on his comrades:

"Don't just stand there! Get moving! Don't just gawp! Don't be useless time-wasters, because you'll never get another chance like this."

So the comrades followed their leader and put their hands to the shovel and swept up whatever sweepings there were. Once Kvachi, like a cat on a hot tin roof, rushed to see Ivan Ivanych Ivanov and appealed to him: "The Whites and the cadets are looting the palace. There are treasures and works of art beyond price in it. Quick, a mandate!"

In five minutes Ivan Ivanych had entrusted Kvachi with a fearsome mandate and a dozen ferocious security officers. Kvachi quickly shoved the mandate in his pocket; it took him half an hour to get his band of men to a palace where the Whites were encircled by the Reds. Kvachi and his comrades joined forces with the armed workers and security men and entered the palace. It was packed full by a mob, some of them armed, some of them not. One man was dragging off a samovar, another was clutching a marble statue, a third was removing the upholstery from a chair, a fourth was wrapping a tapestry round his waist, and others were loading up antique pictures, porcelain vases, crockery, and all sorts of small items, and looking for the exit.

"In the name of the council of workers', peasants' and soldiers' deputies, stop!" screamed Kvachi, reading out his mandate at the top of his voice. Then he gave the red workers and the security men their orders: they drove everyone into the big hall, searched them, and then drove them out. In half an hour the looters had been forced to abandon everything. Kvachi stationed his friends in various places and told the reds:

"Brothers, thank you for saving the people's property. We'll now take care of everything. You're no longer needed. Goodbye."

They locked the doors and wore their hands out working day and night: the valuables were sorted out, put into boxes and chests, and carted off to Kvachi's cellar for "safekeeping." From then on Gintz and a Jewish antique dealer became frequent visitors to that cellar.

Kvachi was now a habitual treasure seeker, saving and protecting it. If the mandate had worked in one place, why shouldn't it work elsewhere? Kvachi tested his cunning and the mandate's power, which turned out to be unlimited and magical. Everyone quaked when they saw that piece of paper, as if it were the black death or a live hand grenade. People automatically bowed their necks and doors opened. Kvachi was quite amazed by the countless treasures so generously strewn about Peter's city.

Once Kvachi recalled the time when he decided to forsake his deceitful habits and sincerely serve the people and the revolution. After recalling it, he justified to Beso his reversion to his old ways:

"It makes no difference, Beso, honest people never amount to anything. Everyone, old or new, around them is robbing and looting: an honest man is left stranded and dies hungry. The new revolution is not going the way I thought it would. It's going to drown in blood and take us with it. We have set out on a very dangerous path, but it's too late to turn back. So the only thing left for us is to get our share and then escape from this hell. You see, Russia is taking on the whole world. When camels fight, the baby camel gets squashed between them. While the fight is going on, we've got to grab everything we can, but we mustn't leave it too late to get out of here."

The Society of Defenders of the Red Revolution expanded

and blossomed. The new rulers had no time to investigate it, so that everything in Kvachi's army went on as Kvachi wanted it to.

But eventually this Society was put on the Smolny Institute's agenda. Kvachi quickly sensed danger and instructed his headquarters:

"We're going to get our necks broken: it's time to slowly dismantle this nest of ours which has kept us nice and warm for a whole year. If a building has a crack in it, you can't stay there any more. Now we've got to get posts. Who knows, we might be better off taking refuge that way. The mandate is so effective that we can take on any posts without pay."

What they resolved, they did. It took Kvachi a week to find them all new chairs to sit on. He had himself appointed as commissar in a major bank, while Sedrak was appointed chief cashier there; Gabo Chkhubishvili was moved to the Red Cross warehouse, Ladi Chikinjiladze was insinuated into the Mint, while Chipi Chipuntiradze, Pavlov, and Bekarev continued their old career in spying and searching.

Beso Shikia took over from Kvachi as the manager of the Society of Defenders of the Red Revolution: he dissolved the society and sold its property, and did so brilliantly in a month.

Kvachi also needed only a month to carry out his plan. Almost every day Beso or Chipi or Ladi would come in to see him and present him with million-rouble "assignation" notes, cheques, or other documents. Kvachi would casually write "Received" on them, and Sedrak, who told everyone else there was no money, would credit all the money to the gang. Chainstein then took it to the stock exchange and in the evening brought back the equivalent in gold and jewels.

Every day, as noon approached, Kvachi would reach for the telephone and have a conversation in thieves' slang:

"Beso, is that you?"

"Yes, it's me."

"Put down five million today."

"All right."

An hour later a demand would go to the bank in the name of Kvachi's society or some other institution.

In the evenings the gang would gather at Kvachi's apartment, exchange news, settle accounts, and set new traps.

Outside the sky might be on fire, the earth might be soaked with blood, the moans of fighters might deafen the streets, and the thunder of guns make the ground shake.

Kvachi and his associates strained their ears and eyes, watching everything anxiously, working deftly: whatever could be grabbed, they grabbed; whatever could be reaped, they reaped; anything that fell, they picked up; they fleeced the fallen, they easily sneaked into cracks, they claimed anything left unclaimed, sometimes taking the owner as well.

Pavlov was just completely at home in his new job: he soon became Kvachi's right-hand man. Not a day passed without Pavlov offering Kvachi a new trick to pull off:

"This is a job we can set up … that one is dangerous … this one will never work … That one they know about … This they don't."

Some time earlier Kvachi had issued an order: "Act so that we can be ready at any time to leave town. A careful man at times like these should always have his horse saddled."

Isaac and Rebecca had been released from prison. They both left straight away for Odessa. Although Kvachi had forgiven them both their weakness, they avoided him, using Bekarev as a go-between to offer their regards and ask him to excuse them. They then both suddenly vanished.

Elena, too, had disappeared.

The government moved to Moscow. Kvachi and his headquarters were supposed to follow, but he delayed, because there were a couple of jobs he had yet to finish.

"Gabo, how's my friend Ganus?" he asked around this time.

"He's just died."

"Of natural causes?" asked Kvachi, astonished.

"I said he's died. If you're eating fruit, you don't ask about the fruit-grower," said Gabo with a smile, as he looked down. Kvachi caught the gist. Gabo had a gold watch on a chain, was holding a gold cigarette case, and his fingers were covered in expensive gleaming rings.

"Good man," said Kvachi approvingly. "I owe you my thanks."

Kvachi and his gang were laying their hands on things more often, grabbing excessive amounts, extracting more, so that in one week they made more than they had up till then. Meanwhile the storm clouds were gathering over Kvachi. There was a menacing smell in the air. There were occasional flashes of lightning. Finally, one evening Chipi Chipuntiradze rushed in to see Kvachi; he was in complete disarray, shouting:

"We're doomed! They've found out everything! Run for your lives! Here, read this!"

They opened the evening paper and read: "The revolution has also been infiltrated by Prince Kvachantiradze, a friend of Rasputin and the Tsar's faithful servant, who has ..."

"Brothers, it's time we went ..." said Jalil, flashing his horse's teeth.

Chipi was followed by Pavlov, who announced curtly and calmly:

"They've found out everything, we must pack now or it's too late."

"Right, in half an hour you're all to be at the station," said Kvachi, giving the order to mobilize.

It all went smoothly. All the gang was at the station in half an hour.

"We're doomed!" Chipi yelled again. "There isn't a train in sight."

"Don't shout, Chipi," Kvachi reassured his panicky spy. "Beso, go and find a train, spare no expense."

Beso came back in ten minutes.

"Two carriages will be ready right now. I don't think a hundred gold roubles is too dear."

"It's not too dear," Kvachi agreed.

"In half an hour a two-carriage train was speeding towards Moscow. All nine of them sat in a saloon carriage, the nine members of the Society of Helpers and Defenders of the Red Revolution who were entrusted with "regulating the movement of trains for revolutionary soldiers."

"Will that mandate still work?" Sedrak asked fearfully.

"It will not only work, it will smash everything!" replied Ladi.

"Who's going to sign it?" Kvachi asked Beso, who was holding the yard-long mandate.

"The revolutionary military committee. Look. There's the seal and everything's as it should be. Read it: 'Rev-Mil-Com'."

"Allah!" exclaimed Jalil, "the strength a piece of paper has in Russia!"

"Now, Jalil: supper!" demanded Kvachi. "Get some good vodka, Crimean wine, and Crystal champagne."

Half an hour later the Georgian "Live a thousand years" song was drowning out the rattle and rumble of the train. Jalil followed that song with a Turkish love song, and after that came "Down the Mother Volga."

In the morning the train approached a station. The gang had a wash. They stretched their limbs languidly and got ready for breakfast. The station, seething with Russian guards, became like a swarm of startled bees, roaring: "It's coming, it's coming!"

When the train reached the platform a sea of men in greatcoats surged forwards, roaring excitedly: "Come on! Take it! Throw them out!"

Soldiers laden with weapons, boxes, rucksacks, and bags

swallowed up the entire train. They rushed the carriages, screaming and threatening, and installed themselves. Some came in through the doors, some squeezed through the windows. Others clutched from behind the soldiers who were tumbling in and pulled off their boots, or stole their luggage.

"Comrades," the soldiers called out. "Why is this scum pushing in?"

"Comrades! Violence will be severely punished!" Kvachi threatened. "We have a mandate which … Now listen, look …"

But nobody wanted to see or hear the mandate. Kvachi's shouts and threats were met by laughter and other threats. Someone called out:

"Comrades! We've had enough of these bourgeois drinking our blood. Enough! Throw them out of the window!"

In two minutes Kvachi and his gang were thrown out of the windows, to the sound of a few thumps, obscene curses, loud laughter, and threats of the firing squad.

"Quick, help me get the luggage, or we're ruined," ordered Kvachi.

They had a hard time of it outside the train, pleading and fawning, promising money and vodka, but they couldn't get back to the carriages. Finally the overcrowded train moved off to the sound of shouts and roars, taking with it the property of Kvachi and his gang—clothes, provisions, money, jewels—all they had worked for and looted, the fruit of past hopes, curses, and tears.

The gang sat in the station hall, their heads hanging low, and wept.

"We're finished, we're finished!" wailed Chipi, his eyes full of tears.

"Oh what an idiot I am! It's what I deserve!" muttered Sedrak, thumping his head with his fist.

"How could we have made God so angry with us? How could we lose all that wealth?" moaned Gabo.

"Ye-e-es, things aren't looking good," Pavlov agreed.

"Our luck's out. Woe to Allah, it's gone," Jalil said, shaking his head.

Beso was cracking his fingers, Ladi Chikinjiladze was crunching the dried fruit left in his pocket, Bekarev was choking in his own cigarette smoke, and Kvachi, as frantic as a wild animal in a cage, ran about, constantly rubbing his furrowed brow. Finally they all fell silent and stared their leader in the eyes. Nobody spoke for a long time, waiting for Kvachi to pronounce their fate.

"How are you, Kvachi?" Beso finally ventured.

"I feel like a dog."

"What do you suggest?"

"Nothing. What did you manage to save in that traveling bag?"

"Nothing much. Seals and rubber stamps."

"You say nothing much? You've saved everything! Good man!"

Kvachi's brow became smooth again, he smiled. Then he gave the comrades encouragement and hope, saying in a firm voice:

"Don't let it get you down, comrades. We'll recover our losses in one month, if our luck doesn't let us down and if God doesn't strike us again. Right, get up! Gather your strength! Follow me!"

"Allah preserve you, prince, Allah preserve you!" exclaimed Jalil, lifting both hands to Allah.

The Story of Samtredidze

Work was in progress in the rooms belonging to the Provincial Executive Committee (ProvExCom). Three men boldly came up to the ExCom's chairman's office. A guard barred their way: "You can't go in. The Committee's in session."

The leader of the three moved the guard aside with one hand, another opened the door and entered. The two others followed. The meeting broke off. The speaker broke off his speech; everyone stared at the newcomers.

"My apologies, comrades!" said Kvachi Kvachantiradze with cool aplomb. "Let me introduce myself. I am Pavle Samtredidze, a member of the Revolutionary Military Council. These are members of my staff: Panov and Shikiants." He pointed to Pavlov and Beso Shikia.

Everyone rushed to their feet and stood to attention. Kvachi adopted an even more sardonic expression and continued:

"Horrible things are happening in your town, and you stand there calmly gossiping. For example, my staff and I came by special train. On the way I was informed that treasonable bourgeois were taking jewelry and gold abroad. I searched them, and the information proved to be true. Of course, I confiscated the valuables, and shot the loathsome traitors on the spot. But right under your noses, at the station, soldiers turned robbers threw us off our train, took everything off us and left, using our train. Comrades, what have you got to say about this?"

The comrades were perturbed. There was a flurry of running about, telephoning, and roaring motor cars.

"Are you the chairman of the *Cheka* secret police?" Kvachi asked one man. "There are nine of us. I shall stay here, take the others with you. Now send a telegram to have this train stopped at a small station, the locomotive detached and sent on its way, to stop the soldiers stealing the train. Do you understand my plan?"

"Yes indeed, I understand, comrade. At the same time I'll send a hundred or so armed men to the train, we'll surround it and ..."

"Right. And take four or five machine guns. When are you going?"

"In an hour. I'm sending the telegram right now."

"Very good. I wish you success. I owe you a favor. Oh, I forgot: here are our mandates."

Kvachi took out half a dozen long mandates and spread them out on the desk. Faced with these fearsome mandates everyone again stood to attention and quaked in their shoes. Nobody dared to pick up and read a mandate. So Kvachi put the papers back in his pocket and said:

"Get to work, then. Goodbye, comrades. Jalil, you were magnificent!"

"Allah's grace be upon you!"

Kvachi took Beso aside and told him: "Now our life is in your hands. I'll fix everything here by the time you're back."

Just two men were left in the office: an indignant Kvachi, and the ProvExCom chairman, standing to attention.

"Sit down, comrade!" Kvachi deigned to say. "Sit down and tell me what's going on in your province."

The chairman had worn himself out talking, but it took only a couple of words for Kvachi to calculate the state of affairs in the province and assess its rulers' work.

"Good, now tell me what your supplies are like. How much wheat, potatoes, flour, sugar, and other provisions?"

When he had an answer, he asked again: "Have you been confiscating merchants' property?"

"A little bit."

"Have you audited the gold and jewelry?"

"Not yet."

"I see you're well behind the capital city. Not that it matters. I'll help you: I'm experienced, so let's work together. You'll soon be trained up. Now listen to me. I need ten or so rooms, three motor cars, a typewriter, office supplies, and furniture. Issue the order."

In two hours three families were evicted from a house on the main street. Kvachi was told: "Your rooms are ready. By evening there'll be a telephone and so on. It's time for dinner. Come and eat with us, comrade."

Kvachi did the ProvExCom chairman the honor of accepting his hospitality, then went to his rooms to lie down and sleep.

The sun was setting when Beso and Jalil woke Kvachi up.

"Get up, Kvachi, we're back. We've got everything back. Not a pin is missing, nothing except the drink. The soldiers finished off all the vodka, brandy, wine, and champagne."

"I hope it did them good. No blood was shed, was it?"

"Not a drop."

"Beso was a very clever man, very," said Jalil.

"Congratulations, Beso and Jalil! Let me kiss you both. I haven't been idle, either: it's all ready." The leader gave them both brotherly kisses.

"You don't need all this, Kvachi. Give it up. We've recovered such a fortune: what more do you want? Let's clear off tomorrow, or … who knows? It's very dangerous," said Beso.

"Let's go, prince, let's go, or Allah will be angry," pleaded Jalil.

"Beso, old man, you've never been able to understand my character. Let me fix one last job, a real man's job: why the hell would I want just to be rich? Someone said, 'Gaining a good name is the best of gains'."

"They'll put us up against a wall, Kvachi."

"They won't be able to touch me! If it comes to that, I myself will put everyone here in front of a firing squad."

The next day Kvachi and his staff moved into their new lodgings. At the same time Kvachi issued orders and instructions. To Pavlov:

"Go back to Petersburg. Organize intelligence-gathering. If we are in any danger, send a telegram saying 'Come back now'."

To the others: "Sedrak, you go to Moscow. Ladi, get yourself accommodation in Smolensk. Periodically you'll all get goods and instructions. Sometimes you yourselves will be sending goods to other places. Beso, organize mandates for them and tell them how to use them. If the whole thing goes belly-up, then we all gather in Rostov."

Beso devoted a whole day to instructing and training the other comrades; the next day, each got down to his own job.

Kvachi had beautifully equipped offices: the chancellery itself took up three rooms. Sentries and couriers stood to attention here and there. Jalil wore a funnel-shaped Budionovka army hat. A typewriter clattered. Every minute the telephone rang. Clients came in great numbers. Beso filtered the clients and managed the office. Chipi Chipuntiradze, Gabo Chkhubishvili, and Bekarev infiltrated the wealthy, looking for clients.

Work expanded in a week like wildfire. Kvachi was sitting like a spider in a city with a network of five railways. Traffic stopped. The railways were paralyzed. Not just grain, but the actual wagons were stolen. The tracks were strewn with smashed locomotives. Every wagon was worth more than human blood: it was Kvachi who burnt the wagons and their food supplies.

Every now and again Kvachi invited the local authorities and told them: "Look, read this." The authority would read a telegram: "To Samtredidze, member of the RevMilCom. Urgently send five wagons flour, five wagons cabbages, same of potatoes and various provisions."

"When will they be ready?"

"Three days."

"I'll despatch them myself: load them, then let me know."

The loaded train would go to Moscow or Petersburg, where it would fall into a pit-trap prepared by Kvachi.

From Smolensk and other cities Kvachi periodically received substantial property which he would within two days turn into gold and jewels. Almost every day Kvachi would set up these frauds, and some merchant, a Spekulov or a Ripoff, would be brought to see him.

"I want five wagons to go to Moscow."

"The price is five hundred gold roubles."

They agreed a price, Kvachi confirmed the order: " ...and I certify that the fifth division is being sent unscheduled five wagons of goods." Spekulov's loaded train would depart the next day for Moscow, with Spekulov on it, and Kvachi's properly signed yard-long mandates. Thanks to these mandates, in Moscow Spekulov was given his property, which Sedrak helped to sell. Then the same mandates and the same Sedrak saw that a loaded train departed from Moscow, carrying a load to be sold by Kvachi. Every now and again Kvachi and the authorities received an order: "Carry out requisition of gold and jewelry (or provisions, or textiles, or other goods), as ordered by member of the Military Council Samtredidze, entrusted with taking requisitioned goods to Moscow."

By now the bellowing and groans of merchants and the wealthy was reaching the heavens: the accumulated goods went to Moscow and Petersburg, where Sedrak and Pavlov welcomed them with open arms.

Kvachi had set little traps at the stations, too. When a train passed through, it was caught in Kvachi's little web. His lads would go round the travelers, searching them, and confiscating forbidden objects. Very often they also took objects that were not forbidden. Every morning the station was filled with the victims' tears. The air was filled with foul language, curses, threats, gasps, weeping, pleas, and imprecations from fleeced travelers. But Kvachi's lads were quite unafraid, for tears and curses turned to gold in their hands and there was no sign of any danger. All around everything was on fire or being demolished, and the sobs and pleas of their crushed victims were drowned out in the storm, just as a cat's mewling is by thunder.

"Kvachi, we've got enough," Beso would warn Kvachi.

"No, hang on a little longer," Kvachi, carried away, would reassure his frightened friend, and went on tirelessly sweeping up, ripping off, fleecing, and grabbing.

Kvachi once did the rounds of a passenger train in person. In one carriage he came upon a dozen genuine comrades, wearing leather jackets, Budionovka funnel-hats, and armed to the teeth. Ivan Ivanych Ivanov was among them, short-sighted, confused, and absent-minded as ever. Kvachi was dumbfounded; they stared at one another, but Kvachi quickly realized that Ivan had failed to recognize him.

"Comrades," Kvachi asked in a polite, but firm voice. "you wouldn't have provisions above the permitted norm, would you?"

"No," replied one of the comrades. "We have a drop of brandy, but …"

The comrades were having dinner: they'd set out black bread, pickled gherkins, a stinking fish, and cold potatoes, with a bottle of brandy.

"Kindly let me have that bottle," said Kvachi, reaching for it.

"Comrade, we haven't drunk it yet," growled the first comrade.

"Don't be so strict," a second comrade begged Kvachi.

"Take it then," said a third comrade, handing the bottle to Kvachi. "Laws are laws, and that's all there is to it. We'll obey you."

"Quite right, comrade," said a fourth. "Can't deny that's true. We were given the decree, so we should be the first to obey it."

Ivan Ivanych took another look at Kvachi, rubbed his forehead, and thought, "I wonder, where have I seen that man?"

The train left. The comrades debated Kvachi's behavior for some time. Some cursed him, others approved of his strictness.

"It was a big mistake of ours not to ask his name," said one. "Men as firm and loyal as him should be cherished."

"I know the man, I recognize him, but …" muttered Ivan Ivanych. "I can't remember where or when I met him. I think … I think …"

He kept rubbing his forehead until they got to Moscow: then he remembered. The moment the train arrived, Ivan quickly leapt out, clapped his hand to his brow and called out: "I've remembered, I've remembered!"

"What? What have you remembered?" everyone asked him.

"I've remembered, I've remembered! Get me some paper quick, a telegram! Arrest that scoundrel, or he'll wreck the country. Quick!"

"Ivan, who's going to wreck the country? Who's got to be arrested?"

"Him, him! The man who took the brandy off us. His name's Kvachantiradze. He has three or five names: Kvachi, Apollo, Napoleon and ... The devil knows who he really is! Anyway, give me paper at once!"

Karapet Shulavriants

It took Ivan Ivanych ten minutes to write an angry telegram at the Moscow station. But Beso Shikia was standing behind him, smiling as he read the telegram over his shoulder, before sending two telegrams of his own—to Pavlov and Ladi—and getting on a special train where Kvachi and the rest of the gang were waiting for him. He was followed straight away by Sedrak, who had left town to look for Kvachi's train. While they embraced and asked after each other, porters filled half the carriage with Sedrak's luggage: wine, a dozen other drinks, provisions, and expensive goods. Then Beso told Kvachi:

"Ivan Ivanych has managed to remember who you are. He's sent a telegram to have us arrested. I've just read it."

"Ha-ha," laughed Kvachi. "Our Ivan Ivanych is too late, far too late. Let them look for me, Sedrak, read this piece of paper and tell me if the *Cheka* is going to get us."

Sedrak read the long mandate, which stated: "Karapet Minasich Shulavriants and his comrades (a dozen names followed) have orders to find and arrest the notorious counter-revolutionary, saboteur, and bandit Kvachi Kvachantiradze, aka Anapodiste, aka Apollo, aka Napoleon, aka Pavle Samtredidze."

"My God," said Sedrak, his jaw dropping. "So you're searching for yourself, then?"

Kvachi Kvachantiradze was searching for himself. When he arrived at one of several towns or stations he immediately went to see the authorities, showed them his yard-long mandate and asks:

"Do you know if this man, Kvachi Kvachantiradze, is in the vicinity?"

Then he asked for lodgings, a telephone, a motor car and looked for some crack to exploit. The routes were cut off. Rostov and other cities were changing from White rule to Red and then went back to the Whites. The bloody quadrille was a never-ending dance.

Kvachi soon hit on his own trail. The *Cheka* was pursuing his every step, sometimes on his tail, sometimes ahead of him. Kvachi used dozens of different tricks. Beso cooked up a dozen new mandates and certificates. They met rarely. There were a few places where they could safely break through the front, but everywhere they came across traps.

Once Jalil told Kvachi: "Boss, Jalil had a very bad dream last night: I hope they don't arrest you."

"Don't worry, Jalil. We'll soon be out of this hell," Kvachi reassured him.

The next day Kvachi and Beso went to the station to reconnoitre the situation. As was their custom, they walked separately to the platform and sniffed the air. Suddenly two men in black leather coats came up to Kvachi on either side with revolvers drawn.

"Hands up! Come with us."

They pushed Kvachi in front of them. Beso went round in front of Kvachi and they exchanged glances. Kvachi smiled slightly.

In the *Cheka* headquarters forms were filled in and Kvachi was put in a cell. An hour later Pavlov approached the *Cheka* chairman: "You should know who I am, comrade: here's my mandate."

The mandate stated that the *Chekist* Silov was entrusted with arresting Kvachantiradze and taking him to Moscow.

"Two people have just been to see me on the same business. Look, read their mandate and the declaration."

"I know."

But Beso still cast an eye over this piece of paper and saw the declaration at the end, saying that the *Chekist* in pursuit knew Kvachantiradze personally, that he had often had conversations with him and had deliberately taken part in his frauds.

"Fine. Is that the man who arrested Kvachantiradze?"

"No, it was one of our agents. I'll question him and then hand him over to ... what's the name? Yes, Chinov. Yes, I'll hand him to Chinov."

"Fine, but I should tell you that I am also under instructions to keep an eye on Chinov and ... investigate a certain case. I'll tell you straight: we don't trust Chinov any more."

"As you like."

"One more thing. I'm looking for a major spy: his trail leads here, to you. I think this is the man you've arrested."

"Surname?"

"Zeitunov."

"We've got no prisoner under that name."

"I expect he's using another surname. Would you let me have a look at the prisoners. I know this Zeitunov."

"By all means."

"One other thing: don't let Chinov know I'm here. If he needs to interrogate Kvachantiradze, I want to be there, too."

"All right."

He rang the bell, passed Pavlov-Silov to a guard and gave the necessary orders.

Pavlov went from cell to cell, inspecting the prisoners. The guard trudged some distance behind him. Pavlov put his eye to a spy-hole: through it he could see Kvachi's nose and eyes.

"Don't worry, I'll get you out. The Moscow *Chekist* Chinov insists he recognizes you personally. Think of something ..." Pavlov whispered as fast as he could to Kvachi.

In less than half an hour Kvachi was brought upstairs. Chinov and Pavlov were sitting behind a desk.

"I had some trouble getting hold of you, comrade Kvachantiradze," a smiling Chinov told Kvachi as he came in. "Please take a seat."

Kvachi was astounded: "What did you say? Kvancharidze? I'm not Kvancharidze. My name is Saropoulo, Mitro Saropoulo, I'm a businessman from Rostov."

"Fine, fine. We know who you are. Confess. Your real name is Kvachantiradze. You do have other surnames: Samtredidze, Shulavriants and … weren't you arrested today?"

"Me? I've been here three months. Who did you want? If it's Kvacharadze … It wouldn't be more than two hours ago that he was brought in, would it?"

Chinov was taken aback. Clearly, he didn't recognize Kvachi.

"Yes, yes, he's the one I want … Him."

"That's the man that was brought to my cell."

"Then there's been a mix-up. I asked for Kvachantiradze to be brought up."

"I don't even look like Kvachantiradze!"

"True … you don't. The devil take him, body and soul. Hey you, comrade!" he called to the guard. "I told you to bring me Kvachantiradze, and you've brought me some Greek. Take this man away and bring me Kvachantiradze. Get it? Kva-chan-ti-ra-dze! Be quick about it."

Kvachi quickly straightened up; his eyes flashed, he struck the desk with his fist and then he told Chinov to his face:

"I'm Kvachantiradze. Yes, I'm your Kvachi Kvachantiradze! I demand you draw up a statement and put in it that you couldn't recognize Kvachantiradze. Be quick. I said, draw up a statement. Go on … Look, we've got witnesses."

The noise brought the *Cheka* chairman in. Chinov was confused: he'd gone too far by adding a little lie to a dozen truths. That lie had tripped him up, and given Kvachi something to hold onto.

The statement was drawn up. Pavlov smiled as he told the *Cheka* chairman: "I told you Chinov wasn't reliable. He's messed things up here, too. There's something fishy about him. I'm off to Moscow tomorrow. I'll take both of them with me, Kvachantiradze and Chinov. Let me have that statement. No, I don't need your guards, I've got four men of my own ... Well, till tomorrow, comrade! Chinov can wait here."

"Till tomorrow, comrade."

Once Pavlov had left, the chairman called a guard and gave him an order: "Chinov is in that room: arrest him."

The next day Pavlov-Silov dressed Bekarev, Chkhubishvili, Jalil, and Chipi in black leather, put Budionovkas on their heads and Mausers on their belts and took the two prisoners from the *Cheka*, surrounding them with his four colleagues, while he led the party. They crossed town, took their seats in a railway carriage, and set off for the north. Once the train was moving, there was nothing but shouts, embraces, kisses, and joyful laughter to be heard in that carriage.

"Well done, Pavle, well done!" they said, re-baptising Pavlov as Pavle and clapping him hard on the back. "You're a genius, a genius."

"From now on you're my blood brother!" Kvachi told Pavlov, as he embraced him. "You saved my life, so it's now all yours."

"True, I contributed a little bit," Pavlov admitted. "But the main person responsible for saving you is this rogue here." Pavlov put a finger on Beso.

"My true friend Beso! Come, come closer!"

And Kvachi hugged his inseparable companion so hard that Beso couldn't breathe.

"That's the sort of comradeship we need," said Chkhubishvili happily.

"Hey," Sedrak said admiringly. "It's a fairytale, a fairytale."

Chipi was fidgeting and giggling like a child; Beso Shikia was smiling gravely, Chikinjiladze was now frowning, and Jalil was opening bottles and periodically raising his hands to the heavens: "*Allah il-allah! Shukur Allaha*!"

Suddenly they remembered about Chinov who was hunched in a corner and watching, his jaws dropping, the prisoners and *chekists* embracing. Kvachi turned to this bemused *chekist*:

"Comrade, you were going to shoot us all; now you're in our clutches. We're not wild animals, so we're not going to hurt you. But we can't let you go. Do you want to come with us to Georgia, or not?"

The *chekist* had already considered his position and worked out a plan of action.

"I couldn't wish for anything better. If you get me out of this hell, I'll be your faithful servant."

"Then come and have a drink of this vodka, to mark our peace treaty."

They made him shake hands, drink, and eat.

"Whatever else he may be, he's a *chekist*, said Kvachi in Georgian. "Chipi, I'm putting this man in your hands. Don't take your eyes off him, day or night, or he'll put one over us."

When they reached a major station Pavlov had the gang's carriage uncoupled and coupled to another train which was heading for the front. After supper Kvachi lit his pipe and said:

"Friends, everything has a beginning and an end. Moderation is a divine grace: we have exhausted our bloody path in life and we have done our revolutionary duty. Until Russia went mad and lost all sense of proportion, we served a common motherland conscientiously. But our fair-haired brothers have gone mad. We've seen so much and experienced such hell, that anyone else in our shoes would have gone mad themselves. But nature has endowed us—thank the Lord—with a sense of proportion, clear minds, and a feeling for reality. We cannot exterminate each other for the sake of abstract hallucinations. If we go on annihilating one another, bears and jackals won't be able to reincarnate our sacred principles over our graves. Jalil, pour me another. Friends! If the Georgian people had never created anything else, just one saying of Shota Rustaveli would prove that Shota and the Georgian people are geniuses."

"What did he say that was so brilliant?" asked Pavle.

"He said: 'Whatever is in the wine-jar will flow out of it'. Wonder at these words and use your wits to apply them to what is happening in Russia today. Whatever is in the Russian soul is flowing out, neither more nor less. Russians have found their soul again. They had forced it into European clothes and plastered it with European cosmetics. They've thrown off the bourgeois-capitalist fog and reverted to their true selves."

"Is that all that's happened?"

"Nothing else. The rest is just words, just words. Words are there to conceal people's thoughts. Words are a cloak to hide the body—nobody knows if the body's beautiful or ugly, white or black, red or yellow."

He downed a glass of port, lit his pipe two or three times more, and turned to Pavlov:

"You Russians must be peculiar. So far nobody has managed to understand your soul and character. I thought Russians were trying to get freedom for themselves. Don't tell me that: they're actually fighting the whole world. This is a fight they are going to lose. The fact that you've been involved in this fantastic struggle won't hurt you, but we Georgians (for some time Kvachi had, instead of disdaining them, taken pride in his origins) are so few that we can be counted on the fingers of one hand. Today's Russia is going to the grave and dragging the tiny handful of Georgians with it. I'm sorry: we may follow you to the edge of the grave, but not into it. If our nice Ivan Ivanych were here, he'd tell me this is a petty-bourgeois attitude. It may well be, but even a petty bourgeois doesn't like being thrown out of his birthplace and being wiped out. This reminds me of our chat last year, brother Pavle. We were both fighting in the rear against Red Russia. Whether we were right or not, we both stopped doing so. I never regret the past, sincerely or insincerely, I fix my mind on the present. But today I'm telling you: brother Ivan, this is as far as I can go with you. Goodbye! May God show you the right way. We have our own motherland waiting for us and calling us."

"That's true, that's true!" exclamations came from all sides.

"In Georgia nobody's going to kill me and I'm not going to kill anybody. We are longing for peace, and here I don't think we'll ever find peace. In any case, in Georgia we all have parents and relatives. It's time we remembered them and tried to help them."

"Let's go, then. We love you. That's right!" Gabo and Sedrak said impatiently.

"To our motherland! To Georgia! Home!" the comrades kept on calling out for some time, downing bottle after bottle, belting out "Live a thousand years!" as the train sped rattling southwards.

A Bloody Battle

"Kvachi, get up! Quick, quick!"

Kvachi leapt up straight away.

"Chinov's got away," Beso informed him.

"We're doomed. Now we really are doomed," shrieked Chipi Chipuntiradze, tearing his hair. "It's my fault, mine. I fell asleep for a minute … The scoundrel gave me the slip, he got away."

"Pack the bags," Kvachi ordered grimly. "Don't take anything you don't need … Ladi, leave that wretched wine … Jalil, throw away those rags … Now, follow me! Guns at the ready."

The gang jumped out of the train into the snow-covered fields, like bedbugs onto a white bedspread. After they'd jumped off, they ran at a trot in single file. It was now daylight and the cloudy sky and boundless snow-covered fields seemed to merge in the distance. The gang, like a line of ants, waded knee-deep in snow, groaning as they struggled onwards. Every now and again they stopped to get back their breath. Kvachi inspected the area through his binoculars, sometimes turning aside, sometimes going straight ahead.

Nobody knew whom they might run into or have to deal with. The endless countryside was so chaotic and anarchic that there were ten enemies of various colors and races for each person. Everyone was fighting everyone: Hetman Skoropadsky, Petliura, Makhno, Antonov, the Germans, the Muscovites, the French, the Poles, the White Volunteers, robbers, deserters, bandits, and marauders. They had all got so confused and entangled with each other that Kvachantiradze had lost his ability to distinguish between enemy and friend.

When the sun was setting they saw smoke. They stopped and sent Bekarev to reconnoitre the village. An hour later he returned.

"There's nobody in the village. But they're expecting the Whites any day: they're not far."

They entered the village and settled in a cottage. They asked after horses, but it seemed that the Reds and the Whites hadn't left a single horse behind. Tired, the comrades ate hot borscht and rested. Bekarev went to the edge of the village on sentry duty.

Kvachi was in a deep sleep when he suddenly heard Bekarev's voice:

"Get up, get up!"

They all rushed towards him: "What's going on? What's happened?"

"They're coming, they're coming!"

"Who? Where from? How many of them?"

"At least forty on horseback. They're taking cover in the gullies. A dozen men are coming towards us from the left."

Pavlov then came in: he had gone into the village to sniff the air.

"Eureka! I've just found two machine guns. The Whites hid

them two weeks ago. They're bringing more."

The friends were joyful, as if a hundred men had come to their aid.

"Right, go outside, or this cage will turn into a real grave," Kvachi called on them as he rushed out of the cottage, looked round, and quickly weighed up and assessed the turn of events. "All right, friends! This is the Day of Judgement. Death in battle is better than death by firing squad. Pavle, you, Bekarev, and Ladi take cover behind this wall and cover that approach, so they won't be able to get us from that direction. Take one machine gun with you. The rest, follow me. Don't waste bullets, don't be too hasty! Take it slowly and bravely."

Three men took cover behind a wall, and the rest sheltered under a hedge with a full view of the open fields and a broad gully. The Reds had tethered their horses in the gully, and were coming in single file on foot up the path, slowly creeping up on the gang.

"Twenty-seven ... twenty-eight ..." Kvachi counted. "All in all, thirty-two, and there are six of us."

"Nine," Gabo told him.

"I don't count the other three: they have their own enemy. As long as we win before nightfall, we'll be out of harm. Right, Gabo! Get behind the machine gun, you know how to use it."

"We're finished, Kvachi," mewled Chipi.

"Shh, son of a dog," said Jalil to silence Chipi.

"God, what's wrong with me?" muttered Sedrak, his teeth chattering. "I must have a fever. My rifle's shaking."

"Don't huddle together," Kvachi told his gang. "Spread out ten paces from each other."

Kvachi had Jalil lie down on his right, and Chkhubishvili sprawled on his left. Beso took one wing, Sedrak squatted on the other.

The Reds stopped and took cover. One of their leaders stepped forward and called out: "Hey you, Kva-chan-ti-ra-dze! Bandit! Surrender."

Kvachi smiled and aimed his rifle. He fired. The red leader waved both arms; his rifle fired, but missed, and he fell on his back. That instant thirty rifles roared from the gully: the bullets hit the hedge like peas. A furious, remorseless battle began.

"Don't shoot at random!" Kvachi periodically ordered. "Aim! Fire! Load!"

"Ha, you sons of dogs! Beggars. *Kırmız shaitan* (Red devils)," mumbled Jalil.

"I've knocked another one out!" Chkhubishvili rejoiced. "That's just the start!"

"Oh no," came a shout from the right wing. Kvachi looked round. Sedrak was hunched, his face in the snow; one hand seemed to be raking snow. Chipi had lowered his head and was angrily firing at the sky.

"Chipi," Kvachi yelled. "Who are you shooting at? Where are you firing? Straighten up, take aim!"

Chipi bent his head even lower, moaned horribly, and fell on his back.

"Jalil!", Kvachi called. "Take the rifles and cartridges off both of them and pass them here. My rifle's so overheated that it's burning my hand."

The Reds suddenly rushed forward, running with shouts of "Hurrah!"

Kvachi, hold out. Kvachi, don't tremble. Be quick! Be brave! Be firm! Don't turn your back on the enemy, or you, your friends, and your booty will all be lost for ever!

"Right, friends!" Kvachi shouted in fury. "Load! Aim! Fire!"

"Rat-a-tat-tat," the machine gun rattled in Gabo's hands.

"Crack-crack-crack," thundered half a dozen rifles.

The devils that possessed Kvachi on Demir-Tepe possessed him again. Earlier he had been so enthralled by the devils that he could no longer understand the object of his madness, but now he was fighting purposefully and seriously for his reputation and his life. No, Kvachi was not ready to die yet. He would not die such an ungodly and ordinary death in some village in the backwoods. Kvachi was not going to die before he had hugged Silibistro and Pupi once more, before he had made a last trip to Kutaisi and Tbilisi, to Saghoria and Mushtaid farm, to the Kakhetian farm and Mtatsminda, before he had done the rounds of Eremo's and Laitadze's inns in Kutaisi, or been to the *Eden* and the *Fantasy* in Tbilisi's Vera gardens, before he'd played a last game of baccarat in the Georgian club and raised such hell that the name of Kvachi Kvachantiradze would be remembered for at least a dozen years, if only in tiny Georgia.

"Load, fire!"

That might not come true: even now in his homeland there was thunder and lightning as his brothers' blood was spilled and a new page in his people's history was being written in fire. No, no! At times like these Kvachi could not stand aside, nor could he die.

"Load! Aim! Fire!"

The yells of "Hurrah" were no longer to be heard under the hedge. The Reds turned and fled. They had left a dozen wounded and dead on a hillock. At the same time the machine gun stopped rattling. Kvachi looked all round. Gabo Chkhubishvili was dying, slumped on his weapon. Both arms were wrapped round the red-hot machine gun, which he had embraced like a much-loved woman. Beso Shikia, as white as the snow all round, was leaning against the hedge, bandaging his wounded shin. Chipi Chipuntiradze was nowhere to be seen.

"Jalil, help Beso."

Kvachi himself ran to find Pavlov. Ladi Chikinjiladze was lying flat on his back. Kvachi put an ear to his chest and examined the wound. He was dead! Bekarev had fallen face down. He too was dead. Kvachi rushed to Pavlov. Pavlov was still breathing and moaning. He was alive! Kvachi carried Pavlov into the cottage and bandaged his wounds. Jalil brought in Beso and called out:

"*Allah il-allah*! The Red devils have gone, Kvachi-*bey*, they've gone. We've won. *Shukur Allah! Shukur Allah*!"

Jalil was smiling; Beso was grimacing with pain. Kvachi sat, his head bowed, weeping for his slain friends. Kvachi forgot the joy of victory. He had lost five comrades, five loyal comrades he had grown up with.

They could no longer return to the motherland or see their mother and father, their relatives and friends again. Poor Ladi! Poor Chipi! Poor Sedrak! Bekarev! Gabo! Everything was lost for them, and they were lost to everyone. Gabo and Sedrak could never again feast in the shade of a walnut tree or bathe in the Liakhvi and Alazan's clear waters, never embrace black-eyed girls, or enjoy the taste of crumbly cheese and Kakhetian wine, chicken, and lamb stew, smoked sturgeon and shashlyk. Their aged parents would wait with anguish for their lost sons and go on writing them tearful letters.

"Jalil", Kvachi asked Jalil with a groan. "Go into the village and get a dozen peasants to dig us graves."

Kvachi went out to take another look at the slain. Only now did he remember that he hadn't caught sight of Chipi. In the heat of battle Chipi had collapsed, as if killed or badly wounded, but now that Kvachi inspected the place where Chipi had fallen he did not see a single drop of blood. There were footprints in the snow: he must be hiding somewhere.

"Chipi, Chipi, where are you? Chipi! Chipi!"

There was no answer. Suddenly an evil doubt sprang up in Kvachi's mind. He rushed straight back to the cottage and looked for their treasure. The luggage had been ransacked. The valuables were nowhere to be seen. While the peasants dug a grave, Kvachi worked himself up into a fury:

"God, the ungrateful dog! The two-faced traitor! Shame on me, if I don't make Chipi's mother weep on his grave."

"Dirty beggar! Dog! *Kurumsag*! (May he wither!)," mumbled

Jalil. "He's not a man, he's a dog, a dog. Jalil wants to drink Chipi's blood. Blood! Just wait ... I'll ..."

The peasants who'd been sent in pursuit of Chipi came back: all traces of him had vanished. It was getting dark when four stiff and bruised corpses were laid to rest in the earth. Kvachi, tears in his eyes, threw a few fistfuls of earth over his friends. Jalil followed suit, sighed deeply, and said: "Allah bless your souls, friends."

After half an hour the graves were filled and marked with crude crosses.

The Reds would probably be returning. Staying in this village would have doomed the survivors. The peasants couldn't help, for they were afraid of their village being ravaged. There was no alternative: Kvachi slung Pavlov, who had recovered consciousness, over his shoulders; Jalil took Beso on his back. They let the peasants have everything else, keeping only a rifle, a hand gun, and cartridges for each man. One peasant led them to the edge of the village and said, "Follow this road, then turn left, then right, and left again, then right again, then go straight on and you'll reach the Whites."

Groaning and tottering, Kvachi and Jalil went on, stopping to wipe away their sweat or to rest, always going on and on. There was nothing to the left or to the right, no road, no path. They often stumbled, plunged into deep snow; sometimes they fell down and had trouble dragging their frozen bodies on. Darkness fell. In the distance a pair of tiny eyes shone, then a horrible howl rang out; an hour later wolves' eyes were flashing on all sides. Whenever Kvachi or Jalil fell, or sat down to rest in the snow, the wolves would boldly approach. At the sound of a rifle shot the vicious animals ran away, only to approach the enfeebled travelers a little later, just as boldly, trailing after them, waiting for their prey to lose its last ounce of strength.

"Hey, he-e-ey!" Jalil and Kvachi shouted from time to time. "Help!"

Their voices died away in the white desert. Nothing and nobody could be seen anywhere. Suddenly Beso heard a yell. A wolf had leapt up and sunk its teeth into Beso, who was riding on Jalil's back. Their hands trembling with cold, Jalil and Kvachi fired their rifles. In the silence the rifles roared like cannon. But the wolves were not afraid. They crouched a little way off and waited for their time to come. When a rifle fired, the wolves jumped to one side, changed places, and crouched again; their eyes shone like candles, and they howled horribly.

"Things are bad, prince," said Jalil. "My hands are very frozen."

"So are mine. I can't fire any more," Kvachi replied.

Is Kvachi Kvachantiradze really to be a wolf's dinner? Who will know, who can count how many dangers he's survived, how often he's escaped choking talons, how many iron traps he's broken free of, slipping away from a bloody end, smashing iron hoops? But now …

The wolves were getting bolder and moving forwards, trotting as they came nearer, within a dozen paces of the exhausted travelers.

Really? Are you going to perish in such a vile way, Kvachi? Is this really how you have to die, with nobody able to find even your bones? Will Silibistro and Pupi really never find out the horrible vengeance taken by treacherous fate?

The wolves were now five paces behind. You could hear them panting and you could see their tongues hanging out.

"He-e-elp! He-e-elp!"

Their yells sounded like groans. Their voices cracked in their throats, their weakened arms no longer obeyed them, their teeth were chattering like the wolves': the metal of their revolvers burnt their hands like fire.

Kvachi, don't tremble! Kvachi, don't break down! Kvachi, summon your strength! Gather all your strength. Keep your eyes vigilant. Be brave, be vigilant! Quick and determined, or this is the hour of your death.

"Hey, sons of dogs! Beggars!" Jalil muttered in Turkish.

Beso and Pavlov, their heads drooping, were sitting between their two comrades, coolly waiting for death to come.

"Kvachi," said Beso. "Kill me. I'd rather die from a bullet than from a wolf's teeth."

"How can you say that, Beso? Just wait …"

That instant a wolf leapt up and a revolver fired. The wolf fell, sprawling next to Kvachi.

"Is it dead, prince, is it dead? Good shot, prince, good shot!" yelled Jalil, who now stood up. "We can go on now, we'll be a long way away by the times the wolves have eaten the dead one."

But Kvachi couldn't stand. He had put all his strength into that revolver shot. They only managed to crawl about twenty paces from the spot. The hungry wolves went straight for their dead comrade and in ten minutes had picked all his flesh. Then they surrounded the travelers again and crouched five paces away. Half an hour passed.

"Jalil, I can't carry on," Kvachi whispered.

"I don't have any strength left," replied Jalil. "We've had it."

"Goodbye, Jalil."

"Don't go to sleep, prince, don't go to sleep," Jalil murmured, as he lay in the snow. In the silence that followed he groaned, "*Allah il-allah*!"

"Goodbye, Beso," Kvachi whispered again.

Beso did not answer. Sprawled on his back, he stared at the stars.

"Pavle!" Pavlov didn't reply, either. He had rolled into a ball with his head on his knees.

"It's over … It's finished … I'm dying … I shall freeze to death, or the wolves will eat me …" Kvachi thought as he sank into a fog of confusion. The doors of his mind shut, he dozed contentedly, and fell into a pleasant delirium. The wolves were getting to their feet preparing for a final leap.

Suddenly, far off, very far off, a gun fired. That moment Kvachi and Jalil summoned their last drop of strength and moved forward. Even Beso opened an eye.

"He-e-elp!" they rasped and croaked.

"Hey, hey, which side are you?" came a reply from some way away.

Long shadows appeared, moving over an enormous white covering. More rifles fired, and again came the call "Which side are you?" The wolves now backed off, then melted into the whiteness and vanished. Ten or so minutes later a dozen Whites appeared before Kvachi, now on his last legs, and his three comrades. Kvachi wept and sobbed for joy:

"Thank the Lord! Thank the Lord!"

"*Allah il-allah*!" mumbled Jalil.

The Whites rubbed their frozen limbs and poured a little vodka down their throats, put the wounded on horseback, and supported Kvachi and Jalil by the arms. Then they went back whence they had come.

Returning to the Motherland and Bringing a Coffin

The next day Kvachi told the White detachment all about what he'd experienced, seen, and heard. The four men were taken to a small town and given hospital beds. Kvachi and Jalil recovered in a week and moved to a hotel; the wounded, Pavlov and Beso, needed longer. Kvachi complained of penury; Chipi's name was never far from his heart or tongue. He kept repeating: "Beso! Jalil! Mark my words: I swear by God and my good name: I shan't rest until I've made Chipi's mother weep over his grave."

After a while Beso and Pavlov were their old selves and left the hospital. All four went to Odessa. Kvachi was immediately reminded of his distant past, the sweet days of his youth, two carefree years, Hofstein, Rebecca, Isaac, Sidorov, Sidorov's daughter Vera, and a hundred other friends and people he then knew. Memories dispersed his worries, he relaxed, and his face lost its tension. He started exploring the city, running about it, sounding things out, and pondering the state of things. But he was not carefree: he walked hunched and gloomy, having spent his day's allowance. Once, when he was distressed by his penury, Beso sat down next to him, took out a handkerchief, and spread it out. The room, Beso and Kvachi suddenly felt illuminated: Beso was holding a radiant white diamond the size of a thrush's egg.

"I've been saving these stones for a rainy day. Take them, they'll come in handy," said Beso.

"Beso, my dear Beso!" exclaimed Kvachi, embracing his friend. "If I weren't Kvachi, I'd certainly want to be a Beso. My dear Beso ..." he said, becoming childlike with joy. He became fidgety and so excited that he left the hotel and went round the restaurants. Then, when he'd quietened down, he went to see the local White general and had a talk with him:

"The Reds are our common enemy. Today they're at your throat, tomorrow it will be Georgia's turn. We are natural allies."

"True," agreed the ally.

"You need soldiers, officers, oil, petrol, and thousands of other things. We want flour and food, so ..."

In two days the general got Kvachi's measure and the next day came to terms with him. While Beso was recovering, Kvachi spent a day and a night out of doors, breathing freely, relaxing in restaurants, spending all night in cafés, gathering news of old friends. Inspector Hofstein was still in his old job, Captain Sidorov was still a captain, and his daughter Vera ... but it was too painful to reopen old wounds.

One evening Kvachi caught sight of a woman in a Sister of Mercy uniform: he immediately recognized his Odessa Vera—short, blonde, and plump. Vera had by her side a ten-year-old black-haired child: Kvachi's. The spitting image of Kvachi! "Who is the father of the unborn child?" Odessa students had asked ten years ago. "Kvachi Kvachantiradze, or Sedrak Havlabariani?" The mystery was then unsolvable, but Kvachi knew then and now knew perfectly well that this black-haired boy was his flesh and blood, his! Kvachi's face turned bright red; the blood rushed boiling hot to his head. He ducked and staggered into a shop.

Several days passed. The friends prepared to depart. Kvachi was alone in the room. Suddenly, Chipi's head and Jalil's hand came through the doorway. Chipi was resisting, clutching the door. But the hand round his neck punched him hard and a crumpled Chipi was hurled into the middle of the room. Then Jalil himself entered, solemnly locked the door, and just as solemnly said:

"Kvachi-*Aga*, I've brought him. You made an oath: now do the deed."

"Chipi," growled Kvachi, taking two leaps towards him.

"Kvachi," mewled Chipi, quivering like an aspen leaf. "I'm … I did wrong … But I've got nothing left, I swear by God, I've got nothing left … They took it off me, they took everything off me. I … I …"

"I know for certain they took it off him, but Chipi's still a swine, so …" Jalil added, rolling up his sleeves.

Kvachi's iron arms sprang forwards of their own accord and began to crack Chipi's neck. At the same instant Jalil leapt up from the ground. After five minutes they left Chipi stretched out on the floor, strangled, his eyes popping.

"Right, Jalil, wrap him up."

"You have to take him to Georgia," said Jalil. "You swore to Allah that his mother has to weep on Chipi's grave, so …"

"I know, I know. Wrap him up. We've got to take him to his mother."

Two days later Kvachi, Beso, and Jalil boarded the *Pushkin* which was heading for Georgia. Captain Sidorov and Kvachi pretended not to know one another. Pavlov was to make his own way to Tbilisi when he finished his treatment: that was what Kvachi and the White general had agreed.

Another week passed. One night the ship docked at Batumi.

Kvachi, Jalil, and Beso, who was still limping, stood on deck and stared at the line of lights.

"Last year Enver Pasha took Batumi ..." Jalil said.

"Well, Jalil? Are you sorry that Batumi is ours again?"

Jalil frowned, flashed his teeth, and stamped his foot:

"No, but ... I'm sorry for the Turks. The English took a lot off them."

Kvachi was no longer listening to him. He was recalling an evening, twelve years ago, when as a young man he stood on the ship's prow and sailed north to win the woman of his dreams and a place in the world. What had Kvachi not undergone in those twelve years? How many countries he traveled to! How many times had merciful fate detained him and then let him go! He, a powerful knight, could have mounted his victorious steed ten or twenty times and returned to his little and impoverished motherland to waving flags, festive welcomes, and roars of applause, and there he would easily have been a big fish in the land. But he had preferred to be a small fish abroad, always fighting danger, pursuing one phantom after another. Oh, why had Kvachi not believed poor Gabo and Sedrak five years ago? Why had he not then bridled his fate's headstrong Pegasus? Why had Kvachi, then rich and healthy, not gone back to his little hearth? Who knows how fortune's wheel might have turned for him and for his other friends, who now, in the freezing cold ... far off, somewhere in the open fields ... lay in the black earth. Only now was Kvachi—depressed, ashamed, empty-handed, and bankrupt—going back to his destitute and decrepit motherland. Twelve years ago, when Kvachi, as if on wings, was sailing off into this sea, the star of his fate smiled at him and promised victory. But now it glimmered faintly and flickered as if about to go out. For some strange reason Kvachi's heart groaned, an odd shame gnawed at this feeble child who had somewhere squandered his youth and his strength, and only now remembered the elderly country that had nurtured him, brought him up, and fed him.

"Kvachi, what's wrong with you?" asked Beso, who could see in the moonlight Kvachi's furrowed brow and quivering lips.

"Nothing ..." Kvachi told him, his voice shaking. "Let's go and pack ... Jalil, come here!"

An hour later, when the travelers set foot on shore, Kvachi bent down to touch his native soil and then put his hand to his lips.

First of all, he wanted to go to his native Kutaisi to see his parents, but the next morning, in the hotel, he realized that Silibistro had bought a fine house in Tbilisi and had moved for good to the capital.

"I expect he used the money I sent him last year from Petersburg to buy it," said Kvachi, turning to Jalil. "Jalil, get the luggage ready, tomorrow we're off to the city."

Jalil packed, then stood awkwardly in front of Kvachi, shrugged and, stumbling, said with a smile: "*Agha*, you're very fine lads, but Jalil has to go away for a while."

"Where to, Jalil? Where are you off to?"

"I've seen an old friend. He's here. He's going to Istanbul. I want to go there: I want to move about a bit, try my luck, then come back to you."

Kvachi thought a while: he was downcast.

"Beso, it's just us two left!" Then he turned to Jalil: "I'll find it hard without you ... But ... since you've thought about it ... go! Go, Jalil. God give you peace!"

"*Chok sag ol* (Be very healthy)! I'm very happy, very. Allah be with you. Salaam, prince, salaam. I'll find you soon, but now I'll go. Be healthy. Salaam, prince."

They kissed one another and parted.

The previous night Kvachi had sent Chipi, in a firmly nailed coffin, to his parents, who had come to Batumi and the next day attended the burial.

"Kvachi, don't go," Beso advised him tentatively.

"An oath has to be kept to the end, Beso!" Kvachi replied coldly. "I have to see his mother weep."

He went and he saw. Chipi's elderly parents could hardly stand for grief. His mother's shrieks reached the heavens, his father muttered something unintelligible.

"He was strangled by ruffians," Kvachi told Chipi's parents. "I had trouble finding his body and getting it out."

Then, at the funeral service, Kvachi began to speak. It was his first speech in the new independent Georgia: resonant, fiery, yet sad.

"Brother Chipi," Kvachi addressed his friend. "You were always a Georgian in heart and soul; you were a Georgian and fought for your motherland. In this fight your infinitely strong heart and crucified life were exhausted. The treacherous enemy perfidiously extinguished your beautiful life, but your pure memory will be immortal in the hearts of your friends and your people, and a grateful motherland will record in letters of gold your crystal-pure name in its chronicles, and it will turn your heroic death into an example for posterity. Meanwhile, unforgettable brother, rest in the black earth, for earth you were and earth you shall become. Whereas we … we …"

Kvachi's soul was overflowing, his words ended in sobs; staggering off, he joined the crowd of mourners.

That day Kvachi ran around Batumi. He discovered old acquaintances and made many new ones. The next morning he got into a train compartment, opened a newspaper, read Chipi's obituary, and recited verbatim his own speech. Beso had exaggerated slightly. The paper read: "Chipi's body was carried by his loyal friend Kvachi in the middle of winter on his back and by sledge from Kiev to Odessa."

Beso Shikia really was a highly skilled man!

CHAPTER SEVEN

Running About on One's Home Ground

Kvachi was in an odd mood: he couldn't settle in his compartment, he was restless, constantly going out into the corridor and chatting to strangers; he would be glued to one window, then switch to the other; he fidgeted, felt surges of joy and laughter, and very often called out:

"Beso, come here! Look: that's Bartskhana ... Up there you can see the Mingrelian fort ... on the right Hamidiye's fort ... Erge fort was on the top of the mountain ... we had a fierce battle with the Turks last year ... apparently, we were badly defeated. Our courage failed us Georgians. We had ten thousand men and two hundred cannon, the Turks had seven thousand men and six little cannon. It was winter. We were in the town and the fort; they were in the forest on the mountain. But they still won."

"What happened, then?"

"Our battle-hardened army just went home. We were tired, so we thought, let others make war. Our government, they say, evacuated all the children. Anyway, our independence began in disgrace, and ..." Kvachi lowered his voice. "It'll be bad if it ends in disgrace, too ... though we don't know yet what's going on here. Let's hang about, find out everything, and then say what we think."

When they passed Kobuleti, Kvachi called out to Beso again:

"Beso, look out of the window! It's the Choloki river. This is where we purged the disgrace of Batumi. Here the Khashuri and Gori men fought the Turks, and we had a great victory. This is where our frontier is now. Here, you see, this side of the river, English soldiers are on guard, but on the other side of the bridge

... Beso! Just look! Beso! Georgian soldiers! Georgian soldiers!"

The deeper the train penetrated into Georgia, the greater became Kvachi's excitement and restlessness.

"We're in Guria now ... Natanebi ... Sajevakho ... Beso, Samtredia! Our own Samtredia! Beso! My heart's beating as if I were going to see a mistress I hadn't seen for ages."

He leapt off the train in Samtredia, ran round the station for ten minutes, and found a dozen old friends, embraced them all, greeting them:

"Hello, Bondo! That isn't Dzalua Dzabuli, is it?! How are you, Isidore? Me? Well, you see I'm back, back for good. I've got to work for Georgia, too. Now I'm off to Tbilisi, but I'll see you Samtredia and Kutaisi people soon ... Regards to all. Well, goodbye for now! Goodbye."

And he leapt onto the moving train. He soon became excited again:

"Beso, the River Rioni! Our Rioni. And there's Kutaisi! Our little Kutaisi! The poor place seems empty! As if all Kutaisi has gone to Tbilisi. All that's left is Eremo's, Laitadze's, and Daniel the Jew's. They seem to have gone broke too: Jews and Rachians don't like partying and singing."

Kvachi had even forgotten to eat and drink. There was nobody in the carriage that Kvachi hadn't got to know and asked for news, new and old.

"What's amazing, Beso, is how we've been cut off from our country, and not heard any proper news for a whole year. If the Moscow papers wrote anything about Georgia, it seems to have been all lies."

"If we'd lived another five or ten years in that bloody country, we still wouldn't have heard the truth."

Kvachi was silent for a while, then he spoke:

"Beso, in just one day something very strange has happened to me. I've remembered my past. I was so cut off from my motherland that—I shan't hide it from you—I was even almost ashamed to be Georgian. I had no faith in my country, in its culture, its language, or its future. When people talked about autonomy for Georgia, I, like others, was against it. I used to say: Georgia would be worse off, it hasn't got the population or the resources. But something has changed in my heart and my head."

"Perhaps because today's Russia has gone mad."

"That can't be the only reason. True, Russia has gone mad. I can't recognize October any more. It wasn't what I expected. It betrayed my hopes, so I betrayed it. Now Russia is plunged in darkness, fathers are killing sons, brothers—brothers, there's famine, freezing cold, and all sorts of epidemics. Russia means to turn the world upside down and is fighting everybody. It has one foot in the grave, and it may soon have both feet in the grave. I say it again: we've followed Russia to the grave, but we shan't follow Russia into it, because we still don't hate ourselves that much. So little Georgia has parted from great Russia. In any case, our people obviously know how to live, they have a sense of moderation, they're sober-minded, and they long to stand on their own feet. They instil faith in me that Georgia can walk on its own, even if on one leg, and will prove to the world that we deserve to live and exist. Just that's enough, Beso, to justify us helping others and building our own home here."

"Yes, but … I'm afraid …" Beso replied hesitantly: he was more cautious, less trusting. "Sharks from all sides are threatening our country."

"White Russia, at least, is doomed. The red bear will soon be clambering up the Caucasus. What are we to do then? I don't know, I don't yet know anything. First I must sound out things and understand what's going on. Then I'll give you an answer. Look, Beso, look! See, Armazi … now Mtskheta! Our old capital Mtskheta, crumbling, decrepit, and moss-eaten over the centuries. Qoranashvili used to say that it was five hundred years older than

Rome. Actually, Beso, find Qoranashvili for me and bring him along tomorrow. I need to begin studying Georgian language, literature, and history ... Take a good look, Beso: there's the Jvari monastery: it's supposed to be the oldest building in Georgia."

Night was falling. From afar Kvachi could spot the lights of Tbilisi; he became even more worked up and excited. Nowhere and never had he felt such a mysterious stirring in his heart and unrest in his soul. He ran along the station platform like an ecstatic child. Getting into the cab, he told the driver: "To Sololaki! At a walking pace!"

After Russia's dead cities, to Kvachi the capital seemed like Paris. The generously lit streets were packed with people, joyfully gossiping and shrieking. In a sea of lights Mount David arose like a gigantic black icon-lamp, crowned with a diadem of stars.

They passed through the long streets of Kukia, crossed Vera bridge, and climbed the road leading to the broad Rustaveli Avenue. Kvachi couldn't settle down:

"Beso, look, look! Here's *Noah's* Hotel ... There's the House of the People. Over there is the River Mtkvari, our Mtkvari. This is the opera ... the drama theater ... Kvasheti church ... the *Orient* hotel. There's the military cathedral, the palace, the museum! It's all ours now, Beso, ours."

Ten minutes or so later, Kvachi rushed like a man demented into his own house and his joyful embraces nearly suffocated his parents—Silibistro, Pupi, as well as Khukhu and Notio. They shrieked and wept or laughed or rushed about aimlessly, or stared, helpless with joy, fussed, bustled, and jabbered.

First Steps

The next day Kvachi did the rounds of ministers and others in authority: "Let me introduce myself: Kvachi Kvachantiradze. I've just returned from the Red hell."

It seemed that even Georgia had heard the loud sound of his reputation from the far north. The loudness was now enhanced by silvery voices. Just as the sun's rays at a distance lose their burning power, so Kvachi's reputation, somewhat stained and sullied in distant Russia, was nicely washed and sparkling clean by the time it got to Georgia.

While Kvachi enjoyed the parental affection and made himself known to the authorities, the highly intelligent Beso Shikia was mobile in the city and made sure never to stop mentioning the name of Kvachantiradze. The news of Kvachi's return went round Tbilisi like a flash of lightning. Everyone everywhere was talking about his reappearance:

"Have you heard the news?" people asked each other in the street, the clubs, theaters, and restaurants. "Kvachi Kvachantiradze has come back."

"Good heavens! Really? Thank God!"

News spread among one group of people like wild fire:

"They say he has forty million cash in Europe's banks," said one man.

"It's not just forty, it's a hundred million!" another corrected him.

"They say he's going to bring the money here and invest it."

"Let me tell you the truth," a third man explained. "He's going to lend the government twenty million to back their bonds, then spend twenty million on roads, forty on electricity stations, another twenty on setting up factories, and ten on student grants, and forty on the army. Believe me, I have this from an unimpeachable source."

Something similar did the rounds of a second group who recalled Kvachi's past:

"Ten years ago Kvachi saved Russia from the predicament it's in today. The Tsar wanted to abdicate. Nobody could change his mind. In the end Kvachi took the job on, and kept the Tsar on the throne."

"In one week he crashed both the London and Paris stock exchanges."

"Enver Pasha took an entire Russian army prisoner, but Kvachantiradze with a handful of Georgians turned the tables on him, captured the Ottoman army, and nearly got hold of Enver Pasha himself."

"That's nothing: they say America sent Russia several ships loaded with arms, but the Germans sank the lot. Kvachantiradze took over the job and brought forty ships in undamaged."

"I'm told he's a very able financier."

"Not just able, he's a real genius."

"The Bolsheviks apparently forced him to work for them. Kvachi was furious and arranged things so that the Moscow government was ruined in just over a week. They saw what he was up to, but he found out first and fled. They say he took five hundred armed men with him. And then his band of men grew to a thousand. They blocked the railways with cannon. Three or five times he took Kiev, Kharkov, and Rostov from the Reds. He was marching on Moscow, but couldn't get Denikin to agree. Denikin was a monarchist, and Kvachantiradze an outright republican. 'If that's how things stand,' said Kvachantiradze, 'to hell with both the Turks and the Reds.' And he turned and left. He wiped out Reds and Turks. He took Odessa by force and got fifteen ships out. These ships are now in Batumi."

"These ships, they say, are carrying enormous amounts of flour and weapons, and he's donated them to Georgia."

"So we'll be eating our fill of white bread soon."

Hopes thus kindled soon fired all the Caucasus. While Beso was stoking the fires so thoroughly, Kvachi was pulling the wool over the authorities' eyes, telling them stories about the Reds and Whites:

"Russia is finished, sir, finished! Even Jesus Christ can't bring it back to life. Red Russia is the wrath of God, and White Russia is God's curse."

Did Kvachi really believe Russia was finished? No, he did not. "It only has to wag its tail, that will be enough for us," he told himself, not daring to say so aloud. because he would be immediately labeled a Red agent, and that would ruin all his plans.

In the evening Kvachi and Beso went all round town.

"Beso, I feel I'm in a real Georgian city. All Imeretia has come here."

At a charitable evening in the Georgian club Kvachi made a generous donation. The pretty waitresses, educated and well-born, in the *Brotherly Comfort* café soon drew him with their friendly chat and courteous behavior. He stumbled upon an evening of the *Blue Horns'* poets in the truly chimerical *Chimerion* wine cellar. The poets greeted him with rams' horns full of wine, gibberish poems, and overblown paeans of praise. They flattered each other with warm words and lavish colorful panegyrics, and smiled broad smiles. True, they and Kvachi were strangers, but the *Blue Horns'* alert ears had heard from afar the thunder of the Georgian knight's reputation, and in the freezing north even Kvachi had heard about the new musical ravings of the brotherhood of modern poets. A bemused Kvachi forked out a generous donation to publish a *Blue Horns* magazine and made several efforts to get out of the vaults where the *Blue Horns* were feasting, but leaving the poets' banquet and surfacing from the vortex of sweet rhymes was not so easy. Finally, as day broke, they helped each other out of this cellar of phantoms. Who led whom, who followed whom and saw them home, nobody now recalls—neither the poets, nor Kvachi.

The next day Kvachi read in the newspapers Beso's concoction: "The famous financier, our fellow countryman Kvachi Kvachantiradze has returned to Georgia. Last year he underwent extraordinary and terrible experiences in the Red hell. We will publish a separate article on this, but now we sincerely wish our famous brother, now embraced by his motherland, rest and fruitful work for the benefit of our people and for the glory of the fatherland."

Such a reception demanded an appropriate response. That same day Kvachi went round the editorial offices, got to know all the print workers, and introduced himself. From then on Kvachi and the newspapers played the same mysterious fraternal tunes, periodically applying ointment to keep their musical instruments smooth and clean.

In one week Kvachi knotted a thousand visible and invisible threads. He smeared himself with honey to make old acquaintances and new friends stick to him like flies. They were all peering into his eyes and pockets, hoping for some miracle. Kvachi, however, went on furiously weaving traps, pulling the wool over the country's eyes, and getting ever closer to the authorities and their money. Qoranashvili gave him lessons in Georgian subjects, Beso Shikia provided reliable information and carried out Kvachi's daily instructions, while the others loyally and selflessly served the common cause, which would any day now expand into a fabulous milch cow for everyone.

Kvachi had fundamentally changed his ploys and his working methods. In Red Russia he had run about like a cat on a hot tin roof and talked non-stop, but here he kept his lips tight shut for now, and rarely went out of doors. It was thanks to Beso Shikia and others, not Kvachi, that thousands of people said thousands of things about him. Who was going to bring white bread to Georgia? Kvachi Kvachantiradze. Who would import from Europe thousands of goods which the Caucasus needed? Kvachantiradze, of course. Who would back our currency, which was depreciating with every day? Kvachantiradze, again. Who would export from the Caucasus all the oil, coal, wool, cotton, tobacco, silk cocoons, timber, wine, and countless other things that had been piling up over five years? Kvachi, Kvachi, only Kvachi. There wasn't a country in Europe or America whose bankers, businessmen, and industrialists didn't know Kvachi and trust him like a brother. Kvachi knew everything. Kvachi could sort everything out. For Kvachi everything was possible.

In the suburb of Sololaki Kvachi was living on the second floor of his own house. No need to be shy, go and take him your wishes, money, and property. Kvachi is a magician. He can turn one rouble into ten. Go on! Don't be shy! Go on. Please do.

People kept coming every day to Kvachi's, where the door never closed. Kvachi himself didn't discuss business much, and that little was vague and imprecise. Kvachi was new to Georgia. He didn't know a lot about the local economy, but what he did know was that you mustn't reveal your ignorance. He promised property owners to sell their property at the highest price, and people with money were promised the highest returns. All you needed to do is set up a joint stock trading and banking company, and invest money. Kvachi's secretaries would tell you the rest and give you every information. For this purpose Kvachi took on three new secretaries—an Armenian, an Azeri, and a Georgian.

Finally, the big game that Kvachi had been waiting for came along. An Englishman, a red-faced John Rawlinson, came to see him. In one hour Kvachi and John did a deal. The money and the general management would be John's, the goodwill, network, technology, and equipment would be Kvachi's.

Neither Kvachi nor John liked delays: it was less than two weeks before the first floor of a building on Freedom Square was adorned by yard-high letters in gold "Sibunion Limited Company", and the "English-Caucasian Bank" was opened on the ground floor.

In a very short time the Caucasus had branches of "Sibunion" and business was booming. Sibunion didn't buy property for cash; you gave it on credit your wool and cotton, tobacco and oil, wine and cocoons. Sibunion trusted you. It would export your goods to

Europe, sell them, and then … settle up with you.

They could hardly keep up with all the goods to be loaded. The warehouses were packed; a hundred or so employees worked at a feverish pace, John Rawlinson rushed to and from Baku and thence to London. Every day the papers printed: "Kvachantiradze has exported twenty thousand bales of wool … has bought sixty thousand bales of tobacco … has imported a hundred thousand bags of flour … has contracted to sell state property … has donated a hundred pounds sterling … has gone … has come … said … expressed the opinion … has received … has gone to see … has held a meeting …"

Pavlov, now well and armed with a mandate from the Whites, soon arrived in Tbilisi and speeded up work. Kvachi fulfilled his promise conscientiously. All he did was endow Pavlov with help, trust, influence, and equipment. "Sibunion" merely traded and carried out commercial contracts. It sent the Crimea officers oil, petrol, olive oil, clothes, and all sorts of goods, big and small. What did Kvachi care if this all went to the White army? Politics was not his business. In return, Kvachi imported white flour and all sorts of provisions. No, Kvachi no longer meddles in politics, although … in the end, he was dragged into it and cheated.

Neither Here nor There

That greedy, mindless, blind bull Denikin turned his forces on Georgia and annexed Abkhazia. At the same time the Reds called from Moscow: "Georgians! Support us! Join us! Let's strike the White general together and throw him back into the Black Sea. Come on, let's begin! Attack!"

What was Kvachi Kvachantiradze to do? He could no longer stand aside, for he was a Georgian. He was a loyal son of Georgia! So, by God's grace, he had to roll up his sleeves, and his heart had to burn with patriotic fervor. He had to recall his heroic deeds on the fabulous plateau of Demir-Tepe and in Russia's boundless fields around Kiev, where his faithful friends now slept eternally. He had to do his duty by his motherland. He hadn't yet fired a rifle or shed a drop of blood for her, nor called with the voice of the hero Qaraman, "Follow me! In line! Quick! Go on! Attack! Hack!"

Be quick, Kvachi, quick. Before the White wave comes and washes away your "Sibunion" and your motherland, which by some mysterious force you have only just come to know, like, and love. What is there to ponder? Why dither? Quick, Kvachi, quick! or ... Why are you swinging like a pendulum? What's shackling you? Why don't you want to help the Reds? Why do you fear their friendly embrace? Will you really have your bones broken? Well then, stand by their side against the mad White bull who is calling on you, who will take you with him and show you how to turn Red Moscow really red, then darken it, and make it white. You don't want that, either? Are you afraid your past sins will be exposed? Is that worth a thought? Who is today without sin? Who is saddled with a past that's cleaner than yours? So get a move on, make your decision, or ...

"The Whites will bring us trouble, the Reds will be just as bad."

Is that your decision? Well, what do you want? Who are you going to run to for shelter? The British?

"Neither one, nor the other. I'm standing aside, I shan't harm or help anyone. I'm nobody's enemy, neither here nor there."

Kvachi, what's wrong with you? What's dulled your famous intuition? Who's killed your unerring instincts? Who or what fateful witch has convinced you that nobody's going to harm you if you don't harm anyone? Who's deceived you? Who's made you write on the highway such childish babbling: "Here sleeps a defenceless lamb. Please don't bother it. Private road: no passage." Suppose people don't bypass you? Suppose someone lays hands on you or smashes your head in and breaks into your house? You'll be amazed, I bet. You'll yell and raise the alarm, I expect. But who's going to help you? The democracies who don't have a single hand gun or a single soldier? Are you relying on democratic yells and cackling? All very well, but you still haven't grasped that even a dozen million windpipes can do nothing but scare the crows and magpies. Haven't you managed to think of anything? You don't dare walk the White road or the Red road? And you don't want to cling to the British coat-tails? So you're afraid of democratic cackling?

"Neither here, nor there!" the parrot repeats.

What are you afraid of, Kvachi? Who's making you hesitate? Are they going to expel you from the party, or snatch a fat piece of dung out of your mouth? Is it because you're afraid that you've lost your ability to speak? If so, fine.

Britain has turned the White bull back and temporarily saved you. But circumstances have changed. Well, take a look: this panicky, beaten, and worn-out bull has been pushed into the Black Sea, while the Red's Budionovka hats are clambering up the Caucasus chain and now looking down at you. Do you see the red flags fluttering on Mt Elbrus, in Dagestan, and on the glaciers? Can you hear the victors' roar? Can you see what Britain is doing? It's gathered all its belongings and has moved from the Caucasus to Batumi, as if vacating this country for someone else to have. Now look to the east, and be amazed: can you see the friendly hands that Moscow, Ankara, Tehran, and Kabul are offering one another? Can you hear the singing of the *Internationale*, the Turkish *shikasta* and *bayat*? There is a hoop of fire around you, Kvachi. Red clouds are gathering overhead, Kvachantiradze! The distant thunder is already audible, red lightning can be seen, a whirlwind of flames is twisting, and any day it will strike. Kvachi, come to your senses. Say goodbye to your phantoms! Let the mist rise. Wake up and run for your life, or it will be too late to gnash your teeth and chew your fingernails.

But Kvachi could not wake up. He was suffering from a strange illness. His observant eyes had a cataract, his trained nose had lost the scent, and his well-scoured brain was befogged. He was squawking mindlessly, like an exhausted old parrot on its wooden perch:

"Neither here, nor there … Neither heat, nor cold … neither Red, nor White … I'll harm nobody, nobody will harm me …"

Kvachi, remember the reason why Buridan's ass died. It was offered barley on one side, and oats on the other: it kept wondering which was better, oats or barley, but couldn't decide. It thought for so long that it kicked the bucket from starvation while choosing. Kvachi, have you got the moral of this fable? Couldn't you understand?

All very well, then. A Red train full of Budionovka hats is slowly and calmly entering Baku, as if Baku were its home. The next day it will change direction and head for Georgia. The roar of battle can almost be heard in the capital. Erevan has turned Red. An arc of fire surrounds Georgia on three sides. The ground Kvachi is standing on is now hot. Red flames come from one side, then from the other.

Kvachi Kvachantiradze! Can you still not understand a thing? Can you not see the gathering thunderclouds? Have you understood and seen? Just about! All very well, then. Now what do you say?

Kvachi runs about like a panicking herald, shouting anywhere his voice can be heard:

"Now come out! Run for your lives! Danger is at our doors! Go! Attack! Hack!"

And you, Kvachi, what do you think? What have you in mind? Why aren't you there, too, where rifles fire and blood is shed? I suppose you have no time. You've done your duty, I suppose. You've sent the army a hundred packs of cigarettes and you're taking your property and precious items to Batumi as quick as you can.

They're a stubborn lot, my God! Some talk as if Kvachi was the equal of Sir Lancelot. Neither Sir Lancelot nor the country has anything to lose, except Sir Lancelot's life, whereas Kvachi is worth ten thousand Sir Lancelots! How can Georgia, Silibistro, and Pupi manage without Kvachi? Who will "fix" a thousand things for posterity, if Kvachi isn't there? In any case, Kvachi has countless possessions which would fall into the hands of the Reds, if he's not there. So Kvachi Kvachantiradze is on the run. He's running off with wealth beyond counting, which the toilers who are running with him want to entrust to his safe-keeping.

The storm passed, leaving deep furrows in Kvachi's mind and brain. Now he had found a peerless remedy: England! The protector! Quick, find a powerful defender, or our days are numbered. Kvachi got down to business: first he talked to his colleague John Rawlinson.

"All right ... Yes," Rawlinson replied curtly and vaguely; he himself had arranged things so that, if need be, he could slip away in just two days, lock, stock, and barrel. Kvachi was in a bad state and sweating hard.

"Listen to me, trust me, friends, or you'll regret it. Everything I've predicted so far has come true. I now say our independence is a fairytale. We children of country bumpkins can't make a state. Our people are leaderless. We have no laws or money. There are forces surrounding us so strong that we daren't even flick a finger at them. Georgia will be split up like Christ's garments. If King Erekle II gave up his crown for the sake of his people, why shouldn't the good-for-nothing squires from Lanchkhuti and Chokhatauri tear their straw scarecrow hats off their own heads?"

What are you getting at, Kvachi? Say what you've got to say. Don't let anyone stop you. Spit it out. Are you afraid of being thrown out of the party again?

"The point, gentlemen, is that we have to get protection from Europe."

Say it straight, Kvachi! Who has to get protection, and how?

"We've got to ask either England or France for protection."

A protectorate? A vassal state? If it were only that. Kvachi can't understand these tricky words. In a nutshell, arrange things so that a European army defends Georgia, or … suppose it doesn't come off …

"If it doesn't, it's best for us to come to terms with the Reds."

How do we come to terms? What do you mean by that, Kvachi? Stop talking in riddles. Put what you have to say clearly and distinctly.

"All right, I'll do so … though … it's not easy to say so, but … since there's no alternative, I tell you we have to put a red flag over the palace and … we have to surrender power to the Reds."

Aha! Kvachi has given his opinion and inner thoughts. Now you can tear him to pieces, or expel him from the party or imprison him!

What did you say, Kvachi? Are you raving mad? How dare you? That's treason, real treason.

Kvachi dared: he told you the truth. Now you know it. He's done his duty.

"I was a fool to caw like a magpie, 'Neither here nor there … I don't like the Whites or the Reds … I won't harm anyone, and nobody is to harm me.' Now I'm telling you: either here, or there; either White, or Red; either London, or Moscow. That's my program today."

Fine, but which way are you going to go, Kvachi? Are you staying, or fleeing? Kvachi can't possibly stay, because the Reds have old scores to settle with him. Whatever happens, Kvachi has to save his property.

Anyone who speaks the truth has to have his horse saddled and ready to go: Kvachi was proof of the proverb. After he had spoken, he was dismissed as a windbag. Some said that he'd gone mad, some even shouted that he had betrayed them. Kvachi's voice died away without response in the desert. This upstart Cassandra was shunned and scorned. Kvachi fell silent and kept his doubts, fears, and opinions to himself.

Kvachi and Beso were present on the day that the last British soldiers were due to leave Batumi. The mute, listless, and wan Britons solemnly boarded their ships. The Georgian army and government, leaping for joy and excited, entered what had been their city with festive yells and roars. Finally the gigantic British flag slowly, gently, gradually descended the tall flagpole. At the same instant the same flagpole had a Georgian tricolor flying from it, again with joyful leaping, and festive yells and roars.

"Now we really are finished," Kvachi told Beso in the restaurant, while all around ecstatic people celebrated at the top of their voices. "Mark my words, Beso, few people understand the meaning of what's happened today. Over there the English ships are sailing away, Europe has gone. We've been abandoned again in Asia. Those ships have taken away our last hope and left us with in-de-pen-dence! Garçon, warm up a bottle of Lafitte ... Look all around you, Beso. They're rejoicing! They're laughing! They're banqueting. Ha-ha-ha! Just ask those idiots why they're laughing. What are they so happy about? Why are they having a party? If they had any brains and could foresee tomorrow, they'd weep bitter tears and be mourning today the grief to come. Today's rulers only think of today and of Kvachi Kvachantiradze, but it will be too late to bite their fingernails. Up till now we had two paths: either Russia or Europe. Now we're left with one: the Moscow path, which is Red and thorny. Garçon, your fruit is no good. Bring us a bottle of champagne and Turkish coffee. Pay attention to one thing, Beso: our enemies are even gladder than we are that the English have gone. In Moscow I expect they're jumping for joy. That's a very bad sign. The Reds are now polishing their weapons and getting ready for war. Qoranashvili told me that our ancestors said, 'When you cannot win, giving way is best for men of honor.'"

"Better to drag off, than to be dragged off," Beso Shikia added.

"That's a good saying, too, Beso. They also said, apparently, 'When the cart overturns, then you can see the road.' God protect us, and may that proverb turn out to be true for us."

"So far it has often turned out true."

"Because we had good cart-drivers. These cart-drivers will crash our broken-down cart into such a ravine that we won't even be able to find the splinters. So far I've been dithering. First I called out, 'Neither here nor there.' That path turned out to be no good. Then I put my hopes on Europe, but nobody trusted me. Now that Europe has gone, all that's left is Europe's observers. They're saying they don't see any difference between a pink and a Red Georgia. That's true, too. So mightn't we as well turn Red? We won't actually lose anything except a few minor enemies, and we will gain quite a lot. We'll have a strong protector and we'll have our own Red government. We'll avoid bloodshed and occupation by a foreign army. Beso, that's the only path open to us now. I'll have to serve that cause, too. If they trust me, that will be very good for everyone; if they don't, to hell with them. I'll have done my duty."

"How about our business?"

"From now on we diversify. I can't become an innkeeper, but big business is finished, or it will be in a day or two. I'm not so crazy as to think anything big can be done again, so I won't get my property ready for the Reds or build them factories. I'll convert everything into jewelry and gold. Garçon, a chair! Do me the honor, minister! Please sit down. Boy, another bottle of champagne, some good fruit, and coffee. Perhaps you'd prefer Cointreau or Chypre, sir? Good, please have some. I'll get you some Chypre, then. We were saying, minister … have some more, sir, do. This is a fine cigar. It has a wonderful smell, and it's not too strong. Here, have a light No, no! Cut it first. Let me have it, I'll cut it … Right. Now light up. Yes, I was saying that today you're rejoicing, while I feel the devil's choking me. Why? I'll tell you."

And he did tell him, point by point, gravely, backing up his statements. When Kvachi finished, the minister screwed up his eyes and then removed the cigar from his mouth, set aside his glass, full of Chypre, and looked at Kvachantiradze, as if the latter were a pig-keeper who had by chance come to the sultan's throne to tell him, "Great Sultan, the wisest thing you can do is kindly vacate that throne and let me be sultan."

From then on Kvachi acquired the reputation of being an agent of Moscow. Kvachi paid no heed at first, saying:

"That's why I advise you to surrender power, so as not to incur Moscow's anger. When the Muscovites come, I'll have to get out of Georgia, because I've got a record of crimes as long as your arm."

Kvachi could only warn people, but his belief was so strong that it made this convinced patriot say the same thing everywhere: in the streets, in private homes, on the square, and to the authorities:

"Come to terms ... surrender power ... end it all peacefully ... don't play with fire, or any day now war will break out. Don't expect help from the democracies. They'll let you down. They'll be no more use than I'd be to the Hottentots or Indo-Chinese. Believe me ... I swear ... listen to me."

But almost nobody believed Kvachi, and those that did couldn't do anything about it. Several times Kvachi was warned that if he didn't shut up, if he liked the Reds that much, they'd expel him from the party and deport him to Red Russia.

At any other time Kvachi would not have shut up or bowed his head. He didn't shut up and hide when the Tsar's government tried to hang him or when Kerensky threatened him. But here in Georgia Kvachi found he was in a blind alley. Could he resist the authorities and support Moscow? No, he dared not: fear of his past sins and some strange force were shackling him. Kvachi wanted peaceful, gentle change. But once it was obvious that such an outcome was impossible, he told his Red friends:

"You at least should believe me, comrades. If the fortress isn't to be blown up from inside, then any day now the job will be easier than emptying this bottle. Just take my life for example. People have suffered for want of leadership, nobody knows now whether we have rule of law or not. They don't even know who has power: the government, the national guard, the party, the city, the national movement, or the bandits. Very soon the people themselves will knock on your door seeking a strong government, peace, and rule of law. I assure you that today's authorities are doing your job better than you can. Don't be impatient, don't be in a hurry. Just bear with things a little longer and it will all happen of its own accord. Let's do the job from inside, don't try anything else, or ..."

Such was the Kvachantiradze path; in his opinion it did not lead to paradise, but it would certainly result in peace.

Finally the authorities were fed up with Kvachi's colorful outlook. Once, when Kvachi overdid his praise of the Reds, a friend told him:

"They've been talking about you: you're expelled from the party."

Kvachi expelled from the party? Big deal! He'd sneaked into the party ten times and sneaked out again ten times. This didn't bother him. He didn't give a toss any more about the party or about friendship with those who were on the way out. They could go to hell.

But Kvachi could no longer stand aside or sit on the fence. So he reinforced the threads binding him to the Reds and remembered Pavlov, who had one foot in the Red camp and the other in the Crimean White camp, and who had placed some of his hopes on Vrangel's army. Not that Kvachi had any faith in that army.

"You are as doomed as we are, friend ..." Kvachi told Pavlov. "At any moment the Reds will throw you into the sea."

True, the Crimean army was soon routed and driven into the sea. Pavlov then came back to Kvachi, who welcomed him like a brother and lodged him nearby, for he would never forget Pavlov's kindness.

It took a month to convert "Sibunion" and its property to jewelry. Kvachi sold his house and kept just an apartment. Silibistro and Pupi complained and pleaded a lot, for all their lives they'd longed for a nest in Tbilisi, but Kvachi easily consoled them for their loss:

"You can see every day that house prices are dropping. Anyway, the Reds are about to come and they'll take the house off us. If they don't come, I'll buy you the house back with the money we got for it."

Kvachi pointed out Khrkhriants's palace, which Silibistro fancied.

"If you ever get me into that house," Silibistro replied, "I'll cross my arms over my chest and die smiling. You know best. Sell."

Kvachi at War

Kvachi was ready to flee when he learned of two events: Khrkhriants was selling his palace and ten thousand bales of wool at rock-bottom prices. Kvachi was like a man possessed. For a long time he waved his arms about and fought the devil's temptations, but finally gave in, saying that if he got the wool down quickly from Tusheti and exported it, he'd make a threefold profit. As for the palace ... oh, that palace! A lovely three-storey palace, with caryatids, bronze balconies, blush-red columns, and marble staircases. Kvachi had never been guided by other people's opinions, but this time he fell for it: he persuaded Beso, Pavlov, Silibistro, and Pupi, bought the palace and the wool and ... burnt both his hands.

When Kvachi and his family moved into the palace they held a house-warming banquet that Kvachi's friends still remember today. Three men went off to Tusheti to fetch the wool. Khrkhriants put Kvachi's gold in his box and left Georgia at a gallop the very next day. A week passed. One morning Beso came running into Kvachi's bedroom to tell him:

"Kvachi, get up! War with the Reds began last night."

"War? Then we've had it."

Yes, Kvachi, just as you feared. Once again your trained instincts dictated the truth to you; once again your tried and tested eye saw into a pitch-dark future and your sharp sense of smell detected gunpowder from afar. But you've still been misled by trusting others. What the hell do you want this palace for now? How will you move so much wool from Tusheti to Batumi in this chaos? There's no point Beso and ten brokers running about. Nobody wants your palace now, and you won't find a buyer anywhere for your wool. Forget the wool and the palace, Kvachi. Collect what you can still lay hands on. Abandon your elderly parents, Kvachi. Their snow-white heads will somehow get through. Khukhu and Notio are on their last legs and any day now will be buried in your absence.

Your motherland? Georgia? What has the motherland given you? What is it to you, or you to it? "Sibunion"? The concessions? Goods exported on commission and a dozen or so dubious jobs? When you did these things abroad, foreigners put juicy morsels in your mouth! Here they didn't make you even a simple district commissar because you didn't belong to the rulers' orthodox church. You predicted the future, you warned the authorities, and did your duty honestly. But nobody believed you. In fact they replied with threats and virtually kicked you out of your own nest. You've done your duty, Kvachi. Take Beso with you, take Pavlov, and take up a life of wandering and heroic machinations. Go, then. Go while there's time and a way out, or you'll be too late and you'll regret it. Move! Fly! Quick, Kvachi, quick!

Why are you roaming the streets like a lost goose, Kvachi? What are you seeking? What are you staring at? What are you amazed at, stunned by? In their very first battle the victorious national guards scattered and went back to town. Are they looking for the way home? That's what amazes you, I expect. Imagine what they'll do if they're defeated!

Some are wearing new boots, but still calling out that they won't go to war unless they're given another pair. They were each given a new pair. They took them to the market and sold them. Now they're demanding a third pair. I imagine you're astonished, Kvachi. Don't be, brother, don't. There are more people who agree with you than you thought. Boots, leaving the battlefield to go home is only a pretext for turning Red. They're not fighting, because they don't want to; they don't want to, because they themselves are Reds, expecting white bread, free sugar, tax-free circulation of goods, lower taxes, destruction, and a Red paradise.

"Where is the army?! Where are our sixty-five thousand men?"

Don't be surprised, Kvachi. Sixty-five thousand was written on paper to get ten times as much money from the treasury and to keep gullible people like you happy.

"In the middle of winter, hungry people with no coats are being taken out to Qaraiaz forest to cut wood for the national guard. Why didn't they dig a single trench near Shavnabada or Tabakhmela?"

"We can't use these English rifles. Why haven't we been instructed how to use them?"

"Our aeroplanes can't fly, they say the propellers are broken."

"The Reds already know our secrets. How? Who told them?"

Calm down, Kvachi, calm down. It's too late now to shriek and tear your hair. You like witty sayings. Remember: "Whatever is in the barrel will come pouring out." Or: "Whatever happens to you, it's all your fault." Or: "When the cart overturns ..."

Kvachi knows these sayings. But his ardent heart still can't take it in.

"This is too much, too much! Such betrayal! Such lies, fooling the country like this! Deceiving oneself and the people so brazenly! Ugh, you scoundrels! Rogues! Pharisees! Treacherous and two-faced liars!"

Kvachi, don't get so heated. Be quiet and calm yourself. A time will come for judgement and settling accounts. Then you can seek out the traitors and tie them to the pillar of shame. But now … you're in imminent danger. Red banners are already flying beneath Shavnabada, over Kojori, and in Vaziani. Stop raging round the city like a bull with its tail up. Hold your tongue, pick up a rifle, duck down, and head in your own way towards the battlefield. Why are you dithering? What's paralyzing you? Pick up your worldly goods and go to the station. Go and don't look back, or you're in trouble.

That's it. It's over. Kvachi can't flee. Kvachi can't carry his shame to the grave. Kvachi has to do his sacred duty and throw the ball back in the enemy's face. He'll show those cowardly laggards how a Kvachantiradze dies for his motherland. Right, Beso. Bring guns and cartridges. Leather coat! Balaclava! Get a motor car! Silibistro, goodbye! Pupi, don't cry! Notio, Khukhu, be quiet. Kvachi has to do his duty. He'll either return victorious or you'll never see your offspring again. Put wine, tea, sugar, bread, pastries, cigars, champagne, sausages, and smoked ham in the car. Goodbye, now! Don't cry, Kvachi's still alive! Beso, get in! Right, to Kojori. "Move! Go faster! Go!"

The muffled thump of artillery, the rattle of machine guns, and the thunder of rifles can be heard from the snowy plateau. Kvachi's motor car emerges from the hairpin bends and approaches the battlefield. Wounded, tired, and sick men are staggering towards him. Some are on stretchers, some are galloping on horseback. Assorted people in assorted uniforms are moving uphill. Some are speeding in motor vehicles, others hurrying on foot. Half an hour later Kvachi reached the Tabakhmela frontline.

"Where is the battlefield?"

Here, Kvachi, here! In front of your very eyes … A hundred yards away. Everyone is running towards the sound of rifle fire, the clash of bayonets, the thunder of cannon, and the frantic yells.

Kvachi, don't lag behind! Have you hurt your foot? Are you limping? Are you hiding in those bushes and shooting from there? Fine, so be it. But don't hit our men. Right, aim!

"Tra-ta-ta. Tra-ta."

You've used five cartridges? Why have you stopped? You can't see anything from here? Then move on, get nearer! God damn it, how cold it's got. Kvachi's fingers are so frozen that he can't reload his rifle. He didn't know it would get so cold, otherwise … Kvachi, a warrior gets hot in war. If you can't fire your gun, then use your bayonet! Come out of the bushes and help your comrades. Right, Kvachi! Go, go! It takes a dozen leaps to be in the middle of the fray. The Budionovka hats have closed in on the cannon. Over here, one man down … another, another, that makes ten! Here, one man is chasing another with a bayonet! Look, right here: two fighters are clashing with swords. What's more, two have hit each other simultaneously with pistols and both have fallen on their backs. Here, three men are grabbing a man on horseback. Kvachi, help them, help them! Yes, jump across! You can fire from there. It's too late: one horseman is already sprawling on the ground.

What's wrong with you, Kvachi Kvachantiradze? What evil spirit has made your heart pound with fear? Who has shackled your limbs? Remember Demir-Tepe! Where are those divine demons who then took you by the arms and sent you flying to the throne of God? Where are the sorcerers who flew you across the fields of Ukraine? Why have they now abandoned you? Now, when you are fighting on your own ground for your own self … Come back, Kvachi, come back! Your soul is desolate, the ice of disbelief has settled in your heart, and doubt is gnawing at your brain … here's your motor car. Get in and go back to Silibistro … Revive Pupi, who has fainted … Calm Khukhu and Notio. Go, Kvachi, go! You were wrong. You shouldn't have come up here. What's happening here is not for you. Go, Kvachi, my boy, go!

25 February and Kvachi Turns Red

Kvachi, wake up! Don't sleep! Can't you hear the tread of a browbeaten army, the clatter of horses' hooves, the motor cars roaring, and the carts squeaking? Kvachi, wake up! The capital is emptying … everyone is going …

The roads to Dighomi and Avchala are packed. Train follows train. Scared women and children stumble hurriedly with bundles on their backs and armfuls of rags through the snow and slush. Kvachi, wake up!

The whole city is on its feet. People wake each other up, bang doors and windows, and call on each other to be on the move. Kvachi! Your palace is on a back street, but this street too is all abuzz. It's now light, past nine o'clock … ten … at any moment the Red Army will enter Tbilisi. Everyone in the city has now packed. The streets are empty. Only here and there can you see passersby with bowed heads and frightened eyes darting about, in a hurry to find a hiding place.

"Kvachi, get up! Kvachi! Kvachi!"

"What's going on? What's happened?"

"What's happened is that our government and army have left town."

"What are you saying, Beso? When? How? Why didn't we hear? Why didn't anyone tell us?"

"Quick, quick! We might just be in time to leave."

"Quick, call for the motor car! Throw in your clothes, a change of underwear, documents. Silibistro! Here's some money … Don't be frightened … Pupi, be quiet! Kvachi is off, but will be helping you. No, no! Kvachi can't take you with him this time … Later, later. Well, goodbye! Beso, Pavle, come on! To the station!"

The last train left as Kvachi arrived: he was too late.

"Driver, to Avchala!"

At Ghele Ravine there was Red cavalry.

"Turn back, turn back! Take a side road! Get a move on! Speed up! Accelerate!"

Kvachi's motor car speeds off. Like an arrow it crosses Vera bridge and shoots off on the military highway. At the White Inn they're stopped.

"Stop! Go back!"

The motor car span round and went back. Kvachi was dumbstruck:

"It's amazing! Why didn't they shoot us on the spot? Why did they send us back?"

"That'll all come in good time," Pavlov assured him. "They're in no hurry. It doesn't matter, all roads have been cut off."

Nobody said a word until they got back home. They were all as white as sheets, expecting some unprecedented and unforeseen horror.

"Kvachi, what do you say?" Beso finally asked Kvachi, who, deep in thought, was pacing the room furiously.

"Say something, tell us what to do," whined Pavlov.

"Speak, son! Kvachi, so, why don't you speak?" Silibistro and Pupi tried to rouse Kvachi from his thoughts.

Kvachi seemed only now to recover his awareness.

"Give me a pack of thick paper and some red ink."

He was brought paper and ink.

"Beso, write in big letters, in Georgian and Russian: 'Union of Friends of Red Georgia' ... Done it? Now take it and stick it to our door ... Wait, let's agree that if anything has to be said, you all say the Union was founded a month ago, I'm the chairman, Beso and Silibistro are on the committee, and the rest of you are members of the union. We have three hundred members. Beso, write the constitution today. You remember the constitution of the Society of Helpers of the Revolution? Bring in anyone you meet and make them sign this piece of paper. We'll get three hundred to sign up in three days, then three thousand. Off you go, Beso: put up this notice and call for the car. Pupi!"

"I'm here, son."

"Take the red edging off my bedspread; bring it here. Quick! Notio!"

"I'm here, too, son."

"Bring my flag, my big national flag, But hurry up! Silibistro!"

"What do you want, son?"

"Bring me a long pole."

Silibistro brought the pole, Pupi the red bedspread edging. Kvachi measured up the broad side of the silk material against the pole and said:

"It fits: even they don't have a silk banner. Right, Pupi, tie it to the pole. Beso, are you back? Now look. They won't have a flag as good as this. I seem to remember we have some gold paper somewhere."

"We've got several reams."

"Cut out a five-pointed star and stitch it to the middle of this flag. Hurry up! Notio, give me the Georgian flag."

He took the two-yard-long national flag off her, tore off the white and the black from the top corner, sewed on a red piece to cover the tear, and in five minutes he'd turned the national tricolor into a shield that suited the new times.

"Pupi, take this flag to the balcony and hang it out. I'll need it later. Who knows when the doorbell will ring? Beso, open the doors."

Kvachi's neighbors came in: Kolia Tsalikadze, Grisha Kalidze, and Volodia Chorishvili. All three were deadly pale and dumbstruck. The moment they came in they rushed to Kvachi.

"Come to your senses, why are you so pale?" said Kvachi angrily. "Don't listen to gossip, nothing's going to happen. I know these people very well. At times like these you've got to be nice to the winners, keep nodding, say 'Yes sir' to them, sing the *Internationale*, and dye your face red, that's all there is to it. Just follow me and do as I do."

All six men squeezed into the motor car. "To Navtlughi!"

Beso Shikia, holding a red flag the size of a blanket, stood next to the driver. When they went up Tsitsishvili Hill Beso was told by Kvachi to start shouting: "Citizens! Gather round! Follow me! Let's meet them: let's greet the new government!"

People gathered in groups, afraid and confused, and gradually followed Kvachi's motor car. The crowd grew. Around Navtlughi a reconnaissance squad of cavalrymen appeared with red banners. The banner and Kvachi's gigantic flag closed in on each other.

"Comrade," Kvachi asked the squad's leader, "we're delegates and we want to welcome the new government, the army commander, and his staff. Can you tell us where to find them?"

"I don't know about any government. The staff is coming up behind me."

"People, get into groups!" Kvachi commanded. "Bring bread and salt here. Market traders, move forward! Businessmen, you stand here … Porters, move over there a bit. Beso, bring me the flag. Right, they're coming: Hurra-a-ah!"

"Hurra-a-ah, hurra-a-ah!" a nervous yell rang out.

"Comrades," Kvachi thunders, standing in his motor car. "You come in peace. Tormented by lawlessness and disorder, the Georgian proletariat has been waiting for three years for the red flag which from today on is establishing workers' rule, the people's freedom, justice, and peace. It is bringing land to the peasant, power to the worker, and brotherhood to everybody. The Social-Democrats and those cannibal chauvinists have gone and won't be coming back. Welcome, comrades! Accept our fraternal greetings and hospitality. We are privileged to have you as our guests. Long live Soviet power, hurra-a-ah!"

Again there was a roar of hurrahs, hats were thrown in the air, and people went back to town. For some days Kvachi rushed about in his motor car, remembering old friends and acquaintances, and willing to make new ones. He met newcomers at the station, or found them somewhere to stay, or got them furniture, or arranged board for them and attended to other details.

Kvachi's life hung by a thread. God forbid anyone who found out or mentioned his heroic deeds, his machinations in Red Russia. Kvachi wasn't afraid of the distant past, because those deeds were concealed behind his "machinations" and his heroism in February 1917. But be careful, Kvachi, this is no time for joking. Your life isn't worth a penny. Don't run around in panic, don't show yourself to everybody, don't proclaim your name loudly, or you'll regret it.

"You're right, Beso," Kvachi said a few days later. "I have to hide in the shadows and stay silent, or I'll be denounced. Let's work quietly, keep our heads down, and get rich. That's our program for now."

Kvachi quietly got down to work and in a few days added a new inscription to the previous one: "Meat for the Red Army."

He chose two influential Reds that he knew and installed them nearby. Just in case, he registered with two small commissions, and had a couple of small mandates to put in his pocket. He could rest easy for a while. Pavlov was avoiding Tbilisi: he'd gone to Tusheti to see to Kvachi's wool. Beso Shikia wormed his way into a commissariat and took on the management of its agricultural department.

In two days the city's atmosphere and pulse had changed. Workers sometimes worked and sometimes marched with red flags; speakers spoke, yardmen swept the yards, cab-drivers drove their rattling cabs, chauffeurs sped around like madmen, deafening the city with their horns and carelessly squashing deafened pedestrians. About a hundred buildings were converted to house government offices. Tbilisi was so packed with newcomers that there was no more room. The city was now like a gigantic, excited beehive, with an endless feast going on, but the bees were preoccupied with finding the best place to feed and a comfortable seat. New people appeared everywhere. People with cellars moved upstairs, and those upstairs moved down instead. Any sealing wax that could be found in the city was used to seal shops, warehouses, and the apartments of those who had fled. Engravers were busy making new stamps and seals, and porters, horses, and oxen were worn out transporting furniture from one apartment to another. Countless people were busy taking stock and carrying out inventories in warehouses and shops, counting up and confiscating goods in front of their downcast and tearful owners. Big houses were transferred to the city and the workers. There was no end now to the stocktaking. Innumerable people were busily entering the city's stocks of paper, books, motor cars, oil, sugar, flour, wire, ironmongery, craftsmen, doctors, engineers, horses, cows, poultry, and a thousand petty and large properties, inanimate and animate, four- and two-legged, into the inventory registers.

Holding his breath, Kvachi was as quiet as a lamb. Everyone seemed to have forgotten his name, his house, and his property. The placard of the "Union of Friends of Red Georgia" still worked and stood outside Kvachi's house like a guardian angel. "Meat for the Red Army", thanks to Silibistro's support, brought in the bacon. But the chairman of "Meat", Kvachi, was summoned to the barracks and shown a carcass of his:

"What is this: ox or buffalo?"

"Ox, though …"

"It's buffalo, isn't it? Show me the papers!"

Why make such a fuss about Kvachi? Leave him alone and he'll leave you alone! A penalty? Fine, go ahead. Goodbye for now. Let them look for someone to replace Kvachi, and that person will bring them cow instead of buffalo, and lamb instead of cow, of course he will.

That day Kvachi, agile as ever, once more slipped out of the noose.

Time passed. The whole country had forgotten the very name of Kvachi. But once they did recall it; some workers turned up at the house to curtly announce: "From now on by order of the municipality this house belongs to the city. How many people live on this floor? None? Nine persons in nine rooms? It's not your property, you'll have to reduce."

They measured the apartment, calculated, assigned five rooms to the nine persons and added: "That's too much for you bourgeois. You've sucked enough of our blood as it is."

"As you like. Many thanks, comrades," Kvachi meekly mewed, agreeing to obey the new leadership, but in his heart he was gnashing his teeth and growling, "Ugh, you bandits! Robbers! I hope God gives me the strength one day to show you my appreciation!"

It was now that Pavlov crept back to town to tell Kvachi: "That's it. It's finished. They took our wool away."

Kvachi hadn't digested this news or voiced a protest, when some workers who had followed Pavlov coolly announced: "Workers are to be moved into this house. Vacate it by this time tomorrow."

Great God! Why are the heavens so angry with Kvachi? By this time tomorrow ... but where was he to move to?

"To Dog's Gorge, we've got you nice little lodgings there."

"In that stinking hole? In those peasant huts? It deserves to be called Dog's Gorge! Well, how many rooms will nine persons get?"

"Three rooms will do you. And that's more than you deserve. You've sucked enough of our blood as it is. Don't touch the furniture, or else ..."

This was unbearable! House, apartment, and wool, too. All that Kvachantiradze had left to lose was his underpants.

"I have two mandates. I work in two commissions."

"Keep your mandates. Don't try to pull the wool over our eyes with them."

"My God, what vile times. Even mandates have lost their power. No, I won't put up with this. Ugh, Khrkhriants: your name's as bad as your nature. Cunning fox! Scoundrel! Pickpocket! I expect you're feasting in Paris or Istanbul on what I sweated to earn. I hope the money kills you."

Really! The apartment belongs to the "Union of Friends of Red Georgia." Kvachi had almost forgotten that detail. He shielded himself with record books and documents concocted by Beso, and added:

"I am the chairman of the committee. Here's Silibistro Kvachantiradze, here's Besarion Shikia: they're committee members, we have been of immeasurable use to the Soviet government, for example ..."

One of the workers cut off Kvachi in mid-flow:

"Give me those papers. They'll be examined by the authorities."

They'd really gone too far. Kvachi couldn't swallow that. He, Kvachi Kvachantiradze, would complain, make a fuss, and have his own way. Dog's Gorge, where there's nothing but chickens, geese, horses, cows, and pigs. That's not the worst of it. Kvachi would move from there the next day, but ten thousand roubles' worth of furniture? That's like the wrath of God, that's a real disaster! No! Kvachi would complain here and now, protest loudly, turn the whole city upside down:

"Beso, go and see Chioradze and get things moving! Silibistro, you know Mzhavadze from Kutaisi? Well, find out where he is and remind him he owes you a favor. Pupi, you visit Shiradze's wife Dzabuli and work on her. I'll do the running round. Right, be quick! Get moving! Don't dawdle, or we'll all be out in the street."

That evening they all came home hopeful. Each one brought a fearsome note, inspiring hope, and promising assistance. The next day Kvachi's apartment was besieged again.

"Right, vacate the premises!"

"I can't let you! See, a commissar's letter … Look, a Communist Party note! Look, a Bolshevik order! I can't let you have it!" Kvachi had sorted the business the previous day. "So you vacate the premises, instead."

They ripped these notes and letters to pieces over Kvachi's head, scattered the pieces of paper over the street, together with a small quantity of his worldly goods. They put those possessions into a lorry and shouted: "Right, to Dog's Gorge."

The battle for the apartment was over. Kvachi had lost. He had been badly defeated. But something much heavier weighed on his heart, and he had to get rid of this weight before it destroyed him for ever. No, resisting was a trick that no longer worked. He had to unsheathe another weapon.

He unsheathed it: he suddenly bowed his proud neck, became as soft as cotton, and with fox-like cunning appealed for pity:

"All right, comrades, all right … As you say. I'm a man of discipline. The workers' wish is my command. I believe in the dictatorship of the proletariat, but … what have you got against that man, that unfortunate worker?" he asked, pointing to Pavlov who, deliberately wearing rags and making himself pathetic, was standing huddled in a corner. Everyone looked at Pavlov. One man asked him:

"Who are you? What are you doing here?"

"Me? I'm … the Union's watchman."

"Yes, he's our Union's watchman," Kvachi confirmed. "Comrades, I beg you, let the Union have this room. It's separate from the rest of the apartment. We shan't get in each other's way."

"But it's a very nice room …"

"It is … it's a good room … my office …"

"But we'll take the furniture off you."

"Whatever you say, but …" Kvachi grimaced. "Let me have this little rug … the one hanging on this wall … Can't you? I'll buy you two just as good in exchange for it. This rug is … a memento of my fiancée. That's all I have left of her after the accident … The poor girl died before her time on this carpet. Yes, my fiancée died on this carpet. All I ask is for you to leave the carpet hanging on this wall for two days. If I don't get you one that is as good or better by the day after tomorrow, then you can take it, and bring shame on this room and on me."

"That's easy. We'll put this carpet on the list. But you, comrade," the man turned to Pavlov, who was hunched in the corner, "stay in this room. Right, let's get it over with. Now get out, and take all your junk with you."

That same day Kvachi and his household found themselves in such a stinking hole that Pupi fainted and Notio shrieked hysterically.

Kvachi's Loyal Service and Rescue by Madame NEP

The next day Kvachi brought the very best carpet for the tenants of his palace; he left the wall carpet where it was. Should he tell Pavlov that an iron safe was installed behind the wall carpet, or that it contained Kvachi's treasure? No, he'd tell him nothing. You can't be too careful. Suppose Pavle found it irresistible? No, no. Kvachi will keep quiet for now, but visit the room to check on the treasure as often as possible.

Beso runs round the estate agents and fixes the problem of finding a nice flat very neatly. Kvachi is gnashing his teeth, Silibistro is muttering, Pupi is weeping bitter tears, and Notio is uttering the blackest curses. Beso had no trouble finding himself a room, but Kvachi … If he were an official, he'd have almost everything—accommodation, water, electricity, potatoes, sugar, bread, and sausages—free of charge. But now Kvachi, as a free man, is outside the law, and deprived of all rights.

Don't snarl, Kvachi. You were baptised in Red water in Russia and learned what a new country is like. So why be surprised? Don't be upset, be welcoming; instead of cursing, get used to the new and adapt to it. That's all there is to it. Well, get to work! Find a way in and out again. Laugh when you feel like crying. Cry when you feel like laughing. Stop frowning, fix your lips in a smile, sweeten your tongue, bow your neck, and accept the yoke of being senior assistant to a junior Party secretary.

Two days later Kvachi had to choose; he didn't know which position to accept: there were five of them. Finally he said:

"I know these bastards. They'll make you a big boss and then appoint five people to spy on you. A decent man like me, however hard I try, won't last two months. Then the *Cheka* comes ... and I'll have had it. No, brother, no, you can't fool me. I'm a little man and I prefer a little job."

Little Kvachi really did choose a little job working in a remote district police force, becoming a full citizen with full rights. A few days later he moved into a flat which he would not have spurned even in earlier times.

Kvachi worked lazily, cautiously, and without enthusiasm. He was a gentle, polite, and kind-hearted commissar. He never exceeded his authority and he avoided rows, he stayed out of the limelight and kept a tight rein on himself. He was being very careful. He walked on tiptoe, talked in whispers and squirmed like a tightrope walker. He kept twenty, rather than two eyes, and ten pairs of ears, rather than one, open. His alert mind never stopped working. Only occasionally, when he came across startled game in the dark, he would crouch like a Red Indian and have the game neatly skinned before it had managed even to squawk or see the hunter's hand. But there was only small game to be had. Kvachi wouldn't bother with sprats, but salmon very seldom strayed into Kvachi's net.

"Careful, Beso, careful," he often told his friend who was involved in everything: management, brokering, and a thousand big and small affairs.

The "Union of Friends" had ceased to exist. Kvachi received a resolution to that effect, but they didn't know about this in Party headquarters. Pavlov was still guarding the Union's room with Kvachi's treasure in Sololaki. Kvachi thought several times of moving it, but dared not do so. He said that those people were bound to search him, that he'd been identified and stripped naked before. So it might as well stay there, where nobody would suspect it was. Beso eventually suggested:

"Kvachi, let's go abroad, or we'll be packed off somewhere."

"Wait, don't be too hasty. Whenever we got a few pennies together in Russia, you told me we had to get away fast. But I didn't believe you. I stayed on another year, and I didn't lose anything."

"What do you mean, you didn't lose, Kvachi? They stripped us of everything on the railway."

"That was just bad luck. The treasure we have in Sololaki will be enough for us to live on, but there are different ways of living. I've got a couple of jobs I've started. Let's finish them and ... then let's see."

These two jobs were followed by four or five new ones, but Kvachi kept repeating:

"Let's finish this one ... Let's just fix this business ... Let's see it through ... Let's do it."

Kvachi lasted barely two months as a commissar. Once they went sniffing round his activities, caught the scent of something, and told him:

"Cut the staff."

Kvachi found another post, and moved to the treasury. That lasted only a month.

"Reduce the staffing!"

Kvachi tried factory management:

"Fire him!"

He got a job in warehousing:

"Dismiss him."

Kvachi kept looking for work, filling in one or two gigantic forms each week. He was asked:

"Father's previous occupation?" Kvachi writes, "Farm laborer."

"Class?"—"Peasant."

"Your revolutionary past?" Kvachi fills a whole page.

"Where were you in February 1917?"—"In the heart of the revolution."

"In October?"—"In Petersburg, on the side of the Reds."

"In which party did you work?"—"In none, but I helped everybody."

"What party do you now belong to?"—"None."

"Which party do you sympathize with?"—"Only the communists."

Kvachi filled in his loyalty questionnaires and wrote letters, but got the same response:

"Throw him out! Dismiss him! Don't touch him with a barge pole!"

What was going on? What had happened? What was behind it all? Why had they got it in for Kvachi? Why were they hounding him? Why was he being chased away everywhere like a dog with distemper? Were they the only people entitled to live in this world? Why wouldn't they tell Kvachi to his face why? Was he a prince? That was a lie. Was he gentry? Sheer rumor. Who ever heard of a Kvachantiradze being a prince or a member of the gentry? Kvachi was a peasant, a real peasant. Ashordia? That was rumor, too. They ought to work out that Kvachi was not even five years old at the time. Made a prince by the Tsar? That wasn't true, either. In Russia every Georgian was called "prince", so Kvachi was stuck with that title too. A lord-in-waiting? Friendship with Rasputin? What unforgiving people! Hadn't Kvachi atoned ten times over for those sins? Hadn't he worked for the revolution? Proof? Witnesses? All very well and good: Kvachi would provide thousands of proofs and would show that …

Be careful, Kvachi. Avoid proofs, because if you get an investigation started, they may accept five proofs, but the sixth they'll delve into; if they look into one room, they'll poke their noses into two or three others; if they undress you, they'll take off your shirt and strip you naked, so that not an inch of you will be hidden. Stay clear of the past, Kvachi. Don't open your heart to anyone, don't undo your clothes, don't put your head in fate's noose, or on the tenth occasion it won't let you slip out, but will grip your neck so hard that your very best tricks will no longer help you.

No, no! Leave Kvachi alone. He doesn't need to work for you, or to please you, or to be a candidate for Communist party membership, or to have a revolutionary reputation. Kvachi has died, he doesn't exist any more. Destroy his case. Tear up his declarations. Put the papers in the stove. That's right ... like that ... Thank you, thank you very much. Now forget the name of Kvachi for ever. Goodbye!

Hail Madame NEP, New Economic Plan! Welcome! Blessed be the day of your birth and the right hand of whoever devised you. The black darkness is lifting. The weather is turning cloudless and sunny. Come, Madame NEP, open the shops, smash the shutters off the inns, start up clubs, relax every day and feast every evening, spin the roulette wheel, deal blackjack cards, buy, sell, lose, win, drink, eat, live and let live!

Kvachi Kvachantiradze! Congratulations on your resurrection. The past has come back for you, your cell doors have been opened. So come on out and enjoy yourself. Show the suckers your tricks and teeth, your iron muscles and nimble feet. Spread your mighty arms wide, make your sparkling brains race, knot your silk threads, set golden traps, and cast your net of deception. Go on, get to work, leap about, enjoy yourself! Go on, neatly! Deftly! Nimbly! Go on! Attack!

Kvachi worked and intrigued so hard that a whirlwind of smoke and dust rose up wherever his feet and hands had been.

"Sibunion" revived, its five departments reopened, and Kvachi got back his army of employees.

"Pavle, move to Baku. You're not known there. Buy their wool, oil, caviar, silk cocoons, and cotton ... Silibistro, move into Pavlov's room and keep an eye on my treasure which is increasing with the frequent donations! Kolia, go to Batumi: it's a real gold mine now. Right, get a move on. Get on with it! Rake it in! Swiftly! Quick! Good man!"

"Jalil, my Jalil. Thank God you're back, come and let me hug you."

"*Allah sana shukur versin, kochi-bey* (You can give thanks to God, boss). It's very good to see you're still alive, very, very good."

"Where have you been, Jalil. Where?"

"I was abroad, I got a bit of money."

"Where abroad, Jalil?"

"Abroad ... I saw a bit of Istanbul, I went to a few other places. *Allah il-allah*! You're alive, prince? *Shukur Allah*!"

"Jalil, do you want to come in with me again?"

"Jalil's your friend. It was very hard for Jalil when he left you. I haven't seen my friend for two years. I asked other people. They said you're fine. So I came."

"Well, welcome back, Jalil. Give me your hand. Now let's go to the club. Follow me."

Kvachi's day and night contained a hundred hours and just as many things to see to: instead of walking he flew, instead of working he whirled like a child's top. Kvachi lived as if a year was but a day and a day but a second. He couldn't go to sleep if he hadn't spent an hour at the roulette wheel or played several rounds of pontoon, if he hadn't had a satisfying supper followed by liqueurs, and if he hadn't squeezed the tender flanks of some blonde or brunette. If Silibistro's son ever lost interest in money and women, he didn't know what would give him so much pleasure. Beso saw to the accounting. The books were chaotic at first, then covered in dust and gnawed by mice. Every day Kvachi received a dozen telegrams: "The dollar is down ... sterling is up ... Sugar is dearer ... Tobacco is cheaper ..."

People ran in and out of Kvachi's office all day, counting or paying in their money, selling and buying. He could hardly keep up with the orders he had to give: "Buy ... sell ... I don't want ... Bring ... Cash ... Count ..."

In the morning Kvachi's till is stuffed: after an hour it hasn't got a single billion roubles or a single dollar, but half an hour later the room is packed to the ceiling with sacks stuffed with vouchers. His clerks work at the sacks, count the money in packs, then load it on carts and exchange it all for one tiny cheque.

Kvachi buys and sells goods he has never set eyes on. He doesn't need to. NEP has revived the old convenient and profitable ways. True, no day passes without a shouting match and an argument breaking out in the office. There are still a lot of troublemakers around. There's nothing they won't dispute with Kvachi. Either his cheque has bounced, or there are a few billion roubles missing from his sacks, or his sugar has got wet, or his textiles turn out to be rotten. Kvachi wasn't on the ship, or traveling in the railway wagon; he didn't pour water on the cotton or mix grit with the wool, or remove money from the sacks: he doesn't even know if the British Bank's cheques are duds. "Send the cheque to London and you'll find out. If it bounces, find John Rawlinson." As for the rest, they can complain to Kvachi if they like, or go to court. You'll wait a year, if not forty, for the case to be decided. "Fine, let's settle. Don't shout and don't swear, or ... Jalil! Show this gentleman the door. Are you still threatening me? You're wasting your time." If you knew the power and influence of Kvachi's pocket, you wouldn't mess about.

What does Kvachi do? Nothing and everything. He buys and sells whatever he can lay hands on: foreign currency, Baku shares, oil fields, state bonds, out-of-date promissory notes, all kinds of economic information, and orders from "State Foreign Trade" for importing and exporting all sorts of goods; he leases buildings without asking their owners, sometimes he sells "air", or even undertakes to do what he cannot carry out, such as demolishing Mt Qazbeg. But that's nothing. He has only to take a deposit and put the money to work: the rest develops all by itself. What Kvachi most likes are trusts, factories, and cooperatives. They combine money, property, and inexperienced people.

Is Kvachi trusted? Of course he is. If he weren't, who could be trusted? He has unlimited property: a palace which, sooner or later, when the Reds go or are overthrown, he will certainly repossess; a beautiful place with a garden in the country near Sukhumi, plantations in Batumi, other people's goods in his warehouses, worthless shares, valuable papers and ... his word of honor. Yes, Kvachi's word of honor which has never been broken or even besmirched.

But somehow a change occurred. Kvachi's office was unexpectedly visited and searched: an enormous amount of foreign currency was confiscated, and Kvachi himself was taken away and asked:

"Are you involved in speculation?"

"I'm a trader. I have a legal right to trade."

"This isn't trade, this is speculation."

"It's trade."

"I said it's speculation."

They sweated for several hours, looking for the boundary between trade and speculation. Finally, Kvachi was told:

"You can go, but if we detain you again ..."

"My money?"

"We're not sending you to Metekhi prison, so be grateful for that."

"I protest."

"Then off you go to Metekhi."

"No, no! Sorry … Sorry. I understand the difference now. I take my words back. Goodbye."

Kvachi was heading for home, clenching his fists, gnashing his teeth, and swearing like a Turk. For a whole week no smile passed his lips and his head stayed bowed: the venom would not dry in his mouth. But Kvachi's head, hands, and feet did not rest for a single hour. Ducking his head, he raced around and "fixed" things extremely cautiously.

In about two weeks Kvachi recovered his losses, resumed his upright stance, and forgot the fine he had paid. But others had not forgotten Kvachi: once again he was collared and once again had his pockets and till emptied.

"Have you been converting foreign currency?"

"Yes, I have."

It was a month before Kvachi emerged from that building, but he overcame his sorrows and left his anger behind. Again, he lowered his bull's neck and went his usual way.

"Beso," he would sometimes tell his loyal friend, "it looks as if there's no point working here any more. You can't take goods out or bring them in, you can't deal in foreign currency. And now they've introduced the gold rouble, we're finished, and can't make a profit changing money. The new laws won't let us touch the trusts, and the banks won't give us credit now. Any day now we'll be choked off. Who knows how many people have gone broke?"

"Let's leave, Kvachi, I said we should leave the country before we die of starvation. Apart from state employees nobody here can make a living."

"Hang on, Beso, hang on. We'll leave when I make up my losses."

But losses followed losses, penalties followed penalties, and there were more spells in Metekhi. Kvachi was going to pieces with every day. First he closed the "Sibunion" office in Baku, then trade stopped in Batumi, and finally Kvachi was beset by so many brakes and hoops that he slammed the doors of his office shut and told Beso:

"Sell everything tomorrow or the day after. Dismiss our employees and tell the customers that 'Sibunion' has closed. That's it. It's all over. It's impossible to work or to live here. Jalil, come here."

From then on Kvachi was a free citizen again. He walked down Rustaveli Avenue with nothing in mind. He spent the nights in clubs and restaurants. He drank, he chased girls, and played cards. Silibistro moved back to Kutaisi, bought a house as old as himself on Balakhvani Street, and settled in. Silibistro urged Kvachi many times to move to Kutaisi, but Kvachi was not yet so old as to go back to a depopulated Kutaisi.

Once, a gloomy Beso entered Kvachi's room. He announced gravely:

"We really are finished now."

"What's going on, Beso?"

"Pavlov has made a run for it."

"What are you saying, Beso?"

"I said he's made a run for it. He packed his bags and went the day before yesterday, apparently."

"Well? And the … the treasure?"

"He opened the safe and took the lot."

Kvachi could not utter a sound, and Beso, too, was struck dumb. Jalil rolled his eyes and waited for an explanation. Finally Kvachi got up and said through clenched teeth:

"Get ready! Jalil, you go to Batumi. Beso, you go up to the Caucasus pass and then on to Rostov. I'm going to Baku. But be quick. We're going today. Ugh, wait till I get you, Pavlov."

Jalil asked: "I don't know, *agha*. What trick has Pavle played?"

"He's stolen, he's stolen the money."

"Stolen the money? Hey, *köpoglu* (son of a dog). Dog! Bastard!"

"Listen carefully," Kvachi instructed the two men. "Don't say a word, don't let the police find out anything, or they'll get wise and finish us off, too. If you find Pavlov, strangle him ... or threaten him, so that he gives you back the treasure at once. Then send a telegram to me straight away. Right, get ready to go."

All three left the same day in three directions in pursuit of Pavlov, who had vanished from the face of the earth.

A week later Kvachi was back in Tbilisi; Jalil also returned to report:

"Pavle's a son of a dog. I couldn't find him."

A week late Beso, too, came back:

"Not a trace of him."

With every day Kvachi became more and more depressed. He was paralyzed by sorrow and impotent with bile. Money lost its value in his eyes; he lost his appetite for life. Occasionally he made a deft leap to grab a purse full of gold, but the next day not a single gold coin was left. He had lost his old genius for making money. He lacked his old refinement, agility, and clear thinking. His mind was often clouded, his eyes no longer focussed, and his machinations now became crude and clumsy.

He could no longer speak about politics; he just thanked God that his past had not been investigated. Finally, Silibistro's son was at such a low point that he began borrowing gold roubles left and right and stopped thinking about tomorrow.

Kvachi's Engagement

"Get in quick!" came an order in Russian.

"Hang on, comrades, it's very dark."

"I said, get in."

Aleksi Iremadze uttered a deep sigh, gathered his courage, and strode through the pitch darkness. In an instant the doors behind him shut, he could hear the click of a key and the heavy tread of the guard's boots. Then everything stopped and there was silence.

Suddenly, far in the depths of the dark pit he heard:

"Hey, who are you?"

Iremadze was relieved. He recovered his voice and croaked like an old man: "I'm … a prisoner. Help me for God's sake, tell me where to go."

"God's got nothing to do with it, nor has the devil."

"For God's sake …" Iremadze gasped.

"I said keep God out of it, but I'll help you if you've got tobacco."

"They took it off me."

"I hope the devil takes them off … Hmm … Whoever you are, listen to me. Follow the wall and count twenty steps. Slowly, the steps are wet. Don't fall or you'll end up in the pit. Well, are you coming?"

"I'm coming …" he said as he counted the steps, "Five … ten … fifteen … twenty. Now, do I go straight on?"

"Stop there. Don't come nearer, or you'll fall down the well."

"What are you saying, brother, what well? What's a well doing here?"

"Don't risk it, or you'll end up dead. There's a pit in the middle of the dungeon, the pit's full of snakes, lizards, frogs, and other devils. Go round it on the right and move along the walls, don't take your hand off the wall, or you're finished. I'm coming to help you. Hey, where are you?"

"I'm here," croaked Iremadze, his trembling body clinging to the damp wall; he muttered: "You don't believe in God … What a disaster! Throwing live people down bottomless pits … for snakes and lizards to eat. God almighty, how dark it is!"

Cautiously, he crept on tiptoe in the darkness, groping with his hands and feet, measuring and testing every inch.

"Careful, brother, careful, or you'll have an accident. This morning an Armenian fell in. Hey, where are you?"

"I'm here … I'm coming."

They bumped into each other in the dark and joined hands.

"Hello."

"God be with you."

"Right, follow me. Careful, don't let go of the wall."

They moved another dozen paces.

"We're safe now. Right, sit down and tell us about it."

"Many thanks. God give you peace. The ground's wet, I'll get a chill."

"The whole dungeon's wet. Sit down, you'll get used to it. Now tell us what's going on in town. I haven't seen the sky for a month."

"Give me a minute, dear chap … You were saying an Armenian fell down the pit this morning …"

Someone giggled at this point.

"Would anyone else fall in?"

"Why are you laughing, you Turk?" the first man retorted. "He's a Turk, his name's Jalil. I asked what you're laughing at."

"A mouse … a mouse chewed my foot. May God eat him."

"Don't take our God's name in vain. If you swear, swear by Allah. So a rat bit your foot? It stole my hat yesterday, it took it down its hole."

"Oh no," Iremadze whined, leaping up: a huge rat had jumped on him.

The two other prisoners laughed so loud that the walls began to shake.

"You may feel like laughing … you're used to it … Don't expect me to laugh," muttered Iremadze.

"Sit down, brother, sit down. You'll have to get used to it. A rat's a nightingale compared to the snakes. What? Were you really afraid? It won't hurt you. Sit between us. Yes, like that! Jalil, warn our new guest in future. It will walk over us. What, the Armenian? Yes, he lost his footing this morning and fell in. Stick to the wall, don't slip down, or … He fell in and that was the end of him. The snakes and other foul things are eating his corpse now. What did you say? Is it deep? I tell you, it's bottomless. Now listen. I'll throw this stone. One, two, three! I've thrown it."

They all held their breath and listened. After a dozen seconds the pebble made a muffled sound, as if it had fallen into a bottomless pit.

"God almighty!" groaned Iremadze.

"So you see, brother. Move three paces from the wall, and you'll move in with my grand-dad and we'll choke on the smell of your corpse."

Iremadze's nostrils twitched.

"Yes, it does smell of corpses. I wonder how many have come to a sticky end …"

"Who's counting? Listen, old man. You've got to learn the rules here. They'll come in handy. Remember: whatever you see or hear, keep it a deep secret. If you ever say a thing, you're finished: they'll arrest you and stick your head down that pit. Got it? Memorized it?"

"God, help me! I've got it, I've memorized it. Thanks very much for the advice. I heard in town that if anyone blurts anything out … anyway, there's a lot of talk about things here."

"The rumors are right, believe me. Whatever you see or hear here is considered a state secret. Idle talk is punished the same as treason or spying. So now you know, old man. The rest is up to you."

"Thanks a lot, dear chap, thanks a lot. Ask me any favor in return. I've never been a talker, so why has God sent me this in my old age?"

"Actually, old man, who are you, and why are you in prison? It's time we got to know each other."

"My name's Iremadze, dear chap, Aleksi Iremadze."

"Aleksi Iremadze! I must be blind! Why didn't you tell me

before, dear man. Oh, this is shameful of me. Aleksi Iremadze in this dungeon?! The father of my Silovan. Oh shame on me, what a wretch I am."

The anonymous chatterbox began busily fussing in the dark, groping with his hands, yelling to the Turk and telling him:

"Jalil, quick! Bring my coat! Here's my coat. Put it under you, Aleksi old man, or you'll catch a chill. What would I tell Silovan if you did? Move over here, old man. I must be blind. Why didn't you tell me before, old man. I nearly threw uncle Aleksi into the pit! Jalil, bring bread, water. What, no more bread? Sorry, old man, a thousand apologies. We can't offer you bread. Oh no, to think I should meet Silovan's father in such a place! Who am I? Silovan's closest and best friend, Kvachi Kvachantiradze. Yes, I'm Kvachi Kvachantiradze. You know a bit about me? Silovan and I lived together in Moscow for five years. Dear Silovan. You couldn't have a better friend in the whole wide world. He's in Germany now, isn't he? I know, old man, I know. I wasn't in town when he left, otherwise we wouldn't have spent a single hour apart. I meant to go to Germany, but couldn't manage it. Dear Silovan, what a lad. What a man! Nobody in Georgia can match him: such a scholar that he was the talk of the whole country. Mark my words, uncle Aleksi. If I've ever misled anyone, don't come near me. My dear old Silovan!"

It took Kvachi about ten minutes to give Iremadze an account of his ten years' friendship and shared life with Silovan, their studies, love affairs, struggles, imprisonment, deportation, return, and a thousand adventures. Who knows how many times Kvachi sacrificed himself for Silovan, how often he had saved Silovani from mortal danger? True, some ten years had passed since Silovan had gone off with his money, but such trivia were not worth mentioning. How much had he lost? Just three hundred roubles. Uncle Aleksi shouldn't bother. Kvachi and Silovan would settle up when the latter returned.

Then more was revealed: Aleksi Iremadze, a respected school-teacher, had been searched ten days previously, and a proclamation was found on him. He insisted that someone had planted the proclamation in his house. The interrogator was sure that Aleksi was distributing proclamations and, because Aleksi wouldn't confess, had punished him by putting him in this dark, damp dungeon. That was all: there was nothing else. What had actually happened? Quite simply: 5 April was the birthday of Elena, Aleksi's unmarried daughter. As always, Aleksi held a supper and had a dozen guests. They had a good time, not leaving until six in the morning.

Aleksi bent down and whispered to Kvachi: "One of them was spying on me, or talked. I'm accused of reading the proclamation at that supper. True, why should I hide anything from a good friend of Silovan? I had several copies, I let my guests have them. Someone decided to ruin me."

Then Kvachi Kvachantiradze told Aleksi about his case, which was much simpler and more straightforward. In spring, at two in the morning, an Armenian was robbed on the road to Tsqneti. A month later Kvachi was "for no reason at all" seized and thrown into this dungeon. He was asked where he was at two a.m. on 5 April. He didn't remember, he was not such a fool as to keep a diary. He'd been thinking for a month, but couldn't remember. They were threatening him with the death penalty. His landlord, the landlord's wife, and the neighbors repeatedly insisted that they remembered very well that Kvachantiradze had not been at home on 5 April: they'd probably plotted to have Kvachantiradze put away, because the three of them were reactionaries, while Kvachi, as the entire country knew, was a revolutionary. He'd been in prison, he'd been in exile, so that was the reason why they sided against him.

It was ridiculous! Accusing Kvachi of robbing a man. All Georgia must be laughing. Did they suppose Silibistro had spent a whole cartload of gold on Kvachi and sent him all over the country, just so he could turn out to be a robber? Who? Kvachi Kvachantiradze? Ha-ha-ha. It was enough to cause an earthquake. Ha-ha-ha!

Kvachi suddenly fell silent, probably plunged into thought. Aleksi started talking to Jalil about the fate of those who were locked up, about the "local" ways, and the pit. Suddenly Kvachi reached out for Aleksi's hand and almost burst into tears.

"Uncle Aleksi, help me, do me a favor."

"How, boy, how?"

"For Silovan's sake, uncle, help me, save me from death. I have elderly parents and a dozen relatives to look after. I'm still young, the same age as your Silovan. This is no time for me to die. I know you won't let me down. I've had it if you don't help me. You can do it, my savior, you can, you can ... Uncle, dear uncle ..."

He kissed Aleksi's hands and wetted them with his tears. Aleksi was moved. Not saying a word, he kissed Kvachi's brow and stroked his hair.

"Tell me, poor boy, tell me if I really can; I'll help you, how could I not? We're Christians, we're brothers. Say how I can help."

"You had a supper on 5 April, didn't you?"

"Yes, 5 April. So?"

"On 5 April I committed ... They claim I robbed that Armenian at two a.m. on 5 April. This is how you can help, uncle, you've got to be a witness for me. Say I was there at the supper. Uncle, for the sake of your gray hair, say that. Then I'll be a slave to you and to Silovan."

"Fine, but ... I had a dozen guests to supper."

"That doesn't matter, uncle, if you go ahead, it will all work out. Listen ... today or tomorrow you'll be released. I'm sure they'll let you go. You've got lots of people to stand up for you and help. When you get out, go and see all your guests and tell them what to say. Some of them may know me anyway. They mustn't let me go down, they must help me. A week after you get out I'll remember that on 5 April I was with you."

"Fine, but ..."

"Bear with me, uncle, bear with me. Tell your guests to say that Kvachi Kvachantiradze was present at that supper. I'm thirty-five, tall, black and curly hair, clean-shaven, clipped moustache, with a scar from a wound on my chin. Don't be afraid, nobody will ever find out that we colluded here. We have different interrogators. So you needn't worry. Now please tell me who your guests were."

"Vano Kaliashvili, Dzuku Pipia ... Beso Gugulia."

"I know Gugulia and Pipia. Who else?"

"Pupi Lomidze, Darispan Shelidze."

"I know both of them, uncle, I do! Who else?"

"Silovan Shiradze ... Mikha Berishvili ... Taso Alavidze ..."

"Uncle, I know nearly all of them. I do!" Kvachi repeated joyfully.

"Good, my lad, good, if they let me out, I'll see everybody and tell them what to do."

Kvachi was leaping for joy, turning his head towards Aleksi, unsure how he could thank him. He was shouting:

"Jalil, you Turk. Don't you know who you're talking to? There's nobody in Georgia so famous and knowledgeable: if you Turks had a man like that, they'd make him Sultan of Turkey. Jalil, come over here, don't let uncle Aleksi fall into the pit, or I'll throw you down to join him. Sorry, uncle, I do apologize. There's no way I can return the favor. Poor me! What a place to meet uncle Aleksi: nothing to eat or drink, or even smoke! What can I do, uncle, if you help me and I get out, it'll be a matter of honor to thank you."

"Don't fret, lad, I'm all right. I can put up with anything. The mice and rats do bother me, otherwise ..."

"Jalil, do something. Don't let a single rat near, or it'll be all your fault. Right!"

"Shoo, shoo, you wretches!" Jalil called out, thumping the ground and mewling like a cat: "Miaow, miaouw, miaouw ..."

They all laughed and joked.

"Jalil, tell uncle Aleksi about your Marusia," said Kvachi, laughing in anticipation.

Jalil was both laughing and groaning, laughing at himself, but striking his forehead as a sign of regret. He said: "What a fool! Stupid, mad Jalil! Stupid fool." But finally he told his story.

Jalil had grown up in Georgia: he'd worked for others, he'd traded, he'd leased a bathhouse, he'd quietly helped the revolution and the Ottomans too. He'd been in Persia in Sattar Khan's forces: the "one-armed Vlas Mgeladze" had enlisted him. Then he went off to trade in Odessa. On the way there he met *agha* Kvachantiradze and stuck with him. After that they traveled the world. Sometimes Jalil stayed behind and went his own way, but wherever Kvachi was, he later found and followed him. He fought in Edirne, in Çatalca, he helped the Arabs in Libya, but the Italians captured him. He got back with his loot and started trading again. Where was he in the World War? He didn't remember well, but summed up: "I was over there and made a bit of money."

Where "over there" was—in the direction of Russia or Turkey—and how he made his "bit of money", Jalil avoided saying.

Later, he'd turned up in Kars as the Russian army was going home. When the Turks took Batumi, Jalil was "close by." When the hero of Baghdad, Halil-Pasha, came to Tbilisi, Jalil went to meet him and offered to serve under him. He knew Nuri-Pasha well, too, as well as Kazim-Bey, and offered to "serve a bit" under them all. Jalil was a fine "fighting lad": young, strong, deft, hardworking, diligent, non-drinking, non-gambling. He did take brandy "as medicine" because he had the "fevers." But he had one big defect: he was too fond of Russian blondes. Blondes made him lose his "wits" many times, caused him regret, cleaned him out, and robbed him. Many times he swore an oath never to come near one again, but he couldn't keep his vow. And it was a blonde that finally broke him.

Two weeks previously, when Jalil was coming down the street, he came across a beautiful blonde "in his doorway." She offered Jalil a very nice Persian shawl. He invited this beauty into his house, served her sherbet and sweets, and then it all happened: laughing, kissing, joking, chasing round the room, panic, and uproar. The beauty from Tambov would not give in to him, Jalil gave her two gold roubles, but even gold didn't work. The woman laughed as she turned Jalil's rooms upside down, roused the neighborhood, excited him, got his blood boiling, "burned" him, wore him out, made him sweat and then ... fled. That same day Jalil was put in the dark dungeon. While he was groping and embracing and kissing her, the blonde Marusia had stolen a piece of paper which Halil-Pasha had given him. In it was written that Jalil was "one of ours", that he had done the Turks "a great service" and he should be "given support." So Jalil was in prison waiting for that "support", but no supporter was in sight. "Uncle is a very good man," and perhaps really would be let out any day. Jalil didn't ask for much: just for him to send a telegram to Baku, Quba Street, to Shahmad Emin-oglu, saying Jalil was "very ill." If he did that, Jalil would remember to the day he died, and "uncle" could demand Jalil's service and loyalty. Jalil was embarrassed to ask: he didn't like to bother "an uncle he didn't know." Finally, he said:

"Uncle, I swear, if Allah showed me the heavens and the earth a second time, I won't forget this service. That's all, I've give you an oath."

Aleksi promised to do what Jalil asked, and Jalil recovered his good mood. He started joking and retelling the Nasreddin stories. In a quiet, sweet voice he sang a *shikasta* and a *bayat*, comforting himself and shedding a few tears at the same time.

When Marusia was mentioned, there was more laughter, mockery, and happy joking in the dungeon. In the end Jalil sighed deeply and said:

"*Allah il-allah*. We're laughing, while Allah sees everything.

Perhaps the devil sent her: go and bring poor Jalil's soul. Perhaps Jalil will go to see Allah tonight ...*Allah il-allah*!"

Jalil's words dried everyone's mouth; they all felt a chill, and their bodies bristled; they fell silent and surrendered to their own thoughts.

A long time passed. Nobody knew whether it was midday or evening, whether it was cold or hot outside, raining, or sunny.

A mouse stole Jalil's hat, ran over Aleksi's chest, and bit Kvachi on the foot. After a while Kvachi's tearful, whispered pleas could be heard:

"Uncle, dear uncle ... You're my only hope while I'm here ... After this I'm your slave, your servant ..."

Uncle Aleksi was muttering: "Yes, lad, yes. I'll do as I promised. Because you've been such a friend to Silovan. You've looked after him so well and been a brother to him."

Kvachi was recalling more and more events which involved Silovan in trouble and Kvachi giving fraternal help.

Suddenly the doors banged. They all pricked up their ears.

"Aleksi Iremadze!"

"I'm here! He's here. Here, here," they repeated in Russian.

"Come out quick," said the guard in Russian.

They all stirred,

"Uncle, my uncle! ... You're my only hope ... Only you ..."

"Yes, lad, yes. Stay calm. I'll do as I promised, goodbye, Kvachi. Goodbye, Jalil."

"Goodbye, goodbye. Jalil, go round me. Careful, uncle, don't fall in the pit, or we're all doomed."

They both laid hands on Aleksi and with great care conducted him to the end of the wall and then led him up the steps.

"Goodbye," groaned Kvachi once more, as he put his lips to Aleksi's hand in the darkness."

Goodbye, uncle," said Jalil. "Don't forget: Quba Street, Mahmud Emin-oglu ... Jalil is very ill."

"Come on out, what's keeping you?" said the guard in Russian.

"Coming, comrade, coming."

Iremadze left. The doors were locked again. Kvachi and Jalil at first laughed sarcastically at the mention of the dungeon's pit, snakes, and other foul creatures, then lay down in separate corners and dreamed prisoner's dreams: warm sun ... happy streets ... people ... beautiful women ... a nicely furnished flat ... friends ... relatives ... a good dinner ... a soft bed ...

Aleksi Iremadze quickly trotted off. He crept like a thief into his own home: his thirty-year-old daughter Elena greeted him with laughter and tears. They hugged each other as if Aleksi had returned from the next world. Aleksi told Elena that he'd been in a nice room all day, and added:

"My girl, I've got to save a very good man from death. Our Silovan had a close and well-known friend, Kvachi Kvachantiradze. They lived five years together in Moscow, in prison and in Siberia. Kvachantiradze several times saved our Silovan from great danger. If I hadn't met Kvachantiradze "there", I wouldn't have come back alive. Now he himself is in danger. He expects to be shot. He's a decent and kind man. Listen to me carefully, my girl. If anyone should ask you, tell them you know him, that on your birthday, 5 April, Kvachantiradze had supper with us and stayed until morning. He's tall, thirty-five years old, dark haired, clipped moustache, and has a scar on his chin. Have you got that?"

"Yes, papa, I'll say that. What will the other guests say?"

"I'm going to see and tell them all now. Let's go together if you like."

"Let's go."

They left. That evening and the next day they went and saw everyone and rehearsed them: "Tall ... black-haired ... has a scar on his chin. A decent and very kind man."

Of course they knew Kvachi. The whole country knows him, everyone.

All the guests consented. Then Aleksi sent a telegram to Baku: "Jalil is very ill. Iremashvili."

A few days later Kvachi was summoned by his interrogator. Greatly heartened, Kvachi rushed into the interrogator's room and called out: "I've remembered, I've remembered!"

"What have you remembered?"

"I finally remembered that from nine in the evening of 5 April until six the next morning I was having supper with Aleksi Iremadze ..." and he gave a detailed description of the supper and a list of all the other guests. "I can name Aleksi Iremadze, his daughter Elena, and ten guests. Please summon and question them all. Draw up a statement."

Kvachi wrote down the story with such ardor, sincerity, and clarity that the interrogator was at a loss what to do. The statement was drawn up and Kvachi went back down to his dark dungeon.

After a few days Aleksi, Elena, and their guests were indeed-summoned. They all gave the agreed evidence that Kvachi had spent the whole night at that supper:

"Kvachi Kvachantiradze? Who doesn't know him! Thirty-five years old, tall, black-haired, has a scar on his chin, right?"

"Yes indeed, he has a scar."

"He spent from nine to six with us. Nobody else apart from him turned up that evening. There wasn't anybody around. We danced, sang, ate, and had a good time.

Twelve people swore, confirmed, and signed the statement.

Two weeks later Kvachi turned up with his luggage at Aleksi Iremadze's house. There was great joy and celebration, with tears, embraces, kisses, and shouts of regret. Aleksi and Elena greeted him like their own son or brother.

"You did right, Kvachi, to come straight to me from that place."

"What could I do, uncle, I didn't want to, I was unwilling to bother you, but I couldn't wait. How could I put off thanking you?"

After a lot of concerned questions and breakfast, Kvachi boldly and coolly told Aleksi:

"Uncle, if you don't take me in, there's nowhere for me to go now. They've taken away my room. You'll have to lodge me for a week and lend me a bit of money. My mother's gone to Sukhumi to buy a house."

"All right, Kvachi, I can let you have my study. How much money do you want?"

"Let's talk Turkish liras or in gold. My clothes have all rotted. My landlord's robbed me, I've lost everything: fine furniture from three rooms, four sets of clothes, three pairs of boots, twelve sets of linen, two full bookcases, and a piano. That adds up to two thousand roubles' losses. I've laid a complaint, I've had the couple arrested; they seem to have found almost everything, but, you know, until the case is dealt with …"

Quite apart from all this, Kvachi had a lot of other wealth: a big palace in Sololaki … even Aleksi knew this palace, probably. Also, he had four fine houses in Batumi and Sukhumi; two had been requisitioned, but he had two left. In addition, he had three orchards in Guria, Mingrelia, and Sukhumi, two sawmills, and a lot of other property, but …

"Let me sum up how I stand today: three employees and a mother, poor old woman, are keeping an eye on all this. I've got more than half of it back, and we'll be given back the rest soon."

What's more, he had due to him two thousand roubles he'd lent to friends. All in all, Kvachi Kvachantiradze could "temporarily" make do with a hundred lira. Aleksi gave him fifty for now, would borrow and give him the rest in the evening. He added:

"Go to the bathhouse now, son, then do the rounds, see your friends, see to your affairs."

That evening Kvachi invited Aleksi and Elena to the cinema, then he took them to the public gardens and treated them to supper. From then on he became a family member; they didn't want to part, and there was nothing to divide them. Kvachi got up first and was never idle in the household for a single hour: he was always attending to something. If something was broken, he mended it or cobbled it together. Aleksi was very grateful to be able to pay off his debt; he unexpectedly received a whole pack of liras and added to Kvachi:

"I've had a small debt repaid, and the rest is profit I made on a deal."

Kvachi and Elena often sat on their own in a corner, or went for a walk. Soon Elena, who was no longer young, changed visibly: she would walk about distracted, forgetting everything, getting easily upset and, for whole hours when Kvachi was out, she sat alone, thinking about something.

Kvachi meant to move to other accommodation soon, but he was not allowed to. He once told Aleksi:

"Uncle, your house used to be worth twenty thousand roubles. Now you'd be lucky to get three thousand."

"Never mind about three, I'd let it go if I were offered two thousand. I'm fed up with this house: it's bled me dry and aged me. It's five years since I've had a penny from it. A third of my income I have to spend on the house. I've meant to sell it for some time, but Elena doesn't want to sell. What can I do? It's her dowry."

"Two thousand a month now, at the very least, will give a thousand profit."

"That's what I say, but what can I do, I'm no businessman, and I haven't got Silovan here."

Kvachi very slowly coaxed Aleksi. Kvachi was expert at business. He had a lot of experience. He had a very good business going in Sukhumi, but he'd had a lot of bother. Now he often bought and sold other people's goods, but still made good money. He had a colleague in the lower market who'd gone bankrupt. He was selling his property at half price, because he was in a hurry. Kvachi and Aleksi should go and take a look.

They did go and take a look. Aleksi brought a dealer he knew with him. The property and a shop really were being sold at half price.

Aleksi pondered. The bankrupt merchant was in a hurry. Kvachi said:

"Make a decision, uncle. I'm putting two thousand lira into the business. I've got a lot of friends who are begging and pestering me."

Elena took Kvachi's side. At first shyly, then persistently, she demanded that the house be sold. Elena would be the accountant, Kvachi would do the trading, Aleksi would manage it overall and inspect the books once a week.

Earlier Elena had clung to the house, and now it was Aleksi. A week later Kvachi took Aleksi and Elena back to the middle market, showed them the former shop, which was full of goods, and announced that he had a half-share in the business. Two men were trading there.

Beso Shikia backed Kvachi up. He gave Kvachi a stuffed envelope:

"Here, Kvachi, take this to the bank. There's exactly three thousand lira. It's on your way, so don't say no."

Kvachi put the envelope in his breast pocket. Aleksi asked him: "What's your daily turnover?"

"In total, it comes to five thousand lira."

"Profit?"

"The net profit would be a third."

When they were going back home, Aleksi lagged behind, walking thoughtfully as he calculated: "That amounts to 150 lira a day, which makes about four thousand lira profit. Four thousand! My share will come to 1,300 lira. Converted to vouchers, that will make … will make …"

It made twenty gold, or two billion paper roubles.

"If we add my two thousand to the capital, the turnover goes up by a third, so the net monthly profit will rise to six thousand. My share will be two thousand, that's seventy lira a day ... God almighty! How will I spend so much money?"

Aleksi at the time was spending sixty liras a month; if he increased his spending five-fold and spent three hundred, there'd still be from 1,500 to 1,700 lira left over. That would make twenty thousand a year, so that he could buy in a year ten houses like the one he now had. If he put all the profit in the business together, it would be forty to sixty thousand lira by the end of the year.

Aleksi's calculations were fuzzy. He was incapable of exact mental arithmetic. He needed pencil, paper, and solitude. He was now a man possessed, and his brain was feverish. He quickened his pace. He was in a hurry to draw up the real accounts. Only when they got home, did he notice that Kvachi was missing: he thought, "He's probably gone to deposit the money in the bank."

He locked himself in his study and got down to the figures. He calculated very carefully, allowing for expenses that reduced the income. But the profit still came to forty thousand liras. He didn't trust himself. He went out and had a chat with some friends. They all said that money traders paid 25-30 percent interest, so trade in goods must give a profit of 40-50 percent. Aleksi came back convinced and more enthusiastic. Now he was impatient for Kvachi to return. He started talking to Elena.

"These days only an idle wastrel hangs on to his house and money," he told her. "They all say that a rouble doubles itself in a month today."

He said about Kvachi: "I've never met a man as decent, hardworking, and diligent as him. He's busy all day, he can squeeze blood from a stone, he makes so much money."

He praised Kvachi for a long time, and then they both went to bed.

Aleksi couldn't get to sleep. He turned like a spit-roast all night, calculating huge profits, thinking how to spend them, or, to scare the devil and bring on sleep, repeating: "Twice two is four … twice three is six … twice six is eight … twice eight is six."

Kvachi didn't come back that night. When Aleksi fell asleep, the cockerels had already crowed for the second time.

The next day Aleksi impatiently waited for Kvachi. Kvachi came for dinner. Elena opened the door and reproached him as strongly—"Where were you?"—as a wife does a husband. Kvachi kissed Elena's hand. Then there was whispering, followed by silence and more whispering. Aleksi coughed and greeted Kvachi. Elena blushed and announced:

"Papa, Kvachi's mother has arrived."

They rejoiced. Kvachi didn't want to bother them, so his mother had stopped with a relative. But, of course, she'd come the very next day to meet them and offer her thanks.

After dinner Kvachi made a brief, curt announcement:

"Uncle Aleksi, it's time I let you know what I've been keeping to myself. Elena, don't go, you should be here to listen. Why should I hide it from you: Elena and I are in love. Give us your blessing."

This was too sudden for Aleksi. He was at first silent, then he blinked, rubbed his eyes and murmured as he embraced one, then the other:

"My dear Elena … My Kvachi … Children … God send you happiness … My children … My dear Elena … My Kvachi!"

Elena burst into tears. Kvachi walked about, erect and proud at having not only saved Aleksi from death, but now having brought unbounded prosperity and happiness to his family. After a little while Kvachi and Aleksi went into the study, where Kvachi said:

"You must give me your word of honor, uncle Aleksi, that you'll keep all this a secret for two weeks. And Elena must keep quiet about it. Later we can celebrate our engagement. I shan't tell my mother. We have to keep it quiet. Don't ask me why. I'll tell you later."

Aleksi gave his word of honor. Then he unburdened himself

of the worries that he had been harboring. He had decided to sell the house, because "in our times only a loser hangs on to both house and money." Kvachi should make him a business partner.

Kvachi thought hard, then beat around the bush. True, business was going very well, but ... His mother had brought five thousand lira, and Kvachi had invested them in the business. Gold was business. Expanding was a good idea, but ... Kvachi was wary: he was very cautious and calculating. It would be bad if ... In a nutshell, he'd think about it.

Finally, Kvachi as good as refused Aleksi's offer, even though the latter was pleading with him. True, the house was Elena's dowry, but as long as Aleksi was alive, he had to live and retire. Kvachi relented. He would ask his other partners. Today? Fine, because Aleksi was in such a hurry, he would give his answer today. The final price for the house? What? Three thousand? No, the house couldn't fetch three thousand now ... All right. Kvachi would look for a buyer. He'd try asking for as much as five, so let the final price be two thousand five hundred.

They drank the health of the betrothed couple. All three rejoiced and celebrated their happiness. Aleksi burst into tears again, Elena was flushed and laughing with joy, while Kvachi kept smiling and looking pleased with himself.

The next day Kvachi brought some Azeri to take a look at the house. They started bargaining hard: the house was praised, criticized, made much of, and belittled. After three days they went to the notary. That evening Aleksi paid out two hundred and fifty gold roubles to Kvachi and was given a signed receipt ...

"Just in case ... who knows, we're only human ..."

"Kvachi Kvachantiradze promises to pay Aleksi Iremadze one third of the profits on turnover and on cash receipts ... I suppose that's how a trading partnership contract is drawn up," Aleksi thought, as he put Kvachi's signed paper in his documents drawer.

Next day Kvachi moved to a new apartment: he found it

awkward to stay with his prospective father-in-law. He then vanished for three days. Elena's face was grim; she didn't know what to do with herself. Aleksi went to the lower market three times, but couldn't find Kvachi or his partner Beso Shikia. In the end Aleksi was told: "We don't know any Kvachi Kvachantiradze."

"What do you mean? Then whose shop is this? What? Shvelia's? And Shikia was just an assistant? And you don't even know where he lives? He's gone to Russia?"

Crazed and stunned, Aleksi staggered back home; tormented by suspicion, his pallid lips whispered: "God almighty! God, spare me the shame and the misfortune … Almighty God … God almighty!"

Aleksi walked up and down Vardisubani Street three times. Kvachi had come down that street. Everywhere he was told:

"He doesn't live here … We don't know him … We haven't heard anything."

Somebody said they'd seen Kvachi playing roulette in the *Arto* club: he was a big client at that club, he spent a lot of money there, and had his eye on a Jewish woman, Rachel. Did Aleksi really not know who Rachel was? The whole of Tbilisi knew. She was the mistress of Janoiani, then of Mamedov, then of some NEP businessman. Now Kvachantiradze had snatched her from all of them. The gamblers all came to life when Kvachi turned up at the club: he didn't sit down to supper until he had a dozen men and women sitting round him.

At nine in the evening Aleksi hung about the doors of the *Arto*. At eleven Kvachi arrived by car at the door. Four people, two men and two women, got out. All four were dressed to kill, so that Aleksi stood aside in embarrassment to let them pass. Then he quickly doffed his hat, went up to Kvachi, who was passing arrogantly, and with a disdainful, embarrassed smile muttered: "Kvachi … Kvachi, my boy …"

Kvachantiradze, barely looking at him, brusquely responded,

"I haven't got time," before mingling with the others.

Neither Aleksi nor Elena slept that night. Embittered and enraged, Aleksi paced the room, brandished his fists, and threatened Kvachi:

"If that's how it is, I'll show you, you scoundrel, you … You deserve a thrashing, you pickpocket! Just you wait … Just you wait …"

The next day Aleksi found out where Kvachi was living and waited outside his house for two hours. Finally, Kvachi emerged. Aleksi blocked his path. They did not exchange greetings.

"I want a couple of words with you … What does this mean?"

"Nothing," Kvachi gravely and calmly replied, with a hint of a smile. "I'm going to start the business I promised shortly."

"What do you mean, start it? Before this you told me that the business was yours and Beso Shikia's!"

"That's not true. I never said that. I said I and Shikia were buying it."

Kvachi wasn't going to listen to Aleksi's protests. Aleksi had lent Kvachi two thousand five hundred roubles, so that was all Kvachi owed him. No more to be said! When was he going to start trading? Soon … He couldn't give the actual date. Shikia had gone to Istanbul to bring goods. If Aleksi couldn't wait and didn't want to be a partner any more, then he could have his money back … When? When Shikia brought the goods back and they'd been sold. That's all there was to it. Why had Kvachi stopped visiting Aleksi and his daughter? A very delicate question … Kvachi found it awkward to talk about, but since Aleksi insisted on knowing, he would say why:

"I didn't know that Elena once had an affair with Vano Khrameli."

"What? That business twelve years ago? Just a simple schoolchildren's infatuation? That's all dead and buried, isn't it?"

Kvachi didn't know, he wasn't sure. Everything might still be

… nobody knows. No! Kvachi's family is too good for him to bring in spoilt goods or cracked vases.

"Are you threatening me again?" asked Kvachi. "Don't forget I was having supper with you on 5 April when you read a proclamation out loud and made a counter-revolutionary speech. Twelve people have confirmed in writing that I was there. What? You didn't read out a proclamation? You didn't make a speech? Four of your guests in the presence of several witnesses have confirmed that you did. Are a dozen witnesses not enough? Didn't you yourself tell me 'down there' in the dungeon? Don't you remember Jalil? He's a witness, too."

Kvachantiradze advised Aleksi to keep quiet, for that would be in Aleksi's own interests. He had great respect for Aleksi, his household, his family, his reputation, but only so far … anyway, it would be best if they both kept quiet. Kvachi was very busy just now: he had urgent things to see to, and he was late, in any case.

"Goodbye. Jalil, let's go."

With haughty strides Kvachi went to his car, where the tall Turk was sitting next to the chauffeur. Proudly stretching inside the car, Jalil smiled at Aleksi. Aleksi went home, more dead than alive.

Elena had virtually stopped eating or speaking to anyone. She stayed in the house, crying, grieving, and silently reproaching her father. Every utterance she made, her sadness and tears penetrated Aleksi's heart like bullets: in a month he had become bent, elderly, white, thin, and shrunken. Every now and again, when he thought about his lost house and his heartbroken daughter, he would become fiery, restless, and hot-tempered: he would race around his room like a madman, brandishing his fists at Kvachi, menacing him: "Just you wait … Just you wait … I'll show you, you scoundrel, you … Just you wait … Just you wait …"

One day the tall Turk came into Aleksi's room:

"Hello, uncle! I'm Jalil," he said, smiling with his walnut-sized eyes and flashing his white horse's teeth.

"Jalil, it's you, is it?" asked Aleksi, his depression lifting.

"It's me Jalil, didn't you recognize me? It was very dark 'down there'."

"Sit down, Jalil, sit down. Tell me how you are."

"*Chok raziam* (Very well), uncle sir. My brother helped me out. He got your telegram. *Chok raziam, chok.* Take this present, uncle sir." Jalil opened a little bundle and spread out a beautiful yard-long rug.

"Jalil, why go to all that trouble? Why was it necessary?"

"Uncle sir, your telegram helped me a lot. Please take it, or I'll be very hurt. Take it, uncle, take it."

Jalil smiled as he begged and pleaded. Aleksi thanked him effusively, gave him tea with brandy to drink, and offered him fruit.

"Now I'm working for Kvachantiradze. He's a good boss. He's got lots of money. He's a joker. He played a nasty joke on you 'down there'; he's tricked others, too. We laughed a lot. Once he fell in the pit himself."

"He fell in? Well, how did he get out again?"

Jalil guffawed: "Uncle sir, Kvachantiradze was joking. There was no pit. Ha-ha-ha."

Aleksi couldn't help comparing this uncouth rough-mannered Turk with the sophisticated, educated Kvachantiradze, and he felt upset, angry, and disturbed. Once Jalil had gone, Aleksi brandished his fists again, muttering: "Just you wait ... just you wait, you pickpocket, you scoundrel. Just wait, just wait."

Very soon the day dawned for Aleksi's revenge and Kvachi's judgement: Kvachi was imprisoned again and thrown into the same dark dungeon with "snakes, lizards, frogs, and other foul things." His partner Shiladze had been arrested a few days earlier and made to confess: Shiladze had said that on 5 April, at two in the morning, he and Kvachi had robbed an Armenian in Vera gardens.

Aleksi rushed round his room anxiously, repeatedly mumbling: "The mills of God grind slowly, but exceeding small … Almighty God! Wondrous are Thy deeds and severe is Thy justice! Now what do you say, you scoundrel, eh? Who's going to help you now? You're not relying on Aleksi Iremadze, are you? I'll help you all right! I'll cast the first stone!"

Aleksi anticipated revenge, but …

Soon Aleksi, Elena, and their ten guests were summoned for the second, third, and fourth time by the interrogator. After that Iremadze stopped his threats. For three months now Aleksi, exhausted and drained, had trotted around his guests and whispered fearfully and timidly in a locked room: "I've given evidence that Kvachi Kvachantiradze that night … in a word, nothing's changed in my evidence … don't let them fool you, nobody must take back their word or confess, otherwise … you know what we'll get for giving false evidence? Anyway, the business of the proclamations will come out, too. True, I let you have the proclamations and I read them to you, I made a speech too, but you listened to me, and you talked and took the proclamations with you."

The twelve witnesses again colluded so that this padlock could never be unlocked, not by pliers, or keys, or threats, or kind words. Day and night Aleksi fussed over the padlock, thought and worried about it every day, pondered, gave everyone instructions and warnings, as he selflessly resisted the investigation with fury, obstinacy, and firmness.

Finally they had their day in court. Twelve witnesses swore an oath and then, from morning till evening they all, as one, repeated firmly, stubbornly, and coolly:

"I know Kvachi Kvachantiradze very well. On 5 April we had supper together at Aleksi Iremadze's … He came at nine o'clock precisely and left at six in the morning. He was very drunk. He never left the room. What did he do? What anyone does at a supper! He chatted, sang, flirted, danced, drank, enjoyed himself …

Yes, I swear to this and confirm it."

And they did confirm it. Shiladze's evidence was disbelieved. It was clearly proven that he wanted to avenge himself on Kvachantiradze and get hold of his money. Twenty witnesses stated that the two men had old scores to settle, that Shiladze received a thousand liras from Kvachi to bring goods from Istanbul, but had apparently squandered the money, so had implicated Kvachi to destroy him, but …

"There is still justice in this world," shouted the lawyer. "Nemesis's iron hand has taken Shiladze by the neck, and he flails about in vain thinking he can sully the innocent name of Kvachantiradze with his filth. Let him be the sole person to bear responsibility. And Kvachi Kvachantiradze must be returned to his honorable mother, his chaste fiancée, and to all those friends who are waiting here for your unbiased verdict. The goddess of justice is blindfolded, but not blind. She has already weighed him in her scales. Gentlemen of the court, give us back this young and thoroughly decent man, this talented, clever, ingenious, and useful member of society. You cannot condemn him. Your hand would tremble and your heart pound," Kvachi's lawyer concluded his speech.

The judges' hearts were in fact pounding and their hands were trembling. Shiladze was doomed; Kvachi boldly descended the court's staircase, smiling for joy. He was accompanied on the left by his "chaste fiancée" Rachel, and on the right by his mother, while his lawyer followed behind. Kvachi shook hands with his friends and relatives on the right and the left, telling them:

"Thank you, friends, many thanks. Almighty God has saved me from danger. Thank you … a thousand thanks."

At the door they all embraced. Suddenly Kvachi bumped into Aleksi and Elena.

"Uncle Aleksi! Miss Elena! … My God …" and he embraced Aleksi and kissed Elena's hand. "Thank you, uncle Aleksi. Thank you, Miss Elena … I thank you from the bottom of my heart. I have done you both wrong. But I hope that you've now forgiven me. In my time a fallen man used to be forgiven for everything. Uncle Aleksi," he said, taking Aleksi aside, "you see what that scoundrel Shiladze did to me. He has reaped what he sowed. He squandered so much of my money and nearly dragged me down with him. Don't worry, uncle Aleksi, God is great. I'll still pay you back what I owe ... I'll pay you soon, very soon ..."

Then he turned to everybody:

"Friends. We should celebrate today the supper of 5 April. I invite you all to come at ten to the *Arto*. You too have to do me the honor, Aleksi, and you, Miss Elena! Again, thanks to everyone and good luck. Right then: this evening at ten I expect you all in the *Arto*.

At the supper to mark the 5 April supper, some smiled, some laughed. Jalil sent the car roaring down the streets. After Kvachi, his "chaste" Rachel, his mother, and lawyer left, the others very slowly dispersed. This supper too went on until six the next morning. Kvachi paid a hundred billion paper roubles.

Afterwards, whenever Elena thought of her lost house, she chewed her fingers with frustration. She would not eat, she stayed in the house, wept, and grieved; Aleksi rushed around his room, brandishing his tired fists at his lost son-in-law, threatening him:

"Wait ... just you wait, you pickpocket, you scoundrel, you ... God is great, and will make you pay ... Wait ... Just you wait ..."

"What a show, what a show," Jalil said whenever he recalled all this.

Rachel's Infidelity

Two mountains can never meet, but two human beings always can. That inexorable proverb proved only too true for Kvachi.

That evening Kvachi had just broken the last thread tying him to Rachel. She was a determined woman. All the possessions which she had got by sweating, heavy breathing, and whimpering or howling were on her person: some on her neck, others on her ears, breast, and fingers. Once Rachel went too far, thanks to Kvachi, and got so drunk that he had trouble getting her upstairs; ten minutes after he got her there, he went back down to the car where Valiko Kalmadze was waiting for him.

"Go, Valiko, go. You're in luck: all Rachel talks about is you."

Valiko had his eye on Rachel and was waiting for his turn, but he was still surprised that Kvachi was authorizing him.

"Do I understand you correctly, Kvachi?"

"Yes, that's what I said. I'm fed up with her, I've gone off her."

Valiko went up to see Rachel, and Kvachi rejoined the company.

The next day a panicky Rachel rushed to Kvachi: "My treasure! My earrings! My rings! They've taken them, they've taken everything!"

"Who? Who took them?"

Rachel didn't know. Either Kvachi, or a servant, or even … Valiko.

"Valiko? Was Valiko with you last night?"

"Yes, he dropped in for a minute." But Rachel didn't remember, because she was very drunk.

For a minute? Ha-ha-ha! Kvachi knew everything, he did. Valiko left Rachel's room at five in the morning. Kvachi had been watching Rachel for some time. This morning the truth finally emerged: "Ugh, you two-faced whore, you lying woman!"

Forgive her, Kvachi, forgive her. Rachel was really drunk. It's your fault that she was unfaithful: yours! Why did you pester her yesterday and make her drink so much champagne?

No, it's all over. There's no more to be said. Kvachi can't forgive infidelity. Blood will have to be shed, blood. There's no point pleading with Kvachi, Rachel. No point wetting your swollen cheeks with tears. In one night you've lost a rich lover and twenty years hard work. It's your fault. You asked for it. You won't be getting drunk again. You'll have to start all over again using the well-worn tools of your trade if you're going to have a secure old age. Don't cry. Your tears won't wash the bile off Kvachi. How about your jewelry? Kvachi will help you. But don't expect anything else from him. He'll help you recover your losses, but on one condition: you keep your mouth shut and don't take it out on Valiko. Valiko is Kvachi's friend and has an unsullied reputation. Don't ruin a young lad, don't bring shame on his respectable parents.

Kvachi and Valiko got down to business. They had trouble coming to an agreement. "Tomorrow or the day after" never ended. Beso was the intermediary, by slowly dripping into Rachel's wan ear the sweet poison: "Rachel, Kvachi is forgetting about your infidelity … Kvachi loves you again … he loves you more than ever. Kvachi will come back to you, for sure, but you must give Valiko the benefit of the doubt and not ruin him … Kvachi will recompense you for your loss, he'll pay you back double."

Kvachi soothed the grief and went back to Rachel. Rachel, he's forgotten your infidelity. Make up, and mend love's broken threads. Compared with Kvachi's love, that jewelry's not worth mentioning. Kvachi has forgotten your infidelity, Rachel. So you, in turn, should forget that thief Valiko and your shoddy baubles. How much were your things worth? Ten thousand? No more? Is it worth ruining Valiko for the sake of a few pennies? Kvachi can repay you that money in a couple of months. He certainly will, certainly. He'll buy exactly the same things, or pay you in cash. So you've made up? You've forgotten the jewelry you've lost and the infidelity? Excellent! Nothing could be better. Peace and love for body and soul, for both of you. Live like brother and sister, husband and wife, as sweetly as Adam and Eve. Whatever you say, in this harsh life all you have left is love and enjoyment. So love one another like doves. Embrace one another like starving wolves, be as cuddly as monkeys, and as randy as cats.

Slow down, Kvachi. Don't be too much in a hurry to break the worn out threads of love, don't be such an oaf as to tear your tired heart from Rachel's bedraggled breast. Be cautious … take your time … gradually … That's right, just pull the threads gently. Today you're ill, tomorrow you can't come to the house to see her, the next day you have urgent business. The following day you're going to Kutaisi, then … Then let Beso take your place in Rachel's bed. No, Kvachi, you're not to shoot Beso! Kvachi, Kvachi! You're not to kill Rachel. Don't kill her. Calm down, Kvachi, calm down … Come to your senses … Your love affair is over. Over forever. Two hearts, once joined, are torn apart. The dove's nest is smashed. Don't cry, Kvachi. Don't cry. Your best friend and your mistress have both betrayed you. Ugh, what snakes' offspring they are. Ugh, treacherous friends. Ugh, ungrateful and two-faced. Goodbye, Rachel! Goodbye, Beso! God help you both. As you have fallen in love, Kvachi won't stand in your way or try to part you. Goodbye … goodbye …

Raking Over the Past, and a Miracle

This terrible event happened on the terrible and unforgettable night when mountain failed to meet mountain, when Kvachi broke with Rachel and then, on his own stairs, bumped into a person he had forgotten.

"Stop! Hands up! Don't move, or I'll finish you off here and now."

Calm down, citizens, take it easy. Kvachi is stopping, of course he is … He's raising his hands, too; he's not moving. Kvachi is unarmed, so he very humbly begs you to lower your guns, or not aim them at him, or there might be an accident … who knows how often these things happen.

"Anyway, who are you? Kvachi Kvachantiradze?"

"That's me. What can I do for you? I don't know you."

"But we know you. However, do you really not recognize me? Well, take a good look at me and try to remember."

God almighty! Five years ago, in Ukraine ... That *chekist* Chinov was watching Kvachi as a cat watches a mouse. He finally caught Kvachi when the latter turned the tables on him and jumped on the cat. That was when Pavlov and Beso performed their brilliant "act": they grabbed Kvachi and got this cat in the trap. Then the *chekist* gave them the slip as they were traveling ... After that furious battle ... slaughter ... blood.

"I had it coming to me," Kvachi growled to himself as he followed the *chekists*. I had a hundred chances to slip away, but put it off each time. I wanted to get four times and five times as much loot. A greedy idiot always loses one when he's trying to catch two. Beso, why didn't you persuade me, why didn't you drag me by force out of this Red "paradise"?

Kvachi was searched, registered, and, an hour later, taken away. Now he had three interrogators going for him. The *chekist* was sitting there too, smiling triumphantly. My God! They seemed to know everything, everything. They'd read his life like a good novel. They moved from page to page, leafing through it. Finally, they said: "Confess."

Instead of replying, Kvachi smiled and asked:

"Just tell me where and how you got all this information."

"Is it true or not?"

"It's worse than the truth. If I'd kept a diary, I couldn't have written better than that."

The three men were flattered by the praise for their clever work.

"Well," exclaimed Kvachi's chief interrogator. "We're professionals."

"Comrades, I'm not exaggerating: I've never seen such a neat piece of work, in real life or in a novel."

"In that case ..."

"In that case, if I sat here thinking for ten years, I couldn't come up with any more. You've got it all written down, everything. Amazing work, amazing. Take a cigarette each, comrades, it's very good tobacco."

"So shall we start writing?"

"Let's begin."

They wrote for three evenings and three mornings. When they finally finished, Kvachi said:

"You don't need me any more. Do take another cigarette each. Take me off to Metekhi prison. It's good tobacco, isn't it. An old general sells it. It's cheap, but it's good. The general lives at 4 St David's Street. I said, you can take me to Metekhi. When my turn comes, you can take me to Saburtalo cemetery."

"Do you think that's how your case will end?"

"Of course, I'm ready for it. I've run out of road. I'm sorry for anyone who hasn't lived, but I've had my share of life and I've taken thousands of shares from others. So my final request is: send me to Metekhi."

"All right, we'll think about it."

They thought about it for a week, then summoned Kvachi and sent him to Metekhi. They brought him to the building that looks out onto the River Mtkvari and the bathhouses. They opened up a cell and at once locked the doors on him. Kvachi stood there, as if struck by lightning. On a bunk in front of him sat Pavlov, staring back open-mouthed.

"Pavle, you? Here?"

Pavle turned his face away, then back and mumbled: "I … I … you …" Tears poured down his moustache and beard. He could not speak. He stood up and wiped his eyes.

"Sit down. Sit down and tell me." Kvachi forced Pavlov to sit, then sat by his side. Pavle again burst into tears and whispered: "Serves me right, it does. That's what traitors deserve. I … you … I'm a real rogue, a real rogue. Any day they'll bump me off … I don't deserve better."

They were silent for a while, then Kvachi put a hand on Pavlov's shoulder, asking him gently: "Pavle, stay calm; tell me how it happened."

"It's simple. We asked you ten times, we asked you a hundred times. We said let's get out of here, let's escape, it's too dangerous."

"True."

"You didn't believe us."

"That's true, too. I didn't believe you, I was out of my mind."

"I couldn't go on my own. I didn't have the money."

"Why didn't you ask me for it?"

"Because … I wouldn't have gone without you. Then I happened to come across the safe fixed in the wall. I opened it and … I broke into it … I couldn't stop myself. I deserve all this, serves me right."

"What then?"

"Then I packed up the treasure and set off for Batumi. Someone had his eye on me on the way there. I got off at Batumi. He was following me. I dodged about, but he kept on my trail. I went to a hotel. He followed me in. I got a room. I hid the treasure quickly in a tall iron stove, covered it in ash, and then moved to a different room. An hour later I was arrested."

Only now did Kvachi pay attention to a second prisoner lying snuffling on another bunk.

"Don't worry," said Pavlov. "That man sleeps so deep even a cannon wouldn't wake him; anyway, he doesn't speak Russian."

"Go on, go on."

"Give me a cigarette first. Thanks. They searched the room where they arrested me, but didn't even look in the other one."

"So the treasure …"

"Is probably still in the stove. It's summer, nobody's going to light a fire. I don't think anyone will think of cleaning out the ash, either."

"They put me in prison. I was in prison in Batumi for two months, then they transferred me here. I wanted to get a message to you, but …"

"But what?"

"Well, I was embarrassed. Several times I meant to, but who could I trust with a message? If I told anyone, he'd go to Batumi himself and grab the treasure. I sat here in torment, waiting for something to happen. I don't even know what I was expecting."

"Today."

Pavlov took heart: "Yes, yes, today, today's lucky coincidence. You'll get out, you'll get out soon and …"

"Take it easy, Pavle, calm down. I'll be leaving here the same way as you. Don't let's deceive each other. We're finished."

"We are," Pavlov agreed.

"We've got to let Silibistro or Beso know about the hiding place. At least they can benefit from it. Now tell me, who is that man stretched out so happily?"

"Him? Some idiot. He was arrested by chance. Any day they'll let him go. He's sick."

"What's wrong with him?"

"Sleeping sickness. He gets up only to eat. I did tell you even a cannon won't wake him."

Kvachi sat by the window, watching the town. Down below, at the bottom of the cliff, he could see a strip of the River Mtkvari where the warm water emerges from the bathhouses; women with their skirts hitched up to their thighs were washing their clothes. On the right he could see Nariqala castle. Underneath its tower and rocks lay the botanical gardens. To the left and straight opposite, donkeys were hauling charcoal and sour cream up and down the mountain paths. On the banks of the Mtkvari an Azeri family was sitting down to tea on a broad balcony. In another house a gramophone was belting out a hoarsely sung *bayat*. Somewhere a broken-down barrel-organ was screeching.

Kvachi sat there contemplating his fate. So here was the place and time that fate had finished its pursuit of Kvachi. This was where the angel of death had caught up with him. This was how his colorful and tortuous life was ending. And how? In such an ungodly, inhuman, and worthless way? Who knows or could count how often he had evaded death by misadventure, how many times he had slipped free of the greased noose. The whole country had been hunting Kvachantiradze down, but he had hidden under a hat of invisibility. He'd evaded German cruisers, he'd been bayoneted and hacked to pieces on Demir-Tepe plateau, but he'd got back on his feet and into the saddle. They'd put up the gallows for him in Peter and Paul prison, but he'd escaped from there, too. In the fields of the Ukraine with nine men he'd defeated forty and broken out of Red traps ten times. But now ... here, in his motherland ... now ... Suppose ...Suppose Kvachi failed to break down another thick wall and melt down another iron cage? God almighty, help Kvachi. All-powerful God, help that unbeliever Kvachi once more. God in heaven, perform one more miracle. Your insatiable Kvachi will return for ever to Your holy kingdom, he will build You three churches, will dutifully magnify Your name, and faithfully serve Your glorious church. God, hear Kvachi's prayer! God, send him a miracle and give your servant Kvachi freedom, life, and happiness.

Kvachi prayed ardently and thought intensely. His brain was on fire. A light appeared on his forehead. Lightning flashed in his eyes. His heart raced and his soul seethed.

Finally he stood up and was rigid. But a smile played on his clenched lips and the furrows on his forehead disappeared. He fell upon the sleeping prisoner and shook him hard.

"Hey you, brother. Get up! Get up! Get up! I said, wake up!"

He turned him over this way and that several times, he pulled his feet, rubbed his ears, and forced his eyelids open.

"I said wake up! I think you've been called. What's your name?

Ah, Ivane? Pavle, write it down. Your father's name? Surname? Chilikashvili? Pavle, write it down! How old are you? Where are you from? Pavle, make sure you get it right. What were you arrested for? Fine. That's all. Nobody was calling for you. Go back to sleep."

Kvachi then turned to Pavlov: "Do you get it? Didn't you? I'll be out in a day or two ... I said, I'll be out! Yes, I will. I will! Can I get you released? Of course I can. But you have to help me. Tell me one thing: do the warders know this prisoner, or not?"

"Nobody knows him. He was brought in the day before yesterday. So far he hasn't been taken into the yard."

"That's very good. Now tell me when are prisoners usually released?"

"In the evening, after nine."

"Very good. Now tell me how I can get hold of some bromine."

"I've got bromine. The doctor gave it to me."

"Really? Then God has heard my prayer. It's three o'clock now. Hey, Ivane! Get up, get up! You're not the only one in this prison, are you? Pavle, lie on your bunk and don't let that idiot come near you. However much he begs you, don't let him lie on his bunk. Hey you, Ivane, I said, get up! There are two bunks here, and three of us. I haven't had a wink of sleep for two days. I'll sleep in the day, you can sleep at night. So get up! It won't break your back! Pavle, wake me up at seven exactly."

Kvachi lay down on Ivane's bunk, while Ivane staggered round the cell, squinting and puffing like a drunken bear. At seven in the evening Pavle woke Kvachi up.

"Brother, you're not ill, are you?" Kvachi asked Ivane.

"Of course I am. I've got a stomach ache."

Stomach? My dear man, why didn't you tell Kvachi? He's a doctor, a famous doctor. He's treated thousands of cases like yours. "Look, we've got the medicine. Pavle, bring that bromine. Now, take that and lie down."

Five minutes later Ivane was snoring happily. Kvachi rushed about nervously. Nine o'clock … ten … eleven … The prisoners due for release were released. The prison's murmurs and buzz gradually died down.

Kvachi can't sleep and won't let poor Ivane sleep. He lies on Ivane's bunk, staring at the ceiling. Only in the evening does he give Ivane Chilikashvili his "stomach medicine" and send him to sleep. He himself gets up at first light and wakes Ivane. Sometimes Ivane lies on the floor, but this is when Kvachi wants to pace up and down the narrow cell. When Ivane is sprawling on the bunk, this is the time when Kvachi wants to sleep. Kvachi takes no exercise and won't let Ivane do so, either. The cell is kept locked. Kvachi is waiting for something, waiting, seething inside and feeling faint at the same time.

He could barely get through the fourth day. For the thousandth time he'd paced the cell. Ivane was hunched against the wall, not daring to lie on the bunk, which Kvachi had taken over.

"Brother, don't lie on my bunk or you'll infect my bedding with lice," said Kvachi.

As soon as it began to get dark, Kvachi gave Ivane the last dose of bromine: "Take it and go to sleep."

Ivane took the bromine and lay down. He slept like the Turkish cemetery at the bottom of the hill, visible from the window. It was eight o'clock. Kvachi, all on edge, ran up and down the cell like a wild hyena. It was half past eight … Nine … Half past nine. Kvachi was in the corridor standing by the window overlooking the courtyard. A prison guard began shouting: "Giorgi Chokrishvili-i-i!"

Instantly several guards' voices echoed: "Giorgi Chokhrishvili! Chokarishvili!" Somewhere a voice came: "Here, here!" Four surnames were read out … five, six, seven. Suddenly the courtyard echoed: "Ivane Chilakashvili! Ivane Sirikashvili! Ivane Lichikashvili!" as the guards repeatedly distorted the name.

"He's here, here," Kvachi yelled in Georgian and Russian, and ran back to the cell. "Pavle, goodbye! Goodbye."

"Goodbye ... for ever ... forever ..." muttered Pavlov, hugging Kvachi and letting tears flow down his cheeks.

The real Ivane Chilikashvili was sleeping like a stone. Kvachi quickly bound up his jaws, chin, and lips with a towel (he had toothache, apparently), rammed his hat down over his eyes, thrust his bundle under his arm, and rushed into the corridor. He hunched his back to make himself look small, dropped his head to his chest, and crossed the yard. By the main gate there was a little room.

"Surname and name?" asked the guard, leafing through a thick book.

"I be Ivane Chilikashvili, your honor," said Kvachi, speaking like a bumpkin.

"How old are you?"

"I think I be thirty years old, your honor."

"Thirty?" asked the prison officer, looking hard at Kvachi.

"I think I be, your honor. I don't rightly know, maybe more, maybe less."

"What's wrong with you, why are you bandaged up?"

"Toothache, your honor," Kvachantiradze-Chilikashvili whined.

"When were you brought to Metekhi?"

"It'd be a week now."

Why was this man going on at Kvachi? Why were his eyes drilling into him like an awl? What did he want from Kvachi?

"Why were you arrested?

"Just because ... They had it in for me, your honor, they said I be ..." Then he bit his tongue, turned bright red and became dumbstruck. The prison guard couldn't take his eye off Kvachi's blushing face and smiled for a while. Then he asked: "Do normal people say 'I be' and 'your honor'? 'I be' ... 'I be' ... hmm ..."

"I be from round here, your honor, but twenty years back I started working for an Imeretian, so I speak their way too."

"Who did you work for?"

"Kvachi Kvachantiradze, your honor."

"I know Kvachantiradze, but not by sight. I've heard of him. He's here now."

"Where, your honor?"

"Here in Metekhi. Didn't you know?"

"They did tell me, your honor, but I haven't seen him."

Kvachi, shut up! Shut up. Stop, you've waded in too far, look out ...

"Kvachantiradze's a big man," said the guard, writing something in his book. "The things they say about him!"

"He be a very big man, sirree, very. But it be a pity he be a goner."

"Be a goner! Not 'be a goner,' 'is a goner ... is a goner'. You've been in Imeretia too long."

"You be right, your honor."

"Take this paper with you, or you'll be arrested again. Now go ..." and he turned to a warder. "Show this man out."

"Thank you, your honor, thank you."

The main gates opened with a great creak. Then a second set of doors ... Then a third ... Kvachi felt giddy. His heart nearly stopped. His brain was feverish. The guards at the doors inspected him as if they knew everything. Now he had to pass a soldier, then cross a narrow street, and go down a steep hill. At the bottom of the prison fortress there were more guards. They looked hard at Kvachi, and he almost broke into a run. Once he'd left the prison area, he crossed a small square, then ran across Avlabar bridge and leapt into a cab.

"To Sioni cathedral!"

The cab went down dark streets, passed Sioni and Anchiskhati church, then Vanki quarter, before climbing up past the sappers' barracks on the banks of the Mtkvari. Then it turned left onto the end of Rustaveli Avenue. The place was accursed: a real trap. Kvachi had to come out into Vera quarter. He couldn't avoid the corner of Vera Hill and Moscow Street, where there were police agents every few feet. A trap, a real trap.

"Hey you, brother, speed up. Make those horses move!"

Kvachi ducked down and made himself as small as he could. His neck sank into his shoulders, his hat was rammed down to his nose, his towel was over his lips, he held his breath, and broke into a cold sweat. Quick, quick! Move! Drive faster! Turn left. Now turn right, right! Stop! From now on Kvachi would go on foot, sneaking in and out, covering his tracks, for you never knew ... you never knew.

"Valiko! Valiko, my friend. Thank the Lord you're there to meet me. But be quick. Get moving! Find Beso and Jalil right now. Beso's in hiding? Do you know where he's staying? Not far? Very good. Well, call him quickly, quick."

"Beso, my dear Beso. My loyal friend. How did I get out? I'll tell you in a minute, in a minute. How are you? How's Jalil? How much money have you got?"

"Good man! Beso, excellent. Well, that's the sort of friend I need. So you were working on getting me out? You were going to smuggle me out of prison? You had everything ready? Many thanks, Beso, many thanks. I got out without your help. But my life is still in your hands, for ever. So you sold my property and turned it into cash, did you? You're already ready to leave, are you? This morning, if need be?"

Beso had come to see Kvachi, and let him, like an older brother, hug him once more. Then he ran off to give Jalil the good news.

"So this is what we'll do," said Kvachi. "Tomorrow at first light you and Jalil bring round the car. We'll take the train at Mtskheta. Dress like workers and peasants, let your beards grow, don't wash your face and hands, in fact make sure they're really dirty, get rid of your European suitcases, those big coffers, and put your dirty linen and ordinary stuff in plain baskets and sacks."

Beso had got nicely written identity papers ready in anticipation.

"Right, until tomorrow morning. Goodbye, Beso, goodbye. Bless you for your loyalty, now and for all eternity. Amen."

Fleeing an Ungrateful Motherland

Dressed up as workers and peasants, Kvachi, Beso, and Jalil went to a Batumi hotel.

"Have you got a room?"

"Yes, sir, of course we have."

"Is room seven free?"

"Seven? No, sir, it's taken."

"Six?"

"Available, sir."

They settled in room six. Beso would sneak in to room seven and sniff it out as well as its occupant. Jalil would go to Nuri market and have a quiet talk with some smugglers, while Kvachi wrote a letter.

"My dear Silibistro and Pupi. Our enemies couldn't break us. I've got away again and proved that anyone who tries to destroy a Kvachantiradze will himself be destroyed, or will burn his hand and make a fool of himself. It will be better if I don't visit Georgia. I've lost everything I ever had there. That's the fate of a small nation. We have to devour each other if we want to be sated. I always told you, Silibistro, that Georgia is too small to contain me. Now it's impossible for me to fix anything for myself here. Trade is impossible, so is manufacture, so is money. I'm not going to be an innkeeper and I won't take up petty thieving. If a man is lucky enough to get three roubles here, he's bound to have two taken off him the next day. I can't live in that sort of atmosphere. I'm off. I haven't been able to come and kiss you goodbye, because I've been in a terrible hurry and I'm dogged by danger. Who knows if I'll ever see this accursed country again. If I didn't have you, I wouldn't even have cause to mention the name of Georgia. I'm going to Istanbul, but my heart is with you. If I get on my feet again, I'll bring you out, because I can't manage without you. I have nobody but you. This letter is wet with tears, as you can see. What can I do, my dear parents, my heart aches, and my eyes are burning. But don't cry for your little Kvachi. He won't go under. He is the son of such parents that he can live at the bottom of the sea and squeeze money out of a stone. But if you're sad, then my life will be bitter. There's no alternative, we have to be patient and endure sorrow for a time. As for the people who've done this to us, I'll have my revenge on them in Istanbul or Paris. I hope God won't let me go to the grave with my anger at people here unavenged, or I'll never have any rest. True, now I remember that when I was in Metekhi I prayed to God and promised to light a candle ..." (Kvachi's three churches had shrunk to one candle). "God helped me. Go and light a little candle on my behalf, since there are no churches in Turkey and I won't be able to do as I promised, and God will be angry with me and will destroy me somewhere. Beso is coming too and sends you all his regards. So goodbye! Goodbye! I kiss you a thousand times, and Khukhu and Notio too. Your unlucky and unfortunate son, Kvachi."

Beso came in with a dozen keys. Jalil also returned, saying:

"I've done everything, boss-*agha*. We can go now. We go tonight."

At dinner-time Beso said: "It's time, Kvachi. The man in room seven has gone out to eat."

Jalil stood guard on the stairs. Beso had no trouble opening room seven. Kvachi rushed to the stove, raked the ashes, and exclaimed:

"I've found it, Beso, I've found it."

In five minutes all three had left the hotel and an hour later, dressed as local Ajarians, had walked out of Batumi. A real Ajarian, silent, quick-footed, and farsighted, led the group. All four had walking sticks, to which their bundles were attached. They passed Stepanov's fort on the right, cut through the undergrowth, came onto the bridge across the Çoruh, and went uphill on the left. For some time they crept along in silence. Finally they came to Simoneti village, sneaked into a small wooden hut, and sat down. The Ajarian vanished. The sun went down, and, when it was night, the Ajarian slipped into the hut to say: "Let's go, sir."

The agile and sharp-sighted Ajarian trotted along like a wolf. Kvachi, Beso, and Jalil followed. The fields gave way to thick undergrowth, which soon was mist-filled forest. The road became a path, and then vanished. The slope was ever steeper. There was no moonlight in the forest. They stumbled in the dark, following each other's shadow. Midnight came. They crossed a ridge and came to the edge of the forest.

"Wait for me here, brothers," said the Ajarian, disappearing into the bushes.

"What do you say, Jalil: they won't catch us, will they?"

"They can't, *agha*. Don't worry, I know the rest of the way."

They were silent, then started whispering. The Ajarian came back with someone else. Again, they set off, walking, stumbling, and sweating. Finally they stopped, rested, and found themselves by a rocky, scrub-covered mountain. They tiptoed cautiously on, then the Ajarian started frequently veering from side to side, checking the surroundings, listening, then coming back and becoming even more wary. At one point they all lay down and crawled along, feeling their way. Finally they emerged into a field. The Ajarian turned towards them:

"Brothers, we're on Turkish soil, no more Russian soil."

The refugees yelled with joy, congratulating one another, and then set off further. They were no longer afraid, so walked carefree.

A light appeared and they headed towards it and entered a small coffeehouse. One Ajarian hid in the darkness. At first light he would set off home, taking two local Laz with him. The Ajarians handed the refugees over to the Laz, took payment, and wished them all a safe journey, slung their smuggled goods over their shoulders and left.

Newcomers soon turned up at the coffee house. One was a mounted policeman, the others were soldiers. The policeman inspected the travelers and asked Jalil in Turkish who they were, where they were going, whether they had passports and permission to enter Turkey. The policeman often mentioned the word "Bolshevik", while Jalil kept repeating "*Kuran ahki! Allah ahki! Man manim allahim*! (Brothers in the Koran, brothers in God, God forbid)" Finally the policeman said: "*Gel, gedah*! (Come with me)"

"Let's go, effendi, let's go to see the officer," said Jalil.

They all left. It was light now. They spent two hours sitting and waiting in a house, guarded by a soldier armed with a rifle. Finally the three were called in:

"*Parlez-vous français, monsieur*?" Kvachi asked the tall officer.

"*Non, non, bilmirim* (I don't know it)," replied the officer, who then started a long chat with Jalil in Turkish. Then the officer said something to the policeman, who searched all three from head to toe, put their treasure and wallets on the table, and then stood back, flashing his eyes. The officer smiled, counted the money, and gloated over the jewelry.

Jalil translated: "Ali Bey says the princes are very rich people."

Kvachi knew that the *bey* would help himself to whatever he liked, regardless; so he decided it was best to get straight to the point.

"Jalil, tell Ali Bey to choose whatever he fancies."

Ali Bey picked out one object: "Ali Bey is very grateful."

"Tell Ali Bey that his gratitude is ten times better than this present."

Ali Bey chose a second and a third piece of jewelry.

"Ali Bey asks whether you are Bolsheviks or not."

"Jalil, tell Ali Bey that the Bolsheviks have put a price of a hundred thousand lira on our heads."

Jalil passed that on. Ali Bey pocketed two big diamonds.

"Ali Bey says that today we are Ali Bey's friends and guests."

"Jalil, tell Ali Bey that only Allah can thank him as he deserves."

"Ali Bey asks if you could lend him a little money."

"Jalil, he can help himself!" Kvachi rasped angrily. "But tell him also that we three are going to Istanbul and, if we don't have enough money for the journey, Ali Bey will have to introduce us to someone who can lend us the money."

Jalil translated. Ali Bey laughed and passed on a reply for Kvachi:

"Ali Bey says that he knows just the right person."

"Who is this person, Jalil?"

"Ali Bey."

Kvachi laughed a hanged man's laugh:

"Jalil, tell Ali Bey that I'll return his money with interest, but if Ali Bey ever comes to Istanbul and wants to enjoy my hospitality, I'll offer him an Arab horse and a Damascus sword that have no equal in Turkey."

Jalil translated this too. Ali Bey just frowned.

"Ali Bey said if you don't want to be his guests, you go to Moscow."

"Jalil, Ali Bey shouldn't have taken offense. I was speaking the truth. I'd rather be a guest of the devil's than of the Muscovites. Our heads, this money, and those jewels can all be *baksheesh* for Ali Bey."

Ali Bey stopped frowning. Then he counted out two thousand lira and proffered them to Kvachi with the words: "*Buyur, effendi* (Please take this, sir)."

Kvachi was Ali Bey's guest that day. They got on like brothers who had not seen each other for ten years. They were kindly and flattering to one another, told their life stories, exchanged addresses, and promised eternal brotherhood and to always keep in touch.

The next day Ali Bey gave Kvachi a written safe conduct, found him horses, gave him an armed escort, and saw him off. Their soldier handed Kvachi to another soldier, and he to a third, and so on to a sixth. A few days later Kvachi entered Trabzon. The local governor received Kvachi just as Ali Bey had done: amicably and politely, but, unlike Ali Bey, he neither lent nor borrowed money from Kvachi. Instead, he made him wait a whole month before giving him permission to leave for Istanbul.

"Thank the Lord," said Kvachi once he had boarded a ship. "We've got very little money left, but …"

"But we've still got our heads on our bodies!" Beso concluded.

"*Shukur Allah*!" Jalil comforted the others. "Istanbul is better than Saburtalo cemetery. *Shukur Allah! Allah il-allah*!"

Reliving Old Times

The three men were on deck as the ship approached the Bosphorus. An American, Watson, was standing next to Kvachi, who had won three thousand dollars off him at bridge the previous night.

"I've walked everywhere round here: I even know that the castle we can see on the left has a Georgian name, *Kari-bche*, 'Ramparts gate.'"

"*Kari-bche*?" exclaimed Kvachi. "That's Georgian, indeed. But why, how?"

"In Byzantine times the Georgians built a monastery here and called it that. Then they built a castle."

Later, when the ship entered the straits, Watson kept pointing to the right and left, constantly talking: "Over there is Rumeli lighthouse ... and there is the Anatolian lighthouse ... On the left is Büyük-Dere ... on the right Anadolu Hisar."

Kvachi had traveled the world and didn't expect to be amazed by anything in Turkey, but he and Beso were entranced by the beauty of the Bosphorus.

"What beauty! How beautiful! What an extraordinary spectacle!" they both kept exclaiming.

"There's Rumeli Hisar," the American continued. "Ortaköy ... Vaniköy." The ship was nearing Istanbul. "That's Çiragan palace ... now Dolma Bahçe palace ... this is the German embassy ... the Mahmudiye mosque; Tophane ... Galata ..."

The ship docked at the port; they all disembarked in Pera and took rooms at the best European hotel.

Kvachi began a new life, but it resembled the old one, before February 1917 and Madame Kerensky, or October and the Red Hell.

Three rooms in a superb hotel, a dozen suits, silk underwear, good food and drink, leisurely walks, cafés, rich entertainment and ... women, women, women—Jewish, Greek, Armenian, Turkish (these in secret dives only), Arab, Syrian, and from every other corner of the Orient. Kvachi had known westerners for a long time. He knew their taste, color, their temperament in love, and their countless flirtatious techniques. Orientals now pleased him more: big-eyed, dark-haired, mysterious, and hot-blooded, as soft as an Angora cat, as lithe as a southern snake, sometimes as restless as an Arab horse, sometimes as lazy as a sated leopard. Their eyes were a dark sea reflecting the trembling planet Mars, their skin was like old ivory, and their lips a newly split pomegranate. Kvachi was no longer his former self: he was now a mature stallion—serious, experienced, and refined. Kvachi now understood Isaac Idelsohn's advice, given to him in the Bois de Boulogne ten years previously. What did the sophisticated Idelsohn say then?

"A young woman is still unenlightened, untrained in the art of love: she is a plant with no roots. A mature woman is a deep-rooted oak. The girl sows, the woman reaps; one is learning, the other teaches; one smiles shyly or giggles or sheds gentle tears, the other laughs loud, or roars and bellows. A girl's caress is a breeze, a woman's—a gale; a girl's passion is a spark, a woman's—smouldering embers; silly girls smell of roses and violets, aroused women smell of marinade and Roquefort cheese."

Now Kvachi understands Isaac's taste. He understands and pushes in everywhere to sniff and seek. He seeks and he finds in abundance.

But, God curse the man who invented money: the liras and dollars are going down the drain. Several times Kvachi skinned Watson and a couple of European losers, but fate was merciless to him: European suckers rarely surfaced in Istanbul or quickly became as devilish as Kvachi. The Turks won't let Kvachi come near, and the local Armenians, Greeks, Jews, and Levantines are themselves trying to get a hand in Kvachi's pocket. What people, my God, these Greeks, Armenians, Jews, and Levantines are! They've all got his measure. Before the lad from Samtredia even opens his mouth, these crooks already know what he has in mind and they answer him in advance. Before Kvachi has even set his trap, they have laid half a dozen traps around him; while Kvachi is still weaving his net, he has been caught in half a dozen of their nets. Kvachi's brain is an open book to them, and they can read it at high speed. His tricks are dry twigs they can snap with two fingers, and his magic is a rotten veil which falls apart by itself. No, here it's impossible to pull a single "trick." Life is impossible in this damned city. So, to Paris, London, or Rome, again. But ... Kvachi won't be allowed into Europe; he won't be given a visa. They probably know who Kvachi Kvachantiradze is, and his enemies will give him no peace here, either.

"So be it!" Kvachi finally said, accepting his new fate. But even in Istanbul living needed money, so that he now bridled himself once he had given a cab driver his last lira.

Istanbul was the émigré capital. In Pera, Russian was more often heard than Turkish. The cafés, restaurants, and night clubs were full of Russian princesses and once important nonentities. Kvachi got used to these places and the people there. He went from one restaurant or café to another, doing something, looking for somebody. Sometimes he found what he was looking for and managed to do a small "job." He would get to know a particular woman, take her off, and hand her over to Watson or some other client. Kvachi had crumbs from the tables of the Watsons, and this was bitter bread. Watson introduced Kvachi to a doctor, and the doctor took Kvachi to see an elderly woman. She examined Kvachi closely, tried him out, and then told him:

"There are a lot of childless women in this city. They've got husbands, but ... you understand?"

Kvachi does, of course. Kvachi is, he assumes, to help these childless couples out. Excellent. "How much?"

"We'll settle on a fee, but you must never reveal a client's identity."

Kvachi is happy to accept this condition, and carry out the work. He does so conscientiously and lives for his new profession every day.

One day Kvachi looked into a tiny little courtyard: "Does a Mister Derbly live here?"

"No, Mister Derbly doesn't live here."

God almighty! Whose voice was that? Who's that standing on the little balcony? Whose is that pile of golden hair? Whose are those deep, twinkling blue eyes? Those lips, just a little worn, but ... They stared at each other for some time. Then a smile played on those lips.

"Rebecca ... Rebecca! Is it you? Is it you?"

"It's me, me. Couldn't you recognize me?"

"My Rebecca ... My Rebby! Rebby!"

Kvachi crossed the courtyard in a few bounds and clutched Rebby to his chest. Rebecca blushed and responded to his burning kiss with a shy kiss; she became embarrassed and confused, and looked over her shoulder. In the little doorway another woman was standing.

"God almighty! Elena … Elena! You're here too? You, too …"

He hugged Elena as well, stuck his lips to hers, and murmured:

"The two of you together … Both in one day, in the same apartment … Double happiness."

"Come in quick … Come in," Rebby said.

They all went into the living room: it was low, dark, and small. Elena's and Rebby's accommodation was imbued with poverty, damp, and sadness. Kvachi looked at both of them carefully. Cheap chintz dresses, both patched; hands scarred by needle pricks, and eyes swollen from lack of sleep. An occasional tear rolled down Rebecca's cheeks.

"Rebby, why are you crying? What's wrong?"

Rebby, tell your troubles to your Apollo. Tell your old friend the reason for your tears. Don't fight shy of Kvachi. He's forgotten your unkindness and your weakness when you couldn't hold out against Pavlov's torture and said what you shouldn't have said. Trust your heart and wash away the poison. Pavlov has met the fate he deserved.

"A month ago he was shot in Tbilisi."

The news gives Rebecca no pleasure. Elena just turned pale. "Yes, actually," Kvachi recalled, "Pavlov and Elena were in love at one point. That was barely four years ago." Elena was nevertheless hurt to the quick: whatever else, Pavlov had been a fine, handsome man. Poor Pavlov.

When they finally trusted their instincts and diffidently asked after each other, Rebecca and Elena told Kvachi their story.

Isaac, Rebecca, Elena, and several of their acquaintances left

Petersburg together five years previously. They ended up stuck at a small railway station near Moscow. The three of them were robbed and left to starve. They went, completely destitute, to Odessa. It took them five months. They begged and got food by doing manual labor. They would describe that terrible journey in detail later. In Kiev they met Wittgenstein. Kvachi would remember the lad who was the unsuccessful Paris rival of the lucky Apollo, wouldn't he?

"I remember him well."

Wittgenstein helped Elena, but he was soon shot.

"Who shot him?"

Who knows? Everyone was shooting and hanging everyone then: Petliura, Skoropadsky, Makhno, the Germans, the Whites, the Reds, and the Greens. Then they got to Odessa. Isaac's and Rebecca's relatives had been stripped of everything. When the Reds began to take the city, the three of them fled to Istanbul. Isaac was an ingenious man.

"What do you mean 'was'? Where is Isaac?" Kvachi asked belatedly.

"The poor man died," said Elena.

Rebecca started to cry again.

Elena continued: "Isaac was clever. He opened a restaurant. It was making a profit. Rebby and I worked there. We could live on our wages. So we lived. Then six months ago Isaac caught a chill and died."

"Poor man," exclaimed Kvachi.

"The restaurant was in debt, so we sold it, but we ended up penniless. Now we stitch and repair underwear for a living, but ... it's no life."

Kvachi then told them the story of his life.

"I lost Chkhubishvili, Sedrak Havlabariani, Chikinjiladze, Chipi Chipuntiradze, and Bekarev, all killed in battle."

"Poor man ... poor man ..." the women echoed repeatedly.

"Bekarev deserved it," exclaimed Rebby. "He put me in prison."

"True. How is Tania?" Elena recalled.

"She died of starvation ..." Kvachi replied gravely.

Elena was upset: "And couldn't you do anything to help?"

"She didn't tell me anything. I wanted to help, but ... She wouldn't accept help from me."

"Ganus and his wife?"

"Ganus was shot. His wife is taking in washing."

They recalled and asked after many more people. Some had perished of famine and spite, some had been slaughtered by others, others were in Russia, Europe, or Istanbul, taking in washing or cleaning shoes or serving in restaurants and cafés, or doing all kinds of heavy manual work, wasting away, and heading for an early death.

Kvachi invited the two women to a restaurant, but they refused with thanks, because neither had a dress fit to appear in. Finally they agreed, and Kvachi trudged after them to a canteen where their impoverished clothes wouldn't stand out.

That evening they found it hard to part.

What path would Kvachi take? How would he act? Would he come round to see the mistresses he had abandoned seven years previously? Was Kvachi obliged to take on these two and have them round his neck? Of course he wasn't. At the time all three had taken what was to be had, given what was to be given, and had then gone their own way, but ... All the same ... we're only human ... who knows?

The next day he invited the two to a sordid nightclub. The customers here were already thoroughly drunk and uninhibited. The music screeched, people splayed their legs and bellies in tangos and belly dances so that even the club's dog was blushing. The customers were served by girls who now and again dragged a drunken customer off into the yard and brought him back a little later.

They sat down and ordered. Kvachi kept his eyes on his

guests, looking at their eyes as at a mirror. What he could clearly see was the impression made by this nightclub. Both Rebby and Elena had worked in a restaurant. Had the restaurant been clean or dirty, shabby or elegant, with girls or without? Were they used to this, or not, were they experienced, or not? Kvachi quickly read the answers in the women's faces: they were only slightly embarrassed by the atmosphere in this club. Excellent. Then they were pretty well broken in.

"Those girls make a lot of money," said Kvachi.

"They do until they get too old," replied Rebby.

"They earn a lot, but it's no fun," added Elena.

"Of course not, it's not easy doing business with these filthy people," Kvachi continued, "but you can find other places, where the setting is nice and the people are clean, rich, and educated. Have a drink, Elena, it's real Chartreuse. The girls there live like princesses. And they end up well off: almost all of them find happiness and get married."

Rebby sighed. Elena smiled secretively. Kvachi went on:

"In the end, to tell you the truth, even these girls don't do as badly as novelists make out. Rebby, why aren't you drinking? Drink it. People always get used to things and adapt. That's their chief weapon and their source of happiness. These girls have a surplus of what millions long for: warm flesh. We have to take account of that. And they don't have the torment of hard work which the rest of humanity has to put up with. They get everything free: a nice flat, plenty to eat and drink, and lovely clothes. If a girl like that uses her wits, puts up with a few things, and avoids any false ideas about herself, at least for a time, she can easily get through it and reach a happy old age. Rebby, drink up! Elena, keep up with us!"

"You need beauty first for that job," said Rebby, sighing again.

"Of course," Kvachi quickly agreed.

"And you need to be young."

"That's not true: what's youth? Some forty-year-old women

are younger than twenty-five-year-olds."

"That's true," sighed Elena.

"Anyway, believe me, in the eyes of men of experience or any maturity, a mature woman has more value than a nubile idiot."

"That's true," Rebby and Elena agreed.

"I also ought to tell you that in a good ... a good house, a good family background, and good education is more valued than beauty or youth. Elena, drink up! Rebby, keep up with us!"

The liqueurs and the passion all round had now fired Rebby and Elena. The men and girls around them were cuddling so boldly and unashamedly that the glasses and furniture were imbued with their lust.

"They're both ready, they're both ripe," Kvachi rejoiced silently, ordering more food and drink: "Garçon, champagne, a lobster and fruit. Bring coffee afterwards."

It was nearly dawn when the three of them returned to their damp room. Kvachi himself was drunk and unable to leave; he had no more strength, so he would sleep at their place. "By God, just sleep! You can put two beds together. Yes, like that. Why are you laughing? What is there to laugh at? There was a time when you were both free with your favors for Kvachi. You knew all about it at the time. Would it do any harm if the three of us had a taste together of past delights? Are you embarrassed? Are you shy with the other there? Now what? We've been together all this time, and now this bourgeois morality? Haven't you managed to rid yourselves of bourgeois habits? Is this so hard for you? Fine. Kvachi will get into bed and fall asleep, and you can go to sleep afterwards, or you needn't sleep at all. Ha-ha. So we've got no alternative? Take your clothes off ... take your clothes off. That's more like it ... That's right. No, no. Elena, don't blow out the candle. You know my habits, you haven't forgotten, have you? Right, come on ... God loves a trinity."

That night Kvachi tested and inspected the two women, as an

experienced hunter tests and tries out a hound. Had Elena put on too much weight? Had Rebby lost too much? Was their skin wrinkled? Were they not agile enough? Had they become too heavy, or slow? They had got a little heavier, but everything else was in order. Good, very good, then. That's excellent.

Cashing in on Old Love, Getting Married, and Ending the Story

Kvachi dug deep in his pockets and found the money to dress his old mistresses. Then one night he took them back to the "house" whose fine qualities he had enumerated the night before. He took Beso and Jalil, too.

The house, big and clean, was brightly lit. Its marble staircase was decorated with rugs, sculptures, and tropical plants. The long hall, full of paintings of naked women and muffled with heavy drapery, was packed with women and guests. At the end of the hall was a red room with an ottoman divan. A woman was sitting, her legs under her thighs, on the divan, and watching as gravely and calmly as a divine Buddha.

Kvachi brought the two women into the red room.

"Liza-*hanım*, may I introduce my sisters. Here's the first … and this is the second."

He reached for Liza's hand and reverently kissed it. Liza-*hanım* was a very stout, squat, and chubby woman of fifty. Her dyed black hair, piled high, was laced with a string of diamonds. She had a bejewelled necklace round her flabby neck, over which her double chin hung. Her enormous bare chest, her broad wrists, and her fingers, as big as cucumbers, were generously studded with rubies, turquoises, emeralds, and amethysts.

Liza examined the two women with her expert eye, as a horse broker examines horses for sale. Finally she rasped in a quiet bass voice.

"Sister," she said to Elena, "your eyes are blacker than jet. They seem to reflect the stars. I can see insatiable desire on your lips. Your breasts haven't shrunk yet, and God has preserved your flesh. I can tell that you are thoroughly well-brought up, well-bred, and refined. Do sit down."

Then she turned to Rebecca:

"Your hair really is golden. Your eyes make me think of the stars, with two pearls shining in the sky. Your lips are like a bleeding wound. You're as elegant as a gazelle, and your body is slim. Your high narrow hips are a rarity in our times. I can tell by your arms and legs that you've got hot blood in your veins. Please take a seat, too. Prince," she turned to Kvachi. "If you don't mind being next to me, sit down on this divan."

She solemnly picked up a silver bell, solemnly rang it, and solemnly told the Arab boy who immediately appeared: "Hussein, four coffees and glasses of Chypre."

They sat, drank, and had a delightful chat.

"I'm a Christian," Liza said with a smile. "There isn't a foreign drop in my Greek blood. My girls (I have twenty-eight of them) just adore me and call me mother. There's never been a single complaint about this house. I have girls of all faiths: they all pray in their own way. I don't interfere with that. I have a room full of presents for my girls. A thousand have left here and a thousand have got married, but they can't forget their Liza-*hanım*. I get about forty letters a day. They get all the food and drink they want, masses of clothes, and endless fun. There's no charge for doctors, lawyers, and servants. What more could they ask for? Nothing. They wait to see who will turn up. In the end they always find him and get married, have children, and live happily. That's Liza-*hanım's* house for you."

This was the nightingale song of Liza-*hanım* who had married off a thousand girls and created a thousand happy families. She sang her own praises, drank, and offered her guests drink. Finally she said:

"My jet-black girl, my golden girl! Go and have a good time. Today you're my guests, tomorrow we'll have another nice little chat."

Kvachi took Rebby and Elena off to the hall, handed them to Beso, and then went back to sit with Liza. He sat so close to her that they could hear each other breathing. Kvachi then asked her:

"What do you say, Liza-*hanım*?"

Liza was silent for a while, then gave an offhand answer.

"The black-eyed one's too fat, the golden-haired one's too old."

"Liza-*hanım*," Kvachi whispered in her ear. "You're fifteen years older than the golden-haired one and, compared to you, the black-eyed one is a skinny child. But, I swear on my life and to God, I still prefer you to any other woman."

He furtively slid his arm over her broad thigh. Liza looked into Kvachi's eyes and gave him a decrepit smile, and tapped him under the chin with her fat index finger, saying:

"Effendi, don't mock me."

"If I were in your bed, I'd prove to you straight away that Prince Kvachantiradze would never stoop to mocking Liza-*hanım*."

"When are you going to prove it?"

"Right now, if you like."

Liza got up and waddled like a goose towards the door. Our Arab horse slowly strode after the goose.

After the "proof" they both came back and resumed their seats. Kvachi had a new pack of banknotes in his pocket, and a gigantic new ring on his thumb. That was the sale price for the two women and the "proof."

Liz-*hanım* folded her legs back into her Buddha pose, while her oily eyes surveyed the hall. Then she said:

"Apollo, your Russian women seem to be doing well. Verochka is very cheerful: look how her lips move. And Katenka is keeping up with her. They're getting the clients to spend a lot."

"How is Nadinka fitting in, Liza-*hanım*?"

"I've hardly ever seen anyone dance like her. You've got a gift for choosing them. Now go, or your friends are going to look at us. Move both of them into my house tomorrow, the house opposite this one. They can live there for the time being, slowly get the hang of things, and then they can move here. I'll see to the rest. Goodbye, my lion. When you're about to leave, come and see me in my room. Come earlier tomorrow."

That was how that night Kvachi turned two superannuated loves into cash and found in Liza-*hanım* a new friend, albeit also superannuated and rusty, but fat and profitable.

Time passed. Kvachi had become a member of Liza-*hanım's* family. His sisters—Rebby, Elena, and half a dozen others—had become Liza's children. Every night Kvachi had to "prove" that he preferred a mature and well-trained woman's roars and guffaws to a silly young thing's whimpering and giggling, while Liza-*hanım's* scent (of Roquefort cheese) drowned out the scent of roses and violets.

Kvachi and Liza-*hanım* would sit on the ottoman divan, helping themselves to coffee, liqueurs, and confectioneries, smoking Egyptian tobacco, having a pleasant chat while watching the rutting in the hall.

Once Liza-*hanım* told Kvachi: "My Apollo, it's time we sorted out business matters: listen to me and think about it. I've got two big houses and a third country place I've just bought in Kadiköy. Also, half of Papadopoulos's firm belongs to me. You know the rest: a luxurious flat, a carriage, a lot of ornaments, and up to two hundred thousand in cash. My annual income is over sixty thousand. My husband died last year, as you know. I've no children, as you also know. My relatives are waiting for me to die, as I've told you. But I've no intention of dying or giving up my business. I love my work and this business: I'm used to it. But working with no man around, especially in this trade, is like being a three-legged horse: you can stumble along, but you can't run away. Anyway, my mourning period is over. I'm not used to being alone. You can see I've got men, young and rich, hovering around me like flies waiting for a response."

They both smoked in silence for a while.

"Have you understood me?" Liza-*hanım* finally asked.

"Liza-*hanım*!" replied Kvachi. "I'm burning with shame, because you said it before I did. I was going to broach the subject tomorrow, but, since you got in before me, I've no alternative: we have to settle things today. Liza-*hanım*! I've told you who I am and what I've been through. I'm a prince, for one thing; secondly, I'm still young at thirty-seven; thirdly, I've got two university degrees; fourthly, because I was brought up in a prince's palace, I have the appropriate tastes and habits; fifthly, the Reds took everything I had, but I still earn money and spend it as I like."

Again, they smoked in silence. Then Kvachi asked:

"Liza-*hanım*, have you understood my answer?"

"I have, my Apollo. A man's pocket has to be full of money, my last husband spent two hundred lira a month."

"Liza-*hanım*!" Kvachi interrupted. "Your husband was no prince, he was older than you, and he was uneducated, so …"

"So you'll have to manage on a thousand lira."

"Liza-*hanım*! I spend three thousand."

"Fifteen hundred will be enough for you."

"Liza-*hanım*!"

"Let's settle things. Two thousand will be more than plenty for you. What's more, I'll take your friends on too, and buy you a motor car instead of the carriage. You can have two riding horses as a bonus. Let's settle: give me your hand."

They shook hands on the deal, embraced, and once more "proved" their eternal friendship.

**
*

Everything goes on as it should in Princess Liza-*hanım* Kvachantiradze's "house." Once night has fallen Liza-*hanım's* thirty girls line up half-naked and spread out in the big hall. The guests gradually assemble.

Finally, Princess Liza-*hanım* waddles out like a goose, folds herself up on the ottoman divan, solemnly freezes like a Buddha idol, and enjoys her children's happiness.

Beso is seated at the cash till. Wearing a red fez, fully armed, with his arms folded, Jalil stands like a pillar at the door.

Kvachi, Liza-*hanım's* husband and the "house" manager, runs round in circles like a lost turkey-cock. He sits down next to his princess, or gives Beso a helping hand, or addresses a couple of words to Jalil, or greets the guests, or looks into the kitchen or the pantry. Kvachi runs round in circles, inwardly growling. Sometimes he lets Beso know of his sorrows and complains like an elderly widow; sometimes he hides furtively in a corner and moans, breaks down, and bursts into tears.

Why are you crying, Kvachi Kvachantiradze? Why is this spirited heart groaning? What clouds your bright eyes? Why is your clear and unfurrowed brow now frowning? What's happened to you, Kvachi Kvachantiradze? All you can eat and drink, every conceivable garment, inconceivable amounts of money, women of your choice, horses and a car, servants and friends, old and new: what are you missing, Kvachi Kvachantiradze? The friends who were slain? You got over that a long time ago. Silibistro and Pupi? They're very well. If you like, bring them out here. Glory and a reputation? You had them, and you yourself discarded them. The motherland's skies and land? Saburtalo cemetery awaits you. So what do you want, Kvachi Kvachantiradze? Endless roaming? Constant fortune-seeking? Running and flying round the world without end? Breaking out of your golden cage and flying off? So what do you want, then?

I don't think you know!

I understand you, Kvachi Kvachantiradze!
I understand you, my Kvachi!
I understand you, my little Kvachi!
I understand … I understand.

GEORGIAN LITERATURE SERIES

The Georgian Literature Series aims to bring to an English-speaking audience the best of contemporary Georgian fiction. Made possible thanks to the financial support of the Georgian National Book Centre and the Ministry of Culture and Monument Protection of Georgia, the Series began with four titles, officially published in January 2014. Available in January 2015 are four new titles, offering readers a choice of Georgian literary works.

GEORGIAN LITERATURE SERIES

Erlom Akhvlediani

Vano and Niko & other stories / Translated by Mikheil Kakabadze

Akhvlediani's minimalist prose pieces are Kafkaesque parables presenting individual experience as a quest for the other. ISBN 978-1-62897-106-4 / $15.95 US

Lasha Bugadze

The Literature Express / Translated by Maya Kiasashvili

The Literature Express is a riotous parable about the state of literary culture, the European Union, and our own petty ambitions—be they professional or amorous.
ISBN 978-1-56478-726-2 / $16.00 US

Zaza Burchuladze

adibas / Translated by Guram Sanikidze

A "war novel" without a single battle scene, Zaza Burchuladze's English-language debut anatomizes the Western world's ongoing "feast in the time of plague."
ISBN 978-1-56478-925-9 / $15.50 US

Tamaz Chiladze

The Brueghel Moon / Translated by Maya Kiasashvili

The novel of the famous Georgian writer, poet and playwright Tamaz Chiladze focuses on moral problems / issues, arisen as a result of the too great self-assuredness of psychologists. ISBN 978-1-62897-093-7 / $14.95 US

Mikheil Javakhishvili

Kvachi / Translated by Donald Rayfield

This is, in brief, the story of a swindler, a Georgian Felix Krull, or perhaps a cynical Don Quixote, named Kvachi Kvachantiradze: womanizer, cheat, perpetrator of insurance fraud, bank-robber, associate of Rasputin, filmmaker, revolutionary, and pimp. ISBN 978-1-56478-879-5 / $17.95 US

Zurab Karumidze

Dagny

Fact and fantasy collide in this visionary, literary "feast" starring historical Norwegian poet and dramatist Dagny Juel (1867-1901), a beautiful woman whose life found her falling victim to one deranged male fantasy after another.
ISBN 978-1-56478-928-0 / $15.00 US

Anna Kordzaia-Samadashvili

Me, Margarita / Translated by Victoria Field & Natalia Bukia-Peters

Short stories about men and women, love and hate, sex and disappointment, cynicism and hope—perhaps unique in that none of the stories reveal the time or place in they occur: the world is too small now for it to matter. ISBN 978-1-56478-875-7 / $15.95 US

Aka Morchiladze

Journey to Karabakh / Translated by Elizabeth Heighway

One of the best-selling novels ever released in Georgia, and the basis for two feature films, this is a book about the tricky business of finding—and defining—liberty.
ISBN 978-1-56478-928-0 / $15.00 US

www.dalkeyarchive.com